STEPHEN JONES lives in London. He is the winner of three World Fantasy Awards, three Horror Writers Association Bram Stoker Awards and three International Horror Guild Awards as well as being a fifteen-time recipient of the British Fantasy Award and a Hugo Award nominee. A former television producer/director and genre movie publicist and consultant (the first three *Hellraiser* movies, *Night Life*, *Nightbreed*, *Split Second*, *Mind Ripper*, *Last Gasp* etc.), he is the co-editor of *Horror: 100 Best Books*, *The Best Horror from Fantasy Tales*, *Gaslight & Ghosts*, *Now We Are Sick*, *H.P. Lovecraft's Book of Horror*, *The Anthology of Fantasy & the Supernatural*, *Secret City: Strange Tales of London*, *Great Ghost Stories* and *The Mammoth Book of Best New Horror*, *Dark Terrors*, *Dark Voices* and *Fantasy Tales* series. He has written *Creepshows: The Illustrated Stephen King Movie Guide*, *The Essential Monster Movie Guide*, *The Illustrated Vampire Movie Guide*, *The Illustrated Dinosaur Movie Guide*, *The Illustrated Frankenstein Movie Guide* and *The Illustrated Werewolf Movie Guide*, and compiled *The Mammoth Book of Terror*, *The Mammoth Book of Vampires*, *The Mammoth Book of Zombies*, *The Mammoth Book of Werewolves*, *The Mammoth Book of Frankenstein*, *The Mammoth Book of Dracula*, *The Mammoth Book of Vampire Stories By Women*, *The Mammoth Book of New Terror*, *Shadows Over Innsmouth*, *Dark Detectives*, *Dancing With the Dark*, *Dark of the Night*, *White of the Moon*, *Keep Out the Night*, *By Moonlight Only*, *Don't Turn Out the Light*, *Exorcisms and Ecstasies* by Karl Edward Wagner, *The Vampire Stories of R. Chetwynd-Hayes*, *Phantoms and Fiends* and *Frights and Fancies* by R. Chetwynd-Hayes, *James Herbert: By Horror Haunted*, *The Conan Chronicles* by Robert E. Howard (two volumes), *The Emperor of Dreams: The Lost Worlds of Clark Ashton Smith*, *Clive Barker's A-Z of Horror*, *Clive Barker's Shadows in Eden*, *Clive Barker's The Nightbreed Chronicles* and the *Hellraiser Chronicles*. You can visit his web site at www.herebedragons.co.uk/jones

Also available

THE MAMMOTH BOOK OF

NEW TERROR

Edited by
Stephen Jones

CARROLL & GRAF PUBLISHERS
New York

Carroll & Graf Publishers
An imprint of Avalon Publishing Group, Inc.
245 W. 17th Street
New York
NY 10011-5300
www.carrollandgraf.com

AVALON
publishing group incorporated

First published in the UK by Robinson,
an imprint of Constable & Robinson Ltd 2004

First Carroll & Graf edition 2004

ISBN 0-7867-1409-3

Printed and bound in the EU

CONTENTS

ACKNOWLEDGMENTS

INTRODUCTION: RECREATING THE TERROR copyright © Stephen Jones 2004.

FRUITING BODIES copyright © Brian Lumley 1988. Originally published in *Weird Tales* No. 291, Summer 1988. Reprinted by permission of the author and his agents, Dorian Literary Agency.

NEEDLE SONG copyright © Gary Hoppenstand 1979. Originally published in *Midnight Sun* Number 5. Reprinted by permission of the author.

TURBO-SATAN copyright © Christopher Fowler 2004.

TALKING IN THE DARK copyright © Dennis Etchison 1984. Originally published in *Shadows* 7. Reprinted by permission of the author.

THE CIRCUS copyright © Sydney J. Bounds 1980. Originally published in *The Thirteenth Fontana Book of Great Horror Stories.* Reprinted by permission of the author and the author's agents, Cosmos Literary Agency.

FOET copyright © F. Paul Wilson 1991. Originally published in *Borderlands 2: An Anthology of Imaginative Fiction.* Reprinted by permission of the author.

This one is for Jay,
part of my extended Chicago family by marriage,
my good friend and drinking companion by choice.

INTRODUCTION

Recreating the Terror

THE FIRST BOOK I ever edited in the hugely successful *Mammoth* series was *The Mammoth Book of Terror* back in 1991.

At the time, I wanted to assemble a hefty, non-themed horror anthology featuring some classic stories by many of the biggest names in the field, along with a scattering of tales that would be original to the book.

The result was more successful than I could have imagined. The volume was reprinted in the UK and went through four printings in the United States. There was also a hardcover version, various budget editions and even an Italian translation. Even more importantly, the book was a precursor to an entire series of *Mammoth* titles that I have continued to edit up to this day.

So when I was offered the opportunity to put together this follow-up volume, I naturally jumped at the chance. There are still many superb stories of horror and dark fantasy that, for one reason or another are not currently in print, or have never been previously published on one side of the Atlantic or the other.

It is therefore my pleasure to welcome back to this volume such esteemed authors as Ramsey Campbell, Basil Copper,

Dennis Etchison, Brian Lumley, Graham Masterton, David J. Schow, Lisa Tuttle and F. Paul Wilson. Although they are no longer with us, R. Chetwynd-Hayes and Karl Edward Wagner are also both remembered with examples of their finest work, which will most likely be unfamiliar to many readers.

Such other respected names as Sydney J. Bounds, Phyllis Eisenstein, Charles L. Grant and E.C. Tubb are also represented with classic tales of unease, and there is more recent or original work from Pat Cadigan, Christopher Fowler, Neil Gaiman, Glen Hirshberg, Caitlín R. Kiernan, Terry Lamsley, Brian Mooney, Kim Newman and Michael Marshall Smith, many of whom were only just starting their professional careers when the first volume of *Terror* was originally published.

Finally, I am delighted to present two powerful collaborations between rising stars Tim Lebbon and Brian Keene and the talented writing team of married couple Tanith Lee and John Kaiine, along with David Case's classic psychological novella "Among the Wolves" which, like all the author's early work, deserves to be back in print again.

So there you have it – another bumper volume of contemporary terror, brought to you by some of the finest writers currently working in horror fiction. And remember, if you enjoyed this volume, then there are many more stories out there just waiting to be told . . .

Stephen Jones
London, England

BRIAN LUMLEY

Fruiting Bodies

BRIAN LUMLEY WAS BORN on England's north-east coast nine
months after the death of H.P. Lovecraft. He claims that is just a
coincidence. He was serving as a sergeant in the Corps of Royal
Military Police when he discovered Lovecraft's fiction while
stationed in Berlin in the early 1960s. After deciding to try his
own hand at writing horror fiction, initially set in HPL's
influential Cthulhu Mythos, he sent his early efforts to editor
August Derleth. The latter's famed Arkham House imprint
published two collections of Lumley's short stories, *The Caller of
the Black* and *The Horror at Oakdene and Others*, plus the short
novel *Beneath the Moors*.

Lumley's many other books include the *Psychomech* trilogy,
Demogorgon, *The House of Doors*, *Fruiting Bodies and Other Fungi*, *A
Coven of Vampires*, *The Whisperer and Other Voices* and *Beneath the
Moors and Darker Places*.

More recent publications include *Freaks*, a collection from
Subterranean Press that includes a new story, and a reprinting
of *Khai of Khem* from Tor Books. Delirium has reissued the first
Hero of Dreams novel in a very limited leatherbound edition, and
the third issue of *H.P. Lovecraft's Magazine of Horror* is a "Brian
Lumley Special" that features two original tales.

These days Lumley is best known as the author of the popular *Necroscope* vampire series. Published in 1986, the first book in the series made him a best-seller all over the world. That initial volume was followed by *Necroscope II: Wamphyri!* (aka *Necroscope II: Vamphyri!*), *Necroscope III: The Source, Necroscope IV: Deadspeak* and *Necroscope V: Deadspawn.* The *Vampire World* trilogy appeared in the early 1990s, and that was followed by the two-volume *Necroscope: The Lost Years*, the three-volume *E-Branch* series, and the collection *Harry Keogh: Necroscope and Other Weird Heroes!* Forthcoming is *The Touch,* a new "E-Branch" spin-off.

In 1998 he was named Grand Master at the World Horror Convention, and *The Brian Lumley Companion,* co-edited with Stanley Wiater, appeared from Tor in 2002.

" 'Fruiting Bodies' won a British Fantasy Award in 1989," reveals the author. "It had some stiff competition and I count myself lucky to have won. Whether it's frightening or not is for you to decide. If it's entertaining, and gives that certain *frisson,* then I'm satisfied.

"One thing's for sure, there isn't any blood here: mushrooms don't bleed."

MY GREAT-GRANDPARENTS, and my grandparents after them, had been Easingham people; in all likelihood my parents would have been, too, but the old village had been falling into the sea for three hundred years and hadn't much looked like stopping, and so I was born in Durham City instead. My grandparents, both sets, had been among the last of the village people to move out, buying new homes out of a government-funded disaster grant. Since when, as a kid, I had been back to Easingham only once.

My father had taken me there one spring when the tides were high. I remember how there was still some black, crusty snow lying in odd corners of the fields, coloured by soot and smoke, as all things were in those days in the north-east. We'd gone to Easingham because the unusually high tides had been at it again, chewing away at the shale cliffs, reducing shoreline and derelict village both as the North Sea's breakers crashed again and again on the shuddering land.

And of course we had hoped (as had the two hundred or so other sightseers gathered there that day) to see a house or two go down in smoking ruin, into the sea and the foaming spray. We witnessed no such spectacle; after an hour, cold and wet from the salt moisture in the air, we piled back into the family car and returned to Durham. Easingham's main street, or what had once been the main street, was teetering on the brink as we left. But by nightfall that street was no more. We'd missed it: a further twenty feet of coastline, a bite one street deep and a few yards more than one street long had been undermined, toppled, and gobbled up by the sea.

That had been that. Bit by bit, in the quarter-century between then and now, the rest of Easingham had also succumbed. Now only a house or two remained – no more than a handful in all – and all falling into decay, while the closest lived-in buildings were those of a farm all of a mile inland from the cliffs. Oh, and of course there was one other inhabitant: old Garth Bentham, who'd been demolishing the old houses by hand and selling bricks and timbers from the village for years. But I'll get to him shortly.

So there I was last summer, back in the north-east again, and when my business was done of course I dropped in and stayed overnight with the Old Folks at their Durham cottage. Once a year at least I made a point of seeing them, but last year in particular I noticed how time was creeping up on them. The "Old Folks"; well, now I saw that they really were old, and I determined that I must start to see a lot more of them.

Later, starting in on my long drive back down to London, I remembered that time when the Old Man had taken me to Easingham to see the houses tottering on the cliffs. And probably because the place was on my mind, I inadvertently turned off my route and in a little while found myself heading for the coast. I could have turned round right there and then – indeed, I intended to do so – but I'd got to wondering about Easingham and how little would be left of it now, and before I knew it . . .

Once I'd made up my mind, Middlesbrough was soon behind me, then Guisborough, and in no time at all I was on the old road to the village. There had only ever been one way in and out, and this was it: a narrow road, its surface starting to crack now, with tall hedgerows broken here and there, letting you look through to where fields rolled down to the cliffs. A beautiful day, with seagulls wheeling overhead, a salt tang coming in through the wound-down windows, and a blue sky coming down to merge with . . . with the blue-grey of the North Sea itself! For cresting a rise, suddenly I was there.

An old, leaning wooden signpost said EASINGH – for the tail had been broken off or rotted away, and "the village" lay at the end of the road. But right there, blocking the way, a metal barrier was set in massive concrete posts and carried a sign bearing the following warning:

DANGER!
Severe Cliff Subsidence
No Vehicles Beyond This Point

I turned off the car's motor, got out, leaned on the barrier. Before me the road went on – and disappeared only thirty yards ahead. And there stretched the new rim of the cliffs. Of the village, Easingham itself – forget it! On this side of the cliffs, reaching back on both sides of the road behind overgrown gardens, weedy paths and driveways, there stood the empty shells of what had once been residences of the "posh" folks of Easingham. Now, even on a day as lovely as this one, they were morose in their desolation.

The windows of these derelicts, where there were windows, seemed to gaze gauntly down on approaching doom, like old men in twin rows of deathbeds. Brambles and ivy were rank; the whole place seemed as despairing as the cries of the gulls rising on the warm air; Easingham was a place no more.

Not that there had ever been a lot of it. Three streets lengthwise with a few shops; two more, shorter streets cutting through the three at right angles and going down to the cliffs and the vertiginous wooden steps that used to climb down to the beach, the bay, the old harbour and fish market; and, standing over the bay, a Methodist church on a jutting promontory, which in the old times had also served as a lighthouse. But now –

No streets, no promontory or church, no harbour, fish market, rickety steps. No Easingham.

"Gone, all of it," said a wheezy, tired old voice from directly behind me, causing me to start. "Gone for ever, to the Devil and the deep blue sea!"

I turned, formed words, said something barely coherent to the leathery old scarecrow of a man I found standing there.

"Eh? Eh?" he said. "Did I startle you? I have to say you

startled me! First car I've seen in a three-month! After bricks, are you? Cheap bricks? Timber?"

"No, no," I told him, finding my voice. "I'm – well, sight-seeing, I suppose." I shrugged. "I just came to see how the old village was getting on. I didn't live here, but a long line of my people did. I just thought I'd like to see how much was left – while it was left! Except it seems I'm too late."

"Oh, aye, too late," he nodded. "Three or four years too late. That was when the last of the old fishing houses went down: four years ago. Sea took 'em. Takes six or seven feet of cliff every year. Aye, and if I lived long enough it would take me too. But it won't 'cos I'm getting on a bit." And he grinned and nodded, as if to say: so that's that!

"Well, well, sightseeing! Not much to see, though, not now. Do you fancy a coffee?"

Before I could answer he put his fingers to his mouth and blew a piercing whistle, then paused and waited, shaking his head in puzzlement. "Ben," he explained. "My old dog. He's not been himself lately and I don't like him to stray too far. He was out all night, was Ben. Still, it's summer, and there may have been a bitch about . . ."

While he had talked I'd looked him over and decided that I liked him. He reminded me of my own grandfather, what little I could remember of him. Grandad had been a miner in one of the colliery villages further north, retiring here to doze and dry up and die – only to find himself denied the choice. The sea's incursion had put paid to that when it finally made the place untenable. I fancied this old lad had been a miner, too. Certainly he bore the scars, the stigmata, of the miner: the dark, leathery skin with black specks bedded in; the bad, bowed legs; the shortness of breath, making for short sentences. A generally gritty appearance overall, though I'd no doubt he was clean as fresh-scrubbed.

"Coffee would be fine," I told him, holding out my hand. "Greg's my name – Greg Lane."

He took my hand, shook it warmly and nodded. "Garth Bentham," he said. And then he set off stiffly back up the crumbling road some two or three houses, turning right into an overgrown garden through a fancy wooden gate recently painted white. "I'd intended doing the whole place up," he said, as I followed close behind. "Did the gate, part of the fence, ran out of paint!"

Before letting us into the dim interior of the house, he paused and whistled again for Ben, then worriedly shook his head in something of concern. "After rats in the old timber yard again, I suppose. But God knows I wish he'd stay out of there!"

Then we were inside the tiny cloakroom, where the sun filtered through fly-specked windows and probed golden searchlights on a few fairly dilapidated furnishings and the brassy face of an old grandfather clock that clucked like a mechanical hen. Dust motes drifted like tiny planets in a cosmos of faery, eddying round my host where he guided me through a door and into his living-room. Where the dust had settled on the occasional ledge, I noticed that it was tinged red, like rust.

"I cleaned the windows in here," Garth informed, "so's to see the sea. I like to know what it's up to!"

"Making sure it won't creep up on you," I nodded.

His eyes twinkled. "Nah, just joking," he said, tapping on the side of his blue-veined nose. "No, it'll be ten or even twenty years before all this goes, but I don't have that long. Five if I'm lucky. I'm sixty-eight, after all!"

Sixty-eight! Was that really as old as all that? But he was probably right: a lot of old-timers from the mines didn't even last *that* long, not entirely mobile and coherent, anyway. "Retiring at sixty-five doesn't leave a lot, does it?" I said. "Of time, I mean."

He went into his kitchen, called back: "Me, I've been here a ten-year. Didn't retire, quit! Stuff your pension, I told 'em. I'd rather have my lungs, what's left of 'em. So I came here, got this place for a song, take care of myself and my old dog, and no one to tip my hat to and no one to bother me. I get a letter once a fortnight from my sister in Dunbar, and one of these days the postman will find me stretched out in here and he'll think: 'Well, I needn't come out here any more.'"

He wasn't bemoaning his fate, but I felt sorry for him anyway. I settled myself on a dusty settee, looked out of the window down across his garden of brambles to the sea's horizon. A great curved millpond – for the time being. "Didn't you have any savings?" I could have bitten my tongue off the moment I'd said it, for that was to imply he hadn't done very well for himself.

Cups rattled in the kitchen. "Savings? Lad, when I was a

young 'un I had three things: my lamp, my helmet and a pack of cards. If it wasn't pitch 'n' toss with weighted pennies on the beach banks, it was three-card brag in the back room of the pub. Oh, I was a game gambler, right enough, but a bad 'un. In my blood, like my Old Man before me. My mother never did see a penny; nor did my wife, I'm ashamed to say, before we moved out here – God bless her! Savings? That's a laugh. But out here there's no bookie's runner, and you'd be damned hard put to find a card school in Easingham these days! What the hell," he shrugged as he stuck his head back into the room, "it was a life . . ."

We sipped our coffee. After a while I said, "Have you been on your own very long? I mean . . . your wife?"

"Lily-Anne?" he glanced at me, blinked, and suddenly there was a peculiar expression on his face. "On my own, you say . . ." He straightened his shoulders, took a deep breath. "Well, I am on my own in a way, and in a way I'm not. I have Ben – or would have if he'd get done with what he's doing and come home – and Lily-Anne's not all that far away. In fact, sometimes I suspect she's sort of watching over me, keeping me company, so to speak. You know, when I'm feeling especially lonely."

"Oh?"

"Well," he shrugged again. "I mean she *is* here, now isn't she." It was a statement, not a question.

"Here?" I was starting to have my doubts about Garth Bentham.

"I had her buried here," he nodded, which explained what he'd said and produced a certain sensation of relief in me. "There was a Methodist church here once over, with its own burying ground. The church went a donkey's years ago, of course, but the old graveyard was still here when Lily-Anne died."

"Was?" Our conversation was getting one-sided.

"Well, it still is – but right on the edge, so to speak. It wasn't so bad then, though, and so I got permission to have a service done here, and down she went where I could go and see her. I still do go to see her, of course, now and then. But in another year or two . . . the sea . . ." He shrugged again. "Time and the tides, they wait for no man."

We finished our coffee. I was going to have to be on my way soon, and suddenly I didn't like the idea of leaving him. Already I could feel the loneliness creeping in. Perhaps he sensed my restlessness or something. Certainly I could see that he didn't want me to go just yet. In any case, he said: "Maybe you'd like to walk down with me past the old timber yard, visit her grave. Oh, it's safe enough, you don't have to worry. We may even come across old Ben down there. He sometimes visits her, too."

"Ah, well I'm not too sure about that," I answered. "The time, you know?" But by the time we got down the path to the gate I was asking: "How far is the churchyard, anyway?" Who could tell, maybe I'd find some long-lost Lanes in there! "Are there any old markers left standing?"

Garth chuckled and took my elbow. "It makes a change to have some company," he said. "Come on, it's this way."

He led the way back to the barrier where it spanned the road, bent his back and ducked groaning under it, then turned left up an overgrown communal path between gardens where the houses had been stepped down the declining gradient. The detached bungalow on our right – one of a pair still standing, while a third slumped on the raw edge of oblivion – had decayed almost to the point where it was collapsing inwards. Brambles luxuriated everywhere in its garden, completely enclosing it. The roof sagged and a chimney threatened to topple, making the whole structure seem highly suspect and more than a little dangerous.

"Partly subsidence, because of the undercutting action of the sea," Garth explained, "but mainly the rot. There was a lot of wood in these places, but it's all being eaten away. I made myself a living, barely, out of the old bricks and timber in Easingham, but now I have to be careful. Doesn't do to sell stuff with the rot in it."

"The rot?"

He paused for breath, leaned a hand on one hip, nodded and frowned. "Dry rot," he said. "Or *Merulius lacrymans* as they call it in the books. It's been bad these last three years. Very bad! But when the last of these old houses are gone, and what's left of the timber yard, then it'll be gone, too."

"It?" We were getting back to single-word questions again. "The dry rot, you mean? I'm afraid I don't know very much about it."

"Places on the coast are prone to it," he told me. "Whitby, Scarborough, places like that. All the damp sea spray and the bad plumbing, the rains that come in and the inadequate drainage. That's how it starts. It's a fungus, needs a lot of moisture – to get started, anyway. You don't know much about it? Heck, I used to think I knew *quite* a bit about it, but now I'm not so sure!''

By then I'd remembered something. "A friend of mine in London did mention to me how he was having to have his flat treated for it," I said, a little lamely. "Expensive, apparently."

Garth nodded, straightened up. "Hard to kill," he said. "And when it's active, moves like the plague! It's active here, now! Too late for Easingham, and who gives a damn anyway? But you tell that friend of yours to sort out his exterior maintenance first: the guttering and the drainage. Get rid of the water spillage, then deal with the rot. If a place is dry and airy, it's OK. Damp and musty spells danger!''

I nodded. "Thanks, I will tell him.''

"Want to see something?" said Garth. "I'll show you what old *merulius* can do. See here, these old paving flags? See if you can lever one up a bit." I found a piece of rusting iron stave and dragged it out of the ground where it supported a rotting fence, then forced the sharp end into a crack between the overgrown flags. And while I worked to loosen the paving stone, old Garth stood watching and carried on talking.

"Actually, there's a story attached, if you care to hear it," he said. "Probably all coincidental or circumstantial, or some other big word like that – but queer the way it came about all the same."

He was losing me again. I paused in my levering to look bemused (and maybe to wonder what on earth I was doing here), then grunted, and sweated, gave one more heave and flipped the flag over on to its back. Underneath was hard-packed sand. I looked at it, shrugged, looked at Garth.

He nodded in that way of his, grinned, said: "Look. Now tell me what you make of this!''

He got down on one knee, scooped a little of the sand away. Just under the surface his hands met some soft obstruction. Garth wrinkled his nose and grimaced, got his face down close to the earth, blew until his weakened lungs started him coughing. Then he sat back and rested. Where he'd scraped and blown the sand away, I made out what appeared to be a grey fibrous mass running at right angles right under the pathway. It was maybe six inches thick, looked like tightly packed cotton wool. It might easily have been glass fibre lagging for some pipe or other, and I said as much.

"But it isn't," Garth contradicted me. "It's a root, a feeler, a tentacle. It's old man cancer himself – timber cancer – on the move and looking for a new victim. Oh, you won't see him moving," that strange look was back on his face, "or at least you shouldn't – but he's at it anyway. He finished those houses there," he nodded at the derelicts stepping down towards the new cliffs, "and now he's gone into this one on the left here. Another couple of summers like this 'un and he'll be through the entire row to my place. Except maybe I'll burn him out first."

"You mean this stuff – this fibre – is dry rot?" I said. I stuck my hand into the stuff and tore a clump out. It made a soft tearing sound, like damp chipboard, except it was dry as old paper. "How do you mean, you'll 'burn him out?' "

"I mean like I say," said Garth. "I'll search out and dig up all these threads – mycelium, they're called – and set fire to 'em. They smoulder right through to a fine white ash. And God – it *stinks*! Then I'll look for the fruiting bodies, and –"

"The what?" His words had conjured up something vaguely obscene in my mind. "Fruiting bodies?"

"Lord, yes!" he said. "You want to see? Just follow me."

Leaving the path, he stepped over a low brick wall to struggle through the undergrowth of the garden on our left. Taking care not to get tangled up in the brambles, I followed him. The house seemed pretty much intact, but a bay window on the ground floor had been broken and all the glass tapped out of the frame. "My winter preparations," Garth explained. "I burn wood, see? So before winter comes, I get into a house like this one, rip out all the wooden fixings and break 'em down ready for burning. The wood just stays where I stack it, all prepared and waiting for the bad weather to come in. I knocked this window out last week, but I've not been inside yet. I could smell it, see?" He tapped his nose. "And I didn't much care for all those spores on my lungs."

He stepped up on a pile of bricks, got one leg over the sill and stuck his head inside. Then, turning his head in all directions, he systematically sniffed the air. Finally he seemed satisfied and disappeared inside. I followed him. "Spores?" I said. "What sort of spores?"

He looked at me, wiped his hand along the window ledge, held it up so that I could see the red dust accumulated on his fingers and palm. "*These* spores," he said. "Dry rot spores, of course! Haven't you been listening?"

"I *have* been listening, yes," I answered sharply. "But I ask you: spores, mycelium, fruiting bodies? I mean, I thought dry rot was just, well, rotting wood!"

"It's a fungus," he told me, a little impatiently. "Like a mushroom, and it spreads in much the same way. Except it's destructive, and once it gets started it's bloody hard to stop!"

"And you, an ex-coalminer," I started at him in the gloom of the house we'd invaded, "you're an expert on it, right? How come, Garth?"

Again there was that troubled expression on his face, and in the dim interior of the house he didn't try too hard to mask it. Maybe it had something to do with that story he'd promised to tell me, but doubtless he'd be as circuitous about that as he seemed to be about everything else. "Because I've read it up in books, that's how," he finally broke into my thoughts. "To occupy my time. When it first started to spread out of the old timber yard, I looked it up. It's –" He gave a sort of grimace. "– it's interesting, that's all."

By now I was wishing I was on my way again. But by that I mustn't be misunderstood: I'm an able-bodied man and I wasn't afraid of anything – and certainly not of Garth himself, who was just a lonely, canny old-timer – but all of this really was getting to be a waste of my time. I had just made my mind up to go back out through the window when he caught my arm.

"Oh, *yes*!" he said. "This place is really ripe with it! Can't you smell it? Even with the window bust wide open like this, and the place nicely dried out in the summer heat, still it's stinking the place out. Now just you come over here and you'll see what you'll see."

Despite myself, I was interested. And indeed I could smell . . . something. A cloying mustiness? A mushroomy taint? But not the nutty smell of fresh field mushrooms. More a sort of vile stagnation. Something dead might smell like this, long after the actual corruption has ceased . . .

Our eyes had grown somewhat accustomed to the gloom. We looked about the room. "Careful how you go," said Garth. "See the spores there? Try not to stir them up too much. They're worse than snuff, believe me!" He was right: the red dust lay fairly thick on just about everything. By "everything" I mean a few old sticks of furniture, the worn carpet under our feet, the skirting-board and various shelves and ledges. Whichever family had moved out of here, they hadn't left a deal of stuff behind them.

The skirting was of the heavy, old-fashioned variety: an inch and a half thick, nine inches deep, with a fancy moulding along the top edge; they hadn't spared the wood in those days. Garth peered suspiciously at the skirting-board, followed it away from the bay window and paused every pace to scrape the toe of his boot down its face. And eventually when he did this – suddenly the board crumbled to dust under the pressure of his toe!

It was literally as dramatic as that: the white paint cracked away and the timber underneath fell into a heap of black, smoking dust. Another pace and Garth kicked again, with the same result. He quickly exposed a ten-foot length of naked wall, on which even the plaster was loose and flaky, and showed me where strands of the cottonwool mycelium had come up between the brick-work and the plaster from below. "It sucks the cellulose right out of wood," he said. "Gets right into brickwork, too. Now look here," and he pointed at the old carpet under his feet. The threadbare weave showed a sort of raised floral blossom or stain, like a blotch or blister, spreading outward away from the wall.

Garth got down on his hands and knees. "Just look at this," he said. He tore up the carpet and carefully laid it back. Underneath, the floorboards were warped, dark-stained, shrivelled so as to leave wide gaps between them. And up through the gaps came those white, etiolated threads, spreading themselves along the underside of the carpet.

I wrinkled my nose in disgust. "It's like a disease," I said.

"It *is* a disease!" he corrected me. "It's a cancer, and houses die of it!" Then he inhaled noisily, pulled a face of his own, said: "Here. Right here." He pointed at the warped, rotting floorboards. "The very heart of it. Give me a hand." He got his fingers down between a pair of boards and gave a tug, and it was at once apparent that he wouldn't be needing any help from me. What had once been a stout wooden floorboard a full inch thick was now brittle as dry bark. It cracked upwards, flew apart, revealed the dark cavities between the floor joists. Garth tossed bits of crumbling wood aside, tore up more boards; and at last "the very heart of it" lay open to our inspection.

"There!" said Garth with a sort of grim satisfaction. He stood back and wiped his hands down his trousers. "Now *that* is what you call a fruiting body!"

It was roughly the size of a football, if not exactly that shape. Suspended between two joists in a cradle of fibres, and adhering to one of the joists as if partly flattened to it, the thing might have been a great, too-ripe tomato. It was bright yellow at its centre, banded in various shades of yellow from the middle out. It looked freakishly weird, like a bad joke: this lump of . . . of *stuff* – never a mushroom – just nestling there between the joists.

Garth touched my arm and I jumped a foot. He said: "You want to know where all the moisture goes – out of this wood, I mean? Well, just touch it."

"Touch . . . that?"

"Heck it can't bite you! It's just a fungus."

"All the same, I'd rather not," I told him.

He took up a piece of floorboard and prodded the thing – and it squelched. The splintered point of the wood sank into it like jelly. Its heart was mainly liquid, porous as a sponge. "Like a huge egg yolk, isn't it?" he said, his voice very quiet. He was plainly fascinated.

Suddenly I felt nauseous. The heat, the oppressive closeness of the room, the spore-laden air. I stepped dizzily backwards and stumbled against an old armchair. The rot had been there, too, for the chair just fragmented into a dozen pieces that puffed red dust all over the place. My foot sank right down through the carpet and mushy boards into darkness and stench – and in another moment I'd panicked.

Somehow I tumbled myself back out through the window, and ended up on my back in the brambles. Then Garth was standing over me, shaking his head and tut-tutting. "Told you not to stir up the dust," he said. "It chokes your air and stifles you. Worse than being down a pit. Are you all right?"

My heart stopped hammering and I was, of course, all right. I got up. "A touch of claustrophobia," I told him. "I suffer from it at times. Anyway, I think I've taken up enough of your time, Garth. I should be getting on my way."

"What?" he protested. "A lovely day like this and you want to be driving off somewhere? And besides, there were things I wanted to tell you, and others I'd ask you – and we haven't been down to Lily-Anne's grave." He looked disappointed. "Anyway, you shouldn't be driving if you're feeling all shaken up . . ."

He was right about that part of it, anyway: I did feel shaky, not to mention foolish! And perhaps more importantly, I was still very much aware of the old man's loneliness. What if it was my mother who'd died, and my father had been left on his own up in Durham? "Very well," I said, at the same time damning myself for a weak fool, "let's go and see Lily-Anne's grave."

"Good!" Garth slapped my back. "And no more diversions — we go straight there."

Following the paved path as before and climbing a gentle rise, we started walking. We angled a little inland from the unseen cliffs where the green, rolling fields came to an abrupt end and fell down to the sea; and as we went I gave a little thought to the chain of incidents in which I'd found myself involved through the last hour or so.

Now, I'd be a liar if I said that nothing had struck me as strange in Easingham, for quite a bit had. Not least the dry rot: its apparent profusion and migration through the place, and old Garth's peculiar knowledge and understanding of the stuff. His — affinity? — with it. "You said there was a story attached," I reminded him. "To that horrible fungus, I mean."

He looked at me sideways, and I sensed he was on the point of telling me something. But at that moment we crested the rise and the view just took my breath away. We could see for miles up and down the coast: to the slow, white breakers rolling in on some beach way to the north, and southwards to a distance-misted seaside town which might even be Whitby. And we paused to fill our lungs with good air blowing fresh off the sea.

"There," said Garth. "And how's this for freedom? Just me and old Ben and the gulls for miles and miles, and I'm not so sure but that this is the way I like it. Now wasn't it worth it to come up here? All this open space and the great curve of the horizon . . ." Then the look of satisfaction slipped from his face to be replaced by a more serious expression. "There's old Easingham's graveyard — what's left of it."

He pointed down towards the cliffs, where a badly weathered stone wall formed part of a square whose sides would have been maybe fifty yards long in the old days. But in those days there'd also been a stubby promontory and a church. Now only one wall, running parallel with the path, stood complete — beyond which two thirds of the churchyard had been claimed by the sea. Its occupants, too, I supposed.

"See that half-timbered shack," said Garth, pointing, "at this end of the graveyard? That's what's left of Johnson's Mill. Johnson's sawmill, that is. That shack used to be Old Man

Johnson's office. A long line of Johnsons ran a couple of farms that enclosed all the fields round here right down to the cliffs. Pasture, mostly, with lots of fine animals grazing right here. But as the fields got eaten away and the buildings themselves started to be threatened, that's when half the Johnsons moved out and the rest bought a big house in the village. They gave up farming and started the mill, working timber for the local building trade . . .

"Folks round here said it was a sin, all that noise of sawing and planing, right next door to a churchyard. But . . . it was Old Man Johnson's land after all. Well, the sawmill business kept going 'til a time some seven years ago, when a really bad blow took a huge bite right out of the bay one night. The seaward wall of the graveyard went, and half of the timber yard, too, and that closed old Johnson down. He sold what machinery he had left, plus a few stacks of good oak that hadn't suffered, and moved out lock, stock and barrel. Just as well, for the very next spring his big house and two others close to the edge of the cliffs got taken. The sea gets 'em all in the end.

"Before then, though – at a time when just about everybody else was moving out of Easingham – Lily-Anne and me had moved in! As I told you, we got our bungalow for a song, and of course we picked ourselves a house standing well back from the brink. We were getting on a bit; another twenty years or so should see us out; after that the sea could do its worst. But . . . well, it didn't quite work out that way."

While he talked, Garth had led the way down across the open fields to the graveyard wall. The breeze was blustery here and fluttered his words back into my face: "So you see, within just a couple of years of our settling here, the village was derelict, and all that remained of people was us and a handful of Johnsons still working the mill. Then Lily-Anne came down with something and died, and I had her put down in the ground here in Easingham – so's I'd be near her, you know?

"That's where the coincidences start to come in, for she went only a couple of months after the shipwreck. Now I don't suppose you'd remember that; it wasn't much, just an old Portuguese freighter that foundered in a storm. Lifeboats took the crew off, and she'd already unloaded her cargo somewhere up the coast, so the incident didn't create much of a to-do in the newspapers. But she'd carried a fair bit of hardwood ballast, that old ship, and balks of the stuff would keep drifting ashore:

great long twelve-by-twelves of it. Of course, Old Man Johnson wasn't one to miss out on a bit of good timber like that, not when it was being washed up right on his doorstep, so to speak . . .

"Anyway, when Lily-Anne died I made the proper arrangements, and I went down to see old Johnson who told me he'd make me a coffin out of this Haitian hardwood."

"Haitian?" Maybe my voice showed something of my surprise.

"That's right," said Garth, more slowly. He looked at me wonderingly. "Anything wrong with that?"

I shrugged, shook my head. "Rather romantic, I thought," I said. "Timber from a tropical isle."

"I thought so, too," he agreed. And after a while he continued: "Well, despite having been in the sea, the stuff could still be cut into fine, heavy panels, and it still French-polished to a beautiful finish. So that was that: Lily-Anne got a lovely coffin. Except –"

"Yes?" I prompted him.

He pursed his lips. "Except I got to thinking – later, you know – as to how maybe the rot came here in that wood. God knows it's a damn funny variety of fungus after all. But then this Haiti – well, apparently it's a damned funny place. They call it the Voodoo Island, you know?"

"Black magic?" I smiled. "I think we've advanced a bit beyond thinking such as that, Garth."

"Maybe and maybe not," he answered. "But voodoo or no voodoo, it's still a funny place, that Haiti. Far away and exotic . . ."

By now we'd found a gap in the old stone wall and climbed over the tumbled stones into the graveyard proper. From where we stood, another twenty paces would take us right to the raw edge of the cliff where it sheered dead straight through the overgrown, badly neglected plots and headstones. "So here it is," said Garth, pointing. "Lily-Anne's grave, secure for now in what little is left of Easingham's old graveyard." His voice fell a little, grew ragged: "But you know, the fact is I wish I'd never put her down here in the first place. And I'd give anything that I hadn't buried her in that coffin built of Old Man Johnson's ballast wood."

The plot was a neat oblong picked out in oval pebbles. It had been weeded round its border, and from its bottom edge to the foot of the simple headstone it was decked in flowers, some wild and others cut from Easingham's deserted gardens. It was deep in flowers, and the ones underneath were withered and had been compressed by those on top. Obviously Garth came here more often than just "now and then". It was the only plot in sight that had been paid any sort of attention, but in the circumstances that wasn't surprising.

"You're wondering why there are so many flowers, eh?" Garth sat down on a raised slab close by.

I shook my head, sat down beside him. "No, I know why. You must have thought the world of her."

"You don't know why," he answered. 'I did think the world of her, but that's not why. It's not the only reason, anyway. I'll show you."

He got down on his knees beside the grave, began laying aside the flowers. Right down to the marble chips he went, then scooped an amount of the polished gravel to one side. He made a small mound of it. Whatever I had expected to see in the small excavation, it wasn't the cylindrical, fibrous surface – like the upper section of a lagged pipe – which came into view. I sucked in my breath sharply.

There were tears in Garth's eyes as he flattened the marble chips back into place. "The flowers are so I won't see it if it ever breaks the surface," he said. "See, I can't bear the thought of that filthy stuff in her coffin. I mean, what if it's like what you saw under the floorboards in that house back there?" He sat down again, and his hands trembled as he took out an old wallet, and removed a photograph to give it to me. "That's Lily-Anne," he said. "But God! – I don't like the idea of that stuff fruiting on her . . ."

Aghast at the thoughts his words conjured, I looked at the photograph. A homely woman in her late fifties, seated in a chair beside a fence in a garden I recognized as Garth's. Except the garden had been well tended then. One shoulder seemed slumped a little, and though she smiled, still I could sense the pain in her face. "Just a few weeks before she died," said Garth. "It was her lungs. Funny that I worked in the pit all those years, and it was her lungs gave out. And now she's here, and so's this stuff."

I had to say something. "But . . . where did it come from? I mean, how did it come, well, here? I don't know much about dry rot, no, but I would have thought it confined itself to houses."

"That's what I was telling you," he said, taking back the photograph. "The British variety does. But not this stuff. It's weird and different! That's why I think it might have come here with that ballast wood. As to how it got into the churchyard: that's easy. Come and see for yourself."

I followed him where he made his way between the weedy plots towards the leaning, half-timbered shack. "Is that the source? Johnson's timber yard?"

He nodded. "For sure. But look here."

I looked where he pointed. We were still in the graveyard, approaching the tumbledown end wall, beyond which stood the derelict shack. Running in a parallel series along the dry ground, from the mill and into the graveyard, deep cracks showed through the tangled brambles, briars and grasses. One of these cracks, wider than the others, had actually split a heavy horizontal marble slab right down its length. Garth grunted. "That wasn't done last time I was here," he said.

"The sea's been at it again," I nodded. "Undermining the cliffs. Maybe we're not as safe here as you think."

He glanced at me. "Not the sea this time," he said, very definitely. "Something else entirely. See, there's been no rain for weeks. Everything's dry. And *it* gets thirsty same as we do. Give me a hand."

He stood beside the broken slab and got his fingers into the crack. It was obvious that he intended to open up the tomb. "Garth," I cautioned him. "Isn't this a little ghoulish? Do you really intend to desecrate this grave?"

"See the date?" he said. "1847. Heck, I don't think he'd mind, whoever he is. Desecration? Why, he might even thank us for a little sweet sunlight! What are you afraid of? There can only be dust and bones down there now."

Full of guilt, I looked all about while Garth struggled with the fractured slab. It was a safe bet that there wasn't a living soul for miles around, but I checked anyway. Opening graves isn't my sort of thing. But having discovered him for a stubborn old man, I knew that if I didn't help him he'd find a way to do it by himself anyway; and so I applied myself to the task. Between the two of us we wrestled one of the two halves to the edge of its base, finally toppled it over. A choking fungus reek at once rushed out to engulf us! Or maybe the smell was of something else and I'd simply smelled what I "expected" to.

Garth pulled a sour face. "*Ugh!*" was his only comment.

The air cleared and we looked into the tomb. In there, a coffin just a little over three feet long, and the broken sarcophagus around it filled with dust, cobwebs and a few leaves. Garth glanced at me out of the corner of his eye. "So now you think I'm wrong, eh?"

"About what?" I answered. "It's just a child's coffin."

"Just a little 'un, aye," he nodded. "And his little coffin looks intact, doesn't it? *But is it?*" Before I could reply he reached down and rapped with his horny knuckles on the wooden lid.

And despite the fact that the sun was shining down on us, and for all that the seagulls cried and the world seemed at peace, still my hair stood on end at what happened next. For the coffin lid collapsed like a puff-ball and fell into dusty debris, and – God help me – *something in the box gave a grunt and puffed itself up into view!*

I'm not a coward, but there are times when my limbs have a will of their own. Once when a drunk insulted my wife, I struck him without consciously knowing I'd done it. It was that fast, the reaction that instinctive. And the same now. I didn't pause to draw breath until I'd cleared the wall and was half-way up the field to the paved path; and even then I probably wouldn't have stopped, except I tripped and fell flat, and knocked all the wind out of myself.

By the time I stopped shaking and sat up, Garth was puffing and panting up the slope towards me. "It's all right," he was gasping. "It was nothing. Just the rot. It had grown in there and crammed itself so tight, so confined, that when the coffin caved in . . ."

He was right and I knew it. I *had* known it even with my flesh crawling, my legs, heart and lungs pumping. But even so: "There were . . . *bones* in it!" I said, contrary to common sense. "A skull."

He drew close, sank down beside me gulping at the air. "The little 'un's bones," he panted, "caught up in the fibres. I just wanted to show you the extent of the thing. Didn't want to scare you to death!"

"I know, I know," I patted his hand. "But when it moved –"

"It was just the effect of the box collapsing," he explained, logically. "Natural expansion. Set free, it unwound like a jack-in-the-box. And the noise it made –"

"That was the sound of its scraping against the rotten timber, amplified by the sarcophagus," I nodded. "I know all that. It shocked me, that's all. In fact, two hours in your bloody Easingham have given me enough shocks to last a lifetime!''

"But you see what I mean about the rot?" We stood up, both of us still a little shaky.

"Oh, yes, I see what you mean. I don't understand your obsession, that's all. Why don't you just leave the damned stuff alone?''

He shrugged but made no answer, and so we made our way back towards his home. On our way the silence between us was broken only once. "There!" said Garth, looking back towards the brow of the hill. "You see him?"

I looked back, saw the dark outline of an Alsatian dog silhouetted against the rise. "Ben?" Even as I spoke the name, so the dog disappeared into the long grass beside the path.

"Ben!" Garth called, and blew his piercing whistle. But with no result. The old man worriedly shook his head. "Can't think what's come over him," he said. "Then again, I'm more his friend than his master. We've always pretty much looked after ourselves. At least I know that he hasn't run off . . .''

Then we were back at Garth's house, but I didn't go in. His offer of another coffee couldn't tempt me. It was time I was on my way again. "If ever you're back this way –" he said as I got into the car.

I nodded, leaned out of my window. "Garth, why the hell don't you get out of here? I mean, there's nothing here for you now. Why don't you take Ben and just clear out?''

He smiled, shook his head, then shook my hand. "Where'd we go?" he asked. "And anyway, Lily-Anne's still here. Sometimes in the night, when it's hot and I have trouble sleeping, I can feel she's very close to me. Anyway, I know you mean well.''

That was that. I turned the car round and drove off, acknowledged his final wave by lifting my hand briefly, so that he'd see it.

Then, driving round a gentle bend and as the old man sideslipped out of my rear-view mirror, I saw Ben. He was crossing the road in front of me. I applied my brakes, let him get out of the way. It could only be Ben, I supposed: a big Alsatian, shaggy, yellow-eyed. And yet I caught only a glimpse; I was more interested in controlling the car, in being sure that he was safely out of the way.

It was only after he'd gone through the hedge and out of sight into a field that an after-image of the dog surfaced in my mind: the way he'd seemed to limp – his belly hairs, so long as to hang down and trail on the ground, even though he wasn't slinking – a bright splash of yellow on his side, as if he'd brushed up against something freshly painted.

Perhaps understandably, peculiar images bothered me all the way back to London; yes, and for quite a long time after . . .

Before I knew it a year had gone by, then eighteen months, and memories of those strange hours spent in Easingham were fast receding. Faded with them was that promise I had made myself to visit my parents more frequently. Then I got a letter to say my mother hadn't been feeling too well, and another right on its heels to say she was dead. She'd gone in her sleep, nice and easy. This last was from a neighbour of theirs: my father wasn't much up to writing right now, or much up to anything else for that matter; the funeral would be on . . . at . . . etc., etc.

God! – how guilty I felt driving up there, and more guilty with every mile that flashed by under my car's wheels. And all I could do was choke the guilt and the tears back and drive, and feel the dull, empty ache in my heart that I knew my father would be feeling in his. And of course that was when I remembered old Garth Bentham in Easingham, and my "advice" that he should get out of that place. It had been a cold sort of thing to say to him. Even cruel. But I hadn't known that then. I hadn't thought.

We laid Ma to rest and I stayed with the Old Man for a few days, but he really didn't want me around. I thought about saying: "Why don't you sell up, come and live with us in London?" We had plenty of room. But then I thought of Garth again and kept my mouth shut. Dad would work it out for himself in the fullness of time.

It was late on a cold Wednesday afternoon when I started out for London again, and I kept thinking how lonely it must be in old Easingham. I found myself wondering if Garth ever took a belt or filled a pipe, if he could even afford to, and . . . I'd promised him that if I was ever back up this way I'd look him up, hadn't I? I stopped at an off-licence, bought a bottle of half-decent whisky and some pipe and rolling baccy, and a carton of two hundred cigarettes and a few cigars. Whatever was his pleasure, I'd probably covered it. And if he didn't smoke, well I could always give the tobacco goods to someone who did.

My plan was to spend just an hour with Garth, then head for

the motorway and drive to London in darkness. I don't mind driving in the dark, when the weather and visibility are good and the driving lanes all but empty, and the night music comes sharp and clear out of the radio to keep me awake.

But approaching Easingham down that neglected cul-de-sac of a road, I saw that I wasn't going to have any such easy time of it. A storm was gathering out to sea, piling up the thunderheads like beetling black brows all along the twilight horizon. I could see continuous flashes of lightning out there, and even before I reached my destination I could hear the high seas thundering against the cliffs. When I did get there –

Well, I held back from driving quite as far as the barrier, because only a little way beyond it my headlights had picked out black, empty space. Of the three houses which had stood closest to the cliffs only one was left, and that one slumped right on the rim. So I stopped directly opposite Garth's place, gave a honk on my horn, then switched off and got out of the car with my carrier-bag full of gifts. Making my way to the house, the rush and roar of the sea was perfectly audible, transferring itself physically through the earth to my feet. Indeed the bleak, unforgiving ocean seemed to be working itself up into a real fury.

Then, in a moment, the sky darkened over and the rain came on out of nowhere, bitter-cold and squally, and I found myself running up the overgrown garden path to Garth's door. Which was when I began to feel really foolish. There was no sign of life behind the grimy windows; neither a glimmer of light showing, nor a puff of smoke from the chimney. Maybe Garth had taken my advice and got out of it after all.

Calling his name over the rattle of distant thunder, I knocked on the door. After a long minute there was still no answer. But this was no good; I was getting wet and angry with myself; I tried the doorknob, and the door swung open. I stepped inside, into deep gloom, and groped on the wall near the door for a light switch. I found it, but the light wasn't working. Of course it wasn't: there was no electricity! This was a ghost town, derelict, forgotten. And the last time I was here it had been in broad daylight.

But . . . Garth had made coffee for me. On a gas-ring? It must have been.

Standing there in the small cloakroom shaking rain off myself, my eyes were growing more accustomed to the gloom.

The cloakroom seemed just as I remembered it: several pieces of tall, dark furniture, pine-panelled inner walls, the old grand-father clock standing in one corner. Except that this time . . . the clock wasn't clucking. The pendulum was still, a vertical bar of brassy fire when lightning suddenly brought the room to life. Then it was dark again – if anything even darker than before – and the windows rattled as thunder came down in a rolling, receding drumbeat.

"Garth!" I called again, my voice echoing through the old house. "It's me, Greg Lane. I said I'd drop in some time . . . ?" No answer, just the *hiss* of the rain outside, the feel of my collar damp against my neck, and the thick, rising smell of . . . of what? And suddenly I remembered very clearly the details of my last visit here.

"Garth!" I tried one last time, and I stepped to the door of his living-room and pushed it open. As I did so there came a lull in the beating rain. I heard the floorboards creak under my feet, but I also heard . . . a groan? My sensitivity at once rose by several degrees. Was that Garth? Was he hurt? *My God!* What had he said to me that time? "One of these days the postman will find me stretched out in here, and he'll think: 'Well, I needn't come out here any more.' "

I had to have light. There'd be matches in the kitchen, maybe even a torch. In the absence of a mains supply, Garth would surely have to have a torch. Making my way shufflingly, very cautiously across the dark room towards the kitchen, I was conscious that the smell was more concentrated here. Was it just the smell of an old, derelict house, or was it something worse? Then, outside, lightning flashed again, and briefly the room was lit up in a white glare. Before the darkness fell once more, I saw someone slumped on the old settee where Garth had served me coffee . . .

"Garth?" the word came out half strangled. I hadn't wanted to say it; it had just gurgled from my tongue. For though I'd seen only a silhouette, outlined by the split-second flash, it hadn't looked like Garth at all. It had been much more like someone else I'd once seen – in a photograph. That drooping right shoulder.

My skin prickled as I stepped on shivery feet through the open door into the kitchen. I forced myself to draw breath, to think clearly. *If* I'd seen anyone or anything at all back there (it could have been old boxes piled on the settee, or a roll of carpet leaning there), then it most probably had been Garth, which would explain that groan. It *was* him, of course it was. But in the storm, and remembering what I did of this place, my mind was playing morbid tricks with me. No, it was Garth, and he could well be in serious trouble. I got a grip of myself, quickly looked all around.

A little light came into the kitchen through a high back window. There was a two-ring gas cooker, a sink and draining-board with a drawer under the sink. I pulled open the drawer and felt about inside it. My nervous hand struck what was unmistakably a large box of matches, and – yes, the smooth heavy cylinder of a hand torch!

And all the time I was aware that someone was or might be slumped on a settee just a few swift paces away through the door to the living-room. With my hand still inside the drawer, I pressed the stud of the torch and was rewarded when a weak beam probed out to turn my fingers pink. Well, it wasn't a powerful beam, but any sort of light had to be better than total darkness.

Armed with the torch, which felt about as good as a weapon in my hand, I forced myself to move back into the living-room and directed my beam at the settee. But oh, Jesus – all that sat there was a monstrous grey mushroom! It was a great fibrous mass, growing out of and welded with mycelium strands to the settee, and in its centre an obscene yellow fruiting body. But for God's sake, it had the shape and outline and *look* of an old woman, and it had Lily-Anne's deflated chest and slumped shoulder!

I don't know how I held on to the torch, how I kept from screaming out loud, why I simply didn't fall unconscious. That's the sort of shock I experienced. But I did none of these things. Instead, on nerveless legs, I backed away, backed right into an old wardrobe or Welsh-dresser. At least, I backed into what had once been a piece of furniture. But now it was something else.

Soft as sponge, the thing collapsed and sent me sprawling. Dust and (I imagined) dark red spores rose up everywhere, and I skidded on my back in shards of crumbling wood and matted webs of fibre. And lolling out of the darkness behind where the dresser had stood – bloating out like some loathsome puppet or dummy – a second fungoid figure leaned towards me. And this time it was a caricature of Ben!

He lolled there, held up on four fibre legs, muzzle snarling soundlessly, for all the world tensed to spring – and all he was was a harmless fungous thing. And yet this time I did scream. Or I think I did, but the thunder came to drown me out.

Then I was on my feet, and my feet were through the rotten floorboards, and I didn't care except I had to get out of there, out of that choking, stinking, collapsing –

I stumbled, *crumbled* my way into the tiny cloakroom, tripped and crashed into the clock where it stood in the corner. It was like a nightmare chain reaction which I'd started and couldn't stop; the old grandfather just crumpled up on itself, its metal parts clanging together as the wood disintegrated around them. And all the furniture following suit, and the very wall panelling smoking into ruin where I fell against it.

And there where that infected timber had been, there he stood – old Garth himself! He leaned half out of the wall like a great nodding manikin, his entire head a livid yellow blotch, his arm and hand making a noise like a huge puff-ball bursting underfoot where they separated from his side to point floppingly towards the open door. I needed no more urging.

"God! Yes! I'm *going!*" I told him, as I plunged out into the storm . . .

After that . . . nothing, not for some time. I came to in a hospital in Stokesley about noon the next day. Apparently I'd run off the road on the outskirts of some village or other, and they'd dragged me out of my car where it lay upside-down in a ditch. I was banged up and so couldn't do much talking, which is probably as well.

But in the newspapers I read how what was left of Easingham had gone into the sea in the night. The churchyard, Haitian timber, terrible dry rot fungus, the whole thing, sliding down into the sea and washed away for ever on the tides.

And yet now I sometimes think: Where did all that wood *go* that Garth had been selling for years? And what of all those spores I'd breathed and touched and rolled around in? And sometimes when I think things like that it makes me feel quite ill.

I suppose I shall just have to wait and see . . .

CHARLES L. GRANT

Needle Song

CHARLES L. GRANT'S CAREER has spanned more than thirty-five years and during that time he has won, among other honours, three World Fantasy Awards and two Nebulas from the Science Fiction-Fantasy Writers Association. A recipient of the British Fantasy Society's Special Award and the Horror Writers Association's Lifetime Achievement Award, he was also named Grand Master at the 2002 World Horror Convention.

A prolific short story writer and novelist, he has cultivated his unique style of "quiet horror" in many novels and collections, including *The Curse, The Hour of the Oxrun Dead, The Sound of Midnight, The Grave, The Bloodwind, The Soft Whisper of the Dead, The Nestling, The Tea Party, The Orchard, The Pet, For Fear of the Night, In a Dark Dream, Dialing the Wind, Stunts, Something Stirs, Jackals, The Black Carousel, Tales from the Nightside, A Glow of Candles* and *Nightmare Seasons*. More recent titles include the first two *X Files* novelizations, *Goblin* and *Whirlwind*, the "Millennium Quartet" inspired by the Four Horsemen of the Apocalypse, and the "Black Oak" series about a security team of paranormal investigators. Grant has also published a number of books under the pseudonyms "Geoffrey Marsh" and "Lionel Fenn".

As an editor he is responsible for two dozen anthologies, including the influential *Shadows* series (twelve volumes) along with *Nightmares, Midnight, Greystone Bay, The Dodd Mead Gallery of Horror* and *Gothic Ghosts* (with Wendy Webb).

With his wife, editor and novelist Kathryn Ptacek, Grant lives in a century-old haunted Victorian house in Sussex County, New Jersey.

"I also write and edit books like this one," explains the author, "ones that if all goes well will give their readers a good dose of the chills, the shudders, and the outright shrieks now and then. After all, if the truth be known, we haven't grown up all that much; the fears we have now aren't the same as they were when we were children, but they're fears just the same. They make our palms sweat, they give us nightmares, and they're sometimes powerful enough to alter our characters."

IN A LIVING ROOM, sparse and battered furniture had been formed into a square so that, in her darkness, the old woman could find them, avoid them without the tap of her probing white-tipped cane. There were neither rugs on the floors nor pictures on the walls, and only a single shadeless lamp. No matter the day or the weather, she always wore the same dress, an oddly shapeless garment whose colors seemed dead for centuries. Her hair was decades long, braided and coiled into a silver basket round the top of her head, and her face and arms and thin-strong legs were shadowed with ancient wrinkles.

But as she sat at her piano, her hands glided out from long, laced sleeves, and they were beautiful.

Eric sat quietly on the family-room floor, his short legs pulled up tight in awkward Indian fashion, his back resting stiffly against the dark oak paneling that covered the walls to the ceiling. His hands, as pinkly puffed as the rest of him, were folded in his lap, and for a moment he smiled, thinking of how his teacher would approve. Caren lay on the overstuffed couch, her white-blonde hair sifting down over her face. One hand dangled almost to the floor, and when, in her sleep, she whimpered once it jerked up to her cheek, touched, and fell again. He was tempted to wake her but didn't want to move, didn't want to whisper. The slightest sound might spoil the battle, might make him miss the music, and then it would be too late.

He stared instead at the walls and the pictures there of his father's favorite game birds. Then he tried to count the floor's black-and-white tiles, but his eyes blurred and he had to shake his head to clear his vision. A fly, perhaps the last of the year, darted across the room, swerved toward him, and made him duck. Automatically, his hands unclenched, remembered, and settled again. His knees ached where he had scraped them the day before. Caren sighed.

Through the two windows above the couch he could see the brown-edged leaves of a ribbon of flowers his mother had planted along the front of the house. They had been green once, like all the others in the neighborhood; watered, dusted with aerosol sprays, and caressed with eyes that loved and appreciated them. By stretching very slightly he could see beyond the single row of faded bricks that separated the garden from the lawn. The grass was hidden, but he knew it was dying anyway, a perfect camouflage for the leaves that sailed from the elms and willows.

I wish I knew what I was doing, he thought as he lowered his gaze to Caren again. I never killed no one before. But I guess it's got to be done or she'll kill us all first. I know it. I know she will.

Visions of his parents, of Caren's, of all the others, lying in the street like so much discarded trash.

Visions of television shows, of movies, of twisted evil women burning at the stake and laughing, having their heads cut off and their mouths stuffed with garlic, fading to corpse-grey dust at the first touch of daylight.

Visions, and it was all supposed to be make-believe, and the witch/vampire/werewolf wounds just makeup that washed off with soap.

A strong gust of wind drummed twigs against the windows, and Caren moaned softly in her sleep. As she rolled over onto her back, Eric wondered if he should have talked to some of the others. But he knew most of them would have been too frightened to do anything but call for their mothers. In fact, Caren was the only one who believed all that he said, and was the only one who was willing to join in the fight.

Maybe, he thought, we're both a little nuts. Even in the stories, vampires only drink blood.

But his father, he recalled, had been complaining about something called deterioration, depreciation, and plummeting values just before he had been hospitalized, and perhaps if Eric understood it more he might be convinced that this was what was killing the street, and all the other streets in all the other towns. He frowned, scratched at his chin, and rhythmically, lightly, thumped his head back against the wall. Maybe. And maybe his father was so involved in just being an adult that he couldn't see what was real anymore. That's what Caren had said after her spaniel puppy had been killed by a driver who hadn't even bothered to stop to say he was sorry.

Murder.

The word popped into his mind unbidden.

"Eric," Caren had said that afternoon, "we can't just break into the house and kill her. How can you kill her?"

"I don't know. Maybe we can find a gun somewhere, knock her out, and I don't know, cut off her head or something."

"You're being silly."

"Kids kill people all the time. I see it on the news at night."

"Big kids," she said, pulling nervously at her hair. "We'll have to think of something else."

"Like what?"

"I don't know, but we'll think of something."

He shifted to ease the discomfort creeping up his back, then rubbed his palms against his thighs. The sun went down unwatched, and the windows went briefly black before reflecting the single light from the floor lamp near the steps. He stretched his legs straight out ahead of him, and his heels squeaked on the tiles. Caren jumped, swung her legs to the floor, and sat up.

"It's okay," he said, grateful for the chance to get to his feet. "Nothing's happened yet. Do you want to sleep some more?"

"No," and her voice was younger, smaller than the size of her dozen years. "Do you think she'll do it tonight? It hasn't been regular for a long time."

Eric shrugged, stretched up to his toes so he could see the house across the street. "Her light is still on."

"It always is. Even in the day."

"You want something to drink? I think Mom left some soda in the kitchen for us."

"No," she said. "I don't want to leave her, not yet. Maybe we should call Jackie and see if she can come over, too."

"She's always crying, Caren. She can't help. Besides, she's too young to understand. We have to do it alone." He placed his hands on his hips, a gesture his father used to indicate finality. "Do you think you can remember enough good things?"

Caren nodded, rubbing at her eyes, then began swinging her legs. The room seemed large with shadows in the corners, but neither of them made a move to turn on the lights embedded in the white ceiling. Instead, they stared at the backless clock on the far wall, and willed the hands to sweep to nine.

Caren marked the seconds by tapping a nail against her palm.

Eric wondered why no one else knew.

The fingers that rested on the keys were like ten wings of five sleeping humming birds, and they were slender and long. They hesitated, as if undecided about waking up and what to do when they did. The ivory was yellowed in blotches and stains, but the velvet-coated hammers were young and deep blue. The old woman breathed deeply to draw in what she felt, assimilated it and translated it to the language of the wings that fluttered now, darted and glided, a polka and waltz, and from the depths of the piano the music came back.

Hawthorne Street was a community unto itself, and no one who lived there would have had it any other way. Along its entire length, all families were neighbors and all children friends. The seasons were shared with garden-hose batons, snow-blower basso; pets roamed free, and every yard but one had a hole in its hedge for the passing of gossip. Tree houses sprouted, sidewalks were chalked, but the unofficial leader was Eric because his home faced the unlucky Number 136. Of all the houses on the street, only this one could not keep a family; three in less than two years, not because it was haunted, but because the people were not able to penetrate the tightly meshed lives of everyone else.

Then, Eric remembered, came last September and the smallest moving van he had ever seen pulled into the ragged blacktop driveway and unloaded: one odd-angled piano a disturbingly deep black, one polished cedar hope chest that took three men to carry, one greying wicker chair slightly unstrung, and a bench of burnished copper. He and Caren had loitered on the curb waiting for signs of children or pets, but there was nothing else in the van, and after one of the men had relocked the front door, it pulled away and did not return.

A week passed, and suddenly Caren had pounded on the front door, dragged Eric into the street. In Number 136, in the dirtstreaked picture window, were wine-red curtains. A light glowed behind them, and no one ever saw it go off. Four days more to a Saturday waiting for autumn, and an old, very old woman appeared on the front lawn. She sat like a weathered totem in the wicker chair, her head covered by a sun hat whose brim dropped to her shoulders. She did nothing but sit. Watch. And sit until dark. Repeated every day until November's cold drove her inside.

One by one, or in reassuring groups, the children passed by, waving, and receiving no response. Eric had been the only one with nerve enough to call her a greeting, but only a breeze moved.

"I think she's blind," he said to Caren on the way to school just before the Thanksgiving holiday.

"Deaf, too," she said, grinning, receiving a grin in return.

And though they pestered their parents daily, they could get no satisfactory answers about the odd woman's origins, her designs, why she never invited anyone in for tea or cookies and soda.

She became, simply, the Old Lady, and a superstition instantly born prevented any of the younger children from passing her house on her side of the street.

And then, one cold and snow-ready night, when Hawthorne Street stayed home and huddled, richly, in front of fieldstone fireplaces and gleaming Franklin stoves, the music began. Precisely at nine o'clock the November chill was warmed by glittering sparks that sifted through the windows and doors and startled the people who heard.

Hey, a circus, Eric thought, running to the living room to look up and down the street.

Hey, Mom, Caren had called, there's one of those guys with the monkey and the thing that you turn.

There was a lullaby, a love song, memories of dance bands, carnivals, and boardwalk calliopes on a hot August night.

For thirty minutes to the second before it stopped, and the notes fell like powdered snow to vanish into the ground.

"Eric?"

He spun around, blinking, then glaring at Caren's silent laugh.

"What's the matter, did I scare you?"

"Not me," he said. "You kind of just snuck up on me, that's all. What's the matter? You need something, or something?"

"I was thinking about the time she came," and she shivered an exaggerated chill, making him laugh. "Remember the time we tried to sneak a look through the back window and Jackie started sneezing because of her hay fever and we didn't stop running until we must have got all the way to the park?"

"I wasn't scared then, either."

"I didn't say you were, silly."

"Then why'd you have to say all that? Don't we have enough troubles?"

"I was just trying to remember, Eric, that's all."

"Okay, I'm sorry, but you'd better save it. I think I can feel it coming."

Remember, he thought in disgust. Just like a girl to waste her time remembering when we got things to do more important. And what good would it do asking for things to be the way they were anyway?

Throughout that winter, it seemed as if what rainbows there were had all spilled into a vast shimmering pot called Hawthorne Street, and all on the heels of the music.

Caren's brother was accepted into a European university with full scholarship honors; Eric discovered he had a natural talent for musical instruments, and horns in particular, and his teacher told him in all honesty that he would someday be famous; Jackie Potter's family won a state lottery and planned a trip across the country during Easter vacation; and there seemed nothing at all wrong in standing by the front window and listening to the piano drawing them closer, stirring their emotions while it accompanied snow onto the lawns, ice into puddles, and guided the wind to cradle dead leaves softly into the gutters. The snowmen were bigger, the snow forts more elaborate, and Eric's father came home twice with promotions and once with a car big enough to hold thousands.

Eric scrubbed his cheeks dryly. It was no good remembering things like that because it wasn't that way anymore, and it was all because of a vampire witch who sucked them dry with her music.

It was April when the weekly concerts stopped, and while most of the people worried for a while, no one thought to visit the old woman to see if there was anything wrong. It was as if the children's superstition had been universally accepted, and when Eric suggested they try again to sneak a look into the Old Lady's house, Caren became angry and told him to leave the poor thing alone.

In May a fire destroyed the oldest house on the street, Caren's brother was arrested for possession of drugs and assault with a deadly weapon, and Eric's grandfather died in the guest room, in his sleep. New grass was planted, was washed away during three consecutive storms that knocked out power for three days, flooded every waterproof cellar, and uprooted a maple that was reputed to have been planted by the town's original settlers.

Caren's puppy died.

Eric's father was forced out of work and into a hospital bed by a series of massive heart attacks.

The elms rotted from the inside, and the willows crawled with worms that soon stopped their weeping.

The music came again, at odd hours for nearly a week, stopped just as abruptly, and what grass was left began dying in the middle of a shower.

All the houses needed painting, gardens weeding, and red brick shaded to brown.

Something had been taken away, something was missing, but few people cared, fewer still knew.

"Hey, listen, if you're going to sleep, I'm going home."

Eric grinned stupidly. He was sitting against the wall again, and his head felt stuffed with cotton like a baby's toy.

"I thought we weren't supposed to be thinking yet."

"Okay, I'm sorry again," he said, crossing the room to sit with her on the couch. "I just can't help it."

"I know what you mean. Do you . . . do you think we can fight her?"

He looked at her carefully before nodding.

"What if we're wrong?"

"We're not, I told you."

"Then let's get going."

The music. It came at them through the dead leaves and grass and age-bent trees. The melody varied, wavered, changed.

"Maybe we should put cotton in our ears or something."

"Eric, I'm frightened."

There was a sliver of a tear in the corner of her eye, and he looked away to avoid seeing it slither down her satin cheek.

"Don't be," he said. "Just remember that time we put the snake in Mrs Green's desk."

"That was dumb."

"It was funny, remember?" He turned back, insistent, a hand reaching to grab her shoulder before it pulled away. "It was funny," he repeated slowly, and took a breath to laugh.

"Sort of," she said, hinting a smile, "but not as much as the picnic we went on with the Potters. Remember how you kept falling on your fat face in that sack race thing? I thought you were going to start digging holes with your nose."

The music, searching for crevices in their conversation, cracks in their memories.

Eric giggled, clamped a hand over his mouth, then leaned back and filled the room with high-pitched laughter.

"You –" he said, gulping for air, "you on that stupid pony. You should have seen your face when the saddle fell off."

Caren winced. "Well, it hurt, dope. Hey, remember the Christmas your father made me that doll? And your mother made all her clothes? I still have it, you know. Of course, I'm too old to play with it, but I like to look at it now and then."

"Good," Eric said, jumping onto the couch to look out the window. "Hey," he shouted, "what about the time we found the bird in the yard."

"Robin."

"Right. Remember how we used the eyedropper to feed it until it learned to fly?"

"A cat could have eaten it," Caren said, shuddering.

"Yeah, but we saved it!"

Eric clambered to the floor and improvised an impatient dance while he slapped at his sides to jog loose more memories, anything at all he could throw at the music.

"Wait a minute," Caren said. "What about the time we went to the beach that summer? You won me an elephant at the stand."

He stopped, almost choking in his desperation to find more words. "Nothing to it," he said finally. "Them bottles is easy to knock down."

Her hands stopped and she pushed herself away from the keyboard. Carefully, with the measured steps of the practiced blind, she crossed the bare floor to the old chest and opened it. With deliberate care she pulled out what was once a large black square of satin. It was covered, now, except for one small corner, with colors that danced, sang in harmony, and laughed; never blending, capturing light, repelling a tear.

"Eric—"
  "Hey, remember—"
  "Eric, it's finished!"
  He blinked, listened, heard nothing, and let his small chest sag in relief.
  "Hey," he said proudly, "we ain't so little, are we?"

She sat on the bench facing the red curtains. Methodically she arranged the satin across her knees, touching each thread line that led to the corner. A needle sharp with use glinted in her right hand, and a single web of many lights dropped from its eye into a plain brown sack at her feet. Then her eyes seemed to clear and she waited, poised, humming arcane tunes to herself and the chest that was filled to the brim with bright on dark.

"You probably think you're pretty smart," Caren said.
  "Sure am. It was my idea, wasn't it? I put it all together and figured out that the Old Lady was taking away all our happiness with that music we was hearing, didn't I? And that's what was making all the bad things happen, right?"
  "Well—"
  "—and didn't I say that we had to show her that we were still doing all right anyway? And now that we did, she'll move away and never come back because we were too much for her. We beat the music."
  "Well, it's done now," she said, and grinned.
  "Sure is," he said, grinning, wiping his forehead with his sleeve.

The needle shimmered, dipped, ready to extend the rainbow.

"When's your mother coming home from the hospital?"
  "I don't know. She said she was going to look in on someone, I don't know who, on her way back."
  They stared at each other across the room, then gathered in air and screeched it out in a victory yell that shattered all their doubts. Eric fetched two cans of soda, opening one and immediately pouring it over Caren's head.
  "I told you I was right, and I was, right?"

Caren grabbed for the other can, but he ducked away. "So what?" she said, laughing. "Nobody's going to believe us. They don't know she was some kind of a witch thing."

"What do you care?" he shouted, leaping onto the couch to avoid her grasp. "We're still heroes. And everything will be all right, you'll see."

The needle darted.

"One of these days," he said, "I'm going to be the world's best trumpet player, and you can come to my opening and tell everyone you know me."

"No thanks," she said. "You look like an elephant with that horn in your mouth."

He laughed, leaped over the arm. But he wasn't fast enough to escape Caren's hand, and in a minute the second container of soda was emptied over his head, and Caren, for good measure, rubbed it in like shampoo.

"I don't care," he shouted. "I don't care."

The corner was nearly finished. She hummed, knowing her fingers would stop in just a minute. Then tie. Bite. And she gathered the cloth to her chest and breathed deeply the musty mausoleum odor of the house. Then she dropped the spectrumed satin into the chest with the others. One day, she thought, she would sew herself a new dress of a thousand colors and be young again. But there was one more town . . .

She locked the chest with a pass of her hand.

And the light went out.

"Hey, we'd better clean this up before your mother gets home."

Eric looked at the still bubbling soda spilled all over the tiles, and he nodded. His arms felt leaden, his legs began to stiffen, and the stuffing in his head wouldn't go away. Caren prodded him again, and he ran toward the stairs, didn't hear her warning yell until it was too late. His foot slid in one of the puddles and, in trying to wave his arms to keep his balance, pitched face forward into the corner with the lamp.

Caren paled when he finally turned around, groaning, and she screamed when he dropped his hands from his face and smeared the blood that ran from his lips.

CHRISTOPHER FOWLER

Turbo-Satan

CHRISTOPHER FOWLER LIVES AND WORKS in central London, where he is a director of the Soho movie marketing company The Creative Partnership, producing TV and radio scripts, documentaries, trailers and promotional shorts. He spends the remainder of his time writing short stories and novels, and he contributes a regular column about the cinema to *The 3rd Alternative*.

His books include the novels *Roofworld*, *Rune*, *Red Bride*, *Darkest Day*, *Spanky*, *Psychoville*, *Disturbia*, *Soho Black*, *Calabash*, *Full Dark House* and *The Water House*, and such short story collections as *The Bureau of Lost Souls*, *City Jitters*, *Sharper Knives*, *Flesh Wounds*, *Personal Demons*, *Uncut*, *The Devil in Me* and *Demonized*. *Breathe* is a new novella from Telos Publishing.

Fowler's short story "Wageslaves" won the 1998 British Fantasy Award, and he also scripted the 1997 graphic novel *Menz Insana*, illustrated by John Bolton.

"'Turbo-Satan' sprang from watching a TV series about tower blocks," recalls Fowler, "and how teenagers were setting up and destroying each other's pirate radio stations on the rooftops.

"I also wanted to do a new 'urban legend' story involving

mobile phones, but needed an unguessable outcome rather than the usual 'then the Devil appears' kind of ending such stories attract.

"Hopefully readers won't be prepared for the punch-line to this!"

IT WAS A SATURDAY afternoon in East London when Mats reordered his world.

Balancing under leaking concrete eaves, looking out on such dingy grey rain that he could have been trapped inside a fish tank in need of a good clean, he felt more than usually depressed. The student curse: no money, no dope, no fags, no booze, nothing to do, nowhere to go, no-one who cared if he went missing for all eternity. He had chosen to be like this, had got what he wanted, and now he didn't want it.

Withdrawn inside his padded grey Stussy jacket, he sat beneath the stilted flats, on the railing with the torn-up paint-work that had been ground away by the block's Huckjam skateboarders who ripped up their own bones more than they flipped any cool moves, because this wasn't Dogtown, it was Tower Hamlets, toilet of the world, arse-end of the universe, and every extra minute he spent here Mats could feel his soul dying, incrementally planed away by the sheer debilitating sweep of life's second hand. London's a great place if you have plans, he thought, otherwise you sit and wait and listen to the clocks ticking. He should never have turned down his father's offer of a monthly cheque.

"You're late," he complained to Daz, when Daz finally showed up. "Every minute we're getting older, every hour passed is another lost forever. Don't you wonder about that?"

"If you think about it you'll want to change things and you can't, so the gap between what you want and the way things actually are keeps growing until you drive yourself insane, so actually no, I don't," said Daz. "Have you got any fags?"

They were first year graphic art students, college locked for the duration of the Christmas break because vandals had turned the place over and all passes had been rescinded until a new security system could be installed. So Mats was sleeping on Daz's mother's lounge sofa because he didn't want to spend Christmas with his parents. Not that they cared whether he showed or not, and Daz's mother was away visiting her boyfriend in Cardiff, possibly the only place that gave Tower Hamlets a run for its money in the race to become Britain's grimmest area.

"It'll be a new year in two days' time, and I have absolute zero to look forward to," Mats complained. "I hate my life. All the crappy art appreciation classes I took at school are never going to give me the things I want. Kids in Africa have a better time than I do."

"I don't think they do, actually," Daz suggested.

The two students had so little in common it was perhaps only proximity that connected them. Mathew's parents were not, in truth, missing him. Having given in to their son for too long, they had allowed him to attend art college in the hope that he would eventually weary of trying to be outrageous. His parents were not outraged, or even vaguely shocked, by his attempts to test the limits of their liberality. If truth be told, they found him rather boring, a bit of an angry student cliché, incapable of understanding that the world's axis was not set through his heart.

Mats considered himself more sensitive than those around him, but his convictions had the depth and frailty of autumn leaves. His parents could see he was adrift but had run out of solutions. They were comforted by the knowledge that he could only fall as far as his trust fund allowed, and were happy to let him get on with the gruesome task of self-discovery. What he really wanted, he told them unconvincingly, was to become a citizen of the world. Finally they shrugged and left him alone.

"The problem is that I haven't been properly equipped to deal with the future," Mats continued, "and there's no nurture system for highly sensitive people."

Daz had heard all this before, and had other things on his mind; his sister was pregnant and broke, his mother increasingly suffered mental problems and was probably going to lose her flat. Oddly, listening to Mats moaning about his life didn't annoy him; it had a curiously calming effect, because his fellow student was so fake that you could make him believe anything. Conversely, Daz attracted Mats because he was real. There was a loose-limbed lying craziness that sometimes took Daz to the brink of a mental breakdown, which was all the more frightening because his nerve endings crackled like exposed live wires. It took guts to be nuts, and Daz was braver than most.

Mats hadn't stopped complaining for almost twenty minutes.

"I mean," he was saying now, "what's the point in creating real art when it's denied an impact? I don't know anything that can change anything."

"I do," said Daz, cutting him off. "I know a trick."

"What kind of a trick?"

Daz jumped up and brushed out his jeans, then headed into the rain-stained block of flats behind them.

"Where are you going?" asked Mats as they moved through the dim concrete bunker that passed for the building's foyer. Daz just grinned, dancing across orange tiles to smack the lift buttons with the back of his fist.

"There's only one place it works," said Daz, stepping into the lift, three narrow walls of goose-fleshed steel that reeked of urine and something worse. He pumped the panel, firing them to the top floor. When they got out, he pushed at the emergency exit and took the stairs to the roof three at a time. Montgomery House was required to keep the door unlocked in case of fire evacuation. Mats didn't like thirty-storey tower blocks, too much working-class bad karma forced upright into one small space, but he felt safe with Daz, who had chased storms from the stairwells since he was two-foot-six.

"Is it cool to be up here?" Mats asked, all the same. The hazing rain had dropped a grey dome over the top of the block. He walked to the edge of the roof and looked down, but the ground was lost in a vaporous ocean.

"There's some kids run a pirate station from one of the flats, that's that thing over there." Daz pointed to the makeshift mast attached to the satellite TV rig propped in the centre of the gravelled flat-top. "Touch their stuff and they'll cut you up. No-one else ever comes up here." The wind moaned in the wires strung between the struts of the satellite mount. Five blocks, all with their own pirate sounds. "When they're not chucking vinyl, they're taking each other's signals down with bolt-cutters. Give me your mobile."

"Fuck right off, I got about three calls left before it stiffs."

"Come on, check this," said Daz, snatching the mobile away from Mats. He flipped it open and punched in 7–2–8–2–6, waited for a moment, held it high, punched in the same numbers again, waited, held it high again, did it twice more, making five numbers five times, then turned the phone around so that Daz could see.

Behind them, the makeshift transmitter released a melancholy hum, like a phasing analogue radio. Mats could feel the crackle of electricity rustling under his clothes, as though he was about to be hit by lightning. Something had happened to the phone's screen; the colours had turned chromatic, and were cascading like psychedelic raindrops on a window.

"You screwed up my phone, man. What did you do?"

"7–2–8–2–6, you figure it out."

"I don't know," Mats admitted, "you paying your congestion charge?" A lame joke, seeing as neither of them owned any kind of vehicle.

"Try texting the number, see what comes up."

Mats went to MESSAGES, and tapped in the digits. "Oh, very mature. How do I clear the screen?"

"Can't, you have to put in a text message to that number to get rid of it."

"What is it, a glitch in the system?"

"Must be, only works on a Nokia, and only when you're near a mast, getting a clear signal."

"I don't get it, what's the point?"

"You didn't type in the text yet."

"Okay." Mats' fingers hovered over the pinhead keys. "I don't know what to write."

"C'mere." Daz pulled him beneath the hardboard shelter beneath the illegal transmission masts. "Ever wonder why ancient curses used to work? 'Cause they're ancient. Victims sickened and died, they wasted away when they discovered they were cursed. Belief, man." He thrust his outstretched fingers at Mats' brain, then his own. "There's no belief anymore, so curses no longer work. Who do you believe now? Do you think God will answer your prayers and sort out your life? No. Do you buy the whole Judeo-Christian guilt-trip? No. Do you believe your computer when it tells you your account's overdrawn? Yes. The new world order can't survive on images of demons and the fiery pit, 'cause we're just slabs of flickering code running to infinity. The only things you have faith in are digitised. Digital society needs digital beliefs. Most people's brains are still hardwired to analogue. Not our fault, that was the world we were born into, but it's all gone now. So change your perception."

Mats glared at the tiny silver handset. "What, with this?"

"What I think? A programmer somewhere spotted an anomaly in his binary world and opened up a crack, a way through.

Then he leaked it. A five-digit number punched in five times, somewhere near a powerful signal, near a transmitter, all it takes to open the whole thing up. Send the message. Make it something that could alter the way you see the world."

"Like what?"

"I don't know, use your imagination."

Mats stared at the falling rain. Unable to think of anything interesting, he typed MY PARENTS LIVE IN A BIG HOUSE IN THE COUNTRY, then sent the message to 7–2–8–2–6.

MESSAGE SENT

"Now what?"

"That's it, dude." Daz was grinning again.

"You *fuck.*" Mats angrily stamped to his feet and shoved his way into the downpour. "You almost had me believing you."

He took the lift to the ground and walked off toward the bus stop, annoyed with himself for being so stupid. While he was waiting for the bus he rang his father, thinking that maybe he could tap his old man for a cheque after all, despite having failed to return home for the holidays. He'd told his mother he couldn't come back for Christmas because there was no God, and how could they all be so fucking hypocritical? He stared absently at the falling rain, waiting for the call to be answered. His mother picked up the receiver. When she realised who was calling, she adopted a tone that let him know she would be displeased with him until they were all dead.

"Just let me talk to Dad."

"You'll have to hold on for a minute, Matthew," she warned. "Your father's in the garden fixing the pump in the pond."

Which was interesting, because they didn't have a pump, a pond or a garden. They lived on the fourth floor of a mansion block in St John's Wood.

"What are you talking about?" he asked.

"The garden doesn't stop growing just because it's raining," she answered impatiently. "Hold on while I call for him."

Mats snapped the phone shut as if it had bitten him. He fell back on the bus stop bench in awe. In the distance, a bus appeared. He felt his flat pockets, knowing there was no more than sixty pence in change. Minimum fare was a pound, and the bus driver got so weird if he tried to use a credit card. Money – he needed money.

It was a good reason to go back and try again.

He ran to Montgomery House and hopped the lift, but found that Daz had left the roof. Stepping out into the rain and flipping open the mobile, he redialled 7–2–8–2–6, adding text: BUS DRIVER GIVES ME TEN POUNDS, punched SEND. Then he shot back down, jumped on the next bus, and waited to see what would happen.

Red doors concertina'd back. The wide-shouldered Jamaican driver had surprisingly dainty hands, which she rested at the lower edge of her steering wheel. She did not move a muscle as he stepped up and stood before her, never raised her eyes from the windscreen before hissing the doors shut. Then she reached into her cash dispenser and handed him two five pound notes as if they were change.

He stayed on until reaching the city, the phone burning a patch in his pocket. Alighting near the Bank of England, he tried to understand what might be happening. Altered perception, Daz had said. Daz, who had not replaced his own mobile since it was stolen, so why hadn't he altered perception to make himself really, really rich?

Why wouldn't you? There had to be some kind of problem with that, didn't there? How specific did you have to be? Tom Thumb's Three Wishes-specific, get the wording exactly right or else you end up with a sausage on your nose? What were the parameters? Was there a downside, some kind of come-uppance for being greedy, for failure to perform a good deed? Did the Devil appear, hands on hips, laughing hard at Man's foolishness? Already he had forgotten talk of binary existence and was replacing it with the lore of fairytales, a language of quid pro quo cruelties, kindnesses and revenges, *because that's what is clearly fuckin' called for in this situation*, he thought, sweating at the seams.

Obviously, he needed to try again. There was a transmitter mast at Alexandra Palace, but what about mobile masts? There had been some kind of argument about placing one halfway up Tottenham Court Road, so that was where he headed next.

He couldn't get high above the ground, but he climbed to the second floor of Paperchase and stood near the rear window, close enough to see the phone mast, hoping it was closer enough to register. Flipping open the mobile, he examined the screen. The pulsing chroma-rain had cleared itself after the transmission of the last message. Suddenly, his sealed existence had unfolded into a world of possibilities. Suppose he

could do anything, anything at all? He could save the world.
End starvation and poverty. Reverse climate change. Bring back
the Siberian Tiger. Build a special community in the Caribbean
where artists from all over the world could live and work
together in peace, free from the pressures of society.

Fuck that shit. What about the things he really wanted?

The exhilaration welled inside his gut as he realised that he
could be a good six inches taller for a start, five-eight to at least
six-two. His height had always bugged him. And a better
physique, get rid of the beer belly. No, wait. He needed to
think carefully before doing anything else. His priorities were
ridiculous and wrong. What he wanted most, what he needed
more than anything, was a girl – no, not a girl, a woman, *Women*.
Lots of them. He wouldn't force them to like him, just provide
them with the possibility. *Wishes go bad when they're forced*, he
thought. But what he really needed was money, lots of money,
because it could buy you freedom. He'd be able to travel,
because that was how to make yourself truly free. Go around
the world and hang out with whomever you liked. It was all a
matter of slipping through the cracks in perception.

Whatever he asked for had to be something he wanted very
badly. As quickly as the possibilities occurred, they faded away,
leaving behind a fog of appalled anxiety. If it was so easy, why
hadn't Daz done it? Why was he still hanging out at his mother's
council flat?

He punched out Daz's number and asked him.

Daz sounded surprised. "That's your perception, Mats. I only
feature in your world as some kind of sidekick, a support to the
main act. But that's not the way I see it from my side, *compadre*.
I'm the big event – you barely exist. You see, once you're *really*
through to the other side, the digital world, that's when you
discover who you should really be, and you're free. You get the
life you always deserved, probably the life you have right now
but simply can't see. Figure it out, Mats, the answer's right in
front of you. Just help yourself." The line went dead. Was he
stifling a laugh as he rang off? It sure as hell didn't sound like
Daz talking. He couldn't usually string two clear thoughts
together without aid.

Mats had walked the upper floor of the store half a dozen
times before he understood what he was supposed to do.
Gardens, buses, looks, girls, money, all small-time stuff, changing single elements, not rewriting the hard drive. He pulled

the phone from his pocket, flipped it open and punched in the number again.

7–2–8–2–6

He watched as the letters came up once more.

S-A-T-A-N

A broadband hotline to the Devil, a kind of turbo-Satan, a programmer's joke, not even that – a child's idea of a secret, something so obvious nobody even thought to try it. *You're supposed to send it to yourself,* he thought, *that's all you have to do, like making a wish.* This time, instead of texting a request, he simply typed in his own phone number, then pressed SEND.

MESSAGE SENT

What now? The screen was teeming with colours once more, but now they were fading to mildewed, sickly hues; something new was at work. For a moment he thought he saw Daz outside the window, laughing wildly at something preposterous and absurd. He felt bilious, as if he had stepped from a storm-shaken boat. The pale beech wood floor of the store tilted, then started to slide away until he was no longer able to maintain his balance.

He landed hard, jarring his arm and hip, but within a second the wood was gone and he had fallen through – he could feel the splinters brushing his skin – until the ground was replaced with something soft and warm. Sand on clay, earth, small stones, heat on his face, his bare legs. His eyes felt as if they had been sewn shut. He lay without moving for a moment, feeling the strange lightness in his limbs. Then he reached out a hand to touch his bruised thigh.

Stranger still. It was not his leg, but one belonging to a child, thin and almost fleshless – and yet he could feel the touch of his fingers from within the skin.

So bright. He could see the veins inside his orange eyelids. Yet there was something else moving outside. He sensed rather than saw them – dozens of black dots bustling back and forth.

He ungummed his eyelids and opened them. Flies, fat black blowflies lifted from his vision in a cloud and tried to resettle at once. He brushed them away with his hand, and was horrified to discover the brown, bony claw of a malnourished child. The effort required to pull himself upright was monstrous. Looking down at his legs, he found that instead of the pre-stressed flares he always wore, his twisted limbs were encased in torn, ancient suit-trousers five sizes too small.

He found himself sitting exhausted beneath a vast fiery sun on a ground of baked mud, waiting for the charity worker in front of him to dole out a ladle of water from a rust-reddened oil drum. Staring down into the opalescent petrol stains on the rancid liquid, he saw his opposite self: an encephalitic head, fly-crusted eyes, cracked thin lips, sore-covered ribs thrust so far forward that they appeared to be bursting from his skin; the knife of perpetual hunger twisting in his swollen stomach. Looking around, he saw hundreds of others like himself stretching off into the dusty yellow distance, the marks of hunger and disease robbing them of any identity. He would have screamed then, if his throat had not been withered long ago to a strip of sun-dried flesh.

Daz made his way along the balcony of Montgomery House, avoiding pools from the dripping ceiling, swinging the cans of beer he had withdrawn from his secret stash behind the bins. He had half-expected Mats to trail him back to the flat, but perhaps he was off sulking somewhere about the phone joke. That was the great thing about people like Mats – you could tell them any old shit, and at some primitive level, even when they said they didn't, they actually believed you. Heart and soul.

DENNIS ETCHISON

Talking in the Dark

DENNIS ETCHISON IS THE winner of two World Fantasy Awards
and three British Fantasy Awards. The late Karl Edward Wagner
described him as "the finest writer of psychological horror this
genre has produced".

Etchison's stories have appeared in numerous periodicals
and anthologies since 1961, and some of his best work has been
collected in *The Dark Country, Red Dreams, The Blood Kiss* and *The
Death Artist*. *Talking in the Dark* is a massive retrospective volume
from Stealth Press marking the fortieth anniversary of his first
professional sale, and *Fine Cuts* is a volume of stories about the
dark side of Hollywood, from PS Publishing.

Etchison is also well known as a novelist (*The Fog, Darkside,
Shadowman, California Gothic* and *Double Edge*) and has pub-
lished the movie novelizations *Halloween II, Halloween III* and
Videodrome under the pseudonym "Jack Martin".

As an acclaimed anthologist, he has edited *Cutting Edge,
Masters of Darkness I-III, MetaHorror, The Museum of Horrors*
and *Gathering the Bones* (with Jack Dann and Ramsey Campbell).

More recently, Etchison has written thousands of script pages
for *The Twilight Zone Radio Dramas*, broadcast world-wide and
available on audiocassette and CD. He also reads his stories

"The Dog Park" and "Inside the Cackle Factory" on *Don't Turn on the Lights! The Audio Library of Modern Horror, Vol. 1.*

"In 2000 I was asked to assemble a retrospective collection of my stories," remembers the author, "to be entitled *A Long Time Till Morning*. This required me to re-read forty years' worth of short stories, and the experience was a shock to the system. They were not at all as I remembered them. Those I had believed were the best now seemed tedious and embarrassingly overwrought, and some of the minor pieces, while not very good stories, contained quirky, idiosyncratic material that surprised and fascinated in ways I could not have anticipated. All of which suggests that we are not reliable, objective judges of even the most important events in our lives at the time we live through them.

"I lived through a lot, some of it not very pleasant, while this story was written at the beginning of the 1980s. But that could be said about any period of my life after the age of five or six, and I suspect the same applies to everyone. My stories usually reflect personal events and obsessions, either directly or met-aphorically. I won't bore you with autobiographical details, except to say that I felt very alone for several years and began to wonder when if ever my real life, the one I had always looked forward to, would begin. Poor me. But the feeling was very real.

"It was difficult to talk about this in a way that might be entertaining or interesting to other people, who surely had problems of their own. Then one day, as is often the case, several unrelated entries from my notebooks suddenly came together, and I began to see a story that might convey some of what I had held inside for so long, in the manner of a song that serves as a vehicle for a singer's deepest emotions. The working title was 'The Sources of the Nile', and it began with my recollections of a well-known (and benign) editor and person-ality in the science fiction field who once took a car trip across America for the sole purpose of meeting fans with whom he had corresponded over the years.

"Victor Ripon's name derives from two waterfalls located on the River Nile, and Gezira, the fictional town in which he resides, refers to a point where the two Niles, the blue and the white, come together, as well as to the school colours in my hometown, where my uncle Harold owned an ice cream parlour called 'The Blue and White' across the street from Stockton High. The naïve, painfully heartfelt words Victor writes to his favourite author, the imaginary Rex Christian, were inspired by actual letters sent to a very real horror writer, containing his readers' comments about a non-fiction book he had published, after he asked me to read and evaluate them in case there were any factual errors that needed to be corrected for the revised edition.

"And the ending is obviously influenced by Nicolas Roeg's *Don't Look Now*, one of my favourite films from the 1970s. By the time my retrospective collection finally came out in 2001 I had retitled it *Talking in the Dark*, after another part of the quotation by Kenneth Patchen that provided the title of this story when it was first published in Charles L. Grant's anthology *Shadows 7*.

"I have since been told that this is a comic story rather than the tragic, heartbreaking metaphor I had intended. Perhaps so. Apparently I'm not the most reliable authority. You will have to go to the source of the Nile, if you can find it, for the final word . . ."

IN THE DAMP BEDROOM Victor Ripon sat hunched over his desk, making last-minute corrections on the ninth or tenth draft, he couldn't remember which, of a letter to the one person in the world who might be able to help. Outside, puppies with the voices of children struggled against their leashes for a chance to be let in from the cold. He ignored them and bore down. Their efforts at sympathy were wasted on him; he had nothing more to give. After thirty-three years he had finally stepped out of the melodrama.

He clicked the pen against his teeth. Since the letter was to a man he had never met, he had to be certain that his words would not seem naive or foolish.

Dear Sir, he reread, squinting down at the latest version's cramped, meticulously cursive backhand. He lifted the three-hole notebook paper by the edges so as not to risk smearing the ballpoint ink. Dear Sir . . .

First let me say that I sincerely hope this letter reaches you. I do not have your home address so I have taken the liberty of writing in care of your publisher. If they forward it to you please let me know.

I am not in the habit of writing to authors. This is the

first time. So please bear with me if my letter is not perfect in spelling, etc.

I have been reading your Works for approximately 6 yrs., in other words since shortly after I was married but more about that later. Mr Christian, Rex if I may call you that and I feel I can, you are my favorite author and greatest fan. Some people say you are too morbid and depressing but I disagree. You do not write for children or women with weak hearts (I am guessing) but in your books people always get what they deserve. No other author I have read teaches this so well. I can see why you are one of the most popular authors in the world. I have all 6 of your books, I hope there are only 6, I wouldn't like to think I missed any! (If so could you send me a list of the titles and where I might obtain them? A S.A.S.E. is enclosed for your convenience. Thank you.)

My favorite is THE SILVERING, I found that to be a very excellent plot, to tell the truth it scared the shit out of me if you know what I mean and I think you do, right? (Wink wink.) MOON OVER THE NEST is right up there, too. My wife introduced me to your novels, my ex-wife I should say and I guess I should thank her for that much. She left me 2½ years ago, took the kids to San Diego first and then to Salt Lake City I found out later. I don't know why, she didn't say. I have tried to track her down but no luck. Twice with my late parents' help I found out where she was staying but too late. So that is the way she wants it, I guess. I miss the kids though, my little boy especially.

In your next book, THE EDGE, I noticed you made one small mistake, I hope you don't mind my pointing it out. In that one you have Moreham killing his old girlfriend by electrocution (before he does other things to her!) while she is setting up their word processor link. Excuse me but this is wrong. I know this because I was employed in the Computer Field after dropping out of Pre-Med to support my family. The current utilized by a Mark IIIA terminal is not enough to produce a lethal shock, even if the interface circuits were wired in sequence as you describe (which is impossible anyway, sorry, just thought you might like to know). Also the .066 nanosecond figure should be corrected . . .

And so on in a similar vein. Victor worked his way through three more densely-packed pages of commentary and helpful advice regarding Rex Christian's other bestsellers, including *Jesus Had A Son, The Masked Moon* and the collection of short stories, *Nightmare Territory*, before returning to more personal matters.

> If you ever find yourself in my neck of the woods please feel free to drop by. We could have a few beers and sit up talking about the many things we have in common. Like our love of old movies. I can tell you feel the same way about such "classics" (?) as ROBOT INVADERS, MARS VS. EARTH and HOUSE OF BLOOD from the way you wrote about them in your series of articles for TV GUIDE. I subscribed so I wouldn't miss a single installment. There are others we could talk about, even watch if we're lucky. I get Channel 56 here in Gezira, you may have heard about it, they show old chestnuts of that persuasion all night long!!
>   If you have not guessed by now, I too try my hand at writing occasionally myself. I have been working for the past 1½ years on a story entitled PLEASE, PLEASE, SORRY, THANK YOU. It will be a very important story, I believe. Don't worry, I'm not going to ask you to read it. (You are probably too busy, anyway.) Besides, I read WRITER'S DIGEST so I know where to send it if and when I succeed in bringing it to a satisfactory stage of completion. But you are my inspiration. Without you I would not have the courage to go on with it at all.

He hesitated before the conclusion, as he had when first drafting it four nights ago. On the other side of the window pane the sky was already smoking over with a fine mist, turning rapidly from the color of arterial blood to a dead slate grey. The sea rushed and drubbed at the coastline a mile to the west, shaking and steadily eroding the bedrock upon which his town was built; the vibrations which reached the glass membrane next to him were like the rhythms of a buried human heart.

> There is one more thing. I have a very important question to ask you, I hope you don't mind. It is a simple thing (to

you) and I'm sure you could answer it. You might say I should ask someone else but the truth is I don't know anyone else who could help. What I know isn't enough. I thought it would be but it isn't. It seems to me that the things we learned up until now, the really important things, and I can tell we've had many of the same experiences (the Sixties, etc.), when it came time to live them, the system balked. And we're dying. But don't worry, I'm a fighter. I learned a long time ago: never give up.

I live in my parents' old house now, so we could have plenty of privacy. In my opinion we could help each other very much. My number is 474–2841. If I'm not here I'll be at the Blue & White (corner of Rosetta and Damietta), that is where I work, anybody can tell you where to find it. I hope to hear from you at your earliest convenience.

Meanwhile, I'm waiting with bated breath for your book of essays, OTHER CEDENTS, they mentioned it on "Wake Up, America" and I can hardly wait! If you care to let me read the manuscript prior to publication I promise to return it by Express Mail in perfect condition. (Just asking, hint hint.) In any event please come by for a visit on your next trip to the West Coast. I hope you will take me up on it sometime (soon!), I really need the answer. We Horror Fans have to stick together. As you said in your Introduction to NIGHTMARE TERRITORY, "It may be a long time till morning, but there's no law against talking in the dark."

> Faithfully Yours,
> VICTOR RIPON

He sat back. He breathed in, out. It was the first breath he had been aware of taking for several minutes. The view from the window was no longer clear. A blanket of fog had descended to shroud all evidence of life outside his room. The puppies next door had quieted, resigned to their fate. Still a hopeful smile played at the corners of his mouth. He stacked and folded the pages to fit the already-stamped envelope. There. Now there wasn't anything to do but wait.

He stretched expansively, hearing his joints pop like dry bones, and his fingernails touched the window. So early, and yet the glass was chillingly brittle, ready to shatter under the slightest provocation.

With any luck he wouldn't have long to wait at all.

The days shrank as the season contracted, drawing inward against the approaching winter. Trees bared stiffening limbs, scraped the sky and etched patterns of stars as sharp and cold as diamond dust above the horizon. Victor got out his old Army jacket. The main house became dank and tomblike, magnifying the creaking of dryrotted timbers. He took to sleeping in the guest cabin, though the portable heater kept him tight and shivering night after night.

He pressed bravely ahead with his story, the outlines and preliminary versions of which by now filled two thick notebooks, reorganizing, redrafting and obsessively repolishing lines and paragraphs with a jeweler's precision.

But it was not good enough.

He wanted the pages to sing with ideas that had once seemed so important to him, all and everything he knew, and yet they did not, and no amount of diligence was able to bring them to life. The story came to be a burden and weighed more heavily in his hands each time he lifted it out of the drawer. After a few weeks he was reluctant to open the desk at all.

He stayed in bed more and slept less, dragging himself up for work each day only at the last possible minute. Nothing except Rex Christian's books held any interest for him now, and he had read them all so many times he believed he knew them by heart, almost as well as his own stillborn effort. Channel 56 exhausted its library of late-night movies and sold out to a fundamentalist religious sect peddling fire and brimstone. The nights lengthened and the long winter closed around him.

Each day, he thought, *I die a little. I must. I get out of bed, don't I?*

Mornings he walked the two miles along the creek into town, reexamining the last few years like beads to be memorized in his pocketed fists before they slipped away forever. He walked faster, but his life only seemed to recede that much more swiftly across the dunes and back to the sea. He could neither hold onto nor completely forget how things had once been. Whether or not they had ever truly been the way he remembered them was not the point. The spell of the past, his past, real or imagined, had settled over him like the shadow of giant wings, and he could not escape.

He submerged himself in his work at the shop, a space he rented for small appliance repair behind the Blue & White Diner, but that was not enough, either. For a time he tried to tell himself that nothing else mattered. But it was an evasion. *You can run,* he thought, *but you can't hide.* Rex Christian had taught him that.

Some days he would have traded anything he owned and all that he had ever earned to wake up one more time with the special smell of her on his pillow – just that, no matter whether he ever actually set eyes on her again. Other days his old revenge fantasies got the better of him. But all that was real for him now was the numbness of more and more hours at the shop, struggling to penetrate the inner workings of what others paid him to fix, the broken remnants of households which had fallen apart suddenly, without warning or explanation.

When not busy at work, the smallest of rewards kept him going. The weekly changes of program at the local movie theater, diverting but instantly forgettable; the specialties of the house at the Blue & White, prepared for him by the new waitress, whose name turned out to be Jolene; and Jolene herself when business was slow and there was nowhere else to go. She catered to him without complaint, serving something, perhaps, behind his eyes that he thought he had put to rest long ago. He was grateful to her for being there. But he could not repay her in kind. He did not feel it, could not even if he had wanted to.

By late December he had almost given up hope.

The weekends were the worst. He had to get out, buttoned against the cold, though the coffee in town was never hot enough and the talk after the movies was mindless and did not nourish. But he could bear the big house no longer, and even the guest cabin had begun to enclose him like a vault.

This Saturday night, the last week before Christmas, the going was painfully slow. Steam expanded from his mouth like ectoplasm. He turned up his collar against an icy offshore wind. There were sand devils in the road, a halo around the ghost of a moon which hung over his shoulder and paced him relentlessly. At his side, to the north, dark reeds rustled and scratched the old riverbank with a sound of rusted blades. He stuffed his hands deeper into his jacket and trudged on toward the impersonal glow of the business district.

The neon above the Blue & White burned coolly in the darkness.

The nightlife in Gezira, such as it was – Siamese silhouettes of couples cruising for burgers, clutches of frantic teenagers on their way to or from the mall – appeared undiscouraged by the cold. If anything the pedestrians scissoring by seemed less inhibited than ever, pumping reserves of adrenaline and huffing wraiths of steam as if their last-minute shopping mattered more than anything else in this world. The bubble machine atop a police car revolved like a deranged Christmas tree light. Children giggled obscenities and fled as a firecracker resounded between lampposts; it might have been a gunshot. The patrol car spun out, burning rubber, and screeched past in the wrong direction.

He took a breath, opened the door to the diner and ducked inside.

The interior was clean and bright as a hospital cafeteria. A solitary pensioner dawdled at the end of the counter, spilling coffee as he cradled a cup in both hands. Twin milkshake glasses, both empty, balanced near the edge. As Victor entered, jangling the bell, the waitress glanced up. She saw him and beamed.

"Hi!"

"Hi, yourself."

"I'll be a few more minutes. Do you mind? The night girl just called. She's gonna be late." Jolene watched him as she cleaned off the tables, trying to read his face as if it were the first page of a test. Her eyes flicked nervously between his.

"Take your time," he said. He drew off his gloves and shuffled up to the counter. "No hurry."

"The movie –?"

"We won't miss anything."

She blinked at him. "But I thought the last show –"

"It starts," he said, "when we get there."

"Oh." She finished the tables, clearing away the remains of what other people could not finish. "I see," she said. "Are – are you all right?"

"Yes."

"Well, you don't sound like it." She looked at him as if she wanted to smooth his hair, take his temperature, enfold him in her big arms and stroke his head. Instead she wiped her hands and tilted her face quizzically, keeping her distance. "How about something to eat?"

"Just coffee," he said. "My stomach's . . ." He sought the precise word; it eluded him. He gave up. "It's not right."

"*Again?*"

"Again." He tried a smile. It came out wrong. "Sorry. Maybe next time."

She considered the plate which she had been keeping warm on the grill. It contained a huge portion of fried shrimp, his favorite. She sighed.

The door jingled and a tall man came in. He was dressed like a logger or survivalist from up north, with plaid shirt, hiking boots, full beard and long hair. Victor decided he had never seen him before, though something about the man was vaguely familiar.

Jolene dealt out another set-up of flatware. He didn't need a menu. He knew what he wanted.

Victor considered the man, remembering the sixties. That could be me, he thought; I could have gone that way, too, if I had had the courage. And look at him. He's better off. He doesn't have any attachments to shake. He opted out a long time ago, and now there's nothing to pull him down.

Jolene set the man's order to cooking and returned to Victor.

"It won't be long," she said. "I promise." She gestured at the old Zenith portable next to the cash register. "You want the TV on?"

She needed to do something for him, Victor realized. She *needed* to. "Sure," he said agreeably. "Why not?"

She flicked a knob.

The nightly episode of a new religious game show, *You Think That's Heavy?* was in progress. In each segment a downtrodden soul from the audience was brought onstage and led up a ramp through a series of possible solutions, including a mock employment bureau, a bank loan office, a dating service, a psychiatric clinic, and, finally, when all else had failed, a preacher with shiny cheeks and an unnatural preoccupation with hair. Invariably this last station of the journey was the one that took. Just now a poor woman with three children and a husband who could not support them was sobbing her way to the top of the hill.

I hope to God she finds what she needs, Victor thought absently. She looks like she deserves it. Of course you can't tell. They're awfully good at getting sympathy . . .

But someone will come down and set things right for her, sooner or later. She'll get what she deserves, and it will be right as rain. I believe that.

But what about the kids? They're the ones I'm worried about . . .

At that moment the door to the diner rang open and several small children charged in, fresh from a spree on the mall, clutching a few cheap toys and a bag of McDonald's French fries. They spotted the big man in the red plaid shirt and ran to him, all stumbles and hugs. The man winked at Jolene, shrugged and relocated to a corner booth.

"Whadaya gonna do?" he said helplessly, "I reckon I gotta feed 'em, right?"

"I'll get the children's menus," said Jolene.

"You got any chili dogs?" said the man. "We came a long way. Don't have a whole lot left to spend. Is that okay?"

"Give them the shrimp," suggested Victor. "I can't handle it."

Jolene winked back. "I think we can come up with something," she said.

The pensioner observed the children warily. Who could say what they might have brought in with them? He obviously did not want to find out. His hands shook, spilling more coffee. It ran between his fingers as if his palms had begun to bleed.

Well, thought Victor, maybe I was wrong. Look at the big guy now. He can't run away from it, either. But it could be he doesn't want to. He's got them, and they'll stick by him no matter what. Lucky, I guess. What's his secret?

Out on the sidewalk passers-by hurried on their way, a look of expectation and dread glazing their eyes. Victor picked up his coffee. It was almost hot enough to taste.

There was another burst of ringing.

He braced himself, not knowing what to expect. He scanned the doorway.

But this time it was not a customer. It was the telephone.

Jolene reached across the counter, pushing dirty dishes out of the way. One of the milkshake glasses teetered and smashed to the floor. At the end of the counter, the pensioner jumped as though the spirit of Christmas past had just lain its withered fingers on the back of his neck.

"What?" Jolene balanced the receiver. "I'm sorry, there's so much – yes. I said yes. Hold on." She passed the phone to Victor. "It's for you," she said.

"It is?"

"Sure is," she said. "I can't tell if it's a—"

"Yes?"

"Victor?"

"Yeah?"

"Vic!" said the reedy voice on the line. "Great to get ahold of you, finally! This is Rex. Rex Christian!"

"Really?" said Victor, stunned.

"Yup. Look, I'll be passing through your town in about, oh, say an hour. I was just wondering. Are you free tonight, by any chance?"

"Uh, sure, Re . . ."

"Don't say my name!"

"Okay," said Victor.

"I'm on my way from a meeting in San Francisco. Traveling incognito, you might say. You don't know how people can be if the word gets out. So I'd appreciate it if, you know, you don't let on who you're talking to. Understand?"

"I understand." It must be hard, he thought, being a celebrity.

"I knew you would."

Victor cupped his hand around the mouthpiece. The old man from the end of the counter fumbled money from his coin purse and staggered out. Victor tried to say the right things. He wasn't ready. However, he remembered how to get to his own house. He gave directions from Highway 1, speaking as clearly and calmly as he could.

"Who was that?" asked Jolene when he had hung up.

"Nobody," said Victor.

"What?"

"A friend, I mean. He . . ."

"He what?"

"I've got to . . . meet him. I forgot."

Her expression, held together until now by nervous anticipation, wilted before his eyes. The tension left her; her posture sagged. Suddenly she looked older, overweight, lumpen. He did not know what to say.

He grabbed his gloves and made ready to leave. She smoothed her apron, head down, hiding a tic, and then made a great effort to face him. The smile was right but the lines were deeper than ever before.

"Call me?" she said. "If you want to. It's up to you. I don't care."

"Jolene . . ."

"No, really! I couldn't take the cold tonight, anyway. I – I hope you have a nice meeting. I can tell it's important."

"Business," he said. "You know."

"I know."

"I'm sorry."

She forced a laugh. "What on earth for? Don't you worry."

He nodded, embarrassed.

"Take care of yourself," she said.

You deserve better, he thought, than me, Jolene.

"You, too," he said. "I didn't plan it this way. Please believe . . ."

"I believe you. Now get going or you'll be late."

He felt relieved. He felt awful. He felt woefully unprepared. But at least he felt something.

All the way home the hidden river ran at his side, muffled by the reeds but no longer distant. This time he noticed that there were secret voices in the waters, talking to themselves and to each other, to the night with the tongues of wild children on their way back to the sea.

Now he considered the possibility that they might be talking to him.

Victor unlocked the old house and fired up the heater. He had little chance to clean. By the time he heard the car he was covered with a cold sweat, and his stomach, which he had neglected to feed, constricted in a hopeless panic.

He parted the bathroom curtains.

The car below was long and sleek. A limousine? No, but it was a late-model sedan, a full-size Detroit tank with foglights.

A man climbed out, lugging a briefcase, and made for the front of the house.

Victor ran downstairs and flung open the door.

He saw a child approaching in the moonlight. It was the same person he had seen leave the shadow of the car. From the upstairs window the figure had appeared deceptively foreshortened.

The boy came into the circle of the porchlight, sticking his chin out and grinning rows of pearly teeth.

"Vic?"

Victor was confused.

Then he saw.

It was not a child, after all.

"I'm Rex Christian," said the dwarf, extending a stubby hand. "Glad to meet you!"

The hand felt cold and compressed as a rubber ball in Victor's grip. He released it with an involuntary shudder. He cleared his throat.

"Come on in. I . . . I've been expecting you."

The visitor wobbled to an overstuffed chair and bounced up onto the cushion. His round-toed shoes jutted out in front of him.

"So! This is where one of my biggest fans lives!"

"I guess so," said Victor. "This is it."

"Great! It's perfect!"

On the stained wall, a grandfather clock sliced at the thick air.

"Can I get you something?" Victor's own voice sounded hollow in his ears. "Like something to drink?"

"I'd settle for a beer. Just one, though. I want to keep a clear head."

Beer, thought Victor. Let me see . . . He couldn't think. He looked away. The small face, the monkey mouth were too much for him. He wanted to laugh and cry at the same time.

"You owe me, remember?"

"What?"

"The beer. In your letter you said—"

"Oh. Oh, yeah. Just a minute."

Victor went to the kitchen. By the time he returned he had replayed his visitor's words in his mind until he recognized the rhythm. Everything the dwarf – midget, whatever he was – had said so far fit the style. There was no doubt about it. For better or worse, the person in the other room was in fact Rex Christian. The enormity of the occasion finally hit him. Setting the bottles on the coffee table between them, he almost knocked one over.

My time has come, he thought. My problems are about to be over. My prayers have been answered.

"This must be pretty far out of the way for you," Victor said.

"Not at all! Thanks for the invitation."

"Yeah," said Victor. "I mean, no. I mean . . ."

And in that instant he saw himself, this house, his life as it really was for the first time. He was overwhelmed with self-consciousness and shame.

"Did . . . did you have any trouble finding the place?"

"Nope. Followed your directions. Perfect!"

Victor studied the virgules in the carpet, trying to find his next words there.

Rex Christian leaned forward in his chair. The effort nearly doubled him over.

"Look, I know what it's like for you."

"You do?"

"Believe me, I do. That's my business, isn't it? I've seen it all before."

Rex sat back and took a long pull from the tall bottle. His Adam's apple rolled like a ball bearing in his throat.

"You must know a lot about people," said Victor.

"Never enough. That's why I take a trip like this, at least once a year." He chortled. "I rent a car, visit folks like you all over the country. It's a way of paying them back. Plus it helps me with my research."

"I see." There was an awkward pause. "You . . . you said you were in San Francisco. On business. Was that part of this year's trip?"

"Right. Nothing beats the old one-on-one, does it?"

So he didn't come all this way just to see me, thought Victor. There were others. "From your writing, well, I thought you'd be a very private person."

"I am! Somebody wants a book, they have to climb the mountain. But when it comes to my fans it's a different story. They're raw material. I go to the source, know what I mean?"

"I used to be a people-person," said Victor, loosening up a bit. He drained his bottle. He thought of going for two more. But the writer had hardly touched his. "Now, well, I don't go out much. I guess you could say I've turned into more of a project-type person."

"Glad to hear it!"

"You are?"

"It just so happens I've got a project you might be interested in. A new book. It's called *A Long Time Till Morning.*"

"I like the title," said Victor. "Excuse me."

He rose unsteadily and made a beeline for the stairs. The beer had gone through his system in record time. When he came out of the bathroom, he gazed down in wonderment from the top of the landing. Rex Christian was still sitting there, stiff and proper as a ventriloquist's dummy. I can't believe this is happening, he thought. Now everything's changed. There he is, sitting in my living room!

His heart pounded with exhilaration.

Let me never forget this. Every minute, every second, every detail. I don't want to miss a thing. This is important; this matters. The most important night of my life.

He bounded down the stairs and snagged two more beers and an opener from the kitchen, then reseated himself on the sofa.

Rex Christian greeted him with a sparkling grin.

"Tell me about your new book," said Victor breathlessly. "I want to hear everything. I guess I'll be the first, won't I?"

"One of the first." The author folded his tiny hands. "It's about an epidemic that's sweeping the country – I don't have the details yet. I'm still roughing it out. All I gave my editor was a two-page outline."

"And he bought it?"

Rex Christian grinned.

"What kind of epidemic?"

"That's where you can help, Vic."

"If it's research you want, well, just tell me what you need. I used to do a lot of that in school. I was in premed and . . ."

"I want to make this as easy as possible for you."

"I know. I mean, I'm sure you do. But it's no sweat. I'll collect the data, Xerox articles, send you copies of everything that's ever been written on the subject, as soon as you tell me . . ."

Rex Christian frowned, his face wrinkling like a deflating balloon. "I'm afraid that would involve too many legalities. Copyrights, fees, that sort of thing. Sources that might be traced."

"We could get permission, couldn't we? You wouldn't have to pay me. It would be an honor to . . ."

"I know." Rex Christian's miniature fingers flexed impatiently. "But that's the long way around, my friend."

"However you want to do it. Say the word and I'll get started, first thing in the morning. Monday morning. Tomorrow's Sunday and . . ."

"Monday's too late. It starts now. In fact it's already started. You didn't know that, did you?" Rex's face flushed eagerly, his cheeks red as a newborn infant's. "I want to know *your* feelings on the subject. All of them." He pumped his legs and crept forward on the cushion. "Open yourself up. It won't hurt. I promise."

Victor's eyes stung and his throat ached. *It starts here,* he thought, awe-struck. The last thirty-three years were the introduction to my life. Now it really starts.

"You wouldn't want to know my feelings," he said. "They . . . I've been pretty mixed up. For a long time."

"I don't care about what you felt before. I want to know what you feel tonight. It's only *you,* Vic. You're perfect. I can't get that in any library. Do you know how valuable you are to me?"

"But why? Your characters, they're so much more real, more alive . . ."

Rex waved his words aside. "An illusion. Art isn't life, you know. If it were, the world would go up in flames. It's artifice. By definition." He slid closer, his toes finally dropping below the coffee table. "Though naturally I try to make it echo real life as closely as I can. That's what turns my readers on. That's part of my mission. Don't you understand?"

Victor's eyes filled with tears.

Other people, the people he saw and heard on the screen, on TV, in books and magazines, voices on the telephone, all had lives which were so much more vital than his own wretched existence. The closest he had ever come to peak experiences, the moments he found himself returning to again and again in his memory, added up to nothing more significant than chance meetings on the road, like the time he hitchhiked to San Francisco in the summer of '67, a party in college where no one knew his name, the face of a girl in the window of a passing bus that he had never been able to forget.

And now?

He lowered his head to his knees and wept.

And in a blinding flash, as if the scales had been lifted from his eyes, he knew that nothing would ever be the same for him again. The time to hesitate was over. The time had come at last to make it real.

He thought: I am entitled to a place on the planet, after all.

He lifted his eyes to the light.

The dwarf's face was inches away. The diminutive features, the taut lips, the narrow brow, the close, lidded eyes, wise and all-forgiving. The sweet scent of an unknown after-shave lotion wafted from his skin.

"The past doesn't matter," said the dwarf. He placed the short fingers of one hand on Victor's head. "To hell with it all."

"Yes," said Victor. For so long he had thought just the opposite. But now he saw a way out. "Oh, yes."

"Tell me what you feel from this moment on," said the dwarf. "I need to know."

"I don't know how," said Victor.

"Try."

Victor stared into the dark, polished eyes, shiny as a doll's eyes.

"I want to. I . . . I don't know if I can."

"Of course you can. We're alone now. You didn't tell anyone I was coming, did you, Vic?"

Victor shook his head.

"How thoughtful," said the dwarf. "How perfect. Like this house. A great setting. I could tell by your letter you were exactly what I need. Your kind always are. Those who live in out-of-the-way places, the quiet ones with no ties. That's the way it has to be. Otherwise I couldn't use you."

"Why do you care what I feel?" asked Victor.

"I told you – research. It gives my work that extra edge. Won't you tell me what's happening inside you right now, Vic?"

"I want to. I do."

"Then you can. You can if you really want it. Aren't we all free to do whatever we want?"

"I almost believed that, once," said Victor.

"Anything," said the dwarf firmly. "You can have anything, including what you want most. Especially that. And what is it you want, Vic?"

"I . . . I want to write, I guess."

The dwarf's face crinkled with amusement.

"But I don't know what to write about," said Victor.

"Then why do you want.to do it?"

"Because I have no one to talk to. No one who could understand."

"And what would you talk to them about, if you could?"

"I don't know."

"Yes, you do."

"I'm afraid."

"Tell me, Vic. I'll understand. I'll put it down exactly the way you say it. You want me to relieve your fear? Well, in another minute I'm going to do that little thing. You will have nothing more to fear, ever again."

This is it, Victor thought, your chance. Don't blow it. It's happening just the way you had it planned. Don't lose your nerve. Ask the question – now. *Do it.*

"But where does it come from?" asked Victor. "The things you write about. How do you know what to say? Where do you get it? I try, but the things I know aren't . . ."

"*You want to know*," said the dwarf, his face splitting in an uproarious grin, "*where I get my ideas?* Is that your question?"

"Well, as a matter of fact . . ."

"From you, Vic! I get my material from people like you! I get them from this cesspool you call life itself. And you know what? I'll never run out of material, not as long as I go directly to the source, because I'll never, ever finish paying you all back!"

Victor saw then the large pores of the dwarf's face, the crooked bend to the nose, the sharpness of the teeth in the feral mouth, the steely glint deep within the black eyes. The hairs prickled on the back of his neck and he pulled away. Tried to pull away. But the dwarf's hand stayed on his head.

"Take my new novel, for instance. It's about an epidemic that's going to sweep the nation, leaving a bloody trail from one end of this country to the other, to wash away all of your sins. At first the police may call it murder. But the experts will recognize it as suicide, a form of *harakiri*, to be precise, which is what it is. I know, because I've made a careful study of the methods. Perfect!"

The underdeveloped features, the cretinous grin filled Victor with sudden loathing, and a terrible fear he could not name touched his scalp. He sat back, pulling farther away from the little man.

But the dwarf followed him back, stepping onto the table, one hand still pressing Victor in a grotesque benediction. The lamp glared behind his oversized head, his eyes sparkling maniacally. He rose up and up, unbending his legs, knocking over the bottles, standing taller until he blocked out everything else.

Victor braced against the table and kicked away, but the dwarf leaped onto his shoulders and rode him down. Victor reached out, found the bottle opener and swung it wildly.

"No," he screamed, "my God, no! You're wrong! It's a lie! You're . . . !"

He felt the point of the churchkey hook into something thick and cold and begin to rip.

But too late. A malformed hand dug into his hair and forced his head back, exposing his throat and chest.

"How does *this* feel, Vic? I have to know! Tell my readers!" The other claw darted into the briefcase and dragged forth a blade as long as a bayonet, its edge crusted and sticky but still razor-sharp. "How about this?" cried the dwarf. "And this?"

As Victor raised his hands to cover his throat, he felt the first thrust directly below the ribcage, an almost painless impact as though he had been struck by a fist in the chest, followed by the long, sawing cut through his vital organs and then the warm pumping of his life's blood down the short sword between them. His fingers tingled and went numb as his hands were wrapped into position around the handle. The ceiling grew bright and the world spun, hurling him free.

"Tell me!" demanded the dwarf.

A great whispering chorus was released within Victor at last, rushing out and rising like a tide to flood the earth, crimson as the rays of a hellishly blazing sun.

But his mouth was choked with his own blood and he could not speak, not a word of it. The vestiges of a final smile moved his glistening lips.

"Tell me!" shrieked the dwarf, digging deeper, while the room turned red. "I must find the perfect method! *Tell me!*"

SYDNEY J. BOUNDS

The Circus

SYDNEY JAMES BOUNDS BEGAN his career by contributing
"spicy" stories to the monthly magazines produced by Utopia
Press in the 1940s. He was soon writing hardboiled gangster
novels for John Spencer under such house names as "Brett
Diamond" and "Ricky Madison", and he contributed short
stories to their line of SF magazines which included *Futuristic
Science Stories, Tales of Tomorrow* and *Worlds of Fantasy.*

He became a regular contributor to such magazines as *New
Worlds Science Fiction, Science Fantasy, Authentic Science Fiction,
Nebula Science Fiction, Other Worlds Science Stories* and *Fantastic
Universe.* However, as the science fiction magazine markets
started to dry up during the 1960s, the author began to notice
the growth of paperbacks. Although he continued to be pub-
lished in such periodicals as *London Mystery Magazine, Vision of
Tomorrow, Fantasy Tales, Fantasy Booklet, Fantasy Annual* and
Fantasy Quarterly, he quickly became a prolific and reliable
contributor to such anthology series as *New Writings in SF,
The Fontana Book of Great Ghost Stories, The Fontana Book of Great
Horror Stories,* the *Armada Monster Book,* the *Armada Ghost Book*
and *Fantasy Adventures.*

Bounds has also pursued parallel careers as a successful

children's writer and a Western novelist for Robert Hale, and in 2003 Cosmos Books issued the first-ever collections of the author's work as two paperback volumes, *The Best of Sydney J. Bounds: Strange Portrait and Other Stories* and *The Wayward Ship and Other Stories*, both edited by Philip Harbottle.

One of the author's best-known stories, "The Circus" was adapted by George A. Romero for a 1986 episode of the syndicated television series *Tales of the Darkside.*

"One of the tricks a writer has for producing a new story is to reverse a standard situation," explains Bounds. "Back in the 1970s, werewolves and vampires were considered evil and words like horror and terror were applied to them. So why not devise a story based on the wonder of the differences in nature? Here it is . . ."

BECAUSE HE HAD BEEN drinking, Arnold Bragg considered it a stroke of good fortune that the accident happened a long way from any main road and the chance of a patrolling police car. He had no exact idea of his location, just that it was somewhere in the West Country.

He was on his way back from Cornwall where he'd been covering a story, an expose of a witches' coven, for the *Sunday Herald.* He drove an MG sports car and, as always with a few drinks inside him, drove too fast. With time to spare, he'd left the A30 at a whim. It was a summer evening, slowly cooling after the heat of the day. The countryside was what he called "pretty", with lanes twisting between hedgerows. He took a corner at speed and rammed the trunk of a tree that jutted into the road around the bend.

Shaken but unhurt, he climbed from his car and swore at a leaking radiator. Then he got back in and drove on, looking for a garage. He found one, a couple of miles further along, next to a pub with a scattering of cottages; there were not enough of them to justify calling them a village.

A mechanic glanced at the bonnet and sniffed his breath. "Ar, I can fix it. Couple of hours, maybe."

Arnold Bragg nodded. "I'll be next door when you've finished."

It was the kind of pub that exists only in out-of-the-way places, and then rarely: a house of local stone with a front room converted as a bar. The door stood open and he walked in past a stack of beer crates. The walls were thick and it was cool inside. On a polished counter rested two casks, one of cider and one of beer. A grey-haired woman sat knitting behind the counter, and two oldish men sat on a wooden bench by the window

Bragg turned on a charm that rarely failed him. "I'll try a pint of your local beer."

The woman laid her knitting aside, picked up a glass mug and held it under the tap; sediment hung in the rich brown liquid.

Bragg tasted it, then drank deeply. "I didn't know anyone still brewed beer like this." He glanced around the room.

"Perhaps you gentlemen will join me?"

"Ar, likely we will, sir. And many thanks."

Bragg's gaze moved on to a poster thumb-tacked to the wall. It had obviously been hand-printed, and read:

CIRCUS
Before your very eyes, werewolf into man!
See the vampire rise from his coffin!
Bring the children – invest in a sense of wonder

As Arnold Bragg stared and wondered if beer had finally rotted his brain, sluggish memory stirred. In his job, he always listened to rumours; some he hunted down and obtained a story. There had been this crazy one, crazy but persistent, of a freak circus that never visited towns but stopped only for one night at isolated villages. He'd come across it first in the fens, then on the Yorkshire moors, and again in a Welsh valley.

The knowledge that this circus was here, now, sobered him. He set down his glass on the counter, unfinished. When he scented a lead, he could stop drinking. And this one was likely to prove the apex of a career dedicated to discrediting fakes and phoneys of all kinds.

He studied the poster carefully. No name was given to the circus. There was no indication of time or place of performance. Still, it shouldn't be hard to find.

He strolled outside, passed the garage where the mechanic worked on his car, and sauntered towards the cottages. A few families, young husbands and wives with their offspring, were walking down a lane, and he followed them. Presently he glimpsed, in the distance, the canvas top of a large tent showing above some trees.

He kept to himself, observing the people on the way to the circus; there was no gaiety in them. With solemn faces and measured step they went, people who took their pleasure seriously.

Beyond a screen of trees was a green field with the big top and a huddle of caravans and Land Rovers. People formed a small queue at an open flap of the tent, where a little old man sold tickets. He sported a fringe of white hair, nut-brown skin and the wizened appearance of a chimpanzee.

Bragg dipped a hand into his pocket and brought out some loose change.

"I don't believe you'll like our show, sir." The accent was foreign. "It's purely for the locals, you understand. Nothing sophisticated for a London gentleman."

"You're wrong," Bragg said, urging money on him. "This is just right for me." He snatched a ticket and walked into the tent.

Seats rose in tiers, wooden planks set on angle-irons. In the centre was a sawdust ring behind low planking; an aisle at the rear allowed performers to come and go. There was no provision for a high-wire act.

Bragg found an empty seat away from the local people, high enough so that he commanded a clear view, but not so far from the ringside that he would miss any detail.

Not many seats were occupied. He lit a cigarette and watched the crowd. Grave faces, little talk; the children showed none of that excitement normally associated with a visit to the circus. Occasionally eyes turned his way and were hastily averted. A few more families arrived, all with young children.

The old man who sold tickets doubled as ringmaster. He shuffled across the sawdust and made his announcement in hardly more than a whisper. Bragg had to strain to catch the words.

"I, Doctor Nis, welcome you to my circus. Tonight you will see true wonders. The natural world is full of prodigies for those who open their eyes and minds. We begin with the vampire."

Somewhere, pipe music played; notes rippled up and down a non-Western scale, effecting an eerie chant. Two labourers came down the aisle, carrying a coffin. The coffin was far from new and they placed it on the ground as if afraid it might fall to pieces.

The pipes shrilled.

Bragg found he was holding his breath and forced himself to relax. Tension came again as the lid of the coffin moved. It moved upwards, jerkily, an inch at a time. A thin hand with long fingernails appeared from inside. The lid was pushed higher, creaking in the silence of the tent, and the vampire rose and stepped out.

Its face had the pallor of death, the canine teeth showed long and pointed, and a ragged cloak swirled about its human form.

One of the labourers returned with a young lamb and tossed it to the vampire. Hungrily, teeth sank into the lamb's throat, bit deep, and the lips sucked and sucked . . .

Bragg stared, fascinated and disgusted. When, finally, the drained carcass was tossed aside, the vampire appeared swollen as a well-filled leech.

The labourers carried the coffin out and the vampire walked behind. Jesus, Bragg thought – this is for kids?

Dr Nis made a small bow.

"You who are present tonight are especially fortunate. Not at every performance is it possible to show a shape-changer. Lycanthropy is not a condition that can be perfectly timed – and now, here is the werewolf."

He placed a small whistle to his lips and blew into it. No sound came, but a large grey wolf trotted into the sawdust ring, moving as silently as the whistle that called it. Slanting eyes glinted yellowish-green. The animal threw back its head and gave a prolonged and chilling howl.

Hairs prickled on the back of Bragg's neck and he almost came out of his seat. He blinked his eyes as the wolf-shape wavered. The creature appeared to elongate as it rose high on hind limbs. The fur changed. Bragg moistened suddenly-dry lips as the wolf became more manlike . . . and more . . . till it was a naked man who stood before them.

An attendant draped a blanket about his shoulders and together they walked off. Blood pounded through Bragg's head; it had to be a fake, obviously, but it was a convincing fake.

"The ancient Egyptians believed in physical immortality," Dr Nis whispered. "They had a ceremony known as the Opening of the Mouth. This ceremony restored to the body, after death, its ability to see, hear, eat and speak. Here now, a mummy from the land of the Pharaohs."

A withered mummy, wrapped in discoloured linen bandages,

its naked face dark-skinned, was carried into the ring. Four jars were placed about it.

"These are Canopic jars, containing the heart and lungs and the viscera of the deceased."

A voice spoke, a voice that seemed to come from the mummy. It spoke in a language unfamiliar to Bragg.

Dr Nis said smoothly: "I will translate freely. The mummy speaks: True believers only are safe here – those who doubt are advised to open their hearts."

Bragg wanted to laugh, but sweat dried cold on his flesh and laughter wouldn't come.

The mummy was carried off.

"We have next," Dr Nis said with pride, "an experiment of my own. Can a corpse be re-animated? Can the component parts of a man be brought together and endued with life? I shall allow you to judge how successful I have been."

A travesty of a man shuffled down the aisle and into the ring. It was hideous. The limbs were not identical; they had not come from the same body. The head, waxen and discoloured, lolled at an angle, as if insecurely hinged at the neck. It lumbered unsteadily around the sawdust ring, and it smelt. The man-thing did not speak; it stumbled over uneven feet, rocking from side to side as it tried to recover balance, and lost its head.

A small gasp was jerked from Bragg's lips as the detached head hit the sawdust and rolled to a stop. The headless cadaver blundered on aimlessly, like a decapitated chicken, until attendants hurried to guide it from the ring.

Bragg felt sick, and his fingers drummed nervously on his knees. Impossible to believe the thing was just a freak; yet he had to believe, or admit the impossible.

Dr Nis looked unhappy. "I must apologize – obviously my experiment is not yet perfected for public viewing. And so we come to our final offering this evening. You all know, if only in a vague way, that before men inhabited this world, the reptiles ruled for millions of years. They were the true Lords of the Earth. Science maintains that they died out before men appeared, but science has been wrong before. There was interbreeding . . ."

The creature that slithered into the ring was about five feet long. It had the general appearance of a man on all fours, but its skin was scaly and iridescent. The hands were clawed, the head narrowed and thrust forward, and a forked tongue hung from the mouth.

An attendant brought a plastic bag and released from it a cloud of flies. The creature reared up, long tongue flickering like forked lightning, catching the flies and swallowing them.

A sick show, Bragg decided; an outrage to perform this sort of thing before children. The catch-phrases of popular journalism ran through his head – "This Show Must Be Banned!"

Pipe music played again, a falling scale. Dr Nis bowed and left the ring. Families rose and filed quietly out, their offspring subdued.

Bragg vaulted into the ring, crossed the sawdust and left by the aisle exit. As he hurried towards the caravans, he saw Dr Nis entering one of them.

The door was just closing when Bragg arrived and leaned on it. Dr Nis turned to peer at him.

"Ah, Mr Bragg, I was half-expecting you. You are, after all, well known in your trade."

Bragg pushed his way into the caravan and felt like a giant in a doll's house; everything seemed smaller, neat and tidy in its appointed place.

"Then you'll know the paper I work for and the sort of thing I write." He couldn't be bothered to turn on the charm. "Tell me – tell the *Herald's* millions of readers – how do you justify your show? Horror for adults – okay, we'll go along with that. But the kids?'

Dr Nis made a small deprecating motion with his hands. "Horror, Mr Bragg? I deplore the term. My life is spent trying to keep alive a faith, a faith in the mystery of Nature. Strange things happen. If a man who believes sees a ghost, is he frightened? Yet a man who disbelieves and comes face to face with one may well die of shock. So perhaps my show serves a useful purpose . . . as for children, what better time to develop a sense of wonder?"

"That's your story – now let's have the low-down on how your gimmicks work."

"Gimmicks?" Dr Nis regarded him calmly. "I assure you I do not deal in trickery. Consider this: who knows you are here? And aren't you just a little bit frightened?"

Bragg flinched. "Who, me? Of a bunch of freaks?" But his voice was edged with doubt.

Dr Nis said, "I do not want the kind of publicity you have in mind, Mr Bragg. I don't think it would serve my purpose." He smiled suddenly, and his smile was not for his visitor.

Arnold Bragg turned. Freaks crowded the door of the caravan: the vampire, the werewolf and the lizard-man. The resurrected man was conspicuously absent.

"I think it would be best if Mr Bragg disappeared," Dr Nis said quietly. "But don't damage his head, please." He looked again at Bragg, his eyes bright and hard.

"You see, Mr Bragg, I believe I have a use for it."

F. PAUL WILSON

Foet

OVER SEVEN MILLION COPIES of F. Paul Wilson's books are in print around the world and he is the author of such best-selling novels as *The Keep* (filmed in 1983) and *The Tomb*. In 1998 he resurrected his popular anti-hero Repairman Jack and recently published the latest volumes in the series, *Gateways* and *Crisscross*. Beacon Films is presently developing Jack into a franchise character.

In 2003, *Midnight Mass* was a micro-budget independent movie adaptation of his vampire story of the same title (with a cameo by the author), released straight to video by Lions Gate Films. More recently he combined the tale with its two prequels, "The Lord's Work" and "Good Friday", and expanded them into a full-length novel.

"In many cases I have no idea where a story comes from," reveals Wilson. "Not so with 'Foet'. It arrived intact while I lay awake after an argument with a woman friend over her fur coat. (Such a deal, she'd bought two.) She wasn't the least bit fazed that anal electrocution is the method of choice for killing minks. Her attitude was: animals are here for our use, to do with as we please. Another woman present agreed.

"My wife Mary squeezed my thigh under the table – her oft-

used technique for warning me to think before igniting my
flame-thrower. (Some nights I'm limping by the time we get
home.) I realized then that you cannot have a serious conversation with some women – not all women, but too many, as
evidenced by the ongoing popularity of fur – about the humane
treatment of animals if vanity or fashion are part of the equation.
(I hear the cries of 'Sexist!' but I speak from experience.)
Fashion and vanity create an ethical blind spot in these women.

"I remember my closing remark before the conversation fled
to more neutral ground: 'You'd probably wear human skin if it
was in vogue!'

"And thus, the story."

DENISE DIDN'T MIND THE January breeze blowing against her
back down Fifth Avenue as she crossed Fifty-seventh Street. Her
favorite place in the world was Manhattan, her favorite pastime
was shopping, and when she was shopping in midtown –
heaven.

At the curb she stopped and turned to stare at the pert
blonde who'd just passed. She couldn't believe it.

"Helene? Helene Ryder, is that you?"

The blonde turned. Her eyes lit with recognition.

"Ohmigod, Denise! Imagine meeting you here! How long
has it been?"

They hugged and air kissed.

"Oh, I don't know. Six months?"

"At least! What are you doing in the city?"

"Just shopping. Accessory hunting."

"Me, too. Where were you headed?"

"Actually, I was looking for a place to get off my feet and have
a bite to eat. I skipped lunch and I'm famished."

"That sounds good." Helene glanced at her watch. A diamond Piaget, Denise noticed. "It's tea time at the Waldorf.
Why don't we go there?"

"Wonderful!"

During the bouncy cab ride down Park Avenue, Denise gave
Helene a thorough twice-over and was impressed. Her blonde
hair was short and fashionably tousled; her merino wool top-
coat, camel's-hair sweater, and short wool and cashmere skirt
reeked of Barney's and Bergdorf's.

Amazing what could happen when your husband got a big

promotion. You could move from Fairfield to Greenwich, and you could buy any little thing your heart desired.

Not that Helene hadn't always had style. It was just that now she could afford to dress in the manner to which she and Denise had always hoped to become accustomed.

Denise was still waiting to become accustomed. Her Brian didn't have quite the drive of Helene's Harry. He still liked to get involved in local causes and in church functions. And that was good in a way. It allowed him more time at home with her and the twins. The downside, though, was that she didn't have the budget to buy what she needed when she needed it. As a result, Denise had honed her shopping skills to the black-belt level. By keeping her eyes and ears ever open, buying judiciously, and timing her purchases to the minute – like now, for instance, in the post-holiday retail slump – she managed to keep herself looking nearly as in style as someone with a pocketbook as deep as Helene's.

And on the subject of pocketbooks, Denise could not take her eyes off Helene's. Fashioned of soft, silky, golden brown leather that seemed to glow in the afternoon sunlight streaming through the grimy windows of the cab, it perfectly offset the colors of her outfit. She wondered if Helene had chosen the bag for the outfit, or the outfit for the bag. She suspected the latter. The bag was exquisite, the stitchwork especially fascinating in its seemingly random joining of odd-sized and odd-shaped pieces. But it was the material itself that drew and captured her attention. She had an urge to reach out and touch it. But she held back.

Later. She'd ask Helene about it during tea.

Sitting here with Helene on a settee along the wall in Peacock Alley at the Waldorf, sipping tea and nibbling on petits fours from the tray on the table before them, Denise felt as if she were part of the international set. The room whispered exotic accents and strange vowels. Almost every nationality was represented – the Far East most strongly – and everyone was dressed to the nines. The men's suits were either Armani or Vacca, and a number of the women outshone even Helene. Denise felt almost dowdy.

And still . . . that handbag of Helene's, sitting between them on the sofa. She couldn't escape the urge to caress it, could not keep her eyes off it.

"Isn't it beautiful?" Helene said.

"Hmmm?" Denise felt a flash of embarrassment at being caught staring, and wondered if the envy showed in her eyes. "The bag? Yes, it is. I don't think I've ever seen anything like it."

"I'd be surprised if you had." Helen pushed it closer. "Take a look."

Soft. That was the first thing Denise noticed as she lifted it. The leather was so soft, a mix of silk and down as her fingers brushed over the stitched surface. She cradled it on her lap. It stole her breath.

"Um . . . very unusual, isn't it?" she managed to say after a moment.

"No. Not so unusual. I've spotted a few others around the room since we arrived."

"Really?" Denise had been so entranced by Helene's bag that the others had gone unnoticed. That wasn't like her. "Where?"

Helene tilted her head to their left. "Right over there. Two tables down, in the navy blue sweater chemise and matching leggings."

Denise spotted her. A Japanese woman, holding the bag on the coffee table before her. Hers was black, but the stitching was unmistakable. As Denise scanned the room she noticed another, this one a deep coffee brown. And she noticed something else – they belonged to the most exquisitely dressed women in the room, the ones draped in Helmut Lang and Versace. Among all the beautifully dressed people here in Peacock Alley, the women who stood out, who showed exceptional flair and style in their ensembles, were the ones carrying these bags.

Denise knew in that instant that she had to have one. It didn't matter how much they cost, this was the accessory she'd been looking for, the touch that would set her apart, lift her to a higher fashion plane.

The Japanese woman rose from her table and walked past. She glanced at Denise on her way by. Her gaze dropped to the bag on Denise's lap and she smiled and nodded. Denise managed to smile back.

What was that? It almost seem as if the women with these bags had formed some sort of club. If so, no matter what the dues, Denise wanted to be a member.

Helene was smiling knowingly when Denise looked back at her.

"I know what you're thinking," Helene sing-songed.

"Do you?"

"Uh-huh. 'Where do I get one?' Right?"

Right. But Denise wasn't going to admit it. She hated being obvious.

"Actually I was wondering what kind of leather it is."

A cloud crossed Helene's face.

"You don't know?" She paused, then: "It's foet."

"*Feet?* Whose feet?" And then Denise realized what Helene had said. "Oh . . . my . . . God!"

"Now, Denise—"

Foet! She'd heard of it but had never thought she'd see it or actually touch it, never *dreamed* Helene would buy any. Her gorge rose.

"I don't believe it!"

Denise pushed the bag back onto the sofa between them and glared at Helene.

"Don't look at me like that. It's not as if I committed a crime or anything."

"How could you, Helene?"

"Look at it." Helene lifted the bag. "How could I not?"

Denise's eyes were captured again by the golden glow of the leather. She felt her indignation begin to melt.

"But it's human skin!" she said, as much to remind herself of that hideous fact as to drag it out into the open.

"Not human . . . at least according to the Supreme Court."

"I don't care what those old farts say, it's still human skin!"

Helene shook her head. "*Fetal* skin, Denise. From abortions. And it's legal. If fetuses were legally human, you couldn't abort them. So the Supreme Court finally had to rule that their skin could be used."

"I know all about that, Helene."

Who didn't know about *Ranieri v. Verlaine?* The case had sent shock waves around the country. Around the *world!* Denise's church had formed a group to go down to Washington to protest it. As a matter of fact—

"Helene, *you* were out on Pennsylvania Avenue with me demonstrating against the ruling! How could you—?"

Helene shrugged. "Things change. I'm still anti-abortion, but after we moved away from Fairfield and I lost contact with our old church group, I stopped thinking about it. Our new friends aren't into that sort of stuff and so I, well, just kind of drifted into other things."

"That's fine, Helene, but how does that bring you to buying something like . . ." She pointed to the bag and, God help her, she still wanted to run her hands over it. "*This!*"

"I saw one. We went to a reception – some fund-raiser for the homeless, I think – and I met a woman who had one. I fell in love with it immediately. I hemmed and hawed, feeling guilty for wanting it, but finally I went out and bought myself one." She beamed at Denise. "And believe me, I've never regretted it."

"God, Helene."

"They're already dead, Denise. I don't condone abortion anymore than you do, but it's legal and that's not likely to change. And as long as it stays legal, these poor little things are going to be killed day after day, weeks after week, hundreds and thousands and millions of them. We have no control over that. And buying foet accessories will not change that one way or another. They're *already dead.*"

Denise couldn't argue with Helene on that point. Yes, they were dead, and there was nothing anyone could do about that. But . . .

"But where do they sell this stuff? I've never once seen it displayed or even advertised."

"Oh, it's in all the better stores, but it's very discreet. They're not stupid. Foet may be legal but it's still controversial. Nobody wants trouble, nobody wants a scene. I mean, can you imagine a horde of the faithful hausfraus from St Paul's marching through Bergdorf's? I mean *really!*"

Denise had to smile. Yes, that would be quite a sight.

"I guess it would be like the fur activists."

"Even worse," Helene said, leaning closer. "You know why those nuts are anti-fur? Because they've never had a fur coat. It's pure envy with them. But foet? Foet is tied up with motherhood and apple pie. It's going to take a long time for the masses to get used to foet. So until then, the market will be small and select. Very select."

Denise nodded. *Select.* Despite all her upbringing, all her beliefs, something within her yearned to be part of that small, select market. And she hated herself for it.

"Is it very expensive?"

Helene nodded. "Especially this shade." She caressed her bag. "It's all hand sewn. No two pieces are exactly alike."

"And where'd you buy yours?"

Helene was staring at her appraisingly. "You're not thinking of starting any trouble, are you?"

"Oh, no. No, of course not. I just want to look. I'm . . . curious."

More of that appraising stare. Denise wanted to hide behind the settee.

"You want one, don't you?"

"Absolutely not! Maybe it's morbid on my part, but I'm curious to see what else they're doing with . . . foet these days."

"Very well," Helene said, and it occurred to Denise that Helene had never said *Very well* when she'd lived in Fairfield. "Go to Blume's – it's on Fifth, a little ways up from Gucci's."

"I know it."

"Ask for Rolf. When you see him, tell him you're interested in some of his better accessories. Remember that: 'better accessories.' He'll know what you're looking for."

Denise passed Blume's three times, and each time she told herself she'd keep right on walking and find a taxi to take her down to Grand Central for the train back to Fairfield. But something forced her to turn and go back for one more pass. Just one more. This time she ducked into a slot in the revolving door and swung into the warm, brightly lit interior.

Where was the harm in just looking?

When he appeared, Rolf reminded her of a Rudolf Valentino wannabe – stiletto thin in his black pin-stripe suit, with plastered-down black hair and mechanical pencil mustache. He was a good ten years younger than Denise and barely an inch taller, with delicate, fluttery hands, lively eyes, and a barely audible voice.

He gave Denise a careful up-and-down after she'd spoken the code words, then extended his arm to the right.

"Of course. This way, please."

He led her to the back of the store, down a narrow corridor, and then through a glass door into a small, indirectly lit showroom. Denise found herself surrounded by glass shelves lined with handbags, belts, even watch bands. All made of foet.

"The spelling is adapted from the archaic medical term," Rolf said, closing the door behind them.

"Really?" She noticed he didn't actually say the word: *foetal.*

"Now . . . what may I show you?"

"May I browse a little?"

"*Mais oui.* Take your time."

Denise wandered the pair of aisles, inspecting the tiers of shelves and all the varied items they carried. She noticed something: Almost everything was black or very dark.

"The bag my friend showed me was a lighter color."

"Ah, yes. I'm sorry, but we're out of white. That goes first, you know."

"No, this wasn't white. It was more of a pale, golden brown."

"Yes. We call that white. After all, it's made from white hide. It's relatively rare."

" 'Hide?' "

He smiled. "Yes. That's what we call the . . . material."

The material: white fetal skin.

"Do you have any pieces without all the stitching? Something with a smoother look?"

"I'm afraid not. I mean, you have to understand, we're forced by the very nature of the source of the material to work with little pieces." He gestured around. "Notice too that there are no gloves. None of the manufacturers wants to be accused of making kid gloves."

Rolf smiled. Denise could only stare at him.

He cleared his throat. "Trade humor."

Little pieces.

Hide.

Kid gloves.

Suddenly she wanted to run, but she held on. The urge passed.

Rolf picked up a handbag from atop a nearby display case. It was a lighter brown than the others, but still considerably darker than Helene's.

"A lot of people are going for this shade. It's reasonably priced. Imported from India."

"Imported? I'd have thought there'd be plenty to go around just from the US."

He sighed. "There would be if people weren't so provincial in their attitudes about giving up the hides. The tanneries are offering a good price for them. I don't understand some people. Anyway, we have to import from the Third World. India is a great source."

Denise picked up another, smaller bag of a similar shade. So soft, so smooth, just like Helene's.

"Indian, too?"

"Yes, but that's a little more expensive. That's male."

She looked at him questioningly.

His eyes did a tiny roll. "They hardly ever abort males in India. Only females. Two thousand-to-one."

Denise put it down and picked up a similar model, glossy, ink black. This would be a perfect accent to so many of her ensembles.

"Now that's—"

"Please don't tell me anything about it. Just the price."

He told her. She repressed a gasp. That would just about empty her account of the money she'd put aside for all her fashion bargains. On one item. Was it worth it?

She reached into her old pocketbook, the now dowdy-looking Fendi, and pulled out her gold MasterCard. Rolf smiled and lifted it from her fingers.

Minutes later she was back among the *hoi polloi* in the main shopping area, but she wasn't one of them. She'd been where they couldn't go, and that gave her special feeling.

Before leaving Blume's, Denise put her Fendi in the store bag and hung the new foet bag over her arm. The doorman gave her a big smile as he passed her through to the sidewalk.

The afternoon was dying and a cold wind had sprung up. She stood in the fading light with the wind cutting her like an icy knife and suddenly she felt horrible.

I'm toting a bag made from the skin of an unborn child.

Why? Why had she bought it? What had possessed her to spend that kind of money on such a ghoulish . . . *artifact*? Because that was just what it was – not an accessory, an artifact.

She opened the store bag and reached in to switch the new foet for her trusty Fendi. She didn't want to be seen with it.

And Brian! Good God, how was she going to tell Brian?

"*What?*"

Brian never talked with food in his mouth. He had better manners than that. But Denise had just told him about Helene's bag and at the moment his mouth, full of food, hung open as he stared at her with wide eyes.

"Brian, please close your mouth."

He swallowed. "*Helene?* Helene had something made of human skin?"

. . .not human . . . at least according to the Supreme Court . . .

"It's called *foet,* Brian."

"I know damn well what it's called! They could call it chocolate mousse but it would still be human skin. They give it a weird name so people won't look at them like they're a bunch of Nazis when they sell it! Helene – how could she?"

. . . they're already dead. Denise . . .

Brian's tone became increasingly caustic. Denise felt almost as if he were talking to her.

"I don't believe it! What's got into her? One person kills an unborn child and the other makes the poor thing's skin into a pocketbook! And Helene of all people! My God, is that what a big pay raise and moving to Greenwich does to you?"

Denise barely heard Brian as he ranted on. Thank God she'd had the good sense not to tell him about her own bag. He'd have been apoplectic.

No doubt about it. She was going to return that bag as soon as she could get back into the city.

Denise stood outside Blume's, dreading the thought of facing Rolf in that tiny showroom and returning her foet, her beautiful foet.

She pulled it out of the shopping bag and stared at it. Exquisite. Strange how a little extra time could turn your attitude around. The revulsion that had overwhelmed her right after she'd bought it had faded. Perhaps because every day during the past week – a number of times each day, to be honest – she'd taken it out and looked at it, held it, caressed it. Inevitably, its true beauty had shown through and captured her. Her initial beguilement had returned to the fore.

But the attraction went beyond mere beauty. This sort of accessory *said* something. Exactly what, she wasn't sure. But she knew a bold fashion statement when she saw one. This however was a statement she didn't have quite the nerve to make. At least not in Fairfield. So different here in the city. The cosmopolitan atmosphere allowed the elite to flash their foet – she liked the rhyme. She could be so very *in* here. But it would make her so very *out* in Fairfield – out of her home too, most likely.

Small minds. What did they know about fashion? In a few

years they'd all be buying it. Right now, only the leaders wore it. And for a few moments she'd been a member of that special club. Now she was about to resign.

As she turned to enter Blume's, a Mercedes stretch limo pulled into the curb beside her. The driver hopped out and opened the door. A shapely brunette of about Denise's age emerged. She was wearing a dark grey short wrap coat of llama and kid over a long-sleeved crepe-jersey catsuit. In her hand was a black clutch purse with the unmistakable stitching of foet. Her eyes flicked down to Denise's new handbag, then back up to her face. She smiled. Not just a polite passing-stranger smile, but a warm, we-know-we've-got-style smile.

As Denise returned the smile, all doubt within her melted away as if it had never been. Suddenly she knew she was right. She knew what really mattered, what was important, where she had to be, fashion-wise.

And Brian? Who said Brian had to know a thing about it? What did he know about fashion anyway?

Denise turned and strode down Fifth with her new foet bag swinging from her arm for all the world to see.

Screw them all. It made her feel good, like she was *some*body. What else mattered?

She really had to make a point of getting into the city more often.

BASIL COPPER

The Candle in the Skull

AFTER WORKING AS A journalist and editor of a local newspaper, Basil Copper became a full-time writer in 1970. His first story in the horror field, "The Spider", was published in 1964 in *The Fifth Pan Book of Horror Stories*, since when his short fiction has appeared in numerous anthologies, been extensively adapted for radio and television, and collected in *Not After Nightfall, Here Be Daemons, From Evil's Pillow, And Afterward the Dark, Voices of Doom, When Footsteps Echo, Whispers in the Night* and *Cold Hand on My Shoulder*.

Along with two non-fiction studies of the vampire and werewolf legends, his other books include the novels *The Great White Space, The Curse of the Fleers, Necropolis, The Black Death* and *The House of the Wolf.* Copper has also written more than fifty hardboiled thrillers about Los Angeles private detective Mike Faraday, and has continued the adventures of August Derleth's Sherlock Holmes-like consulting detective Solar Pons in several volumes of short stories and the novel *Solar Pons versus The Devil's Claw* (actually written in 1980, but not published until 2004 by Sarob Press with an Introduction by the late Richard Lancelyn Green).

The Hallowe'en story that follows has not been reprinted since its original appearance twenty years ago . . .

I

"IT'S HALLOWE'EN TOMORROW," Kathy said.

Her father looked at her sharply. The little girl sat in the window seat watching the cold October wind send leaves whirling and scraping down the sidewalk beyond the broad strip of lawn which separated the house from the street.

Kathy was ten now, small for her age, but with a rather strange, intense little face below the shock of blonde hair. Her eyes were the most extraordinary thing about her, Martin felt. They were a vivid violet colour which seemed to penetrate deep within one; in fact, even though he was her father, she gave him an uneasy feeling sometimes. It was almost as though she could sense his thoughts.

And that would never do, he felt, turning back to his work at the desk, answering the question with some banality, uneasily aware of Charlotte moving about somewhere upstairs in one of the cavernous rooms of the big, old frame house.

Martin signed the cheque with a brittle scratching of the pen which seemed to echo unnaturally loudly above the soft crackle of the log fire which burned in the brick Colonial fireplace. He was again aware of the little girl's murmured remarks in the background.

"What was that?" he remarked irritably, clipping the cheque to the account and sealing it in the envelope.

Kathy still sat with her cheek pressed against the pane, watching the dusky street outside with rapt intensity.

"I'm going to have a nice skull," she said firmly. "With a candle inside it. Better than the other children on the block."

Martin bit back his first startled remark. He remembered then she had been talking about Hallowe'en. Tomorrow was the 31st.

He supposed she would dress up in sheets and wear a scary mask like the other youngsters and make the round of the neighbourhood houses on a trick or treat expedition. How tiresome it all seemed, though once, many years ago, he had enjoyed it. Now he had other preoccupations.

"That will be nice, dear," he said absently.

The little girl turned to him and gave a smile of great sweetness.

"A beautiful skull," she said dreamily. "A skull for Hallowe'en."

Martin bit back his rising irritation. He again turned to the desk, keeping his nerves under control with difficulty. There was something strange about the child; he hesitated to use the term, even within the secret recesses of his own heart, but supernatural was not too strong a description. The child was an odd and unlikely fruit of a union such as his and Charlotte's; the only thing that had kept them together in twenty years of a lacerating marriage.

But it was all over. He would lose Janet if he hesitated any longer. He had everything planned. He stared down at the green leather surface of the desk, clasping his hands to prevent them trembling, biting his lips until the blood came. There was no other way. He had decided to murder his wife.

II

He had thought it all out extremely carefully. It wanted only the necessary resolve on his part. Janet had given him that. With her delicate, esoteric beauty and warmth, her vibrant personality, and smouldering sensuality, she epitomised everything Charlotte should have been and wasn't. Charlotte was cold, bitter and revengeful; she suspected his affair with Janet even if she didn't actually know.

That suspicion had merely sharpened the knife and given a little extra venom to the barbs of her conversation; the war had gone on for long years, festering beneath the surface even when it did not blaze into open resentment. It was time to end it all.

Martin glanced over at the innocent figure of his daughter, who had now turned her face to the window again. He was a clever man; a brilliant chemist with a multi-national corporation who had an almost limitless future. But that future was now threatened. Janet was fifteen years younger than he. She would not wait for ever. She had hinted as much. One of these evenings she might even come to the house.

Martin saw her three nights a week; it was a situation which might have continued for a long time in his case. It was not good enough for Janet. She had put the germ of the idea in Martin's mind, innocently enough. If only Charlotte would disappear, she had said. From that one remark had grown Martin's plan. And he had not breathed a word of his scheme, even to Janet.

He knew how to make people disappear; chemically, at least. He had a fully equipped workroom in the cellar with laboratory facilities. Discreetly, late at night, he had been moving in drums of chemicals, carried from the city in the boot of his car. They had been purchased through his corporation and, due to the manipulation of invoices between one company and another, would now be untraceable.

He had asked Charlotte to come down there before dinner, to discuss something important with him; he often worked at home. The suite of rooms below was warm and well equipped; there would be nothing to arouse her suspicion. They often talked – or rather argued – there.

Martin caught a bitter smile on his mouth in the gracious oval mirror opposite; was conscious at the same moment that Kathy's strange violet eyes were watching him. It was almost as though every evil thought in his head was exposed to that candid gaze. He changed his expression to normal, waited until the child had turned away again.

Kathy was the problem. She and her mother were very close. She would be immediately suspicious at Charlotte's disappearance. She would be at school early in the morning of course; the housekeeper usually got her breakfast and saw her to the bus. Charlotte always slept late and she and Martin had long occupied separate rooms.

Kathy would be in bed before nine o'clock tonight. After tomorrow Kathy would not matter. She might be suspicious but she was a mere child and in no position to prove anything. Janet would not want her custody; that was for certain. Perhaps his brother-in-law and his wife would take her. That was a problem best left for the future.

He glanced at his watch surreptitiously; his nerves were raw and it would not do to let the child see his rising agitation. Children missed nothing; she might persuade her mother not to come down below this evening. That would throw out the whole timetable. He had spent six months screwing himself to this point. He could not go through it again.

The steel tank had been filled that morning. He could not keep its contents there indefinitely. The vapour given off would start to corrode material in the workshop. It had to be this evening. He would have an hour at least. The housekeeper had gone to the cinema and would not be back until at least ten-thirty.

Martin shifted violently in his chair as a faint screaming came from the boulevard. An open tourer drifted by, its rear seats filled with weirdly attired teenagers. Kathy was kneeling up excitedly on the window seat now.

"Hallowe'en! Hallowe'en!" she chanted.

Martin swallowed, fighting to control his nerves. The child got up and came toward him. Her eyes seemed to fill the whole immensity of the room and he felt dizzy for a moment. He was becoming overwrought. He must watch his nerves. Especially in the difficult days to come. There were bound to be police inquiries; there always were in the case of missing persons.

Martin had a plausible story prepared; Charlotte would be visiting relatives, which would give him time enough. Time to drain the contents of the tank; he would not make the mistake of emptying it into the drains. He would convey the sludge in the original drums to a garbage tip at the edge of the city and empty it out gallon by gallon, making sure there were no identifiable remains. He had thought it through very carefully.

He frowned at the child, who watched him with those large accusing eyes. Martin was vaguely aware that she had never liked him. He did not care for her if the truth were known; she was too much like Charlotte in her nature. Vindictive and spiteful; even a child could show these traits in a dozen ways without displaying open hostility. Kathy was a strange, deceitful child. Martin would have to watch her. Someone with her alertness and gift for being in the wrong place at the wrong time could upset all his plans.

She leaned toward him, her head on one side.

"It will soon be Hallowe'en!" she breathed.

The man was startled by the sudden staccato beat of footsteps at the side of the house. The child had heard them too and glanced quickly at a shadow passing the window.

"You'd better hurry! Mummy is going down to the workroom!"

III

Martin went down the steps hurriedly, his heart thumping irregularly in his chest, a dull rage against the child in his heart. He had sent her to bed quickly. The plan was not working. It might even have to be postponed. Firstly, Kathy had seen her mother on her way to the outside steps. Perhaps Charlotte had gone out without him knowing.

And she was almost an hour early. Everything was falling apart and his nerves were ragged as he got to the shadowy corridor at the foot of the stairway. He had left the lights off. For his own purposes, of course. But one had to be careful here; the steps branched off to the old wood-store at the right.

There was a sheer drop to concrete here which was dangerous. He had been meaning to have it railed off for years but had never gotten around to it. It would have been the ideal solution to his problems but Charlotte would never come this way to the cellar; she always went around to the side of the house and down the shallow flight of steps to the outside door there.

He hoped she would not go through into the main laboratory; then he remembered he had kept it locked. He suddenly felt giddy again. He leaned against the wall for a moment. He recalled Kathy's eyes. Their strange, violet gaze seemed to haunt him. He pulled himself together, descending the remaining steps carefully. He was himself once more by the time he found his way to the room where he worked on his experimental theories.

The door was ajar and the small radio he kept there was playing dance music loudly. That was one of the things which irritated him about Charlotte. Even in small matters her habits made his nerves raw. But things could not have been more propitious this evening. Apart from the problem of Kathy. He looked in quickly. Charlotte was sitting at the desk with her back to him, going through some papers he kept there. He was committed now.

He had the iron bar from the bench. In two steps he was at her side. Before she could turn the heavy metal was descending. He caught her at the nape of the neck, as he had planned. She was already dead before he began dragging the body out to the laboratory. It was the work of a few moments to carefully immerse her, still fully clothed, in the tank, making sure none of its lethal contents slopped.

He did not stop but fled from the place, locking the door behind him. He did not know how he came there but presently he awoke to find himself at his desk in the living room. He was perspiring heavily, his pulse racing, his face white and curiously elongated in the mirror. He glanced at his watch, saw with a shock that only some two minutes had passed since he went to the cellar.

He held the dial to his ear. It had not stopped. Then he heard the brittle clatter of footsteps passing along the concrete path at the side of the house. His heart froze. Had he slept then and dreamed of the horrible event in the workroom below? Had he to go through it all again? He got to his feet, conscious of Kathy's strange eyes boring into his own.

No, he had not been mistaken. His wife's footsteps were real enough; the clock in the corner went on ticking gently. It showed the same time as his watch. He almost expected to see his daughter's ethereal-looking form huddled in the window seat but there was nothing there. He remembered then she had gone to bed.

He crossed the room quickly, made his way to the door which led to the cellars, his brain confused and bewildered. Charlotte was dead; there was no doubt about that. There were cobwebs on the front of his suit where he had descended the steps some time ago. But it could not have taken less than two minutes. The thing was impossible.

He must have been mistaken about the footsteps. Perhaps some child on a Hallowe'en prank had passed on the sidewalk. That must have been it. He was halfway down the steps now, the light from the hall door above sending yellow beams down the wooden stairway. He had forgotten the light switch in his agitation.

"Martin! Martin. Where are you?"

His heart turned to stone in his chest. There was no mistaking Charlotte's voice. His mind must be going. He knew her body was already dissolving within the tank. The blow alone would have killed her instantly.

The voice went on calling his name imperatively. He went down hurriedly, his nerves aflame as though the acid were eroding them too. He had to know whether he had been dreaming or something unexplainable had happened in the cellar. He ran down quickly, careless now, a great roaring in his ears.

Too late he realised he had mistaken his direction on the landing in the dark. His feet encountered empty space. He had time only for a mumbled cry as he descended into the darkness where the concrete floor awaited.

IV

"It's Hallowe'en tonight," Kathy said.

She sat on the floor in front of the window seat, busy with her preparations for the evening, intent on the contents of a big cardboard box. On the boulevard outside the dusk was falling almost imperceptibly on the facades of the houses opposite; the automobiles cutting red trails with their rear-lights in the gathering darkness.

Charlotte sat at her husband's desk, uneasily conscious of her daughter's strange violet eyes regarding her from beneath the mass of blonde hair.

"What did Daddy say?" she asked impatiently for perhaps the tenth time that day.

Martin's inexplicable disappearance was only one of several things that were disturbing her thoughts. She had been through the wardrobe and none of his clothes or his suitcases were missing. When he was called away on urgent business he usually left a note or telephoned her from the office.

"Perhaps Daddy and Auntie Janet have run off together," the child said maliciously.

Charlotte was shocked at the vehemence and the understanding in her daughter's tones. It was evident that she knew a great deal more of what went on around her than her parents had ever guessed.

But she gave a bright, false smile that matched her daughter's own.

"What an extraordinary thing to say! What makes you think that, dear."

The child went on fiddling with something in the big cardboard box by her side. Around were spread the strange paraphernalia of the Hallowe'en ritual. White sheets that looked at though they had been taken from her narrow bed; some stumps of red wax candles; an old lantern from the garage that had been tied with string to the end of a broken-off tree-branch.

Charlotte looked on absently, her thoughts elsewhere. Her lips curved bitterly. It would solve a good many of her problems if Martin and Janet had run off somewhere. She had forgotten how many weary years the problems involved in his treachery had flourished like a rank weed in their marriage.

She again caught a faint thread in the child's prattle,

prompted by a band of youngsters passing the window, lanterns already lit. The blurred chant of "Trick or treat!" died off round the next corner, chopped into segments by the rising wind that gusted at the windows. The fire flickered, sending weird shadows over the furniture until she got up to switch on the ceiling lights.

All Hallows' Eve. It was a strange custom, she reflected, her calm gaze fixed on her daughter's deliberate and methodical actions. A small rose of fire came to life in the corner by the window seat, made a warm glow in which Kathy's absorbed face was silhouetted against the darkening window panes. The child had lit one of the red candles in its metal holder.

"Be careful," Charlotte warned.

Her daughter turned innocent eyes upon her and once again the mother was struck by the strange, almost baleful glance that had the power to draw even an adult up short.

There was an ethereal quality about Kathy sometimes that was a little unnerving. Charlotte's interest aroused, she walked over from the light switch.

"What have you got there?"

Kathy smiled one of her sweetest smiles.

"A skull. I'm going to put a candle in it."

Charlotte gave the girl an incredulous look.

"A skull! Where did you get it? Is it made of candy?"

Kathy ignored her questions. She was again absorbed in the cardboard box, her fingers rustling mysteriously among folded twists of paper. She held up the candle, dripping the burning tallow below the edge of the box.

Charlotte was held halfway across the room, her attention focused on the child's intent activity. Kathy lifted the object now. Charlotte gave a gasp. The thing was certainly – she was going to say lifelike – but that was absurd under the circumstances. It was a small, beautiful, highly polished skull; delicately made and apparently that of a woman.

Charlotte waited breathlessly as the girl fixed the candle, manipulating it delicately through one of the eye-sockets.

"Don't you think it looks like Auntie Janet?" the child said.

Charlotte was astonished; she supposed the exquisitely modelled artefact was made of spun sugar, probably purchased at some establishment which specialised in such macabre aspects of Hallowe'en. Her throat tightened and her breath came fast and shallow.

There was an amazing resemblance to Janet now that the child came to mention it. Janet had a small, delicate head, almost like some ancient Egyptian queen. There was one tiny blemish which would have revealed the absurdity of the suggestion, but Charlotte remained where she was; pinned there by some sudden, overmastering emotion.

Kathy had lit the candle again now, the skull a subtle shell of growing radiance through which the eye-sockets and the teeth gleamed eerily.

"It gives a lovely light!" the child piped excitedly.

Charlotte fought down her nervous qualms. She recalled Edna St Vincent Millay's lines. It did give a lovely light.

Kathy had twisted the skull, so that the light gleaming from the jagged orifices threw uneven shadows on the wall. She cradled her soft cheek against the white bone, posing for her mother's approval.

Charlotte stared at the candle in the skull, its small halo of orange flame making little fretwork patterns on the girl's cheek, shimmering on the golden mass of hair.

"It's Hallowe'en tonight!" Kathy said.

RAMSEY CAMPBELL

The Chimney

RAMSEY CAMPBELL HAS BEEN named Grand Master by the World Horror Convention and received a Lifetime Achievement Award from the Horrors Writers Association.

His latest supernatural novel, *The Overnight,* is now available from PS Publishing, Tor Books has reprinted his landmark collection *Alone With the Horrors,* and a new edition of his Arkham House collection *The Height of the Scream* was recently reissued by Babbage Press. An original ghost story, "The Decorations", appeared in a limited edition from Sutton Hoo Press of Winona for Christmas 2004, and the author is currently at work on a new novel, *Secret Stories.*

"I see from the ledger I used as a diary in those days that 'The Chimney' was conceived on Christmas Day 1972," recalls Campbell, "after (but presumably not related to) my first viewing of Nigel Kneale's *The Stone Tape.* To quote the notes:

"*Child afraid of Santa Claus . . . Perhaps from a very early age has associated horror with the large fireplace in his bedroom? His parents tell him of Santa Claus . . . But when they tell him the truth about SC, the horror comes flooding back . . . And something's always moving in there toward Christmas . . . He sees it emerge each year: but this year he sees it in more detail . . .*

"I sketched some other details, including the final apparition, and there the material appears to have lain until I was looking back in search of story ideas in June 1975. The tale was written in a little over a week, from the 20th to the 27th of that month. By gum, the energy of the young! I don't think I could be so productive these days.

"It wasn't then apparent to me that the story was disguised autobiography – about my relationship with my father, who was an unseen and hence monstrous figure who lived in my house throughout my childhood. I still recall realizing this as I read the tale to a gathering at Jack Sullivan's apartment in New York.

"It was also there that I discovered how funny a story it was, but well before the end the laughter ceased."

MAYBE MOST OF IT was only fear. But not the last thing, not that. To blame my fear for that would be worst of all.

I was twelve years old and beginning to conquer my fears. I even went upstairs to do my homework, and managed to ignore the chimney. I had to be brave, because of my parents – because of my mother.

She had always been afraid for me. The very first day I had gone to school I'd seen her watching. Her expression had reminded me of the face of a girl I'd glimpsed on television, watching men lock her husband behind bars; I was frightened all that first day. And when children had hysterics or began to bully me, or the teacher lost her temper, these things only confirmed my fears – and my mother's, when I told her what had happened each day.

Now I was at grammar school. I had been there for much of a year. I'd felt awkward in my new uniform and old shoes; the building seemed enormous, crowded with too many strange children and teachers. I'd felt I was an outsider; friendly approaches made me nervous and sullen, when people laughed and I didn't know why I was sure they were laughing at me. After a while the other boys treated me as I seemed to want to be treated: the lads from the poorer districts mocked my suburban accent, the suburban boys sneered at my shoes.

Often I'd sat praying that the teacher wouldn't ask me a question I couldn't answer, sat paralysed by my dread of having to stand up in the waiting watchful silence. If a teacher shouted at someone my heart jumped painfully; once I'd felt the stain of

my shock creeping insidiously down my thigh. Yet I did well in
the end-of-term examinations, because I was terrified of failing;
for nights afterwards they were another reason why I couldn't
sleep.

My mother read the signs of all this on my face. More and
more, once I'd told her what was wrong, I had to persuade her
there was nothing worse that I'd kept back. Some mornings as I
lay in bed, trying to hold back half past seven, I'd be sick; I
would grope miserably downstairs, white-faced, and my mother
would keep me home. Once or twice, when my fear wasn't
quite enough, I made myself sick. "Look at him. You can't
expect him to go like that" – but my father would only shake his
head and grunt, dismissing us both.

I knew my father found me embarrassing. This year he'd had
less time for me than usual; his shop – The Anything Shop,
nearby in the suburbanised village – was failing to compete with
the new supermarket. But before that trouble I'd often seen
him staring up at my mother and me: both of us taller than him,
his eyes said, yet both scared of our own shadows. At those times
I glimpsed his despair.

So my parents weren't reassuring. Yet at night I tried to stay
with them as long as I could – for my worst fears were upstairs,
in my room.

It was a large room, two rooms knocked into one by the
previous owner. It overlooked the small back gardens. The
smaller of the fireplaces had been bricked up; in winter, the
larger held a fire, which my mother always feared would set fire
to the room – but she let it alone, for I'd screamed when I
thought she was going to take that light away: even though the
firelight only added to the terrors of the room.

The shadows moved things. The mesh of the fireguard
fluttered enlarged on the wall; sometimes, at the edge of sleep,
it became a swaying web, and its spinner came sidling down
from a corner of the ceiling. Everything was unstable; walls
shifted, my clothes crawled on the back of the chair. Once,
when I'd left my jacket slumped over the chair, the collar's dark
upturned lack of a face began to nod forward stealthily; the
holes at the ends of the sleeves worked like mouths, and I didn't
dare get up to hang the jacket properly. The room grew in the
dark: sounds outside, footsteps and laughter, dogs encouraging
each other to bark, only emphasised the size of my trap of
darkness, how distant everything else was. And there was a

dimmer room, in the mirror of the wardrobe beyond the foot of the bed. There was a bed in that room, and beside it a dim nightlight in a plastic lantern. Once I'd wakened to see a face staring dimly at me from the mirror; a figure had sat up when I had, and I'd almost cried out. Often I'd stared at the dim staring face, until I'd had to hide beneath the sheets.

Of course this couldn't go on for the rest of my life. On my twelfth birthday I set about the conquest of my room.

I was happy amid my presents. I had a jigsaw, a box of coloured pencils, a book of space stories. They had come from my father's shop, but they were mine now. Because I was relaxed, no doubt because she wished I could always be so, my mother said "Would you be happier if you went to another school?"

It was Saturday; I wanted to forget Monday. Besides, I imagined all schools were as frightening. "No, I'm all right," I said.

"Are you happy at school now?" she said incredulously.

"Yes, it's all right."

"Are you sure?"

"Yes, really, it's all right. I mean, I'm happy now."

The snap of the letter-slot saved me from further lying. Three birthday cards: two from neighbours who talked to me when I served them in the shop – an old lady who always carried a poodle, our next-door neighbour Dr Flynn – and a card from my parents. I'd seen all three cards in the shop, which spoilt them somehow.

As I stood in the hall I heard my father. "You've got to control yourself," he was saying. "You only upset the child. If you didn't go on at him he wouldn't be half so bad."

It infuriated me to be called a child. "But I worry so," my mother said brokenly. "He can't look after himself."

"You don't let him try. You'll have him afraid to go up to bed next."

But I already was. Was that my mother's fault? I remembered her putting the nightlight by my bed when I was very young, checking the flex and the bulb each night – I'd taken to lying awake, dreading that one or the other would fail. Standing in the hall, I saw dimly that my mother and I encouraged each other's fears. One of us had to stop. I had to stop. Even when I was frightened, I mustn't let her see. It wouldn't be the first time I'd hidden my feelings from her. In the living-room I said "I'm going upstairs to play."

Sometimes in the summer I didn't mind playing there – but this was March, and a dark day. Still, I could switch the light on. And my room contained the only table I could have to myself and my jigsaw.

I spilled the jigsaw onto the table. The chair sat with its back to the dark yawn of the fireplace; I moved it hastily to the foot of the bed, facing the door. I spread the jigsaw. There was a piece of the edge, another. By lunchtime I'd assembled the edge. "You look pleased with yourself," my father said.

I didn't notice the approach of night. I was fitting together my own blue sky, above fragmented cottages. After dinner I hurried to put in the pieces I'd placed mentally while eating. I hesitated outside my room. I should have to reach into the dark for the light-switch. When I did, the wallpaper filled with bright multiplied aeroplanes and engines. I wished we could afford to redecorate my room, it seemed childish now.

The fireplace gaped. I retrieved the fireguard from the cupboard under the stairs, where my father had stored it now the nights were a little warmer. It covered the soot-encrusted yawn. The room felt comfortable now. I'd never seen before how much space it gave me for play.

I even felt safe in bed. I switched out the nightlight – but that was too much; I grabbed the light. I didn't mind its glow on its own, without the jagged lurid jig of the shadows. And the fireguard was comforting. It made me feel that nothing could emerge from the chimney.

On Monday I took my space stories to school. People asked to look at them; eventually they lent me books. In the following weeks some of my fears began to fade. Questions darting from desk to desk still made me uneasy, but if I had to stand up without the answer at least I knew the other boys weren't sneering at me, not all of them; I was beginning to have friends. I started to sympathize with their own ignorant silences. In the July examinations I was more relaxed, and scored more marks. I was even sorry to leave my friends for the summer; I invited some of them home.

I felt triumphant. I'd calmed my mother and my room all by myself, just by realising what had to be done. I suppose that sense of triumph helped me. It must have given me a little strength with which to face the real terror.

It was early August, the week before our holiday. My mother was worrying over the luggage, my father was trying to calculate his accounts; they were beginning to chafe against each other. I went to my room, to stay out of their way.

I was halfway through a jigsaw, which one of my friends had swapped for mine. People sat in back gardens, letting the evening settle on them; between the houses the sky was pale yellow. I inserted pieces easily, relaxed by the nearness of our holiday. I listened to the slowing of the city, a radio fluttering along a street, something moving behind the fireguard, in the chimney.

No. It was my mother in the next room, moving luggage. It was someone dragging, dragging something, anything, outside. But I couldn't deceive my ears. In the chimney something large had moved.

It might have been a bird, stunned or dying, struggling feebly – except that a bird would have sounded wilder. It could have been a mouse, even a rat, if such things are found in chimneys. But it sounded like a large body, groping stealthily in the dark: something large that didn't want me to hear it. It sounded like the worst terror of my infancy.

I'd almost forgotten that. When I was three years old my mother had let me watch television; it was bad for my eyes, but just this once, near Christmas . . . I'd seen two children asleep in bed, an enormous crimson man emerging from the fireplace, creeping towards them. They weren't going to wake up! "Burglar! Burglar!" I'd screamed, beginning to cry. "No, dear, it's Father Christmas," my mother said, hastily switching off the television. "He always comes out of the chimney."

Perhaps if she'd said "down" rather than "out of" . . . For months after that, and in the weeks before several Christmases, I lay awake listening fearfully for movement in the chimney: I was sure a fat grinning figure would creep upon me if I slept. My mother had told me the presents that appeared at the end of my bed were left by Father Christmas, but now the mysterious visitor had a face and a huge body, squeezed into the dark chimney among the soot. When I heard the wind breathing in the chimney I had to trap my screams between my lips.

Of course at last I began to suspect there was no Father Christmas: how did he manage to steal into my father's shop for my presents? He was a childish idea, I was almost sure – but I was too embarrassed to ask my parents or my friends. But I wanted not to believe in him, that silent lurker in the chimney;

and now I didn't, not really. Except that something large was moving softly behind the fireguard.

It had stopped. I stared at the wire mesh, half expecting a fat pale face to stare out of the grate. There was nothing but the fenced dark. Cats were moaning in a garden, an ice-cream van wandered brightly. After a while I forced myself to pull the fireguard away.

I was taller than the fireplace now. But I had to stoop to peer up the dark soot-ridged throat, and then it loomed over me, darkness full of menace, of the threat of a huge figure bursting out at me, its red mouth crammed with sparkling teeth. As I peered up, trembling a little, and tried to persuade myself that what I'd heard had flown away or scurried back into its hole, soot came trickling down from the dark – and I heard the sound of a huge body squeezed into the sooty passage, settling itself carefully, more comfortably in its burrow.

I slammed the guard into place, and fled. I had to gulp to breathe. I ran onto the landing, trying to catch my breath so as to cry for help. Downstairs my mother was nervously asking whether she should pack another of my father's shirts. "Yes, if you like," he said irritably.

No, I mustn't cry out. I'd vowed not to upset her. But how could I go back into my room? Suddenly I had a thought that seemed to help. At school we'd learned how sweeps had used to send small boys up chimneys. There had hardly been room for the boys to climb. How could a large man fit in there?

He couldn't. Gradually I managed to persuade myself. At last I opened the door of my room. The chimney was silent; there was no wind. I tried not to think that he was holding himself still, waiting to squeeze out stealthily, waiting for the dark. Later, lying in the steady glow from my plastic lantern, I tried to hold on to the silence, tried to believe there was nothing near me to shatter it. There was nothing except, eventually, sleep.

Perhaps if I'd cried out on the landing I would have been saved from my fear. But I was happy with my rationality. Only once, nearly asleep, I wished the fire were lit, because it would burn anything that might be hiding in the chimney; that had never occurred to me before. But it didn't matter, for the next day we went on holiday.

My parents liked to sleep in the sunlight, beneath newspaper masks; in the evenings they liked to stroll along the wide sandy streets. I didn't, and befriended Nigel, the son of another family who were staying in the boarding-house. My mother encouraged the friendship: such a nice boy, two years older than me; he'd look after me. He had money, and the hope of a moustache shadowing his pimply upper lip. One evening he took me to the fairground, where we met two girls; he and the older girl went to buy ice creams while her young friend and I stared at each other timidly. I couldn't believe the young girl didn't like jigsaws. Later, while I was contradicting her, Nigel and his companion disappeared behind the Ghost Train – but Nigel reappeared almost at once, red-faced, his left cheek redder. "Where's Rose?" I asked, bewildered.

"She had to go." He seemed furious that I'd asked.

"Isn't she coming back?"

"No." He was glancing irritably about for a change of subject. "What a super bike," he said, pointing as it glided between the stalls. "Have you got a bike?"

"No," I said. "I keep asking Father Christmas, but—" I wished that hadn't got past me, for he was staring at me, winking at the young girl.

"Do you still believe in him?" he demanded scornfully.

"No, of course I don't. I was only kidding." Did he believe me? He was edging towards the young girl now, putting his arm around her; soon she excused herself, and didn't come back – I never knew her name. I was annoyed he'd made her run away. "Where did Rose go?" I said persistently.

He didn't tell me. But perhaps he resented my insistence, for as the family left the boarding-house I heard him say loudly to his mother "He still believes in Father Christmas." My mother heard that too, and glanced anxiously at me.

Well, I didn't. There was nobody in the chimney, waiting for me to come home. I didn't care that we were going home the next day. That night I pulled away the fireguard and saw a fat pale face hanging down into the fireplace, like an underbelly, upside-down and smiling. But I managed to wake, and eventually the sea lulled me back to sleep.

As soon as we reached home I ran upstairs. I uncovered the fireplace and stood staring, to discover what I felt. Gradually I filled with the scorn Nigel would have felt, had he known of my fear. How could I have been so childish? The chimney was only a passage for smoke, a hole into which the wind wandered sometimes. That night, exhausted by the journey home, I slept at once.

The nights darkened into October; the darkness behind the
mesh grew thicker. I'd used to feel, as summer waned, that the
chimney was insinuating its darkness into my room. Now the
sight only reminded me I'd have a fire soon. The fire would be
comforting.

It was October when my father's Christmas cards arrived, on
a Saturday; I was working in the shop. It annoyed him to have
to anticipate Christmas so much, to compete with the supermarket. I hardly noticed the cards: my head felt muffled, my
body cold – perhaps it was the weather's sudden hint of
winter.

My mother came into the shop that afternoon. I watched her
pretend not to have seen the cards. When I looked away she
began to pick them up timidly, as if they were unfaithful letters,
glancing anxiously at me. I didn't know what was in her mind.
My head was throbbing. I wasn't going home sick. I earned
pocket money in the shop. Besides, I didn't want my father to
think I was still weak.

Nor did I want my mother to worry. That night I lay slumped
in a chair, pretending to read. Words trickled down the page; I
felt like dirty clothes someone had thrown on the chair. My
father was at the shop taking stock. My mother sat gazing at me.
I pretended harder; the words waltzed slowly. At last she said
"Are you listening?"

I was now, though I didn't look up. "Yes," I said hoarsely,
unplugging my throat with a roar.

"Do you remember when you were a baby? There was a film
you saw, of Father Christmas coming out of the chimney." Her
voice sounded bravely careless, falsely light, as if she were
determined to make some awful revelation. I couldn't look
up. "Yes," I said.

Her silence made me glance up. She looked as she had on
my first day at school: full of loss, of despair. Perhaps she was
realizing I had to grow up, but to my throbbing head her look
suggested only terror – as if she were about to deliver me up as a
sacrifice. "I couldn't tell you the truth then," she said. "You
were too young."

The truth was terror; her expression promised that. "Father
Christmas isn't really like that," she said.

My illness must have shown by then. She gazed at me; her lips
trembled. "I can't," she said, turning her face away. "Your
father must tell you."

But that left me poised on the edge of terror. I felt unnerved, rustily tense. I wanted very much to lie down. "I'm going to my room," I said. I stumbled upstairs, hardly aware of doing so. As much as anything I was fleeing her unease. The stairs swayed a little, they felt unnaturally soft underfoot. I hurried dully into my room. I slapped the light-switch and missed. I was walking uncontrollably forward into blinding dark. A figure came to meet me, soft and huge in the dark of my room.

I cried out. I managed to stagger back onto the landing, grabbing the light-switch as I went. The lighted room was empty. My mother came running upstairs, almost falling. "What is it, what is it?" she cried.

I mustn't say. "I'm ill. I feel sick." I did, and a minute later I was. She patted my back as I knelt by the toilet. When she'd put me to bed she made to go next door, for the doctor. "Don't leave me," I pleaded. The walls of the room swayed as if tugged by firelight, the fireplace was huge and very dark. As soon as my father opened the door she ran downstairs, crying "He's ill, he's ill! Go for the doctor!"

The doctor came and prescribed for my fever. My mother sat up beside me. Eventually my father came to suggest it was time she went to bed. They were going to leave me alone in my room. "Make a fire," I pleaded.

My mother touched my forehead. "But you're burning," she said.

"No, I'm cold! I want a fire! Please!" So she made one, tired as she was. I saw my father's disgust as he watched me use her worry against her to get what I wanted, his disgust with her for letting herself be used.

I didn't care. My mother's halting words had overgrown my mind. What had she been unable to tell me? Had it to do with the sounds I'd heard in the chimney? The room lolled around me; nothing was sure. But the fire would make sure for me. Nothing in the chimney could survive it.

I made my mother stay until the fire was blazing. Suppose a huge shape burst forth from the hearth, dripping fire? When at last I let go I lay lapped by the firelight and meshy shadows, which seemed lulling now, in my warm room.

I felt feverish, but not unpleasantly. I was content to voyage on my rocking bed; the ceiling swayed past above me. While I slept the fire went out. My fever kept me warm; I slid out of bed and, pulling away the fireguard, reached up the chimney. At the length of my arms I touched something heavy, hanging down in the dark; it yielded, then soft fat fingers groped down and closed on my wrist. My mother was holding my wrist as she washed my hands. "You mustn't get out of bed," she said when she realized I was awake.

I stared stupidly at her. "You'd got out of bed. You were sleepwalking," she explained. "You had your hands right up the chimney." I saw now that she was washing caked soot from my hands; tracks of ash led towards the bed.

It had been only a dream. One moment the fat hand had been gripping my wrist, the next it was my mother's cool slim fingers. My mother played word games and timid chess with me while I stayed in bed, that day and the next.

The third night I felt better. The fire fluttered gently; I felt comfortably warm. Tomorrow I'd get up. I should have to go back to school soon, but I didn't mind that unduly. I lay and listened to the breathing of the wind in the chimney.

When I awoke the fire had gone out. The room was full of darkness. The wind still breathed, but it seemed somehow closer. It was above me. Someone was standing over me. It couldn't be either of my parents, not in the sightless darkness.

I lay rigid. Most of all I wished that I hadn't let Nigel's imagined contempt persuade me to do without a nightlight. The breathing was slow, irregular; it sounded clogged and feeble. As I tried to inch silently towards the far side of the bed, the source of the breathing stooped towards me. I felt its breath waver on my face, and the breath sprinkled me with something like dry rain.

When I had lain paralysed for what felt like blind hours, the breathing went away. It was in the chimney, dislodging soot; it might be the wind. But I knew it had come out to let me know that whatever the fire had done to it, it hadn't been killed. It had emerged to tell me it would come for me on Christmas Eve. I began to scream.

I wouldn't tell my mother why. She washed my face, which was freckled with soot. "You've been sleepwalking again," she tried to reassure me, but I wouldn't let her leave me until daylight. When she'd gone I saw the ashy tracks leading from the chimney to the bed.

Perhaps I had been sleepwalking and dreaming. I searched vainly for my nightlight. I would have been ashamed to ask for a new one, and that helped me to feel I could do without. At dinner I felt secure enough to say I didn't know why I had screamed.

"But you must remember. You sounded so frightened. You upset me."

My father was folding the evening paper into a thick wad the size of a pocketbook, which he could read beside his plate. "Leave the boy alone," he said. "You imagine all sorts of things when you're feverish. I did when I was his age."

It was the first time he'd admitted anything like weakness to me. If he'd managed to survive his nightmares, why should mine disturb me more? Tired out by the demands of my fever, I slept soundly that night. The chimney was silent except for the flapping of flames.

But my father didn't help me again. One November afternoon I was standing behind the counter, hoping for customers. My father pottered, grumpily fingering packets of nylons, tins of pet food, Dinky toys, babies' rattles, cards, searching for signs of theft. Suddenly he snatched a Christmas card and strode to the counter. "Sit down," he said grimly.

He was waving the card at me, like evidence. I sat down on a shelf, but then a lady came into the shop; the bell thumped. I stood up to sell her nylons. When she'd gone I gazed at my father, anxious to hear the worst. "Just sit down," he said.

He couldn't stand my being taller than he was. His size embarrassed him, but he wouldn't let me see that; he pretended I had to sit down out of respect. "Your mother says she tried to tell you about Father Christmas," he said.

She must have told him that weeks earlier. He'd put off talking to me – because we'd never been close, and now we were growing further apart. "I don't know why she couldn't tell you," he said.

But he wasn't telling me either. He was looking at me as if I were a stranger he had to chat to. I felt uneasy, unsure now that I wanted to hear what he had to say. A man was approaching the shop. I stood up, hoping he'd interrupt.

He did, and I served him. Then, to delay my father's revelation, I adjusted stacks of tins. My father stared at me in disgust. "If you don't watch out you'll be as bad as your mother."

I found the idea of being like my mother strange, indefinably disturbing. But he wouldn't let me be like him, wouldn't let me near. All right, I'd be brave, I'd listen to what he had to say. But he said "Oh, it's not worth me trying to tell you. You'll find out."

He meant I must find out for myself that Father Christmas was a childish fantasy. He didn't mean he wanted the thing from the chimney to come for me, the disgust in his eyes didn't mean that, it didn't. He meant that I had to behave like a man. And I could. I'd show him. The chimney was silent. I needn't worry until Christmas Eve. Nor then. There was nothing to come out.

One evening as I walked home I saw Dr Flynn in his front room. He was standing before a mirror, gazing at his red fur-trimmed hooded suit; he stooped to pick up his beard. My mother told me that he was going to act Father Christmas at the children's hospital. She seemed on the whole glad that I'd seen. So was I: it proved the pretence was only for children.

Except that the glimpse reminded me how near Christmas was. As the nights closed on the days, and the days rushed by – the end-of-term party, the turkey, decorations in the house – I grew tense, trying to prepare myself. For what? For nothing, nothing at all. Well, I would know soon – for suddenly it was Christmas Eve.

I was busy all day. I washed up as my mother prepared Christmas dinner. I brought her ingredients, and hurried to buy some she'd used up. I stuck the day's cards to tapes above the mantelpiece. I carried home a tinsel tree which nobody had bought. But being busy only made the day move faster. Before I knew it the windows were full of night.

Christmas Eve. Well, it didn't worry me. I was too old for that sort of thing. The tinsel tree rustled when anyone passed it, light rolled in tinsel globes, streamers flinched back when doors opened. Whenever I glanced at the wall above the mantelpiece I saw half a dozen red-cheeked smiling bearded faces swinging restlessly on tapes.

The night piled against the windows. I chattered to my mother about her shouting father, her elder sisters, the time her sisters had locked her in a cellar. My father grunted occasionally – even when I'd run out of subjects to discuss with my mother, and tried to talk to him about the shop. At least he hadn't noticed how late I was staying up. But he had. "It's about time everyone was in bed," he said with a kind of suppressed fury.

"Can I have some more coal?" My mother would never let

me have a coal-scuttle in the bedroom – she didn't want me going near the fire. "To put on now," I said. Surely she must say yes. "It'll be cold in the morning," I said.

"Yes, you take some. You don't want to be cold when you're looking at what Father – at your presents."

I hurried upstairs with the scuttle. Over its clatter I heard my father say "Are you still at that? Can't you let him grow up?"

I almost emptied the scuttle into the fire, which rose roaring and crackling. My father's voice was an angry mumble, seeping through the floor. When I carried the scuttle down my mother's eyes were red, my father looked furiously determined. I'd always found their arguments frightening; I was glad to hurry to my room.

It seemed welcoming. The fire was bright within the mesh. I heard my mother come upstairs. That was comforting too: she was nearer now. I heard my father go next door – to wish the doctor Happy Christmas, I supposed. I didn't mind the reminder. There was nothing of Christmas Eve in my room, except the pillowcase on the floor at the foot of the bed. I pushed it aside with one foot, the better to ignore it.

I slid into bed. My father came upstairs; I heard further mumblings of argument through the bedroom wall. At last they stopped, and I tried to relax. I lay, glad of the silence.

A wind was rushing the house. It puffed down the chimney; smoke trickled through the fireguard. Now the wind was breathing brokenly. It was only the wind. It didn't bother me.

Perhaps I'd put too much coal on the fire. The room was hot; I was sweating. I felt almost feverish. The huge mesh flicked over the wall repeatedly, nervously, like a rapid net. Within the mirror the dimmer room danced.

Suddenly I was a little afraid. Not that something would come out of the chimney, that was stupid: afraid that my feeling of fever would make me delirious again. It seemed years since I'd been disturbed by the sight of the room in the mirror, but I was disturbed now. There was something wrong with that dim jerking room.

The wind breathed. Only the wind, I couldn't hear it changing. A fat billow of smoke squeezed through the mesh. The room seemed more oppressive now, and smelled of smoke. It didn't smell entirely like coal smoke, but I couldn't tell what else was burning. I didn't want to get up to find out.

I must lie still. Otherwise I'd be writhing about trying to

clutch at sleep, as I had the second night of my fever, and sometimes in summer. I must sleep before the room grew too hot. I must keep my eyes shut. I mustn't be distracted by the faint trickling of soot, nor the panting of the wind, nor the shadows and orange light that snatched at my eyes through my eyelids.

I woke in darkness. The fire had gone out. No, it was still there when I opened my eyes: subdued orange crawled on embers, a few weak flames leapt repetitively. The room was moving more slowly now. The dim room in the mirror, the face peering out at me, jerked faintly, as if almost dead.

I couldn't look at that. I slid further down the bed, dragging the pillow into my nest. I was too hot, but at least beneath the sheets I felt safe. I began to relax. Then I realised what I'd seen. The light had been dim, but I was almost sure the fireguard was standing away from the hearth.

I must have mistaken that, in the dim light. I wasn't feverish, I couldn't have sleepwalked again. There was no need for me to look, I was comfortable. But I was beginning to admit that I had better look when I heard the slithering in the chimney.

Something large was coming down. A fall of soot: I could hear the scattering pats of soot in the grate, thrown down by the harsh halting wind. But the wind was emerging from the fireplace, into the room. It was above me, panting through its obstructed throat.

I lay staring up at the mask of my sheets. I trembled from holding myself immobile. My held breath filled me painfully as lumps of rock. I had only to lie there until whatever was above me went away. It couldn't touch me.

The clogged breath bent nearer; I could hear its dry rattling. Then something began to fumble at the sheets over my face. It plucked feebly at them, trying to grasp them, as if it had hardly anything to grasp with. My own hands clutched at the sheets from within, but couldn't hold them down entirely. The sheets were being tugged from me, a fraction at a time. Soon I would be face to face with my visitor.

I was lying there with my eyes squeezed tight when it let go of the sheets and went away. My throbbing lungs had forced me to take shallow breaths; now I breathed silently open-mouthed, though that filled my mouth with fluff. The tolling of my ears subsided, and I realised the thing had not returned to the chimney. It was still in the room.

I couldn't hear its breathing; it couldn't be near me. Only that thought allowed me to look – that, and the desperate hope that I might escape, since it moved so slowly. I peeled the sheets down from my face slowly, stealthily, until my eyes were bare. My heartbeats shook me. In the sluggishly shifting light I saw a figure at the foot of the bed.

Its red costume was thickly furred with soot. It had its back to me; its breathing was muffled by the hood. What shocked me most was its size. It occurred to me, somewhere amid my engulfing terror, that burning shrivels things. The figure stood in the mirror as well, in the dim twitching room. A face peered out of the hood in the mirror, like a charred turnip carved with a rigid grin.

The stunted figure was still moving painfully. It edged round the foot of the bed and stooped to my pillowcase. I saw it draw the pillowcase up over itself and sink down. As it sank its hood fell back, and I saw the charred turnip roll about in the hood, as if there were almost nothing left to support it.

I should have had to pass the pillowcase to reach the door. I couldn't move. The room seemed enormous, and was growing darker; my parents were far away. At last I managed to drag the sheets over my face, and pulled the pillow, like muffs, around my ears.

I had lain sleeplessly for hours when I heard a movement at the foot of the bed. The thing had got out of its sack again. It was coming towards me. It was tugging at the sheets, more strongly now. Before I could catch hold of the sheets I glimpsed a red fur-trimmed sleeve, and was screaming.

"Let go, will you," my father said irritably. "Good God, it's only me."

He was wearing Dr Flynn's disguise, which flapped about him – the jacket, at least; his pyjama cuffs peeked beneath it. I stopped screaming and began to giggle hysterically. I think he would have struck me, but my mother ran in. "It's all right. All right," she reassured me, and explained to him "It's the shock."

He was making angrily for the door when she said "Oh, don't go yet, Albert. Stay while he opens his presents," and, lifting the bulging pillowcase from the floor, dumped it beside me.

I couldn't push it away, I couldn't let her see my terror. I made myself pull out my presents into the daylight, books, sweets, ballpoints; as I groped deeper I wondered whether the charred face would crumble when I touched it. Sweat pricked my hands; they shook with horror – they could, because my mother couldn't see them.

The pillowcase contained nothing but presents and a pinch of soot. When I was sure it was empty I slumped against the headboard, panting. "He's tired," my mother said, in defence of my ingratitude. "He was up very late last night."

Later I managed an accident, dropping the pillowcase on the fire downstairs. I managed to eat Christmas dinner, and to go to bed that night. I lay awake, even though I was sure nothing would come out of the chimney now. Later I realized why my father had come to my room in the morning dressed like that; he'd intended me to catch him, to cure me of the pretence. But it was many years before I enjoyed Christmas very much.

When I left school I went to work in libraries. Ten years later I married. My wife and I crossed town weekly to visit my parents. My mother chattered, my father was taciturn. I don't think he ever quite forgave me for laughing at him.

One winter night our telephone rang. I answered it, hoping it wasn't the police. My library was then suffering from robberies. All I wanted was to sit before the fire and imagine the glittering cold outside. But it was Dr Flynn.

"Your parents' house is on fire," he told me. "Your father's trapped in there. Your mother needs you."

They'd had a friend to stay. My mother had lit the fire in the guest-room, my old bedroom. A spark had eluded the fire-guard; the carpet had caught fire. Impatient for the fire engine, my father had run back into the house to put the fire out, but had been overcome. All this I learned later. Now I drove coldly across town, towards the glow in the sky.

The glow was doused by the time I arrived. Smoke scrolled over the roof. But my mother had found a coal sack and was struggling still to run into the house, to beat the fire; her friend and Dr Flynn held her back. She dropped the sack and ran to me. "Oh, it's your father. It's Albert," she repeated through her weeping.

The firemen withdrew their hose. The ambulance stood winking. I saw the front door open, and a stretcher carried out. The path was wet and frosty. One stretcher-bearer slipped, and the contents of the stretcher spilled over the path.

I saw Dr Flynn glance at my mother. Only the fear that she might turn caused him to act. He grabbed the sack and, running to the path, scooped up what lay scattered there. I saw the charred head roll on the lip of the sack before it dropped within. I had seen that already, years ago.

My mother came to live with us, but we could see she was pining; my parents must have loved each other, in their way. She died a year later. Perhaps I killed them both. I know that what emerged from the chimney was in some sense my father. But surely that was a premonition. Surely my fear could never have reached out to make him die that way.

PHYLLIS EISENSTEIN

Dark Wings

PHYLLIS EISENSTEIN HAS BEEN writing professionally since 1971, both on her own and in collaboration with her husband Alex. She has published seven novels: *Born to Exile, Shadow of Earth, Sorcerer's Son, In the Hands of Glory, The Crystal Palace, In the Red Lord's Reach* and *The City in Stone,* as well as some three dozen novellas and short stories in the fantasy, horror and science fiction genres.

Her short fiction has been nominated for the Hugo and Nebula awards five times, and her first collection, *Night Lives: Nine Stories of the Dark Fantastic,* appeared in 2003.

Since 1989, Eisenstein has been an adjunct professor in the Fiction Writing Department of Columbia College, Chicago, teaching science fiction and, more recently, fantasy. In the late 1990s she edited two volumes of *Spec-Lit,* an anthology series showcasing the work of her students.

"At the time I wrote 'Dark Wings'," the author remembers, "I thought it was inspired by one of my favourite Robert Heinlein stories. Only later did I realize that it also had roots in a *Galaxy* cover I saw in my childhood.

"The original painting for that cover, by Ed Emshwiller, now resides in the Eisenstein art collection. But to say more about

either of those sources would be to say too much, and identify-
ing them must be left as an exercise for the reader.''

THE HOUSE SEEMED LARGE and empty now that her parents
were dead. And yet it was also so soothingly quiet that Lydia
would sometimes just stand in the high-ceilinged dining room
and relish the silence. No shrill voice came floating from the
upper story, no gravelly, grating one from the oak-paneled
study, no orders, demands, advice, admonishments. The electricity was gone from the air, leaving nothing but solitude.

She had dreamed of such peace, dreamed as the years and
her youth ebbed away, eroded by a struggle she was too weak to
win. Dutiful and self-sacrificing, people had called her – nurse,
maid, cook, buffer between her parents and the outside world.
But behind her back, she knew, they had clucked their tongues
over the poor, dried-up spinster. What did they know of the
guilts and fears that her parents had instilled in her, of the
elaborate net of obligation they had spun about her, till she was
bound to them with ties that only death could sever. And death
had come, at last, like a knight on his pale charger, and borne
away two coffins that set her free. Still, people clucked their
tongues, because Lydia lived much as before, alone in her
parents' house, alone in her heart. If anything, she was quieter
than ever.

Yet some things had changed for her. She painted a great
deal more these days, uninterrupted. She had moved her
studio from the basement to the big bedroom upstairs, where
the light splashed in from windows on three sides. On fine days,
she would open those windows and let the sea air wash away the
smell of paint. In the evenings she walked by the shore, sharing
it with tourists and young lovers, and there were no responsi-
bilities to call her home at any particular time. Some nights, she
would be there long after the noises of traffic had faded to
nothing, till only the bell of a distant buoy remained for
company. She hardly thought about anything at those times,
only enjoyed the dark and the starlight on the waves, and the
blessed, blessed silence.

On one such night she saw the bird for the first time. The
moon had risen as she watched, its light splashed like a pale
and shimmering highway crossing the restless ocean toward
Europe. Like a shadow upon that path, the bird caught her eye,

its dark wings limned by silvery radiance. For a moment, it glided over the waves, pinions motionless in the still night air, and then it swooped upward and vanished in the darkness.

She stood awhile by the shore, straining her eyes for another glimpse of the creature, hoping it would wheel and make a second pass over the glittering water. It was a hawk of some sort, perhaps even an eagle – size and distance were deceptive out over the ocean, where there were no references to judge by. She wanted it to be an eagle, for they were rare in these parts, and protected. She had only seen a live eagle here once before, when she was a small child. But though she waited till the moon was high and shrunken, she saw the bird no more, though perhaps she heard the beat of its wings far above her head. Or perhaps she only heard the cool surf beating at the rocks below her feet. At night, by the sea, time, distance, and direction all seemed to muddle together, playing tricks on the eyes, the ears, and the mind.

At home, she could not sleep for thinking about the bird, and before dawn she was in the studio by yellow, artificial light, with a fresh canvas and dark acrylic pigments spread over her palette. Swiftly, she recreated the impression of the scene, the silver moonpath, the dark bird an instantaneous silhouette, and all surrounded by an impenetrable black that seemed to suck light away from the hard, sharp stars. Blue-black she used, instead of true black – Prussian Blue, that velvety shade so dark that only a careful eye could tell it from black, but warmer somehow, softer, deeper. The sky and the bird, Prussian Blue. But when dawn added its radiance to her lamps, she saw that she had not captured the mood of that moment. The canvas was dull and dim. Her dilated pupils had perceived a patch of luminous, ethereal night in a vaster darkness, but the paints had given her only the latter.

Light, she thought, as she cleaned the palette and brushes. Light. But all she could remember was the plumage of the bird, blacker than black under the silver moon.

She slept.

Later in the day, she walked down to the shore, earlier than usual. This time she carried binoculars, hurriedly purchased in town, and she scanned the seaward sky from north to south, searching for a familiar silhouette. Gulls she saw, gulls in plenty, soaring, swooping for food, perching on rocks. Fat gulls, grey on top and white beneath. But no hawks, no eagles. She turned the binoculars westward, toward the rooftops of the town, just visible beyond the intervening trees. She saw flecks that might be pigeons, crows, even sparrows, near and far. Ordinary birds. Nowhere did she see the short head, broad tail, and flared wings that marked her quarry.

She ate a quick dinner and returned to the painting by the waning, rosy glow of dusk. One could not evoke the depths of night, she thought, under a bright sun. She lightened her palette, reworked the moon and sea and even the dark air between them, trying to capture the radiance against which the bird had seemed so intense a shadow. Past midnight, she realized that there was a contradiction in her mind, a double image of that instant, in which the sky was bright and dark at the same time. She could feel it, but the painting was only a poor reflection of that feeling, two dimensional, and – by now – muddy. She cleaned the palette and brushes and set the canvas aside against the wall. Stifling a yawn, she mounted a fresh, blank canvas on the easel.

The bird this time, nothing else. She sketched quickly, placing tail and flared pinions, adding details that she felt rather than remembered. The light was moonlight of course, but there was no sky, no ocean, only the dark wingspan and the merest suggestion of curved beak and piercing eye. And when she reached the limits of both her recollection and her invention, she went downstairs to the study and looked eagles up in the encyclopedia. She knew now that it had been an eagle; she wouldn't allow it to be anything else. The encyclopedia illustrations gave her some inspiration and corrected a few of her assumptions, and she hurried back upstairs to make adjustments.

By dawnlight again, she viewed her new effort with a critical eye. She had never painted birds before; at most, they had been pieces of background in her few landscapes, a brushstroke or two in the sky. The black eagle showed her lack of familiarity with his kind; he was naive and awkward, though bold. If she squinted, she could see a family resemblance to the bird on the back of a dollar bill.

At twilight, she walked by the shore, searching the darkening sky for him, staying on till the moon was high, that night and many after. Night upon night, as the moon waned and the stars brightened by contrast. Night upon night, in fair weather and foul, when the waves were slick as glass, when the waves were wild things clutching for the sky. She waited for another glimpse, straining at clouds or a late gull or a speck of flotsam on the water. She waited late, late, and past midnight she returned home and worked on one or the other of the paintings, striving to recreate the bird.

She had never gone to town much, less since the deaths of her parents. Now she had no use for the place at all; she had her groceries delivered and paid her bills by mail. Every scrap of her spare time was spoken for, by paint or binoculars, or the sleep that she grudgingly allowed herself. Only the postman saw her, dropping off a few bills, catalogues, advertisements a couple of times a week. And the people who walked by the sea. But the weather was beginning to grow chilly for both tourists and lovers; soon the moon waxed full again, and only Lydia stood on the shore to watch it touch the waves with silver.

She heard the bird now, sometimes – she was sure of that, though she never saw his broad, dark wings. She heard him beat the air once, twice, high above her head, and then there was silence as he soared and she stared upward, trying to pierce the blackness with her human eyes. She thought he could probably see her well enough, eagles' eyes being so much sharper than humans', and she tried to imagine how she must appear to him – her face a pale speck amid the darkness of rocks and scrubby grass. A small thing, earthbound, of no significance to a creature who sailed the dark ocean of air. What would it be like, she wondered, to have wings and look down upon the creatures who could only walk?

The paintings had proliferated by this time. They lined the studio, view after view of the subject she had seen only once. Yet there was a clear image of him in her mind's eye, as if she could reconstruct his whole form from the sound of his wings. His eye, she knew, was golden, like a great amber bead set above the corner of his beak. The beak was dark as his plumage, like polished jet. And to display their true span, the great black pinions would require a canvas larger than any Lydia had ever worked. She contemplated ordering the proper size from Boston, stretching it and preparing it herself. She measured the door of the studio, to be sure the finished product could be carried out of the room, and then she made the phone call.

Autumn was waning by the time the painting was well-begun. The sea breeze that washed her studio was chill by day now, and gusty, though she still opened the windows to it, and painted wearing an old sweater. When she walked by the shore, she could see scarlet leaves floating among the restless waves. The color of the ocean was changing, too, and the color of the sky; the daytime world was beginning to grey out for winter. Only at night were the changes invisible. At night the buoy still clanged far out on the water, and the moon still splashed its shimmering highway to Europe almost at Lydia's feet. At night, ebony wings beat the air, and Lydia strained for a glimpse, just a single brief glimpse, of the bird that glided somewhere, somewhere, in the vast, unchanging darkness.

The days grew shorter, as the chilling wind ruffled the waves to a restive froth, and the nights were long – long for walking by the choppy water, long for painting by lamplight. Lydia slept the whole short day through now, seeing the sun only at dawn and dusk. The bird preferred the night hours, and Lydia had begun to understand that preference. Day was jarring, stark, revealing too much of reality. Night was kind and soothing, hiding the world's flaws in velvet. At night, Lydia could look into her dimly lit mirror and see the girl she had once been, the girl whose skin bore no sign of wrinkling, whose hair was yet untouched by grey, whose life still lay ahead of her. That girl could walk on the shore and dream dreams; she could look upon the moonlit highway to Europe and imagine herself traveling it, light as a feather, eastward, over the horizon.

She finished the painting half a dozen times. At dawn she would step back from it, cock her head to one side, and nod to herself. She would clean the brushes and palette carefully, then, and go to bed satisfied. But when she woke a dusk, the light of the setting sun showed her flaws, approximations, incompleteness, and she would eat a quick breakfast and go out to the shore again, in search of her model, and inspiration. Inspiration she would find, in the clang of the buoy or the whisper of the wind, or the faint rustle of wingbeats high, high. But the model would not show himself, not even his shadow, and she would return home and work determinedly through the dark hours until she laid the brushes aside again, come dawn.

Half a dozen times, she finished, and slept, and then one blustery sunset found her with nothing left to do.

Not that the painting was perfect. She eyed it critically from every angle, brushes poised in her fingers, palette in the crook of her arm. She approached it several times, as if to lay another stroke upon the canvas, then drew back. The paint was very thick in some places. But she knew another layer would not make it better. The painting was beyond her ability to improve. She set her brushes aside and went out to walk.

Lydia understood the limits of her skill. She did not expect the canvas to be a photographic reproduction of the image in her mind's eye. She knew she would have to be satisfied with the faintest hint of the beauty and grace and power of the original. And down by the shore, in the pale light of the full moon, she had to weep for her own limitations. She wept, and she shivered a little because the night was very chill, and her coat was not quite heavy enough.

High above her head, she heard his wings.

She knew the sound instantly and looked up, straining to pierce the darkness, her tears a chilly patch upon each eye, blurring her vision for a moment. As a blur, she saw him silhouetted against the moon, and then she blinked and brought him into sharp focus. He was poised above the shimmering path that the moon laid down on the surface of the sea, his great wings motionless as he glided lower, lower, almost touching the white-topped waves. An eagle – yes, she had been right all the time, right in every detail, even to the amber eye that glittered with moonlight, glittered as it regarded her.

He swooped toward her, his great dark wings blotting out the moon, the sky, the world. She gazed at him in wonder, in adoration; the painting had not matched his true size, not remotely. He was the grandfather of eagles, she thought – the god of eagles. She felt a great gust of air as he hovered over her a moment. And then, as delicately as she might cradle a kitten, his great talons locked about her waist and hips. Her hair blew wild as his pinions cupped air to rise again, and then her feet floated free of the earth. Upward they soared – upward, and the rushing wind was a tonic to Lydia's soul. She felt light, young, and beautiful as the bird himself. Looking down, she could see the silver moonpath flowing far below.

Eastward they flew. Eastward toward Europe.

As the first rays of sunlight spread out over the ocean, Lydia saw the island. The only land visible from horizon, to horizon, it was dominated by a huge mountain, and as they drew closer, she realized that the summit of that mountain was their destination. This did not surprise her; where else, she reasoned, would an eagle rest?

Closer still, and she saw the nest, big as her parents' house, built of bushes and driftwood and spars from sailing ships, some with ropes and tattered canvas still clinging to them. And then, at the last moment, just before her feet touched the soft, shadowed interior of the nest, just before they brushed the lining of feathers torn from the bird's own downy breast, and his mate's, she struggled. Poor dried-up spinster, she struggled – weakly – as she fell toward those small, dark, gaping beaks.

GRAHAM MASTERTON

Reflection of Evil

GRAHAM MASTERTON RETURNED TO Britain in 2002, after living in Cork, Ireland, for four years, where "the silver rain and the golden silence were highly conducive to writing". While there, he was honoured for his fund-raising for the Irish Society for the Prevention of Cruelty to Children.

His latest novels include *Swimmer*, the Edgar Award-shortlisted *Trauma*, *The Hidden World* (which began life as a story he told to Irish Traveller children in his local library), *A Terrible Beauty* (set in County Cork), *The Doorkeepers*, *The Devil in Grey* and *Unspeakable*. The author's 1998 thriller *Genius* (originally published under the pseudonym "Alan Blackwood") was re-issued in hardcover, and Telos Publishing also issued a special 25th anniversary edition of his debut horror novel, *The Manitou*. He is currently working on a sequel, which the author describes as "Native American terror with knobs on."

An abridged version of the following story originally appeared on the BBC's horror website with illustrations by veteran artist Frazer Irving. It was also broadcast on BBC7 digital radio, read by Jamie Bamber. This marks the story's first appearance in print.

"I have been fascinated by mirrors ever since my mother

read me *Alice Through the Looking-Glass* when I was very young," recalls Masterton. "Lewis Carroll's idea that something different was happening in a mirror-world, if only you could see it, both alarmed and excited me, and I used to spend hours with my cheek pressed against the mirror in my grandparents's house, trying to see the strange and different garden which I was convinced existed just beyond the reflected back door.

"My novel *Mirror* told the story of a young boy whose murder was witnessed by a mirror, but I returned to the subject of reflected evil after reading a poignant story called 'The Lady of Shalott', about a small crippled girl in New York who (like Tennyson's Lady of Shalott) could only see the outside world by means of her mirror.

"I wrote three different stories on the same theme, including this one."

IT WAS RAINING SO hard that Mark stayed in the Range Rover, drinking cold espresso straight from the flask and listening to a play on the radio about a widow who compulsively knitted cardigans for her recently-dead husband.

"It took me ages to find this shade of grey. Shale, they call it. It matches his eyes."

"He's dead, Maureen. He's never going to wear it."

"Don't be silly. *Nobody* dies, so long as you remember what they looked like."

He was thinking about calling it a day when he saw Katie trudging across the field toward him, in her bright red raincoat, with the pointy hood. As she approached he let down the window, tipping out the last of his coffee. The rain spattered icy-cold against his cheek.

"You look *drowned*!" he called out. "Why don't you pack it in?"

"We've found something really exciting, that's why."

She came up to the Range Rover and pulled back her hood. Her curly blonde hair was stuck to her forehead and there was a drip on the end of her nose. She had always put him in mind of a poor bedraggled fairy, even when she was dry, and today she looked as if she had fallen out of her traveler's joy bush and into a puddle.

"Where's Nigel?" he asked her.

"He's still there, digging."

"I told him to survey the ditches. What the hell's he digging for?"

"Mark, we think we might have found Shalott."

"What? What are you talking about?"

Katie wiped the rain from her face with the back of her hand. "Those ditches aren't ditches, they used to be a stream, and there's an *island* in the middle. And those lumps we thought were Iron Age sheep-pens, they're stones, all cut and dressed, like the stones for building a wall."

"Oh, I *see*," said Mark. "And you and Nigel, being you and Nigel, you immediately thought, 'Shalott!' "

"Why not? It's in the right location, isn't it, upstream from Cadbury?"

Mark shook his head. "Come on, Katie, I know that you and Nigel think that Camelot was all true. If you dug up an old tomato-ketchup bottle you'd probably persuade yourselves that it came from the Round Table."

"It's not just the stones, Mark. We've found some kind of metal frame. It's mostly buried, but Nigel's trying to get it out."

"A *frame?*"

Katie stretched her arms as wide as she could. "It's big, and it's very tarnished. Nigel thinks it could be a mirror."

"I get it . . . island, Camelot, mirror. *Must* be Shalott!"

"Come and have a look anyway. I mean, it might just be scrap, but you never know."

Mark checked his watch. "Let's leave it till tomorrow. We can't do anything sensible in this weather."

"I don't think we can just *leave* it there. Supposing somebody else comes along and decides to finish digging it up? It could be valuable. If we *have* found Shalott, and if it *is* a mirror –"

"Katie, read my lips, Shalott is a myth. Whatever it is you've dug up, can't you just cover it up again and leave it till tomorrow? It's going to be pitch dark in half an hour."

Katie put on one of those faces that meant she was going to go on nagging about this until she got her own way. They weren't having any kind of relationship, but ever since Katie had joined the company, six weeks ago, they had been mildly flirting with each other, and Mark wouldn't have minded if it went a little further. He let his head drop down in surrender, and said, "Okay . . . if I *must.*"

The widow in the radio-play was still fretting about her latest sweater. "He's not so very keen on raglan sleeves . . . he thinks they make him look round-shouldered."

"He's dead, Maureen. He probably doesn't *have* any shoulders."

Katie turned around and started back up the hill. Mark climbed down from the Range Rover, slammed the door, and trudged through the long grass behind her. The skies were hung with filthy grey curtains, and the wind was blowing directly from the north-east, so that his wet raincoat collar kept petulantly slapping his face. He wouldn't have come out here at all, not today, but the weather had put him eleven days behind schedule, and the county council were starting to grow impatient.

"*We're* going to be bloody popular!" he shouted. "If this *is* bloody Shalott!"

Katie spun around as she walked, her hands thrust deep in her duffel-coat pockets. "But it could be! A castle, on an island, right in the heart of King Arthur country!"

Mark caught up with her. "Forget it, Katie. It's all stories – especially the Lady of Shalott. Burne Jones, Tennyson, the Victorians loved that kind of thing. A cursèd woman in a castle, dying of unrequited love. Sounds like my ex, come to think of it."

They topped the ridge. Through the misty swathes of rain, they could just about make out the thickly-wooded hills that half-encircled the valley on the eastern side. Below them lay a wide, boggy meadow. A straggling line of knobbly-topped willows crossed the meadow diagonally from south-east to north-west, like a procession of medieval monks, marking the course of an ancient ditch. They could see Nigel about a quarter of a mile away, in his fluorescent yellow jacket and his white plastic helmet, digging.

Mark clasped his hands together and raised his eyes toward the overbearing clouds. "Dear Lord, if You're up there, please let Nigel be digging up a bit of old bedstead."

"But if this *is* Shalott—" Katie persisted.

"It *isn't* Shalott, Katie. There is no Shalott, and there never was. Even if it *is* – which it isn't – it's situated slap bang in the middle of the proposed route for the Woolston relief road, which is already three-and-a-half years late and six-point-nine million pounds over budget. Which means that the county council will have to rethink their entire highways-building plan, and we won't get paid until the whole mess has gone through a full-scale public enquiry, which probably means in fifteen years' time."

"But think of it!" said Katie. "There – where Nigel's digging – that could be the island where the castle used to stand, where the Lady of Shalott weaved her tapestries. And these were the fields where the reapers heard her singing! And that ditch was the river, where she floated down to Camelot in her boat, singing her last lament before she died!"

"If any of that is true, sweetheart, then *this* is the hill where you and I and Historic Site Assessment Plc went instantly bankrupt."

"But we'd be *famous*, wouldn't we?"

"No, we wouldn't. You don't think for one moment that *we'd* be allowed to dig it up, do you? Every medieval archeologist from every university in the western hemisphere would be crawling all over this site like bluebottles over a dead hedgehog."

"We're perfectly well qualified."

"No, darling, we're not, and I think you're forgetting what we do. We don't get paid to find sites of outstanding archeological significance interest, we get paid *not* to find them. Bronze Age buckle? Shove it in your pocket and rediscover it five miles away, well away from the proposed new supermarket site. An Iron Age sheep pen, fine. We can call in a JCB and have it shifted to the Ancient Britain display at Frome. But not Shalott, Katie. Shalott would bloody sink us."

They struggled down the hill and across the meadow. The rain began to ease off, but the wind was still blustery. As they clambered down the ditch, and up the other side, Nigel stood up and took off his helmet. He was very tall, Nigel, with tight curly hair, a large complicated nose, and a hesitant, disconnected way of walking and talking. But Mark hadn't employed him for his looks or his physical co-ordination or his people skills. He had employed him because of his MA Hist and his Dip Arch & Landscape, which were prominently displayed on the top of the company notepaper.

"Nigel! How's it going? Katie tells me you've found Shalott."

"Well – *no* – Mark! I don't like to jump to – you know – *hah!* – hasty conclusions! Not when we could be dealing with – *pff!* I don't know! – the most exciting archeological find *ever*! But these *stones*, look!"

Mark turned to Katie and rolled up his eyes in exaggerated weariness. But Katie said, "Go on, Mark. *Look.*"

Nigel was circling around the rough grassy tussocks, flapping his hands. "I've cut back some of the turf, d'you see – and – underneath – well, *see*?" He had already exposed six or seven rectangular stones, the color of well-matured Cheddar cheese. Every stone bore a dense pattern of chisel-marks, as if it had been gnawed by a giant stone-eating rat.

"*Bath* stone," said Nigel. "Quarried from Hazlebury most likely, and look at that jadding . . . late thirteenth century, in my humble opinion. Certainly not cut by the old method."

Mark peered at the stones and couldn't really see anything but stones. "The old method?"

Nigel let out a honk of laughter. "Silly, isn't it? The *old* method is what quarrymen used to call the *new* method – cutting the stone with saws, instead of breaking it away with bars."

"What wags they were. But what makes you think this could be Shalott?"

Nigel shielded his eyes with his hand and looked around the meadow, blinking. "The *location* suggests it, more than anything else. You can see by the way these foundation-stones are arranged that there was certainly a tower here. You don't use stones five feet thick to build a single-story pigsty, do you? But then you have to ask yourself *why* would you build a tower here?"

"Do you? Oh yes, I suppose you do."

"You wouldn't have picked the middle of a valley to build a fort," said Nigel. "You would only build a tower here as a folly, or to keep somebody imprisoned, perhaps."

"Like the Lady of Shalott?"

"Well, exactly."

"So, if there was a tower here, where's the rest of it?"

"Oh, pilfered, most likely. As soon its owners left it empty, most of the stones would have been carried off by local smallholders, for building walls and stables and farmhouses. I'll bet you could still find them if you went looking for them."

"Well, I'll bet you could," said Mark, blowing his nose. "Pity they didn't take the lot."

Nigel blinked at him through rain-speckled glasses. "If they'd done that, *hah*! we never would have known that this was Shalott, would we?"

"Precisely."

Nigel said, "I don't think the tower was standing here for very long. At a very rough estimate it was built just before 1275, and most likely abandoned during the Black Death, around 1340."

"Oh, yes?" Mark was already trying to work out what equipment they were going to need to shift these stones and where they could dump them. Back at Hazelbury quarry, maybe, where they originally came from. Nobody would ever find them there. Or maybe they could sell them as garden benches. He had a friend in Chelsea who ran a profitable sideline in ancient stones and 18th century garden ornaments, for wealthy customers who weren't too fussy where they came from.

Nigel took hold of Mark's sleeve and pointed to a stone that was still half-buried in grass. There were some deep marks chiseled into it. "Look – you can just make out a cross, and part of a skull, and the letters DSPM. That's an acronym for medieval Latin, meaning '*God save us from the pestilence within these walls.*'"

"So whoever lived in this tower was infected with the Black Death?"

"That's the most obvious assumption, yes."

Mark nodded. "Okay, then . . ." he said, and kept on nodding.

"This is very, very exciting," said Nigel. "I mean, it's – well! – it could be *stupefying*, when you come to think of it!"

"Yes," said Mark. He looked around the site, still nodding. "Katie told me you'd found some metal thing."

"Well! *Hah!* That's the clincher, so far as I'm concerned! At least it *will* be, if it turns out to be what I think it is!"

He strode back to the place where he had been digging, and Mark reluctantly followed him. Barely visible in the mud was a length of blackened metal, about a metre-and-a-half long and curved at both ends.

"It's a fireguard, isn't it?" said Mark. Nigel had cleaned a part of it, and he could see that there were flowers embossed on it, and bunches of grapes, and vine-tendrils. In the center of it was a lump that looked like a human face, although it was so encrusted with mud that it was impossible to tell if it was a man or a woman.

Mark peered at it closely. "An old Victorian fireguard, that's all."

"I don't think so," said Nigel. "I think it's the top edge of a mirror. And a thirteenth century mirror, at that."

"Nigel . . . a *mirror*, as big as that, in 1275? They didn't have glass mirrors in those days, remember. This would have to be solid silver, or silver-plated, at least."

"Exactly!" said Nigel. "A solid silver mirror – five feet across."

"That's practically unheard of."

"Not if *The Lady of Shalott* was true. She had a mirror, didn't she, not for looking at *herself*, but for looking at the world outside, so that she could weave a tapestry of life in Camelot, without having to look at it directly!

" '*There she weaves by night and day*
A magic web with colors gay.
She has heard a whisper say
A curse is on her if she stay
     To look down to Camelot.

"*But moving through a mirror clear*
That hangs before her all the year,
Shadows of the world appear . . . ' "

Katie joined in.

"*And in her web she still delights*
To weave the mirror's magic sights
For often thro' the silent nights
A funeral, with plumes and lights
     And music, went to Camelot."

"Top of the class," said Mark. "Now, how long do you think it's going to take to dig this out?"

"Oh . . . several weeks," said Nigel. "Months, even."

"I hope that's one of your University of Essex jokes."

"No, well, it has to be excavated properly. We don't want to damage it, do we? And there could well be other valuable artifacts hidden in the soil all around it. Combs, buttons, necklaces, who knows? We need to fence this area off, don't we, and inform the police, and the British Museum?"

Mark said, "No, Nigel, we don't."

Nigel slowly stood up, blinking with perplexity. "Mark – we

have to! This tower, this mirror – they could change the entire concept of Arthurian legend! They're archeological proof that the Lady of Shalott wasn't just a story, and that Camelot was really here!"

"Nigel, that's a wonderful notion, but it's not going to pay off our overdraft, is it?"

Katie said, "I don't understand. If this *is* the Lady of Shalott's mirror, and it's genuine, it could be worth *millions!*"

"It could, yes. But not to us. Treasure trove belongs to HM Government. Not only that, this isn't our land, and we're working under contract for the county council. So our chances of getting a share of it are just about zero."

"So what are you suggesting?" said Nigel. "You want us to *bury* it again, and forget we ever found it? We can't do that!"

"Oh, no," Mark told him, "I'm not suggesting that for a moment." He pointed to the perforated vines in the top of the frame. "We could run a couple of chains through here, though, couldn't we, and use the Range Rover to pull it out?"

"What? That could cause *irreparable* damage!"

"Nigel – everything that happens in this world causes irreparable damage. That's the whole definition of history."

The rain had stopped completely now and Katie pushed back her hood. "I hate to say it, Mark, but I think you're right. *We* found this tower, *we* found this mirror. If we report it, we'll get nothing at all. No money, no credit. Not even a mention in the papers."

Nigel stood over the metal frame for a long time, his hand thoughtfully covering the lower part of his face.

"Well?" Mark asked him, at last. It was already growing dark, and a chilly mist was rising between the knobbly-topped willow-trees.

"All right, then, bugger it," said Nigel. "Let's pull the bugger out."

Mark drove the Range Rover down the hill and jostled along the banks of the ditch until he reached the island of Shalott. He switched on all the floodlights, front and rear, and then he and Nigel fastened towing-chains to the metal frame, wrapping them in torn T-shirts to protect the mouldings as much as they could. Mark slowly revved the Range Rover forward, its tires spinning in the fibrous brown mud. Nigel screamed, "*Steady! Steady!*" like a panicky hockey-mistress.

At first the metal frame wouldn't move, but Mark tried pulling it, and then easing off the throttle, and then pulling it again. Gradually, it began to emerge from the peaty soil which covered it, and even before it was halfway out, he could see that Nigel was right, and that it was a mirror – or a large sheet of metal, anyway. He pulled it completely free, and Nigel screamed, "*Stop!*"

They hunkered down beside it and shone their flashlights on it. The decorative vine-tendrils had been badly bent by the towing-chains, but there was no other obvious damage. The surface of the mirror was black and mottled, like a serious bruise, but otherwise it seemed to have survived its seven hundred years with very little corrosion. It was over an inch thick and it was so heavy that they could barely lift it.

"What do we do now?" asked Katie.

"We take it back to the house, we clean it up, and we try to check out its provenance – where it was made, who made it, and what its history was. We have it assayed. Then we talk to one or two dealers who are interested in this kind of thing, and see how much we can get for it."

"And what about Shalott?" asked Nigel. In the upward beam of his flashlight, his face had become a theatrical mask.

"You can finish off your survey, Nigel. I think you ought to. But give me two versions. One for the county council, and one for posterity. As soon as you're done, I'll arrange for somebody to take all the stones away, and store them. Don't worry. You'll be able to publish your story in five or ten years' time, and you'll probably make a fortune out of it."

"But the island – it's all going to be lost."

"That's the story of Britain, Nigel. Nothing *you* can do can change it."

They heaved the mirror into the back of the Range Rover and drove back into Wincanton. Mark had rented a small end-of-terrace house on the outskirts, because it was much cheaper than staying in a hotel for seven weeks. The house was plain, flat-fronted, with a scrubby front garden and a dilapidated wooden garage. In the back garden stood a single naked cherry-tree. Inside, the ground-level rooms had been knocked together to make a living-room with a dining area at one end. The carpet was yellow with green Paisley swirls on it, and the furniture was reproduction, all chintz and dark varnish.

Between them, grunting, they maneuvered the mirror into the living-room and propped it against the wall. Katie folded up two bath-towels and they wedged it underneath the frame to stop it from marking the carpet.

"I feel like a criminal," said Nigel.

Mark lit the gas fire and briskly chafed his hands. "You shouldn't. You should feel like an Englishman, protecting his heritage."

Katie said, "I still don't know if we've done the right thing. I mean, there's still time to declare it as a treasure trove."

"Well, go ahead, if you want Historical Site Assessment to go out of business and you don't want a third share of whatever we can sell it for."

Katie went up to the mirror, licked the tip of her finger and cleaned some of the mud off it. As she did so, she suddenly recoiled, as if she had been stung. "*Ow*," she said, and stared at her fingertip. "It gave me a shock."

"A shock? What kind of a shock?"

"Like static, you know, when you get out of a car."

Mark approached the mirror and touched it with all five fingers of his left hand. "I can't feel anything." He licked his fingers and tried again, and this time he lifted his hand away and said, "Ouch! You're right! It's like it's *charged*."

"Silver's *very* conductive," said Nigel, as if that explained everything. "Sir John Raseburne wore a silver helmet at Agincourt, and he was struck by lightning. He was thrown so far into the air that the French thought he could fly."

He touched the mirror himself. After a while, he said, "No, nothing. You must have earthed it, you two."

Mark looked at the black, diseased surface of the mirror and said nothing.

That evening, Mark ordered a takeaway curry from the Wincanton Tandoori in the High Street, and they ate chicken Madras and mushroom bhaji while they took it in turns to clean away seven centuries of tarnish.

Neil played *The Best of Matt Monro* on his CD player. "I'm sorry . . . I didn't bring any of my madrigals."

"Don't apologize. This is *almost* medieval."

First of all, they washed down the mirror with warm soapy water and cellulose carsponges, until all of the peaty soil was sluiced off it. Katie stood on a kitchen chair and cleaned all of the decorative detail at the top of the frame with a toothbrush and Q-tips. As she worried the mud out of the human head in the center of the mirror, it gradually emerged as a woman, with high cheekbones and slanted eyes and her hair looped up in elaborate braids. Underneath her chin there was a scroll with the single word *Lamia*.

"Lamia?" said Mark. "Is that Latin, or what?"

"No, no, *Greek*," said Nigel. "It's the Greek name for Lilith, who was Adam's first companion, before Eve. She insisted on having the same rights as Adam and so God threw her out of Eden. She married a demon and became the queen of demons."

He stepped closer to the mirror and touched the woman's faintly-smiling lips. "Lamia was supposed to be the most incredibly beautiful woman you could imagine. She had white skin and black eyes and breasts that no man could resist fondling. Just one night with Lamia and *pfff!* – you would never look at a human woman again."

"What was the catch?"

"She sucked all of the blood out of you, that's all."

"You're talking about my ex again."

Katie said, "I seem to remember that John Keats wrote a poem called *Lamia*, didn't he?"

"That's right," said Nigel. "A chap called Lycius met Lamia and fell madly in love with her. The trouble is, he didn't realize that she was a blood-sucker and that she was cursed by God."

"Cursed?" said Katie.

"Yes, God had condemned her for her disobedience for ever. 'Some penanced lady-elf . . . some demon's mistress, or the demon's self.'"

"Like the Lady of Shalott."

"Well, I suppose so, yes."

"Perhaps they were one and the same person . . . Lamia, and the Lady of Shalott."

They all looked at the woman's face on top of the mirror. There was no question that she was beautiful; and even though the casting had a simplified, medieval style, the sculptor had managed to convey a sense of slyness, and of secrecy.

"She was a bit of a mystery, really," said Nigel. "She was supposed to be a virgin, d'you see, 'yet in the lore of love deep learnèd to the red heart's core.' She was a blood-sucking enchantress, but at the same time she was capable of deep and genuine love. Men couldn't resist her. Lycius said she gave him 'a hundred thirsts.' "

"Just like this bloody Madras chicken," said Mark. "Is there any more beer in the fridge?"

Katie carried on cleaning the mirror long after Mark and Nigel had grown tired of it. They sat in two reproduction armchairs drinking Stella Artois and eating cheese-and-onion crisps and heckling *Question Time*, while Katie applied 3M's Tarni-Shield with a soft blue cloth and gradually exposed a circle of shining silver, large enough to see her own face.

"There," she said. "I reckon we can have it all cleaned up by tomorrow."

"I'll give my friend a call," said Mark. "Maybe he can send somebody down to look at it."

"It's amazing, isn't it, to think that the last person to look into this mirror could have been the Lady of Shalott?"

"You blithering idiot," said Nigel.

"I beg your pardon?"

Nigel waved his can of lager at the television screen. "Not you. Him. He thinks that single mothers should get two votes."

They didn't go to bed until well past 1:00 a.m. Mark had the main bedroom because he was the boss, even though it wasn't exactly luxurious. The double bed was lumpy and the white Regency-style wardrobe was crowded with wire hangers. Katie had the smaller bedroom at the back, with teddy-bear wallpaper, while Nigel had to sleep on the sofa in the living-room.

Mark slept badly that night. He dreamed that he was walking at the rear of a long funeral procession, with a horse-drawn hearse, and black-dyed ostrich plumes nodding in the wind. A woman's voice was calling him from very far away, and he stopped, while the funeral procession carried on. For some reason he felt infinitely sad and lonely, the same way that he had felt when he was five, when his mother died.

"Mark!" she kept calling him. "*Mark!*"

He woke up with a harsh intake of breath. It was still dark, although his travel clock said 07:26.

"Mark!" she repeated, and it wasn't his mother, but Katie, and she was calling him from downstairs.

He climbed out of bed, still stunned from sleeping. He dragged his towelling bathrobe from the hook on the back of the door and stumbled down the narrow staircase. In the living-room the curtains were drawn back, although the grey November day was still dismal and dark, and it was raining. Katie was standing in the middle of the room in a pink cotton nightshirt, her hair all messed up, her forearms raised like the figure in *The Scream*.

"Katie! What the hell's going on?"

"It's Nigel. Look at him, Mark, he's dead."

"What?" Mark switched the ceiling-light on. Nigel was lying on his back on the chintz-upholstered couch, wearing nothing but green woollen socks and a brown plaid shirt, which was pulled right up to his chin. His bony white chest had a crucifix of dark hair across it. His penis looked like a dead fledgling.

But it was the expression on his face that horrified Mark the most. He was staring up at the ceiling, wide-eyed, his mouth stretched wide open, as if he were shouting at somebody. There was no doubt that he was dead. His throat had been torn open, in a stringy red mess of tendons and cartilage, and the cushion beneath his head was soaked black with blood.

"Jesus," said Mark. He took three or four very deep breaths. "Jesus."

Katie was almost as white as Nigel. "What could have *done* that? It looks like he was bitten by a *dog*."

Mark went through to the kitchen and rattled the back door handle. "Locked," he said, coming back into the living-room. "There's no dog anywhere."

"Then what—?" Katie promptly sat down, and lowered her head. "Oh God, I think I'm going to faint."

"I'll have to call the police," said Mark. He couldn't stop staring at Nigel's face. Nigel didn't look terrified. In fact, he looked almost exultant, as if having his throat ripped out had been the most thrilling experience of his whole life.

"But what did it?" asked Katie. "*We* didn't do it, and Nigel couldn't have done it himself."

Mark frowned down at the yellow swirly carpet. He could make out a blotchy trail of footprints leading from the side of the couch to the centre of the room. He thought at first that they must be Nigel's, but on closer examination they seemed to be far too small, and there was no blood on Nigel's socks. Close to the coffee-table the footprints formed a pattern like a huge, petal-shedding rose, and then, much fainter, they made their toward the mirror. Where they stopped.

"Look," he said. "What do you make of that?"

Katie approached the mirror and peered into the shiny circle that she had cleaned yesterday evening. "It's almost as if . . . no."

"It's almost as if *what?*"

"It's almost as if somebody killed Nigel and then walked straight into the mirror."

"That's insane. People can't walk into mirrors."

"But these footprints . . . they don't go anywhere else."

"It's impossible. Whoever it was, they must have done it to trick us."

They both looked up at the face of Lamia. She looked back at them, secret and serene. Her smile seemed to say *wouldn't you like to know?*

"They built a tower, didn't they?" said Katie. She was trembling with shock. "They built a tower for the express purpose of keeping the Lady of Shalott locked up. If she was Lamia, then they locked her up because she seduced men and drank their blood."

"Katie, for Christ's sake. That was seven hundred years ago. That's if it really happened at all."

Katie pointed to Nigel's body on the couch. "Nigel's dead, Mark! *That* really happened! But *nobody* could have entered this room last night, could they? Not without breaking the door down and waking us up. *Nobody* could have entered this room unless they stepped right out of this mirror!"

"So what do you suggest? We call the police?"

"We *have* to!"

"Oh, yes? And what do we tell them? 'Well, officer, it was like this. We took a thirteenth-century mirror that didn't belong to us and The Lady of Shalott came out of it in the middle of the night and tore Nigel's throat out?' They'll send us to Broadmoor, Katie! They'll put us in the funny farm for life!"

"Mark, listen, this is real."

"It's only a story, Katie. It's only a legend."

"But think of the poem, *The Lady of Shalott.* Think of what it says. '*Moving thro' a mirror clear, that hangs before her all the year, shadows of the world appear.*' Don't you get it? Tennyson specifically wrote *through* a mirror, not *in* it. The Lady of Shalott wasn't looking *at* her mirror, she was *inside* it, looking out!"

"This gets better."

"But it all fits together. She was Lamia. A blood-sucker, a

vampire! Like all vampires, she could only come out at night. But she didn't hide inside a coffin all day . . . she hid inside a mirror! Daylight can't penetrate a mirror, any more than it can penetrate a closed coffin!''

"I don't know much about vampires, Katie, but I do know that you can't see them in mirrors.''

"Of course not. And this is the reason why! Lamia and her reflection are one and the same. When she steps out of the mirror, she's no longer inside it, so she doesn't appear to have a reflection. And the curse on her must be that she can only come out of the mirror at night, like *all* vampires.''

"Katie, for Christ's sake . . . you're getting completely carried away.''

"But it's the only answer that makes any sense! Why did they lock up the Lady of Shalott on an island, in a stream? Because vampires can't cross running water. Why did they carve a crucifix and a skull on the stones outside? The words said, *God save us from the pestilence within these walls.* They didn't mean the Black Death . . . they meant *her*! The Lady of Shalott, Lamia, *she* was the pestilence!''

Mark sat down. He looked at Nigel and then he looked away again. He had never seen a dead body before, but the dead were so totally dead that you could quickly lose interest in them, after a while. They didn't talk. They didn't even breathe. He could understand why morticians were so blasé.

"So?'' he asked Katie, at last. "What do you think we ought to do?''

"Let's draw the curtains,'' she said. "Let's shut out all the daylight. If you sit here, perhaps she'll be tempted to come out again. After all, she's been seven hundred years without fresh blood, hasn't she? She must be thirsty.''

Mark stared at her. "You're having a laugh, aren't you? You want me to sit here in the dark, hoping that some mythical woman is going to step out of a dirty old mirror and try to suck all the blood out of me?''

He was trying to show Katie that wasn't afraid, and that her vampire idea was nonsense, but all the time Nigel was lying on the couch, silently shouting at the ceiling. And there was so much blood, and so many footprints. What else could have happened in this room last night?

Katie said, "It's up to you. If you think I'm being ridiculous, let's forget it. Let's call the police and tell them exactly what happened. I'm sure that forensics will prove that we didn't kill him."

"I wouldn't count on it, myself."

Mark stood up again and went over to the mirror. He peered into the polished circle, but all he could see was his own face, dimly haloed.

"All right, then," he said. "Let's give it a try, just to put your mind at rest. *Then* we call the police."

Katie drew the brown velvet curtains and tucked them in at the bottom to keep out the tiniest chink of daylight. It was well past eight o'clock now, but it was still pouring with rain outside and the morning was so gloomy that she need hardly have bothered. Mark pulled one of the armchairs up in front of the mirror and sat facing it.

"I feel like one of those goats they tie up, to catch tigers."

"Well, I wouldn't worry. I'm probably wrong."

Mark took out a crumpled Kleenex and blew his nose, and then sniffed. "God, what a terrible smell."

"That's the blood," said Katie. Adding, after a moment, "My uncle used to be a butcher. He always said that bad blood is the worst smell in the world."

They sat in silence for a while. The smell of blood seemed to be growing thicker, and riper, and it was all Mark could do not to gag. His throat was dry, too, and he wished he had drunk some orange juice before starting this vigil.

"You couldn't fetch me a drink, could you?" he asked Katie.

"Ssh," said Katie. "I think I can see something."

"What? Where?"

"Look at the mirror, in the middle. Like a very faint light."

Mark stared toward the mirror in the darkness. At first he couldn't see anything but overwhelming blackness. But then he saw a flicker, like somebody waving a white scarf, and then another.

Very gradually, a *face* began to appear in the polished circle. Mark felt a slow crawling sensation down his back, and his lower jaw began to judder so much that he had to clench his teeth to stop it. The face was pale and bland but strangely beautiful, and it was staring straight at him, unblinking, and smiling. It looked more like the face of a marble statue than a human being. Mark tried to look away, but he couldn't. Every time he turned his head toward Katie he was compelled to turn back again.

The darkened living-room seemed to grow even more airless and suffocating, and when he said, "*Katie . . . can you see what I see?*" his voice sounded muffled, as if he had a pillow over his face.

Soundlessly, the pale woman took one step out of the surface of the mirror. She was naked, and her skin was the color of the moon. The black tarnish clung to her for a moment, like oily cobwebs, but as she took another step forward they slid away from her, leaving her luminous and pristine.

Mark could do nothing but stare at her. She came closer and closer, until he could have reached up and touched her. She had a high forehead, and her hair was braided in strange, elaborate loops. She had no eyebrows, which made her face expressionless. But her eyes were extraordinary. Her eyes were like looking at death.

She raised her right hand and lightly kissed her fingertips. He could feel her aura, both electrical and freezing cold, as if somebody had left a fridge door wide open. She whispered something, but it sounded more French than English – very soft and elided – and he could only understand a few words of it.

"*My sweet love,*" she said. "*Come to me, give me your very life.*"

There were dried runnels of blood on her breasts and down her slightly-bulging stomach, and down her thighs. Her feet were spattered in blood, too. Mark looked up at her, and he couldn't think what to say or what to do. He felt as if all of the energy had drained out of him, and he couldn't even speak.

We all have to die one day, he thought. *But to die now, today, in this naked woman's arms . . . what an adventure that would be.*

"Mark!" shouted Katie. "Grab her, Mark! Hold on to her!"

The woman twisted around and hissed at Katie, as furiously as a snake. Mark heaved himself out of his chair and tried to seize the woman's arm, but she was cold and slippery, like half-melted ice, and her wrist slithered out of his grasp.

"*Now,* Katie!" he yelled at her.

Katie threw herself at the curtains, and dragged them down, the curtain-hooks popping like firecrackers. The woman went for her, and she had almost reached the window when the last curtain-hook popped and the living-room was drowned with grey, drained daylight. She whipped around again and stared at Mark, and the expression on her face almost stopped his heart.

"*Of all men,*" she whispered. "*You have been the most faithless, and you will be punished.*"

Katie was on her knees, struggling to free herself from the curtains. The woman seized Katie's curls, lifted her up, and bit into her neck, with an audible crunch. Katie didn't even scream. She stared at Mark in mute desperation and fell sideways onto the carpet, with blood jetting out of her neck and spraying across the furniture.

The woman came slowly toward him, and Mark took one step back, and then another, shifting the armchair so that it stood between them. But she stopped. Her skin was already shining, as if it were melting, and she closed her eyes. Mark waited, holding his breath. Katie was convulsing, one foot jerking against the leg of the coffee-table, so that the empty beer-cans rattled together.

The woman opened her eyes, and gave Mark one last unreadable look. Then she turned back toward the mirror. She took three paces, and it swallowed her, like an oil-streaked pool of water.

Mark waited, and waited, not moving. Outside the window, the rain began to clear, and he heard the whine of a milk-float going past.

After a while, he sat down. He thought of calling the police, but what could he tell them? Then he thought of tying the bodies to the mirror, and dropping them into a rhyne, where they would never be found. But the police would come anyway, wouldn't they, asking questions?

The day slowly went by. Just after two o'clock the clouds cleared for a moment, and the naked apple-tree in the back garden sparkled with sunlight. At half-past three a loud clatter in the hallway made him jump, but it was only an old woman with a shopping-trolley pushing a copy of the *Wincanton Advertiser* through the letterbox.

And so the darkness gradually gathered, and Mark sat in his armchair in front of the mirror, waiting.

> *"I am half-sick of shadows, said*
> *The Lady of Shalott."*

E.C. TUBB

Mirror of the Night

E.C. TUBB IS PROBABLY BEST known as a science fiction author. Since 1951, he has published more than 120 novels, plus 230 short stories in such magazines as *Astounding, Analog, Authentic, Galaxy, Nebula, New Worlds, Science Fantasy, Vision of Tomorrow* and, in more recent years, *Fantasy Annual* and *Fantasy Adventures*. His work has also been translated into more than a dozen languages.

His long-running "Dumarest of Terra" series of science-fantasy novels ran to thirty-one volumes from DAW Books, and a further entry in the series was published by New York small press imprint Gryphon Books after first appearing in a French translation.

Since then, he has published two supernatural swords and sorcery novels, *Death God's Doom* and *The Sleeping City*, a new SF novel *Footsteps of Angels*, and an original *Space: 1999* novelization, *Earthbound*. *The Best Science Fiction of E.C. Tubb* is a recent retrospective collection.

Interspersed with Tubb's many SF short stories of the 1950s and early '60s were a smaller number of supernatural stories, many of them written under pseudonyms. The best of these were reprinted in 2003 by Sarob Press in the hardcover collection *Mirror of the Night*. Originally published in 1998, the title story marked the author's first return to horror fiction in more than twenty years.

"You think and brood and odd things seem to come together to form a logical whole," explains Tubb. "A strained marriage and an effort to make repairs. A journey into unfamiliar places. The emotive strain building and the biological facet enhanced as the man wants, desperately, to gain a measure of independence and respect. An illustration, perhaps, of the awesome power held by every woman over the man who adores her.

"And then the all-too familiar compliment paid by almost every man to every attractive woman: 'You look ravishing my dear. You look good enough to eat.'

"Sometimes, in the right circumstances, a man might mean exactly what he says . . ."

THUNDER MADE A FITTING accompaniment; sonorous echoes rolling from the surrounding hills, the fitful glare of lightning dancing like silver ghosts on the shadowed peaks. Savage brilliance which threw into sharp detail the massed vegetation, the winding road, the branches which, almost meeting from side to side, made a laced canopy overhead and enhanced the Gothic mystery of the terrain.

One Stephen Aldcock appreciated and would have used earlier in his career. It gave an added dimension to the trip he was making into the Appalachians following narrow, unmarked and near-forgotten roads, the wheels of the car bouncing into ruts, the sides lashed by hanging fronds.

A journey Diane wasn't enjoying. She hadn't spoken since he'd switched off the radio. Trying to argue she had met defeat and now sulked in silence wreathed by a haze of smoke. Yet he had been right to insist; the region held an atmosphere of its own and the noise had been a distraction.

Glancing at her he tried to explain.

"We're travelling back in time," he said. "Into the past when people lived close to nature. This region has hardly changed since the settlers first came. Try to imagine it," he urged. "They had to move along narrow paths winding between scattered habitations. These woods would have sheltered all kinds of danger and travellers would have been attacked, ripped, clawed, shot, stabbed, left to lie bleeding on the ground. Think of being injured, lying out there in the woods with night closing in just as it is now. Hurt, knowing you're alone with death very close. Knowing too that something could be watching you. Something inhuman."

"You're sick," she said. "Crazy."

"It happened."

"Sure it happened." She lit another cigarette. "No matter what you imagine somewhere, at some time, it has happened. So people died out here – so what?"

"Can't you feel it? The atmosphere? The magic?"

"I feel cold," she snapped impatiently. "I feel hungry and tired and cramped. I need a good meal, a bath, a warm bed. How much longer are you going to amuse yourself by dragging me around these godforsaken roads?"

She had no imagination, but he had known that when he married her. Then it hadn't seemed important and he had traded compatibility for appearance. She had dazzled him with her physical beauty and he had lusted after the prize. Now, too often, he regretted having won it.

Patiently he said, "Try harder, darling. Look at these hills, each as old as time. Listen to the thunder. Feel the atmosphere of the place. It's odd. Strange. As if aliens had landed here eons ago and performed mysterious rites to unknown gods. See!" He pointed to a distant rift, one suddenly touched by the glare of lightning. "Beyond that cleft could lie a forgotten village in which at each sunset, a sacrifice is made. A hen or a rat, maybe, but once a year something larger. A dog, a goat, even a girl. A real, live unblemished virgin!"

"Stop it!"

"You wouldn't qualify, of course, not as a virgin. But they'd settle for your beauty."

She snapped, savagely, "That's enough of this stupid talk. Writers are supposed to be a little crazy but this is too much. If you're trying to frighten me you're wasting your time. Now let's get back to civilization and find a decent motel."

It wasn't that easy. As the night closed around them he realised they were lost. The road he followed branched into smaller tracks and, choosing one at random, he drove down a path on which it was impossible to turn.

As Diane complained he said, quickly, "This must lead to a farm. When we reach it there'll be room to turn. Just sit and relax."

Several minutes later, without warning, the path opened to reveal the totally unexpected.

"No!" Braking he leaned forward to stare at what lay ahead. "I don't believe it!"

"A house! Stephen, it's a house!"

A mansion set against a wall of trees. A tall building with twisted chimneys and arched windows now illuminated by the glare of headlights and the flashes of lightning accompanying the growing fury of the storm. An old house that squatted like a decaying beast beneath sagging eaves. One with warped frames and scabs of lichen, flaking bricks and mouldering tiles. The relic of a bygone age; the path they had followed the remains of a once-tended drive.

"A house," she said again. "There must be people." Then, as he made no effort to move, "See if we're welcome. Find out where we are. Ask if you can use the phone."

She'd turned on the radio by the time he returned, the sound fuzzed and distorted. Thunder rolled as he switched it off. As it faded she said, "Well?"

"No luck."

"What?"

"The place is empty," he explained. "Deserted. I couldn't get an answer and saw no signs of life. It must have been abandoned years ago. We'll have to keep moving."

The car moved forward as he engaged the drive, swinging wide to avoid a pool, straightening to sweep the house with searchlight clarity.

"Wait!" Diane caught at his arm. "I saw something in an upper window. A face. It looked like a face."

"A reflection."

"A face," she insisted. "Someone is watching us."

He grunted, making no comment, fighting the wheel as the car skidded towards the pool. Rain hammered on the roof, gushed over the windscreen, churned the ground to mud as the storm, breaking, filled the air with noise and fury. Abruptly he braked and cut the ignition.

"Stephen?"

"We'll have to take shelter in the house. This rain will wash out the roads. If we get wrecked no one will ever find us. Get to the door. I'll follow after I switch off the lights."

"Can't you leave them?"

"And run down the battery? Not a chance. The lightning will guide us. Hurry!"

She ran, long legs flashing, her coat lifted to protect her hair.

He followed after collecting the bag of provisions from the boot; cans of meat, crackers, pickles, pate and some wine. Items picked up at a local store as a bribe in return for directions. A place a county away now. A world.

The door, sheltered by a weathered portico, had defied her attempts to open it. With sudden impatience he lifted his boot and slammed it against the lock. Wood splintered, yielded beneath a second onslaught, the door opening with a creak of hinges. Air gusted from the dark interior, chill, tainted with a sickly odour.

"Quick." Stephen led the way. "Inside."

Lighting illuminated the interior with stroboscopic flashes; a wide hall, bare boards, stairs that wound upwards, doors that were closed, a box on which rested a stub of candle. It flared to life as Diane set fire to the wick. From the walls faces stared with brooding hostility.

Lifting the candle Stephen examined the framed portraits. All were of men and bore a common likeness; the jowls heavy, the lips full, the chin deeply cleft. Some wore wigs, others had ribboned hair, some were proudly bald. Their eyes seemed to move in the flickering light.

"It's cold." Diane shivered. "Can't we light a fire?"

"Not here." The gaping fireplace held nothing but dust and wind carried rain through the open door. "I'll look upstairs. Shut the door and find the lights."

There were no lights; the house had never been wired for electricity or piped for gas and any lamps had long since vanished. There were no more candles but Stephen found a bowl of grease that held a wick. It threw a guttering light and emitted a noisome odour. Hastily he extinguished it.

"We'll make do with the candle. There's a room upstairs with a fireplace and a few chairs the looters didn't take. They'll do for fuel."

"Looters?"

"Owners, then, I don't know. Whoever cleared this place. Relatives, friends, debtors, thieves, who can tell?" He paused on the stairs and looked at the portraits. "This must have been a family home but they died out long ago. No modern costumes, see? The land gave out and the money, and the workers would have left. The owners would have clung on from habit and pride. A decaying aristocracy drifting into incest, perver-

sion, degeneracy. Winding up as idiots. Dying out in the end.
It's an old story."

Diane said, thoughtfully, "Why didn't they sell the portraits?
If they had to get rid of everything else then why keep them?
Why leave them here?"

"For the same reason you leave headstones in a graveyard.
Fear. Respect – this was their home, remember. In a way it still
is." Chuckling he added, "I've an idea. Let's invite them to
dinner. Take them upstairs. It'll add to the adventure. Come
on, darling, help me."

"No." She didn't want to touch the portraits. "Do it if you
must. I'll start the fire and set the table."

There was no table, only a section of the floor, the bright
labels of the provisions a glaring contrast to the warped and
time-stained boards. The wine had come with plastic cups.

Stephen poured, solemnly lifted his container and bowed to
the row of faces he had set against a wall.

"To your very good health, my lords. I salute you!"

Diane watched, not amused. It was more idiocy to add to the
rest; the tiresome journey, the search for ancient places, his
interest in the house, the ridiculous urge that had made him
bring the mouldering portraits into the room. Not all of them,
most still remained in the hall, but those he had chosen seemed
to have a special vibrancy.

"Here!" Stephen offered her wine. "It's your turn to make a
toast."

"Must I?"

"Not if you don't want to. But drink it anyway, it'll help you to
relax."

Accepting the container she stepped towards the window
and looked out into the night and the storm. It had yet to ease
and distant flashes walked on the hills and thunder echoed like
gunfire. She drank and turned, quickly, suddenly startled. Wine
splashed over her hand.

"Is something wrong?" Stephen, at her side, was concerned.

"It's nothing. I just – it's nothing."

"You saw something," he said. "Look." Turning her to face
the window he said, "You saw me. My reflection. Did you think I
was a ghost?"

Pale against the night he could have been but, if so, she was
another. Reflections caught in the mirror the window had
become. Two figures almost of an equal height, his thinner,

older, hers making no secret of her sex. As she watched she saw his hand rise, move, felt the touch of his fingers, the pressure of his flesh, the yielding of her own.

"My darling," he murmured. "You are beautiful."

A long moment in which she felt herself begin to respond then the glare of lightning destroyed the reflections and the blast of thunder made the floor quiver and the flames dance in the grate. Flames that died as the candle died.

"Damn!" Stephen poked at the embers. "I can't eat in the dark. We'll have to use the bowl."

The one filled with a rancid grease which yielded an odour which now oddly seemed less repugnant than earlier. By its light he opened cans and packets and dispensed the food. Eating he looked at the row of painted faces again lifting his container of wine in a silent toast. One in which Diane refused to share. The faces were too alive, the eyes gloating as they followed her every move, the lips moist, the teeth gleaming.

"Stephen, they're horrible! Turn them to the wall!"

"Why? Don't you like an audience?"

"What do you mean? Damn you, answer me!"

Her anger startled him. "Mean? Nothing. It's just that you're fond of making an entrance. To be the centre of attention. Most beautiful women are. Like flowers they love the sun."

Flattery but she was worthy of it and was it flattery to tell the truth? She was beautiful and, sitting on the floor before where she sat in the only remaining chair, he could appreciate the curved perfection of her body. Mentally he assessed it as the wine warmed him with a pungent glow.

"Stephen?" Diane was staring at him, her mouth tense. "Your eyes – is anything wrong?"

"No."

"Your expression. I've never seen you look like that. What's the matter?"

"Nothing is the matter. I was just looking at you and thinking of the early days of our marriage and remembering just how lovely you are." Smiling he reached towards her, touched her, fingers running over the smooth contours of her calves and thighs. "You look wonderful, darling."

And was wonderful in a variety of ways. He felt her withdraw from the touch of his hand as his mind filled with bizarre images. What games had the owners played? Isolated in the hills how had they amused themselves? Bonded servants chased

and slaughtered in a travesty of the hunt? Nubile girls tormen-
ted, beaten, whipped, flayed and used as objects of sexual
gratification? Things easy to believe; the painted faces held a
demented perversion. What would they have thought of Diane?
Her physical attraction?

"Stephen!"

Her tone snapped him from his reverie.

"Sorry." He found the wine and drank from the bottle
ignoring the cups as he did the portraits. "I was thinking about
something."

"Tell me about it."

"This is a vacation, darling, so why not enjoy it?" Rising, he
moved to stand behind her, his hands dropping to her
shoulders, moving lower in an intimate caress. "Two people,"
he whispered. "Lost in the hills. An old deserted house. The
storm. A perfect setting for them to perform the act of love that
confirms their union. Please, darling, I need you."

"Are you crazy!" Twisting in his arms she glared her distaste.
"You want to use me? Here? Not on your life!"

Once she hadn't been so particular. His hands cradled
softness as thunder blasted the air with force enough to shake
the window.

"See, my darling? The gods are with me. They demand we
perform the ancient rite."

"You're drunk."

"I've had a drink," he admitted. "But that has nothing to do
with it. I want to make love to you. Here and now." His fingers
closed with sudden, hurtful strength. "Damn it, woman, you're
my wife!"

"Don't be an animal." She rose, breaking his grasp as she
stepped aside. "You think I'd do that? On the floor? Before
them?" She gestured at the portraits, her painted nails looking
as if tipped with flame. "Look at them! Degenerates! Filthy
lechers! Scum!"

"They're only paint and canvas. If you want I'll turn them to
face the wall."

"Won't that spoil your fun?" She glared her anger. "Is that
what you really want? To have others watch while you kiss and
grope and slobber? You disgust me! Get out! You drunken
pervert! Get away from me! Leave me alone!"

He went with the wine, weaving down the stairs and into the
hall, the gloom, the watchful eyes of painted faces. To a window

where he stared into darkness, his features reflected in the pane. To a spot on the floor where he sat and leaned his back against a wall. To finish the wine. To close his eyes. To sleep. To dream.

The house became alive with whispering susurrations. Figures moved, stepped from their frames, followed the steps of an elaborate saraband. All were men. No women. This house belonged to men and he felt a part of it. Felt he had returned to something he had once known. A companionship that embraced him with its comfort. The storm murmured in the distance, walking the sky on feet of lightning, talking in the voice of thunder. He stirred in his sleep as the dream turned into nightmare.

The figures became ghosts, which merged into him, sinking into his body as if he were a sponge absorbing their souls. They became him and he became a host to them all. Together they roved through the house and, as they roved, hunger came to join them.

A blast and the house shook to the dying fury of the storm and abruptly he was in a small, familiar room. One flanked by painted faces, the litter of a picnic spread before them. He wasn't alone.

Before him, facing him, a naked figure with a cleft chin and heavy jowls stooped and lifted things high into the air their juices dappling his face and head with carmine smears. Scraps that had been torn from something lying on the floor, which had once been round and smooth with velvet skin and nails the colour of flame. Something that was now red all over.

Diane, her stomach ripped open, intestines spread in greasy ribbons. The proud breasts missing from the wall of her chest. Flesh torn from her buttocks, back, the soft flesh of her thighs. Delicacies to feed a degenerate appetite. All illuminated by the guttering flame of a wick set in a bowl of rancid, human fat. Light which shone on the prominent teeth of the ghoul as it feasted on the body of the dead.

Stephen cried out and lunged forward and saw the creature lunge in turn as they both snatched at the lamp. The flame vanished with the breaking of the bowl to leave only darkness and the crystalline shatter of the window it had broken. The mirror of the night.

BRIAN MOONEY

Maypole

BRIAN MOONEY'S FIRST PROFESSIONAL sale was to *The London Mystery Selection* in 1971. Since then, his fiction has been published in such anthologies and magazines as *The Pan Book of Horror Stories, Dark Voices, The Mammoth Book of Werewolves, The Mammoth Book of Frankenstein, Final Shadows, Dark Horizons* and *Fiesta*.

His adventures of the psychic detective Reuben Calloway have appeared in *Dark Detectives, Shadows Over Innsmouth, The Anthology of Fantasy & the Supernatural, Cthulhu: Tales of the Cthulhu Mythos #2* and *Kadath,* and the author is currently working on a new tale featuring the character.

"The idea for 'Maypole' came to me during a rail journey," recalls the author, "and was just one of those odd chains of thought which lead to inspiration. The train passed a field where a solitary tall post or stake had been driven into the ground. Several children were chasing each other around this post and it occurred to me that they had a ready-made Maypole for May Day.

"This led me to remember something I had once read about the possible origin of the Maypole and in turn, the wonderful 'What if . . .?' question popped into my mind. I pulled out a large notebook I had in my case and by the time I reached my destination, I had roughed out the opening section of the story.''

DEATH'S EMISSARIES CAME FOR Thomas Comstock a few minutes before midnight on a fine spring evening. The limping man was there, as was the man with the blemished face. The two were overshadowed by their companion, the giant. The three were expected and Comstock received them with joy in his heart.

When the men arrived, one of them gave a sharp rap on the front door of the tied cottage and they entered unbidden. Comstock had prepared himself in the ordained fashion and he awaited them in his cramped living room.

The mantel above the open fireplace was littered with tacky souvenirs and a wall-mounted pendulum clock ticked away the minutes of Comstock's life. A battered Welsh dresser, its shelves crammed with paperback Westerns, stood against one wall, while at the opposite was a folded dining-table with two ill-matched chairs. A greasy black leather sofa faced the television and the floor was covered with a threadbare carpet. Amidst this mundane clutter, the men's garb was incongruous and anachronistic.

The three newcomers were clothed in ankle-length white gowns, secured at the waist with silken cords, and their brows were adorned with circlets of some silvery metal.

In contrast, Thomas Comstock wore a coarse shift, several pieces of sacking loosely sewn together with light thread, which reached no further than his knees. His thick, reddish hair was crowned with a wreath woven from young oak leaves.

The men nodded to each other but there was silence between them. All the visitors pressed Comstock's hand and the biggest man patted him gently on the shoulder before indicating that they should go. Comstock was careful to turn off the light before he left the cottage.

The air was sweet and mild after several days of warm weather but Comstock was unable to suppress a slight shiver. The giant saw and once more gave him a reassuring pat.

About half-a-mile distant, across the flat landscape, the angular shapes of village dwellings were silhouetted against a star-bright sky, the chunky tower of an ancient church looming

above all the others. There was a lazy breeze and Comstock
thought that he could hear the creaking of the old sign at the
pub. In the east, a rising full moon was shedding its mellow light
over fields and hedgerows.

They moved with slow but purposeful steps towards the
moon, the limping man and his disfigured companion flanking
Comstock, each lightly clasping one of his elbows.

The more than seventy-eight-inch bulk of the giant trod
closely behind them. All knew that Comstock would not flee
but each man was deeply imbued with a sense of occasion.
More than that, though. They were not merely an escort: they
were also there to impart, by their presence and touch, some of
their strength to Comstock. At times such as this, even the most
stalwart man needed the strength of his friends.

When at last they reached the appointed place – a large and
freshly-ploughed field – a small crowd of some thirty to forty
people awaited them. Many held fiery torches and all but one
wore long white robes. The exception was a woman lightly
gowned in floating, pale-green chiffon which did little to
conceal her slim body. A garland of wild flowers rested upon
her cascade of ash-blonde hair and from a fine gold cord about
her waist was suspended a sickle, its curved blade gleaming. As
Comstock's escort faded back into the crowd, the green-clad
woman and two handmaidens advanced to greet him.

The woman took both of Comstock's hands in hers, and he
gazed at her with uncritical adoration, thinking as always how
very beautiful she was.

"Welcome to this place, Thomas," she said. "Do you come
here of your own free will?"

"I come most willingly, Mother Priestess," the man replied,
rural burr contrasting strongly with her educated tones.

"Then hail and farewell, Thomas." She moved closer, kissed
him on the mouth, then seized and ripped his garment, tearing
away the flimsy threads and leaving him naked. In the pallid
moonlight and the light shed by the flickering torches, his
muscular torso and limbs spoke of peasant vitality and his
erection appeared to be enormous.

The handmaidens began to caress Comstock's body with
light, butterfly strokes and the priestess gently clasped the rigid
penis. Her fingers were long and elegant, her manipulations
soft and skilled. Thomas Comstock's face was a graven mask of
fierce pride.

The woman's movements were languid at first, then became more urgent as the man's breathing quickened. Suddenly he ejaculated, semen spurting silver in the moon's glow. The surrounding men and women echoed Thomas Comstock's cry of ecstasy as if they too had climaxed. The priestess genuflected, tenderly cupping his testicles and the still engorged and throbbing phallus in her left hand. Then with a swift upward stroke of the sickle she scythed Thomas Comstock's genitals from his body!

A single shriek of anguish was torn from the man's throat to be almost drowned by the shout of exultation which burst forth from the onlookers.

For several seconds, or for a thousand years, Comstock just stood there, gouts of blood spilling in a grisly second orgasm, spilling onto the seed he had shed and soaking with it into the soil. Then, despite his agony, he began to run about the field, splashing his blood until his run became a stagger and his stagger a series of stumbles. He fell to his knees with head bowed, as if to watch his own life flood out.

The priestess ran to Comstock, to kneel and cradle his head against her breasts, a living and pagan Pietà. He raised a tortured face to her and his voice was just a whisper. "Was I worthy?"

Love shone from her eyes and her kiss was light upon his cheek. "The most worthy of all, Thomas," she assured him.

He smiled a tired smile and nodded his thanks. Then he held his head back, exposing his throat for the final merciful stroke of the sickle.

Several men came and lifted his body with reverence, bearing it face down about the field so that as much as possible of the rich earth was sanctified by his precious blood.

Anthea Moore took a surreptitious glance at her wristwatch. About ten minutes to go. Too late to start something completely fresh but she could give them a minor research project. The question was, what? Well, May Day was coming up – something to do with that, perhaps? She turned back to the twenty-odd teenagers who made up her folklore and mythology class.

Anthea had been sceptical when a friend, the principal of a sixth-form college, had approached her with the idea of conducting a class once or twice a week.

"Modern teenagers won't be interested in folklore," she had said.

"Don't be cynical," her friend had replied. "Give it a try and be surprised."

So she had given it a try and had been happily surprised. Her students were aged between sixteen and eighteen, all of them studying subjects such as literature, history and religious studies. They seemed to enjoy Anthea's class although she was unsure whether it was because of the subject or because of the fund of often-bloody anecdotes she could tell them or because they were proud of being taught by a genuine published writer.

"Listen carefully," she said. "Beltane, Lughnassadh, Samhain and Imbloc." They goggled at her and at the alien-sounding words. She snatched up a piece of chalk and printed the four words on the blackboard. "Those were the four great festivals of the Celtic year. You may not know much about the Celts but you've almost certainly heard of their priests, the Druids. Take a note of those names, discover what you can about them and we'll discuss your findings at the next session. See if you can link them to any of the Christian festivals or folk celebrations. If you look at the right sources, you'll probably discover that by our standards the Druids were not nice people."

"In what way, Miss Moore?" Stumps of pencil and nibbled pens were poised over dog-eared notebooks.

Anthea smiled. So many of them reminded her of her own younger self. "Well, in common with many ancient religions, fertility rites were important to the Celts for a good planting and a good harvest. The Druids tried to ensure their harvests were good by sacrificing human beings.

"The popular concept now of Druids is of a bunch of harmless eccentrics who gather together every once in a while to worship at Stonehenge."

She paused to write the word "Stonehenge" on the board and drew an immense question mark behind it. "I don't know if anyone has bothered to tell the modern Druids but their predecessors are unlikely to have worshipped at Stonehenge. For a start, Stonehenge predates the first Celtic invasion of Britain by at least a thousand years and probably much longer; and secondly, the Druids venerated trees – the woodlands were their preferred places of worship."

"You mentioned human sacrifice, Miss Moore," said a stout

youth with thick glasses, "Aren't you going to tell us about that?"

"I might have expected *you* to pursue that one, Charles," grinned Anthea. "I had noticed the latest Stephen King among your books."

She waited for the smattering of laughter to die down and then continued, "Some of you may have heard of the Wicker Man. The Druids built great wickerwork cages, often in human form, in which they would burn living slaves and captive enemies."

"Oh, is that all?" said a disappointed Charles.

"No, that's not all," Anthea told him. "I think you're all mature enough to be told about the Corn King . . . even you, Charles.

"The Corn King was selected from among the most physically strong and most ferocious fighters in his tribe and was often – dare I mention it? – the most sexually potent man in the community. He was the Celtic stud." She raised a hand to quell the sniggers. "Many social wild animals know instinctively that it can benefit the herd or pack if the genes only of the most powerful male are passed on. Many pre-Christian pagan tribes had the same instinct. The Corn King was *literally* a stud. It is believed that the Celts willingly gave the Corn King access to their wives, and if a child resulted from the union then it was treated as the husband's own. I think this could possible be the origin of the changeling legend."

"Nice work if you can get it." Tim Finnegan was what American students would call a "jock", an all-round athlete and self-appointed God's gift to women. He waggled lascivious eyebrows at several girls nearby.

One of them sighed. "And to think Miss Moore believes we're *all* mature."

Anthea nodded at the boy. "Yes indeed, Tim, nice work if you can get it. But I'm not so sure you'd like it."

"Try me," Tim laughed.

"Okay, submit your application through the usual channels," Anthea said, "but read the job description very carefully. The Corn King reigned for a single year. At the end of that time he was sacrificed to ensure the fertility of the fields. He might be skinned alive or have his throat cut or be dragged by horses – anything at all to give his blood to the land. Now that you know what it entails, Tim, how soon can you start?"

Mocking shouts were interrupted by the bell signalling the period's end. "Right, that's it for now," Anthea told them. "Please leave quietly and enjoy the short break. I'll see you soon, and don't forget—" She tapped the four words on the blackboard.

"You going anywhere good for the break, Miss?" someone asked as they gathered their books together.

"I'm getting into my car and I'm going to drive around looking for interesting May Day customs," Anthea said. "I don't know where yet, but the weather has been very good recently and I hope to have a pleasant trip."

Famous last words, thought Anthea Moore ruefully. She was sitting in her car staring out at a grey-white cocoon of fog which surrounded her.

She had decided on East Anglia for her holiday drive. There was an out-of-the-way village called Bresslingham Market which was said to have some very interesting old May Day revels. There might just be the basis for an article or the start of a book there.

The weather had started out well – "Bright periods," the radio weather forecast had promised – but conditions had worsened gradually after she had driven off the A11 onto the secondary road system which would bring her to Bresslingham Market.

The change had started with a sudden dip in temperature. There had been nothing disturbing in that. After all, cold snaps in late April and early May are only to be expected, particularly in the eastern counties. Anthea had turned up the car's heating system and was soon warm. Then thin tendrils of mist had started to creep across the broad, flat farmlands, climbing the low hedgerows and sliding through shallow ditches towards the road until the whole day was wrapped in a light monochrome shawl.

Still, it wasn't too bad. Visibility was down to several hundred yards and the car's headlights were well able to deal with that. Anthea had slowed down to compensate for her unfamiliarity with the convolutions of the narrow country road. Thank God, she had encountered very little traffic and she guessed that most drivers stuck to the main roads. After all, this part of East Anglia was sparsely populated.

And then without warning Anthea Moore had found herself

in the middle of the thickest fog she had ever seen. She reduced her speed even more, down to about ten miles an hour, leaning forward with her face almost touching the windscreen in a vain attempt to see through the murk ahead. The wipers clacked back and forth but made little difference to the viscous droplets which smothered the vehicle.

Fate had been reserving its dirtiest trick. One moment the car was crawling ahead and then, for no apparent reason, it just stopped. The engine seemed to be running sweetly and then . . . silence.

"*Shit!*" muttered Anthea Moore.

There was a minor consolation. She was on a straight run of road which stretched for some distance ahead and so there was little chance of an accident. Unless the oncoming driver was a road maniac, she realized, and there were plenty of those on the loose. She steered as far in to the left as the narrow road would permit and applied the handbrake.

For several minutes she tried the ignition and pressed the gas-pedal. Nothing, save for some odd choking noises from the engine. For the first time ever, Anthea regretted that she knew so little about the working of cars. But this was supposed to be one of the most reliable small cars on the road. "Excuses don't start engines," she told herself. "Decide what you're going to do."

Expert opinion was that a woman finding herself in this position should lock herself in the vehicle and await the next police patrol. Trouble was, this particular good advice was aimed at women stranded on motorways, not on very minor roads in the middle of nowhere. The police patrol around here was likely to be a bicycle-riding bobby who passed by once every three or four months.

Anthea consulted her road atlas but it was of little help. She could see where she had left the major road and she was able to pinpoint Bresslingham Market in relation to that junction. But she had little idea of how far she had travelled through the thickening murk. The town could be around the next bend or it could be an hour away at fog speed. God, in this blinding mess she could well have driven *through* the town and never have realized it.

Decisions, decisions! She could stay here in the car, cold, miserable and hungry, for any length of time. Alternatively, she could get out and walk and hope that she would soon arrive at

Bresslingham. She glanced at her wristwatch. Two o'clock. At least it was still daylight (*ha, ha*). Anthea reached into the back seat for her overnight bag. Her suitcase could wait until she returned with help. She took a flashlight from the glove compartment.

She carefully locked the car door and began to walk. The idea of the walk itself did not bother her. She often walked for pleasure and she was wearing sensible shoes. But the fog was heavy and damp, clinging to her as she moved, and all sound – even that of her own footsteps on the road – was muffled. Anthea felt as if she was treading the depths of a lifeless sea.

Perhaps ten minutes passed and Anthea began to imagine things. Or, rather, she hoped that she was only imagining things. The fog, as if sentient and inimical, seemed to press closer. The woman's spine began to itch with a sensation of being silently watched. Several times she wanted to whirl about and scream into the gloom but controlled herself. It's natural to be apprehensive in this situation, she told herself fiercely. Succumb to panic and you've really got problems.

She used the flashlight sparingly, switching it on briefly and casting the beam around. She got the impression that the hedges bordering the road were becoming higher and Anthea was sure that she could hear strange rustlings coming from within their depths. Another flick of the torch's button and – *What was that?* That silent, flitting shadow just beyond the beam's edge?

Anthea stood still and took deep breaths to calm herself, suffering a coughing fit for her pains. Bloody fool, it was a fox or something. Wasn't it?

An unexpected chattering noise from behind made her spin about. *That wasn't imagination!* The beam of light punched into the haze. Nothing. Another animal? Anthea shifted the torch to her shoulder like a cudgel. "Who's there?" she called out. "I know you're there. Be careful, I'm armed!"

There was an empty feeling in her stomach and her heart beat more rapidly as she backed away, staring into the fog, wary for the unseen pursuer. She could neither see nor hear anything and relaxed slightly. And bumped straight into something behind her.

Anthea whirled, ready to lash out with the flashlight. Then she gasped and laughed weakly. Her assailant was a wooden post. Anthea leaned against it, giggling. She had often prided herself on her strong nerves but this fog had cut her down to size.

A wooden post. Could it be . . . ? Anthea grinned and shone her torch upwards. Yes, it was. A signpost. An arm, pointing the way she was heading, carried the legend, BRESSLINGHAM MARKET 7. Great! Then she noticed the second pointer, indicating a road off to the left. Anthea strained on tiptoes to see it.

The letters were rather more worn that those on the main arm but Anthea deciphered them as NAYSHAM $\frac{3}{4}$. So, there was a village or hamlet called Naysham nearby. Anthea had never heard of it, nor could she recall noticing it in the road atlas. But it was much nearer than Bresslingham and she was sure that at least she could find shelter until the fog lifted. Feeling much happier, she walked on and within a few minutes found the side road to Naysham. Giving a little sigh of relief, Anthea stepped out briskly.

The fog still clung to her in soggy caress and there were still noises in the hedgerows but Anthea did not care. She was no longer facing the unknown: the fog was just fog, the noises just natural noises. Within a few minutes she was even whistling.

At last through the denseness she began to make out the shapes of low buildings, a corner here, an odd line of thatching there, an occasional low gleam of light-bulbs within cottages. Then she saw the most welcome thing of all, a mirage-like haze of blue. She approached carefully until the blue shape solidified into an old-fashioned carriage lamp surmounting a sign which announced POLICE.

Anthea grinned and punched the air before pushing her way through a heavy door and into the friendly warmth of a gas-fire and the welcome glow of electric light. Her way was barred by an oak counter on which stood a gleaming brass bell. Anthea gave a tentative tap and there was a friendly jingling noise.

A voice from somewhere towards the rear of the building roared out, "Now which of you lot's daft enough to come out on an afternoon like this? Just hang on a minute!" Despite the volume of the bellow, the voice sounded amiable enough.

Anthea heard the flushing of a toilet followed by the running of a tap. Then the biggest man she had ever seen strolled into the lobby, drying his hands on a piece of rough towelling.

"Where's the bloody fire then –?" He stopped, embarrassed. "Oh, sorry, Miss. Thought it was one of the neighbours." He ran a huge hand across a stubble of grey hair and gave Anthea an awkward grin. The policeman had an ugly, craggy face which Anthea thought oddly attractive. "We don't see many strangers here in Naysham," the man continued. "What can I do for you?"

Anthea told the man her name and explained her predicament. The police officer nodded. "You poor lass. Rotten thing to happen. We do get these sudden fogs around here at this time of the year. Well, we're only a small village but we've got all that's needed to help you out.

"There's Dick Brand who owns the filling station and garage, although he'll not be able to do anything for you until the weather clears. I'll fix that for you as soon as I can. Then we've got a nice little pub here, The Maypole. They don't normally cater for travellers but there are a couple of spare rooms. It's clean and comfortable and I know Reg Feltham and his missus'll be glad to put you up for the night. I'll take you over there now if you'll just give me a minute to get my jacket. I'm Constable Lewis, by the way – Jack to my friends."

They stepped out into the bone-gripping damp and cold. Anthea shivered. Jack Lewis, buttoning his tunic, said, "Don't worry, Miss Moore, soon have you comfortable." He sniffed at the air. "This'll be clear, probably by tonight sometime, tomorrow morning at the latest. Here, lass, give me that little bag of yours. And you'd better take my arm. Don't want to lose you as soon as we've found you."

Anthea did as bid. She was above average woman's height but the policeman was a good head and shoulders taller than she. The kind of man a girl feels safe with, she thought. Then, what do you mean, girl? You're thirty-two and self-sufficient. Well, not this afternoon, you're not. She chuckled.

"What's funny?" asked Jack Lewis.

"Oh, me," said Anthea. "I've always been full of spit and independence and then a few noises in the hedgerows this afternoon and I came near to panic."

"Understandable," the man said. "The countryside's not so peaceful as townsfolk think and this fog would confuse anyone. This way, Miss."

They crossed the road. The half-seen shape of a squat grey shadow triggered a memory for Anthea. "Am I imagining things or is that a genuine Saxon church?"

"Yes, Miss, St Alaric's. Believed to date from the ninth

century and we're very proud of it. And here's The Maypole.
You can just about see the inn sign."

Anthea looked up, following his pointing finger. The sign
was old and ill-painted and she could see little more than a pale
shaft which could have been anything. There were marks which
might have represented dancing figures but the dirt of ages
made this uncertain.

Jack Lewis opened a low door and allowed Anthea to pre-
cede him. He had to bend to follow her. Anthea found herself
in the warm fug of a public bar, redolent with the rich odours of
strong ale and tobacco. The floor was of stone flags, the walls
and ceiling smoke-darkened. A cheerful fire roared in an
inglenook, its flames reflecting in the burnished surfaces of
brass and copper artefacts dangling from blackened beams.
Furniture was sparse, a few high-backed settles around the walls
and several wooden stools and chairs by the fireplace. Two
elderly men, retired farm labourers perhaps, sat at the bar,
drinking pints and playing cribbage. They had probably been
coming in here for years and were not to be put off by a little
fog. Anthea smiled at them. The Maypole was not the sort of
place she would normally have chosen – wine bars being her
preferred watering-holes – but in her present mood it seemed
to be the most welcoming room she had ever seen.

A skinny man with side-whiskers stood behind the bar
polishing glasses. He wore a chequered shirt and a chequered
waistcoat, both loud and in clashing colours. The whiskered
man looked up as Anthea and the policeman entered. "Hello,
Jack. Usual?" Although speaking to Lewis, he stared at Anthea
with unabashed curiosity.

"Nothing thanks, Reg," the police officer said. "Wonder if
you've got a room for Miss Moore here? Her car broke down
and she's stranded in the fog."

"But of course," the publican replied, manner instantly full
of bonhomie. "I'll just call the wife."

"I'll leave you with Reg then, lass." Jack Lewis grinned at
Anthea. "I'll arrange for your car to be fixed in the morning.
Hope I'll see you again before you go on your way."

Twenty minutes later Anthea had signed the register and was
relaxing by a cosy gas-fire in the small chintzy bedroom to
which she had been shown by a fat and chuckling Mrs Feltham.
She had been served toasted ham sandwiches, a pot of tea and a
large brandy – "On the house, my dear, to get the chill out of

your bones." The deep armchair was soft and comfortable and Anthea dozed.

She was jerked from sleep by a steady knocking at the bedroom door. For a moment she was disorientated, wondering where she was. Anthea glanced at her watch. She had been asleep for a couple of hours. There was a stale taste in her mouth and she drained the dregs of cold tea. It helped a little.

She had a fuddled impression of a disquieting dream but was unable to recall details. There had been half-seen figures in a fogscape and there had been some sort of tall column. Phallic symbol? Wonder what Freud would make of that? She shook her head. Of course, the answer was obvious. She had had an anxious time this afternoon and now she was lodged at The Maypole pub. She had probably been dreaming of the fog and the old inn-sign. Phallic symbol was right. She glanced towards the latticed window. The fog outside was still thick.

The knocking continued. Anthea pulled herself from the armchair and went to open the door.

The tall woman who entered was dressed for bad weather in the countryside – waxed jacket, green gumboots, man's tweed cap – but there was no disguising her striking beauty.

"Hello. Do forgive the intrusion. We don't get many strangers in Naysham, you know."

Anthea took the proffered hand. "Anthea Moore," she replied.

"I know. I peeked in Feltham's register. Tell me, are you the Anthea Moore who wrote *Ancient Cultures* and *From Dark Memory*? You are? I'm so pleased." The woman gave a bright smile. "I'm sorry. I must seem very rude. My name's Melissa Taybourne. If I were a man, I suppose you'd say I was the squire in these parts.

"Jack Lewis came to see me about something and mentioned that a young woman was stuck here. I wandered over out of curiosity to find out about you. Imagine my pleasure when I saw your name. I thought it was too good to be true that you should be one of my favourite writers on folklore. Anyway, regardless of who you had been, I intended to offer you dinner this evening. Bonny Feltham's a dear but her cooking leans towards the homely. Do say you'll accept. And I'll insist that you sign my copies of your books."

Anthea laughed. "In the circumstances, I can't refuse," she said. "And I would have been at a loose end. Pubs aren't much

in my line and I haven't even got a decent book in my overnight
bag. Of course I'll come to dinner, and thank you."

Melissa Taybourne nodded. "Good. About seven o'clock
then. Feltham will show you how to get to my home. It's only
a few minutes walk."

When Anthea descended a few minutes before seven, Reg
Feltham was waiting for her at the foot of the narrow staircase.
"This way, Miss. I've got strict orders from Miss Melissa to get
you to her house." He led the way to the front door, moving
with a peculiar strutting gait as if one leg was slightly longer
than the other. "Fog's lifted a fair bit," he added. "reckon it'll
be clear later tonight."

He was certainly right in part. Although the air was still misty,
visibility was now several hundred yards. Reg Feltham pointed
down the street. "Go back the way you came here," he
instructed. "Past the church, across the road and it's the big
detached house a little way beyond the police station. You can't
miss it. Enjoy your evening, now."

Anthea found the house easily. As she passed through the
gateway, the front door was flung open and Melissa Taybourne
was there to greet her. "I hope you don't mind, but I've invited
another guest," she said as she took Anthea's hand to draw her
into the house. "Our rector, Mr Luckhurst, is another folklore
enthusiast and he'd not forgive me if he missed the chance to
meet you. He's in here, in the sitting-room."

It was a comfortable, chintzy room and logs crackled and
blazed in the fireplace. A thin man in clerical garb leaned
against the mantel, sipping from a glass of sherry. His face, in
profile, was fine and sensitive-looking, with fine lines radiating
from the corner of eyes and mouth. Sandy-white hair, a trifle
too long, maybe, was brushed straight back from his brow.

"Rector," Melissa Taybourne called. "Come and meet Anthea Moore."

The man turned towards them and Anthea struggled to keep
from gasping. The rector's features, so pleasing in profile, were
marred by a purple, warty birthmark which clung like a cancer
to the left side of his face. But his handshake was warm and dry
and reassuring and his voice, as he greeted Anthea, was
pleasantly deep and soothing, exuding charm.

Dinner was served in a small, panelled dining-room, the only
illumination coming from tall white candles in a silver cande-
labra. "I don't usually put on the dog like this," laughed

Melissa Taybourne. "But it is good to have a new guest. We tend to be very insular in Naysham."

Anthea enjoyed the meal and the conversation. It quickly became evident that neither Melissa Taybourne nor the rector were claiming devotion to folklore for the sake of politeness and entertainment. Both were knowledgeable and Mr Luckhurst was scholarly in his approach to the subject.

Over coffee, the rector said, "Although we're grateful for your presence here, Miss Moore, what on earth could have brought you to this remote place?"

Anthea drained her cup and accepted a refill from her host. "I just suddenly decided to come to Bresslingham Market for the holiday. I wanted to witness their May Day celebrations."

"They are interesting," said Luckhurst. "But before travelling on you must come and see our own modest maypole ceremony. We hold it very early in the morning, so there will be no bar to your continuing on to Bresslingham once your car is mobile again."

"Yes, do. It would be a pleasure to have you attend," added Melissa Taybourne. "Hardly anyone but the villagers come and we could do with some new blood."

"I'd like that," said Anthea. "I wonder why I've not heard of this village and its May celebration."

"As I said earlier, we tend to insularity. I can't think of anyone in the village who'd want tourists tramping everywhere."

"I concur," said the Reverend Luckhurst. "You must promise, Miss Moore, that if you write about us you will give the village a fictitious name."

A light ground mist lingered when Anthea finally left Melissa Taybourne's house, but above the sky was speckled with stars. "It looks as if it will be fine tomorrow," observed the rector. "That'll be good for the maypole ceremony."

"We'll call for you early, Anthea," said Melissa Taybourne. "You'll find the ceremony unusual but I hope interesting. We'll involve you so that you don't feel left out of it. Good night and sleep well."

Anthea walked back towards the pub, mellowed by fine food and feeling pleasantly tired. As she neared St Alaric's she heard a creaking noise, as if of a door opening on rusty hinges, and there was a glimmer of scarlet light spilling from the church. A huge shadow detached itself from the church doorway and turned towards The Maypole. It had to be the policeman, Jack Lewis.

Anthea almost called out a greeting, then checked her tongue. She couldn't put a finger on it, but there was something almost furtive about the way Lewis was moving, as if he had something to be ashamed of and wished to sneak away unseen.

As Anthea drew abreast with the church, she noticed that a sliver of ruddy light still fell across the footpath and that the main entrance door had been left slightly ajar. She pushed gently until the door was no more than wide enough to admit her. Anthea found herself in a small porch.

Keeping as quiet as possible, she closed the door behind her. The red light was from an oil-lamp hanging from the ceiling and beyond was another doorway. Venturing on, Anthea came into a cramped and claustrophobic nave, the walls bleak and moist. The nave, like the porch, was lit by a pendant red lamp. There were no pews as such, just a few time-polished wooden forms on the stone floor.

Down to the left was a wall broken by a low archway. Remembering what she did of Saxon architecture, Anthea knew that through the archway she would find the chancel. She tiptoed to the archway and had to stoop slightly to pass through.

The chancel was deeply shadowed, being lit only by two candles on the small altar. As Anthea straightened, she noticed something which made her catch her breath. It was the marble outline of something – someone – lying still upon the altar. Anthea put her hand to her lips to stifle a giggle. Of course, it was an effigy. But then, she wondered, did Saxon churches ever have commemorative effigies? She could not quite recall.

For some reason, she suddenly wanted to run away; only her enquiring mind prevented her from doing so. She took several deep breaths and approached the altar slowly. When she was what was there. Anthea moaned softly and bit fiercely on the knuckles of her right hand.

The man was naked and there was no doubt that he was dead. His face was peaceful but beneath that mask of serenity an appalling, mirthless crimson grin split his throat. That was not all. Anthea's eyes, taking in detail piecemeal, wandered to a dreadful raw wound at the groin. Then, most terrible of all –

Anthea wanted to be sick and only with great effort managed

to swallow the rising vomit. The hands were crossed on the corpse's broad chest and below them the genitals had been placed on the abdomen in such a way that they appeared raised and offered.

Shaking, Anthea backed away until she was brought up short by the wall between chancel and nave.

Her thoughts tumbled. What was going on in this place? With those frightening wounds, the dead man had to have been murdered. And it followed that Jack Lewis must be involved somehow, the way he had appeared to slink away from the church. If the victim had been slaughtered by – what? a maniac? – then the place would be crawling with police and the killing would have been he talk of the village. Perhaps Jack Lewis was the maniacal killer. But then, leaving his victim in the church like this meant that others would be in on the secret . . .

Anthea felt giddy. She ducked under the archway and fled the church. Outside, the mist had finally dispersed but in her distraught state she hardly noticed. She was aware that the village street was empty and she made a dash for the pub, flinging back the door which led into the public bar.

The bar was almost full and the hubbub of talk and laughter ceased as Anthea crashed into the room. She stood there, trying to catch her breath, and everyone turned to look at her. A huge figure moved from a dim corner into the light to confront her. It was Jack Lewis, a pint glass almost hidden in his fist.

"Why, Miss Moore, is anything wrong?" The policeman's voice was kind and concerned.

Lips tight, she backed away a little and shook her head. Seconds later she managed to speak, doing her best to sound calm. "No, I'm just a bit more tired than I realized and I feel a bit unwell. I'll go to my room."

"I'll get the missus to bring you up some cocoa, shall I?" offered Reg Feltham.

"Thank you, no," said Anthea. To her own surprise she managed to sound normal. "I just need sleep. I'll see you in the morning."

Anthea turned and left the public bar, walking up the stairs as slowly as she dared. Once in the room she locked the door and removed the key from the lock. She noticed strong iron bolts at both top and bottom of the door and she rammed them closed. There was a murmuring noise from below, as if things were getting back to normal in the bar. Or were they discussing her odd behaviour?

A worrying thought came to her. Had she left the church door open when making her frantic escape? If so, Lewis and any accomplices he might have would realize that she knew their terrible secret. Going to the window, she looked out into the street. It was still empty. From where she was she could not see the church doorway. She pulled the weighty velvet curtains closed. This at least gave her a feeling of security and safety.

Anthea had stopped smoking some years previously but now she felt the urgent desire for a cigarette. She slumped into the armchair and thought.

There was no doubt that she must get away from Naysham as soon as possible. Tonight was certainly out, even though the fog had evaporated. She didn't know the area and could easily become lost. And yet if she stayed, would Lewis try to come for her in the early hours? The room door seemed to be solid enough and she doubted that the man could get in without rousing the rest of the pub. But suppose that they were all in on it? *Stop it now!* she scolded herself – you're becoming paranoid.

The best thing to do, Anthea concluded, would be to stay awake all night and make her getaway at first light. At this time of the year, that should be a little after four-thirty. She was fairly fit and seven miles was not so far. By the time the village came to life she could be in Bresslingham Market, reporting the savage murder to the police there.

The thought of using the bed was attractive but Anthea resisted temptation. She turned the chair to face the door and then snuggled into it, trying to make herself as comfortable as possible. She prepared to face a long night.

Anthea awoke with a slight cry. She fumbled with her watch, pressed the stud which illuminated the dial. Almost five-twenty. Stiffly, body protesting, she uncurled herself from the armchair and tottered to the window. God, she felt as if she had been on an all-night bender. The old brass rail squealed as she pulled apart the curtains.

The room was flooded with the saffron glow of early sunlight. Anthea opened the window a little, peering out with caution. The village was quiet and she could neither see nor hear any sound of life. Now was the time to be gone.

She wrote a cheque to cover her night's lodging and clipped it to the bedspread with a safety-pin. Stealthily, Anthea drew the bolts and unlocked the door. She listened for a moment but The Maypole was still. Taking up her shoes in one hand and her overnight bag in the other, she left the room and crept downstairs.

As she descended, imagination took over again. The pub door would be locked by an ancient iron key which was kept beneath the landlord's pillow while he slept. She would not be able to escape the place . . .

She need not have worried. The door was fastened by a simple Yale lock. Anthea left the premises and pulled the door shut behind her.

They were waiting for her at the first corner. There were four of them: Melissa Taybourne, Lewis, the rector and the publican. "Why, Anthea," said the woman. "Don't tell me that you meant to leave us without witnessing our May celebrations?"

Shocked, Anthea lost power of movement and her case slipped from her hand. Jack Lewis stepped forward to pick it up. "I'll look after this for you, Miss Moore."

Anthea stared at the four. The men wore flowing white robes while Melissa Taybourne, hair loose and flowing, was clearly naked beneath her flimsy green gown. But it was the scintillation of early sunlight on the sickle at Melissa's belt which caught and held the eye rather than her lovely form.

"The maypole's not very far away, Anthea," Melissa said. "Just a short walk. I'm sure that if you're not feeling well these gentlemen will lend you support."

Reverend Luckhurst took Anthea's left arm in a firm grip. "It will be a pleasure, Miss Moore," he said. Reg Feltham, with a friendly nod, grasped Anthea's other arm.

"Shall we go?" asked Melissa Taybourne.

Anthea stumbled along with them, any will to resist drained from her. She became aware of a noise from somewhere ahead. It sounded like singing and clapping.

She had her first glimpse of the maypole at a distance and her mind tried to tell her that it was all right, that everything was normal after all. The singing came from a crowd of villagers while others were dancing around the maypole in threes, each middle dancer holding the ribbon which spiralled around the tall shaft. It was just a simple village tradition.

Then as they drew near, Anthea knew that it was not all right.

There was something truly strange about the dancers, or at least about the ribbon holders.

The flanking pair of each trio wore the long white robes but the middle dancers, men and women, were naked. And the ribbons were wrong. They were not gay strips of multi-coloured bunting but thick and greasy-looking, aberrant purple-grey coils.

And then Anthea saw that the naked dancers' chests and bellies were spattered with what seemed to be red paint, and seconds later she knew that it was not paint and that they were not holding the ribbons but that the ribbons protruded from their lower bodies and were growing longer as they stumbled about the maypole.

"You're all insane," Anthea whispered.

Melissa Taybourne smiled and shook her head. "What is insane about propitiating the old gods of the land as our ancestors did?" She waved an elegant hand at the dancers. "These are all volunteers. Thomas Comstock – you saw him in the church, Anthea – gave his blood for the fertility of the land but he has left his seed in many wombs. The ceremony of the maypole is to ensure the fertility of that seed."

"And you were sent to us for a purpose, Miss Moore," said Jack Lewis. "From time to time it is only good and proper that an outsider be brought into our rites. Fresh blood, you know, can only be beneficial to the community."

"We thought that you, Anthea, of all people would understand this," said the rector.

Anthea wanted to scream but she could only whimper. With firm gentleness her escort led her to the maypole. They cut away her clothing until she was quite naked, after which Melissa Taybourne went to work with the sickle.

Then Anthea was able to scream.

TERRY LAMSLEY

Under the Crust

TERRY LAMSLEY WAS BORN in the south of England but lived in the north for most of his life. He currently resides in Amsterdam, Holland.

His first collection of supernatural stories, *Under the Crust,* was initially published in a small paperback edition in 1993. Originally intended to only appeal to the tourist market in Lamsley's home town of Buxton in Derbyshire (the volume's six tales are all set in or around the area), its reputation quickly grew, helped when stories from the book were included in two of the annual "Year's Best" horror anthologies.

The book was subsequently nominated for no less than three prestigious World Fantasy Awards, with the story reprinted here eventually winning the award for Best Novella. Ramsey Campbell accepted it on the author's behalf, and Lamsley's reputation as a writer of supernatural fiction was assured.

In 1997, Canada's Ash-Tree Press reissued *Under the Crust* as a handsome hardcover, limited to just five hundred copies and now as sought-after as the long out-of-print first edition. A year earlier, Ash-Tree had published a second, equally remarkable collection of Lamsley's short stories, *Conference With the Dead:*

Tales of Supernatural Terror, and it was followed ⅰ.
collection, *Dark Matters*.

More recently, he has had stories in *By Moonlight On*
Turn Out the Light and *Taverns of the Dead*, and a new nov
appears in *Fourbodings* from PS Publishing.

"Dove Holes is a real place," reveals Lamsley. "People living
there, not having much else to do a lot of the time, were in the
habit of packing their families in the car, at weekends and
holidays, to have a day out rummaging about on the large Council
tip on the edge of the village. Rumour had it that rich people
from Buxton sometimes dumped valuable antiques there.

"To get into the main part of the tip you had to have some
bona fide waste material of your own to deposit, though a lot of
people brought out a lot more rubbish than they took in. Or so
I was told. Whatever the truth of this, I have seen long queues of
cars lined up at the entrance on sunny days. The Victory Quarry
was much as I described it, at the time of writing."

MAURICE BEGAN TO FEEL ill as he came off the Chapel-en-le-
Frith by-pass and drove up the A6 to Dove Holes. His palms
were damp, and his hands slithered on the steering wheel. He
was trying to grip too hard to compensate for a feeling he had
that if he didn't do so, his hands would start to tremble. Also, he
was having trouble with his vision. The edges of things were
hazy, and patches of blue sky that showed through the gaps in
the high, blousy clouds, looked far too bright, like neon light
shining off painted metal. He wanted to stop, but was caught in
a line of lorries, and there was nowhere to pull off the road that
he could remember. He wiped his hands on his shirt. They
became sticky again at once. There was a droning sound
somewhere. He wasn't sure if it was coming from the car
engine or inside his skull.

He blinked and shook his head in consternation. He had
been feeling uneasy all day, all week even, and there was plenty
in his life to feel uneasy about, but he had thought he was fairly
fit. Now, it seemed, his body was going to let him down, and
play host to some sickness, on top of everything else. He
slammed the steering wheel with the heel of his hand in
disgust, wound down the side window a couple of inches,
and leaned forward tensely against his seat-belt.

As he drove through the tight, dusty village of Dove Holes he

started to experience a sensation of more general disorienta-
tion. He saw a narrow turning forking to his left and, on
impulse, took it much too fast. The unfamiliar road curved
and dipped between two low stone walls and, hardly slowing at
all, he rocketed along it for a few hundred yards, feeling almost
helpless, as though the car had taken possession of him. He
made an effort of concentration, to gain control of the vehicle,
but a square, dark shape sprang up to the right of him, as
though it had pounced out of the earth, and plunged towards
him. He swung the car to the left to avoid whatever it was – it
seemed to be a huge black, windowless van – and rode wildly up
and along a low, steep, grassy bank. He sensed, rather than saw,
the other driver staring down at him. The car scraped against a
wall and he had a vague impression of stones tumbling away
into the field beyond. The car pulled up sharp at last, its front
end pointing up to the sky.

Maurice glanced back to see what had happened to the other
vehicle, but it had vanished. Could anything that size, travelling
that fast, not have gone off the road?

Then he recalled that the van, or whatever it was, had made
no attempt to avoid him. It had taken no evasive action in the
seconds it had been visible, as though the driver had not even
seen him! Thoughts of insurance bleeped on and off in his
mind as he freed his seat-belt buckle, opened the door, and
stumbled out onto the road.

There was a strong, gusting wind blowing. He gulped air
desperately through his half-open mouth, feeling its cold shock
on his lungs, and cursed the world in general.

"Food poisoning!" he thought. The meal earlier on, at the
reception. Something – the chicken? the pork pies? – had
tasted strange, but he had eaten it anyway, in his hunger. The
contents of his stomach flipped over painfully, causing him to
double up over the car bonnet.

He forced himself upright and went to inspect the damage.
One of the front lights was smashed, the left wing dented, and
there were scratches, some deep, along that side. He'd lost a lot
of paint. Still, it could have been worse. The wall he had hit
some dozens of yards back must have been ready to collapse, or
the car would have been in a very bad way.

He sat down on the grass bank and waited for his heart to
stop racing. His head felt clearer, but things still didn't look
quite right; the world was still hazy and slightly out of kilter.

Next to him the car clicked and sighed as the engine cooled. After a while he glanced underneath to check that nothing was leaking, got back inside, and carefully backed onto the tarmac. He continued along the little back road at about ten miles an hour until a further spasm in his stomach made him shut his eyes in agony, and he had to stop again.

He got out, slammed the door behind him, and looked around.

He was near the top of a hill. Open countryside lay spread around him on all sides. Ahead of him a row of scraggy, dark-leafed trees stretched to the right towards acres of torn-up fields and pyramids of raw earth; a scene of tortured ugliness. In front of them a deeply scarred path of churned mud led to a set of old diggings, called the Victory Quarry, that had partly been turned into a tip by the Borough Council. A multitude of large skips, painted drab brown, sprawled away at all angles beyond the end of the line of trees; a porta-cabin guarded the entrance at the other side. A skimpy gate of wire grill on an iron frame gaped wide to give access to dust carts and private vehicles arriving from time to time with cargoes of every kind of rubbish.

He wandered down the path, thinking he would take advantage of the shelter of the trees to relieve his bladder.

It was not easy going. The mud was scored with the tyre-marks of huge machines, which had to be stepped in and out of with care. The rain of the previous weeks had sunk deep, turning the mangled soil oleaginous, but the mix of sunshine and strong wind of the last three days had formed a crust overall that looked solid, but gave way under his feet, precipitating him awkwardly into the mire below. His light town shoes became heavily caked with clumps of dirt, like thick black paste, and his progress was marked by an uneven sequence of gross squelching sounds that complemented the sensations he was experiencing in his belly.

He grabbed at a half-broken branch and pulled himself along it into a space between two trees. He noticed that their trunks on the pathward side had been hacked and wounded by passing vehicles. Great scabs of bark were missing, revealing the plants' fibrous flesh. Crosses, in faded orange paint, had been daubed on the trees, presumably to indicate that they were to be preserved. Stumps of others, less fortunate, remained here and there, like the broken pillars on tombs.

Immediately at the rear of the trees, shrubs and flowers grew in the shaded dimness. He stepped a little way in among them, relieved himself, and stopped to wipe the mud from his shoes with a clump of grass.

Above him, something moved heavily among the branches. For moments there was silence, then the bird, or whatever it was, shifted clumsily again. It made a sudden, rattling, cackling sound that made him start. "Like the noise a toy machine gun would make if it laughed!" he thought, and wondered at his own wild simile. But it was reasonably accurate. There was something taunting and mechanical in the creature's call that unnerved him in his weakened, jittery state. He looked up in the direction of the sound, but the sun was shining directly through the leaves above him, punching blinding slivers of light through an otherwise featureless silhouette. It was impossible to distinguish anything in particular.

There was movement above again. A shower of twigs descended around him, and something else fell, that hit the ground by his feet. After the briefest hesitation, when he felt a stab of regret that he had ever stepped in among the trees, he bent down and picked it up. It was a purple-brown, egg-shaped object, a little more than three inches long. Surprisingly heavy, and icy cold, it looked more like some kind of fruit, but not, he thought, edible. There was something distinctly unappetising about it. It looked old; dry; preserved.

After rolling it on his palm, Maurice went back onto the path again to get a better look at it.

Both ends were quite smooth, with no indication that they had ever been joined to any plant.

"Not a seed," he thought. "And not an egg; far too heavy and too hard. Anyway, an egg would have smashed on its fall from the tree." He pressed harder and harder, and it seemed to give a bit. He closed both hands over it, to obtain more pressure, and gripped them together.

The thing burst and his hands slammed shut on what was left.

He felt something moving in his two-handed fist. He opened his hands and saw what seemed to be a myriad of tiny, dark creatures running out onto his fingers and up his wrists. He held his hands up to his eyes. He was not sure if what he could see was a multitude of tiny entities moving together, as though with one mind, or a single creature made up of almost microscopic sections. Both his hands were covered, as though by thin gloves. He became aware of a slightly painful sensation in the affected areas, and brushed his hands together. After a few moments of vigorous washing motions the "gloves", and the pain, began to subside. Whatever had come out of the egg turned to dust that blew away in the wind as it fell.

A mottled, bruise-like stain remained to mark where the contents of the object had spread. He tried rubbing his hands in the grass, but without effect. The stain seemed indelible.

His skin itched. His hands and wrists looked horrible, as though his skin was diseased. Rubbing them fretfully against each other, he peered up into the trees again.

He saw a branch sway down, as though something was walking along it.

He picked a large stone out of the mud and threw it at where he judged the source of the movement to be.

There was a commotion among the leaves and the harsh, cackling sound recommenced with a vengeance. Nearby, all along the line of trees, other, presumably similar creatures, took up the call. Their combined din became a terrible cacophony. Large sections of all the trees began to heave agitatedly. In his almost-hysterical state of confusion Maurice thought he could see thin arms waving and gesticulating among the branches.

He turned and ran, but in the wrong direction, away from his car. He realized his mistake almost at once, but dared not stop.

Once, he glanced to the left. Behind the trees, in among the shrubs and bushes, spidery shapes seemed to be scuttling up out from between the roots buried there. He got the impression that they were moving along parallel to him. Their movements were slow, but so were his, hampered as he was by the deep tyre tracks and the clinging mud.

He reached the porta-cabin. A shuttered window was open on the side. He ran to the far end, where he could see the edge of the lowest of a set of wooden steps protruding. The door above the steps was open, held back against the wind with a twist of wire. He collapsed on his knees on the steps and looked into the cabin. A young skinhead with a tattooed scalp, in overalls and a black donkey-jacket, sat at an improvized desk, stirring the contents of a mug with one hand and clutching a coverless paperback in the other. The young man regarded him inquisitively over the book, which he lowered a couple of inches.

Maurice got awkwardly up off the steps, turned, and looked back into the trees. He realized the scolding sounds had stopped. The trees swayed gently, normally, in the wind. As far as he could see, nothing moved among them that should not. The mud lane leading to the road was empty.

"What have you got?" a voice asked from inside the cabin. It was a tired, old man's voice.

He turned and looked at the skinhead, who shrugged, and gestured back over his shoulder.

Half way into the cabin, on a pile of filthy mattresses, lay an elderly, whiskery man, also in overalls. He was on his side, with his head propped in his hand.

"Is it household? Garden? That sort of thing?" the old man demanded.

"I'm sorry . . . ?" said Maurice, uncomprehendingly.

"Yer rubbish," said the young man irritably. "What is it?" He sneered at the muddy, frightened man in front of him, who could only press his hand against his brow and shake his head.

"Bloody Hell!" the skinhead said, "what we got here?" and held the tattered book up to his face in a contemptuous, dismissive gesture.

The old man turned and sat up. "You got any rubbish to deposit at this tip, or haven't you?" he asked.

"Oh, I see what you mean! No, I haven't."

"Then why are you here? What can we do for you? This is Council land, you know. Private."

"Well, to tell the truth, my car had a bump on the road back there. Nothing serious. I'm a bit shaken. Thought I'd get some fresh air to clear my head. Is that okay?"

"No harm in that," the old man conceded. "As long as you don't hang about. Trouble is, we get people in scavenging. Can't have that, for health reasons. Know what I mean?"

"Yes, I do," said Maurice vaguely. "I won't be long."

He stumbled as he walked away towards the tip.

Behind him, the skinhead said, "Pissed!"

"As a rat," the old man agreed.

Maurice didn't want to go back past the trees. He didn't feel ready for that. Perhaps he could find another way out onto the road? He looked around. The whole area was enclosed by wire fences, as far as he could see, and he was in no mood to climb over them. He was barely able to walk, to keep upright, as it was.

He wandered into a mangled landscape of many levels. The earth rose and fell away in strange, half-related planes, like a cubist composition. Rough roads of cinders swooped up to sudden edges that led nowhere, or down and around to pools of oily, glinting rainwater and randomly dumped heaps of soil or refuse. It seemed that whole buildings had been dropped from the sky. Piles of bricks, toys, carpets, plaster, furniture, in violent juxtaposition, were dotted everywhere, and mounds the size of small hills, the remnants of unimaginable ruins, formed miniature alpine chains down into the old, unused quarries. All was covered by a dust-crested crust of varying thickness that split under him as he walked. His footprints behind him oozed fleshy mud.

Paper and plastic scraps drifted endlessly across the site in the wind. Occasionally, larger segments of light-weight litter broke loose from the clotted mass and carved into the air, scaring up flocks of shrieking gulls and starlings. Smoke, or steam, puffed up mysteriously from various points, as though a huge engine was building up pressure deep under the earth. A machine made a pumping, clunking sound somewhere out of sight, and the strident alarm of a reversing earth-moving vehicle called out every few minutes from some hidden excavation.

He almost tumbled into a deep hole, about two feet wide. It reached diagonally down, like a giant rabbit's burrow, into the compacted garbage. At first he thought that someone had been tunnelling, for some unimaginable reason, but noticed that loose matter from underground had been pushed up around the lip of the hole, as though it had been dug out from under. He found other similar holes. He knelt beside one, and peered down into it. Buried wires, wooden laths, and plastic pipes had been torn apart by some powerful, or desperate, digging. He couldn't even guess at why the holes were there.

He wandered aimlessly amid the desolation, stumbling like a blind man searching for his lost stick, until he came to the edge of one of the so far unused quarries. Down inside it there was a small lake of pure, shining water reflecting the scudding clouds and the vivid blue of the sky. The sides of the quarry were steep, bare cliffs, or slopes of tumbled stone covered with blossoming shrubs and rich grass. To Maurice, it glowed and beckoned like the Promised Land. He looked for a way down into this pleasant place, but saw that he would have to walk a long

way round to gain access. Too tired and depressed to make the
effort, he sat down on a chunk of creamy marble, part of an old
fireplace, to review his situation.

He still felt wretched. His body ached. Obviously, he needed
to get to a doctor. He hoped that, when he got back to his car,
he would be able to drive. It was only three miles into Buxton,
but somehow, that sounded like a long way. He dreaded the
thought of the journey.

He sat for a while, still as a stone, trying to read his own mind,
to make sense of his recent experiences.

He seemed to be gazing out from some painful place deep
within his skull.

The landscape in front of him, beyond the quarry, had a
hectic look. Cars passing on the A6 chased each other viciously,
the sound of their passage an angry, waspish buzz. Sheep,
grazing in the long sweep of fields that climbed up the side
of Combs Moss to the rough crest of crags called Black Edge
and Hob Tor, looked like fat, lazy maggots browsing on a green
corpse. The hurtling clouds cast swooping shadows, like dark
searchlights, across the pastures. He felt that he had slipped
into another reality, similar to, but alarmingly unlike, the one
he had previously inhabited.

Disgusted with the increasingly morbid turns his mind was
taking, he got to his feet and looked back the way he had come.
In spite of the indications of activity suggested by the various,
continual mechanical noises, he had seen nobody since he had
left the two men in the porta-cabin. Now his eye caught the
movement of five long-shadowed shapes moving slowly towards
him across an area strewn with household waste. The figures
stooped from time to time to lift objects from the ground, and
stood still, heads down, as though inspecting their finds. Then,
they would either drop whatever they had discovered, or walk
over to one of their number who was awkwardly hauling a little
cart of some kind, and carefully place their discoveries inside it.
Their movements were even-paced, and languid to the point of
listlessness.

With the low sun behind them, it was impossible to make out
details of their features. He thought that two of them, including
the smallest, who was tugging the cart in some sort of harness,
were female. He got the impression they were dressed rather
quaintly. As they got nearer, he could hear their voices, quiet
and even-toned, like people at prayer. Presumably, they were

discussing the treasures they were finding. They gave no indication that they were aware Maurice was there until the tip of the hugely extended shadow of the most forward of them touched his feet. Then that figure stopped, raised his right hand to his shoulder, and the others behind him ceased all movement, as though they had become unplugged from their energy source. The man at the front raised his hand even higher, with his index finger close to his brow, and tapped a battered cap lodged above his ear, in an antiquated gesture of respect.

Maurice, embarrassed and irritated by the subservient gesture, which he automatically assumed was one of mock humility, found himself lost for a suitable response. He said, "Hello there!" in the tone he would use to greet one of his colleagues, met by chance on the streets of Manchester.

"I wish you a good day," said the man who had touched his cap, then, after the slightest pause, he added, "Sir." His voice was strangely accented, but there was no note of mockery in his unassuming tone.

Maurice looked hard at him, trying to read his expression, but the man's face was in shadow, and he was too far away. There was a similarity in the posture of the five people, and Maurice was sure that they were a family. They all had a similar shape and stance. The woman pulling the cart was older than the other female, and he guessed she was the wife of the man who had addressed him, who had the air of a paterfamilias. The other three appeared to be in their late teens.

Their stillness (they remained static as waxworks) and their dumb silence as he stared at them, quickly got on Maurice's frazzled nerves.

"They're wondering what I'm doing here," he thought. "I must appear very odd to them. It's obvious why they're here; they're scavenging, but what the hell can they hope to find that's worth taking away? Can people be so desperate, that they have to search in this foul place for the battered, useless things that others have thrown away?"

And; "yes," he thought, "they do look that abject."

Tired of standing pointlessly in silence, Maurice decided to return to his car. He set off in a line wide of the right of the group who, to his surprise, began themselves to move. They went to their cart and began sorting through its contents.

"Sir," called the man. "Would you be at all interested in

anything we've got here? Come and see. We've a few choice
articles." He held some object up. "Look at this. This is for you,
sir, don't you think? This is something you should have."

Maurice glanced across, and shook his head. He couldn't
make out what the man had in his hand, and, for some reason,
he was glad of that. "I have to go," he called, and quickened his
stride.

"Give us a chance sir," the man pleaded, in his odd accent.
"Just look what we've got here. You'll curse yourself, if you
don't."

"That he will," called a female voice, in a kind of soft wailing
drawl. "You'll curse yourself later sir."

Maurice hurried on, almost at a run. They continued to call
after him, but he couldn't hear what they said. He looked back
a couple of times. They seemed to be following him, but he was
well ahead of them, and the distance was widening.

The porta-cabin was shut when he reached it. He looked at
his watch. It was almost seven, hours later than he thought!
Where had the time gone?

He didn't look at the line of trees as he passed, but something in them called out its chattering, scolding cry.

He drove home along the empty back lanes slowly and
furtively, glancing in his rear view mirror every few moments.

Maurice's wife was a hypochondriac. In the three years of their
marriage she had built up an impressive collection of pills and
potions for all her ills, real and imagined. They filled two
drawers of a medium-sized chest in the bathroom. She kept
alphabetical lists of them, stating what each one was good for.

Next morning, after a troubled night, Maurice browsed
through the lists, selected four bottles, and gulped down a
possibly dangerous mix of medication. He checked his post
(more confirmation from the bank of what he already knew; he
was on the brink of bankruptcy) then went to see if he had been
faxed any better news. He found more of the same.

He sat for a while in the cold grey computer-dominated
room he used as an office, listening to a CD of natural and
electronic sounds his wife had bought him to help him relax
after he had told her they were going broke. She had left him
three weeks later.

The pills started to work, and he fell into a deep sleep. The
doorbell rang twice before he was even half awake.

He got to his feet too quickly. The room wobbled under him. His eyes wouldn't focus, and his mouth tasted and felt like the inside of a carpet sweeper. The bell rang again. Whoever it was, was in a bloody hurry! He glanced at himself in a mirror as he passed along the hall, and hated what he saw.

The front door was a fancy affair with beaded glass panels, and lots of expensive brass fittings. He had seen one like it on a backdrop representing the Ugly Sisters' house in a pantomime version of *Cinderella* at the Buxton Opera House. It represented the taste of the house's previous occupant. What he liked about it was that you could get a good idea who was on your front step through the glass without being seen and, if expedient, could take evasive action. He was finding he had to do that more often recently.

This time however, his caller was standing well back, and was just a thin blur.

As soon as he opened the door a man stepped off the drive and held a card up in Maurice's face. The card was a dirty, eggy yellow and bore a tiny photograph of someone who may have been the person holding it. It was creased in a hundred places, as though its owner had used it to practise origami. Maurice didn't even try to read what was printed on it.

"I've been unemployed," the man on the step said, "and I'm trying to do myself a bit of good. Trying to help myself." He had a pallid, pinched boy's face, with small features and a gap between his eyes so wide it seemed to be an effort for him to see straight. His head kept drifting evasively round from side to side. He looked in need of a lot of square meals. He could have been any age between fifteen and fifty. He poked the card down into his shirt pocket and started to open a cheap, bulging plastic sports bag.

"No thanks," said Maurice, "I never buy anything at the door." He began to push the door shut.

"You never do?" echoed the man in a bewildered tone. "But I'm trying to keep myself, I'm not just sitting back. It's to make a living."

Maurice was about to say something like, "That's highly commendable, but no thank you," when he realized that the man had an unusual accent; one that he had heard before; yesterday, in fact! The pills had blurred his mind, or he would have noticed it at once. He looked keenly at the man and, yes! he could have been one of the people he had seen scavenging at the tip. He couldn't be sure, but he had the stance, the pleading, praying voice. He had opened the zip along the top of the bag and was pulling things out – a child's shoe, a partly melted and twisted comb, a two-foot length of hose-pipe, a battered, lidless coffee jug, a tangle of used bandage . . .

"Is any of this any use to you?" the man asked, like a child or a simpleton, totally unaware of the inappropriateness of his words and actions. He spread the bandage out along his arm, as though it were particularly worthy of attention.

Maurice looked at the dirty, bloodstained strip of muslin, and hoped that he was asleep and dreaming. He placed a hand over the sports bag to stop the emergence of more items. "You couldn't have followed me here," he said. "No one did; I watched the road. How did you find me?"

"Were you lost?" the man asked, puzzled. He didn't seem to be joking.

The pointless, silly question enraged Maurice. He growled something like "Get out!" and was about to slam the door shut with his foot when the man slid his thin fingers round inside the doorframe.

Maurice strode onto the step. He grabbed the intruder's wrist, and hauled him to the front gate. The man's loose skin slid back alarmingly along his almost fleshless bones. He put up no resistance. He was surprisingly lightweight. He made sad, bleating sounds. He was searching automatically in his bag with his free hand. As Maurice forced the man out onto the pavement, he was aware that something was pushed into his jacket pocket. He gave the man a final shove on the back, to get him on his way, and marched back into his house.

He waited a few moments, then glanced out of a window to check that his visitor had gone.

The creature was on his knees, carving something on the wooden gatepost with a pen-knife.

Maurice's frayed patience stretched and snapped. He ran out and kicked the man on the upper arm. He felt and heard something break inside the shirtsleeve. Turning an anguished face towards him, looking totally lost and confused, the man reached up and seemed to be trying to protect his whole body with a single, upraised, skinny hand. Feeling furiously disgusted with himself and the pathetic being in front of him, Maurice kicked out again. The heel of his shoe hit the man in the breastbone, and his chest gave way. Maurice felt his foot sink in, and he was reminded of the sun-dried crust he had broached with every step he had taken at the tip.

Evidently, unsurprisingly, the man had had enough. He lurched away, clutching his bag in front of him with both arms. He sounded as though he were choking. He didn't look back.

Maurice bent down to see what he had been carving on the post. Underneath a deeply scored, slightly wavy line was a matchstick figure with over-long legs, rudimentary arms, and a tiny head, in a breaststroke posture. He seemed to be swimming downwards.

Some sort of hex, thought Maurice, contemptuously. A tinker's curse! He spat on the crude drawing, and went indoors.

He was horrified at what he had just done. He was still experiencing the sensation of the second kick; of feeling the man's chest caving in under his foot.

He went into his office, sat in the armchair he kept there for visiting business associates, and pulled out from his pocket the little parcel that had been pushed into it. He unknotted some thin string tied around it and removed a layer of charred newspaper. Underneath was a grubby pale-pink plastic box such as a child might keep cheap jewellery in. He pressed it open with his thumbs. Inside, in a bed of more crumpled half-burned paper, was a purple-brown egg like the one he had burst. He placed it carefully on his desk. He spread his hands out in front of him and studied them. The blotchy stains had almost gone, but the skin still looked chapped and raw.

After a while, he got up and turned on all the machines in his high-tech office. He had the latest of everything a computer could do to assist him with his work. He was continually updating his equipment. To stay ahead in his field, he had invested a fortune, and what he produced was acknowledged to be the most advanced work of its kind in the country.

Even so, he had gone bust; he was ruined.

When everything was on and running, the room was full of the soft humming sound that sometimes soothed him. But not this time. He went around the house in search of a strong drink.

Before he had located a bottle, phone bells rang all over the house. He went to the nearest receiver, a black, Bakelite antique, hesitated for seconds, obscurely reluctant to answer at all, then snatched it up.

It was Neville Gale, one of the partners in his firm calling, ostensibly, to commiserate with Maurice on the departure of his wife. He soon got round to the real subject on his mind however; the failure of their business. Maurice was aware that Gale blamed him for much that had gone wrong, and could tell by his tone that the man wanted to scream and swear down the phone at him like a drunken football fan. But he wouldn't ever do that. Old Nev was far too civilized.

Maurice listened to Gale's reasonable despair for some time, then shouted, "It's too late Nev; I'm sunk, and you're sinking. We're all going under, and there's not a thing we can do to stop it. We're in very deep shit, so get used to the idea, and get off my back!"

He slammed the phone down.

Then, feeling the need to make one more gesture of finality, he picked the instrument up and hurled it at the wall.

Maurice went into his back garden. He poured a heap of charcoal into the middle of the barbecue, placed the egg-like thing on top, and pressed it down a little so it couldn't roll off. He sprayed the pyre with "Betterburn" lighting fluid from a dispenser, and set a match to the lot. He stood well back, half expecting a small explosion, or even a big one. The egg burned slowly, and made a lot of smoke. It hissed and spluttered like breakfast in a pan, emitting tiny crimson flames. When it had almost gone, he poked the ashes and returned to the house for an hour. When he came back, there was no trace of the egg.

He swallowed another mouthful of medicaments, got in his battered car, and drove to Dove Holes the way he had come back last time, along the side lanes.

As he approached the entry to the tip he saw a huge black van – the one that had forced him off the road, he was sure! – gliding out through the gates. It turned into the road and moved away from him very fast. Thinking about his insurance again, like a drowning man clutching at the proverbial straw, he pushed down the accelerator. He was determined to overtake and stop the van.

He made some progress; got a bit closer.

The van was as large as any he had ever seen. It was quite smooth, with no visible panel joins, and was completely un-marked. He couldn't even see a number plate. It was a miracle the driver was able to steer anything that size round the sharp bends in the narrow lane. He had trouble keeping his own vehicle on the road, and had to slow down. He was astonished to see the van draw away from him until it was almost out of sight. In seconds he was at a crossroads on the A6 in the centre of Dove Holes, and there was no sign of the van in any direction. He gave the steering wheel a characteristic, ineffectual thump with the heel of his hand, and swore. Then he turned round and drove back to the tip.

He sensed he was being watched as he walked past the line of trees but did not go to investigate what might be observing him. Half-formed shapes moved stealthily among the shrubs behind the trees, that he tried not to see.

He made his way through the mud to the porta-cabin. Inside, the old man was alone, spread out on his multi-mattress bed. He jumped when Maurice banged on the open door, and sat up.

"What you got?" he said automatically, like a talking machine. Then he recognised Maurice, and got to his feet. A deeply uneasy expression appeared on his face, that he tried to conceal by turning away.

Maurice, not quite sure what he *was* doing there, felt slightly foolish. At last he said, "I wonder if you can help me? I want some information about the scavengers on the tip. I met some people out there, and one of them must have followed me home. At least, I think he was one of them. Turned up on my door step and started pestering me."

"That's nothing to do with me," the man said sullenly.

"I realize that," Maurice said, "but I thought you might know who they are. They don't seem like locals, the ones I met. They spoke differently, they acted differently; do you know what I mean?"

"Perhaps," the man said. "I don't talk to them. I keep away. I'd do the same, if I were you. Let them get on with it."

"Get on with what?"

The man shrugged. He filled an electric kettle from a plastic bottle and plugged it in a socket close to the floor. Slowly, and somewhat clumsily, he went through the motions of setting up a brew of tea. Maurice noticed he only washed out one mug. "Where's your friend?" he asked, "the lad who was with you before?"

"Jed? He went out to scare them off, the scavengers. Hours ago." The old man squinted up at Maurice from under his creased, dirt-smeared brow. "He's not come back. I think he's jacked in the job. He said he was pissed off working here. The place gave him the creeps; got on his nerves. It gets on mine too, but I can't just bugger off. He can get another job, at his age, if he's lucky, but I can't." He spooned sugar angrily into his mug, spilling a trail of white crystals along the newspaper that served as a cloth on the ancient ironing board that was his table. "I'm stuck here," he concluded.

Lost for words, Maurice gazed around the interior of the cabin. It was stacked with rescued furniture and other junk. An artificial Christmas tree, its branches bent and draped with fragments of faded tinsel, lay on the ground at his feet. Rolls of worn carpet were lined up along one wall and bursting suitcases and boxes, packed with god-knows-what rubbish, were piled everywhere. An old tin bath was full of bones! Maurice was startled to see, among them, two skulls. He must have gasped, because the old man looked up from pouring his tea.

"Christ!" Maurice said, stepping towards the tub. "Where did they come from?"

A concatenation of expressions passed over the man's face; annoyance, anxiety, confusion, fear, and others indefinable. He lifted his mug in both hands and sipped his drink. "They were dug up," he said reluctantly at last. "Out there." He pointed beyond the line of trees opposite the cabin.

"But they're human remains, surely?" said Maurice.

"Some of them are," the man admitted, "and some of them aren't."

Maurice squatted down next to the tub. "I see what you mean," he said. Many of the bones were undoubtedly human, but others were far too long and thin, like the leg bones of an ostrich, or some huge bird. He picked one up. It was extraordinarily light, as though it was made of paper.

"Never mind them," the old man said irritably, and threw a blanket over the bath tub. "That's all going to be taken care of. They're all going back."

"But have you notified the relevant authorities?" Maurice said, awkwardly aware of the foolish pomposity of the phrase. "I mean, people may have been murdered and their bodies concealed there."

"Look," the man said sharply. "Mind your own business, if you know what's good for you! Keep your nose out. I know what I'm doing. No one's been murdered; at least, not recently."

"Then you know whose bones they are?"

"I've been told."

"I still think you should tell the police."

"And have the bloody place closed down? And lose my job? That's what would happen! That's a graveyard out there, and a very old one. The place would be crawling with bloody priests and what-you-call-its? . . . archy . . . ?"

"Archaeologists?"

"Those are the buggers. They'd love this place, if they got to know about it, but they're not going to. When the lads started digging up those bones with the J.C.B., Mr Mycock, our gaffer, said to keep it quiet, if we wanted to stay in work, and we have done. There's only a few of us knows about it, and it's going to stay that way. You start blabbing about it, and it's your fault if we lose our jobs! You wouldn't want that, would you?"

"No," said Maurice, thinking about the imminent loss of his own livelihood, "perhaps not."

"Never mind perhaps," the man growled.

"At least you can tell me about it," Maurice added, "if I promise to keep the information to myself."

"I don't know much," the man admitted, "just what old Mr Snape told me. He knows all the history of this area. Got loads of books about it. Goes about with a metal detector all the time. He's found a lot of stuff. There was a thing about him in the paper not long ago. He found the remains of a village or something, up on Combs Moss. Well, I told him about it, because he's done me favours, bought bits from me that have turned up at the tip, and given me a good price. He'll keep his mouth shut, I know."

The old man scratched his chin anxiously, as though he wasn't quite as confident as he sounded, or perhaps he had lice in the stubble of his beard.

"So whose graveyard is it?" Maurice asked, wanting to get to the nub of the matter.

"Some miners. Hundreds of years ago. It's a local legend, according to Mr Snape. He's read about it in one of his old books. They were digging, and they found something they weren't looking for, deep underground, not far from where we are now. Some sort of cave, I suppose it was, though they thought they'd dug their way down into hell. They had a name for it; they called it 'The Devil's Spawning Ground'. They found things there, and saw things that scared the daylights out of

them, but I'm not sure what. They brought out some objects
that looked like eggs and, would you believe it? they started
eating them. It was a bad year, the crops must have failed, Mr
Snape thinks, so they were all starving. They'd eat anything, in
those days, of course."

"They were poisoned?" Maurice ventured, thinking he
could foresee the end of the tale.

"Not exactly. It wasn't like that. Something dreadful did
seem to happen to some of them at once; though old Snape
says he thinks that part of the story was probably just invention.
Something to do with the 'folk imagination'. He says when one
strange thing happens, people add an extra half-dozen other
things in the telling to spice it up. And you can't believe tales of
men and women turning into something else, can you? Into
tall, thin, spidery things, overnight?"

Maurice shook his head, but peered uneasily out towards the
line of trees.

The old man slung the dregs of his tea out the door and wiped
his shirt front round the rim of his mug. "As for the others," he
continued, "for a while, nothing happened to them. Then they
started changing, behaving different. They developed nasty
habits, and people roundabout didn't like them."

"What sort of habits?"

"I don't know. Mr Snape didn't want to go into that side of
things. He's like that; he doesn't talk about anything unpleasant. He just said that people started avoiding them, and for
good reason."

"They became isolated."

"That's it. Formed their own little community. That got a
name too. They called it Devil's Hole. Old Snape thinks, over
the years, it got shortened to Dev's Hole, then the locals forgot
the original name, and it got twisted to Dove Holes, but I don't
know about that. Anyway, things went on without too much
trouble, until some of the miner's wives started having babies.
The kids weren't right at all, and the women tried to hide them.
There was something unpleasant about them."

"You don't know what?"

The old man shook his head. "Snape wouldn't say. But they
were bad enough to force the miners and their families up onto
Combs Moss, out of the way, where they couldn't be seen. They
built a little village of sorts, the one Mr Snape found the
remains of." The old man took a step towards the door and

pointed a grubby hand at the lines of rock that marked Black Edge and Hob Tor. "Just there, I think.

"It seems they made a deal with the other villages hereabouts to keep out of their way, in exchange for food and other things they needed to survive. They used to send a few people down from the Moss with hand carts, to collect stuff. That went on for years, then those children I mentioned started to get loose, started roaming about the country side. It seems they looked very strange. People didn't like the look of them at all. And bad things happened."

Once again, Maurice would have liked more details, but the old man was plainly unable to provide them, so he didn't interrupt. The story, odd, even outlandish as it was, had the ring of truth, and was exacerbating a feeling of unease that had dominated Maurice's mind and body since just before the accident, prior to his first visit to the tip. He was still feeling wretchedly ill, and the medicine wasn't working.

"Things got so bad," the old man continued, "that one day, people for miles around got together, went up onto Combs Moss, and slaughtered everyone there, kids and all. They brought the bodies down and buried them all in a pit they dug here, near the cave they'd found. They sealed off the cave and filled in the diggings that led to it."

"And those were the people whose remains you've found?"

"So Mr Snape says. If anyone knows about these things, it's him. It seems right, as though there may be some truth in it, when you look at some of those bones."

Maurice glanced down at the blanketed bath tub, and imagined the peculiar things hidden there. "You should put them back," he said. "I'll help you. They should be reburied, right now, at once." Suddenly, he was convinced that such action was urgent and necessary.

At first, perhaps from simple laziness, the old caretaker was reluctant to cooperate. He shook his head and made a woofing noise, as though he was being intolerably harassed. "Never mind that now—" he said, but Maurice decided to act.

He pushed his way deeper into the cabin and lifted the tub of bones up to his chest. He was a big man; the sort few people would choose to argue with, and the old man decided.

"Come with me," Maurice ordered. "There's a spade over there. Bring it with you. And show me where they found these bones."

The old man trudged ahead, slithering from time to time, as did Maurice, on the mud under the dried earth crust. He stopped at a spot quite undistinguished by any obvious mark, apparently at random, and pointed down at the ground. "Here," he said.

"Are you sure?" Maurice asked, suspiciously.

The old man nodded emphatically, and repeated, "Here, or hereabouts."

Maurice took the spade and began to dig. It was hard work. He had to cut through a mesh of impacted household waste that lay deep under the thick, heavy mud. He was sweating in streams, probably from fever as much as from his exertions. He paused from time to time to wipe his brow, and noticed small groups of people standing immobile in the distance. They seemed to be observing him, though he could not be sure.

"Are those men who work with you?" he asked his companion.

The old man glanced around, obviously not liking what he saw. "No, that's them," he said. "The scavengers."

"And who are they?" Maurice asked, as he resumed digging.

After a while, after quite a long pause, the old man said, "I think you know as well as I bloody do," and shuffled off towards the cabin. Maurice did not try to stop him.

When he had dug a shapeless hole about three feet deep, and about twice the volume of the tin bath, he poured the bones carefully into it and spread the blanket over them. He shovelled the mix of garbage and earth back on top of them quickly.

When he had finished he slung the shovel over his shoulder and traipsed back towards the cabin. The groups of people appeared to have moved nearer, but were still not close enough to be seen clearly. Their faces were pale, featureless blobs. Some of them, he noticed, had very long arms and legs, but tiny bodies. The harder he stared, the stranger some of them became.

He thought he must be hallucinating; his fever was raging; he needed more medication.

His foot struck something. It looked like ivory, but was probably yellow plastic bleached by the sun. Curious, he bent and tried to pick it up. It would not move. He dug his fingers down around its curved surface and pulled hard. It moved up slightly, and he realised he was holding a bone. It looked very much like a human femur. He straightened up and twisted round, studying the surface of the ground about him intensely. Here and there other whitish lumps protruded. He stalked over to the nearest and gave it a prod with his shoe. It was another bone. He quickly identified half-a-dozen more, within a ten yard circle of the first he had found. Some of the bones were . . . unusual.

A feeling of despair washed over him. He was convinced there were hundreds more of them, scattered out there in the tip. For a reason he could not isolate or understand, the knowledge appalled him. He panicked.

He left the spade on the ground and ran to the porta-cabin. The door and the window were both shut. The door was locked. Maurice was convinced the old man was in there; had deliberately shut himself in. He banged the door with his fist like a fool, and shouted. When he tired of this he trudged bleakly back to his car.

Before leaving, he took one last look round at the tip. There was nobody there. The scavengers had gone.

He wondered where.

He was having a bad night.

He had gone to bed early, at nine-thirty, after taking a cocktail of his wife's pills and potions, washed down with a beaker of whisky. He had slept like a dead thing for about an hour, then had jerked awake as though someone in the room had shouted. Perhaps he had shouted. His dreams had been that bad.

Once awake, he felt terribly disappointed. He had expected to be knocked out well into the next day, but was aware his mind would permit him no more rest. He longed for sleep. He was stuck instead with a nervous, infuriating weakness.

He pitied himself. He felt like a tiny child locked in a cold, dark place as a punishment for something he had not done. He was alone there. He was alone in the world.

His loneliness was something he had been trying to avoid, to bury away deep in his mind. He had been partially successful in doing this, but the knowledge of his solitariness, of his lack of friends, and now of even a wife, had festered there. Now, under pressure of the strange events of the day, and of his sickness, his isolation had burst out, and bloomed in his brain like a huge and hideous flower.

He needed to talk to someone, needed sympathy, and help of some kind.

But he had no one to turn to, no real friends. Previously, all his social life had involved his business associates. He had been closest to the other partners in the company they had created together, but they were the last people he wanted to talk to now. He had no children, his parents and other relatives were dead or estranged, and he had never joined things. He didn't play golf, perform in amateur theatricals, or belong to the Rotarians like Neville bloody Gale.

"God," he thought, "I am pitiable!"

Then, "No, make that pathetic."

He lay alone with this insight and other thoughts, at times almost dozing, for some hours, until his doorbell rang. Someone seemed to have their finger glued to the buzzer. The single ring went on and on. Every nerve in Maurice's body jangled with it.

He sat up, switched on the bedside light, and grabbed his watch. It was ten past two in the morning.

The ringing stopped at last.

He thought he heard a thump on the door.

His house, in spite of the fact it was second hand, was one of the most recent of its kind built in Buxton. It was big, pretentious, had been very expensive, but the walls and ceilings were thin. Sound travelled from room to room without hindrance. A radio playing softly in the kitchen could be heard clearly in the bathroom one floor up at the other end of the house. Maurice was sure someone was doing something to the front door; perhaps forcing the lock.

He sneaked downstairs in his dressing gown, shaking with sickness and, yes – he acknowledged – fear, as well!

The street light outside cast enough illumination for him to make out the shape of a figure on the other side of the distorting glass in the front door. Well enough for him to be sure that his visitor earlier in the day, who he had kicked, had returned. The man was bending forward, pushing clumsily at his letterbox, trying to get something through. Part of a small package and the tips of two fingers and a thumb protruded through the slot.

Maurice went and picked up the telephone he had flung at the wall in rage after his conversation with good old Neville Gale.

The ancient instrument had survived in one piece. It was satisfyingly heavy. He went to the door, held the phone up high, and brought it down with brute force on the letterbox.

There was a sound from beyond the door that made Maurice drop the phone and hide his face in his hands. It was a wail of pain, outrage, and despair, and somehow it expressed, with acute accuracy, the fears, thoughts and emotions that had been haunting him that night, and during the recent past. It gave voice to them exactly. It was as though his own soul stood out there, lost, alone, and in great agony. Maurice felt a sickening mixture of compassion and self-pity.

He *was* sick. He tried to reach the washing-up bowl in the kitchen, but didn't make it.

After he had cleaned himself up, he forced himself to inspect the letterbox, expecting to see blood. There was none. Fragments of charred newspaper were caught in the flap, nothing else.

"No finger-tips," he thought, "thank God!"

On impulse, he turned the locks, shot back the absurd, over-ornate bolts, and opened the door wide. He peered out at his morbidly tidy garden (his one hobby) and found it empty. All was quiet.

His cat ran urgently towards him across the road, then changed its mind, and scampered back. Something behind the privet hedge, near the spot where the cat had changed direction, moved heavily, shaking the bushes. Maurice stared hard, but could see nothing through the darkness under the tight, trimmed leaves.

A shadow passed swiftly across his lawn towards the house, as though a large bird had passed above.

But that was impossible! Nothing had moved below the streetlight, that could cast a shadow!

Then he saw something tall and thin, like the trunk of a narrow tree, in his neighbour's garden. He was sure it had jerked into brief motion; had scuttled quickly a little closer, then gone still.

It did it again, seeming to cover ten feet of ground in a split second. It was now close enough for Maurice to form some idea about what manner of creature it was.

It had many legs.

Maurice ran inside and slammed the door. He locked and bolted it. The doorbell was operated by batteries. He removed them and put them into the pocket of his dressing gown. He sat on the stairs watching the front door for ten minutes, waiting for the bell to ring. He knew that it couldn't, but thought perhaps it would.

He ran upstairs and threw himself into bed. He lay face down, with a cushion over his head, cocooned in his sheets and blankets.

Later, he heard a movement on the roof. Something had climbed up there, and was making its way along the gable above his bedroom. It made harsh, scratching sounds on the tiles, and dislodged some of them. Maurice heard them crashing down into his garden. From the sounds, he judged that whatever it was had clambered out to a position just above his window.

As if to confirm this speculation, there came a loud, spasmodic tapping on the glass.

Maurice half sat up. He was glad that his curtains were pulled shut. As he stared at them, the window behind was shattered and one of them twitched open. A long, grey, scrawny limb, perhaps an arm, but without a proper hand on the end of it, waved a little bundle at him. It dropped the bundle and withdrew.

There were more scampering sounds from above as Maurice fled from the room.

He didn't go near the packet; he thought he knew what was in it.

Something he didn't want.

He locked himself in his office, turned all his equipment on, and played the CD his wife had given him, of soothing natural and artificial sounds, as loud as he could stand it. It had no calming effect, but it drowned out other noises. Maurice sat perfectly still in the one comfortable chair until daybreak.

Then he dressed and went out to his car.

To his surprise, hundreds of birds were singing enthusiastically all round him. It was the dawn chorus. It was just like the sounds on the CD he had been playing, and it scared him stiff.

He got hurriedly into his car and drove towards Dove Holes again.

When he reached the entry to the Victory Quarry he found the tip was closed. A heavy chain, joined at the ends by a fat padlock, was looped through the metal grill on the gates.

He remembered then that it was four-thirty on a Saturday morning. The tip would be shut for another forty-eight hours at least.

He got out of his car and pushed the gates hard with the heel of his shoe. They hardly moved. He climbed back into the driving seat, backed the car away as far as he could, keeping in line with the gate, then accelerated straight down the centre of the access path.

The chain and lock held when the car hit, but the hinges on the left split from the concrete gatepost, and the gates whipped up over the bonnet. Something smashed the windscreen, which fell in fragments on his lap. The car slewed round out of control when he applied the brakes, and tobogganed along on top of the crust of dried mud which opened behind him like a huge wound. The line of trees flashed by as the vehicle spun. The air was full of flying earth, scraps of refuse, and noise.

The rear left side of the car smacked against the right front end of the porta-cabin which reared up under the impact. It did not topple over, but jumped some distance out of its original position. The side caved in and the door flew wide open.

Maurice sat stunned in the driving seat. He didn't seem to have hurt himself in the crash. He felt nothing except numb, possibly from all the pills he had been taking. Too many, maybe. He noticed his reactions were slowed down and movements faltering. His fingers felt wooden as he fumbled with the clip of the seatbelt. The door lock was jammed and he couldn't open it. He crawled over the passenger seat and let himself out that way, emerging face down and on his hands.

He stood up, shook himself, and climbed onto one of the big skips to take stock of his situation.

Although the sun was hardly up, the landscape was bathed in clear, soft, almost creamy light. There were shreds of thin cloud squatting on the fields that clung to the sides of Combs Moss, and frozen billows of morning mist hovered above the surfaces of the small lakes that had formed, over the years, in the quarry bottoms. Something in motion caught his eye, running away from him along a line of wall, but he realized at once, from its russet coat, that it was only a large fox. There were rabbits, too, munching the tall grass around the edges of the tip. The air smelt clean and dry, as he imagined desert air must.

Except for the regular clanking and glugging of a distant

pump engine somewhere down in the old diggings, all was stillness and silence.

Nothing moved or made a sound in the line of dark trees.

He clambered over the broken steps leading up to the cabin, and went inside.

The pile of mattresses had fanned out like a pack of cards. The old caretaker was spread-eagled across them on his back. His face looked raw, and was mottled with dark stains like those that had remained on Maurice's hands after he had crushed the egg-like object he had found. The man looked dead, but wasn't. A heartbeat was just detectable under his overalls, and he was drawing rasping breath through his mouth. Maurice tried to rouse him, but soon gave up. The man seemed in a trance, or coma.

Many of the piles of cases and boxes scattered along the length of the cabin had toppled over and burst open. Maurice was not surprised to see that some of them had been packed with bones, and that two of them contained dozens of the eggs wrapped in scraps of grubby paper and plastic. Bundles of the long, thin bones, tied like firewood with electric cable, were revealed behind a half-fallen rubber sheet.

Maurice left the cabin and wormed his way back into his car. He tried the engine. It started without trouble and he found he was able to back the vehicle away from the cabin. He drove cautiously down into the tip. Something under the chassis was grating against the wheels, but he didn't give it a thought.

The cinder path took him past a high wire fence marking no apparent boundary. Twice he stopped to look round, hoping to catch sight of some of the scavengers, but there was no one else about at all, he was soon convinced of that.

In one of the deeper sections of the recent workings he nosed the car out over what appeared to be dried mud; but the caked surface broke and the vehicle tipped forward alarmingly. The back wheels spun strands of slime, like black mucus, out behind.

He could not reverse out. The car was sinking. Oily stuff oozed in through the bottoms of the doors around his feet.

He awkwardly hauled himself out the passenger door again, and abandoned the car. He walked back the way he had come, out of knee-deep, liquid filth, then climbed up to the top of one of the highest mounds of builder's rubble. The position gave him a view over most of the tip. He noticed little clouds of smoke or steam were starting to drift up from the surface in various places, as though fires had been started underground. He went to investigate.

The smoke, for that was what it was, was coming up through some of the tunnel-like holes he had noticed on his first visit. It was slightly scented, not unpleasantly, and had a greenish tinge. He wandered round for a while, peering down into the openings, then sat down next to a large hole that was not emitting smoke. He could hear a sound deep down in the tunnel, a regular heavy pounding, like the bass line of a musical composition. He leaned out over the hole and cupped his ear with his hand. He thought he could hear other sounds down there, like snatches of a whispered conversation.

He was propped up on one arm with his hand outstretched on the encrusted mud. Suddenly, as he adjusted position, the surface gave under his weight and he dropped into the tunnel clumsily. He lay still for a moment, winded. Then, instead of drawing back out again, he tentatively reached down even further. The tunnel was quite wide enough for him to squirm into. It descended at an angle of about thirty-five degrees to the surface; a comfortable angle to slip down.

And, he judged, not so steep that he could not make his way back out again without too much trouble, if he had to.

It was not absolutely dark down there; there seemed to be some source of dim light ahead of him. Feeling his way carefully and methodically, he lowered himself into the ground. When he felt his feet slip over the lip of the tunnel, he had a momentary doubt about the wisdom of what he was doing, which he forced himself to ignore.

Moving with great caution, he descended perhaps forty or fifty feet down the narrow passage without much trouble.

The tunnel got a little less steep after a while, however, and became narrower, and he found he was having to make more effort to make any progress. Also, the air was getting musty and unpleasant to breathe.

He rested, and began to worry about the sides of the tunnel collapsing on him. He would suffocate. No one knew he was there, or would come looking for him.

Total loneliness stabbed up inside him again, with an accompanying, enervating, surge of self-pity.

Although he was strong, he was not at all fit, and what he was doing, in his condition, seemed suddenly crazy.

He was just about to start wriggling back out when he saw and heard a motion in front of him.

Something reached out of the dark ahead, and clasped his hand. It was a thin, dry, loose-skinned hand, and it took a powerful hold on his. His fingers were crushed painfully together. Whoever was in front of him began to retreat, pulling him further down the tunnel. He tried to resist, but discovered he was at the end of his strength. He plummeted lower very fast, hurting himself against stones and other objects that protruded from the sides of the crudely dug hole.

He tried to keep his free arm bent across his face to protect it, but smashed his elbow against something sharp.

He thought whoever was pulling him was whispering something earnestly to him, that he could not catch. After a while he gave up trying to hear and started howling with pain.

Something hit him hard above the right eye. He became unconscious.

There were voices in the air around him. He knew they were conversing together, not trying to communicate with him. The words they used sounded like a distorted jumble of heavily accented English that he was too weak to make the effort to understand. He lay quite still for what could have been a long time, with his eyes shut. He slept, then woke when he felt himself being lifted and moved. He was lowered to the ground with a bump that hurt. He was vaguely aware of forms and figures moving away from him. He slept again.

He woke to absolute silence.

It seemed that he was blind. He passed his fingers over his eyes and felt a sticky crust covering the top half of his face, welding his eyelids shut. He scratched at his eyes with both hands, and was relieved when the substance began to crumble away. He managed to get his eyes open and saw, as he had suspected, that it was dried blood.

He turned over on his side and tried to get to his feet. Sharp pains shot through his body, causing him to yell. From the sound of his voice, he knew he was enclosed in a small space. He collapsed into a sitting position, and looked about him.

The circular, domed compartment had walls of smoothly worked bare rock. A pale illumination, falling from a number of narrow tunnels that led diagonally up and out, from positions about three feet from the ground, showed him he was alone. Except for himself and a number of piles of the egg-like objects that were now familiar to him, resting in nests of rubbish, the room was empty. He crawled about, trying to ignore the pain in his probably broken left arm, and inspected the nests. They were about two feet in diameter, and made of the shredded, entangled remains of the sort of refuse he would have expected to find in a dustbin.

He touched some of the eggs. They looked slightly different from the ones he had seen previously. They were very warm. He felt them quiver slightly under his finger tips. Their shells were soft. They had a peculiar, pleasantly spicy smell that made him feel hungry. His stomach growled, and he tried to remember when he had last eaten. He had no idea how long he had been underground but, from the sharp, agonizing pangs in his belly, he'd been there some considerable time.

The eggs looked more and more appetising the longer he studied them. "If they taste anything like as good as they smell," he thought, "they would be delicious." He picked up a handful and, with great difficulty, resisted trying to eat one.

He put five of them in the inside pocket of his torn and filthy jacket, and scrambled into one of the passages leading out.

They all pointed upwards.

Presumably, if he kept going, sooner or later, he would reach the surface.

He thought he was going to die down there.

The tunnels looped and twisted off in all directions. There were places where they forked and, when they did, he always chose the path that had the steepest gradient upwards. It didn't seem to matter as, round the first bend, he frequently found himself almost falling along a stretch that took him diagonally down again. The illumination in the passages was always up ahead; somehow he could never discover its source. He was always blundering on towards the light.

From time to time he stopped to doze, then started awake and continued on. His mind was empty; his brain felt as raw as his hands. He was bleeding from dozens of small wounds. He was drenched in the sweat of fever.

When he saw a clear, whiter light ahead, he stopped because it was hurting his eyes. He lay with his chin on the ground while his sight adjusted, and the awareness that what he was looking at might be daylight gradually dawned upon him.

Strangely, he felt no elation. He felt resentment.

"About bloody time," he thought.

He hesitated before completing the last stretch, unaccountably reluctant to get to the surface, now that he was almost there. Something about the quality of the light caused him some trepidation; it was eerie, and not quite right.

It was like moonlight, but far too bright.

The world he emerged into was well-lit, but there was no sun shining. There was no moon, either. Above him stretched an empty, cold, silvery sky.

The topography of the landscape around him was recognizable, but was stripped of its familiar features. The shape of Combs Moss loomed unmistakably ahead of him, but the walls and fields along its sides were gone. What remained looked like a hill of lead. Everywhere, as far as he could see, the land was smoothed off into planes of grey that gave an impression of impenetrable solidity.

When he saw the dark line of trees and the porta-cabin where he had expected them to be, he felt a surge of wild hope.

The huge black van was parked between them! Its back was open. It was parked at an angle to his line of vision, so he could only see a little way inside it. He could see nothing there but shadows.

He started to run towards the van. He hurt in every limb, and stumbled like a drunk with a wooden leg, but he had discovered a resource of determination and energy at the sight of the van. It seemed to represent his last, best hope.

When he was about fifty yards from the vehicle a figure jumped to the ground out of the back and disappeared round the side farmost from him. Maurice shouted wordlessly and made frantic efforts to run faster. He thought he heard a door slam. An engine started. The back of the van started to close automatically; a black door descended smoothly, slowly, and silently.

Maurice tried to scream. He was crying, and waving and flapping both his arms to get attention. His feet were getting heavier every step he took.

The van jerked once, then moved away. It accelerated. Maurice continued trying to run to catch it, but gave up when the vehicle vanished over the crest of a hill.

Finally exhausted, he fell to his knees.

He was facing the line of trees. They were almost leafless now, and he could see, perched on the branches, some of the things that he had not seen clearly before. They were busy at some task, flittering about individually and in groups.

Perhaps they had seen him. One of them called out what could have been a chattering, imbecilic greeting.

A number of them ventured forward out of the trees. Moving in fits and starts, they came towards him, spreading out as they did so.

The closer they got, the worse they looked.

Maurice knew he could not move another step. Resigned, he sat and waited for them.

Remembering he was hungry, he pulled one of the eggs from his pocket and put it in his mouth. Keeping his gaze steadily on the creatures, who were almost upon him, he bit down hard on the egg.

Later.

He was lying down, so he stood up.

He opened his eyes, and found he could see round in all directions at once.

But he could not see directly up or down.

He tried to touch himself, to find out what he was, but he had lost the use of his arms, if he still had any.

He was hungry, but there was nothing anywhere that looked like food. Then he realized he had no mouth.

He stretched his many legs experimentally. He discovered he could move easily across the crusted surface of the earth, with almost no effort.

He made a clattering sound by rattling parts of the top of his body.

He waited.

Then, feeling deeply anxious, he scuttled towards the line of trees to join the others of his kind.

"At least," he thought, "I shan't be alone."

But, when he reached the trees, he realized they had been dead for a long time.

The place was deserted.

LISA TUTTLE

Tír Nan Og

LISA TUTTLE WAS BORN in Houston, Texas, but has lived in Britain since 1980. She worked as a journalist for five years on a daily newspaper in Austin and was an early member of the Clarion SF Writer's Workshop. She sold her first story in 1971 and won the John W. Campbell Award in 1974 for best new science fiction writer.

Her first book, *Windhaven*, was a 1981 collaboration with George R.R. Martin, since when she has written such novels as *Familiar Spirit*, *Gabriel: A Novel of Reincarnation*, *Lost Futures*, *The Pillow Friend* and *The Mysteries*. A new novella, *My Death*, recently appeared from PS Publishing, and her short fiction has been collected in *A Nest of Nightmares*, *A Spaceship Built of Stone and Other Stories*, *Memories of the Body: Tales of Desire and Transformation* and *Ghosts & Other Lovers*. The latter volume, plus another collection entitled *My Pathology*, have recently been released as e-books.

Tuttle's other works include the Young Adult novels *Snake Inside*, *Panther in Argyll* and *Love On-Line*. She is also the author of the non-fiction guides *Encyclopedia of Feminism*, *Heroines: Women Inspired by Women* and *Mike Harrison's Dreamlands*, the erotic fantasy *Angela's Rainbow*, and she has edited the acclaimed horror anthology by women, *Skin of the Soul*, and the anthology of erotic ambiguity, *Crossing the Border*.

"There's not a lot I can say about this story," admits the author. "I'm not myself a cat person, and never set out to write a cat fantasy, but a few years back I realized that three friends of mine, all single women of a certain age who lived in New York City with their cats, had stopped complaining about their unsatisfactory sex-lives and the lack of decent men, and seemed utterly content with their situation.

"As I speculated on possible reasons for the change, this story suggested itself. Of course, it is a total fiction, and you should not think for a moment that any of the characters or events portrayed here have even the slightest basis in fact.

"But I would say that, wouldn't I?"

PEOPLE CAN CHANGE. People *do*. But some things remain the same – like my love for you. Once upon a time, when I first fell, I told you what we could have together was not exclusive and would not last forever. I never used the l-word, and I drew away a little, disbelieving or offended, when you did. I told you, quite honestly, that I had no desire for children, and no use for a husband of my own. I was quite happy to share you with your wife.

It's not surprising if you never understood how much I loved you when I took such care to disguise my deepest feelings. I was a woman with a past, after all. A woman of a certain age, happiest living on my own (well, with a cat) and with plenty of lovers already notched into my belt.

I was past forty when I met you, and the easy-loving days of my youth, when the times between men were measured in days or weeks rather than months or years, were gone. I had been celibate for more than six months when I met you. I was feeling a little desperate, and I fell for you hard.

You probably won't believe that, if you remember how hard I made you work to get me. Once I saw I'd caught your attention – the space between us seemed charged, remember? – I became distant, ironic, cool. I treated you with a casualness that bordered on the insulting. I was so desperate to be wanted that I didn't dare let you suspect. Nothing drives people away more than neediness. And then, after we had become lovers, once you were well and truly caught, I guess it became a sort of habit, the way I was with you, as if you were an irritation to me, as if I suffered you to make love to me now and again as a very great favor.

But our affair went on for nearly seven years. Think of it. And eventually, our positions became reversed. I was no longer the less-loving, the more-loved – that was you. You grew tired of my undemanding presence, and called me less, or made excuses at the last minute to cancel a date. Did you really think I wouldn't mind? That I might even be grateful to lose you? That it wouldn't nearly destroy me?

Well, as I said before, people change. I might have shrugged and cut my losses – dropped you before you could formalize our break – and bounced back in my thirties, but, pushing fifty, the loss of you was the loss of the last of my youth, practically the loss of life itself.

I was surprised by how hard it hit me. If I couldn't win you back, I was going to have to learn some new way of living, to cope with my loss.

I thought about my friends. Over the years that once large throng of independent single women who had comprised the very core of my city, my emotional world, had been whittled away by marriage, parenthood, defection to other parts of the country, and even death. Three remained, women I had been friends with for nearly thirty years, whom I saw regularly and thought of as "like me". Janet was an artist, Lecia was a writer and Hillary was a theatrical agent. We had similar emotional histories and similar lifestyles, in our small apartments with our cats, in love with men who saw us in the time they could carve out from their real lives with their wives and children else-where. Over the years we had kept each other going, cheered and commiserated with each other, staying loyal to a certain vision of life while the men, the cats, the jobs and other details changed.

Now that I thought about it, though, I realized that I alone of the sisterhood still had a lover. The other three were all "between men" – and had been for at least two years. What's more, they seemed content. In the old days, celibacy would have been a matter for complaint and commiseration. I couldn't think of the last time we'd had a good moan about the perfidy of men, or a plotting session devoted to fixing up someone with Mr Right. Bits of subliminal knowledge, mem-ories of certain looks, words unspoken, hints, fell together in my mind. I scented a conspiracy. They knew something that I didn't. And I needed help.

I went to see Lecia. Our friendship was based on straight-forwardness, intellectual discussions, a liking for the same books, an interest in both philosophy and gossip. I felt we were a lot alike, and I knew I could be straight with her. When we were settled with our cups of decaffeinated *latte*, I asked if there was a man in her life.

She chuckled and gave me a funny, assessing look over her cup. "No one except James."

James was her cat, purring in her lap. Lecia lived near Washington Square, and the cat had turned up in her life a few years earlier just after she'd embarked on her project of reading or rereading the entire works of Henry James.

"How long has it been since you split up with . . . ?"

"Three years."

"And there hasn't been anybody since?"

She shook her head.

"And it's all right? You don't miss . . . all that?"

Her mouth quirked. "Do I look frustrated?"

I gave her a careful inspection and shook my head. "You look great. Really relaxed. Is that the yoga? Hormones?" Lecia, who was a few years older than me, had elected to go for HRT when the menopause hit.

She chuckled. "I think it's contentment."

"You do seem happy, which is hopeful. But – wasn't it hard at first?"

"What's all this about?" she asked. "William? Has William—"

I shook my head. "Not yet. He hasn't said anything, but . . . I think he's met someone, or if he hasn't, he's looking. He's tired of me, I can feel it."

"Poor baby."

She sounded so detached, as if she'd never had to worry about being left by a man in her life. It annoyed me, because I remembered when things had been otherwise. Three years ago. What was the guy's name? Jim. His marriage had ended, his affair with Lecia continued, and then he'd been offered a job in Albuquerque – and he'd taken it, just like that. Not that she would have, but he didn't even ask Lecia if she'd go with him. She had been devastated. Looking at her now, remembering her face distorted with tears and the sympathetic tension in myself, I could hardly believe it was the same woman.

"How long did it take you to get over Jim?" I asked. "Did you just decide to give up on all men after he left?"

"Something like that. I decided . . . I decided I'd never be at the beck and call of another man. I was going to be in control from then on, and get what I wanted, take what I wanted – ouch!" James went flying off her lap. Lecia put her hand to her mouth and licked the scratch. She grinned crookedly. "Well, of course, there's got to be give and take in any relationship. There's bound to be conflict sometimes. But why let *him* make all the rules, call the shots, decide to leave you?"

"Are we talking about me or you? I mean, you said – *are* you seeing someone?"

She wouldn't meet my eyes. "You see me as I am, a woman alone except for her cat. And her women friends. You're the one with man-problems."

"And you've solved yours. So what do you advise me to do? Drop him before he drops me?"

"Only if that's what you want."

"It's not. I want *him.*" To my annoyance, tears came to my eyes. "And if I can't have him, well . . . then I want to be happy without him. The way you seem to be." I pressed harder, trying to make her acknowledge me and my right to know. "You and Janet and Hillary . . . you all seem so content to be alone. What's your secret?"

She looked at me, but there was a reserve, a withholding, in her eyes. "You should get a cat; then you wouldn't be so lonely."

"I have a cat."

"Oh, yes, I was forgetting Posy." She looked across the room at James, who was sitting in the corner washing his privates. I looked at Lecia's face, which had gone soft, dreamy and sensual, and suddenly I saw that face on a woman lying naked on a bed, with the cat between her legs.

The grossness of my imagination shocked me. I felt too embarrassed to stay longer. Lecia's serene contentment certainly didn't have its source in bestiality. I was agitated not only by the unwanted pornographic fantasy, but also by the certainty that there was something which Lecia did not trust me enough to share.

I didn't go home when I left her, but instead walked down to Tribeca, to the newish high-rise where Janet had her apartment. It was still Saturday morning, and I was betting I'd find her in. She was, working on one of her intricate black and white illustrations. Although she was trying to make a deadline, she seemed pleased for an excuse to take a break.

"Red zinger, lemon and ginger, or peppermint tea?" she asked as I followed her back to the kitchen. Grey the cat was sleeping on top of the refrigerator. He opened one eye to check us out, then shut it again.

"Red zinger, please." I watched Janet closely as she made the tea. She was slim and strong and she moved lightly as a dancer, humming under her breath. If I hadn't been there she would probably have been talking to herself, I decided, but apart from the scattiness which she'd always had, she looked serene and positively bursting with good health.

"Do you mind being celibate?" I asked her.

She looked at me sharply. "Who says I'm celibate?"

"Oh. Well, when was the last time you had sex?"

Spots of red appeared high on her cheekbones. "That's kind of a personal question."

"I know. I thought we knew each other well enough after all these years to get kind of personal . . ." Janet was one of the most highly sexed and sexually experienced women I knew, and she'd never been one to keep quiet about the most intimate details. She'd said nothing to me about sex or even romance for so long that I had assumed that there'd been no men in her life since the disappearance of Leland.

"Let's go sit on the couch."

"Goody." When we were settled, I said, "So there is somebody? What's the big secret? Who is he?"

"Do you have some reason for wanting to know? Apart from prurient curiosity?"

I laughed. "Prurient curiosity was good enough in the past. Look, as far as I knew, after Leland dumped you there wasn't anybody. For, what is it, two years?"

"Not quite."

"Whatever – in all that time, as far as I know, you haven't gotten involved with anybody else, and it seems like you haven't wanted to, either. Same as Lecia. You seem so calm, so happy. I want to know your secret, because I have this awful feeling that William's fixing to dump me, and the way I feel now, it'll just kill me. If I can't keep him, I need to know how to survive – more than survive – without him."

Her eyes searched my face. "You love him?"

"Oh, God. Yes. More than anyone I've ever – yes."

"Could you live with him?"

I hesitated. "I don't know. It's never been an option. He's tired of me, anyway. If I pushed him, now, or tried to make him choose between me and his wife, I'd lose him for sure. I can put up with sharing, with uncertainty – I've done that for years. If I've lost him, though – what I really want is to be okay about it. Like you and Lecia and Hillary. You seem so together, like you know something. You do, don't you? There is a secret?"

She gave the tiniest nod, then shook her head as if frantically trying to cancel it.

"There is! Oh, God, I can't believe you know something and you haven't told me. You and Lecia – I thought we were friends! What did I do to you?" We stared at each other like two kids on a playground, one the betrayer, one the betrayed, and I saw my anguish get to her. She couldn't resist the claim of friendship.

"You didn't come with us," she said in a low, pleading voice. "I know it wasn't your fault, but that's why, that's the only reason. If you'd been with us, you'd know, too. We swore we'd never tell anyone else." She hesitated, convincing herself. "But you're not just anyone else – you should have been with us. It was meant for you, too. I'm sure I'm right. Wait, look, I'll draw you a map." She got up and went to her drawing table, found a piece of light card which was just the right size, and began to sketch and write something on it, muttering to herself. Then she presented it to me.

"What's this?"

"It's where you have to go." She leaned close and spoke very low, although we were alone. "Take William. Any excuse, a nice hike in the country, just get him there, find the fountain, and make him drink. *Not* you. Just him. If you can't get him to drink there, take a flask and make sure he drinks it later, when you're alone together."

I'd known Janet to be loopy sometimes – she was the fey and temperamental artist, she believed in angels, fairies, witchcraft, magic, anything going, really. For a time she had lived in an occult spiritual commune upstate somewhere.

"And what happens then?" I asked.

"Shh! Just do it. I really shouldn't be telling you. Now, go." She pushed me toward the door, and I went without protesting that I hadn't had my cup of Red Zinger.

I looked at the card when I was in the elevator. The directions were to the Adirondacks, to the middle of nowhere, halfway up the side of a mountain where there was a magical fountain . . .

Then I remembered. The fountain. Three years ago, the others had gone on a camping trip, to a "magical place" with a "special fountain" that Janet had learned about in her commune days. It was meant to be a spiritual retreat and a bonding experience for us four friends. Only the night before we were to leave I ate a bad shrimp, and so while my friends were hiking through the woods I was laid up at home with a case of food poisoning.

Something had happened to them, something they had never told me about, but which explained their solitary contentment.

Outside, I crossed the street and walked past a couple of still unconverted warehouses with trucks in front and big, sweaty men unloading boxes and shouting at each other. I walked past, around, through them like a ghost. I can't say I missed the whistles and sexual commentary my presence would once have inspired, but just then I could have done without the reminder that I was an aging, invisible woman.

A garish green poster, plastered on a wall, caught my eye. It had a spiral pattern and the only words I could read at a distance were TIR NAN OG. That was what the Celts called the Land of the Ever Young, but probably it was the name of a band or a club – my not knowing, my recognizing it only as a reference from an ancient culture, was just another proof of how out of it, how past it, I was.

This was not my city anymore, I thought. This was not my country. The problem was, I didn't know where else I could go, or what else I could be, now that I was no longer a young and beautiful immortal.

I looked at the card again. If it was the fountain of youth, why shouldn't I drink it? Why should I give it to my lover? Janet had been so definite. But what did it do? If it was supposed to make your man love you again, why had Leland and Jim disappeared?

Well, I had asked a question. Now I must make what I could of the answer.

You were swept away, you were charmed, by my sudden insistence on a weekend away. It had been a while since I'd swept you off your feet. You were intrigued, too, because it was

so unlike anything we'd done together before. A day of hiking
in the mountains! As an excuse, I'd claimed that I needed to
check on the existence of a spring-fed fountain mentioned in
one of the books we were going to publish. You had so little
notion of what a book-editor did, and, really, so little interest,
that you believed what I said without question. I didn't ask what
you'd told your wife.

At first it was like old times. The strain that had been between
us disappeared, and we laughed a lot and touched each other
as you drove us out of the city in the freshness of early morning.
But the farther I got from the city and the world I knew, the
more uneasy I felt. What was I doing? I'm a good walker, but
only in the city, when there is some point to it, things to look at,
places worth going to. I don't like the country. It bores me and
it makes me nervous; okay, there have to be farms, and places
for wild animals and plants, but I don't see the point of it for *me*.
As for this magic fountain – did it follow that because I believed
in romantic love I'd also believe in magic? I wasn't Janet – what
sort of desperation had made me believe in her magical
fountain?

Naturally, I took it out on you. Your enthusiasm began to
irritate me. What were you getting so excited about? A walk in
the country? I didn't like hiking, why didn't you know that? You
wanted me to be something I wasn't; you would have preferred
someone else. Before long and I'm sure to your complete
mystification we were arguing.

By the time we reached the place where Janet had indicated
we should leave the car, we were barely speaking to each other.
You cheered up a little once you were out of the car, lacing on
your new Danish hiking boots and inhaling the clean, cool air,
but I felt an undissolved lump of dread sitting heavily in my
stomach. But I was determined to go through with it now. I
couldn't imagine how getting you to drink some water would
result in my feeling better, but I would try.

I am a good walker in the city, but I wasn't used to hills, or to
pathways slippery with pine needles, damp leaves, loose rocks.
Nor could I keep up the pace you set. I had to keep stopping to
catch my breath; I had to keep calling you back. At first
solicitous, you quickly became impatient.

"If we don't get a move on we won't even make the summit
before dark, let alone get back down to the car again."

"We don't need to go to the summit," I pointed out. The

idea filled me with exhausted horror. "Just to the fountain, and that shouldn't be much farther, as far as I can make out from this map . . ." Squinting at it, it occurred to me that scale was not Janet's strong point.

You were as baffled by me as I was by you. What was the point of going only halfway up a mountain? "Come on, it's not that hard a climb."

"But I don't want to go to the top." I couldn't keep the irritating whine out of my voice. "Will, I'm worn out already. I want to stop at the fountain and have a picnic and a rest before we go back."

Your face began to cloud, but then it cleared. "Okay. You stay at the fountain and rest. I'll climb to the summit alone and then come back for you."

I didn't like the idea much, but sometimes you have to compromise.

We reached the fountain a few minutes later. First we heard the cool, gurgling sound of water, and then we found the source, hidden beneath a curtain of ferns and ground-ivy. I pulled back some of the greenery to reveal the smooth rim of a stone bowl that caught the water flowing up from underground. There was a channel that sent the overflow spilling into a small, bright stream that raced away over a rocky bed down the hillside.

"Want a drink?" I asked.

"From that?" You frowned.

"Better than recycled city water," I tempted. "This is exactly the sort of stuff that gets bottled and sold to people like you in restaurants."

"I might try it when I come back. I don't want to stop just now. You'll be all right?"

"What about our picnic?"

You sighed. "The sooner I go, the sooner I'll be back. You can eat some of this stuff while you're waiting for me, if you want. I'll just take a candy bar and my water flask." Then you dropped a kiss on my head, determined not to be caught and delayed by anything as time-consuming as a real embrace.

For a while, I sulked, counting the minutes, wondering how long it would take you to get there and back again. I wished I'd brought a book. With nothing else to occupy me, I poked around the fountain, uncovering more of it from the encroaching plants. I scraped away the furry moss and found a figure

carved in *bas-relief*: a cat, it looked like. Then there were
markings that might have been writing, but the letters appeared to be Greek, which I can't read. It could have been
graffiti left by fraternity boys from Syracuse or Cornell.

I was thirsty. The trill of water made the feeling worse. I
fetched my little plastic bottle of Evian and drank half of it.
More out of boredom than hunger I ate lunch, and finished off
the Evian. Then I filled the bottle from the spring: my insurance in case I couldn't get you to drink *in situ*. Then I sat down
in the sun with my back against a rock and waited for you.

I fell asleep and woke disoriented, hot and dry-mouthed. I
thought that someone had been watching me and laughing,
but that was only the music of the fountain. I was still alone, and
really thirsty. I reached for the Evian bottle and then stopped,
remembering that I had refilled it from the fountain. I licked
dry lips and looked at my watch, which turned out to have
stopped some hours earlier. The battery had been running
down all day and I hadn't noticed except to think how slowly
time was passing.

Where were you? I felt as if I had been sleeping for hours.
What if you had fallen and hurt yourself, what if something
awful had happened? I called your name, but the sound of my
own voice echoing off the rocks in the empty air gave me the
creeps. I advised myself to sit quietly and wait for you. If only I
wasn't so thirsty!

It was late September and the day was pleasantly cool, but the
sun blazed down, making me hot. I wondered if I could be
suffering from sunstroke. I plunged my hands and arms up to
the elbow in the fountain to cool myself, and dabbed water on
my face. I had never been so thirsty in my life. What if I just wet
my lips? But I needed a drink.

I longed for you to come back and save me with the dull, flat,
safe city water in your flask. But you didn't come and didn't
come and finally I couldn't bear my thirst any longer and I
drank.

That was the best water I ever tasted. I drank and drank until
my stomach felt distended. I felt content and at peace with the
universe, without worries. I was no longer thirsty and no longer
too hot. The sun felt good. The smooth rock where I had rested
before was still warm with the sun, so I curled up there and went
to sleep.

I was awakened by the sound of you calling my name. I

opened my eyes and stretched, and you turned and looked straight at me, but the worry didn't leave your face, and you didn't stop calling. Were you blind? I got down and went over and pressed myself against you.

"Well, hello. Where'd you come from?" You began to stroke me. "Have you seen my girlfriend? I guess she got fed up waiting and decided to hike back to the car alone. Only, if she did that, why'd she leave her stuff?"

I wanted to explain, but no matter how I purred and cried and stropped myself against your legs, you just didn't get it. Are women more intuitive than men, or what? I followed you to your car but you wouldn't have me.

One of the sheriff's men took me home with him after a day spent searching the mountainside for me. You did the decent thing, regardless of the trouble it would make for you, and reported me missing.

After many adventures I made my way back to Manhattan, and to Washington Square, and Lecia's little apartment. I don't think she recognized me; at any rate, she shooed me off with a shocking lack of compassion. I hung around anyway, to give her another chance. Maybe she'd put together my reported disappearance with the sudden appearance of a strange cat. I found a position on a fire-escape which gave me a view into her living-room window, and I hunkered down and waited. As soon as I saw her getting ready to go out I'd make for her door and strop her ankles and purr like an engine. She wouldn't be able to resist me forever. So she had a cat already; why shouldn't she have two?

I watched and waited and finally, after moonrise, I saw James the cat turn, in the magic circle of Lecia's arms, into the man who was her lover.

Finally I understood the secret of the fountain, and knew that my only hope was to find you. If you want me, you can have me again. For you, I've left the city. For you, I'll live in the suburbs. By day, I'll be the family cat. But at night, in your arms, secretly, while your wife sleeps unknowing, I'll be your lover. You can make me change, if only you want me.

R. CHETWYND-HAYES

A Living Legend

RONALD CHETWYND-HAYES DIED in 2001. He started writing fiction in the early 1950s, and his first published book was the science fiction novel *The Man from the Bomb* in 1959. His second novel, *The Dark Man* (aka *And Love Survived*), appeared five years later.

While looking on a bookstall in the early 1970s, Chetwynd-Hayes noticed the profusion of horror titles and submitted a collection of his own stories, which eventually appeared in paperback as *The Unbidden*. Becoming a full-time writer, he began producing a prolific number of ghost stories and sedate tales of terror, many tinged with his disarming sense of humour.

Known as "Britain's Prince of Chill", his stories were widely anthologized and collected in such volumes as *Cold Terror, Terror by Night, The Elemental, The Night Ghouls and Other Grisly Tales, The Monster Club, The Cradle Demon and Other Stories of Fantasy and Horror, The Fantastic World of Kamtellar: A Book of Vampires and Ghouls, A Quiver of Ghosts, Tales from the Dark Lands, Ghosts from the Mist of Time, Tales from the Haunted House, Dracula's Children, The House of Dracula* and *Shudders and Shivers*. More recently his work has been compiled in *The Vampire Stories of R. Chetwynd-Hayes* (aka *Looking for Something to Suck and Other*

Vampire Stories), *Phantoms and Fiends, Frights and Fancies* and *Ghosts and Ghouls: The Best Short Stories of R. Chetwynd-Hayes*, while the anthology *Great Ghost Stories* is edited by Chetwynd-Hayes and Stephen Jones.

The movies *From Beyond the Grave* (1973) and *The Monster Club* (1980) were both adapted from his work. In the latter, based on probably his most successful book, the author himself was portrayed by veteran horror actor John Carradine.

In 1989 he was presented with Life Achievement Awards by both the Horror Writers of America and the British Fantasy Society, and he was the Special Guest of Honour at The 1997 World Fantasy Convention in London.

As the author once remarked: "I like to think I write stories for the future. There's just a chance that someone putting an anthology together will find one of my old stories and slip it in. And so I shall live again. In that respect, I suppose being a writer is very much like being a vampire."

WILFRED FRAZER HAD BEEN feature editor of *The Daily Reporter* for more years than I had lived and stated that he hated his job with a hatred that passed all understanding; but he was very good at it. He had the knack of spotting a potential human interest story from the morass of rumour, conjecture and wishful thinking that was dumped on his desk each morning. He motioned me to a chair, then pushed a pair of horn-rimmed spectacles up over his thinning grey hair.

"Young Radcliffe, you're a clever, well educated lad, tell me what you know about Caroline Fortescue."

I shrugged and rummaged around in that mental lumber room that we all have tucked away at the back of our brains.

"A late Victorian lady novelist. Is ranked a little lower than Dickens, but is possibly on equal terms with Thackeray. She rocketed to fame with *Carriden's Ridge* in 1888; a three-volume novel that has been the bane of every schoolboy's life ever since. This was followed by eleven more books of equal length, the last being *Moorland Master* published in 1911. Her style is a bit heavy going, but most critics regard her as a literary genius."

Frazer nodded. "Fine. Proper little know-all, aren't you? What about the woman herself?"

"Ah! That's another matter entirely. She seems to have gone to a lot of trouble to keep herself out of the limelight. No one seems to know anything about her. Her real name, when she was born – when she died. Complete mystery."

Frazer permitted himself a pale smile.

"She didn't."

"Didn't what?"

"Die. According to my informant, a female who was employed around the house, Caroline Fortescue is still alive."

I sat upright and gave a passable imitation of William the Conqueror being told that a man with an arrow in his eye was banging on the front door. I did some complicated arithmetic. "It's now 1975 – if she was twenty in 1888 – Good God! – she'd be a hundred and seven!"

"Not impossible," Frazer pointed out. "But my ex-employee says she's much older than that. She puts her at around a hundred and seventeen. Again I say – not impossible. Isn't there a chap in America who's still belting around at a hundred and thirty-five?"

I communed with my soul before nurturing a germ of hope.

"God! Suppose it's true!"

"Precisely. Imagine finding a live and kicking Charles Dickens and getting the dope from the great man's mouth as to how *Edwin Drood* was intended to end." He pushed a scrap of paper across the desk. "Here's the address. Ye olde manor house down in a place called Bramfield. Get your body down there and if the old girl is still with us and if she can still talk, bring me back an interview that will set the Thames on fire. Take as long as you like. I want a series that'll run for three weeks. Afterwards we'll think about a book."

"Suppose it's all moonshine?" I asked.

"Then you've had a nice day in the country. Do you good. But I've got a hunch about this one. I think we may have something."

"But a hundred and seventeen!" I objected. "It must take all her time merely to breathe."

"Moses was doing all right at a hundred and twenty. If she can't talk use your imagination. Just bring back her mark on a blank sheet of paper."

I arrived at Bramfield Station the following afternoon and went straight to the village post office, that being if my experience was any criterion, the fount of all local gossip. I pushed open a narrow door and entered a shop equipped with an L-shaped counter; the smaller portion protected by a grill which had an oval opening in the lower centre. A smallish woman with red hair and inquisitive eyes shuffled forward and asked:

"Yes, sir, was there something?"

I gave her the full effect of a crooked, rakish smile which I had borrowed from Errol Flynn.

"Yes, can you kindly direct me to Bramfield Manor?"

She frowned and appeared to give the question more consideration than it deserved. Finally she nodded.

"Ain't heard it called that for many a year. Never have any mail you see and the rightful name has sort of got lost. The Old House we calls it in these parts. The property of old Lady Bramfield. Although whether she's still around, I wouldn't like to say. Certainly she ain't been buried to my knowledge."

I assumed a slightly worried expression.

"Surely there can't be any doubt that the – old lady – is still alive? I've been sent down to investigate the claim of a former maid who says she's owed a week's wages."

The pale blue eyes were suddenly alight with an almost evil gleam of curiosity and the head jerked as though issuing an invitation for me to clamber over the counter. The voice sank to a loud whisper.

"That must have been that blonde huzzy who Jenkins drove to the station, with her packed bag on the front seat. When he came in for the provisions and suchlike, I managed to get out of him, that she'd been caught going through some private papers. That's all he'd tell me. Very close is Jenkins."

"This . . . Jenkins . . . ?"

"Used to be butler donkeys' years ago. Now he's all there is. Except when that woman was there. Lordy, I'd give anything to know the rights of it. The old place is falling to bits. Young man, if you ever get past the front door, it would be a mercy if you'd pop back in here and tell me what's what."

"But first," I prompted, "I must get there. Now if you'll kindly tell . . ."

"Ah! Turn right and walk down the main street, then turn left, cross the stile and cut across Five Acre Field until you reach Miles Lane. Turn left and two miles further on you'll come to Manford Bridge which you can't miss because it's got a broken wall on one side. A mile or so on and you'll reach Bramfield Walk. A hundred yards to the left are the Old House iron gates. One's fallen down. The house is at the end of the drive."

"A taxi . . . ?"

"Young man you appear to have a stout pair of legs. It's a nice walk so long as you keep clear of Mr Masterton's bull. Now heed me. Even if you don't get into the house, keep your eyes open and let me know what you see. If the old lady is still about, she might be looking out of a window or something."

I admitted that was a remote possibility, then asked:

"When did you last see Lady Bramfield?"

One not over clean hand went up and began to scratch her head.

"Now you have me! Must have been when I was a child. Over thirty years ago. And I remember she looked old then. She can't still be alive."

The sun was setting when I finally reached the tree lined road that was presumably Bramfield Walk. In fact it was little more than a narrow lane that ran straight as an arrow's flight from the distant main road to the rusty, reeling iron gates. One had not quite fallen down, having been saved from this ultimate indignity by a bottom hinge that somehow kept the top bars from touching the ground. To the right crouched the ruins of a once handsome lodge; beyond a meandering drive, its unpaved surface covered with a profusion of tall grass and wild flowers, flowed like a wind teased river, between tall slender poplars that reached up green clad arms, as though begging alms from the sun.

I passed the ruined lodge and entered a land where poets commune with long forgotten gods and lovely dark-eyed nymphs ride in on the night wind. Not a leaf stirred, although the grass rippled beneath my feet: the total silence suggested it might be masking a phantasmagoria of subtle sounds that would be meaningless to anyone not versed in their tonality. Presently the drive emerged into a vast semi-circular space that lay before a large, grey-stoned house.

Two storeys high. Twin rows of deep set mullioned windows. A flight of steps leading up to a double, weather-stained oak, iron-studded door. A tapering steeple reared up from imitation turrets on either side. The windows did not – or so it seemed – reflect the sunlight: the house – or so it seemed – did not cast a shadow. A familiar house – yet so strange and sinister.

I ascended the steps and entered a large, marble columned portico, then rapped on one door, there being so far as I could see, neither knocker, bell-pull nor exterior handle. Almost at once the left door opened and a tall, lean old man with a sad, lined face bowed his white head and asked:

"How can I help you, sir?"

I said – words flowing from my tongue in an unruly stream:

"I am looking for Caroline Fortescue . . . the Caroline Fortescue . . . who I believe is Lady Bramfield. Will you kindly ask Lady Bramfield if she will receive me?"

The deep-set, dark eyes, glittered and after an interval the strangely husky voice manufactured a reply.

"It is to be regretted, sir, that her ladyship cannot entertain visitors. She is well advanced in years, you understand. Beyond the frontiers of normal human existence."

"So I have been given to understand. Around one hundred and seventeen."

Even then I was prepared for an emphatic denial, but the old man merely bowed his head and said: "We are all as old as time permits, sir. But age consumes – burns up the essential essence. It is to be hoped you have not travelled far."

I was being given the polite brush-off, but I had to get into that house and come face to face with the incredible. Bribery was out of the question, but a veiled threat might be an answer.

"You discharged a maid – a woman who told my editor an astounding story. If it is true she will be paid not to disclose the whereabouts of this house to anyone. Always supposing I get exclusive rights for publication. But if she is allowed to approach the popular press . . ." I shrugged my shoulders. "Half of Fleet Street will be pounding on this door and screaming their questions to high heaven."

The frail mask of imperturbability trembled and I caught a brief glimpse of naked fear.

"We have nothing to hide. That women – creature – was an inveterate liar."

"Then you deny that Lady Bramfield is Caroline Fortescue?"

The man was incapable of telling a direct lie; could only give an evasive answer that was more revealing than a straightforward admission.

"I can only repeat, sir – this is the home of Lady Bramfield."

God forgive me for I told a deliberate lie; made a promise that I had no means – or intention – of keeping.

"If you will let me in, let me interview Caroline Fortescue, I will make certain that the story is not published while she lives."

He shook his head several times, then reluctantly retreated a few steps, a move that I interpreted as an invitation to enter. The hall looked like something from a horror film; age darkened panelling lined the walls, the high windows were so covered with grime and cobwebs, the few items of furniture – an oak settle, two or three massive armchairs and a large credence table – could barely be seen through the ensuing gloom. A wide staircase curved its way up to a landing that surrounded the hall on three sides, part of which had most probably once served as a musicians' gallery.

The old man led me past the staircase and through a doorway situated in the far right hand corner and into a room that was an oasis in that place of dust, neglect and gloom. It was comfortably, even luxuriously furnished; fitted carpet, a settee that looked as if it might be transformed into a spacious bed, deep armchairs and a drop leaf table, not to mention several gilt framed paintings that hung on plush-wallpaper covered walls.

The old man lowered himself into a chair and after motioning me to one opposite, emitted a deep sigh. "We have retreated over the years. Closed up most of the house and concentrated our forces into three rooms. This one, the kitchen and her ladyship's bedroom. Not counting the bathroom of course. I was trained to keep clean. But her ladyship had not bathed for sometime. There are many intimate duties that I am called upon to perform, but . . . That is why I engaged that woman." He again shook his head. "A serious mistake. But it never occurred to me that – that creature would pry into her ladyship's private papers."

"Integrity is dead," I murmured.

"You may well say so, sir."

I edged my chair forward. "You are Mr Jenkins?"

"Just Jenkins, sir. Only the lower servants called me Mr Jenkins in the old days. And then only when I was elevated to the post of butler. Even my late wife called me Jenkins for the entire of our married life. No disrespect was intended, in fact you might say it was a kind of title. When her ladyship was young – or younger than she is now, – she used to say: 'Jenkins, you're one of nature's noblemen.' " He chuckled, a low rasping sound that threatened to disintegrate into a cough. "She liked her little joke."

He lapsed into a thoughtful silence and I waited patiently for the floodgates of memory to open. I tried to imagine what it was like living in this great barn of a house, with no one to talk to, but that old-old woman – and shuddered. Presently that harsh, cultivated voice spoke again.

"I did not know she was Caroline Fortescue until after his old lordship died. Her father you understand. In the Bramfield family, when there is no heir, the title descends through the female line. Her ladyship never married. Perhaps no man could possibly measure up to those heroes she invented. After long and deep reflection I think that was more than possible. She was a great writer, wasn't she, sir?"

"Almost if not quite," I answered as truthfully as I could.

"Most of the critics thought so. Did you know that some thought she was a man? True. The trouble she went to making certain no one found out who Caroline Fortescue really was. Used to ride ten miles once a week to Tuppleton to collect correspondence from her publishers and such like."

"Did her publishers know?" I enquired.

He shook his head. "No, sir. She used another name for her correspondence. Cookham, I believe it was. It was part of her agreement with them that no one would ever try to find out her true identity."

"But why the secrecy? Most women would revel in being a world-famous authoress."

Jenkins actually grinned. Bared his discoloured teeth and crinkled his face into an almost impish grin.

"Why indeed, sir. I think it was this way. She wanted to share her make believe world, but she didn't want it invaded. I'm no hand in expressing myself and that's the best way I can describe it. For her writing a novel was a very personal business, for imagination will only go so far and she had to put a lot of herself into it. Sometimes all of herself – if you follow me. Her ladyship was every man, woman and child who walked through those dozen books."

"The soul bared and sent forth into the world, sliced and packed?" I suggested.

"Nicely put, sir, although I'm not all that sure what it means. But I know there's a question you're dying to ask. How old am I? Am I right?"

Although I had not given the matter any thought, I nodded.

"Yes, if you don't mind telling me."

He laughed, his former reticence now replaced by a kind of senile gaiety. "Bless you I don't mind at all, sir. I'm eighty-five.

Coming up to eighty-six. Her ladyship was thirty-two when I was born. In this very house."

"You don't look it," I said with all sincerity. "I would have placed you in the early seventies."

The compliment (if such it was) pleased him and he expanded, began to regard me with an expression that suggested growing approval. Presently he leaned forward and asked in a harsh whisper:

"Would you like to have a little peep at her ladyship?"

I nodded vigorously. "I would indeed. Will . . . will it be all right?"

"So long as we're quiet. Time for me to look in on her anyway. But it's not one of her good days. I could tell that this morning. Not a movement – not so much as an eye flicker."

Jenkins got up and together we went back into the hall, then up the great staircase and on to the landing. He stopped at the first door, the one facing the stairs, and tapped gently on the top left panel. He looked back over one shoulder.

"She can't hear of course, but I couldn't enter her room without first knocking. It wouldn't be respectful."

He had worn a deep groove in his life that made certain his route to the grave was straight and narrow. After placing a slightly tremulous forefinger to his lips, he opened the door and preceded me into the room beyond. The smell was stomach heaving. The sweet, cloying stench of body decay. It was well established as though the walls, items of furniture had become deeply impregnated, before being heated up by the coal fire that spluttered and roared from an ornate iron grate. Jenkins handed me a large red handkerchief and whispered:

"Keep that pressed to your nose, sir. You'll become acclimatized to the smell after a bit."

I greatly doubted if that were possible, but curiosity made me advance a few steps further into the room, for there was a distinct feeling I had slipped back in time and was now in an ill-smelling pocket of history that must be explored even if I choked in the process. I gave the room a quick glance. A large fourposter bed that rightfully belonged to a museum; ancient padded chairs with faded brocade covering; shelves that hid two walls, packed with books – and any number of bound manuscripts. The bed was neatly made – and empty. My head jerked from left to right, my eyes seeking that which my brain did not wish to see.

A chaise-longue was situated in front of the fire with its raised back towards us, concealing whosoever or whatever it supported. Jenkins tiptoed across the room and peered downwards, a gentle smile transforming his face into that of a benign male nurse. His loud whisper drew me reluctantly forward.

"As I thought, sir, she's asleep. You can come and have a little peep, but quietly if you'd be so kind."

I imitated his tiptoe approach, feeling like a frightened child who is trying not to awake a sleeping cobra. I kept my eyes firmly riveted on Jenkins and did not look down until I had all but bumped into him. All that remained of Caroline Fortescue was dreadful. A tiny skeleton covered with wrinkled, grey skin. At least that was the first impression. Later when I had found the courage to examine her more thoroughly I realized that ingrained dirt was responsible for the greyish hue and the skin resembled crumpled parchment that had been draped over the bones by a careless taxidermist. There must have been a veneer of flesh beneath, but one had to accept such a supposition on trust.

A few white hairs clung to an obscenely gleaming skull, a few more sprouted from the sunken chin; dark eyes were half covered by lids that appeared to have lost the ability to open or close. The hands were hideous claws, the backs ridged by black swollen veins. I could not detect the slightest sign of life. She was attired in a rusty black gown that covered her from neck to ankles, while her feet were encased in grey woollen stockings.

When I was in a condition to speak I whispered: "Do you have to attend to all of her needs? Feeding, toilet requirements . . . ? You know what I mean."

He sighed gently. "As much as possible. Her intake is very small. A little warm milk laced with glucose. Poured slowly from a feeding cup. There's little discharge. Moving her is a very delicate business."

I had to ask the question. "Wouldn't she be better off dead? That . . . that is nothing more than a slowly rotting corpse."

Jenkins slowly turned his head and I stared into eyes that glittered with sullen, old man's rage. His harsh voice seared my brain.

"How dare you suggest such a thing, sir? Her ladyship is very much alive – possibly more than you or I. There may be a slow decay, but it has been going on for a very long time. On her good days she's lively enough. That she is."

A wave of excitement drove the repulsion, the body-numbing horror into temporary retirement – and I gasped:

"You mean that . . . she can hold an intelligent conversation?"

"When she so wishes. So mind your tongue, sir, and be respectful when you talk of her ladyship." His anger went as quickly as it had come and he once again became the model servant, the solicitous nurse, displaying a kind of coy tenderness that was slightly nauseating. He addressed the bundle of skin-wrapped bones.

"I will come back, my lady, in about an hour. In time to serve dinner. Just finish your little snooze."

Having delivered this final instruction he again laid a finger on his lips, then began to tiptoe back towards the door, while I followed with my normal flat-footed steps. I could see no reason for these elaborate anti-noise precautions; it was doubtful if the explosion of a ten ton bomb would awaken Caroline Fortescue before she was ready. Always supposing she ever woke at all.

We returned to Jenkins's room, where I ventured to make a request that I had no reason to suppose would be granted.

"Would it be possible for me to stay here for a few days?"

Jenkins screwed up his face into an expression of deep concentration, before nodding slowly.

"I cannot believe her ladyship would object, sir. After all you have given your word not to reveal anything you see or hear during her lifetime. And to be frank, I will not be sorry to have some company. Lately I've got into the habit of talking to myself: and that's a bad sign."

I hastened to express gratitude. "That's very kind of you and I promise not to be a nuisance in any way. And of course, I'm quite willing to pay . . ."

He raised an admonishing forefinger. "That's out of the question, sir. You are her ladyship's guest. I will open up one of the smaller rooms and do my best to make you comfortable. If you would care to sit with her ladyship for a few hours, I will be grateful."

That was the entire purpose of the exercise, although how long I could stand that infernal stench was a matter for conjecture.

Jenkins insisted I share his dinner and I must say he did himself well. Roast lamb, succulent baked potatoes and Brussels sprouts, followed by an excellent college pudding. We also shared a bottle of excellent claret, a smooth gentle vintage that sent a golden glow coursing through my veins and enabled me to view the grim prospect of spending several hours in that stinking room with something akin to equanimity. Jenkins did not stop talking for the entire of the meal, his brain releasing little snippets of information, the importance of which did not register until long afterwards.

"A sheltered life," he said, sipping from his glass. "Never went out into the world. Private tutors, a select circle of friends that was never enlarged. As each one died, no one came to replace them. His old lordship was the same. Content to vegetate here and between them they invented a wonderful country where all problems could be solved by arranging words in a certain way. By the time she was a grown woman, she could no more face the real world, than pigs can fly. Do you follow me, sir?"

I nodded happily and refilled my glass.

"Absolutely. Another Emily Bronte."

He smiled benignly. "I am glad to learn you are a well read gentleman, sir. But whereas Miss Bronte – a rather coarse writer in my opinion – portrayed Gondal in one novel, her ladyship spread her kingdom over twelve. That's what made them so successful. Readers without thinking much about it, recognized a familiar country. That place, sir, that we all dream about, where we can control our destinies, correct awful mistakes by a mere effort of will." He leaned across the table and stared at me with a strange intensity. "You must understand, sir. No matter what you see or hear – you must understand. Understanding smothers fear."

I tried to reassure him, although the effect of three glasses of that fine old wine was beginning to bemuse my senses.

"I understand. Shut up here for a lifetime, it stands to reason that the seed of genius would blossom into a flourishing flower." I felt quite proud of this piece of imagery and repeated the last two words. "Flourishing flower."

"You have a mastery of words, sir," Jenkins stated. "As befits a writing gentleman. But do you appreciate the situation? The gentlemen callers never made the grade, if I make myself clear. The heroes in those books, sir, they always measured up to expectations. Any little faults could always be ironed out. Erased by a well-turned sentence, glossed over by a flow of polished adjectives. The same could be said for the rest of

us. Servants are only perfect in fiction and truly loving
parents can only be found in well written books. Reality is
studded with nasty little rocks, fantasy is as smooth as a well
mown lawn.''

"True." I nodded. "You are a veritable well of profundity,
Jenkins. But books are merely the depository of crystalised
thoughts, while reality is a seething cauldron of disgusting facts.
He who faces facts goes mad; he who takes refuge in the twilight
of fantasy is insane. You can't win. What about another glass of
claret?''

Jenkins rose rather unsteadily to his feet and suppressed a
hiccup. "Thank you, sir, but it's time for her ladyship's dinner.
Will you do me the honour of your company?''

Her ladyship's dinner consisted of warm milk and glucose
and was served from a vessel with a long spout. This Jenkins
carried, with suitable gravity, on a silver tray up the staircase
and into Lady Bramfield's room. By now I was at a loss as to how
to designate the bundle of skin wrapped bones that lay on the
chaise longue: Lady Bramfield, Caroline Fortescue or that
horrible thing I would rather not look at. Jenkins appeared
not to be bothered by any such doubts, for he bowed and
announced:

"Dinner is served, my lady," and placed spout to feeding
hole. The immediate result was electrifying. Without actually
waking up all that remained of Caroline Fortescue, writer of
genius, peer of Dickens, Thackeray, Hardy and Emily Bronte,
took on a kind of grotesque life. Greedy, sucking, gasping life.
What served for lips clamped round the spout, and I witnessed
a sucking, bubbling, body writhing absorption of nourishment.
Although a lot seemed to me wasted as the white liquid
dribbled down her ladyship's chin and formed a little pool
in the hollow below her throat.

Jenkins kept dabbing her with a red handkerchief.

I watched Caroline Fortescue dine for perhaps a full minute
before running out on to the landing, where I was violently sick
on the doubtlessly priceless, but faded carpet.

Jenkins prepared a room – made up the bed and opened the
windows – that was two doors from Lady Bramfield's own.

I fell into an uneasy sleep in complete darkness and awoke in
full moonlight. There were no curtains to the windows, for this
was a room – according to Jenkins – that had not been used for

half a century. Every item of furniture stood out in stark relief; the massive mahogany wardrobes, their long mirrors slabs of blazing light; the dressing table that crouched like some ill-shaped beast in the far corner; a tallboy that reared up against a side wall, creating an oblique shadow that tapered to a sharp point on the dust-infested carpet.

There was a complete absence of sound. It was as though the universe had yet to be born and my tiny atom of awareness was floating on an unlimited sea of nothing. The room, the furniture, even the moon, were only reflections of what would be in some far off time. Then I was rocketed into the present. Sound was reborn.

Running footsteps in the corridor that lay beyond the closed door, accompanied by a trill of laughter. I did not move for a long while, trying to analyse the sounds. Swift, light foot treads, girlish laughter. A running girl that laughed.

I climbed out of bed and put on a thick satin dressing gown that had been supplied by Jenkins, then – not without some trepidation – went out into the corridor. Here the moonlight was only permitted entry through a solitary window situated at the far end; three quarters of the passage mocked a low wattage bulb that created a tiny oasis of yellow light in a desert of writhing shadows. A long way off a door groaned the protest of oil starved hinges, suggesting that someone had pushed it stealthily open – and I, fired by that damnable curiosity that has reputedly killed many cats, stepped fearfully forward – on naked feet   to investigate.

I came to the landing and looked down into the darkened hall. Not there. The lower part of the house slept the sleep of centuries. I turned left and roamed through the shadow congested bowels of Bramfield Manor, seeking a rational explanation. Presently I was rewarded by seeing a wedge of light that sliced through an eternity of darkness and revealed a partly open door.

As I crept nearer I again heard that trill of girlish laughter, a sound that brought some measure of reassurance and a promise of an exciting adventure. Why should I be frightened of a girl, even if she was mad enough to go running through an old, darkened house? When I reached the door I pushed it fully open and attempted to record the entire contents of the room in one swift glance.

Sheet shrouded furniture basking in brilliant moonlight.

Dust-carpeted floor, cobweb-festooned windows – and a young girl standing by a white marble fireplace.

She alone merited my entire attention. Tall for a girl, perhaps five foot nine, slender, attired in a flowing white dress, long black hair framing a pale oval face. A face that had a beauty that one sometimes dreams about, but rarely sees. Large, dark blue eyes fringed by long lashes, a straight nose and a full-lipped mouth that was now parted in a mischievous smile. When she moved the gown slid off one creamy shoulder – and the vision of virginal beauty was complete. Her voice was captivating, enhanced by a slight lilting tone.

"Hello, who are you?"

It took some little while for my voice to rediscover its normal function. "I might ask the same question. I'm a guest – well sort of. But unless old Jenkins has been singularly remiss, you must be an intruder."

She stopped in front of one window looking so young, appealing and unattainable in the moonlight. "I am – in a way. It's fun to roam through old houses at night, don't you think? Chase your shadow by moonlight. Listen to the voices of those who were once and are no more. One has to be slightly mad to enjoy night running."

"But where do you come from?" I asked.

She jerked her head back in a most enchanting fashion.

"Back there – in the woods. I live with my parents in a sweet little cottage. You must come and see us. In the daytime when the sun sends golden spears down through the whispering leaves." She lowered her voice to a whisper. "Nothing dies there, you know. How can it? Nature is eternal. Is and ever will be."

Despite the ambiguity of her words, her demeanour was flirtatious, tantalizing as though she were deliberately trying to draw me into a meaningless, but purposeful argument. I said:

"You are most certainly mad. What would your parents say if they knew you were talking to a strange man in an old house?"

She giggled. "They'd have a fit. Mother in particular would take me to task most severely, but be most understanding afterwards. But when you meet them don't mention where we became acquainted. What the ear doesn't hear, the heart won't grieve over. Has anyone told you that you are very handsome?"

"No one," I replied. "But I'm telling you that you are very beautiful."

She nodded with evident satisfaction. "I'm so glad you think so. That means we're both beautiful people. Wonderful. I don't like ugly men. As for that matter I don't like ugly women either. I always say – if you have a face that frightens horses, then stay at home. My word, but you have a most wonderful smile!"

I bared my teeth into an even wider grin and wondered why I had not been long ago enraptured by my reflection in the shaving mirror. "You are a lovely liar. Now I must see you home. How did you get in anyway?"

She shrugged. "Oh, there's always an unlocked door, an unlatched window. But you can't see me home because you're not wearing shoes. But you may see me to the front door."

Side by side we went out into the dark passage, only it did not seem so dark anymore, then wended our way back to the landing, while she talked in that enchanting lilting tone that sent a tingling tremor along my nerve grid and aroused sleeping memories of something that had happened long ago. In another lifetime.

"I think we'd better say we met in the lane and you had hurt your ankle and I tied it up for you with my handkerchief. And being a perfect gentleman – which of course you are – you are calling to thank me for my kindness. That sounds nice, doesn't it?"

"But it's not true," I protested.

"Nonsense. Truth is what the majority believe and the minority cannot disprove. A little while ago you said I was mad . . ."

"But delightfully so," I interrupted.

"Of course. But surely you realise that madness is the sanity granted to the selected few. To really enjoy life you must turn the world upside down and not be in the least worried if people are shocked at what you say and do. Do you think I'm a genius?"

I nodded gravely. "No doubt of it."

"I think so too. That's why I talk sideways and only those who have a sense of the ridiculous understand me. Have you a sense of the ridiculous?"

"Maybe. But I still don't understand what you're talking about."

She looked up at me and her eyes glittered in the gloom.

"Think about it. You will."

We descended the stairs and into the hall; I saw the front door was slightly ajar, allowing a sliver of moonlight to paint a stripe of silver light across the floor. When I opened the door to its fullest extent and stood to one side, she went out on to the top step; became glimmering white and faintly disturbing. But her dazzling smile and above all that enchanting voice, succeeded in reestablishing a measure of reassurance.

"I am going straight home now, but you must visit us tomorrow. I will tell Mummy and Daddy to expect you, which I am sure will cheer them up a great deal. They don't have many visitors."

"How far away is your house?" I enquired.

"Not far. Just cross the drive and follow the path through the woods. You'll find our cottage in a clearing."

She descended the steps, then walked slowly across the drive while my bemused brain tried to determine why I should be suddenly attacked by a fit of violent trembling. There was something wrong about that graceful, receding figure, but I could not at that time decide what it could be. Then she entered the shadow cast by the first tree and after turning and giving me a parting wave, disappeared from my sight.

I closed the door and went back to my room, there to lie sleepless on that vast bed, racked by both fear and excitement. I was somewhat relieved to discover that the eerie silence had been dispelled by any number of normal sounds; the distant hoot of an owl, the murmur of breeze-teased leaves, the occasional creak of contracting floorboards.

Presently a black cloud bank obliterated the revealing moonlight and the ensuing darkness did little to comfort, but in the space which separates one thought from the next, I slipped into the pit of oblivion and knew no more until Jenkins roused me. He placed a silver tray on the bedside cabinet and inclined his head.

"Good morning, sir. I trust you slept well. I have taken the liberty of bringing a light breakfast to your room. I remember from the old days that gentlemen appreciate these little attentions."

I sat up and sensed the day was already well advanced.

"There was really no need for you to go to all this trouble."

"No trouble at all, sir. On the contrary. It is a positive pleasure to have a guest in the old place again. It is a beautiful day and I am delighted to say her ladyship is more like her old self. I do think this is going to be one of her good days. She's quite lively."

I found this hard to believe but could do no less than crease my face into an inane grin and express counterfeit delight.

"That's marvellous! Absolutely marvellous! When will it be convenient for me to see her?"

Jenkins hesitated before replying. "I was wondering, sir, if you would be so kind as to sit with her later on this morning. When it's one of her good days I don't like leaving her alone and it is necessary for me to go down to the village. This will be an excellent opportunity for you to have a little chat – hold an interview, I believe you call it."

Hope raised a tiny head and I said: "She really can talk then?"

"Did I not say so, sir? How remiss of me. When you have finished breakfast you'll find the bathroom down the corridor. Razors, toothbrushes and such like are in the wall cabinet. I will await your pleasure, sir."

The bathroom was lined with teak, the bath tub encased in rosewood; but hot water came from a comparatively new wall heater that looked very much out of place. In a cabinet I found several bone-handled toothbrushes, a jar of pink tooth powder and a leather case that contained seven cut-throat razors, each one embossed with a day of the week on its ebony handle. A shaving mug, brush and cylinder of soap completed this collection of Victorian toiletry. Having shaved (with difficulty) and bathed I returned to the bedroom and found my suit had been sponged and pressed, my shirt washed and my shoes cleaned.

When I entered Jenkins' room I found him sitting in an armchair, wearing a black overcoat and bowler hat, nursing a voluminous shopping bag on his lap. He rose and smiled bleakly.

"Ah, there you are, sir. Now you are here I'll pop down to the village. Look in on her ladyship whenever it's convenient. She is expecting you."

"Right. Will you be long?"

"Not more than an hour, sir. But there's no need for you to be concerned: her ladyship has been attended to."

I quickly decided not to think about that statement, then – just as he reached the doorway – asked the question that demanded a satisfactory answer.

"Jenkins, are you aware that a young girl roams this house at night?"

He became as a man who has been robbed of all movement by a certain combination of words. I heard his voice; low – tremulous.

"Indeed, sir! Would she have been a young person in a white dress?"

"Yes. A very beautiful girl. Apparently she lives in a cottage in the woods. With her parents."

He turned his head and spoke slowly, seemingly jerking each word out with great difficulty.

"I know of . . . this . . . young person, sir. It might be well . . . if you . . . did not encourage her. Make no contact . . . whatsoever. Above all . . . I beg of you . . . do not touch her. Never . . . never touch her."

I tried to laugh, but the effort all but choked me. Instead I managed to ask:

"Why not? Who is she?"

"Please don't ask questions, sir. Don't make me regret allowing you to enter this house. Just ignore . . . forget and never touch. Do what I do . . . turn your back and walk away." His voice rose to a near scream. "Shut your eyes, block up your ears and try hard to understand."

He went into the hall, shoulders squared, bag gripped firmly in his right hand, frozen fear expressed in every line of his upright figure. I waited for the sound of the front door closing, before making my way to Caroline Fortescue's bedroom.

I steeled myself to endure that awful stench, but found it less pungent than the day before. The creature on the chaise longue looked much the same; motionless, eyes partly open and betraying no sign of life. So much for Jenkins' assertion that she was awake and expecting me. After watching her for a few minutes, I went over to the book shelves and began to examine the bound manuscripts.

Without doubt they were priceless. Written in a clear, round hand, with a space between each line so as to leave room for corrections, here were the original manuscripts of the literary masterpieces that had enthralled three generations. I turned over the pages of *Moorland Master* and marvelled at the concentration and sheer energy that writing something like a quarter of a million words with a pen and ink, must have involved. But of one thing I was certain. Every book had been a labour of love. The faultless penmanship, the neatly ruled out words of lines, with the substituted prose written above, testified to the masochistic pleasure that is the reward for arduous work well done. A sheet of faded blue notepaper had been pinned on page one and on this was written in the same clear style:

Life is what you make it

A simple philosophy and one easy to follow for a rich young lady in the nineteenth century. I closed *Moorland Master* and was reaching for the next manuscript when a low, almost masculine voice made me jerk round in sudden alarm.

"Young man, come here."

It took courage to approach the chaise longue, then look down at Caroline Fortescue. She had not moved, the eyes were still half closed, but the mouth was wide open, as though the lower jaw had dropped. I managed to say:

"I'm Brian Radcliffe . . . a . . . a guest in your house."

The rasping voice spoke again, but I could detect no movement either of the mouth or tongue. I could only suppose she had taught herself to speak with the stomach muscles, but each word was pronounced with precision.

"Of course, I had forgotten. I am inclined to be absent-minded these days. Time has become fluid, it ebbs and flows so that today often merges with yesterday. More, it sometimes recedes beyond yesterday. I daresay you are confused."

I shook my head. "No . . . that is to say I am trying to understand."

"That is fortunate. Poor Jenkins only thinks he understands. But our time is short for I shall soon drift away and next time we meet . . ." She paused and I heard a ghost of a chuckle. "I'll not be entirely myself. There is a question you wish to ask me."

I swallowed and tried to select one question from an entire army. "Yes, why did you stop writing after 1911?"

"Because there no longer existed the need to write books. I was able to live them. If that is an unsatisfactory reply, I can only add – think on what you have already seen and heard. Then you will . . . There is I believe a feeding cup nearby."

I looked around and saw the china vessel with a long spout standing on the mantel shelf and on taking it down found it contained a small amount of the white liquid.

"Yes, I have it here."

"Then be so kind as to pour liquid nourishment into my mouth. I am conscious of a drying up, purely illusory no doubt, but no less real."

With an unsteady hand I poured enriched milk into that gaping hole, then withdrew the cup when the mouth filled. Little riverlets of white moisture spilled over and ran down the chin, but the remainder gradually disappeared, although I could not detect any sign of swallowing. The stuff seemed to be merely sinking down her throat. The harsh voice spoke again.

"Thank you. But I fear the result is not satisfactory. I am slipping away again . . . slipping away. Remember not to . . . to . . . or all will be . . . lost . . . lost . . ."

I waited for a long time, hoping (but dreading) she might speak again, but although the mouth remained open, no further sound came from it. Presently the door opened and Jenkins came tip-toeing across the room, his face lit by a gentle smile.

"Did you have a chat with her ladyship, sir?"

I nodded. "Yes, we had a brief but interesting conversation. But, Jenkins, how does she talk? Her mouth . . ."

"No questions if you please, sir. Now I see her ladyship has gone back to sleep. Splendid. I've prepared a light lunch, so if you would care to come downstairs, we'll leave her to rest."

I did not encourage the old man to speak during lunch for there was a distinct feeling that if I pressed him too hard, he would tell me something I did not want to hear. In this I was aided by his built-in compulsion not to speak when a *superior* displayed signs of wishing to remain silent, and this I did by frowning when he so much as cleared his throat. At last the meal ended and I volunteered to help him wash up, a suggestion he dismissed with something akin to horror.

"I'll take a little walk," I said quietly, almost daring him to make any objection. "Just a stroll round the grounds."

His head was averted when he answered. "An excellent idea, sir. But it might be well if you kept to the drive. The woods are dangerous at this time of year. The undergrowth conceals boggy patches that can trap the unwary. I entreat you, sir. Keep out in the open."

"I will not take any unnecessary risks," I promised.

As I walked across the drive I knew he was watching, darting from window to window and possibly sighing with relief when I turned right and skirted the woods, wading through knee high grass until I came to an overgrown hedge that was breached by an old stile. This I climbed, then after making certain that I could not be seen from the house, entered the woods.

Dense undergrowth impeded progress, whippy twigs stung my groping hands as though some rustic deity were trying to protect its gloomy retreat from invasion. I veered left looking for the path my nocturnal visitor had taken the night before. Eventually I stumbled on to it; a barely perceptible parting that ran through stunted ferns and crumbling leaf mould; a ghost path which had died long, long ago.

To this day I am not certain how long I followed that narrow, almost non-existent trail, but suddenly I found myself facing a large clearing in which stood a snug, red-bricked cottage. It was familiar, yet more than a little disturbing. I tried to remember where I had seen such a cottage before, but could only conjure up mental pictures torn from brightly illustrated books, last seen before cosy nursery fires. Woodland cottage, elderly loving parents, a beautiful daughter who held intimate conversations with loquacious rabbits and other members of the animal kingdom.

A sloping red-tiled roof, two windows up and two down, a green door in the centre; a crazy paved path that divided a flower-rich garden; all protected by a white picket fence broken by a green gate. Dazzling white curtains masked the windows, flaming red geraniums enhanced the lower window sills, while blue smoke drifted up from two squat chimney pots.

Fear – apprehension – flowed back before a feeling of supreme contentment, creating the ridiculous impression that I – a wanderer on the vast plains of time – had at last come home. But below the surface, under the crust of self-deception, unwelcome knowledge seethed and threatened to manifest as indisputable fact. But I also knew with an unquestionable certainty, that in this place fantasy and reality were but two meaningless words man had created for his convenience. The truth was much more complicated.

I opened the gate, closed it carefully behind me, then walked slowly up the path and mounted the single, hearth-stoned step. I tapped on the green door and waited with keen expectancy for someone to welcome me. The door drifted open and I looked upon the model parents; those that we, when young and

misunderstood, always wished for but rarely, if ever had. The
woman could have been a youthful fifty or a mature forty;
auburn hair, gentle dark eyes and a smiling mouth – the eternal
mother for a perpetual child. The man! Those who can, think
of Ronald Colman – handsome, grey-haired, urbane, neither
young or old; a man of the world who had the ability to dismiss
fear with a single word, banish doubt with a charming smile.

It was he who stretched out a long-fingered hand and said:

"Why, it must be the young man who is staying at the big
house! Cathy has been on tenderhooks all day. Come in, my
dear fellow. I am so pleased to see your ankle is better."

Mother blushed and appeared quite willing to kiss me if
given the least encouragement; and both made me feel like the
prodigal son arriving home for his share of the fatted calf.

I was drawn into a narrow passage, then ushered into a
comfortable parlour (that definition came most easily to mind)
that smelt faintly of warm damp and the cloying aroma of
decay. But there the bright red wallpaper looked as if it had
been recently put up, the furniture newly purchased from a
Victorian store, the patterned carpet delivered that morning
from the factory.

Mother gave me a wonderful smile and motioned me to a
deep fat armchair, while Father stood in the doorway and
called out:

"Cathy, come down, dear. Your friend has arrived."

I did not hear her descend the stairs, neither did it seem
possible she had time to do so, for almost at once my moonlight
girl was following her father into the room, her face enhanced
by a faint blush. She said: "Hello, how is your ankle?" and
promptly sat down in a chair opposite mine. Without hesitation
I replied: "Much better thank you. It was so kind of you to help
me," and actually seemed to remember having my swollen
ankle bound with a large silk handkerchief. But from then on I
began to experience great concern about what I had done and
said since entering the house, and what I might do in the
immediate future. For example: I could remember Father
stretching out his hand, but I could not remember if I had
shaken it or not. For some reason this seemed to be very
important. Maybe because Jenkins' instruction kept crashing
across my brain. "*Make no contact . . . whatsoever.*"

Was sitting on a chair making contact? I gently pounded the
arm of my chair with a clenched fist. It seemed solid enough,

and that which the senses record must be real. Three pairs of eyes watched me; Mother kindly, father expectantly, Cathy lovingly. Father spoke:

"We are so glad you came. It is very lonely sometimes."

Mother expelled a deep sigh. "We could not live without Cathy, but she needs new material. I think that's what I mean."

Cathy's lilting voice made me start.

"What is the use of a book unless it has printed pages? Would you like to stay with us forever?"

Truth wore a shroud as she hammered on the door of my brain, but I refused to admit her; face the grotesque dream. That lilting voice went on and on.

"Fiction can only flourish in the garden of fact. Even my genius cannot snatch fantasy out of the air. And there must be romance. A beautiful young man who comes walking down the lane. He's lost I think and is limping. Or maybe he's escaped from a prison in which he was unjustly confined, or jilted by a girl in that cruel outside world. But here – in this refuge from ugly reality – he will find his true love. They will make unsullied love in the melancholy purple twilight and send beautifully composed dialogue drifting up to the dark dome of heaven. They will never grow old, not even when the sun reaches out and consumes its children."

Mother and Father had become as two wax statues that sat perfectly still with kindly smiles etched on their flawless faces. But Cathy moved. She stood up and stretched out slender arms. I did not surrender immediately for were there not three words blazoned across my brain in letters of fire? DO NOT TOUCH. But why? Could it be that long ago the original Cathy used to torment those *gentlemen callers*; flirt, tantalize, promise with her eyes, then draw back in pretended or real fear when they stepped over the line which separates reality from make believe? *"Don't touch me. Don't ruin the dream."*

Sex creates. Frustrated sex still creates.

Fear made the hair of the back of my neck bristle; anger, unreasoning rage drove me forward – straight into those outstretched arms.

That lovely face was transformed into a mask of naked terror and my God how she screamed. For a brief moment I clasped a slender body in my arms, gazed into wide, wide open eyes and tried to smother that unending scream with my mouth. Then suddenly it seemed as if a mighty cold wind came roaring

through the woods; it blew away the cottage walls, turned the
furniture into scattered rocks; and sent me hurtling down into
a bottomless pit.

When I recovered consciousness and had climbed up onto a
strangely shaped boulder that had been so recently, a fat, deep
chair, I was at last able to gaze upon the naked face of truth. I
will be haunted by that ghastly knowledge until the day I die
and it is one of the reasons why Wilfred Frazer never got his
world-shattering story and why I am writing it now. Perhaps
when it is once committed to paper I will be granted some
peace of mind.

The old house basked in the afternoon sun, its upper
windows gleaming slabs of light, that to the fanciful might
have resembled the eyes of a mythological monster newly
awakened from a century-long sleep. When I emerged from
the woods and began to cross the drive, my shadow elongated
and went streaking out before me, as though it could not wait
for me to enter the house. It was then that I realized what had
been so dreadfully wrong with Cathy when she crossed the
drive in moonlight.

She had not cast a shadow.

Even from the hall I could hear the harsh sobbing, punctuated by an occasional wailing cry. I walked slowly up the stairs,
then entered the room where the remains of Caroline Fortescue, Lady Bramfield lay upon the great four-poster bed.
Jenkins was on his knees beside it, mourning his dead.

I said quietly: "When did she really die, Jenkins?"

He looked at me reproachfully with tear filled eyes.

"When you broke the dream, sir. When you touched. I
warned you, sir. Do not touch, I said. Do not touch. You killed
a living legend."

I went over to the bed and looked down at the thing attired
in a rusty black gown. Where the eyes had been there were now
two gaping holes. A wave of anger made me shout:

"You lie, Jenkins. Lie to me – lie to yourself. She died long
ago."

He shook his head violently and pounded the bed with
clenched fists. "No . . . no . . . you're wrong. She was more
alive than you or I, or anyone who walks the earth today. She
created her own world . . ."

I grabbed his coat collar and pulled him to his feet. I placed my mouth within a few inches of his ear and whispered the awful truth. "Listen to me . . . don't pull away, shut your eyes or plug your ears. That lovely creature that roamed this house at night, ran laughing along the passages, lived with make believe parents in a woodland cottage – that wasn't the real ghost. Was it, Jenkins? Eh? That was how Caroline Fortescue saw herself – as maybe she once was. No, the real ghost was somewhere else. Where was that, Jenkins? Tell me."

When he struggled and cried out I released him and he fell across the bed. Suddenly I was very tired and wanted to be far away from this house of death. I spoke quietly.

"Her dream world was so real she could not leave it, not even after death. So . . . so . . . she haunted her own corpse. Some personality fragment was able to delay decomposition, simulate the need for nourishment and dominate you, the necessary attendant. I don't know how much longer this pretence could have gone on. Until you died possibly, for only you could maintain the great illusion. But before I go, satisfy my curiosity. How long has she been dead?"

Jenkins got up and wiped his eyes on the sleeve of his jacket. "Thirty years, I think. Her decline was gradual, but I have not detected a heart beat for at least twenty years. But I never really admitted that, sir. I couldn't."

I left Bramfield Manor and made my way towards the main gates without so much as a backward glance. I did not pay a visit to the inquisitive post mistress, but caught the first train to town. I told Frazer the truth: Caroline Fortescue had been dead for years and there was no story worth writing.

A week later Bramfield Manor burnt to the ground. Whether this was the result of an accident, or Jenkins had decided to turn the house into one vast pyre, including himself as a funerary sacrifice, is a matter for interesting conjecture. Certainly two charred skeletons were laid side by side in Bramfield churchyard.

I sometimes wonder if Jenkins would have considered this arrangement disrespectful.

DAVID J. SCHOW

Wake-Up Call

DAVID J. SCHOW'S COLLECTION of essays from *Fangoria* magazine, *Wild Hairs*, won the 2001 International Horror Guild Award for Best Non-fiction.

The author's more recent books include a new collection of living dead stories entitled *Zombie Jam*, the short novel *Rock Breaks Scissors Cut*, and a new mainstream suspense novel, *Bullets of Rain*. His earlier collections *Seeing Red* and *Crypt Orchids* have been reissued in new editions, and he edited *Elvisland*, a landmark collection of John Farris's short fiction for Babbage Press.

Schow lives in the Hollywood hills and continues to collect anything and everything to do with The Creature from the Black Lagoon.

As the author observes: "Zombie fiction has become a subgenre. People know zombies, now, the way everybody knew what a vampire was, twenty years ago. Zombie fiction, like it or not, for better or worse, has arrived . . . and this probably isn't the last you'll see of it."

I OPENED MY EYES. It hurt. Someone was speaking.

"Welcome to Phase Two debriefing, Mr Maxwell."

Here is my last memory:

Not drunk, and in complete possession of my senes, I perform the ritual. That's what it feels like – a ritual. Thousands before me have executed similar moves under comparable circumstances, in an equivalent state of mind. First consideration: hardware. I had chosen a classic, the military-issue Colt. 45 semi-auto, a golden oldie with a venerated history. For those of you who don't know much about firearms, this pistol, originally made for the US Army, is designated the M1911A1. The standard clip is seven-plus-one, though larger magazines are obtainable. "Seven-plus-one" means seven cartridges in the clip with an extra round already chambered. If you wish to find out more about the damage index of various bullet types or need a lot of tech stuff, that information is abundantly available; I know enough to make the device work. Second consideration: The note. The inevitable note. The who, what, why and where of suicide. I had a single glass of white Bordeaux while composing it. Whoever discovered my reeking corpse, exsanguinated, cheesy clumps of hair and brain stuck to the walls and hardening on the carpet, would have to reconcile the ghastly display with my carefully-considered farewell memo. The stench of evacuated bowels and exposed organs, the nakedness of decay. Humidity and maggots. What farewell prose could out-vote that sad horror? I checked my gun a dozen times, finished my wine, and completed my note, blaming no one. Then I stuck the muzzle in my mouth and blew off most of the back of my head with a soft-nosed hollow point, for maximum reliability.

Then I woke up.

"Mr Maxwell? Ah. Glad to see you're back with us. My name is – it's okay, Mr Maxwell, you can open your eyes. It might sting a little bit. But it won't harm you."

I tried to track the voice and realized I was strapped into a sort of dentist's chair, reclined, with a lot of leads trailing to beeping machines. But this was not a hospital. I could taste blood in the back of my throat.

"You're probably a little bit thirsty, too," said the voice. Sitting on a stool overseeing my position was a young woman in a smock. She had brilliant grey eyes, strawberry blonde hair, and an abundance of freckles. Her face was compressed and her haircut was not complimentary – she was more of a sidekick type, short and a bit stocky, cute instead of attractive. Eyeglasses on a chain. A bar-coded ID tag dangled from her pen pocket. "My name is Bonnie and I'm your caseworker. This is your preparation for what's called a Phase Two debriefing; you might have heard of it, or read about it."

She tipped a pleated paper cup of water to my lips. My wrists were restricted. The water tasted too cold and invasive. I felt weary.

"I know you feel like you want to go to sleep Mr Maxwell—" she consulted her clipboard. "Orson. But you can't become unconscious as long as you're hooked up, and we need to review a few details before we move on."

"I don't understand." My voice felt arid and abraded. I felt around inside my mouth with my tongue. No hole. I fancied I could still taste the lubricant and steel of the gun barrel. The egress where it had spit a bullet into my head was patched with something smooth and artificial.

"That's why we're here," said Bonnie. "Standard orientation for wake-ups. That's what we call revised suicides – wake-ups."

"Revised?"

"Yes. All wake-ups are selected on the basis of their stats and records. I'm not here to judge, just to prepare you for your reinsertion into the work force. You'll have a meeting with an actual counselor later."

"Excuse me, Miss . . . Bonnie, I haven't heard about this, or read about it, and I don't know what you're talking about. I do know that I feel terrible; I feel worse than I've ever felt in my life, and I don't want to answer any questions."

She smiled and attempted to soften her manner by about a third of one degree. "Please try to understand. I know this is confusing and you probably are in some bona fide physical pain. But by killing yourself – committing suicide – you have forfeited any protest. You *have* to co-operate. It'll seem difficult, for example, when you walk for the first time. But if you don't want to walk, they'll *force* you to walk, anyway. It helps to think of yourself as a newborn, not whatever person you used to be. You do not retain rights, as you understood them."

"I forfeited them."

"Correct. Now we try to minimize the discomfort of wake-up as much as we can, but ultimately, you'll have to do what they'll say until your obligations are discharged."

"Wait, wait . . ." My skull felt like a crockpot of acid, broken glass and infection. "What about my head?"

"That's sealed with a polymer cap. Your structural damage has all been repaired."

"What obligations? Do I have to *pay* for all this?"

"Look," she said, leaning closer. "We're not supposed to

discuss this with wake-ups. Counselors usually deal with inauguration. I don't know anything about you, other than you wound up here. I don't know what you did or why they picked you. I'm just here to smooth your transition into a wake-up."

"Why am I here?"

She sighed and made sure the door to our room was closed before she spoke. "Most of the wake-ups? They killed themselves, or arranged accidents, to avoid substantial debt. That's why they started the program: too many people were in arrears. Too much debt, foisted off onto relatives who couldn't pay. Scam artists and fraudulent insurance claims that paid off triple on accidental death. It was like an open faucet of money, and eventually, it needed to be fixed. That's why the government endorsed the wake-up program."

Death was no longer the end of the billing cycle, apparently. I said, "How?"

"That's a little mysterious, too. Your engrams are sort of flash-frozen. But it also involves voodoo, magic, and that's the part the mission breakdown never mentions, because I think they're just a little embarrassed to have to resort to a combination of science and sorcery. The process was sped up, then simplified, then streamlined, until we have the system we have now. We process dozens of wake-ups per day."

"What do you do with them?"

"Assignments are the responsibility of the individual counselor," she said. "Mostly it's industrial labor, from what I hear."

"You mean like slaves?"

Her expression pinched and she exhaled in a snort. Obviously, she was running out of time. She probably had to get another wake-up in here and start her spiel according to a clock. "Try not to think of it that way. Remember, you divested yourself of human rights when you—"

"Yes, I'm sure it's all nice and legal," I said. "But what about my identity? My home? My relatives? My stuff?"

"That's just it." She lent me a tiny grimace. "You're not supposed to remember any of that. Maybe your name, maybe a few basic residual facts . . . but you're talking in whole sentences. Most wake-ups act severely autistic, or comatose, or zombiatic. They told us the personality prints through in one out of a thousand clients." It was clear she now suspected somebody of fudging the curve.

"Well, then, I'm a special case and we should—"

"No." She overrode me. "There can't be any special cases."

"Who says so?" I felt twinges of remote-control strength in my arms, my legs. Perhaps if I could keep her talking long enough, I'd muster enough energy to be more assertive.

She showed me her clipboard, helplessly. "*They* do."

That's when my quiet time was up.

Another chair (more upright), another set of straps (stronger), and a conference desk. The whole sterile set-up resembled an interrogation cubicle. My counselor was named Eddin Hockney. He did not introduce himself, but had a sizable nameplate on his desk. He had attempted to avert his pattern baldness by shaving his head – and, it seemed, polishing and hot-waxing it as well. Watery brown eyes; thick spectacles; he was short and sciurine. His eyes darted furtively from detail to detail like some forest creature anxious to hoard nuts. His speech was better-rehearsed and more non-stop; as Bonnie had said, sped-up, simplified, streamlined.

"Surely you must agree that lost revenue via self-termination has always been an increasing problem," Hockney said, not looking at me in particular, not searching me for signs of comprehension, just spilling out his rationale. "The data prove it. People try to – eh, do away with themselves, and stick *anyone* else with the bill. Old lovers. Ex-spouses. Heirs. Employers. Banks. Well, the credit companies just wouldn't put up with it anymore. A country can't function without viable credit and liquid assets. Do you know that some people actually *run up* their credit to the limit while they're planning on killing themselves all along? And they expect to just skate on picking up the tab, their responsibility. Well, no longer." He flipped pages, apparently disgusted by me.

"I don't suppose—"

"Aht-aht-aht!" he overrode. "I don't care. You have no rights. What I do see is an outstanding cumulative debt of $178,000. That gets you a standard Class Two work package – twenty years."

I hadn't put anything in my suicide note about monies owed, or regretting my expenditures.

"It's basically robotic manual labor. You don't retain any higher functions. If you *think* you do . . . well, those will fade."

"What happens after twenty years?"

"Huh. Then you get to have a funeral. Cost is pre-figured into the package."

It was not my bad finances that drove me to take my own life, but – possibly – the reduction of my character to no more than the sum of my debts. The badgering, the hectoring, the humiliation. The exponentially increasing lack of human connection in a world where *everyone* was the sum of their debts. "Death" and "debt" sounded alike for a reason, I concluded.

If what Hockney was saying was true, then I'd spend two decades lifting or slinging or swamping or whatever, losing pieces of the memory of my life every heavy step of the way. My wives, my lovers. My joys and ambitions. My concepts of beauty, or what was fair. My despair, which had driven me to purchase a handgun for several hundred dollars on credit. Pain, and my mistaken notion of how it might be ended.

But I didn't forget.

I didn't forget that finest day of my life came unexpectedly in late 1990s, and that I realized what a flawless moment it had been, only in retrospect. Like most people. I didn't forget abysmal black mood that prompted me to pick up gun. I didn't forget that Victor Hugo wrote: *Supreme happiness of life is conviction that we are loved.*

Other things slipped away gradually.

My taskwork was in a large industrial foundry, using a ring-shank-handled skimmer over a crucible of ferrous lava that was channeled to several behemoth injection-molding machines. I live at foundry with other wake-ups. Constant labor is only interrupted by replenishment time: six hours of rest and an orally-pumped diet of fecal paste. Bodies relax, but no here sleeps. Sleep would provide oblivion. We are either awake, or *more* awake.

In this environment, flesh of wake-ups becomes tempered like steel, all leathery callus. No need for safety goggles, helmets, outerwear. Air swims with free silica and lead dust. Soluble cutting oils contain nitrosamines, which are carcinogenic. There's sulfuric acid, mercury, chlorinated solvents, potassium cyanide, xylene, carbon monoxide, infrared radiation, nickel carbonyl, toxic plaster, ethyl silicate. In this atmosphere, hexamethylenetetramine decomposes to formaldehyde. We can receive thermal burns from spattered pours. If molten metal slops on floor, heat will vaporize water in cement, causing steam explosion. Sharp objects. Falling and crushing hazards. I do not know these things. I read them, on warnings for supers, who are normal humans. I can still read.

I can read control number on forehead of wake-up working next to me. 730823. Used to be black man, half his head gone, replaced by a mannequin blank – half his number is printed on plastic, half tattooed on flesh. A tear falls from his single eye and makes a white path through black soot. When I weep, my tears leave black trails on white skin. My number is 550713.

Children work here. Ex-kids. Not suicides. Others, who damned sure didn't kill themselves. Victims of others. I think supers are lying about program for wake-ups.

We cannot feel sparks of forge, though they hit us and sizzle.

I think: *We are not supposed to be able to read, or feel, or cry, or remember.* But I do.

And if I do, big vat of steel below might be crucible not of rebirth, but of re-death. I am special case. Exception. Maybe exceptional enough to will my foot closer to edge. Drop isn't far.

Very odd, to submerge in metal hot enough to instantly vaporize my eyes . . . and feel nothing. Hot solar light and shock of obliteration.

Then a voice, saying, "Welcome to Phase Three debriefing, Number 550713."

KARL EDWARD WAGNER

The Fourth Seal

KARL EDWARD WAGNER WAS one of the genre's finest practitioners of horror and dark fantasy, and his untimely death in 1994 robbed the field of one of its major talents.

Born in Knoxville, Tennessee, Wagner earned his M.D. from the University of North Carolina School of Medicine in 1974 and trained as a psychiatrist before becoming a multiple British Fantasy and World Fantasy Award-winning author, editor and publisher. His early writing included a series of fantasy novels and stories featuring Kane, the Mystic Swordsman. His first novel, *Darkness Weaves With Many Shades* (1970), introduced the unusually intelligent and brutal warrior-sorcerer, and Kane's adventures continued in *Death Angel's Shadow, Bloodstone, Dark Crusade* and the collections *Night Winds* and *The Book of Kane*. More recently, the complete Kane novels and stories have been brought together in two volumes by Night Shade Books as *Gods in Darkness* and *Midnight Sun*.

He edited three volumes of Robert E. Howard's definitive Conan adventures and continued the exploits of two of Howard's characters, Conan and Bran Mak Morn respectively, in the novels *The Road of Kings* and *Legion from the Shadows*. He also edited three *Echoes of Valor* heroic fantasy anthologies and a collection of medical horror stories, *Intensive Scare*. He took over the editing of *The Year's Best Horror Stories* in 1980 and for the next fourteen years turned it into one of the genre's finest showcases.

Wagner's own superior short horror tales were collected in *In a Lonely Place, Why Not You and I?* and *Unthreatened by the Morning Light*. A tribute collection entitled *Exorcisms and Ecstasies* was published in 1997.

"Health is such a chancy thing," explained the author. "And so precious.

"That's why there are doctors.

"That's why you go to them.

"But you are *afraid* of them. Afraid of their offices and hospitals. Afraid of their questions and examinations. Afraid of their poking and probing. Afraid of their pills and needles. Afraid of their scalpels and sutures. Afraid of lying helpless and naked beneath the sterile murmur of fluorescent lights.

"Helpless.

"Can you understand their jargon, their professional aloofness? The half-hearted words, distracted frowns, and flutter of charts and lab reports? The impersonal cluster of peering faces over your bed?

"Best not to try. Just lie there and trust. And pray. What's your choice?

"But then . . .

"Suppose the doctor *isn't* just what you imagined?

"You're lying there on the bed, vulnerable and half-naked in a humiliating hospital gown.

"You see, scalpels don't care who they cut.

"And no one ever gets well in a hospital.

"You're never closer to death. Never more helpless. This is *real* terror.

"Trust me.

"I'm a doctor."

I

"I HAD A FRIEND at St Johns you would have liked to have met," observed Dr Metzger. "At least the idea you've brought up reminds me of some of our old undergraduate bull sessions."

"Bull sessions?" responded Dr Thackeray, his frosty brows wavering askance.

Geoff laughed easily. "Never underestimate the value of a liberal arts background, Dr Thackeray. St Johns men could find loftier subjects to drain a keg of beer over than the matter of a cheerleader's boobs – especially with cheerleaders in short supply.

"No, Kirk Walker was something of a medievalist – and certainly a romanticist. Fancied himself the last of the Renaissance men, or some such, I imagine. Anyway, he used to put away booze like a Viking raiding party, and often he'd kick around some impossibly half-assed ideas. Argue them with dignified tenacity through all our hooting – and you were never sure whether he was serious, or handing us another piece of outrageous whimsy.

"But one of the points he liked to bring up was this idea that modern science, as we call it, isn't all that modern. Maintained that substantial scientific knowledge and investigation have existed on a recondite basis since early history – and not just as hocus-pocus and charlatanry."

"As I have suggested," Dr Thackeray nodded, drawing on his cigar and tilting his padded desk chair a fraction closer to over-balance.

"Pity Kirk isn't here to talk with a kindred soul," Geoff Metzger continued. "He used to drag out all manner of evidence to support his claim. Go on about Egyptian artifacts, Greek thinkers, Byzantine and later Roman writings, Islamic studies after the Roman Lake changed owners, Jewish cabalism, secret researches by certain monks, on through the Dark Ages and into the so-called Renaissance – even threw out bits of Chinese history. He'd go wild talking about the *quattrocento* and the *cinquecento* and dozens of Italian names no one else had heard of – then Central Europe and France and England, and people like Bacon and Paracelsus and Albertus Magnus. That was really the astonishing thing. I mean, all of us at St Johns were supposed to be well read and well versed in the classics and those great and mouldy books, but Kirk was something else. God knows how much that guy must have read!"

"Your friend Walker sounds like a man I ought to meet," Dr Thackeray broke in.

Metzger's face saddened. "I'm sorry to say you can't. Quite a tragic story about old Kirk. He went on to med school after St

Johns, too – some big Southern school of notable reputation. Wasn't happy there for some reason, and ran afoul of the administration. Left after a rather stormy scene. Died not long thereafter – Hodgkins, I believe. Everyone felt bad about it at the time."

"A pity."

"Yes, it was. I must say I'm surprised to find someone of your position giving credence to such similar ideas. Guess maybe we took Kirk more lightly than we might have. Still, he was always one for elaborate jokes. Strange guy." Geoff's eye fell to wandering along the impressively filled shelves which lined Dr Thackeray's office. These walls of conglomerate knowledge – concentrated to blocky solidity, properly bound and systematically shelved – exuded the weighty atmosphere of learned dignity that one expected for the sanctum of the Chairman of the Department of Medicine.

"And why did your friend believe this unsuspected depth of scientific knowledge was kept in secret?" the older man asked carefully.

"Kirk was vague," returned Metzger, downing his acrid coffee before it got colder. A grimy residue stained the bottom of the Styrofoam cup, and he reflected bitterly that hospital coffee deteriorated with every medical center he came to.

"He had several reasons, though. For one thing, he'd argue that our basic conception of the past comes through writings of the past, and that these writers viewed their world from their own particular set of terms. The idea of progress – in fact, the conception of *science* as we understand it – is a relatively modern development of thought. In another age this was altogether different. To the bulk of the populace, scientific knowledge would have been no more than a pointless exercise, useless to them. What would a serf care about a microscope? It wouldn't clothe and feed him. What would an intellectual care about the discovery of microorganisms? Plagues were the punishment of God or the work of Satan.

"And the language of the day was totally different; there simply were no words – nor even systems of thought – to convey scientific conceptions. Thus every man who studied the stars was an astrologer, while the thoughtful investigator of elemental or molecular structure was only another alchemist seeking to create gold. And to be sure, many of these men were only superstitious dabblers in the occult. With the ignorance or even hostility of most writers of the day, fool and genius were lumped together, and the early scientist was categorized as being in league with the devil. He was ignored and mocked at best, more often persecuted by the authorities of the land. We know of several brilliant thinkers who were condemned to the stake for their efforts – or had near misses, like Galileo.

"It is any wonder then that Walker's protoscientists kept their work secret, shared their discoveries only with a select brotherhood? At least, that was Kirk's theory."

Dr Thackeray considered his cigar. "Interesting. And, as you say, tragic. Medicine needs men of his caliber – and men like yourself, Dr Metzger."

Geoff smiled at the compliment. Coming from the Grand Old Man, it meant a lot. "I consider myself fortunate to be associated with the medical center here."

"Good. And I'll say that we're all delighted you decided to join us. You're a capable man, Dr Metzger; your record is brilliant. Those of us who have watched you feel certain you'll go far in medicine – farther, perhaps, than you might imagine."

"Thank you, sir."

"Not at all. I'm merely stating facts. I knew your father during my residency, you know, and he was a splendid physician himself. So I'm pleased that you decided to take a position here at the Center. It's good to learn the facilities are up to your expectations, and that you're getting your lab set up to suit you."

He gestured toward the sheaf of papers Geoff had carried with him. "I like the way you've drawn this together. I'd say it's dead certain the grant will go through."

"I'm counting on it, sir."

Dr Thackeray brandished his cigar. "Oh, it will. It will. You've stated the scientific aspects of it beautifully – and now we'll handle the political end of things. Politics, as you'll learn, count for a great deal. A very great deal, Dr Metzger."

"No doubt," laughed Geoff drily.

It had been a good move, thought Metzger, pausing to look over his new lab facilities. A damn good move. He could make his name here at the Center.

It was a heady feeling to be in charge of his own research project – a major project at the medical center of considerable renown – and still a young man by his colleagues' standards. But Geoffrey Metzger was inured to honors.

He was, after all, the Center's prize catch – hotly contested for by any number of major institutions. Head of his class at St Johns and at Harvard Medical School, and he could have been one of the youngest men to finish, if he had not chosen the round-about course of a liberal arts education, a few sojourns in Europe, and a combined M.D.-Ph.D. (biochemistry) program at Harvard. Afterward he had taken his pick of the most prestigious internships and residencies, finishing as chief resident in one of the nation's best hospital centers. Then a stint with the Public Health Service in the poverty belt – in effect voluntary, since his family connections were sufficient to keep him out of military service.

An uncle with a governorship, a brother doing Very Well in the vice-presidential ladder of a Very Big corporation, and a "good marriage", socially. Another brother was becoming known in legal medicine, and his father-in-law was partner in a string of ENT clinics in Detroit. Medicine had called members of his family for several generations. Geoff had himself followed his father into internal medicine. His father, very influential in the A.M.A., had been supposedly slated for its top post at the time of his death from a coronary.

A good record, as Dr Thackeray had observed. And no reason why it should not continue to shine. Metzger's previous research work – extending back to his undergraduate days and assuming considerable stature during his residency – had led to numerous publications and no little acclaim. Clearly he was a man who was going places, and the Center was quite proud when he accepted their extremely generous offer. They had given him a free hand in a superbly equipped lab in their newest research facility, with a position as attending physician on the medical staff. And they had made it plain that this was merely a start for him, that there shortly would be important vacancies in the hierarchy of the Center . . .

Yes, it had been a damn good move.

Geoff grimaced and crumpled his Styrofoam cup. And one of the first additions to his lab equipment was going to be a private coffee urn.

II

"Did you notice that ring Sid Lipton had on last night?" asked Gwen.

"What?" Geoff, a persistent headache reminding him of the cocktail party at Trelane's the night before, was trying to watch the morning news.

"Sid had on a sort of signet ring," Gwen persisted. "Did you notice?"

"What? No, guess I didn't."

"It was an ornate silver ring with a large black onyx, I think. Into the onyx was set a kind of silver medallion or seal. It looked like a fraternity ring or something, but I couldn't place it. I thought maybe you knew what it was."

"Haven't noticed it. Dr Lipton's usually scrubbed for surgery whenever I see him – or always looks that way. Don't think I've ever seen him wear anything on his hands but rubber gloves."

"Want some more orange juice? Well, it was strange, because when I went to the girls' room I passed Sid and Brice Thackeray in the hall, and Brice seemed like he was upset or something because Sid had on the ring."

"Upset?"

"Well, maybe not. But they were talking over something in a not-very-casual manner, and it seemed like the ring was part of it. They stopped when I walked by and moved back in with the party. Did you see that slutty dress Tess Gilman had on?"

"Huh? No."

"I'll bet. A see-through blouse with her figure! You could see where her body stocking had padded inserts. And all you men ogling her like she was Raquel or somebody."

"Gwen, I'm trying to listen to the news."

Her face tightened. "Screw the news! You spend all day between the hospital and your damn lab, and when you do get home in time to talk, all you do is tell me about the hospital, tell me about your research. Damn it, you might at least try to pay a little attention to me over the breakfast table!"

"Sweetheart, they're talking about Senator Hollister. He had a CVA last night and died. Forgive me if I find the death of the front-running liberal candidate for the next Presidential election of somewhat greater interest than your rehash of the highlights of another boring cocktail party!"

"Well I'm sorry if you find spending an evening with your wife boring!" she returned hotly.

The news moved on to the latest catastrophe in Pakistan.

"Gwen, honey, that wasn't what I meant."

"Well, goddamn it, Geoff! You don't have to brush off everything I say. I put up with that miserable last year of Harvard, and then your internship in that filthy city – gone all the time, and home every other night just to sleep. Then that endless residency period, when everything was supposed to get better and you'd have more free time – but you didn't, because you were doing work on your own in that lab. And Jesus, that miserable stay in the heartland of coal mines and grits while you played the medical missionary! And all this was supposed to lead up to when you could be the big man in the big medical complex, and name your own hours, and pay some attention to me for a change. Remember me? I'm your wife! Would you like to stuff me away with some of those damn virus cultures you're forever playing with!"

I've heard this before, thought Geoff, knowing that he would hear it again. And she wasn't being all that unfair, he also realized. But he was running late, and this lingering hangover left him in no mood to talk things out again.

"Honey, it happens that I'm at a crucial stage right now, and I really have to keep at it," he offered by way of reconciliation. "Besides, we went to the cocktail party at Trelane's last night, didn't we? We were together then, weren't we?"

"Big deal," Gwen sniffled. "It was a lousy party. All you talked about was medicine."

Geoff sighed, and glanced at his watch. "Look, I don't want to make this sound too dramatic, but what I'm working on now could be big – I mean *big*. How big it might be I haven't even told my colleagues – I don't want to look like a fool if it doesn't work out. But, honey, I think it is going to work out, and if it does, I'll have made a breakthrough like no one since . . . Well, it will be a breakthrough."

"Swell! You mean you'll have discovered a whole new way to implant zits on a monkey's navel, or some other thrilling discovery that all the journals can argue about!" Gwen was not to be placated.

Giving it up, Geoff bent to kiss her. She turned her face, and he got a mouthful of brown curls. "Baby, it really could be big. If it is, well, things could get a whole lot different for us in a hurry."

"I'll take any change – the sooner the better," she murmured, raising her chin a little.

"Trust me, sweetheart. Hey look, you were fussing about your party dress last night. Why don't you go out today and pick out a new one – something nice, whatever you like. OK?"

"Mmmff," decided his wife, letting him kiss her cheek.

"What news today?"

Geoff glanced up from his stack of electron photomicrographs. "Oh, hi, Dave." And to atone for the trace of irritation in his voice, he added, "Have a cup of coffee?"

"Muchos grassy-ass," his visitor replied, turning to the large coffee urn Geoff had inveigled for his lab. He spooned in half a cupful of sugar and powdered cream subsitute, and raised the steaming container immediately to his lips – one of those whose mouths seem impervious to scalding temperatures.

"Don't know why it is, but even when you brew your own, it ends up tasting rancid like all other hospital coffee," Geoff commented, half covering his pile of photographs.

"Unh," Dr Froneberger acceded. "Know what you mean – that's why I gave up drinking it black. Rot your liver if you don't cut it with powdered goo. I think it's the water. Hospital water is shot full of chemicals, rays, gases, dead bugs. Very healthfully unhealthful.

"What you got there, Geoff?" he queried, moving over to the desk.

Reluctantly, Metzger surrendered the photomicrographs. Froneberger's own lab was at the other end of the hall, and it would be impolitic to affront his neighbor. Still, he vaguely resented the frequent contacts that their proximity afforded. Not that Dave was any more than ordinarily obnoxious, but the other's research with influenza viruses impinged closely enough on some areas of his own work to raise the touchy problem of professional jealousy.

"Unh," Froneberger expounded, tapping a hairy finger across several of the photos. "Right here, buddy. I can see it too. You got that same twisted grouping along the nuclear membrane, and on these two you can definitely see the penetration. And you can make a good argument with this one that here's the same grouping on the chromosome. Hey, this is good stuff you're getting here, Geoff buddy."

"I think I'm making some progress," offered Metzger testily, rankled at the other's appropriation of data he had spent countless hours working toward. It would never do for Froneberger to insinuate himself into this thing with matters such as they were.

"Where's it leading you, buddy? Got anything backing this besides what the editors like to brush off as 'artifacts of electron microscopy'?"

"I couldn't say," Geoff replied evasively. "I'm getting some new data off these labeled cultures that may lead somewhere."

"May, and again may not, that's the way it always is. I know the feeling, believe you me. Been a few times, buddy, when I damn near thought I . . . But, hell, maybe all the cherries will roll up for you this time, you never know. Looks impressive so far, my fran. Could be we're hearing the Nobel boys sniffing outside the door."

"I think that's your telephone."

"Shit, it is that. And my secretary's on break. Better catch it. Chow!" He lumbered off.

"Damn!" Geoff breathed, resorting his photographs with fumbling touch.

III

"Too late for you to help him, eh?"

"How's that?" Geoff looked up from his evening paper and turned toward the man who was seating himself opposite him. It was Ira Festung, who busily rearranged his cafeteria tray, smiling cheerfully as he smothered his hospital pot roast in catsup. He should have taken the paper back to the lab to finish reading, Geoff reflected. He had promised Gwen he would be home before too late, and he could lose half an hour trying to break away from the garrulous epidemiologist.

"I noticed you were reading the headlines about the Supreme Court Justice," said Dr Festung, doing nothing to clarify his greeting.

"I was," Geoff admitted, glancing again at the lead article, which told of Justice Freeport's death from cancer that morning. "Freeport was a good man. The second justice to die in the last few months, and both of them liberals. They'll have a hard time replacing them – especially with the Administration we have right now."

Festung snorted into his ice water. "Oh, they'll probably find another couple Commies to fill their seats. Don't see how you can seriously regret Freeport and Lloyd, after the stands those leftists took on socialized medicine. Sure it sounds great to be the bleeding-heart humanitarian, but tell me how much of this fancy research you'd be doing as a salaried pill-pusher. Hell, look at the disaster in Britain! Is that the kind of medical care you want to dish out to the public?"

If this got started again, Geoff knew he could plan to spend the whole evening in the hospital cafeteria. And afterward he'd have a sore throat, and his grey-haired colleagues would shake their heads condescendingly and despair of his political judgment.

"What did you mean by what you said when you sat down?" he asked instead, hoping to steer the epidemiologist away from another great debate.

"That?" Festung wiped catsup from his full lips.

Whiskers, and he'd look like President Taft, Metzger decided.

"Well, Freeport had multiple myeloma, and from what I hear, aren't you about to come up with the long-sought breakthrough in cancer?" Festung's watery eyes were suddenly keen.

Goddamn that sonofabitch Froneberger! Geoff fought to hold a poker face. Let word go around that the Boy Wonder thought he had a cure for cancer, and he'd be a laughingstock if this research didn't pan out!

"Oh, is that the scuttlebutt these days?" He smiled carefully. "Well, I'm glad to hear somebody has even greater optimism for my project than I do. Maybe I ought to trade notes with him."

"If we didn't have rumors to play with, wouldn't this medical center be a dull place to live," Dr Festung pronounced.

Geoff laughed dutifully, although he had his own opinion of the back-stabbing gossip that filled so many conversations here.

"Waste of time trying to cure cancer anyway," the epidemiologist continued. "Nature would only replace it with another scourge just as deadly, and then we'd have to begin all over again. Let it run its course and be done, I say."

"Well, that's your specialty," Geoff said with a thin smile, uncertain how serious his companion meant to be taken.

"Common sense," confided Festung. "Common sense and

simple arithmetic – that's all there is to epidemiology. Every Age has its deadly plague, far back as you care to trace it.

"The great plagues of the ancient world – leprosy, cholera, the Black Death. They all came and went, left millions dead before they were finished, and for most of them we can't even say for certain what disease it may have been."

"Those were primitive times," Geoff shrugged. "Plagues were expected – and accepted. No medicine, and filthy living conditions. Naturally a plague would go unchecked – until it either killed all those who were susceptible, or something like the London Fire came along to cauterize the centers of contagion."

"More often the plagues simply ran their course and vanished." Dr Festung went on in a tone of dismissal. "Let's take modern times, civilized countries, then – after your London Fire (actually it was a change of dominant species of rat) and the ebbing of the bubonic plague. Comes the Industrial Revolution to Europe, and with it strikes smallpox and then tuberculosis. A little later, and you get the picture in this country too. OK, you finally vaccinate against smallpox, but what about TB? Where did TB come from, anyway? Industrialization? No sir, because TB went on the wane at the height of industrialization. And why did it? Biggest killer of its day, and now it's a rare disease. And you know medicine had damn little to do with its disappearance. Then influenza. Killed millions, and not just because medical conditions weren't what we have now. Hell, we still can't do much about the flu. Froneberger tells me his research indicates there are two or three wholly new influenza strains 'born' (if you will) each year – that we know about. Hell, we still aren't really sure what strain was the great killer at the early part of the century. And talk about confusion, why, when you say 'flu,' you can mean anything from several bacteria to any number of viral strains and substrains."

"Well, how about polio?" challenged Metzger, digging for a cigarette. Festung hated tobacco smoke.

"Polio? Exactly. Another killer plague that appeared from nowhere. Sure, this time we came up with a vaccine. But so we know where it went – where did polio come from, though? Each generation seems to have its nemesis. When I was your age, the big killer was stomach cancer. Like bad weather, we talked a lot about stomach cancer, but nothing much was ever done, and it faded into the background just the same. Instead, we had heart disease. Now there's the number one killer for these many years – the reason for billions of government dollars doled out for research. And what have we really done about it? Dietary fads, a few ghoulish transplants, and a pile of Rube Goldberg gadgetry that can keep things pumping for a few extra years. Sum total: too close to nothing to bother carrying. But that's all right too, because now heart disease is on the way out, and for now our great slayer of mankind is cancer.

"History and figures tell the story, young man. Cancer is here for the moment. And maybe all your research will do something about it, then more likely it won't. But it doesn't matter in the long run, because cancer will have its heyday and fade like its predecessors at the scythe handle, and then we'll find something new to die of. Wonder what it'll be."

"Someone else's worry that's what it'll be. I suppose, as they say, you got to die of something." Geoff pushed his chair back from the table. "Meanwhile I'll chase after today's problems. And one of the most immediate concerns a scintillation counter run that ought to be gone through by now. See you, Ira."

"Sure. Hey, how about leaving that paper, if you're finished reading it."

Dr Thackeray was waiting in the lab when Geoff returned. The Great Man was leaning over Metzger's desk, idly looking through several days' loose data and notes. A long white lab coat, stylishly ragged after the Center's peculiar snobbery, covered his sparse frame. A little imagination and he could make a good Hallowe'en phantom, mused Geoff, watching the blue cigar smoke swirl about his hawklike face.

Geoff stepped into his office alcove. "Keeping late hours, Dr Thackeray?" The Chairman of Medicine has no first name within the walls of his domain.

"Good evening, Dr Metzger," returned his superior. "No, not particularly. I wanted to see how things were going with you, and I felt it likely you'd still be here. Your devotion to your work has caused some comment – even among our staff. Most commendable, but I hope you aren't working yourself into an early grave."

"I'll manage," Geoff promised. "I feel like I'm really getting somewhere right now though, and I hate to let up."

"Yes. I see you've made progress, Dr Metzger." His eyes

black in the sterile glare of the fluorescents, Dr Thackeray let his gaze gesture about the crowded laboratory. "Very significant progress in the year you've been with us here at the Center."

Geoff framed his words with care. "I don't like to put myself down as saying – even off the record – just how far what I'm doing here might lead, Dr Thackeray. You've seen what I've accomplished so far, read the preliminary reports. But in the last few months I've . . . well, made a few unexpected breakthroughs. I think I know what it will mean, but I want absolute evidence to substantiate my findings before I speculate openly with regard to what I've learned. Forgive me if this seems melodramatic, but I've no desire to be labeled a fool, nor would I care to bring derision upon the Center."

"Again commendable, Dr Metzger. I appreciate your position, naturally. As you know, there's been some speculation among the staff relating to your most recent work – enough that some of us can understand what you're trying to lead up to."

"I'm making no preliminary claims," Geoff repeated. "Between the two of us, I feel certain of my ground. But too many over eager researchers have gone off half cocked and regretted it when their errors were immediately apparent to more careful workers."

"To be sure!" Dr Thackeray turned his piercing eyes into Geoff's. "I truly admire your discretion. Untold damage might result from foolish disclosures at this point. I agree."

"Thank you, sir."

"Not at all." Dr Thackeray waved his hand. His expression darkened. "It's because of the position you find yourself in right now that I've left these two papers on your desk."

Surprised, Geoff noticed for the first time the two dull black binders waiting beside a tangle of data tapes. Their vinyl covers bore no title – then, on closer glance, he was aware of a tiny silver seal embossed on either spine.

"It required considerable effort to obtain those two copies," Dr. Thackeray advised. "Needless to say, I'll expect you to examine them with care – the data is confidential, of course – and return them to me when you've finished. Reading them is explanation enough for the present, so I'll say no more for now.

"I think you'll want to discuss your thoughts on this with me.

How about tomorrow morning at 8:00? I think you will have read through them to your satisfaction by then."

"Certainly," agreed Metzger in bewilderment. "If you feel this is important to my project . . ."

"It's extremely important, Dr Metzger, I assure you. Very well, then. We'll talk this over at eight."

With a bizarre sense of foreboding, Geoff took up the first of the black folders.

IV

Dr Thackeray's secretary was not present when Metzger entered the Department of Medicine offices the following morning – his nerves jagged after a sleepless night. Since he knew he was expected, he knocked and entered the Chairman's office. *Sanctum sanctorum,* soul of the Center, he thought with a tinge of hysteria.

"Dr Thackeray, I've been trying to get in touch with you all night . . ." He halted, startled to find the Chairman of Surgery seated within.

"It's all right, Dr Metzger," pronounced Dr Thackeray. "Dr Lipton is a party to . . . this matter we have to discuss."

Numbly Geoff dropped into the room's vacant chair. The two older men faced him with carefully composed mien – eyes alert as birds of prey.

Geoff thumped a fist against the black vinyl folders in his lap. "God, it's all here!" His eyes were feverish. "Everything I've done, all I'd hoped to establish – a number of aspects I'd never considered!"

Dr Thackeray nodded, eyes unblinking.

"Well, Christ, where did you get this? If you knew someone else was working in my field, why didn't you tell me earlier? Hell, this is too important for professional jealousy. I'll gladly share any of my data with these researchers. To hell with who gets official credit!"

His voice began to shake. "This research – this information! My god – it means a definite cure for almost every form of human cancer! Why, this delineates each etiological factor involved in cancer – pinpoints two definite stages where the causative agent can be destroyed, the disease process completely arrested! This research marks the triumph of medicine over leukemia, most of the systemic dysplasias – individual organ involvement will be virtually eradicated!"

"Quite true," Dr Lipton agreed. His long surgeon's fingers toyed with the silver-and-onyx ring he wore.

"Well, no more suspense, please! Whose work is this? Where's it being done?" Geoff's excitement was undiminished by the coolness of the other two physicians.

"One paper was prepared from the work of Dr C. Johnson Taggart," Dr Thackeray told him.

"Taggart? No wonder it's . . . But Taggart died ten years ago – brain tumor! You mean they've taken this long to piece together his notes?"

"The other paper, as you've noticed, is considerably older. Most of it was the work of Sir David Aubrey," Dr Thackeray concluded.

Geoff stared at them to determine whether they were playing some horribly sick joke. "Aubrey died at the turn of the century."

"True again. But he was responsible for most of the pioneer work in this field," Dr Lipton added with a tone of reproof.

The overweighted shelves of accumulated knowledge seemed to press down on Geoff's soul. A windowless room in the center of the complex, like a chamber of the vast heart of some monstrous entity. "I don't understand," he whispered in a choked voice. "Why hasn't this information been used before now? Why were millions left to die?"

"Perhaps the world wasn't ready for a cure to cancer," Dr Thackeray replied.

"That's . . . that's insane! I don't understand," quavered Geoff, noticing now that Dr Thackeray wore a ring similar to Dr Lipton's. There was a seal set into the onyx. He had seen it before. It was stamped on the spines of the black binders.

"You can understand," Dr Thackeray was saying. "This will be strange – traumatic perhaps, at first. But think carefully. Would it be wise to circulate a total cure for cancer just now?"

"Are you serious? You can't be! The lives, the suffering . . ."

"The price of power, Dr Metzger. The price of power – just as every empire is built upon the lives and suffering of the expendable." Dr Lipton's voice was pitiless as the edge of his scalpels, excising without rancour the organism's defective tissue.

"Think of cancer in more rational terms," Dr Thackeray

went on. "Have you any conception of the money invested every day in cancer research, in treatment of cancer patients? It's incalculable, I assure you. Do you think the medical profession can sacrifice this wealth, this enormous power, just for a humanitarian gesture?"

"But a physician's role is to heal!" screamed Metzger, abstractly noting how thoroughly the endless shelves muffled sound.

"Of course. And he does heal," put in Dr Lipton. "But where would a physician be if there were no sickness to be healed?"

They were mad, Geoff realized. Or he was. He had been overworking. This was a dream, a paranoid fantasy.

This knowledge made him calmer. He would follow this mad logic – at least until he could be certain with whom the insanity lay. "But some diseases are eradicated," he protested.

"When they become expendable," Dr Thackeray told him. "Some, of course, simply die out, or fall victim to nonmedical intervention. Others we announce a cure for – makes the profession look good. The world has restored faith in medicine, praises its practitioners, and pours more money into research. The prestige a physician enjoys in the community is an essential factor to us."

Lipton's frown furrowed into his close-cropped hair where it grew low on his brow. "And sometimes we slip up, and some fool announces a major cure without our awareness. Thank God, there's less of that now with the disappearance of independent research. As it is, we've had some damn close calls – took a lot of work to discredit a few of these thoughtless meddlers."

Geoff remembered some of them. And now he knew fear. Fear greater than his dread of insanity; fear that these men were all too sane. "I suppose something can happen to some of these researchers who might cause difficulty."

"You make it sound like a line from a gangster movie, but yes," Dr Thackeray acknowledged. "Quite a number of them die from some sudden illness, and the scientific community regrets that they left their brilliant promise unfulfilled."

"It's a way of avoiding other dilemmas as well, as I think you'll follow me," Dr Lipton growled. "Meddlers who become aware of our existence. Fools who would destroy the medical profession with Communistic laws and regulations, endanger the social structure with ruinous legislation.

"And don't look shocked, young man. Think instead just what kind of doctor you might be right now, if some of these late and unlamented wild-eyed liberals could have done all they intended to this country and to the medical profession."

"Murder . . ." breathed Geoff weakly.

"Not actually," Dr Thackeray broke in. "After all, as physicians we have to see human society as a living organism. The social organism is subject to disease just like any other entity. To be trite, it isn't murder to excise a cancerous growth. Regulation treatment – sometimes drastic treatment – is essential if the organism is not to perish. This is the rationale behind all forms of government; the alternative is chaos. I think you'll agree that an educated elite is best suited to direct the social destiny of us all. After all, an epithelial cell is scarcely suited to handle the functions of a nerve cell. It functions smoothly, dies when its time comes – all because the brain, of which it has no conception, directs its course. How else would you have it?"

"You can't suppress medical knowledge indefinitely," Geoff returned defiantly. "Someday someone will eradicate cancer. They were aware of its etiology as far back as Aubrey. . . ."

"Certainly."

"In fact, it's amazing that Aubrey understood cancer so thoroughly – considering the relatively crude apparatus of the day."

Dr Thackeray smiled. "Ah, but we've talked earlier about the possibility of what I believe you termed 'recondite scientific knowledge.' And besides, Aubrey had several advantages over moderns as to the matter of his starting point."

Horror was damp on Metzger's face. The air was stifling, charged with hideous revelation. "You said he was a pioneer. . . ."

"Yes," Lipton rumbled impatiently. "A pioneer in the *development* of the disease process."

"Oh my god," whispered Geoff. "*Oh my god!*"

"I know this is a great deal to comprehend," Dr Thackeray offered sympathetically. "But use your intelligence. To have significant power, a physician must have an essential role – and what is more compelling than the power of life and death? If there were no diseases, there would be no need for physicians. Therefore at certain times throughout history it has been necessary to develop and introduce to the general population new forms of disease."

"But accidental deaths – traffic accidents . . ." Geoff countered, striving to follow his resolve to argue the situation by their own insane reasoning.

Dr Lipton laughed shortly. "If you only knew half our efforts toward keeping cars and highways unsafe! Or the medications we release for the public to abuse. Or the chemical additives we've developed . . ."

"*Who? Who are you?*" His nerve was going to shatter in another instant. This dispassionate, insane . . .

"There are a number of us," Dr Thackeray announced. "A small, highly select order of medicine's elite. An ancient order, I might point out. After all, the art of medicine is as old as human suffering, is it not?

"And of course, our order has grown in power with the passage of time. Today, our society is custodian of an astonishing body of medical and scientific knowledge; our research facilities are the best in the world. We have a certain hierarchy – democratically established, of course – to oversee our operations, direct the use of our wealth, to make those decisions vital to maintaining the order's power and security.

"And naturally you can see why we've been so interested in you, Dr Metzger."

Under their relentless stare, Geoff struggled desperately to maintain exterior calm, while underneath his mind grappled with ideas too nightmarish for conception. "What do you want from me?" he grated, dreading the answer.

"Come now, young man," Dr Thackeray spoke reassuringly. "This isn't a high tribunal. We wish to bestow a great honor upon you – an honor reserved for only those most worthy. We want you to join in our order."

"This is insane, of course," Geoff murmured without conviction. "You want me to become part of a society of inhuman despots? God! This is the most debased treachery to mankind that any mind could ever conceive!"

"It will take a certain period for your thinking to adjust to this new awareness," Dr Lipton interceded with some rancour. "It might change matters if you knew your father was one of us."

"I can't believe that!" But from the dim recesses of his memory came the phantom image of a ring he once saw his father wear – a black onyx ring, set with a peculiar signet.

"True, nonetheless," Dr Thackeray said. "I knew him well. His untimely death was a great setback to us."

"So 'untimely death' can even strike your council of petty gods!"

"There are occasional power struggles within our . . ." Dr Lipton began. He was silenced by a glare from Dr Thackeray.

"Naturally we protect ourselves from our own, ah, methods," Dr Thackeray proceeded. "As a member of our order, you will have access to medical techniques beyond the dream of those outside. Only rarely does something untoward occur."

"Why did you pick me?"

"That should be obvious. It was essential to stop your present line of research, certainly. But that could have been a simple matter. No, we've had our attention on you for a great while. As I say, your father was high in our order. Your family connections are invaluable. Your own contributions to medicine would have singled you out, even had your background been quite plebeian. You're a brilliant man, Dr Metzger. It would be difficult to postulate a candidate better qualified for membership in our order."

"I suppose I'm immensely flattered."

"You should be," the surgeon growled.

"And you shall be," Dr Thackeray assured him. "You will naturally want a certain length of time to consider. This is quite understandably a devastating blow to your past conceptions and ideals. We are pleased to offer you time to consider, to reevaluate your position in light of this new awareness. You're an intelligent man, Dr Metzger. I feel certain your decision will be the rational one – once you've had time to reconsider your former prejudices and misconceptions."

"Suppose I decide to tell the world of your unspeakable conspiracy?"

"Who would ever believe you?"

"It's not that unusual for an overwrought researcher to suffer a nervous collapse," Dr Lipton told him. "In such cases, immediate institutional treatment is available. We become very sympathetic, and work very hard to help our stricken fellow – but I'm afraid our cure ratio is somewhat grim."

Geoff remembered, and fear tightened a chill coil around his heart. "I have to think," he muttered, his thoughts searching frantically for some release to this nightmare. "God, I have to think!"

"Of course." Dr Thackeray's smile was one of paternal sympathy. "We'll wait for your decision."

Not very many minutes after Geoff Metzger had dazedly fled Dr Thackeray's office, a section of the book-lined wall pivoted open. The two noted physicians looked expectantly to the heavy-set man who waited within the hidden niche.

"Well, Dr Royce?"

The eminent psychiatrist grimly studied the monitoring devices focused on the room's vacant chair.

"No," he pronounced.

V

By habit Geoff stumbled back to his lab. A wounded beast returns to his lair, he thought morbidly.

None of his lab workers had appeared. No doubt they had been instructed to take a day off. His phone worked – at least there was a dial tone. But then they couldn't disconnect every phone in the Center. Besides, who could he tell? Gwen? She might believe him. More likely she'd call a psychiatrist at the first discreet moment. And even without believing him, her knowledge would endanger her life as well.

It was monstrous. Surrounded by a sterile labyrinth of tile and cinderblock and stainless steel, shelves of gleaming lab equipment, banks of humming research apparatus – watchful in the dead white glare of the fluorescents . . . God, he'd never realized how sinister a research lab could be. Suddenly he felt like some ancient sorcerer, surrounded by the abhorrent paraphernalia of his evil delvings – a sorcerer who had suddenly succeeded with his conjurations, who now held the bleak knowledge of what demonic powers had claimed his soul.

To become a partner in this inhuman conspiracy was unthinkable. Perhaps its arrogant, ruthless rationality would appeal to certain of his colleagues. But never to him. He could never endure the knowledge of so monstrous a betrayal. He would not become traitor to mankind.

The alternative? Death, almost certainly. Countless others had died for suspecting, for so much as entertaining ideas which might lead to exposing this secret order. *He knew.* They would show him no mercy. What chance did one man have against a hidden society that had held remorseless power for centuries?

There was a slim chance. His only chance. He might pretend to aquiesce. He could agree to join them in their dread order. Of course, they would suspect; he would be carefully watched. But in time they would accept him. For such enormous stakes he could afford to bide his time, wait patiently for years perhaps. During that period he could plan, build up unassailable evidence, learn their names – lay preparations for the day when he might expose their dark treason to the unsuspecting world . . .

"Hey, buddy, you look gloomy. Wife troubles, I bet. They don't go for their man spending all his time with the test tubes, I should know. How about some coffee?" Dave Froneberger was grinning at him, already fiddling with the urn.

Geoff blinked at him dumbly. After the ordeal of these last few hours, Froneberger with his insinuating banalities and petty gossip seemed almost an ally. Perhaps he could be one.

"Thanks, Dave," he muttered, accepting the Styrofoam cup. He was too shaken even to feel his customary disgust with the bitter coffee. Yes, Froneberger with his prying interest in his research might be an ally. At least he could be one other party to this new cancer data. They couldn't murder and discredit the entire Center staff.

"You know, Dave," Geoff began. "I'm glad you dropped by just now. It strikes me that your own research is similar to mine in enough aspects that you might have some fresh insight into some problems I've run into. If you'd care to take time, I'd like to go over some of my notes with you, and see what you think."

"I don't think you'll have time," smiled Froneberger. He reached for Geoff's empty coffee cup, dropped it into a pocket of his lab coat.

"What do you mean?" asked Geoff thickly, coughing suddenly. There was pain deep, deep in his throat. Another racking cough filled his mouth with blood.

And he knew what Froneberger meant.

TANITH LEE
& JOHN KAIINE

Unlocked

TANITH LEE BEGAN WRITING at the age of nine and she published three children's books with Macmillan in the early 1970s. She became a full-time author in 1975, when DAW Books published her novel *The Birthgrave* and followed it with twenty-six other titles.

She has now written and published around seventy novels, nine collections and more than 200 short stories. Her work has been translated into sixteen languages and she also had four radio plays broadcast during the late 1970s and early '80s, and scripted two episodes of the cult BBC-TV series *Blake's 7*. She has twice won the World Fantasy Award for short fiction and was awarded the British Fantasy Society's August Derleth Award in 1980 for her novel *Death's Master*. In 1998 she was short-listed for the Guardian Award for Children's Fiction for her novel *Law of the Wolf Tower*, the first volume in the "Claidi Journal" series.

Her more recent books include *Piratica*, a pirate novel for young adults, and its forthcoming sequel *Piratica II: Return to Parrot Island*. *Lionwolf: Cast a Bright Shadow* and *Here in Cold Hell* are the first two volumes in an adult fantasy series set in a world ruled by magic and mysticism, while *Metallic Love* is a sequel to her 1981 novel *The Silver Metal Lover*.

Two works of lesbian fiction, *Fatal Women* and *Thirty-Four* are published by Egerton House, as is the detective novel, *Death of the Day*. She has also contributed a creepy, contemporary romance novella to *When Darkness Falls*, published by Harlequin.

Tanith Lee lives with her husband, the writer and artist John Kaiine, on the south-east coast of England.

"John and I haven't written many stories actually together," explains Lee. "We wrote our first, however, a macabre and colourful piece called 'Iron City' in 1987, although this has since been mysteriously misplaced . . .

"Anyone who has seen much of my work knows I often acknowledge plot or story ideas from John. In the instance of 'Unlocked', it began with John's writing of the journal and grew further from my own abiding fascination with France, plus our mutual obsession with madness and/or asylums – see my *Book of the Mad* and John's metaphysical thriller *Fossil Circus*."

> *I kissed thee ere I kill'd thee, no way but this,*
> *Killing myself to die upon a kiss.*
> —Shakespeare: *Othello*

THE TOWERS AND TURRETS of St Cailloux, so thin and dark against the terrible sky – I only saw them once. It was not possible to make out the bars, nor to hear the cries. The lawns were shaven, and the trees had the controlled shapes into which they had been carefully cut, restrained by wire. Behind, far off, the mountains, broken and unruly.

Some old chateau, so it looks to be, and must have been, once. No longer.

Now it houses the ones who scream and are kept in by bindings and bars and bolts.

I only saw it once. And that was in a photograph.

When they took me to see the land, they explained all over again, as the lawyer had in the town, that the house was "lost".

The land was a shambles too, under that bone-dry sun. Tares and weeds, as in the Bible. And the magnificent old cherry trees, all swarmed with serpents of ivy, although the little apple orchard had no snakes. There could be real snakes underfoot. They warned me. In the black ruin of the house, a glimmer of motion, sun catching something – pale, shimmering.

What a dreadful place. I want only to sell it, although I doubt it will bring in any money.

At the inn or hotel or whatever it thinks itself to be, an old man brought me a parcel, like a peculiar present.

"What's this?" I tried to be pleasant, though he had suspiciously refused to sit down and ignored my offer of a glass of wine.

"Her book."

"I see. Whose book?"

"Hers. Madame Ysabelle."

"Ah – that's the diary, then."

"Her book," he said, put it on the table, nodded angrily – they are all angry with me, the foreigner from the city who has inherited a piece of their landscape, which is the whole world. The two old servants had been sent away before her death. That is a blessing. I can imagine how *they* would have been with me.

"It was found under a stone?" I asked. "By the hearth."

"What kept it," he said.

After he had gone, I unwrapped the paper and took out the diary. It is black and stained, the binding flaking away. But the stone had protected it, as he said. Something ironic in that, almost a pun—

I opened the cover and saw, in a brownish ink, the characters of my distant relative, Ysabelle, the ornate handwriting so encouraged in her youth. But she had only been thirty-two when she died. No doubt a great age here in the country. An old maid. But I had seen her picture. Quite tall, full-figured, with tight corsetted waist. Hair very dark. Long-fingered hands, and an oval face on a long smooth throat. Dark eyes that gave nothing away, by which I mean *gave* nothing, pushed it toward one.

The writing said, *My Book*. Private, in the manner of a young girl. She had never married, "Madame" the rude courtesy of this primitive area, never allowed courtship, which was blamed on her father. After his death, alone in her white house, all wood, as they do it here, with only the thinnest veneer of dropping plaster. A grape vine growing over the terrace, and the cherry trees raising their gnarled hag's arms, that in spring are clothed in blossom like a young girl's skin.

By local standards too old then, Ysabelle, for wooing. At twenty, here, they gave up such hopes, unless she was a widow and wealthy, and really, despite the land, the two servants, there was no money in her family.

I flicked through the pages. I did not particularly want to know her. Although her diary had survived, and insistently they had awarded it to me.

Here and there a sentence: "Nightingale in cherry tree. It kept me awake all night. Exquisite song, save when it stops to imitate an owl it has heard in the woods." Or, "Mireio says there are no eggs today." Or, "The wind has been blowing. Has made my head ache and my eyes." Then, this sentence: "I cut open an apple, seeds, the white flesh inside, the juices, white as wine, nobody has witnessed this before."

How odd. What a curious thing to say. Had Ysabelle, who seemed to have gone mad, never supposed anyone, not even Eve, had cut open an apple before?

Then I read, "The red apples all white inside. The leaves are dead, too hot, shrivelling the blooms, too passionate a heat. Bells toll in the next valley. Seeds and tears, poppy dreams. Summer, hot, heat, the stifling heat. I dream of clouds. This brightness hurts me. The silver that the locket is made of – where from? Taken from earth, like black-berries, cherry trees, grapes, peeling birch. Everything will burn. It is holding its last breath, blooming with the threat of death. Foxgloves."

I put the diary down. It had felt hot in my hands. Smoke rose from it in my imagination.

Walking across to my trunk, I rummaged inside, and pulled out the other thing they had given me, the buckled, shapeless mass of the locket.

Why foxgloves, Ysabelle? It must be the old country superstition, not the poison which also gives life, but the black fox – cipher for Satan – who leaves his mark there, because he is the ghost of a lover.

Was her secret here in this diary, then, and did they all know it, all these walnut-brown people of the valleys and slopes, who rose with the sun and slept when it fell, and would tell me nothing, and not even drink a glass of wine with me?

I opened the diary in another place and read, "I saw them today. They were on the road in their little trap with the pony. *He* sits upright like a stupid rock. She leans, looking this way, that way. Burning hair. Her hair is the sun, but only if the sun is

pale as the moon. I waved. And she saw me, and waved too. *He*
stared, then nodded, a king. Ernst and Hāna. She had a purple
ribbon in her chignon, but her hair is so massive, it drooped on
her slender neck, shoulders. Purple like a wound in all that
blonde.''

Under this, Ysabelle, dimly related to me by the wedlock of
an unknown aunt, had drawn a line of vine leaves, rather well,
in her brown ink that perhaps had been dark when she used it.

Beneath, she writes: ''Hāna, Ariadne, Dionysos. Holy.''

And then: ''Ernst. What a boring statue of shit.''

This startles me, and I laugh. *Ysabelle,* such *unfeminine* language. But it is her private book.

Even so, I suddenly think her modern, ahead of her time.
This boldness in an old unmarried woman. And she is so coarse
about Ernst . . . does she secretly like him?

The next paragraph only says, ''I shall send Jean to advise
him about the horse.''

I put the diary by my bed. Then, in the furtive manner of this
place, pushed it *under the mattress.* I should read more in bed
that night.

Arriving back in my room quite early, for they lower their lamps
at nine o'clock, and yawn, and shuffle, and frown at you – I sat
perversely with the diary, leafing through it, so reluctant to start
at the beginning. Surely I shall be bored. What is there here to
read? The reflections of an unbalanced, lonely woman, possibly
obsessed by her new foreign neighbours, this exciting Ernst
made of shit and the woman, his sister, with all that pale hair . . .

Then something, no, let me be honest, I know precisely what,
and it is prurient, ghoulish, makes me turn to the last page.
Beyond this page lies the drama of death. The fact that the
house of white wood burned, leaving only its hearths and stone
floors, and two tall stone chimneys, and Ysabelle's bones, and
her diary safe under the hearth stone. Bones and stones. Her
neighbours were gone by then, Ernst, Hāna, to their separate
places. And by the time of the fire, those who would speak of it,
had thought Ysabelle mad. The hot weather was not kind to
women. The horrible wind that blew from the mountains. The
roar of light from their flanks, that had been visible too from
the house, and still is from its ground. She had set fire to the
house in her craziness, Ysabelle. It was only the kindness of the
priest that allowed her Christian burial. She might, after all,

have knocked over a lamp. And everything was so dry, flaring up at once—

Was there even a lock on the diary, which the heat from above caused to melt?

Who else has read this book? Who else began by reading the last page first?

"I have a lock of your hair. I cut it from you as you slept. I kissed you there, where the scissors met. You never noticed it had gone. It is all I have of you, your hair. Blonde spirals in a silver locket.

"The locket is cold between my breasts. Cold in the heat. Perhaps it is the heat of the locket which feels cold, as they say witches screamed, when they were burning alive, of the agony of the great terrible freezing coldness. I sweat silver. Your curled hair next to my heart.

"But we are monkeys, not angels.

"Yesterday, when I returned to the old white house, I saw it freshly, as if I had never lived here, or had been away some years. Whose house is that one? Ysabelle's. She lives alone. Truly alone now, for in the town I saw the lawyers, and settled a sum of money on Jean and Mireio. At dawn today, I dismissed them. She was sulky and angry, and he accused me of sending them away because he had tried to shoot the nightingale. Secretly, they were pleased, talking together when they thought I did not hear, of the tobacconist's shop they plan to start together in the next town. Here, a cooking pot and broom are all that remain of them, all they deigned to leave me.

"My new, empty house. I have always liked it. Liked it too well to leave. Nothing has changed since the days of childhood. The peeling painted wooden walls, ivy in the cherry trees – now and then cut back, always returning – the well of broken stone. Such pretty neglect. But yes, the view has changed, the land shrunk and the sky grown. There are no clouds, now.

"I dream of clouds, as indeed I dream of you. Great black clouds to cover the sun, stormy skies to quell this heat. There has been no rain for many months, and I have heard a rumour too, of a goat sacrificed in the woods – killing to bring rain, blood for water.

"I have a lock of your hair. And *this*. I have this, but this is not you. No. How well I remember when it was. For it was the very same height as you, and broader perhaps, than your delicate, slender frame, like a spilling of your soul in silver. How we sat, night after night, brushing your hair, this entity of you, comb-ing it out, both of us marvelling, for I *made* you marvel at the wonder of it that you had never seen it was. Combing, braiding, playing, plaiting with ribbons, silks, the nights you wore it loose, for me, around you like – a shroud. Oh, Hāna. Your hair.

"I have made it into a noose, threaded, sewn with faded mauve. A noose is all now it is worthy to be, this, that was your wedding train. Life, that will be death.

"They call the asylum also the Valley of Wolves – St Stones, St Cailloux. A sort of pun. And this is, too, for I shall put it under the stone of the hearth, and who knows who will ever find it, my Book. But I hope they will, for I want them to know, yes, even if they rage and curse, I want them to know of you. And that my last thought will be of you, dying on a kiss. Good night, Hāna."

For weeks, the valley and the village were alive with gossip concerning the strangers, who were strange in all ways – educated, and not badly off, from another planet – that is, another country – and unrelated even in the faintest sense, to anyone of the locality.

The village people spied on the newcomers, and presently told each other that here was Madame Ysabelle's chance. For the foreign householder, Monsieur Ernst, was unwed, not poor, nor very young, and of the same social class as Madame Ysabelle, who after all, was not bad-looking, and had her land, if only she would bother to see it worked. The single potential stumbling block might be Monsieur Ernst's sister, also unmar-ried, who lived with and looked after her scholarly brother, in just the same way as Ysabelle had looked after her scholarly father until his death, three years before. The sister was old, so the spies decided, who had only seen her from a distance. She had white hair. These females were often the very worst, and the evidence suggested she must have kept him from union before.

The two houses, though, were only half an hour's walk from each other. One day or another, the man and the woman must meet.

It was a fact, there were dual elements in the village, indeed in all the villages and farms of the region. A sort of peasant bourgeoisie existed, gossipy, religious, caste-conscious, exact-ing. But, too, there was the more feral peasant blood, which had other values, and was considered little better than a pack of

wild beasts. These latter had actually troubled properly to see
Mademoiselle Hāna – she was yet young enough for that, twenty-
four years, which to them looked nineteen. Two men had
carried boxes to the house of Monsieur Ernst. A woman had
brought eggs, and later come to see to the washing. These
people knew quite soon that it was the brother who was the stiff
one. If he had not married, it was because he had never seen a
woman he liked sufficiently. And his sister gave him the best of
care – she was what the middle shelf of the region would have
termed *devoted*. To the "wild beasts", perhaps, she was dutiful,
and this while she was not the sort of girl who would be
naturally constrained. She too had vestiges of the wild woods,
where once witches had danced with flowers in their hair, just
as they had ridden from the mountains on their broomsticks
not thirteen years before.

Of Ysabelle also this wild quality might have been noted, in
her girlhood. They had seen her, wandering the fields with
blood-red poppies in her basket. Or watching the moon from
her window while her clever father pored over his books.

To the Wild Beasts, Hāna did not represent an obstacle nor
Ernst a rescue. Although they were not insensible to ideas of
rescue and obstacle in the arrival of the foreign couple.

Ysabelle met Ernst one morning. He was riding along the
lane, or road, that ran by the wall of the garden at the front of
her house, and she was standing there with Mireio, over the
scattered feathers of a chicken some fox had taken in the night.

Mireio was cursing the fox, and promising that Jean would
set a trap, and Ysabelle impatiently was desiring that rather
than do this, the house of the chickens should be repaired.

They argued in the way old servant women did with mistresses they had known as children, and youngish mistresses
with old servant women who had almost been their mothers but
were not.

Ernst stopped the trap, and frankly watched, in cool amusement.

When Ysabelle looked, he raised his hat and introduced
himself.

Doubtless he could see the old servant eyeing him, evaluat-
ing him, but with Ysabelle there was none of that. As he had
heard, she was educated and well-bred, and he liked the look of
her, her coal-black hair softly but neatly dressed, her dark dress,
still in part-mourning apparently, for an adored, respected

father. Her lush figure, too, her graceful features, her sensitive, noble hands.

She answered him politely.

Ernst said, with his perfect command of language and dialect, "I hope my sister may come over and visit you? Of course, there's no one else suitable for her to see, for miles. She's an absolute angel to me. I want her to be happy, but how can a woman be happy with no other women sometimes to chatter to?"

Ysabelle dipped her raven-coloured eyes. She did not smile. As she was doing this, Mireio said, aggressively, "There is the duck, Madame. I said it was too much for us. But for a proper supper for three, it would be perfect."

Ernst let out a roar of laughter. This was as good as a comedy at the theatre, and really he had no objection to sitting over a good country meal, and looking at Ysabelle, and watching her come around to him.

"Well, I should be honoured," he said, "but Madame hasn't yet asked me."

Ysabelle glanced at him. No smile. Quiet as silence. She said, however, "Mireio has decided you must taste her cooking. Please come and taste it."

They agreed an evening, and Ernst rattled away to the town, whistling, and that night told his sister they were to meet a true witch of a woman, who, he was sure, had already laid a spell on him, because he was going to take with them a bottle of his best wine.

"When I first saw you tonight, with the sun just down and the moon just risen, I was so angry and nervous. The stupid supper. Not since my father had I had to suffer in that way. When he died, the freedom gave me wings. And now, I should be trapped, as Jean wished to trap the poor fox, gnawing through my paws to get away. Seeing you, I hated you. You. One entire second, that I will never forget or forgive. I hated your freshness, your glow, your light-coloured hair, your face, eager to be liked, and nervous too, I am sure. Hated you. I punished myself later, when you were gone. I went upstairs and said to myself in the mirror, you hated her. And I slapped my own face, hard, and left a red mark that lasted two hours. I know, I was awake so long."

Ernst made the meal "go", talking all the while, a sort of lecture. He was studying many things, philosophical, medical, and had also an interest in fossils, many examples of which he would find, he said, in the local countryside, for it was rich in them. Hāna, of course, did not understand these interests. "She calls me to task, and says I march about all day, obsessed by stones. *Stones*, Madame Ysabelle. I ask you."

Ysabelle looked at Hāna, and Hāna said, softly, with her slight accent, her slight always half-stumbling in the new language, "Oh, but I know they're – wonderful, Ernst. I do. I only wish I could have seen them – when they were alive. The big animals like dragons, and the little insects."

"She is a tyrant. She also insists archeology is tomb robbery," said Ernst.

Ysabelle said, "Mademoiselle Hāna would prefer to travel in time."

"Yes," said Hāna, "to go back and see it as it was."

"She reads that sort of nonsense," he said.

Ysabelle said, "But monsieur, you know what we women are. Creatures of feeling, not intellect."

"That takes a clever woman to say," gallantly declared Ernst. He added, "Of course, I've heard of your father. I read a book of his. An excellent mind."

"Thank you. He was much admired."

"You must miss him."

"Yes," she said, "every day."

And turning, as Ernst applied himself again to the duck, Ysabelle saw Hāna stare at her almost with a look of fear.

Later Ysabelle took Hāna to inspect the garden, to show her womanly things, domestic herbs, the husbandry of the grape-vine, the moon above a certain tree.

Hāna said abruptly, "You take a risk, Madame."

"Oh? In what way?"

"Making fun of him. He has a horrible temper."

"Yes, I'm sure that he does."

"He doesn't see it now, what you're doing—"

"I'll be more careful."

"Please. Because I'd hate there to be a rift."

"Since you have no other female companions."

"Of course I do," said Hāna. "There are lots of woman here I like very well. He's often away on his business, things to do with his money, and clever papers he's written. Then I sit on the wall of the court with the servant girl, shelling peas, giggling. We take off our shoes."

"I'm sure that is a risk, too."

Hāna said nothing.

Then she said, "We've been to many places. I like this valley." Though her delivery was still hesitant, it was now a fluent, unafraid hesitancy.

The moon stood in the top of the birch, which held it like a white mask upon feathers.

Hāna lifted her face. She was so pale, her white skin and lightly-tinted mouth. Her eyes were dark, although not so dark as Ysabelle's. As Hāna tipped back her head, Ysabelle, who had drunk Ernst's very strong wine, had a momentary irrational fear that the incredible weight of Hāna's chignon would pull back and dislocate her slender neck. And throwing out one hand, she caught the back of Hāna's head in her palm, as a woman does with a young child or baby.

Hāna said nothing, resting her head, so heavy, the massy cushion of silken hair, on Ysabelle's hand.

They gazed up at the moon, at the mask which hid the moon, which might itself in reality be a thing of darkness, concealing itself for ever from the earth.

"I've never seen so much hair," said Ysabelle presently.

"Yes, it makes my head ache sometimes. I wanted to cut some of it once. But Ernst told me that was unfeminine."

"What nonsense. Your brother's a fool. I'm sorry. Even so, you shouldn't – no, you should never cut your hair. Your hair isn't like any other hair. Your hair is – *you*."

Hāna laughed.

Ysabelle in turn felt frightened. She said, "What nonsense *I'm* talking." And took the girl back into the house, which Ernst was filling, as the father had done, with the headachy lustre of cigars.

They left at midnight, a city hour, not valued in the country.

Exhausted, Ysabelle went upstairs, and Mireio, hearing her pace about, nodded sagely, rightly believing her mistress was disturbed by new and awful terrors, tinglings, awakenings, amazements.

Ernst was delighted when Hāna began to spend time with Ysabelle at the white wooden house, among the cherries. She was always returned early enough to greet him, if he had been absent in the town. She made sure as ever that the servants saw to his comforts. When once or twice he slyly said to Hāna, "What do you talk about, you two women, all those hours? Daydreams, and those books of yours, I expect." Hāna replied seriously, "Sometimes we talk about you." "*Me?* What place can a humble male have in your games?" But he needed no answer and was gratified, not surprised, by Hāna's lie. She had learned to be careful of him from an immature age, upbraiding him only in the proper, respectful, foolish, feminine way, desisting at once when chided. She was used to extolling his virtues, praising his achievements and being in awe of them. Even her perhaps-feigned loyalty she had learned to temper, for once, when a rival at his university had, he said, stolen a passage from his paper, and Hāna had asserted that the man should be whipped, Ernst had replied sharply that this might be so, but he did not expect *her* to say it. Hāna had been taught that men were not to be questioned, save by other men. For though some men were base, a woman could not grasp what drove them to it.

All *this* Hāna had relayed to Ysabelle, it was true. And so, in a way, they *had* spoken of Ernst.

"My mother died when I was four," said Hāna, "but I had a kind nurse. I miss my mother still, do you know, I dream of her even now. She'd come in from some ball or dinner and her skirts would rustle, and she smelled of perfume and there was powder on her cheek, as on the wings of the butterflies that Ernst kills."

"I killed my mother," said Ysabelle. Hāna gazed, and Ysabelle added, "I mean, when I was born. Of course, as I grew, I had to take her place in many ways, for my father. For other consolations, he went to the town."

Hāna lowered her eyes. They were a deep shadowy brown, like pools in the wood where animals stole to slake their thirst.

They walked about the countryside, the two women. They picked flowers and wild herbs, and later, mushrooms. They talked the sort of talk that Ernst would have predicted. Of memory and thought and feeling and incoherent longings. They sometimes laughed until their waists, held firm in the bones of dead whales, ached. They read books together aloud. Even, they shelled peas and chopped onions on the broad table, Mireio scolding them as if they were children. She would spoil it soon enough, saying, "Monsieur must come tomorrow or next day. This pork will just suit him." She was ready always with her invitations to Ernst, was Mireio, and he eager to accept them. *Ysabelle*, he remarked to himself, *has that woman very well primed*. He did not mind a little connivance, though, aimed at himself. Ysabelle herself would not be too forward, and she would not anticipate, daughter of a free-thinking intellectual as she was, anything he did not want to give.

But too, she must be parched, surrounded by the local males, such swinish illiterates. How she must look forward to the sound of *his* step, *his* voice, after all that girlish twittering. And she had a lovely bosom, he had seen the white upper curves of it in her once-fashionable country evening gown, and her firm white arms. Her hair smelled of the rose-essence with which she rinsed it. And there was the smell of cherries always in the house now, somehow inciting. He would like to take a bite, there was no denying it.

"He'll be gone – oh, two nights, three. He said, I might ask you to stay with me."

"Did he."

"Have I offended – I hoped – you see, when he's not there, you've no idea, Ysabelle, our maid, Gittel, is so funny—"

"I prefer not to leave my house. But you're welcome to stay with *me*. I'm afraid—" Ysabelle hesitated. She paled, which, in the candlelight, hardly showed, "We would have to share the bed. The other rooms aren't properly cared for. But this bed is very large. It was my mother's when my father – you understand. A large, ample couch. It's strange. My servants are going away too. A visit I promised them. Gone for two nights. But we would manage, wouldn't we?"

Hāna's face. An angel announcing peace to all the world. "But I wouldn't – annoy you?"

Now Ysabelle, stumbling with a familiar language, her own. "Annoy – I – enjoy your company so much."

"I remember my mother," Hāna said, "before she died. Late, she'd wake me. She used to give me sweets, and play with me, all sorts of silly games, how we laughed. And she'd hold me in her arms. She said, We are two little mice, my love. When the cat's from home, the mice will dance."

"Wine and opium. A dream of pearls. Hidden things. Clasp. Hinges. Unhinged. Open. The quiet shout, my cherry blossom. How we sat, that night. And you loosed your hair. My pearl, shut away, the hair in the locket – your little river – my river in the time of drought. The making of your sweet rain. My souvenir. A wedding train, it swept to the floor. Tread on my heart and break it. Your arms – flung up in abandon, your impatient body, waiting. You had fallen asleep, your face hidden in hair, your legs pale, ghostly in the candlelight. I drew nearer, and the candle with me, flickering, threw shadows dancing between your thighs. I grew jealous of light. I inhaled you there, breathed you in. Kissed you and kissed you again, bathed in the little rivers of you. The heat of the candle was stifling, agonising. We blew the flame away with our mouths. We embraced darkness, drank the night. Oh, Hāna. Hāna, Hāna.''

Hāna was at the door in the stillness of the hot evening. The nightingale was already singing, and the sun hung low, the sky a choked pastel blue, as in a faded painting.

On the terrace, Hāna paused.

"May I step over?"

Ysabelle laughed. She was unsettled, vivid and anxious. "Like the ghost? If I ask you in, will you haunt me?"

"No, I shall be circumspect."

"Come in. Haunt my house."

The rooms smelled of the absence of things. The absence of the servants, gone to their family of a hundred nieces and grandsons in the town. The absence of cooking. It was very hot, and the wooden parts of the building creaked. Ysabelle had lit a lamp in her sitting room, and another in the kitchen, and the strings of onions glowed like red metal. In a vase stood three white flowers. She poured from the bottle of wine. They drank. And Hāna came and kissed her, a fleeting little trustful kiss, at the corner of the mouth.

"Such fun," said Hāna.

"Oh, my child," said Ysabelle, and a well of sadness was filled.

"No. We're sisters. My mother is your mother. And Ernst—"

"Ernst," said Ysabelle, looking into her glass.

"Ernst never was born," said Hāna. And her face was wicked, pitiless. "It was you. We two. You can be the clever one. And I'll look after you."

"I'm not clever."

"Yes."

The light was darkness. The sky a blue jewel in every narrow window. The nightingale sang a thousand and one songs, like Scheherazade, never repeating itself.

They made an omelette with fresh herbs and mushrooms, and ate two loaves of the coarse good bread. They opened another bottle, and made the coffee which had come from the town, seething it like soup, and adding cream and cognac.

They talked. Whatever do women talk of? Such non-sense. Of life and death, of the soul, of the worlds hidden behind the woods, the mountains, the sky, the ground. Of God, of – love.

"Did you never love anyone?" asked Hāna.

"No."

"Your – father."

"How could I love him? He simply always inexorably was, like the year, the day. An hour. An hour without end. Do you love your brother?"

"I – feel sorry for him."

Ysabelle – laughed. A new laugh. Bitter? Stern?

"But he can do anything," said Ysabelle.

"He – does not – *see*," said Hāna. "He breaks the stone and the fossil is there. But he sees only this. Not what it was. Its life. And medicine – experiments – he has done things with small animals – and there is a horrible man he consorts with, a sort of doctor. And the butterflies on pins. Their patterns. But not – not what they are. He doesn't see God."

"Do you?"

"Oh yes," said Hāna, simply, quiet, a truthful child.

"Then what does God seem to be?"

"Everything. All things."

"A man. A king. A lord."

"No," said Hāna. She smiled. "Nothing like that."

When they went up to bed, dousing the lamps, carrying the fat white candle, their bodies moved up the stairs as if all matter had been freshly invented. Night, for example. The stars between the shutters. The cry of the fox from far away. The far shapes of the mountains on the dark. The dark. The furniture. Clothes. Bodies. Skin.

"Will you take down your hair?"

"Yes. Then I'll plait it. There's such a lot. I'll tie it up close so it won't trouble you."

Ysabelle said, "May I watch you?"

In the candlelight Hāna, a portrait, pale as alabaster,

and gems of gold in her eyes. "Oh *yes*. I used to watch my mother."

In the old story, the basket issues ropes of silver, and the silver flows on. Or the silver water leaps from the rock, and never stops.

Pins came out, and combs. The two ribbons were undone. Hāna, unwinding from her head the streams of the moon. On and on. Flowing. Never stopping.

The hair poured, and fell, and fell, and hung against the floor, just curling over there. A heavenly veil.

"Oh Hāna," said Ysabelle. "Your hair."

"Too much."

"No. Don't plait it – *don't*. Haven't you ever known?"

Under the sheath of hair, so simple to undress unseen. The train of an empress, when seated, spreading in folds. Standing again, veiled in the moon, she climbs into the wide bed. But lying back, the sea of moonlight parts.

"I'm so sleepy," says Hāna. She yawns. She starts to speak, and sleeps.

Her upturned breast. What is it like? So soft, so kind, like a white bird, sleeping. And her hollow belly, and her thighs. And the mass of her silver hair, even in her groin, thick and rich and pale as fleece. The scent of her which is thyme and lilies – and – something which *lives*, and is warm.

Ysabelle stands. Locked. Her clasped hands under her chin. The voiceless weeping runs down her face as hot as blood.

But where the candle falls. Is it possible that you can steal a kiss, and not wake Beauty?

"Please – forgive me—"

"But it's so lovely. Don't stop—"

"I can't—"

The nightingale sings. Hāna – sings.

"I never—"

"But you must have—"

"No. What is it? Oh – so wonderful—"

"You don't hate me—"

"I love you. Is it possible – could it happen again?"

"Yes."

"And for you?"

"Oh, yes, for me. Touch – there. Can you tell?"

"But – it's like the fountain in the Bible, springing forth. I used to think that must be tears. But it's this—"

"Hāna—"

"You're so dark. Oh I love you. I can see you in the dark. Blow out the light."

Blow out the light . . . Put out the light . . . *I kiss'd thee ere I kill'd thee.*

He was pleased that evidently they had had a nice time together. He liked them to get on. He questioned his sister, trying to elicit some news of what had been said – of him. Hāna hinted a little, only that. Sly thing. He could picture it, these women, and Ysabelle sighing over him, and Hāna telling foolish stories admiringly, secretively, the way women did. His university glories, his boyish foibles, his favourite toy – they had that look now, of confidences exchanged.

It was afternoon, and Ysabelle and Hāna sat in the sitting room of Ernst's house on the slope.

They were rather stiff and upright, as Ernst was. They drank a tisane, and looked at the view, for soon he would arrive home from his fossil hunt along the edge of the mountains.

The mountains loomed here. At the white house, on such a hot day, they were more a presence of burning light in the windows. Mireio had, as she always did in summer, moved two or three pictures in glass away from the reflection – some superstition that Ysabelle had never questioned, in all her thirty-two years.

But the mountains were oppressive, in this other spot. They turned the sun off in one direction, and cast a sort of shade.

Ysabelle said softly, "If I had you alone, heaven knows what I'd do to you."

"How startled I should be."

"I'd nibble at you like a lettuce."

"If only you could."

They saw him on the path, dwarfed by distance, tiny, big and towering, sunburnt, carrying some trophy.

They turned into two whale bones, corsetted tight, dead and hard and upright.

He entered. The door slammed, and the servant girl, Gittel, ran up, noise, fluster, and then he was in the room, enormous, and he must be welcomed and begged to tell his wishes, and send to heat the kettle, the coffee must be prepared. And look, here were the almond cakes bought especially, as he liked them, and some pâté that had been kept untouched and cool in the stone larder.

Would he sit? No. Was he tired? No. But surely, he must be tired a little, after so long an excursion? No. One saw how he watched, amused, the fuss. How strong and brave he was, to have walked so long and still be walking about, and to have broken this rock which now he put down on the table there. How astonishing. How erudite he was, to have found it. To have known where.

He spread the broken halves and showed the fossil, the little images, turned to stones, curling and perfect, ammonites, molluscs, from a sea long gone, in this afternoon of drought. "Look here." They clustered for the lesson. So impressed by him, gasping. "Nobody has witnessed this before," he said.

It was true. They could not argue with him.

Later, alone a moment, she cut the apple, showed it to Hāna. "Nobody," said Ysabelle, "has witnessed this before."

"But, it's only an apple. Many people—"

"Not *this* apple. Nobody, save you and I, have witnessed the inside of *this* apple, before."

"Oh Ysabelle. You're too clever – I'm afraid—"

"Yes, yes, my darling. So am I."

This is Ernst's house. Against the shadow mountains.

In the evening, after the thick soup and the cheese and wine, his cigars, and looking at the brown mass settling on the sides of the heights. Darkness will come. Cannot be held back. Nobody has witnessed this before, not *this* night.

"Oh, my good friend, yes, Le Ruc. Of course, he has his life's work at St Cailloux. A genius," said Ernst, who had made the evening 'go', speaking, entertaining them, and even, in the case of Ysabelle, perhaps able to teach her somewhat. She was promising, Ysabelle. She might write up his notes for the paper on ammonites of the region. A fine clear hand. Her father was to be congratulated posthumously. "I've mentioned, he's fascinated, Le Ruc, by the surgical procedures of Ancient Egypt. But also of course by the most modern inventions. The X-ray now, what a wonder."

"Seeing inside," Hāna said after, another moment alone, "Nothing is to be private."

But Ernst said, "We can't pretend to be delicate. We're monkeys, not angels. Descended from the apes. Not even *you* are an angel, Ysabelle." He raised his glass, "So your appearance must be deceptive."

"Ernst telling us," Ysabelle, writing later, in her clear hand, "with such costive glee, of a machine which can see the very bones *inside* a body. Nothing is left secret. And the fossils, asleep for centuries. What a pillager he is, raping his way over the foothills."

Taken home, in the trap. Ernst had insisted. Hāna left behind. Ernst. The moon high. They have sacrificed a goat in the woods for rain. The blood has splashed the moon. There are marks on it.

"Ysabelle."

She sits silent, listening. At last she says, "Ernst – you flatter me. But – you frighten me, Ernst. I've never known a man so – powerful – so very *wise*. Even my father."

"Ysabelle, don't be afraid of me. What has my intellect to do with this? You inflame me, Ysabelle."

"No, Ernst. I'm unworthy of you. I couldn't bring myself – you'd be disappointed – how could I bear that? You would come to despise me. Oh, ten years ago, perhaps. Not now."

"Don't suppose, Ysabelle, I'm done with you. I shan't give up."

"Please. My dear friend. You must."

"One kiss."

"No, Ernst. I must be firm. What would you think if I had no honour?"

In the house of white-painted wood, retching into the iron sink, spitting the bitter bile, his wine.

He is tickled now. Soon he will be disillusioned.

"Hāna, can't we fly away on the white angel wings of your hair?"

Ernst's house stands there, at the top of the valley. It is well-maintained and there are many rooms. In the courtyard, the well has sweet water, which has almost run dry. It was once, this house, the domicile of a rich aristocrat. But that was long ago, before men learned they were descended from monkeys.

Shutters hang by the windows, the colour the mountains become in the sinking heat of evening.

Ysabelle looks at this house. Now she is often here. *He* has insisted. She must stay here, tonight. *He* must be the dominant one, not Ysabelle, who is a woman. There are more comforts here. And Hāna need not travel.

Ysabelle does not like the house. It seems to her, everything is held inside this building, confined. Just as the land confines the valley. The clouds confine the rain.

But they – can make rain.

In the midst of arid dry compression, the spring leaps forth. Oh, yes, even once when he was below, doing one of the things he does, something with knives or pins, pushing him from thought, in the upper room, clinging, and that enough—

But tonight, in the hot-brown, baked-closed-shutness of the house. For the cat is away. The cat is away again for one more night.

Let us dance. I walked here, dancing. Never before has anyone witnessed the cream of your thighs, the fleece of silver-gold – I cut a curl, two, three, from this sacred place, as you slept, and the god slept inside you. I – robbed you – did I? Did I? No, not robbery. Only too shy to say. One day I will confess, show you. Ysabelle that you call clever. I clipped the little curls and put them in this locket of silver, snapping shut the face of it upon my souvenir. Its hinges . . . Unhinged.

I have a lock of your hair in my locket, cold between my breasts, or is it boiling hot? I cut the curls so carefully I did not even wake you. Your gardens – your sweet breasts, small as a girl's, your perfect face in its wreathes of angel wings. The centre of your life, your womb, behind its treasury silver-golden gate, soft as ermine.

The house is watching, as Ysabelle climbs towards it, but she thinks that is only Hāna, watching from the upstairs window, where she has strewn perfume in the bed.

Night after night, you loosed your hair. That greater river – dry, yet feeling wet to my thirst. But here there is no smell of cherries ripening. This house of his smells masculine, except for the sanctuary of your room, with the wild flowers in the vase, and the chocolate standing in its pot. You are my cherry-fruit.

"He went to that awful – to the asylum."

"St Cailloux? St Stones . . ."

"That man – Le Ruc – Ernst is intrigued by the – what does he say? – the *so-interesting* patients. By the operations Le Ruc discusses with him and wants to carry out. These disgusting things he says the physicians of the pharoahs did—"

"Why are you talking of *him*?"

"I don't know."

"It's because we are here. Tomorrow, after he comes back – make some excuse . . . I know, I shall forget my basket. Then you must bring it to me. Such a womanly thing. How can I manage without it."

"He'll say I should send Gittel."

"*Bring* Gittel. She and Mireio love gossiping."

"Perhaps. He's irritable. He calls you *Juno*. What is that?"

"The wife of the king of the gods in Ancient Rome. She was frosty, sour. A nag – that dreadful thing women do because men won't listen."

"Then he's asked you for favours?"

"Oh—"

"And you put him off. Ysabelle!"

"What? Do you want me to say yes?"

"No – *no* – but he's so proud—"

"He's a monster. He'll grow tired of hunting me."

"He has begun to dislike you. Tonight he said to me, *Be careful what you say to her.*"

"Then – I must flatter him more. Oh God," said Ysabelle, "I'd even accept his caresses, if it were the only way."

They sat in silence. Why was the silence so strange? Of course, here there was no nightingale.

"Perhaps," said Ysabelle, "I can contrive to put some stupid pretty woman in his way, one that won't recoil."

"Sometimes . . ." said Hāna, "when I was only ten, I had little breasts, and he tried and tried to see them. When I wouldn't, he made up a story about me to our father. I don't know what Ernst said, but my father had my nurse tie my hands together every night for three months. She used to cry as she did it. But she'd never explain."

Ysabelle got up. Before she could prevent herself, she retched violently. Hāna rushed to her. At the touch of Hāna the sickness was gone.

"Dionysos," said Ysabelle, "the god of wine and madness, the breaker of chains – do you see sometimes, in the woods, the pine cones piled up together into the form of another cone, the drawing of an eye on a tree or rock – that's the Eye of the Mother, whom Dionysos sometimes represents. And they killed two goats, and they poured wine. Let's run away, Hāna."

"How can we?" said Hāna.

It was true. They were immovable, fixed. One to the man, his life. The other to a place. They did not properly see this, how they had been warped to fit and nailed home. And yet escape was closed by a deep invisible wall.

Ysabelle thought, Perhaps he'll die. An accident, thrown from the trap as the pony bolts at a flash of lightning, clap of moistureless thunder from the mountains. Or too much drink, a haemorrhage.

But Hāna kisses her breasts and Ysabelle melts like wax, and flows down into the rose-red fire.

Their clothes thrown away, murmuring in the stillness, cries choked back, not even a nightingale to shield them with her noisy song.

Hinges. Unhinged.

A locket? A door? Madness?

The story, told locally, clandestinely, was that Ernst returned unexpectedly, after all, that night – perhaps a quarrel with his friend? The house was in darkness and silence, and so he went up quietly to bed, which does not seem very like him, one would imagine actually he would make a disturbance, rouse everyone up, want things done. Or could he have been suspicious?

Passing – on tiptoe? Surely not – the door to Hāna's room, he heard them whispering, and the creak of the wooden bed.

He flung the door wide on its hinges and found them naked, hair down, uncorsetted, undone – his sister Hāna and Madame Ysabelle.

This is not the case.

Ernst rode home in the trap at about nine in the morning, from his country breakfast with Le Ruc. There had been no quarrel, for Ernst and Le Ruc enjoyed a perfect mutual respect and approbation, tinctured pleasantly for each by a wisp of well-concealed tolerance; he for Ernst's slight blindness to the essentials of science, since Ernst was so bound up in theory, nature and the world; Ernst for Le Ruc's slight blindness to theory, nature and the world, since Le Ruc was absorbed utterly by science.

Ernst was not in an ill mood. Only the idea of Ysabelle's having stayed with his sister that night was a small but tart irritant, that had begun to work on him directly he brought the trap on to the rough road, and saw her house before him under the mountains.

Ysabelle was a tease, or a fool. He was beginning, frankly, to notice the failings she had pointed out to him in herself, the elements that made her, she said, unworthy of him. Her "fear" of him he was not, now, so certain of. For fear, to women, was of course a powerful aphrodisiac. It had seemed to him, some four days previously, that this might be the real fount of her desires – to be physically mastered. And so, entering her home on the pretext of requiring eggs from Mireio's hens, he had ended by pressing Ysabelle harshly to the wall of her white wooden sitting room, brutally kissing her mouth, penetrating it with his tongue, while with his free hand he mounded her skirt and squeezed, through layers of clothing, her most interesting feature.

She had somehow got away from him, and stood panting, her face as white as a china plate, her eyes inflamed. This might be arousal, and he approached her again, at which she hoarsely said, "I won't be responsible for any harm." And pulled a fire-iron up from the stone hearth.

"If you keep on like this," he said, "you'll put me off."

"Get away from me," she cried, like a peasant. But then she shook herself and said, putting down the nasty-looking implement, "Excuse me, Ernst. But I'm not for you. I can't – expose myself to the tragedy of losing you, once you tire of me. You know how women are. This sort of liaison – will mean so much more to me."

"I'd think, from another woman, this was a demand for a bourgeois marriage."

Ysabelle threw back her head and laughed. She was hysterical and unappealing. Women were unhinged, one knew this, at certain times more so, and she was approaching that age when they were at their worst.

Why had he fancied her? Well, this was a barren spot.

He himself laughed shortly. "Then, good morning."

Outside, Mireio came sidling with a basket of eggs. It seemed to him she leered at his reddened mouth. Doubtless that other bitch thought she could get more out of him by frustrating him, but he was not of that sort. Besides, if ever he were to marry, he would want youth, for sons, and some money, too.

His annoyance with Ysabelle did not abate as, mentally, he cast her off. He supposed this was a sexual matter. She had led him on, now would not accomodate him as she had hinted she would.

He did not like her. No. He would rather she did not come any more into his house. And Hāna must be warned. Hāna was too trusting, and such women as Ysabelle were not to be trusted. Particularly by their own sex, for women were faithless, and nowhere more so than with each other, filling each other's heads with idiocy, always jealous, treacherous.

Seeing presently his own country house from the trap, Ernst thought that perhaps they might go back to the city. Le Ruc could be invited to stay there, in a proper flat, say, with amenities, and efficient servants. Or perhaps not, for Hāna might well make eyes at him, as she had done before with their few male visitors, afterwards making out they had frightened her – familiar tale!

Some way still from Ernst's house, the pony, unsatisfactorily also his property, cast a shoe.

Ernst got out, and stood cursing, damning the beast. Then he left it there, and went on foot towards his home, where Gittel must be sent to fetch a man for the horse from the village.

So, he approached, walking, in a morning loud with bird song – even the nightgales that, here, had not used their voices through the night. A church bell was tolling too, in the next valley. This was for a burial.

He saw them in a little nook, between the wall and a leaning wild cedar. Hāna's hair was partly unpinned, but Ysabelle was dressed for her journey home along the upper valley. She wore her dark gown, as usual. She looked quite conventional, and conceivably, if he had met her like this, returning from the visit, as he would have done, a minute later, he would have thought her in fact very plain, of very little importance to himself.

But now she moved to his sister Hāna, and concealed yet not concealed, down on the road, unannounced by the wheels of the trap and the pony's homecoming trot, he watched them. He saw how they grew together, breast to breast, their arms around each other's necks, thigh to thigh, lip to lip. They were an image and an image in a mirror, clasped.

Really, it was not much. Women kissed. Friends might kiss. And yet, this *passion*. Smoke rose from their skins, the air about them trembled as later in the day the heat of the drought would make it do.

Ernst ran. He ran straight at them. They heard him then, his gallop over the track, his blundering rush across the little scattered stones, and the dust rose round him. He was a whirlwind. He thrust them apart as they were themselves thrusting apart. Ysabelle fell back into the bole of the tree, slipped down it, sat in the dust, staring. Hāna he slapped, once, twice, across her face.

He was roaring, like a lion, like a bull—

His words – were there any words? Oh yes, jargon of streets and alleys, epithets old as humankind. But words? Were there any? Are there any, for such rage?

Hāna attempted to speak. He raised his hand to strike her again and Ysabelle, staggering up, caught his arm, hung on it, and so he flung her off, sprawling again, and this time heard her thin quick cry of pain.

Now language assembled itself. Not whores – madwomen. They were mad. Their brains – diseased.

He swept up Hāna and bore her off. Suddenly, it was so very visible, the differences in their size and strength, as if he and she were beings of two unlike species.

Her arms outstretched, she called to Ysabelle – "No, don't try to stop him—" And Ysabelle, her knee twisted by the violence of her fall to boneless water, could only lie on her side, as if indolent, observing this, observing Hāna borne along in a cloud of dust and hair, into the brown masculine house that smelled of maleness and cigars. While another cloud, purple as Hāna's ribbons, covered the screech of the sun.

Ysabelle walked home. That is, she limped, crawled. She fainted three times, the pain was so great. Finally she dropped on the road before her own house, and Mireio, who saw it, brought Jean, who carried Ysabelle inside. Thus, both women were carried into a house by a man, and helpless.

"I fell, and twisted my leg."

This was exact, if not decorous. Or true.

As she lay on her bed, her knee packed with the poultices of herbs, tightly bound, and beating like a drum, sometimes leaning to vomit in a chamber-pot, Ysabelle turned over in her mind what she should do. But she was feverish, and could not be sure what had happened. How could Ernst have deduced, from their parting embrace, so much? Yet he had. Indeed, it could not be denied. Of course, any woman who rejected him must be – unnatural. Already condemned. Hopeless.

She would have gone to his door, limping, crawling, but the girl, Gittel, had run out. Gittel, terrified, heaving Ysabelle up and bending under her weight like a young willow. Her thick accent: "Go – go, Madame. She'll calm him. She always does, the four years I'm with them."

And Gittel had pushed Ysabelle away. And from the male house, no sound issued. The birds sang on. The clouds passed intermittantly across the sun. Eclipses.

It was Ysabelle he would condemn. She was a witch who had seduced—

Hāna, so ignorant, naïve, unable to judge, to see the deadly snare—

He would reprimand and instruct. He might be cruel. He might strike her again, and lock her up in her room. Then he would come here. Ysabelle, her brain white with the lights that splashed over her eyes, formulated what she must do. "Oh Ernst – Ernst – after our last time together – I thought you loathed me. Don't you know how women sometimes *pretend* – so foolish – she let me, out of pity – she let me make-believe – that she was *you*!"

And then, stroking him, begging him to take her, his stinking filthy body, his disgusting tongue, and worse, the rest – the rest. But Ysabelle would have it all, she would do anything. For that way, she could protect – she would even take his member, as she had heard tell a prostitute – a *mad* prostitute presumably – would do, take it into her mouth – and choking down her revulsion, moaning as if with joy, become his utter slave.

She would die for him, if she must.

Hāna . . .

Mireio said to Jean that she thought that bad man, Monsieur Ernst, had led Ysabelle a dance, and cast her off. No matter. If there was a pregnancy, it could be dealt with . . . Mireio was skilled. But after all the good food they had wasted on him – the devil.

Jean shrugged. None of this concerned him. A little over a hundred years before, these rich people would have been put under a honed blade. That would have settled their minds wonderfully.

Ysabelle tossed between oblivion and awareness. She thought the pillow was Hāna, because some of Hāna's sweet scent had been left there. She thought the acid voluptuous aroma of the cherries, plucked by Mireio, or bleeding in the grass, was the sharp catch of Hāna's personal perfume in the moments of her ecstasy.

In her fever, Ysabelle spasmed in a deathly pleasure.

When the fever broke, pale and shuddering, Ysabelle sat by the window.

The nightingale still sang. She heard it all night long, as the swelling of her leg waned with the moon.

"No rain," said Mireio.

Seven days passed, and then, Ysabelle went to her writing table, and began to try to compose a letter to Ernst. It was to be a love letter, confessing she could not bear not to see him. That his disapproval broke her heart. He had witnessed her ultimate foolishness, kissing his sister, locked in a female fantasy that Hāna was himself. Would he forgive her, come to her? She did not want marriage, never had, but to lose his regard – it burnt her away, like the summer leaves.

As she was writing this letter, over and over, attempting to make it right, Ernst's letter to Ysabelle arrived, along with a package, its contents also wrapped over and over, in expensive paper from the city.

"My dear Friend," he began, "Ysabelle: I know what worry you must have endured, and as soon as the burden upon me was eased, I sat down to write to you. We both of us care for Hāna so deeply. Let me assure you at once that now the terrible insanity which overwhelmed her has been alleviated. Could you see her, as I did, two days ago, look into her face, clear of all shadow and every frightful thing, you would know, as I do, that this was for the best.

"You will understand, that morning I calmed her as well as I might. Luckily, I keep some opiates by me, for use in certain of my experiments. These rendered Hāna her first peace, and after that I was able to convey her to St Cailloux. Here my friend, Le Ruc, took charge of her at once.

"She had by now awoken, and on feeling her pulse, which was so rapid, he declared immediately this was enough to inform him such a passionate heart was unnatural, and could do her only harm. He confided to me that, in the Dark Ages, she would have been supposed possessed by the Devil. But he is a man of science. The 'Devil' is merely in her mind, its disorder. He acted before nightfall.

"I will not describe to you the operation, the details might alarm you, and besides you would not understand it. It involves certain nerve fibres in the frontal portion of the brain. A delicate pruning away. My magnificent friend, he made the tender incision. He is adept, and although Hāna was his very first subject, the success with her has made him sanguine for the help of others.

"It was a practice in Ancient Egypt, studied by him closely. Curious to think, that when they lay Hāna in the tomb at last, she too will bear this same scar upon her forehead and her skull, as did those persons in that land of pyramids.

"Ah, Ysabelle. Dear sister. If you could see her. She is like a little child again. Everything is new to her. The flight of a bird startles, even that. She does not move from her chair. A picture of repose, her drooping head, her folded hands. Le Ruc says she does not quite know me – I fear she would not know you at all. But when I ask her to smile for me, she does. She will be well cared for, there. And though I must soon be gone from this country, Le Ruc will take thought for her like his own. As indeed, he does for all his charges in that place.

"A note on my gift, which accompanies this letter. You will have realized, it is her hair, which of course, for such medical attention, had to be cut off entirely. All the shining locks. It seemed to me you might value them, dear Ysabelle, as you did when you were to her her closest and most intimate friend.

"Beyond this, my kindest wishes for your continued good health and the ending of your local drought.

"Your brother, if so I may call myself:

"Ernst."

In her diary, her Book, Ysabelle wrote, "I sent for the old man, the charcoal burner they call *Doggy*. Having given him some coins, he went for me to the place, which he names Wolf Valley. He was the only one I could trust. He, and his kind, keep away from the village. He has under his shirt an amulet, dried sticks twisted in a knot. Near dawn, he came back. He had said there he was an old servant, and asked for her. Expectedly, they would not let him in, but said she was in the care of Dr Le Ruc, and he need have no fears. When Doggy said, as I told him to, that he hoped she was better, they laughed. He caught a glimpse of others, at some windows. Their heads were shaved. One was wrapped up tight, and seemed to have no arms. The old man was brave. They hate that place."

Under this Ysabelle, or something, has scrawled in a running jagged line:

Heart burst stifle and drown in blood

Perhaps a curse, or a wish for self.

There are records from the asylum. One may see them, if the tactic is carried out properly. There is a note on a woman, called only by her Christian name, to "protect" her. "Hāna, the prey of uncontrollable, obscene and perverse desires, a danger to herself and others." The operation, "The last possible resort" and "practised among the ancients", was a "success".

Before the final page, Ysabelle sets out for herself some instructions on how best to hang herself. The strong beam in the lower room that faces the afternoon glare of the mountains, and will hold her weight, which, she admits, is much less, as she cannot eat. Mireio and Jean will be sent away with a settlement of money, as the last page also explains. The hair, a dead thing, still with its stranded mauve ribbons that she herself had helped, that morning of the ending, to tie there, is to be strongly plaited, not as before, woven, not with silk, but some coarse twine, to make it sure. And she will be naked, lest the rigidity of her clothes impedes her.

Ysabelle understands, from her reading, that few people die quickly when hanged. They are choked and strangle. In this way, the hair will throttle her, and as she kicks and gags in instinctive physical panic, her soul will remember that it is Hāna who is killing her, as she has killed Hāna. She affirms she will wear the silver locket with Hāna's sexual hair. She has polished the metal.

She says, as if she has forgotten it was mentioned before, and as she says again, too, on the last page, that she has heard of a goat being sacrificed to bring rain.

After that, she says the nightingale has flown away.

Then she says she has finished.

After which, there is the last page.

There are some further pages after that, blank, obviously.

Inevitably, one fills them with the mind – the presumed hanging, the woman choking and kicking, rocked violently from side to side in the white vacant empty house, then only turning, slowing, still, a pendant, while the mountains and the sun stare in. After which, as it seems almost supernaturally, fire catches the house, and burns it to the ground, leaving only the puns – St Cailloux – of the lower stone floors and stone chimneys and the stone hearths, and the stone under which the book is, until the old man, maybe Doggy, fetches it out and brings it here, to me.

In a year's time, a peasant, travelling up the lane on foot, will pause by the ruin of the house. The land by then will have been sold off, but no one, as yet, come to restore or change it. The untended cherry trees will be leafy yet, although one or two will have succumbed to the ivy, with here and there a green young fruit hard among the foliage.

The man, a stranger, will not be troubled by any stories of the region, and going into the ruin, will poke about, since sometimes, in this way, he has found useful things others have overlooked. He will find, however, nothing, and so sit down by a stone, part of one, now collapsed, chimney. He will eat his olives and bread. Then he will fall asleep, for the sun will be again very hot.

When he wakes it will be to great alarm. Across from him, in the wild grass, a small fire will have started. He must leap up to put it out, and do so quickly. For in this weather, another summer drought, fire is the fiercest enemy.

This man is canny. When once he has dealt with the danger, he will find a soreness at his chest, and looking down, where hangs the little silver cross given him as a boy, he will come to see at once what has happened, for he has heard of it before.

An hour after, in the village, he will tell his tale over his wine, and so unravel the mystery of Madame Ysabelle's house. The truth will not make any difference to her burial place, in fact, will only consolidate her rights to holy ground, since no one has generally told the plan of suicide written in her diary.

Now they will say without compunction, that some object – a glass, or mirror, carelessly left by the departing servants – caught the harsh light from the mountains, and cast it off in a ray against the wooden wall. The concentration of this burning-glass presently sent the tinder of the drought-dry house up in a conflagration.

Most of that will be true. Not quite all. For it was no picture or glass that caused the focus of an incendiary ray, the lighting of a death pyre. It was the polished silver locket that lay pendant on the breast of Ysabelle's hanged corpse, once she had stopped moving, once she hung quite still, a pendant herself, naked silver on a silver chain of hair, from the beam above.

I have a lock of your hair.
I cut
It from you as you slept.
I kissed you there,
Where
The scissors met.
You never noticed it had gone.
It is all I have of you,
Your hair.
Blonde spirals in
A silver locket.

NEIL GAIMAN

Closing Time

NEIL GAIMAN HORROR-HOSTED the Fox Channel's *13 Nights of Fear* during the fortnight before Hallowe'en 2004 and got to introduce movies from inside a coffin. He thought it was cool.

His 2002 novel *American Gods* won science fiction's Hugo Award and horror's Bram Stoker Award, while *Coraline*, a dark fantasy for children which he had been writing for a decade, was a huge success on both sides of the Atlantic and even managed to beat its predecessor in the awards stakes.

On the illustrated front, his first *Sandman* graphic novel in seven years, entitled *Endless Nights*, is published by DC Comics and illustrated by seven different artists; *1602* is a new alternate history mini-series from Marvel, and he has collaborated with artist Dave McKean on the children's picture book *The Wolves in the Walls*.

As well as all the above, the *New York Times* best-selling author has somehow also found the time to make a short vampire film entitled *A Short Film About John Bolton*, and he has recently started writing a new novel, with the working title of *Anansi Boys*.

"'Closing Time' is set in a real place," Gaiman reveals. "It was called the Troy Club, and I still run into people who used to drink there (including the editor of this anthology). It was written for Michael Chabon's *McSweeney's Mammoth Book of Thrilling Tales*. I asked him what genre story he'd like, and he asked for a ghost story, and since many good ghost stories are also club stories I decided to set it in one.

"I set out to write an M. R. James ghost story, and wound up having written something more like a Robert Aickman strange story."

THERE ARE STILL CLUBS in London. Old ones, and mock-old, with elderly sofas and crackling fireplaces, newspapers, and traditions of speech or of silence, and new clubs, the Groucho and its many knock-offs, where actors and journalists go to be seen, to drink, to enjoy their glowering solitude, or even to talk. I have friends in both kinds of club, but am not myself a member of any club in London, not any more.

Years ago, half a lifetime, when I was a young journalist, I joined a club. It existed solely to take advantage of the licensing laws of the day, which forced all pubs to stop serving drinks at eleven p.m., closing time. This club, the Diogenes, was a one-room affair located above a record shop in a narrow alley just off the Tottenham Court Road. It was owned by a cheerful, chubby, alcohol-fuelled woman called Nora, who would tell anyone who asked and even if they didn't that she'd called the club the Diogenes, darling, because she was still looking for an honest man. Up a narrow flight of steps, and, at Nora's whim, the door to the club would be open, or not. It kept irregular hours.

It was a place to go once the pubs closed, that was all it ever was, and despite Nora's doomed attempts to serve food or even to send out a cheery monthly newsletter to all her club's members reminding them that the club now served food, that was all it would ever be. I was saddened several years ago when I heard that Nora had died; and I was struck, to my surprise, with a real sense of desolation last month when, on a visit to England, walking down that alley, I tried to figure out where the Diogenes Club had been, and looked first in the wrong place, then saw the faded green cloth awnings shading the windows of a tapas restaurant above a mobile phone shop, and, painted on them, a stylized man in a barrel. It seemed almost indecent, and it set me remembering.

There were no fireplaces in the Diogenes Club, and no armchairs either, but still, stories were told there.

Most of the people drinking there were men, although women passed through from time to time, and Nora had recently acquired a glamorous permanent fixture in the shape of a deputy, a blonde Polish emigré who called everybody "darlink" and who helped herself to drinks whenever she got behind the bar. When she got drunk, she would tell us that she was by rights a countess, back in Poland, and swear us all to secrecy.

There were actors and writers, or course. Film editors, broadcasters, police inspectors and drunks. People who did not keep fixed hours. People who stayed out too late, or who did not want to go home. Some nights there might be a dozen people there, or more. Other nights I'd wander in and I'd be the only person there – on those occasions I'd buy myself a single drink, drink it down, and then leave.

That night, it was raining, and there were four of us in the club after midnight.

Nora and her deputy were sitting up at the bar, working on their sitcom. It was about a chubby-but-cheerful woman who owned a drinking club, and her scatty deputy, an aristocratic foreign blonde who made amusing English mistakes. It would be like *Cheers*, Nora used to tell people. She named the comical Jewish landlord after me. Sometimes they would ask me to read a script.

The rest of us were sitting over by the window: an actor named Paul (commonly known as Paul-the-actor, to stop people confusing him with Paul-the-police-inspector or Paul-the-struck-off-plastic-surgeon, who were also regulars), a computer gaming magazine editor named Martyn, and me. We knew each other vaguely, and the three of us sat at a table by the window and watched the rain come down, misting and blurring the lights of the alley.

There was another man there, older by far than any of the three of us. He was cadaverous, and grey-haired and painfully thin, and he sat alone in the corner and nursed a single whisky. The elbows of his tweed jacket were patched with brown leather, I remember that quite vividly. He did not talk to us, or read, or do anything. He just sat, looking out at the rain and the alley beneath, and, sometimes, he sipped his whisky without any visible pleasure.

It was almost midnight, and Paul and Martyn and I had started telling ghost stories. I had just finished telling them a sworn-true ghostly account from my school days: the tale of the Green Hand. It had been an article of faith at my prep school that there was a disembodied, luminous hand that was seen, from time to time, by unfortunate schoolboys. If you saw the Green Hand you would die soon after. Fortunately, none of us were ever unlucky enough to encounter it, but there were sad tales of boys there before our time, boys who saw the Green Hand and whose thirteen-year-old hair had turned white overnight. According to school legend they were taken to the sanatorium, where they would expire after a week or so without ever being able to utter another word.

"Hang on," said Paul-the-actor. "If they never uttered another word, how did anyone know they'd seen the Green Hand? I mean, they could have seen anything."

As a boy, being told the stories, I had not thought to ask this, and now it was pointed out to me it did seem somewhat problematic.

"Perhaps they wrote something down," I suggested, a bit lamely.

We batted it about for a while, and agreed that the Green Hand was a most unsatisfactory sort of ghost. Then Paul told us a true story about a friend of his who had picked up a hitchhiker, and dropped her off at a place she said was her house, and when he went back the next morning, it turned out to be a cemetery. I mentioned that exactly the same thing had happened to a friend of mine as well. Martyn said that it had not only happened to a friend of his, but, because the hitchhiking girl looked so cold, the friend had lent her his coat, and the next morning, in the cemetery, he found his coat all neatly folded on her grave.

Martyn went and got another round of drinks, and we wondered why all these ghost-women were zooming around the country all night and hitchhiking home, and Martyn said that probably living hitchhikers these days were the exception, not the rule.

And then one of us said, "I'll tell you a true story, if you like. It's a story I've never told a living soul. It's true – it happened to me, not to a friend of mine – but I don't know if it's a ghost story. It probably isn't."

This was over twenty years ago. I have forgotten so

many things, but I have not forgotten that night, nor how it ended.

This is the story that was told that night, in the Diogenes Club.

I was nine years old, or thereabouts, in the late 1960s, and I was attending a small private school not far from my home. I was only at that school less than a year – long enough to take a dislike to the school's owner, who had bought the school in order to close it, and to sell the prime land on which it stood to property developers, which, shortly after I left, she did.

For a long time – a year or more – after the school closed the building stood empty before it was finally demolished and replaced by offices. Being a boy, I was also a burglar of sorts, and one day before it was knocked down, curious, I went back there. I wriggled through a half-opened window and walked through empty classrooms that still smelled of chalk dust. I took only one thing from my visit, a painting I had done in Art of a little house with a red doorknocker like a devil or an imp. It had my name on it, and it was up on a wall. I took it home.

When the school was still open I walked home each day, through the town, then down a dark road cut through sandstone hills and all grown over with trees, and past an abandoned gatehouse. Then there would be light, and the road would go past fields, and finally I would be home.

Back then there were so many old houses and estates, Victorian relics that stood in an empty half-life awaiting the bulldozers that would transform them and their ramshackle grounds into blandly identical landscapes of desirable modern residences, every house neatly arranged side by side around roads that went nowhere.

The other children I encountered on my way home were, in my memory, always boys. We did not know each other, but, like guerrillas in occupied territory, we would exchange information. We were scared of adults, not each other. We did not have to know each other to run in twos or threes or in packs.

The day that I'm thinking of, I was walking home from school, and I met three boys in the road where it was at its darkest. They were looking for something in the ditches and the hedges and the weed-choked place in front of the abandoned gatehouse. They were older than me.

"What are you looking for?"

The tallest of them, a beanpole of a boy, with dark hair and a sharp face, said "Look!" He held up several ripped-in-half-pages from what must have been a very, very old pornographic magazine. The girls were all in black and white, and their hairstyles looked like the ones my great-aunts had in old photographs. The magazine had been ripped up, and fragments of it had blown all over the road and into the abandoned gatehouse front garden.

I joined in the paper chase. Together, the three of us retrieved almost a whole copy of *The Gentleman's Relish* from that dark place. Then we climbed over a wall, into a deserted apple-orchard, and looked at it. Naked women from a long time ago. There is a smell, of fresh apples, and of rotten apples mouldering down into cider, which even today brings back the idea of the forbidden to me.

The smaller boys, who were still bigger than I was, were called Simon and Douglas, and the tall one, who might have been as old as fifteen, was called Jamie. I wondered if they were brothers. I did not ask.

When we had all looked at the magazine, they said, "We're going to hide this in our special place. Do you want to come along? You mustn't tell, if you do. You mustn't tell anyone."

They made me spit on my palm, and they spat on theirs, and we pressed our hands together.

Their special place was an abandoned metal water tower, in a field by the entrance to the lane near to where I lived. We climbed a high ladder. The tower was painted a dull green on the outside, and inside it was orange with rust that covered the floor and the walls. There was a wallet on the floor with no money in it, only some cigarette cards. Jamie showed them to me: each card held a painting of a cricketer from a long time ago. They put the pages of the magazine down on the floor of the water tower, and the wallet on top of it.

Then Douglas said, "I say we go back to the Swallows next."

My house was not far from the Swallows, a sprawling manor house set back from the road. It had been owned, my father had told me once, by the Earl of Tenterden, but when he had died his son, the new earl, had simply closed the place up. I had wandered to the edges of the grounds, but had not gone further in. It did not feel abandoned. The gardens were too well-cared for, and where there were gardens there were gardeners. Somewhere there had to be an adult.

I told them this.

Jamie said, "Bet there's not. Probably just someone who comes in and cuts the grass once a month or something. You're not scared, are you? We've been there hundreds of times. Thousands."

Of course, I was scared, and of course I said that I was not. We went up the main drive, until we reached the main gates. They were closed, and we squeezed beneath the bars to get in.

Rhododendron bushes lined the drive. Before we got to the house there was what I took to be a groundskeeper's cottage, and beside it on the grass were some rusting metal cages, big enough to hold a hunting dog, or a boy. We walked past them, up to a horseshoe-shaped drive and right up to the front door of the Swallows. We peered inside, looking in the windows, but seeing nothing. It was too dark inside.

We slipped around the house, into a rhododendron thicket and out again, into some kind of fairyland. It was a magical grotto, all rocks and delicate ferns and odd, exotic plants I'd never seen before: plants with purple leaves, and leaves like fronds, and small half-hidden flowers like jewels. A tiny stream wound through it, a rill of water running from rock to rock.

Douglas said, "I'm going to wee-wee in it." It was very matter of fact. He walked over to it, pulled down his shorts and urinated in the stream, splashing on the rocks. The other boys did it too, both of them pulling out their penises and standing beside him to piss into the stream.

I was shocked. I remember that. I suppose I was shocked by the joy they took in this, or just by the way they were doing something like that in such a special place, spoiling the clear water and the magic of the place; making it into a toilet. It seemed wrong.

When they were done, they did not put their penises away. They shook them. They pointed them at me. Jamie had hair growing at the base of his.

"We're cavaliers," said Jamie. "Do you know what that means?"

I knew about the English Civil War, Cavaliers (wrong but romantic) versus Roundheads (right but repulsive), but I didn't think that was what he was talking about. I shook my head.

"It means our willies aren't circumcised," he explained. "Are you a cavalier or a roundhead?"

I knew what they meant now. I muttered, "I'm a round-head."

"Show us. Go on. Get it out."

"No. It's none of your business."

For a moment, I thought things were going to get nasty, but then Jamie laughed, and put his penis away, and the others did the same. They told dirty jokes to each other then, jokes I really didn't understand at all, for all that I was a bright child, but I heard them and remembered them, and several weeks later was almost expelled from school for telling one of them to a boy who went home and told it to his parents.

The joke had the word *fuck* in. That was the first time I ever heard the word, in a dirty joke in a fairy grotto.

The principal called my parents into the school, after I got in trouble, and said that I'd said something so bad they could not repeat it, not even to tell my parents what I'd done.

My mother asked me, when they got home that night.

"Fuck," I said.

"You must never, ever say that word," said my mother. She said this very firmly, and quietly, and for my own good. "That is the worst word anyone can say." I promised her that I wouldn't.

But after, amazed at the power a single word could have, I would whisper it to myself, when I was alone.

In the grotto, that autumn afternoon after school, the three big boys told jokes and they laughed and they laughed, and I laughed too, although I did not understand any of what they were laughing about.

We moved on from the grotto. Out into the formal gardens, and over a small bridge that crossed a pond; we crossed it nervously, because it was out in the open, but we could see huge goldfish in the blackness of the pond below, which made it worthwhile. Then Jamie led Douglas and Simon and me down a gravel path into some woodland.

Unlike the gardens, the woods were abandoned and unkempt. They felt like there was no one around. The path was grown-over. It led between trees, and then, after a while, into a clearing.

In the clearing was a little house.

It was a play-house, built perhaps forty years earlier for a child, or for children. The windows were Tudor-style, leaded and criss-crossed into diamonds. The roof was mock-Tudor. A stone path led straight from where we were to the front door.

Together, we walked up the path to the door.

Hanging from the door was a metal knocker. It was painted crimson, and had been cast in the shape of some kind of imp, some kind of grinning pixie or demon, cross-legged, hanging by its hands from a hinge. Let me see . . . how can I describe this best: it wasn't a *good* thing. The expression on its face, for starters. I found myself wondering what kind of a person would hang something like that on a playroom door.

It frightened me, there in that clearing, with the dusk gathering under the trees. I walked away from the house, back to a safe distance, and the others followed me.

"I think I have to go home now," I said.

It was the wrong thing to say. The three of them turned and laughed and jeered at me, called me pathetic, called me a baby. They weren't scared of the house, they said.

"I dare you!" said Jamie. "I dare you to knock on the door."

I shook my head.

"If you don't knock on the door," said Douglas, "you're too much of a baby ever to play with us again."

I had no desire ever to play with them again. They seemed like occupants of a land I was not yet ready to enter. But still, I did not want them to think me a baby.

"Go on. *We're* not scared," said Simon.

I try to remember the tone of voice he used. Was he frightened, too, and covering it with bravado? Or was he amused? It's been so long. I wish I knew.

I walked slowly back up the flagstone path to the house. I reached up, grabbed the grinning imp in my right hand and banged it hard against the door.

Or rather, I tried to bang it hard, just to show the other three that I was not afraid at all. That I was not afraid of anything. But something happened, something I had not expected, and the knocker hit the door with a muffled sort of a thump.

"Now you have to go inside!" shouted Jamie. He was excited. I could hear it. I found myself wondering if they had known about this place already, before we came. If I was the first person they had brought there.

But I did not move.

"*You* go in," I said. "I knocked on the door. I did it like you said. Now *you* have to go inside. I dare you. I dare *all* of you."

I wasn't going in. I was perfectly certain of that. Not then. Not ever. I'd felt something move, I'd felt the knocker *twist* under my hand as I'd banged that grinning imp down on the door. I was not so old that I would deny my own senses.

They said nothing. They did not move.

Then, slowly, the door fell open. Perhaps they thought that I, standing by the door, had pushed it open. Perhaps they thought that I'd jarred it when I knocked. But I hadn't. I was certain of it. It opened because it was ready.

I should have run, then. My heart was pounding in my chest. But the devil was in me, and instead of running I looked at the three big boys at the bottom of the path, and I simply said, "Or are you scared?"

They walked up the path towards the little house.

"It's getting dark," said Douglas.

Then the three boys walked past me, and one by one, reluctantly perhaps, they entered the playhouse. A white face turned to look at me as they went into that room, to ask why I wasn't following them in, I'll bet. But as Simon, who was the last of them, walked in, the door banged shut behind them, and I swear to God I did not touch it.

The imp grinned down at me from the wooden door, a vivid splash of crimson in the grey gloaming.

I walked around to the side of the playhouse and peered in through all the windows, one by one, into the dark and empty room. Nothing moved in there. I wondered if the other three were inside hiding from me, pressed against the wall, trying their damnedest to stifle their giggles. I wondered if it was a big-boy game.

I didn't know. I couldn't tell.

I stood there in the courtyard of the playhouse, while the sky got darker, just waiting. The moon rose after a while, a big autumn moon the colour of honey.

And then, after a while, the door opened, and nothing came out.

Now I was alone in the glade, as alone as if there had never been anyone else there at all. An owl hooted, and I realized that I was free to go. I turned and walked away, following a different path out of the glade, always keeping my distance from the main house. I climbed a fence in the moonlight, ripping the seat of my school shorts, and I walked – not ran, I didn't need to run – across a field of barley stubble, and over a stile, and into a flinty lane that would take me, if I followed it far enough, all the way to my house.

And soon enough, I was home.

My parents had not been worried, although they were irritated by the orange rust-dust on my clothes, by the rip in my shorts. "Where were you, anyway?" my mother asked.

"I went for a walk," I said. "I lost track of time."

And that was where we left it.

It was almost two in the morning. The Polish countess had already gone. Now Nora began, noisily, to collect up the glasses and ashtrays, and to wipe down the bar. "*This* place is haunted," she said, cheerfully. "Not that it's ever bothered me. I like a bit of company, darlings. If I didn't, I wouldn't have opened the club. Now, don't you have homes to go to?"

We said our goodnights to Nora and she made each of us kiss her on her cheek, and she closed the door of the Diogenes club behind us. We walked down the narrow steps past the record shop, down into the alley and back into civilisation.

The underground had stopped running hours ago, but there were always night buses, and cabs still out there for those who could afford them. (I couldn't. Not in those days.)

The Diogenes Club itself closed several years later, finished off by Nora's cancer, and, I suppose, by the easy availability of late-night alcohol once the English licensing laws were changed. But I rarely went back after that night.

"Was there ever," asked Paul-the-actor, as we hit the street, "any news of those three boys? Did you see them again? Or were they reported as missing?"

"Neither," said the storyteller. "I mean, I never saw them again. And there was no local manhunt for three missing boys. Or if there was, I never heard about it."

"Is the playhouse still there?" asked Martyn.

"I don't know," admitted the storyteller.

"Well," said Martyn, as we reached Tottenham Court Road, and headed for the night bus stop, "I for one do not believe a word of it."

There were four of us, not three, out on the street long after closing time. I should have mentioned that before. There was still one of us who had not spoken, the elderly man with the leather elbow-patches, who had left the club when the three of us had left. And now he spoke for the first time.

"I believe it," he said, mildly. His voice was frail, almost apologetic. "I cannot explain it, but I believe it. Jamie died, you know, not long after father did. It was Douglas who wouldn't go back, who sold the old place. He wanted them to tear it all down. But they kept the house itself, the Swallows. They weren't going to knock *that* down. I imagine that everything else must be gone by now."

It was a cold night, and the rain still spat occasional drizzle. I shivered, but only because I was cold.

"Those cages you mentioned," he said. "By the driveway. I haven't thought of them in fifty years. When we were bad he'd lock us up in them. We must have been bad a great deal, eh? Very naughty, naughty boys."

He was looking up and down the Tottenham Court Road, as if he were looking for something. Then he said, "Douglas killed himself, of course. Ten years ago. When I was still in the bin. So my memory's not as good. Not as good as it was. But that was Jamie all right, to the life. He'd never let us forget that he was the oldest. And you know, we weren't ever allowed in the playhouse. Father didn't build it for us." His voice quavered, and for a moment I could imagine this pale old man as a boy again. "Father had his own games."

And then he waved his arm and called "Taxi!" and a taxi pulled over to the kerb. "Brown's Hotel," said the man, and he got in. He did not say goodnight to any of us. He pulled shut the door of the cab.

And in the closing of the cab door I could hear too many other doors closing; doors in the past, which are gone now, and cannot be reopened.

PAT CADIGAN

It Was the Heat

PAT CADIGAN IS A two-time winner of the Arthur C. Clarke
Award and the author of fifteen books. Her fiction is included
in many anthologies, including *The Mammoth Book of Best New
Horror* and *The Year's Best Fantasy and Horror* series, *The Mammoth
Book of Vampire Stories by Women*, *Dark Terrors 3: The Gollancz Book
of Horror*, *The New English Library Book of Internet Stories*, *The Ex
Files: New Stories About Old Flames*, *Disco 2000*, *Dying For It: Erotic
Tales of Unearthly Love* and *A Whisper of Blood*, and her short
stories have been collected in *Patterns*.

Born in Schenectady, New York, and formerly a resident of
Kansas, she now lives and works in North London.

" 'It Was the Heat' was the first thing I wrote as a full-time
professional writer," Cadigan explains. "It was also my love
letter to the city of New Orleans, which is one of the most
gorgeous and inspiringly decadent (or decadently inspiring)
places I've ever visited.

"While almost all the locations are real, nothing like the
events in the story ever happened to me in New Orleans; not
even something as stultifyingly commonplace as a trashy fling
in a cheap hotel room. However, on a wander through the
French Quarter, it's easy to imagine all kinds of things. And a

little jambalaya helps to stir things up even more. Personally, I recommend it.''

IT WAS THE HEAT, the incredible heat that never lets up, never eases, never once gives you a break. Sweat till you die; bake till you drop; fry, broil, burn, baby, burn. How'd you like to live in a fever and never feel cool, never, never, never.

Women think they want men like that. They think they want someone to put the devil in their Miss Jones. Some of them even lie awake at night, alone, or next to a silent lump of husband or boyfriend or friendly stranger, thinking, *Let me be completely consumed with fire. In the name of love.*
    Sure.
    Right feeling, wrong name. Try again. And the thing is, they do. They try and try and try, and if they're very, very unlucky, they find one of them.

I thought I had him right where I wanted him – between my legs. Listen, I didn't always talk this way. That wasn't me you saw storming the battlements during the Sexual Revolution. My ambition was liberated but I didn't lose my head, or give it. It wasn't me saying, *Let them eat pie.* Once I had a sense of propriety but I lost it with my inhibitions.
    You think these things happen only in soap operas – the respectable, thirty-five-year-old wife and working mother goes away on a business trip with a suitcase full of navy blue suits and classy blouses with the bow at the neck and a briefcase crammed with paperwork. Product management is not a pretty sight. Sensible black pumps are a must for the run on the fast track and if your ambition is sufficiently liberated, black pumps can keep pace with perforated wing-tips, even outrun them.
    But men know the secret. Especially businessmen. This is why management conferences are sometimes held in a place like New Orleans instead of the professional canyons of New York City or Chicago. Men know the secret and now I do, too. But I didn't then, when I arrived in New Orleans with my luggage and my paperwork and my inhibitions, to be installed in the Bourbon Orleans Hotel in the French Quarter.
    The room had all the charm of home – more, since I wouldn't be cleaning it up. I hung the suits in the bathroom,

ran the shower, called home, already feeling guilty. Yes, boys, Mommy's at the hotel now and she has a long meeting to go to, let me talk to Daddy. Yes, dear, I'm fine. It was a long ride from the airport, good thing the corporation's paying for this. The hotel is very nice, good thing the corporation's paying for this, too. Yes, there's a pool but I doubt I'll have time to use it and anyway, I didn't bring a suit. Not that kind of suit. This isn't a pleasure trip, you know, I'm not on vacation. No. Yes. No. Kiss the boys for me. I love you, too.

If you want to be as conspicuous as possible, be a woman walking almost late into a meeting room full of men who are all gunning to be CEOs. Pick out the two or three other female faces and nod to them even though they're complete strangers, and find a seat near them. Listen to the man at the front of the room say, *Now that we're all here, we can begin* and know that every man is thinking that means you. Imagine what they are thinking, imagine what they are whispering to each other. Imagine that they know you can't concentrate on the opening presentation because your mind is on your husband and children back home instead of the business at hand when the real reason you can't concentrate is because you're imagining they must all be thinking your mind is on your husband and children back home instead of the business at hand.

Do you know what *they're* thinking about, really? They're thinking about the French Quarter. Those who have been there before are thinking about jazz and booze in go-cups and bars where the women are totally nude, totally, and those who haven't been there before are wondering if everything's as wild as they say.

Finally the presentation ended and the discussion period following the presentation ended (the women had nothing to discuss so as not to be perceived as the ones delaying the after-hours jaunt into the French Quarter). Tomorrow, nine o'clock in the Hyatt, second floor meeting room. Don't let's be too hung over to make it, boys, ha, ha. Oh, and girls, too, of course, ha, ha.

The things you hear when you don't have a crossbow.

Demure, I took a cab back to the Bourbon Orleans, intending to leave a wake-up call for 6:30, ignoring the streets already filling up. In early May, with Mardi Gras already a dim memory? Was there a big convention in town this week, I asked the cab driver.

No, ma'am, he told me (his accent – Creole or Cajun? I don't know – made it more like *ma'ahm*). De Quarter always be jumpin', and de weather be so lovely.

This was lovely? I was soaked through my drip-dry white blouse and the suitcoat would start to smell if I didn't take it off soon. My crisp, boardroom coiffure had gone limp and trickles of sweat were tracking leisurely along my scalp. Product management was meant to live in air conditioning (we call it climate control, as though we really could, but there is no controlling this climate).

At the last corner before the hotel, I saw him standing at the curb. Tight jeans, red shirt knotted above the navel to show off the washboard stomach. Definitely not executive material; executives are required to be doughy in that area and the area to the south of that was never delineated quite so definitely as it was in this man's jeans.

Some sixth sense made him bend to see who was watching him from the back seat of the cab.

"Mamma, mamma!" he called and kissed the air between us. "You wanna go to a party?" He came over to the cab and motioned for me to roll the window all the way down. I slammed the lock down on the door and sat back, clutching my sensible black purse.

"C'mon, mamma!" He poked his fingers through the small opening of the window. "I be good to you!" The golden hair was honey from peroxide but the voice was honey from the comb. The light changed and he snatched his fingers away just in time.

"I'll be waiting!" he shouted after me. I didn't look back.

"What was all that about?" I asked the cab driver.

"Just a wild boy. Lotta wild boys in the Quarter, ma'am." We pulled up next to the hotel and he smiled over his shoulder at me, his teeth just a few shades lighter than his coffee-colored skin. "Any time you want to find a wild boy for yourself, this is where you look." It came out more like *dis is wheah you look.* "You got a nice company sends you to the Quarter for doin' business."

I smiled back, overtipped him, and escaped into the hotel.

It wasn't even a consideration, that first night. Wake-up call for six-thirty, just as I'd intended, to leave time for showering and breakfast, like the good wife and mother and executive I'd always been.

*   *   *

Beignets for breakfast. Carl had told me I must have beignets
for breakfast if I were going to be New Orleans. He'd bought
some beignet mix and tried to make some for me the week
before I'd left. They'd come out too thick and heavy and only
the kids had been able to eat them, liberally dusted with
powdered sugar. If I found a good place for beignets, I would
try to bring some home, I'd decided, for my lovely, tolerant,
patient husband, who was now probably making thick, heavy
pancakes for the boys. Nice of him to sacrifice some of his
vacation time to be home with the boys while Mommy was out
of town. Mommy had never gone out of town on business
before. Daddy had, of course; several times. At those times,
Mommy had never been able to take any time away from the
office, though, so she could be with the boys while Daddy was
out of town. Too much work to do; if you want to keep those
sensible black pumps on the fast track, you can't be putting
your family before the work. Lots of women lose out that way,
you know, Martha?

I knew.

No familiar faces in the restaurant, but I wasn't looking for
any. I moved my tray along the line, took a beignet and poured
myself some of the famous Louisiana chicory coffee before I
found a small table under a ceiling fan. No air-conditioning and
it was already up in the eighties. I made a concession and took
off my jacket. After a bite of the beignet, I made another and
unbuttoned the top two buttons of my blouse. The pantyhose
already felt sticky and uncomfortable. I had a perverse urge to
slip off to the ladies' room and take them off. Would anyone
notice or care? That would leave me with nothing under the
half-slip. Would anyone guess? There goes a lady executive with
no pants on. In the heat, it was not unthinkable. No underwear
at all was not unthinkable. Everything was binding. A woman in a
gauzy caftan breezed past my table, glancing down at me with
careless interest. Another out-of-towner, yes. You can tell – we're
the only ones not dressed for the weather.

"All right to sit here, ma'am?"

I looked up. He was holding a tray with one hand, already
straddling the chair across from me, only waiting my permission to sink down and join me. Dark, curly hair, just a bit too
long, darker eyes, smooth skin the color of over-creamed
coffee. Tank top over jeans. He eased himself down and smiled.
I must have said yes.

"All the other tables're occupied or ain't been bussed, ma'am. Hope you don't mind, you a stranger here and all." The smile was as slow and honeyed as the voice. They all talked in honey tones here. "Eatin' you one of our nice beignets, I see. First breakfast in the Quarter, am I right?"

I used a knife and fork on the beignet. "I'm here on business."

"You have a very striking face."

I risked a glance up at him. "You're very kind." Thirty-five and up is striking, if the world is feeling kind.

"When your business is done, shall I see you in the Quarter?"

"I doubt it. My days are very long." I finished the beignet quickly, gulped the coffee. He caught my arm as I got up. It was a jolt of heat, like being touched with an electric wand.

"I have a husband and three children!" It was the only thing I could think to say.

"You don't want to forget your jacket."

It hung limply on the back of my chair. I wanted to forget it badly, to have an excuse to go through the day of meetings and seminars in shirtsleeves. I put the tray down and slipped the jacket on. "Thank you."

"Name is Andre, ma'am." The dark eyes twinkled. "My heart will surely break if I don't see you tonight in the Quarter."

"Don't be silly."

"It's too hot to be silly, ma'am."

"Yes. It is," I said stiffly. I looked for a place to take the tray.

"They take it away for you. You can just leave it here. Or you can stay and have another cup of coffee and talk to a lonely soul." One finger plucked at the low scoop of the tank top. "I'd like that."

"A cab driver warned me about wild boys," I said, holding my purse carefully to my side.

"I doubt it. He may have told you but he didn't warn you. And I ain't a boy, ma'am."

Sweat gathered in the hollow between my collarbones and spilled downward. He seemed to be watching the trickle disappear down into my blouse. Under the aroma of baking breads and pastries and coffee, I caught a scent of something else.

"Boys stand around on street corners, they shout rude remarks, they don't know what a woman is."

"That's enough," I snapped. "I don't know why you picked me out for your morning's amusement. Maybe because I'm from out of town. You wild boys get a kick out of annoying the tourists, is that it? If I see you again, I'll call a cop." I stalked out and pushed myself through the humidity to hail a cab. By the time I reached the Hyatt, I might as well not have showered.

"I'm skipping out on this afternoon's session," the woman whispered to me. Her badge said she was Frieda Fellowes, of Boston, Massachusetts. "I heard the speaker last year. He's the biggest bore in the world. I'm going shopping. Care to join me?"

I shrugged. "I don't know. I have to write up a report on this when I get home and I'd better be able to describe everything in detail."

She looked at my badge. "You must work for a bunch of real hardasses up in Schenectady." She leaned forward to whisper to the other woman sitting in the row ahead of us, who nodded eagerly.

They were both missing from the afternoon session. The speaker was the biggest bore in the world. The men had all conceded to shirtsleeves. Climate control failed halfway through the seminar and it broke up early, releasing us from the stuffiness of the meeting room into the thick air of the city. I stopped in the lobby bathroom and took off my pantyhose, rolled them into an untidy ball and stuffed them in my purse before getting a cab back to my own hotel.

One of the men from my firm phoned my room and invited me to join him and the guys for drinks and dinner. We met in a crowded little place called Messina's, four male executives and me. It wasn't until I excused myself and went to the closet-sized bathroom that I realized I'd put my light summer slacks on over nothing. A careless mistake, akin to starting off to the supermarket on Saturday morning in my bedroom slippers. Mommy's got a lot on her mind. Martha, the No-Pants Executive. Guess what, dear, I went out to dinner in New Orleans with four men and forgot to wear panties. Well, women do reach their sexual peak at thirty-five, don't they, honey?

The heat was making me crazy. No air-conditioning here, either, just fans, pushing the damp air around.

I rushed through the dinner of red beans and rice and hot sausage; someone ordered a round of beers and I gulped mine down to cool the sausage. No one spoke much. Martha's here, better keep it low-key, guys. I decided to do them a favor and disappear after the meal. There wouldn't be much chance of running into me at any of the nude bars, nothing to be embarrassed about. Thanks for tolerating my presence, fellas.

But they looked a little puzzled when I begged off anything further. The voice blew over to me as I reached the door, carried on a wave of humidity pushed by one of the fans: "Maybe she's got a headache tonight." General laughter.

Maybe all four of you together would be a disappointment, boys. Maybe none of you know what a woman is.

They didn't look especially wild, either.

I had a drink by the pool instead of going right up to the hotel room. Carl would be coping with supper and homework and whatnot. Better to call later, after they were all settled down.

I finished the drink and ordered another. It came in a plastic cup, with apologies from the waiter. "Temporarily short on crystal tonight, ma'am. Caterin' a private dinner here. Hope you don't mind a go-cup this time."

"A what?"

The man's smile was bright. "Go-cup. You take it and walk around with it."

"That's allowed?"

"All over the Quarter, ma'am." He moved on to another table.

So I walked through the lobby with it and out into the street, and no one stopped me.

Just down at the corner, barely half a block away, the streets were filling up again. Many of the streets seemed to be pedestrians only. I waded in, holding the go-cup. Just to look around. I couldn't really come here and not look around.

"It's supposed to be a whorehouse where the girls swung naked on velvet swings."

I turned away from the high window where the mannequin legs had been swinging in and out to look at the man who had spoken to me. He was a head taller than I was, long-haired, attractive in a rough way.

"Swung?" I said. "You mean they don't any more?"

He smiled and took my elbow, positioning me in front of an open doorway, pointed in. I looked; a woman was lying naked on her stomach under a mirror suspended overhead. Perspiration gleamed on her skin.

"Buffet?" I said. "All you can eat, a hundred dollars?"

The man threw back his head and laughed heartily. "New in the Quarter, aintcha?" Same honey in the voice. They caress you with their voices here, I thought, holding the crumpled go-cup tightly. It was a different one; I'd had another drink since I'd come out and it hadn't seemed like a bad idea at all, another drink, the walking around, all of it. Not by myself, anyway.

Something brushed my hip. "You'll let me buy you another, wontcha?" Dark hair, dark eyes; young. I remembered that for a long time.

Wild creatures in lurid long dresses catcalled screechily from a second floor balcony as we passed below on the street. My eyes were heavy with heat and alcohol but I kept walking. It was easy with him beside me, his arm around me and his hand resting on my hip.

Somewhere along the way, the streets grew much darker and the crowds disappeared. A few shadows in the larger darkness; I saw them leaning against street signs; we passed one close enough to smell a mixture of perfume and sweat and alcohol and something else.

"Didn't nobody never tell you to come out alone at night in this part of the Quarter?" The question was amused, not reproving. They caress you with their voices down here, with their voices and the darkness and the heat, which gets higher as it gets darker. And when it gets hot enough, they melt and flow together and run all over you, more fluid than water.

What are you doing?

I'm walking into a dark hallway; I don't know my footing, I'm glad there's someone with me.

What are you doing?

I'm walking into a dark room to get out of the heat, but it's no cooler here and I don't really care after all.

What are you doing?

I'm overdressed for the season here; this isn't Schenectady in the spring, it's New Orleans, it's the French Quarter.

What are you doing?

I'm hitting my sexual peak at thirty-five.

"What are you doing?"

Soft laughter. "Oh, honey, don't you know?"

*   *   *

The Quarter was empty at dawn, maybe because it was raining. I found my way back to the Bourbon Orleans in the downpour anyway. It shut off as suddenly as a suburban lawn sprinkler just as I reached the front door of the hotel.

I fell into bed and slept the day away, no wake-up calls, and when I opened my eyes, the sun was going down and I remembered how to find him.

You'd think there would have been a better reason: my husband ignored me or my kids were monsters or my job was a dead-end or some variation on the mid-life crisis. It wasn't any of those things. Well, the seminars *were* boring but nobody gets that bored. Or maybe they did and I'd just never heard about it.

It was the heat.

The heat gets inside you. Then you get a fever from the heat, and from fever you progress to delirium and from delirium into another state of being. Nothing is real in delirium. No, scratch that: everything is real in a different way. In delirium, everything floats, including time. Lighter than air, you slip away. Day breaks apart from night, leaves you with scraps of daylight. It's all right – when it gets that hot, it's too hot to see, too hot to bother looking. I remembered dark hair, dark eyes, but it was all dark now and in the dark, it was even hotter than in the daylight.

It was the heat. It never let up. It was the heat and the smell. I'll never be able to describe that smell except to say that if it were a sound, it would have been round and mellow and sweet, just the way it tasted. As if he had no salt in his body at all. As if he had been distilled from the heat itself, and salt had just been left behind in the process.

It was the heat.

And then it started to get cool.

It started to cool down to the eighties during the last two days of the conference and I couldn't find him. I made a half-hearted showing at one of the seminars after a two-day absence. They stared, all the men and the women, especially the one who had asked me to go shopping.

"I thought you'd been kidnapped by white slavers," she said to me during the break. "What happened? You don't look like you feel so hot."

"I feel very hot," I said, helping myself to the watery lemonade punch the hotel had laid out on a table. With beignets. The sight of them turned my stomach and so did the punch. I put it down again. "I've been running a fever."

She touched my face, frowning slightly. "You don't feel feverish. In fact, you feel pretty cool. Clammy, even."

"It's the air-conditioning," I said, drawing back. Her fingers were cold, too cold to tolerate. "The heat and the air-conditioning. It's fucked me up."

Her eyes widened.

"*Messed* me up, excuse me. I've been hanging around my kids too long."

"Perhaps you should see a doctor. Or go home."

"I've just got to get out of this air-conditioning," I said, edging toward the door. She followed me, trying to object. "I'll be fine as soon as I get out of this air-conditioning and back into the heat."

"No, *wait*," she called insistently. "You may be suffering from heat-stroke. I think that's it – the clammy skin, the way you look—"

"It's not heatstroke, I'm freezing in this goddam refrigerator. Just leave me the fuck alone and I'll be *fine!*"

I fled, peeling off my jacket, tearing open the top of my blouse. I couldn't go back, not to that awful air-conditioning. I would stay out where it was warm.

I lay in bed with the windows wide open and the covers pulled all the way up. One of the men from my company phoned; his voice sounded too casual when he pretended I had reassured him. Carl's call only twenty minutes later was not a surprise. I'm fine, dear. You don't sound fine. I am, though. Everyone is worried about you. Needlessly. I think I should come down there. No, stay where you are, I'll be fine. No, I think I should come and get you. And I'm telling you to stay where you are. That does it, you sound weird, I'm getting the next flight out and your mother can stay with the boys. You stay where you are, goddamit, or I might not come home, is that clear?

Long silence.

Is someone there with you?

More silence.

I said, is someone there with you?

It's just the heat. I'll be fine, as soon as I warm up.

*   *   *

Sometime after that, I was sitting at a table in a very dark place that was almost warm enough. The old woman sitting across from me occasionally drank delicately from a bottle of beer and fanned herself, even though it was only almost warm.

"It's such pleasure when it cool down like dis," she said in her slow honeyvoice. Even the old ladies had honeyvoices here. "The heat be a beast."

I smiled, thinking for a moment that she'd said *bitch*, not *beast*. "Yeah. It's a bitch all right but I don't like to be cold."

"No? Where you from?"

"Schenectady. Cold climate."

She grunted. "Well, the heat don't be a bitch, it be a beast. He be a beast."

"Who?"

"Him. The heat beast." She chuckled a little. "My grandma woulda called him a loa. You know what dat is?"

"No."

She eyed me before taking another sip of beer. "No. I don't know whether that good or bad for you, girl. Could be deadly either way, someone who don't like to be cold. What you doin' over here anyway? Tourist Quarter three blocks thataway."

"I'm looking for a friend. Haven't been able to find him since it's cooled down."

"Grandma knew they never named all de loa. She said new ones would come when they found things be willin' for 'em. Or when they named by someone. Got nothin' to do with the old religion any more. Bigger than the old religion. It's all de world now." The old woman thrust her face forward and squinted at me. "What friend *you* got over here? No outa-town white girl got a friend over here."

"I do. And I'm not from out of town any more."

"Get out." But it wasn't hostile, just amusement and condescension and a little disgust. "Go buy you some tourist juju and tell everybody you met a mamba in N'awlins. Be some candyass somewhere sell you a nice, fake love charm."

"I'm not here for that," I said, getting up. "I came for the heat."

"Well, girl, it's cooled down." She finished her beer.

Sometime after that, in another place, I watched a man and a woman dancing together. There were only a few other people on the floor in front of the band. I couldn't really make sense of the music, whether it was jazz or rock or whatever. It was just the man and the woman I was paying attention to. Something in their movements was familiar. I was thinking he would be called by the heat in them, but it was so damned cold in there, not even ninety degrees. The street was colder. I pulled the jacket tighter around myself and cupped my hands around the coffee mug. That famous Louisiana chicory coffee. Why couldn't I get warm?

It grew colder later. There wasn't a warm place in the Quarter, but people's skins seemed to be burning. I could see the heat shimmers rising from their bodies. Maybe I was the only one without a fever now.

Carl was lying on the bed in my hotel room. He sat up as soon as I opened the door. The heat poured from him in waves and my first thought was to throw myself on him and take it, take it all, and leave him to freeze to death.

"Wait!" he shouted but I was already pounding down the hall to the stairs.

Early in the morning, it was an easy thing to run through the Quarter. The sun was already beating down but the light was thin, with little warmth. I couldn't hear Carl chasing me, but I kept running, to the other side of the Quarter, where I had first gone into the shadows. Glimpse of an old woman's face at a window; I remembered her, she remembered me. Her head nodded, two fingers beckoned. Behind her, a younger face watched in the shadows. The wrong face.

I came to a stop in the middle of an empty street and waited. I was getting colder; against my face, my fingers were like living icicles. It had to be only 88 or 89 degrees, but even if it got to ninety-five or above today, I wouldn't be able to get warm.

He had it. He had taken it. Maybe I could get it back.

The air above the buildings shimmied, as if to taunt. Warmth, here, and here, and over here, what's the matter with you, frigid or something?

Down at the corner, a police car appeared. Heat waves rippled up from it, and I ran.

"Hey."

The man stood over me where I sat shivering at a corner table in the place that bragged it had traded slaves over a hundred years ago. He was the color of rich earth, slightly built with carefully waved black hair. Young face; the wrong face, again.

"You look like you in the market for a sweater."

"Go away." I lifted the coffee cup with shuddering hands. "A thousand sweaters couldn't keep me warm now."

"No, honey." They caressed you with their voices down here. He took the seat across from me. "Not that kind of sweater. Sweater I mean's a person, special kinda person. Who'd you meet in the Quarter? Good-lookin' stud, right? Nice, wild boy, maybe not white but white enough for you?"

"Go away. I'm not like that."

"You know what you like now, though. Cold. Very cold woman. Cold woman's no good. Cold woman'll take all the heat out of a man, leave him frozen dead."

I didn't answer.

"So you need a sweater. Maybe I know where you can find one."

"Maybe you know where I can find *him*."

The man laughed. "That's what I'm sayin', cold woman." He took off his light, white suitcoat and tossed it at me. "Wrap up in that and come on."

The fire in the hearth blazed, flames licking out at the darkness. Someone kept feeding it, keeping it burning for hours. I wasn't sure who, or if it was only one person, or how long I sat in front of the fire, trying to get warm.

Sometime long after the man had brought me there, the old woman said, "Burnin' all day now. Whole Quarter oughta feel the heat by now. Whole *city*."

"*He'll* feel it, sure enough." The man's voice. "He'll feel it, come lookin' for what's burnin'." A soft laugh. "Won't he be surprised to see it's his cold woman."

"Look how the fire wants her."

The flames danced. I could sit in the middle of them and maybe then I'd be warm.

"Where did he go?" The person who asked might have been me.

"Went to take a rest. Man sleeps after a bender, don't you know. He oughta be ready for more by now."

I reached out for the fire. A long tongue of flame licked around my arm; the heat felt so good.

"Look how the fire wants her."

Soft laugh. "If it wants her, then it should have her. Go ahead, honey. Get in the fire."

On hands and knees, I climbed up into the hearth, moving slowly, so as not to scatter the embers. Clothes burned away harmlessly.

To sit in fire is to sit among a glory of warm, silk ribbons touching everywhere at once. I could see the room now, the heavy drapes covering the windows, the dark faces, one old, one young, gleaming with sweat, watching me.

"You feel 'im?" someone asked. "Is he comin'?"

"He's comin', don't worry about that." The man who had brought me smiled at me. I felt a tiny bit of perspiration gather at the back of my neck. Warmer; getting warmer now.

I began to see him; he was forming in the darkness, coming together, pulled in by the heat. Dark-eyed, dark-haired, young, the way he had been. He was there before the hearth and the look on that young face as he peered into the flames was hunger.

The fire leaped for him; I leaped for him and we saw what it was we really had. No young man; no man.

The heat be a beast.

Beast. Not really a loa, something else; I knew that, somehow. Sometimes it looks like a man and sometimes it looks like hot honey in the darkness.

What are you doing?

I'm taking darkness by the eyes, by the mouth, by the throat.

What are you doing?

I'm burning alive.

What are you doing?

I'm burning the heat beast and I have it just where I want it. All the heat anyone ever felt, fire and body heat, fever, delirium. Delirium has eyes; I push them in with my thumbs. Delirium has a mouth; I fill it with my fist. Delirium has a throat; I tear it out. Sparks fly like an explosion of tiny stars and the beast spreads its limbs in surrender, exposing its white-hot core. I bend my head to it and the taste is sweet, no salt in his body at all.

What are you doing?

Oh, honey, don't you know?

I took it back.

In the hotel room, I stripped off the shabby dress the old woman had given me and threw it in the trashcan. I was packing when Carl came back.

He wanted to talk; I didn't. Later he called the police and told them everything was all right, he'd found me and I was coming home with him. I was sure they didn't care. Things like that must have happened in the Quarter all the time.

In the ladies' room at the airport, the attendant sidled up to me as I was bent over the sink splashing cold water on my face and asked if I were all right.

"It's just the heat," I said.

"Then best you go home to a cold climate," she said. "You do better in a cold climate from now on."

I raised my head to look at her reflection in the spotted mirror. I wanted to ask her if she had a brother who also waved his hair. I wanted to ask her why he would bother with a cold woman, why he would care.

She put both hands high on her chest, protectively. "The beast sleeps in cold. *You* tend him now. Maybe you keep him asleep for good."

"And if I don't?"

She pursed her lips. "Then you gotta problem."

In summer, I keep the air-conditioning turned up high at my office, at home. In the winter, the kids complain the house is too cold and Carl grumbles a little, even though we save so much in heating bills. I tuck the boys in with extra blankets every night and kiss their foreheads, and later in our bed, Carl curls up close, murmuring how my skin is always so warm.

It's just the heat.

TIM LEBBON
& BRIAN KEENE

Fodder

TIM LEBBON HAS WON two British Fantasy Awards and a Bram
Stoker Award, and his work (including the following story) has
been optioned for the screen on both sides of the Atlantic.

His books include the novels *Face, The Nature of Balance,
Mesmer, Until She Sleeps, Dusk, Desolation* and *Into the Wild Green
Yonder* (with Peter Crowther), plus the novellas *Naming of Parts,
White, Exorcising Angels* (with Simon Clark), *Changing of Faces*
and *Dead Man's Hand*. Lebbon's short fiction has been coll-
ected in *As the Sun Goes Down, White and Other Tales of Ruin* and
Fears Unnamed.

Brian Keene is a winner of the Bram Stoker Award and the
author of *The Rising, Terminal, City of the Dead* and other novels.
His short fiction has appeared in numerous magazines and
anthologies, and is collected in *No Rest at All, No Rest for the
Wicked* and *Fear of Gravity*. He contributed one half of the
Earthling Publications chapbook *The Rise and Fall of Babylon*
back-to-back with John Urbanick, and he is also the fiction
editor of *Horrorfind.com*.

"I've written several stories based during the First World
War," reveals Lebbon, "and this is one of my favourites. The

scale of that destruction, that waste of life, that slaughter, has always had a profound effect on me, and when Brian and I worked on this story I read quite a bit around the subject. I felt terrible for giving those poor soldiers something even more awful to deal with than the hell of the trenches, but it all came together for me with the end of the story, and that wide-ranging twist on events."

" 'Fodder' was a real treat to write," Keene admits. "Tim is not only one of my best friends – he's also an author that I have an enormous amount of respect for. I knew that in collaborating with Tim, I would have to be on top of my game. We originally wrote the story for a William Hope Hodgson tribute anthology, and the character of William was based (very) loosely on him. We both had relatives that served during the First World War, so we wanted to touch on that. We also wanted to add the very real element of the flu bug that killed tens of thousands of people at the end of the war."

> "What passing-bells for these who die as cattle?"
> —Wilfred Owen

THE SUN WAS ALREADY scorching, yet Private William Potter's watch showed only nine o'clock. The straps of his knapsack chafed his skin as he walked. He tried to ignore the protests from his aching muscles, but his blistered feet were balls of flame, and his neck was burned lobster-red. He had never felt so exhausted.

The remaining men of the British 3rd Infantry shuffled southward. Swirling clouds of dust, kicked up by their boots, marked their passage along the road towards Argonne. Around them, the beet fields had come to life with the buzzing chatter of insects and the birds' morning chorus, interrupted only by muffled booms from the front; intermittent, yet always present. The sounds of battle were drawing closer with every step.

William blinked the sweat from his eyes and listened to the symphony around him, losing himself in the strange beauty of the moment. The strings and brass of the remaining wildlife accompanied the angry percussion of man. A new poem began to suggest itself to him then, and he longed for a sheet of paper and a pen to write it down. He was away pondering the first line when he slammed into Liggett.

"You, Bollocks," the irate Corporal spat in his thick Cockney accent? "why don't you watch where yer going?"

"Sorry, Liggett," William mumbled apologetically. "I was listening to the birds."

"Oh yeah, listening to the birds, were you? Walking around with your bloody head in the clouds more like." He stopped to rescue his dropped cigarette from the dirt.

"He's right, William," laughed Winston. "Keep going like you are, you'll float above this mess one day."

"Leave him be," Morris said, coming to his friend's defence. "You can laugh all you want now, but William will have the last laugh when he writes a book about all of this."

"Not if he gets his head blown off first," Liggett mumbled, "and that's exactly what'll happen if he don't join the rest of us back down here on earth." His mood did not improve when he found the cigarette in a small, brown puddle. "Look at this," he gasped. "The only bit of water on this whole bleeding road, and Potter makes me drop my last ciggie in it!"

"Can we have a break, Crown Sergeant?" Winston called out to the large man ahead of him.

Crown Sergeant Sterling paused and looked back at the four men. "I suppose you lads will be wanting tea next then?"

"No, Crown Sergeant, it's just that we haven't stopped since . . ." Winston's voice trailed off, lost in the warbling of the birds.

William closed his eyes and unbidden images of the last battle flooded in, the horrors of close-quarter bayonet fighting, the brutal, terrified expressions on their enemies' faces that meant *It's you or me.* Hideous memories of how Dunhill and the others had died.

Sterling softened. The past was haunting him as well.

"I guess we could all do with a break," he said quietly. "Right then! We'll rest here and carry on just before sunset. Should be there within another couple of hours."

Gratefully the exhausted men unslung their knapsacks, rested their rifles upright to keep them clean and sank to the ground. William felt his muscles knotting into cramps, and he spent long minutes stretching the pain away. He did not mind the cramps. He could deal with them. There were far worse pains he had seen other people suffering, indignities visited upon them by murderous Man . . .

"What will we do when we reach the forest, Crown Sergeant?" Morris asked.

The big man drank deeply from his canteen before answering. "Find out if any of the other lads made it out alive," he answered grimly. "See if we're the lot of it. If so, we'll fall in with the French and the Yanks until we reach the Hindenburg line. The Yanks are sure to have a radio. I'll get advisement from headquarters on what we're to do."

"If it's all the same to you, Crown Sergeant," Winston joked, "I'll just walk on to London. I've seen enough to the Hun and I'd like to hear a bit more about this Chaplin fellow."

"That's very noble of you, Private," Sterling said with a humorless grin. "But I'm guessing you'll stay with the rest of us."

"Who is this Chaplin bloke anyhow?" asked Morris. "I heard some boys from the Royal Fifth speaking of him as well."

"A politician, I should guess," Liggett said. "One of the bastards . . ."

They chatted, bantered, avoiding any subject close enough to remind them of the war. William tuned them out because he so liked to watch, to see the way their eyes changed when the spoke of home, to sense the relaxation settling into their bones when they could forget the fight, even for a moment. Fighting men, he thought, were as close to the basis of the human animal as could be. Every emotion was emphasized, every thought clear, the fear and the hope and the dread actually *felt*, not just thought.

"Penny for your thoughts, William," Morris said.

William started, realized he had been drifting away, although to where he had no idea.

"I'm not sure I could articulate them properly," he said, pausing to think for a moment. He was aware that the others were silent now, watching him. "Have you noticed the birds and the insects all around us?"

"I hadn't given it much thought," Morris admitted, fishing through his knapsack.

"There's a war going on all over, happening in their very home, yet they stay. They adapt. They sing along with the sounds of the artillery. Remember when we saw the tanks?"

Morris nodded. Then he frowned.

William wondered if they were remembering the same thing. There had been more of them then, of course. They'd been farther north, securing a bridge to provide safe passage for the armored column. It was the first time any of them had actually seen the new form of weaponry. The tanks had been slow, ponderous things. Even Crown Sergeant Sterling, a career soldier, marvelled at the sheer destructive force the machines bespoke.

As the column had rolled safely across the bridge and chewed its way through a field on the other side, a herd of deer stood watching from the treeline.

"Those deer adapted as well," William said to the seated men. "Something new had entered their home and they investigated, then dismissed it. The sound of artillery echoes off the hills, and the birds become accustomed to it so quickly. I was just wondering . . . how does nature accept the changes?" He shook his head. "How long before it *refuses* to accept them?"

He kicked at the dirt under his feet, and wondered whether it was the dust of dead men.

"And just look at the new ways we've devised to kill each other: the machine-gun; the tank; poison gas! The press calls this the war to end all wars. We hurtle toward our date with destiny, our date with the future. Yet what do we really know of the world we live on? What mysteries of nature have eluded our grasp? What do we truly know of this planet's inhabitants? I wonder what other creatures have adapted to this chaos . . . creatures we don't even know about yet. After all, this is their home too. We're the intruders here. We're the murderers."

"Well, that may be," Morris replied, "but it's not very well our choice." He fished around in his rucksack and pulled out a faded photograph. A young woman stared back at him. He sighed deeply.

"You miss her," William stated.

"Oh aye, I miss her terribly," Morris whispered. "But it's more than that."

"What?"

The men were silent, none of them looking at Morris, all of them waiting to hear what he had to say.

"I'm sure I'll never see her again."

There was something wet and red in the middle of the trench. William stepped over it as he ran. Behind him, Brown was still screaming.

Dunhill was holding something ropy and glistening. As William raced toward him Dunhill held up his cupped hands in a plea for help, and the shining strands spilled out into the mud.

William knelt to help him, the mud squelching around his knees. Desperately, he grabbed at the soldier's innards, clawing his hands as they slipped through his fingers and into the dirt.

He scraped at the mud. A pair of yellow eyes stared up at him. They blinked.

"*Everything* has adapted, William," Dunhill spat, a crimson froth forming on his mouth. "Known, and not yet known."

Morris careened around the corner then, running at the two men squatting in the muck. Behind him came the Hun, bayonets gleaming in the moonlight.

"William!" Morris screamed as a blade sprouted from his chest. "Are you writing this down?"

The Germans trampled over him, bearing down on William. The eyes in the mud blinked again, then narrowed. William struggled to rise and two gnarled hands burst from the earth, grasping his shoulders in a fierce grip.

"William!"

He opened his eyes with a gasp. Morris was shaking him.

"Come on then, time to get up. Something's happening."

"I was dreaming," William said breathlessly, looking around in confusion. "Dunhill . . ."

"I dreamed about him too," Morris said, nodding his head sadly. "I imagine we'll dream it forever."

"No," William insisted, "this wasn't just the battle, not just what happened to Dunhill. There was something in the earth."

"Look lively, lads," Sterling hissed. "We've got company."

A thick fog had descended over the countryside, obscuring the beet fields and the road in front of them. William glanced at his watch. It was nearly sundown. Already the gloom was pervasive, the mist swallowing what little sunlight was left.

Something was coming toward them.

"Off the road," Sterling commanded in a harsh whisper.

They scrabbled into the bushes as the disembodied sounds of many booted feet approached.

"Bloody hell," Liggett muttered, "if it's a fight they want, we'll give it to them."

"Quiet," Morris whispered.

Out of the fog a column of men appeared. French infantry. A slackness pervaded their tattered ranks. The soldiers looked exhausted, covered with dust and dripping with sweat. Gloomy and silent, the procession passed by their hiding place.

Sterling called out a challenge and the ranks halted. They stared at the soldiers in the ditch, showing no hint of surprise. In halting French, Winston conversed with them. Then they shuffled onward.

"What news?" Sterling asked him.

"I'm not sure, Crown Sergeant," Winston replied, a look of confusion on his face. "Apparently, a major offensive is about to begin in the Argonne trenches. But they're not participating. They're leaving this area."

"Deserting," Liggett snapped. "How do you like that?"

"No," Winston countered, "that's what doesn't make sense. They said that they just had an encounter in a village up the road here. I couldn't understand it though. My French is lacking. Something about the dead in the ground."

"What do we do, Crown Sergeant?" William asked.

Sterling shrugged. Shouldered his knapsack. Slapped a fat fly from his cheek. "We move on."

Edging along the fog enshrouded road, they encountered the sad dregs of a fleeing army. Soldiers and civilians passed by in disorder and panic; women carrying children in their arms and pushing them in small carriages; young girls in their Sunday best; boys and old men hefting all sorts of pointless artifacts of their safe life before the war. Soldiers slumped on peasant carts, gazing at nothing.

An infantryman galloped by on an officer's horse. Spying them, he dismounted and threw his arms around the animal's neck. He gasped something in French and then dashed off into the fields.

"What did he say?" asked Liggett.

"He thanked it for saving his life," Winston replied.

"That's an officer's horse," Sterling observed. "The fellow fled on his captain's horse!"

Another soldier paused to speak to them.

"Ask him why it is he doesn't have a rifle, knapsack, or equipment," Sterling told Winston.

Winston listened to the soldier's reply and then translated. "He says he lost them swimming across the Meuse."

"Bollocks," Liggett replied critically. "His clothes are dry!

Here we are, fighting for their country, and they flee like schoolchildren!"

Darkness encircled them like a steel trap as they approached the village. The procession had trickled down to a few stragglers, the last of whom approached them through the dispersing mist. He bore the rank of officer and greeted them in English.

"Where are you going?" Sterling inquired. "We're on our way to the Argonne forest. Do you know what's happening there?"

"I wish only to be away from this cursed ground," the Frenchman replied.

"But sir," Sterling said, fighting hard to hide his exasperation, "why have you left your unit?"

"I am a company commander," he stated proudly. Then he cast his eyes to the ground. "And my company's only survivor."

"But what the hell happened?" shouted Sterling.

"I can speak no more of this place. Let me by!"

The Frenchman brushed past them and William caught a brief glimpse of the tears streaking his grimy face. Then he vanished into the dark along with everyone else.

Face set with steely determination, Crown Sergeant Sterling motioned them onward. With the sounds of the battle drawing closer – the noise of death seemed to be carried further by the night – they entered the village.

Nothing remained save for a few crumbling walls. The five men walked slowly, rifles at the ready, their hearts hammering with fear. The road was paved with rubbish: linens and undergarments; litters of clothing; letters; burst mattresses and eiderdowns; fragments of furniture and shattered pottery.

And the dead lay everywhere.

Retching, William stumbled across five corpses in a tattered heap, all of them children, all of them hugging each other for comfort in death. Farther along lay a young mother and her two daughters, all dressed in their Sunday best, their faces forever frozen in an horrific visage.

Morris placed a comforting hand on William's shoulder as the young man heaved into the dust.

"What do you think happened here?" William rasped.

"I don't know. They don't seem burned or shot. Yet most have been—" The private's answer was cut short by a piercing squeal from behind a ruined building, followed by a guttural grunt.

William jumped to his feet and dashed after Morris and Sterling.

Another squeal ended abruptly as a rifle echoed in the darkness.

They rounded the corner and halted in shock. In what had once been a courtyard, bodies had been stacked like cordwood, limbs flung out in deathly abandon. Pigs wandered through the pickings, feasting on human flesh.

Winston sighted and squeezed the trigger. A second bloated beast sagged to the ground, ignored by its brethren. Liggett was frantically reloading, his efforts punctuated with more swearing.

"Stand down," ordered Sterling. "If there're snipers about, you'll bring them down on our heads!"

Liggett cursed again and brought the rifle up to his shoulder, drawing a bead on the nearest swine.

"Stand down, Corporal! That's an order, Liggett!"

The shaken Corporal looked at them, and in the moonlight William noticed the tears of rage and bewilderment that streaked the dust on his face.

"This isn't right," Winston exclaimed. "It's not natural!"

Sterling stepped forward to survey the makeshift abattoir. "I spent twenty years on the farm, lads," he said quietly. "And I never saw pigs do this. They'll eat most things, but . . ."

"Crown Sergeant," called Morris. "Come and look at this!"

He was standing before a small mound of dirt. The men approached, wondering what new horror was about to be revealed. Slowly, they took their places next to Morris.

In the ground before them was a gaping hole. The yawning entrance led down into the earth, disappearing from sight. A peculiar smell wafted from the chasm. It reminded William of pig iron and summer storms.

"What do you make of this, then?"

"Artillery," Winston answered, the word almost forming a question. "The Germans must have shelled the village."

"No," Sterling countered, "this was no explosion, we can all see that. This was dug. See that dirt? This tunnel was made from beneath the ground, not from above."

"Well then what in bloody hell was it?" Liggett stammered.

"Something else. I don't know what."

"Perhaps the Germans have some new tunnelling machine," William offered.

"There you go, thinking you're bleeding Jules Verne again," growled Liggett. "Pull your head out of yer arse, William!"

"Leave him alone," Morris retorted and stepped toward the surly Corporal.

"Enough!" shouted Sterling, his voice echoing in the silent streets. "The Devil take you all, that's enough! Whatever made this hole, whatever atrocity occurred in this village, we won't solve anything by standing here. Let's move on!"

Shaken, they departed from the village, stepping gingerly over the scattered corpses. The road wound on, cresting a hilltop a few kilometres away. Stealthily, they crept over the hill and looked down upon the valley of the Argonne Forest.

Away in the distance, the trees stood silent watch over the battlefield. The valley was a labyrinth of trenches, both German and Allied. To William, it looked as if ants had burrowed through the vast field, leaving no acre untouched. Ghostly fires dotted the landscape, as soldiers from both sides huddled in the mud while darkness closed upon them.

A maze of barbed wire surrounded the trenches, and they picked their way carefully through it.

William was struck by the silence engulfing the valley. During a battle, when the heavy field guns, rifles, and machine guns were all booming at the same time, the noise was so tremendous that it seemed beyond the limits of human endurance. Amidst a storm of steel and fire, the riot of battle would change in character, volume and tempo; rising and falling with alternating diminuendo and crescendo in both a hurrying and slackening pace. Relentless, the deafening volley of reports had always sounded to William like the clattering of a clumsy and lumbering wagon, jolting heavily over the frozen ruts of a rough country lane. Sometimes it reminded him of the brisk hammering of thousands of carpenters and riveters. Or it could have been the rumbling of hundreds of heavy goods trains, thundering and bumping over uneven points in the line and meeting head on in a hideous collision.

But even more awful than that hellish cacophony were the sudden and unexpected silences, which made William hold his breath and wait for the storm to start again.

It was this silence that greeted them as they entered the trench system. And William finally gasped a new breath, because the barrage had truly halted. For a time, at least.

The ground was a heavy, impermeable clay that had been

gouged and displaced in a series of tunnels and ditches. Thick mud puddles filled every hole and depression, forming a sticky mire for them to flounder through.

"Halt," called a voice from the darkness. "Who goes there?"

Sterling brought up a hand, stopping them as they slogged through the water. "Who do you think? The bloody Red Baron?"

"I've got to ask. Wh-who goes there?"

William could just make out the young private who had issued the challenge, a skinny chap barely old enough to shave, with a uniform caked onto his body like a second skin. His eyes seemed far too big for his face. His rifle was shaking, the butt clinking against the lad's belt buckle.

"We're from the 3rd," Sterling said. "Any good down here?"

"Good," the boy said blankly. "Don't be daft. How could anything be good?"

William frowned. He had seen many strange things during his last four months in France, but the private's nonchalance when addressing the Crown Sergeant was something new and unsettling.

The boy lowered his rifle and slumped back against the side of the trench. He seemed to merge with the ground, such was his grubby appearance. William wondered if he'd ever move again, or would he be sucked into the trench wall, subsumed into the churned mud of the battlefield like so many of his mates?

Sometimes, they left dead men on the edge of the trench because they absorbed more bullets.

"Come on, you lot," Sterling said. "Let's get some grub inside us, then I'd better track down someone in charge."

The young soldier began to laugh. It was a sickly sound, like gritty oil being poured through a sieve; more a hiss than a chuckle. "In charge," he said. "In bloody charge!" He laughed again, but never once looked at William or his friends. He stared through them and beyond, as if he were talking to someone else entirely. As they shrugged past him, his laughter broke into a rapid volley of violent sneezes.

They slopped through the trench, up to their knees in muddy water most of the time, feces or rotten food floating on its soupy surface. William closed his eyes for a few seconds every now and then, navigating by sound alone, and tried to imagine the summery meadow back home. He could find the smells of flowers and the sounds of birds, the feel of grass beneath his hands and the sense of one of the girls from the village sitting primly by his side . . . but he could not see it. Even when he tried to make-believe, he could not see it.

Still, he had to try. Anything was better than this. Even despair was better than this hell beyond despair.

Again his mind drifted back to the previous battle. He thought of the wounded soldier left out in no-man's land because it gave the enemy snipers something to shoot at. Dunhill.

"This'll do," Sterling said from somewhere up ahead.

William opened his eyes. The Sergeant had paused in a much wider area of trench, two further burrows running away left and right. Straight ahead, a depression had been carved from the earth and covered with roughly chopped branches and shattered tree trunks. It was flooded but there were seats gouged into the walls, an unopened crate of rations, and a dead soldier bobbing facedown in the water.

No one liked to touch a dead man. Some thought death was catching, like bad luck or a cold.

"I'm not going in there, with him like that," Liggett said. "Someone should bury the poor sod."

"Go on then," Winston mumbled, just loud enough for the others to hear.

"You do it," Liggett said. "You and Morris drag him out of there and—"

"No way I'm touching him!" A cigarette dropped from Morris's lips as he spoke.

"Just stop it," William sighed, shaking his head. He felt like crying. He often felt like crying, and when he thought it would really help, he did. When it was dark mostly, the night lit only by the intermittent flashes of the guns. It was yet another thing he envied the animals; they would never have cause to despair at the savagery of their own race.

He pushed past the bickering men, glanced at Sterling, and then stepped into the depression in the earth. The soldier was very heavy, weighted down with water, his rifle strap still tangled around one arm—

"Oh Christ!" William gasped as the body flipped over.

The dead soldier had no face.

There was a hint of eye cavities, a hole in his head where his nose should be, but all other features had been destroyed.

William closed his eyes and tried to dream of the meadow as he dragged the body into the trench. He left it against the sidewall. And he could sense everything of home apart from what it looked like.

"What did that?" Sterling whispered later.

William glanced at his Sergeant, unable to find an answer, unwilling to look.

Sterling's gaze did not falter. "That dead chap over there. What did it to him?"

"A shell. A bullet. I don't know." William shrugged. "Perhaps he blew his own head off."

"You know what I mean, Potter, I've seen enough dead men, so have you. His face was taken off after he died."

Yes, thought William, *I had thought that. I've tried to forget it, but it is what I thought at first.* He wished he could lose the memory of the man's ruined face as easily as he had mislaid the image of home.

"Rats," he said quietly.

And then the first barrage of the night began.

The walls of the trench were shaking. Not just vibrating, but actually *moving*, shedding clumps of dirt as if there were something inside trying to break out. Shells staggered the trenches, some of them striking home in sickening explosions of water and smoke and flesh. The sky was blinking at them with each burst of energy, clouds grey against the night, moon barely peering out at the slaughter its erstwhile worshippers were committing. While down here Man was busy racing to his death, in the heavens time was frozen.

William ran through the trenches. Flowering eruptions of mud splashed the landscape, the ground shook, water sloshed around his feet, men shouted, men screamed, shells screamed, Morris shouted at him: "It's all over now, William! The poem's ending now!"

William reached a section of trench that had been blown to smithereens. It looked like a giant hand had scooped up a thousand tons of mud, men, weapons, timber and water, then flung them back at the ground. He saw the bottom half of a body protruding from a bank of earth . . . its feet were shaking, trouser legs rippling and ripping as something pulled it further in.

Then he was out of the trenches and into no-man's land, and everything was being destroyed. In a swirl of colors – apple blossom and setting sun and poppy red – he caught a glimpse of rolling hillsides of gorse and grass. He could smell the loamy scent of moorland in the air, taste summer on the breeze, see sheep boiling the hills higher up . . . and the artillery barrage blew it all apart.

Something grabbed his feet and he looked down.

There was a girl wrapping herself around his lower legs, working herself tight like a snake. He could not recall her name, but he knew that she worked in the baker's shop back home. He thought that perhaps he had loved her at one time.

She looked up at him. "Come home, my darling, my sweet. Come back to the valley. We so need a poet." But then the ground broke apart as another shell struck home, and the girl vanished into mud, and the night was completely dark at last.

There were explosions and shrieks, but they were muffled. Something had a hand clamped across his mouth and nostrils, over his ears, arm pressing into his throat and choking off the scream he was desperate to vent. He sucked in a difficult breath and smelled mud and rot and age. Filthy water seeped into his mouth and trickled down his throat, like an icy finger tracing his lifeline straight to his heart.

He wondered how long he had been buried down here. Sometimes a barrage would seem to go on forever, so it could be anything from seconds to days. He hurt all over, but he could still shift his limbs, he could still *feel* the hurt. That was a good sign, at least.

He pushed his arms and legs, shoved out from where he was curled up like a sleeping baby, trying to distinguish up from down. Fresh air suddenly washed across his face, a cool night kiss tainted with a tang of smoke and its constant companion, death. William pushed some more, heaving with his shoulders, dragging himself from beneath the showering of mud and into the waterlogged trench.

He could not help rolling into the water. He closed his eyes and held his breath, stood quickly, shaking off the rancid mess like a wet dog.

Confusion settled upon him. Where the hell was he? Where were the others, just what had happened?

And then he saw.

Liggett had never been a polite man, but now his arrogant self was spread around the remains of the trench. There were bits and pieces here and there, but it was his head that William recognized, face reddened by blast-heat but still undeniably Liggett. Whatever blood had leaked from him had been consumed by the earth. Here, everything was a constant shade of dirt.

A line of inhuman creatures walked across the shattered horizon. Humped, slow-moving, paying hardly any attention to the massive conflict around them . . . and then William saw that they were medics evacuating no-man's land of the injured and dead. It took him only seconds to identify them, but in that time his imagination had given them glowing red eyes and a lumbering, hippopotamus gait.

He shook his head, looked back down at Liggett. He tried to imagine the dead corporal blinking, his severed arm waving. Grotesque and insensitive, perhaps, but sometimes the craziest notions kept William alive. Thinking about odd things meant, ironically, that he could forget about a whole lot more.

"Potter!" someone shouted.

William ducked as a new volley of shells fell a hundred yards away, then the voice called out again.

"Potter! Over here!"

He tried discerning which direction the voice was coming from, then made his way along the ruined trench. Mud sucked at him, the collapsed walls loose and moist. The night was almost permanently lit now by a flurry of flares. One of the sides must be charging across no-man's land in the wake of the barrage . . . and sure enough, the cackle of machine-gun fire commenced out of sight, mowing down soldiers in hysterical patterns.

William kept low. Above the background roar of the battlefield he heard the bee-buzz of bullets tearing the air overhead. And above even that, the cries of already-forgotten men falling into freshly-blown graves.

"Potter!"

It was Winston. He was huddled at a junction of two trenches, hunched down like a beggar-boy on a London street. Something stirred at his feet, a shape whipping back and forth in the wet mud like a landed fish.

"It's Crown Sergeant Sterling. We were running for help after the shell fell, we'd lost you and Liggett—"

"Liggett's dead."

"Oh." Winston paused briefly, but death was no surprise. He went on: "We only got this far. The tail end of that first volley caught us here, and . . . look. Look, Potter!"

Those last words were cried, not spoken, and in the mono-tone of the flare light Potter could see Winston's eyes. They glittered, but there were no tears. And then he looked at where Winston was pointing.

Sterling was stuck up to his waist in a hole in the trench bottom. Water swilled around his chest. His eyes bulged from his face, his arms skitted across the surface of the water as he twisted . . . or was twisted by something, because he was dead. He was as dead as anyone William had seen, his throat was gone, the front of his uniform was glistening a different wetness to the rest of the place, a rich syrupy mess in the sodium glare of flares.

"What the hell . . ."

"I've tried to pull him out, but he won't budge."

"He's dead," William said.

"No, no, he can't be, he's trying to get out. Look, if we grab an arm each—"

"He's dead!" William frowned, closed his eyes and strove for home. Even trying to do so calmed him, though the image was as elusive as ever. He supposed it could be worse. It could be that he *was* able to think of the valley where he was born, like imagining the purity of Heaven in a never-ending Hell. Small mercy.

A shape leapt across the trench.

Another, merely a shadow blocking out the star- and flare-light, following the first into no-man's land.

"Winston!" William hissed.

"I dropped my rifle," Winston gasped, voice barely audible now that a new barrage had begun to shake the ground.

This time, William thought the shells were aimed in a different direction. Something felt different; not better, just different. A new kind of promised pain.

"Me too. Get down, and—"

Something else leapt, hit the wall of the trench and slithered down into murky water.

William froze. The soldier was yards from him, struggling to bring his rifle to bear, whining deep down in his throat like a dreaming dog. His nose was running, his mouth slack and dribbling dark saliva onto his tunic. He sneezed.

"Wait, who are you?" William said, more to establish a language than anything else.

"What are you?" the man shouted.

"William Potter, 3rd Infantry."

The man laughed and lowered his rifle. "You'd best follow me then, or they'll get you too."

"Is there an offensive? Are we storming the Hun's trenches? In the night, with a barrage still underway?"

The man shook his head and slumped back against the rough earth, letting its slickness lower him into a sitting position. All the time he talked he looked back the way he had come. And he kept his rifle pointed that way, too . . . back at their own lines.

"Who cares about the Hun?," he said. "Who fucking cares? And the barrage? We're not shelling the enemy, you fool. We've turned the guns around to—"

Winston screamed. It was a sudden, irrational exhalation of terror and pain, heartfelt and automatic. By the time William had spun around, his friend was already splashing on his stomach in the bottom of the trench, hands and feet throwing up fans of dirty water. He hadn't been hit by a bullet or shrapnel; whatever had struck him down was still happening, still whipping his body back and forth.

"Winston!" William shouted.

"Don't bother," the soldier said, his voice high pitched and insane, and he fired his rifle along the trench at Winston.

William took one step to tackle him, and then something else happened. He felt it first, a vibration more frequent and intense than the regular *thud* of explosive shockwaves. This was machines churning underground, or something rolling over. He paused and looked along the trench . . . and the knee-high water began to swill and flow, down into several holes that had opened beneath their feet.

William leapt at the trench wall and grabbed hold of something hanging down from above. He looked up into the blank eyes of a dead soldier, his extended arm William's lifeline, his hand cold and hard. Looking back down he saw Sterling disappear underground with a squelch, and Winston drifting to one of the holes and remaining there, half in, half out, filthy water flowing by him.

In seconds, the trench had emptied of water. Six inches of

mud was all that remained; that and humped bodies here and there, rotting, disintegrating already. There were also the pits, each of them steaming and spitting sprays of water into the illuminated night.

He recalled the hole they had seen in the decimated village . . . and the smell that had come from it.

This tunnel was made from beneath, Sterling had said. Well, now the Sergeant knew just where they led.

William hauled himself out of the trench before he could see what emerged from the holes.

Once on top, he lay flat out and searched for the soldier who'd fallen in moments before. But the madman was already dodging his way into the murk of no-man's land, rifle thrown away, arms held wide as if craving a liberating spray of bullets across his chest.

William thought to call after him but knew it would do no good. He was mad. Everyone was mad. Maybe there was a poem there somewhere, but who would be left to read it? Madmen? He laughed, and the sound of his own lunatic giggle perturbed him greatly.

More men came from behind, scrambling over the trench, some of them falling in and never reappearing. There were noises from down there now, shouts and shots and the sound of flesh finding its doom.

Ahead of him, certain death under a hail of enemy fire.

Behind him, dead friends and dying men, dying in ways he could not properly describe or even imagine. From the sounds drifting from the trench . . . the terrible screams suddenly cut off, the crunching of bones being snapped and pulled apart . . . his choice had already been made.

It was war, after all.

William stood and ran into a storm of lead.

Liggett was following him. His various dismembered parts skipped and dodged shattered tree trunks and fallen bodies. One remaining arm hauled his torso through the mud, and his head moved by rolling itself forward. Its mouth was wide open, trying to scream, but it had no neck or throat.

"Help me!" Liggett croaked nonetheless.

William slowed to a halt. Bullets whipped the air around him, slamming into bodies and sending them toppling down to add to the muck. He was in what had once been a forest. Now it was merely another part of the mud, with strangely contorted stumps seeking their lost heads.

"Help!" Liggett rasped as the first of his parts dashed past William.

Dreaming. He had to be dreaming. He could smell home here, not war and death. He could taste honey on the air, not cordite and blood and smoke.

He looked back from where Liggett had fled.

Dreaming.

Strange shapes lumbered from the smoke, slopping through the mud but unhindered by it. Indeed, these things seemed to flow with the filth, not struggle against it. They looked like the stretcher-bearers he had seen earlier, but as they approached he saw that there was no likeness there. None at all.

Dreaming . . . please God, let me be dreaming.

The demons had yellow eyes.

William came to in a flooded shell hole. At first he though he was alone, but then he saw the dead men keeping his night company. He lay in a horrible mire of flesh and blood.

He shuddered, a tortured sigh escaping his cracked lips. The battle continued around him, but now the fighting was more scattered. In the midst of the tumult, he could hear the steady *tac-tac-tac* of the German machine guns, spreading death precisely and methodically. William reflected on how the emotions of the man behind the weapon never hindered its evil effects. The machine gun was new to this world, yet it could have been created and directed by some ancient, scheming spirit of destruction.

Grabbing a rifle from the clutches of a corpse, he peered cautiously over the edge of the crater. The dream lingered with him, the glint from the creatures' yellow eyes as they lumbered toward him like misshapen men . . .

He was in the middle of no-man's land.

And something was charging his position.

Screaming, William pulled the trigger and was greeted with an empty click.

The thing drew closer, its harsh and ragged breath echoing in the darkness. Ducking back down William flailed in the water, searching wildly for another weapon. His hand closed on something round and he brought it up to the surface – he had to, he could not help himself – and an eyeball stared back at him from his glistening palm.

He screamed again.

The shriek was answered from above.

The thing towered over the shell hole, darkness enshrouding its body like a blanket. William scuttled backward like a crab as a guttural laugh mocked him. The thing cocked its head, surveying him calmly.

It's a man . . . it's a man . . . it's got to be a man . . . !

A flare popped half a mile away, throwing a sheen of sickly light over the scene.

Its body was pale and bloated, the skin mottled like melted cheese or wax. The creature bent at the knees and leapt, landing in the hole but not sinking into the mud. It snarled at him. Its fetid breath fogged the air between them.

It was not a German. It was not a man. Men didn't have yellow eyes.

Or tusks.

Scampering up the slope, William fled across the field with the howls of the creature nipping at his heels. He risked a glance to see if it was gaining. Blessed relief washed over him when he noticed that the thing hadn't left the hole.

He heard the ripping sounds, and the chewing. It was feeding.

He turned and ran into the night. The air exploded and burned around him as he dashed across the field and back into the labyrinthine trenches. Leaping over a sandbagged parapet, he saw hunched forms moving in the darkness below. He jumped another trench, missing his mark and clawing wildly at barbed wire as he slid down.

A cluster of German and French troops struggled against one another, not in battle, but in flight. Even as he watched the mud erupted before them, spewing earth and water skyward. William turned and ran before he could see what had caused it.

The earth was giving up its secrets.

The trench crossed another, then another, and soon he was lost in the intersections. The Argonne battlefield was a cacophony of hellish sound now, gunfire and explosions punctuated by cries of agony and other, less human exhortations.

Above him, out in front of the barbed wire, a man was being torn apart. The attacker ripped the victim's arm from its socket. Brandishing the bloody trophy like a club, he began to beat the other man mercilessly. He sank into the mud, raised his remaining arm in a feeble attempt to ward off the blows.

The victor *squealed* in delight.

William continued moving, never willing to stop, always fearing that to halt would be to give in . . . give in to whatever had taken possession of this battlefield.

He reached an empty portion of the trenches and slowed for a moment, gasping for breath. The sounds continued from all around him. The air was heavy with the stench they had first encountered in the village.

Around a dogleg in the trench, footsteps approached.

William looked to his left and saw a thick, yellowish-green cloud veiling the night sky. He wondered if the forest and trenches were on fire. Perhaps that would be good. Maybe flame would purge this place of all its ills, both manmade and . . . other.

The footsteps grew closer, falling faster.

Dizzy, William struggled to remain standing. His throat burned as pain lanced into his chest. His eyes watered. Breathing became difficult . . . and then impossible. He spat blood; crimson frothed on his agonized lips.

Something raced at him along the trench.

"William!" It growled his name, voice horribly distorted, inhuman.

Then he saw that the thing was Morris, a wound on his scalp bleeding freely and matched by a gash in his side.

"William!" his friend screamed again through his mask, and then he was there, catching him as he fell.

"Morris . . ." he coughed. "Hurts."

"Gas. They've gassed the trenches. Come on, we've got to keep moving."

"The Sergeant . . . Winston . . . Liggett . . . they're dead," William spat.

"We're all dead, William," Morris answered as he dragged him through the mud, away from the cloud.

Through the haze, William saw that his friend's hair had turned white.

And then he knew no more.

The grass in the meadow was cool. Beads of dew still clung to the green blades. Wetness also coated William's face as he sobbed quietly, his knees drawn up to his head and his notebook discarded beside him.

"Why do you cry, William?"

The voice startled him. He looked up and saw beauty.

It was the girl from the baker's, her head surrounded by an aura from the bright sun. Light gleamed from her golden tresses as she sat next to him. He remembered her name now. Clarice. She was . . . had been . . . his girlfriend. How could he have forgotten?

Slowly, as if surfacing from a dream, it was all starting to come back. He knew why he was crying. He'd had this conversation before.

"My father is butchering Onyx today," he said quietly as she took his hand. "I know he's only a silly cow, but . . ."

"You've grown fond of him," Clarice finished.

"Well, yes," William agreed. "I've looked after him since he was a calf. I can understand why father must do it, but it all seems so bloody unfair. Onyx has lived his life, day after day, never knowing why he really existed: for food. What kind of fate is that?"

"That is simply the way of things, my love," she answered softly. "There's too much of the poet in you. He's just a cow. We raise cattle to eat. That's why they exist."

"Is that the only reason?" William retorted. "Aren't they intelligent creatures, living things? Maybe they have hopes and dreams? How would you feel if you lived your life only to end up on someone's supper table? It's not fair, Clarice. Onyx is nothing more than fodder."

"Maybe we all are, William," she stated simply. "Come, would you like to see your home?"

"Yes!" William cried. "I'd like that very much. I can't seem to remember it properly at all."

They walked hand in hand through the pasture, the roof of the farmhouse looming just over the hill. They passed through a grazing herd of Holsteins.

"Mind the dung," William warned her, stepping lightly.

Then he stopped, terror rooting him to the spot.

A monstrous bull gazed at him with Sterling's face. "We're all fodder, lad," said the Crown Sergeant, slowly chewing his cud, a bulbous wound opening in his side.

"That's right, William," echoed Winston, his teats swollen with milk as he tore ravenously at a patch of grass. "It's the way things work. We exist to provide sustenance to the planet."

"We're germs," Liggett mooed through a splitting throat.

"I don't understand," William gasped.

"Perhaps you are not meant to," said a voice from behind him.

Clarice had vanished. William turned and saw Morris, buried up to his waist in the soft earth of the meadow.

"The earth still has secrets, William," he said gravely, sinking deeper into the loam. "Buried forever and never meant to be seen. Not by us."

"Come, William," his father cried from over the hill. "Bring the cattle. It's time for the slaughter."

Liggett, Winston and Sergeant Sterling began to snort in agony. Then William was sinking into the earth as well, struggling desperately as he watched the tufts of Morris's hair sink below.

It's a dream, I know it's a dream because his hair turned white back at the front.

William opened his mouth to scream and the earth rushed in. Above him, the slaughter began anew.

He tried to scream again, but his mouth was still blocked. Something long and cold was stuck in his throat. It was connected to . . .

He gagged, grasping the thing and pulling the cadaverous fingers from his mouth. Gasping for breath, he panicked when he found he couldn't move. He turned his head to the right and Morris's glazed eyes stared back at him, unblinking and filled with blood. A warm and sticky fluid dripped onto his forehead. Something heavy lay on top of him.

Bodies, he realized. He was buried beneath bodies. Muck and water covered most of his form, leaving his shoulders and head above, but the night was hidden from view. The echoes of the artillery blast still ricocheted through his mind, even though it could have been minutes or hours ago.

Something landed nearby with a heavy splash and a grunt, and then, for a few brief moments, there was silence. William held his breath and strained to hear or see, but his world had contracted to this; a claustrophobic stench of fresh blood and turned earth, and a cloying darkness caused by the shadows of the dead. He whispered Clarice's name . . .

And then something started ripping and tearing at the bodies around him.

It's time for the slaughter, he heard his father say again.

Something stopped him from crying out. At the time he

thought he was being calm and cautious, but later – when he was walking across a shattered, silent landscape with only the dead and unwanted as company – he realized that it was outright terror.

He was frozen stiff by fear.

Animal sounds of feeding, the snap of bones, wet sucks as bodies were hauled from the mud . . . whole or in pieces . . . gulping and retching. And in the background there was still gunfire, still the occasional thud of an artillery shell finding a home somewhere, but it no longer had the sound of a full-blown battle. Now, it was more like a skirmish.

Soon, with the sounds seeming to grow nearer as the thing ate its way down to him, the gunfire ceased altogether.

But the fighting continued. William heard shouts and screams, feet splashing through water and mud, bodies hitting the ground. At one point, he heard the Lord's Prayer chanted frantically in German. A horrific squeal sent him into a shiver. He clenched his fists and bit down on his lip, tasting blood, desperate to remain still lest the gorging thing sensed him down here.

He realized that he could see it, now. The body above him shifted and jerked as mouthfuls were taken from it. Its head snapped back and crunched into William's nose. His eyes watered, his face caught fire, but he remained still. He should be playing dead, he knew, holding a breath, narrowing his eyes so that light could not glint from the moisture there . . . but he could not close his eyes because he could see the thing, and the horror of it forbade him any solace.

Its mouth was the worst because it was surrounded by flecks of blood and clots of meat. The pale snouted nose leaked copiously over its fleshy lips and chin, diluting dead men's blood and sending it spraying into the air every time the thing moved its blocky jaws. A second before William finally managed to close his eyes, it sneezed.

Retreating into his own mind – trying to escape, to find beauty in his memories – William felt the warmth of alien fluid spatter across his face and run, slowly, down over his split lips.

He imagined blood gushing from a slaughtered bull's throat.

He tasted the vile mucus of the creature, the salty blood of the dead men, and the alkaline fear that was his own.

Daylight woke him. If the corpse had still lain atop him, he may well have remained there until his own body weakened and died, cosseted within his own strange dreams. But the dead soldier had been ripped up and scattered. The sun found William's face and gave him back his life.

He struggled from the loose earth and the body parts that surrounded him, trying not to look too closely. His hands found some horrendous things as he tried to haul himself upright. They were all cold.

An eerie silence hung over the battlefield. There were no whistles or whispers, no crackle of gunfire, no shouting or groaning or screaming from no-man's land. There was not even a breeze to rustle by his ears. Nothing. And as William dragged himself from the collapsed trench that had so nearly been his grave, he saw why.

Everyone was dead.

Never had he seen human destruction on this scale. The landscape around him was carpeted with corpses, piled two or three deep in places, all of them mutilated and tattered by whatever had killed them. Both armies must have abandoned their trenches to fight in the open . . . but fight whom? Not each other, he knew that. He had heard tales about the Hun, seen caricatures of them before he came to war, but the ones he had seen since then . . . the ones he had killed . . . had all looked exactly like him.

The things doing the killing last night were not even human.

William picked his way between corpses, but it soon became too much to look down all the time. So he strode, arms swinging, every fourth or fifth step finding something soft to walk on. He closed his eyes for minutes at a time, mindless of the danger of flooded shell-holes or barbed wire. He had faced much, much worse.

On the backs of his eyelids he saw perfection, beauty, Utopia: the valley back home that could not possibly be as wonderful and innocent as he saw it now, but in his mind's eye it was still the ultimate aim for his poor wandering self. He could smell it and taste it, and he could see it as well, every detail clear and defined, every rolling field—

He wondered what might live beneath his father's farm.

He had to get back to his lines, warn them, tell them there was something here worse than the Hun. He had seen and heard thousands die, but he could save many more if he hurried. There was so little time. It was midday already. He did not want to be out here after dark.

William sneezed twice and spat out a great clot of mucus. A parliament of rooks feeding on a horse's bloated corpse took to the air.

He wiped his nose with a muddy sleeve. His head had begun to throb and his joints were stiffening with every step.

Damn. After all this, he was coming down with the 'flu.

MICHAEL MARSHALL SMITH

Open Doors

MICHAEL MARSHALL SMITH IS a novelist and screenwriter who lives in north London and Brighton with his wife Paula and two cats. His first novel, *Only Forward,* won the August Derleth and Philip K. Dick awards. His second, *Spares,* was optioned by Steven Spielberg and translated in seventeen countries worldwide, while his third, *One of Us,* was optioned by Warner Brothers.

His most recent books, *The Straw Men* and *The Lonely Dead* (aka *The Upright Man*), were published under the name "Michael Marshall" and have been international best-sellers. He is currently writing a third volume in the series.

Smith's short stories have won the British Fantasy Award three times, and are collected in *What You Make It* and the International Horror Guild Award-winning *More Tomorrow & Other Stories.* Six of his tales are currently under option for television.

"I'd been nursing the underlying idea for this story for quite a while," reveals the author, "waiting to find a way to get into it: I am someone who will watch wacky home video programmes on television and spend as much time looking at the details in the houses, at the hints of other lives, as I do laughing at the people falling over. Then one afternoon I happened to walk past a nice, normal house in our neighbourhood, and I thought 'Wouldn't it be odd to just walk up that path, knock on the door and walk in.'

"Thankfully I only did it in a fictional reality . . ."

NEVER BEEN GREAT AT planning, I'll admit that. Make decisions on the spur of the moment. No forward thought, unless you count years of wondering and speculating – and you shouldn't, because I certainly don't. None of it was to do with specifics, with the mechanics of the situation, with anything that would have helped. I just went and did it. Like always. That's me all over. I just go and do it.

Here's how it happened. It's a Saturday. My wife is gone for the day, out at a big lunch for a mate who's getting married in a couple weeks. Shit – that's another thing she'll have to . . . whatever. She'll work it out. Anyway, she got picked up at noon and went off in a cab full of women and balloons and I was left in the house on my own. I had work to do, so that was okay. Problem was I just couldn't seem to do it. Don't know if you get that sometimes: just can't apply yourself to something. You've got a job to do – in my case it was fixing up a busted old television set, big as a fridge and hardly worth saving, but if that's what they want, it's their money – and it just won't settle in front of you as a task. No big deal, it wasn't like it had to be fixed in a hurry, and it's a Saturday. I'm a free man. I can do anything I want.

Problem was that I found I couldn't settle to anything else either. I had the afternoon ahead, probably the whole evening too. The wife and her pals don't get together often, and when they do, they drink like there's no tomorrow. Maybe that was the problem – having a block of time all to myself for once. Doesn't happen often. You get out of the habit. I don't know. I just couldn't get down to anything. I tried working, tried reading, tried going on the web and just moping around. None of it felt like I was doing anything. None of it felt like *activity*. It just didn't feel like I thought it would.

I don't like this, I thought: it's just not *working out*.

In the end I got so grumpy and restless I grabbed a book and left the house. There's a new pub opened up not far from the tube station, and I decided I'd go there, try to read for a while. I stopped by a newsagents on the corner opposite the pub, bought myself a pack of ten cigarettes. I'm giving up. I've been giving up for a while now – and sticking to it, more or less, just a few here and there, and never in the house – but sometimes you've just got to have a fucking cigarette. Sometimes the giving up is worse for you than the cigarettes themselves. Your concentration goes. You don't feel yourself. The world feels like it's just out of reach, as if you're not a part of it any more and not much missed. The annoying thing is that anyone who knows you're not smoking tends to think that anything that's wrong with you, any bad mood, any unsettledness, is just due to the lack of cigs. I was pretty sure it wasn't nicotine drought that was causing my restlessness, but so long as I was out of the house I thought I might as well have a couple.

When I got to the pub – which we called the Hairy Pub, because it used to be covered in ivy to the point where you couldn't actually see the building underneath – it wasn't too crowded, and I was able to score one of the big new leather armchairs in the window, right by a fucking great fern. The pub never used to be like this. It used to be an old-fashioned, unreconstituted boozer, and – as such – a bit shit. I like old-fashioned pubs as much as the next man, but this one just wasn't very good. Now they've got posh chairs and a cappuccino machine and polite staff and frankly, I'm not complaining. They cut off all the ivy and painted it black and it looks alright. Whatever. The pub's not really relevant. I sat there for an hour or so, having a couple of coffees and smoking a couple of my small packet of cigarettes. Each one caused me a manageable slap of guilt, as did the chocolate powder sprinkled on the cappuccinos. I've been on the frigging Atkins diet for a month, to cap it all, which means, as you doubtless know, no carbohydrates. None. "Thou shalt not carb," the great Doctor proclaimed, and then died. Chocolate is carbs, as – more importantly – are pizza, pasta and special fried rice, the three food groups which make human life worth living, the triumvirate of grubstuffs which make crawling out of the swamp seem worth it. That month has seen me lose a big six pounds, or, put another way, one point something pounds a week, while not being able to eat anything I like. It's crap. Anyway.

I tried to read, but couldn't really get into my book. Couldn't get into a newspaper either. My attention kept drifting, lighting on people sitting in clumps around the pub, wondering what they were doing there on a Saturday afternoon. Some looked hungover already, others were in the foothills of starting one for Sunday. They were all wearing their own clothes and had their hair arranged in certain ways, which they were happy with, or not; some had loud laughs, others sat pretty quietly. The staff swished to and fro – most of them seem to be rather gay, in that pub: not something that exercises me in the least, merely making a factual observation. I've often wondered what it's like, being gay. Different, certainly. The music was just loud enough to be distracting, and I only recognised about one song in three. I could see other people tapping their feet, though, bobbing their heads. The songs meant something in their lives. Not in mine. I wondered when they'd first heard it, how come it had come to be a part of them and not me. I looked at my coffee cup and my book and my little pack of cigarettes and I got bored with them and myself, and bored with my trousers and thoughts and everything else I knew and understood. Custom had staled their infinity variety. Custom was making my hands twitch.

In the end I got up and left. I stomped back out onto the street, caught between wistful and depressed and pissed off. Then I did something I wasn't altogether expecting. Instead of walking straight past the newsagent, I swerved and went back in. I went straight up to the desk and asked for a pack of Marlboro Lites. The guy got it, and I paid for them. Emerged back onto the street, looking at what I held in my hands. Been a long, long time since I'd bought a pack of twenty cigarettes. It's like that with everyone these days – you check, in the pubs and bars, everyone's smoking tens now, just to prove they're giving up.

But you can give up giving up, you know. You can choose to say one thing instead of the other, to say the word "twenty" instead of "ten". That's all it takes. You're not as trapped as you think you are. There are other roads, other options, other doors. Always.

I crossed the street at the lights and then, instead of walking back the way I'd come (along the main road, past the station), I took a turning which led to a shortcut through some quiet residential streets. It's pretty hilly around where I live now,

though if you're on the way back from the pub then you're
walking down for most of the way. My first right took me into
Addison Road, which is short and has a school on one side.
Then I turned left into a street whose name I'm not even sure
of, a short little road with some two storey brick Victorian
houses on either side. At the bottom of it is Brenneck Road, at
which point I'd be rejoining the route I would have taken had I
gone the other way.

I was walking along that stretch of pavement, halfway between here and there, halfway between one thing and the
other, when I did it.

I turned left suddenly, pushed open the black wooden gate I
happened to be passing, and walked up to the house beyond it.
Don't know what number it was. Don't know anything about
the house. Never noticed it before. But I went up to the door
and saw that it was one house, not divided up into flats. I
pressed the buzzer. It rang loudly inside.

While I was waiting I glanced back, taking a better look at the
front garden. Nothing to see, really – standard stuff. Tiny bit of
grass, place for the bins, a small tree. Manageable.

I turned when I heard the sound of the door being opened.

A young woman, mid-twenties, was standing there. She had
shoulder length brown hair and a mild tan and white teeth. She
looked nice, and pretty, and I thought okay – I'm going to do it.

"Hello?" she said, ready to be helpful.

"Hi," I replied, and pushed past her into the house. Not
hard, not violent, just enough to get past her.

I strode down the hallway, took a quick peek in the front
room (stripped pine floors, creamy-white sofa, decent new
widescreen television) and went straight through to the kitch-
en, which was out the back. They'd had it done, got some
architect or builder to knock out most of the wall and replace it
with glass, and it looked good. I wanted to do something like
that at home, but the wife thought it would be too modern and
"not in keeping with a Victorian residence". Bollocks. It looked
great.

"Just a bloody minute . . ." said a voice, and I saw the woman
had followed me in. She looked very wary, understandably.
"What the hell are you doing?"

I glanced over her shoulder and saw the front door was still
open, but first things first. I went over to the fridge – nice big
Bosch, matt silver. We've got a Neff. One of those retro ones, in

pale green. Looks nice but holds fuck all. This Bosch was full to the brim. Nice food, too. Good cheese. Pre-cut fruit salad. A pair of *salmon en croûte*, tasty, very nice with some new potatoes, which I saw were also there ready to go. Cold meats, pasta salads, da da da. From Waitrose, supermarket of choice. Wife always shops at Tescos, and it's not bad but it's not half as good.

"Nice," I said. "Okay. Did you buy all this? Or was it your fella?"

She just stared at me, goggle-eyed, didn't answer. But I knew it was her, just from the way she looked at it. She blinked, trying to work out what to do. I smiled, trying to reassure her it was all okay.

"I'm going to call the police."

"No you're not," I said, and smacked her one.

It wasn't hard, but she wasn't expecting it. She staggered back, caught her leg on one of the chairs around the table (nice-looking chairs, kind of ethnic, oak) and fell back on her arse. Head clunked against the fridge. Again, not hard, but enough to take the wind out of her sails for a second.

I checked the back door – shut, locked – and then stepped over her down the hallway and to the front. A woman with a pram was passing by on the pavement. I gave her a big smile and said good afternoon and she smiled back (what a nice man) and then I shut the door. Went to the little table, grubbed around a second, and came up with a set of keys, and a spare. Locked the front door. Went into the front room to check: all windows shut and secured, and here's a couple who stumped up for double glazing. Good for keeping the heat in. Good for keeping the noise in too, I'm afraid.

Went upstairs, had a quick check around. We're secure. Okay. Excellenta.

Back in the kitchen the woman is pushing herself to her feet. As I come in she skitters away from me and slips (nice clean floors), ends up on her bum again. She makes a strange little noise and her eyes are darting all over the place.

"Now listen," I said. "Listen carefully. This is not what you think. I am not going to hurt you unless I have to."

"Get out," she screamed.

"No, I'm not going to do that," I said. "I'm going to stay here. Do you understand?"

She just stared at me, breathing hard, building up to scream again. She was cowering over by the microwave (matt silver again, nice consistent look throughout the whole kitchen area, there's some thought gone into all this).

"Screaming really isn't going to help," I said. It's not that I mind the sound, particularly, but there's a lot of glass out the back and one of the neighbours might hear. "It's just going to piss me off, and I can't see why you'd want to do that. Just not in your best interests, to be honest. Not at this stage."

Then I saw what she was doing, and had to go quickly over there. She had her mobile phone in her hand, hidden behind the microwave, and was trying to activate a speed-dial number.

I grabbed it off her. "I like that," I said. "Really. I do. I like the idea, I like the execution. Nearly worked. Like I said, I admire it. But don't *ever fucking do anything like that again.*"

And then I hit her. Properly, this time.

It's a funny old thing, hitting women. Frowned upon, these days. And, so like everything else you're not supposed to do, it feels like a big old step when you do it. Like you're opening a door most people don't have the courage to go through. You don't know what's on the other side of this door. There's a chance, admittedly, that it won't be anything good. But it's a door, see? There must be *something* on the other side. It stands to reason. Otherwise it wouldn't be there. And if you don't open some of those doors, you're never going to know what you missed.

She fell over and I left her there. I went around the house, collecting up the normal phones. Don't want to break them, but I put there somewhere she's not going to find them.

I feel both good and bad by this stage. Everything's gone fine, would be according to plan if there'd ever been one. Everything's cool, and I'm quietly confident and excited. I love it. But something tells me something's not right yet. I don't know what it is. Can't put my finger on it.

So I ignore it. That's what I do. I just think about something else. I made a cup of tea, stepping over her where she's lying on the floor, and I put a big old couple of spoonfuls of sugar in it. It's much nicer that way, if the truth be told. I checked the woman was still breathing – she was – and then went into the front room.

Then I sat on the sofa, and got busy with her phone.

I looked through the address book on it, and found a few obvious ones. "Mum Mobile", not hard to work out who that is, is it. Few girls' nicknames, obviously good friends. And one that is a single letter, "N". I'm guessing that's her boyfriend (no wedding ring but everything about this house says two people live here) and I also go out on a limb and opt for "Nick". She doesn't look like she'd be going out with a Nigel or Nathaniel or Norman (got nothing against those names, you understand, just she isn't the type). So first I send a quick text message to "N".

Then I dial "Mum Mobile".

It rings for a few seconds and then a middle-aged woman's voice says "Hello, darling". I didn't say anything, obviously. I just listen to this woman's voice. She says hello a few times, sounding a bit confused, irritable, worried. Then she puts the phone down.

It's enough. I've heard enough to get an idea of what she's like, which is all I want. After all, it wouldn't be realistic for a boyfriend never to have heard his mother-in-law's voice. So then I send her a quick text, saying the number got dialled by accident, everything's fine, and I (or of course, *she*, so far as her Mum knows) will call her properly later.

A minute later a text comes back saying OKAY, LOVE. Sorted.

Fifteen minutes later, "N" arrives at the front door, blowing hard. He lets himself in with his key. He runs towards the living room, expecting to see his girlfriend lying there naked and waiting. That, after all, is the impression I/she gave in the text.

He never even saw me behind the door. She did, unfortunately. I saw her wake up as I was straddled over him, and I know she saw the brick come down with the blow that did for him. Shame, for any number of reasons. Transition should be much smoother than that, and she's just going to feel alienated.

But at least I've got his wallet now, which will come in handy. Credit cards, driving licence, the lot. And guess what? He *was* a Nick. Just goes to show.

I know what I'm doing.

She's up on the second floor now. Her name's Karen, I know now. Which is a nice name. I've been practising saying it, in lots of ways. Happy ways, mainly; plus a few stern ways, just in case. Not sure where she is just at this second, but I'm guessing the bathroom. A door that can be locked. She's likely to start screaming again, in a while, so I'm going to have to work out what to do about that. Not all double-glazed up there. Last bout I covered with turning the television up loud. Limit to how many times I'm going to be able to do that. But who knows what the limits are? They're not as tight as you'd think. You can hit people, it turns out. You can listen to music you've never heard of, and learn to like it. You can choose not to give a shit what dead Mr Atkins said: you actually can eat potatoes if you feel like it – just like we're going to a little later on, when Karen calms down and we can sit like proper mates and have our supper.

For the time being I'm just going to sit on this nice sofa and smoke all I want and watch TV programmes I've never seen before. Judging by all the videos, Karen and Nick like documentaries. Better get used to that. Never been one for that kind of thing myself, but it's nice to have a change. For it all to be different. For it to be someone else's life, and not the same old shit of mine, the same old faces, the same old everything. I see later there's one of those home video programmes on, too. I love those. They're my favourite. I love seeing all the houses, the gardens, the wives and dogs. All of the different lives. Superb. If I get bored, I'll just text a few of her friends.

I was worried earlier, but I'm not now. What I felt was just a little niggle of doubt. Gone now. If you've got what it takes, everything's possible. I have high hopes, to be honest. I'm going to like being Nick. The woman's nice-looking. Much better than the last. From what I can make out, Nick was an estate agent. Piece of piss. I could do that – whereas, if I'm honest, I was crap at repairing televisions. Couldn't pick it up in two days, that was for sure. Wouldn't have been long before people started ringing me up, coming round, wanting their televisions back and spotting I wasn't the bloke they left them with and that they weren't fixed. Wasn't a stable life. Just as today, ten minutes after I left the house, a car will have come around expecting to pick up the woman, to take her out to a wonderful lunch with champagne and laughs. I knew about that. It was on their calendar, on the side of that retro fridge. Kind of forced my hand. Two days is a very short life and I didn't want to leave so soon, but I couldn't have talked my way out of that.

She hadn't worked out anyway. Didn't want a new start. Just wanted what she'd had.

Doesn't matter. I like a change. This life, I think it could be different. Could go on for longer. Well . . . to be honest, you only ever get about three, four days. But this will definitely be easier than the last one. More relaxing.

No sign of kids, for a start.

CAITLÍN R. KIERNAN

Andromeda Among the Stones

CAITLÍN R. KIERNAN WAS born in Ireland and now lives in Atlanta, Georgia. She has published five novels: *Silk, Threshold, The Five of Cups, Low Red Moon* and, most recently, *Murder of Angels,* and her short fiction has been collected in *Tales of Pain and Wonder, From Weird and Distant Shores, Wrong Things* (with Poppy Z. Brite) and *To Charles Fort, With Love.* She is currently writing her sixth novel, *Daughter of Hounds.*

Kiernan has a great affection for the sea, although her stories might lead you to believe otherwise.

As the author explains: "This short story is the third in a trilogy that began with 'A Redress for Andromeda' and also includes 'Nor the Demons Down Under the Sea'. All these stories centre on the Dandridge House and the fate of Meredith Dandridge, but I think 'Andromeda Among the Stones' is by far the most effective and fully realised of them all. This is me playing with the short story as epic, something I've been reluctant to do for much of my writing career.

"The story was written in October 2002 and was composed entirely to *Empires* by VNV Nation (Metropolis Records, 2000)."

"I cannot think of the deep sea without shuddering . . ."
—H. P. Lovecraft

I

October 1914

"IS SHE REALLY AND truly dead, Father?" the girl asked, and Machen Dandridge, already an old man at fifty-one, looked up at the low buttermilk sky again and closed the black book clutched in his hands. He'd carved the tall headstone himself, the marker for his wife's grave there by the relentless Pacific, black shale obelisk with its hasty death's head, and his daughter stepped gingerly around the raw earth and pressed her fingers against the monument.

"Why did you not give her to the sea?" she asked. "She always wanted to go down to the sea at the end. She often told me so."

"I've given her back to the earth instead," Machen told her and rubbed at his eyes. The cold sunlight through thin clouds enough to make his head ache, his daughter's voice like thunder, and he shut his aching eyes for a moment. Just a little comfort in the almost blackness trapped behind his lids, parchment skin too insubstantial to bring the balm of genuine darkness, void to match the shades of his soul, and Machen whispered one of the prayers from the heavy black book and then looked at the grave again.

"Well, that's what she always said," the girl said again, running her fingertips across the rough-hewn stone.

"Things changed at the end, child. The sea wouldn't have taken her. I had to give her back to the earth."

"She said it was a sacrilege, planting people in the ground like wheat, like kernels of corn."

"She did?" and he glanced anxiously over his left shoulder, looking back across the waves the wind was making in the high and yellow-brown grass, the narrow trail leading back down to the tall and brooding house that he'd built for his wife twenty-four years ago, back towards the cliffs and the place where the sea and sky blurred seamlessly together.

"Yes, she did. She said only barbarians and heathens stick their dead in the ground like turnips."

"I had no choice," Machen replied, wondering if that was the truth, exactly, or only something he'd like to believe. "The sea wouldn't take her, and I couldn't bring myself to burn her."

"Only heathens burn their dead," his daughter said disapprovingly and leaned close to the obelisk, setting her ear against the charcoal shale.

"Do you hear anything?"

"No, Father. Of course not. She's dead. You just said so."

"Yes," Machen whispered. "She is." And the wind whipping across the hillside made a hungry, waiting sound that told him it was time for them to head back to the house.

This is where I stand, at the bottom gate, and I hold the key to the abyss . . .

"But it's better that way," the girl said, her ear still pressed tight against the obelisk. "She couldn't stand the pain any longer. It was cutting her up inside."

"She told you that?"

"She didn't have to tell me that. I saw it in her eyes."

The ebony key to the first day and the last, the key to the moment when the stars wink out, one by one, and the sea heaves its rotting belly at the empty, sagging sky . . .

"You're only a child," he said. "You shouldn't have had to see such things. Not yet."

"It can't very well be helped now," she answered and stepped away from her mother's grave, one hand cupping her ear like maybe it had begun to hurt. "You know that, old man."

"I do," and he almost said her name then, Meredith, his mother's name, but the wind was too close, the listening wind and the salt-and-semen stink of the breakers crashing against the cliffs. "But I can wish it were otherwise."

"If wishes were horses, beggars would ride."

And Machen watched silently as Meredith Dandridge knelt in the grass and placed her handful of wilting wildflowers on the freshly-turned soil; if it were spring instead of autumn, he thought, there would be dandelions and poppies. If it were spring instead of autumn, the woman wrapped in a quilt and nailed up inside a pine-board casket would still be breathing. If it were spring, they would not be alone now, him and his daughter at the edge of the world. The wind teased the girl's long yellow hair, and the sun glittered dimly in her warm brown eyes.

The key I have accepted full in the knowledge of its weight.

"Remember me," Meredith whispered, either to her dead mother or something else, and he didn't ask her which.

"We should be heading back now," he said and glanced over his shoulder again.

"So soon? Is that all you're going to read from the book? Is that all of it?"

"Yes, that's all of it, for now," though there would be more, later, when the harvest moon swelled orange-red and bloated and hung itself in the wide California night. When the women came to dance, then there would be other words to say, to keep his wife in the ground and the gate shut for at least another year.

The weight that is the weight of all salvation, the weight that holds the line against the last, unending night.

"It's better this way," his daughter said again, standing up, brushing the dirt off her stockings, from the hem of her black dress. "There was so little left of her."

"Don't talk of that here," Machen replied, more sternly than he'd intended, but Meredith didn't seem to have noticed, or if she'd noticed, not to have minded the tone of her father's voice.

"I will remember her the way she was before, when she was still beautiful."

"That's what she would want," he said and took his daughter's hand. "That's the way I'll remember her, as well," but he knew that was a lie, as false as any lie any living man ever uttered. Knew that he would always see his wife as the writhing, twisted thing she'd become at the last, the way she was after the gates were almost thrown open and she placed herself on the threshold.

The frozen weight of the sea, the burning weight of starlight and my final breath. I hold the line. I hold the ebony key against the last day of all.

And Machen Dandridge turned his back on his wife's grave and led his daughter down the dirt and gravel path, back to the house waiting for them like a curse.

II

November 1914

Meredith Dandridge lay very still in her big bed, her big room with its high ceiling and no pictures hung on the walls, and she listened to the tireless sea slamming itself against the rocks. The sea to take the entire world apart one gritty speck at a time, the sea that was here first and would be here long after the continents had finally been weathered down to so much slime and sand. She knew this because her father had read to her from his heavy black book, the book that had no name, the book that she couldn't ever read for herself or the demons would come for her in the night. And she knew, too, because of the books he had *given* her, her books – *Atlantis: The Antediluvian World* and *The World Before the Deluge* and *Atlantis and Lost Lemuria*. Everything above the waves on borrowed time, her father had said again and again, waiting for the day when the sea rose once more and drowned the land beneath its smothering, salty bosom, and the highest mountains and deepest valleys became a playground for sea serpents and octopi and schools of herring. Forests to become Poseidon's orchards, her father said, though she knew Poseidon wasn't the true name of the god-thing at the bottom of the ocean, just a name some dead man gave it thousands of years ago.

"Should I read you a story tonight, Merry?" her dead mother asked, sitting right there in the chair beside the bed. She smelled like fish and mud, even though they'd buried her in the dry ground at the top of the hill behind the house. Meredith didn't look at her, because she'd spent so much time already trying to remember her mother's face the way it was *before* and didn't want to see the ruined face the ghost was wearing like a mask. As bad as the face her brother now wore, worse than that, and Meredith shrugged and pushed the blankets back a little.

"If you can't sleep, it might help," her mother said with a voice like kelp stalks swaying slowly in deep water.

"It might," Meredith replied, staring at a place where the wallpaper had begun to peel free of one of the walls, wishing there were a candle in the room or an oil lamp so the ghost would leave her alone. "And it might not."

"I could read to you from Hans Christian Andersen, or one of Grimm's tales," her mother sighed. " 'The Little Mermaid' or 'The Fisherman and his Wife'?"

"You could tell me what it's like in Hell," the girl replied.

"Dear, I don't have to tell you that," her ghost mother whispered, her voice gone suddenly regretful and sad. "I know I don't have to ever tell you that."

"There might be different hells," Meredith replied. "This one, and the one Father sent you away to, and the one Avery is lost inside. No one ever said there could only be one, did they? A hell for the dead German soldiers and another for the French, a hell for Christians and another for the Jews. And maybe another for all the pagans—"

"Your father didn't send me anywhere, child. I crossed the threshold of my own accord."

"So I would be alone in *this* hell."

The ghost clicked its sharp teeth together, and Meredith could hear the anemone tendrils between its iridescent fish eyes quickly withdrawing into the hollow places in her mother's decaying skull.

"I could read you a poem," her mother said hopefully. "I could sing you a song."

"It isn't all fire and brimstone, is it? Not the hell where you are? It's blacker than night and cold as ice, isn't it, Mother?"

"Did he think it would save me to put me in the earth? Does the old fool think it will bring me back across, like Persephone?"

Too many questions, hers and her mother's, and for a moment Meredith Dandridge didn't answer the ghost, kept her eyes on the shadowy wallpaper strips, the pinstripe wall, wishing the sun would rise and pour warm and gold as honey through the drapes.

"I crossed the threshold of my *own* accord," the ghost said again, and Meredith wondered if it thought she didn't hear the first time. Or maybe something her mother needed to believe and might stop believing if she stopped repeating it. "Someone had to do it."

"It didn't have to be you."

The wind whistled wild and shrill around the eaves of the house, invisible lips pressed to a vast, invisible instrument, and Meredith shivered and pulled the covers up to her chin again.

"There was no one else. It wouldn't take your brother. The one who wields the key cannot be a man. You know that, Merry. Avery knew that, too."

"There are other women," Meredith said, speaking through gritted teeth, not wanting to start crying but the tears already hot in her eyes. "It could have been someone else. It didn't have to be my mother."

"Some other child's mother, then?" the ghost asked. "Some other mother's daughter?"

"Go back to your hell," Meredith said, still looking at the wall, spitting the words like poison. "Go back to your hole in the ground and tell your fairy tales to the worms."

"You have to be strong now, Merry. You have to listen to your father and you have to be ready. I wasn't strong enough."

And finally she did turn to face her mother, what was left of her mother's face, the scuttling things nesting in her tangled hair, the silver scales and barnacles, the stinging anemone crown, and Meredith Dandridge didn't flinch or look away.

"One day," she said, "I'll take that damned black book of his and I'll toss it into the stove. I'll take it, mother, and toss it into the hearth, and then they can come out of the sea and drag us both away—"

But then her mother cried out and came apart like a breaking wave against the shingle, water poured from the tin pail that had given it shape, her flesh gone suddenly as clear and shimmering as glass, before she drained away and leaked through the cracks between the floorboards. The girl reached out and dipped her fingers into the shallow pool left behind in the wicker seat of the chair. The water was cold and smelled unclean. And then she lay awake until dawn, listening to the ocean, to all the unthinking noises a house makes in the small hours of a night.

III

May 1914
Avery Dandridge had his father's eyes, but someone else's soul to peer out through them, and to his sister he was hope that there might be a life somewhere beyond the rambling house beside the sea. Five years her senior, he'd gone away to school in San Francisco for a while, almost a year, because their mother wanted him to. But there had been an incident and he was sent home again, transgressions only spoken of in whispers and nothing anyone ever bothered to explain to Meredith, but that was fine with her. She only cared that he was back and she was that much less alone.

"Tell me about the earthquake," she asked him, one day not long after he'd returned, the two of them walking together along the narrow beach below the cliffs, sand the color of coal dust, noisy gulls and driftwood like bones washed in by the tide. "Tell me all about the fire."

"The earthquake? Merry, that was eight *years* ago. You were still just a baby, that was such long time ago," and then he picked up a shell and turned it over in his hand, brushing away some of the dark sand stuck to it. "People don't like to talk about the earthquake anymore. I never heard them say much about it."

"Oh," she said, not sure what to say next but still full of questions. "Father says it was a sign, a sign from—"

"Maybe you shouldn't believe everything he says, Merry. It was an earthquake." And she felt a thrill then, like a tiny jolt of electricity rising up her spine and spreading out across her scalp, that anyone, much less Avery, would question their father and suggest she do likewise.

"Have you stopped believing in the signs?" she asked, breathless. "Is *that* what you learned in school?"

"I didn't learn much of anything important in school," he replied and showed her the shell in his palm. Hardly as big around as a nickel, but peaked in the center like a Chinaman's hat, radial lines of chestnut brown, and "It's pretty," she said as he placed it in her palm.

"What's it called?"

"It's a limpet," he replied, because Avery knew all about shells and fish and the fossils in the cliffs, things he'd learned from their father's books and not from school. "It's a shield limpet. The jackmackerel carry them into battle when they fight the eels."

Meredith laughed out loud at that last part, and he laughed, too, then sat down on a rock at the edge of a wide tidepool. She stood there beside him, still inspecting the shell in her hand, turning it over and over again. The concave underside of the limpet was smoother than silk and would be white if not for the faintest iridescent hint of blue.

"That's not true," she said. "Everyone knows the jackmackerel and the eels are friends."

"Sure they are," Avery said. "Everyone knows that," but he was staring out to sea now and didn't turn to look at her. In a moment, she slipped the shell into a pocket of her sweater and sat down on the rock next to him.

"Do you see something out there?" she asked, and he

nodded his head, but didn't speak. The wind rushed cold and damp across the beach and painted ripples on the surface of the pool at their feet; the wind and the waves seemed louder than usual, and Meredith wondered if that meant a storm was coming.

"Not a storm," Avery said, and that didn't surprise her because he often knew what she was thinking before she said it. "A war's coming, Merry."

"Oh yes, the jackmackerel and the eels," Merry laughed and squinted towards the horizon, trying to see whatever it was that had attracted her brother's attention. "The squid and the mussels."

"Don't be silly. Everyone knows that the squid and the mussels are great friends," and that made her laugh again. But Avery didn't laugh, looked away from the sea and stared down instead at the scuffed toes of his boots dangling a few inches above the water.

"There's never been a war like the one that's coming," he said after a while. "All the nations of the earth at each other's throats, Merry, and when we're done with all the killing, no one will be left to stand against the sea."

She took a very deep breath, the clean, salty air to clear her head, and began to pick at a barnacle on the rock.

"If that were true," she said, "Father would have told us. He would have shown us the signs."

"He doesn't see them. He doesn't dream the way I do."

"But you told him?"

"I tried. But he thinks it's something they put in my head at school. He thinks it's some kind of trick to make him look away."

Merry stopped picking at the barnacle because it was making her fingers sore, and they'd be bleeding soon if she kept it up. She decided it was better to watch the things trapped in the tidepool, the little garden stranded there until the sea came back to claim it. Periwinkle snails and hermit crabs wearing stolen shells, crimson starfish and starfish the shape and color of sunflowers.

"He thinks they're using me to make him look the other way, to catch him off his guard," Avery whispered, his voice almost lost in the rising wind. "He thinks I'm being set against him."

"Avery, I don't believe Father would say that about you."

"He didn't have to say it," and her brother's dark and shining eyes gazed out at the sea and sky again.

"We should be heading back soon, shouldn't we? The tide will be coming in before long," Meredith said, noticing how much higher up the beach the waves were reaching than the last time she'd looked. Another half hour and the insatiable ocean would be battering itself against the rough shale cliffs at their backs.

" 'Wave after wave, each mightier than the last,' " Avery whispered, closing his eyes tight and the words coming from his pale, thin lips sounded like someone else, someone old and tired that Meredith had never loved. " 'Till last, a ninth one, gathering half the deep and full of voices, slowly rose and plunged roaring, and all the wave was in a flame—' "

"What's that?" she asked, interrupting because she didn't want to hear anymore. Is it from Father's book?"

"No, it's not," he replied, sounding more like himself again, more like her brother. He opened his eyes and a tear rolled slowly down his wind-chapped cheek. "It's just something they taught me at school."

"How can a wave be in flame? Is it supposed to be a riddle?" she asked, and he shook his head.

"No," he said and wiped at his face with his hands. "It's nothing at all, just a silly bit of poetry they made us memorize. School is full of silly poetry."

"Is that why you came home?"

"We ought to start back," he said, glancing quickly over his shoulder at the high cliffs, the steep trail leading back up towards the house. "Can't have the tide catching us with our trousers down, now can we?"

"I don't even wear trousers," Merry said glumly, still busy thinking about that ninth wave, the fire and the water, and Avery put an arm around her and held her close to him for a moment while the advancing sea dragged itself eagerly back and forth across the moss-scabbed rocks.

IV

January 1915
Meredith sat alone on the floor in the hallway, the narrow hall connecting the foyer to the kitchen and a bathroom, and then

farther along, all the way back at the very rear of the house, this tall door that was always locked. The tarnished brass key always hung on its ring upon her father's belt, and she pressed her ear against the wood and strained to hear anything at all. The wood was damp and very cold and the smell of salt water and mildew seeped freely through the space between the bottom of the door and the floor, between the door and the jamb. Once-solid redwood that had long since begun to rot from the continual moisture, the ocean's breath to rust the hinges so the door cried out like a stepped-on cat every time it was opened or closed. Even as a very small child, Meredith had feared this door, even in the days before she'd started to understand what lay in the deep place beneath her father's house.

Outside, the icy winter wind howled, and she shivered and pulled her grey wool shawl tighter about her shoulders; the very last thing her mother had made for her, that shawl. Almost as much hatred in Merry for the wind as for the sea, but at least it smothered the awful thumps and moans that came, day and night, from the attic room where her father had locked Avery away in June.

"There are breaches between the worlds, Merry," he had said, a few days before he picked the lock on the hallway door with the sharpened tip-end of a buttonhook and went down to the deep place by himself. "Rifts, fractures, ruptures. If they can't be closed, they have to be guarded against the things on the other side that don't belong here."

"Father says it's a portal," she'd replied, closing the book she'd been reading, a dusty, dog-eared copy of Franz Unger's *Primitive World.*

Her brother had laughed a dry, humourless laugh and shaken his head, nervously watching the fading day through the parlour windows. "Portals are built on purpose, to be used. These things are accidents, at best, casualties of happenstance, tears in space when one world passes much too near another."

"Well, that's not what Father says."

"Read your book, Merry. One day you'll understand. One day soon, when you're not a child anymore and he loses his hold on you."

And she'd frowned, sighed, and opened her book again, opening it at random to one of the strangely melancholy lithographs, "The Period of the Muschelkalk [Middle Trias]."

A violent seascape and in the foreground a reef jutting above the waves, crowded with algae-draped driftwood branches and the shells of stranded mollusca and crinoidea, something like a crocodile that the author called *Nothosaurus giganteus* clinging to the reef so it wouldn't be swept back into the storm-tossed depths. Overhead, the night sky a turbulent mass of clouds with the small, white moon, full or near enough to full, peeking through to illuminate the ancient scene.

"You mean planets?" she'd asked Avery. "You mean moons and stars?"

"No, I mean *worlds*. Now, read your book and don't ask so many questions."

Meredith thought she heard creaking wood, her father's heavy footsteps, the dry ruffling of cloth rubbing against cloth, and she stood quickly, not wanting to be caught listening at the door again, was busy straightening her rumpled dress when she realized that he was standing there in the hall behind her, instead. Her mistake, thinking he'd gone to the deep place, when he was somewhere else all along, in his library or the attic room with Avery, braving the cold to visit her mother's grave on the hill.

"What are you doing, child?" he asked her gruffly and tugged at his beard; there were streaks of silver-grey that weren't there only a couple of months before, scars from the night they lost her mother, his wife, the night the demons tried to squeeze in through the tear and Ellen Dandridge had tried to block their way. His face grown years older in the space of weeks, dark crescents beneath his eyes like bruises, the deep creases in his forehead, and he brushed his daughter's blonde hair from her eyes.

"Would it have been different, if you'd believed Avery from the start?"

For a moment he didn't reply and the silence, his face set as hard and perfectly unreadable as stone, made her want to strike him, made her wish she could kick open the rotting, sea-damp door and hurl him screaming down the stairs to whatever was waiting for them both in the deep place.

"I don't know, Meredith. But I had to trust the book, and I had to believe the signs in the heavens."

"You were too arrogant, old man. You almost gave away the whole wide world because you couldn't admit you might be wrong."

"You should be thankful that your mother can't hear you, young lady, using that tone of voice with your own father."

Meredith turned and looked at the tall door again, the symbols drawn on the wood in whitewash and blood.

"She can hear me," Meredith told him. "She talks to me almost every night. She hasn't gone as far away as you think."

"I'm still your father, and you're still a child who can't even begin to understand what's at stake, what's always pushing at the other side of—"

"—the gate?" she asked, finishing for him and she put one hand flat against the door, the upper of its two big panels, and leaned all her weight against it. "What happens next time? Do you know that, Father? How much longer do we have left, or haven't the constellations gotten around to telling you that yet?"

"Don't mock me, Meredith."

"Why not?" and she stared back at him over her shoulder, without taking her hand off the door. "Will it damn me faster? Will it cause more men to die in the trenches? Will it cause Avery more pain than he's in now?"

"I was given the book," he growled at her, his stony face flashing to bitter anger, and at least that gave Meredith some mean scrap of satisfaction. "I was shown the way to this place. They entrusted the gate to me, child. The gods—"

"—must be even bigger fools than you, old man. Now shut up and leave me alone."

Machen Dandridge raised his right hand to strike her, then, his big-knuckled hand like a hammer of flesh and bone, iron-meat hammer and anvil to beat her as thin and friable as the veil between Siamese universes.

"You'll need me," she said, not recoiling from the fire in his dark eyes, standing her ground. "You can't take my place. Even if you weren't a coward, you couldn't take my place."

"You've become a wicked child," he said, slowly lowering his hand until it hung useless at his side.

"Yes, Father, I have. I've become a *very* wicked child. You'd best pray that I've become wicked enough."

And he didn't reply, no words left in him, but walked quickly away down the long hall towards the foyer and his library, his footsteps loud as distant gunshots, loud as the beating of her heart, and Meredith removed her hand from the door. It burned very slightly, pain like a healing bee sting, and when she looked at her palm there was something new there, a fat and shiny swelling as black and round and smooth as the soulless eye of a shark.

V

February 1915

In his dreams, Machen Dandridge stands at the edge of the sea and watches the firelight reflected in the roiling grey clouds above Russia and Austria and East Prussia, smells the coppery stink of Turkish and German blood, the life leaking from the bullet holes left in the Serbian Archduke and his wife. Machen would look away if he knew how, wouldn't see what he can only see too late to make any difference. One small man set adrift and then cast up on the shingle of the cosmos, filled to bursting with knowledge and knowing nothing at all. Cannon fire and thunder, the breakers against the cliff side and the death rattle of soldiers beyond counting.

This is where I stand, at the bottom gate, and I hold the key to the abyss . . .

"A *world* war, father," Avery says. "Something without precedent. I can't even find words to describe the things I've seen."

"A world war, without precedent?" Machen replies skeptically and raises one eyebrow, then goes back to reading his star charts. "Napoleon just might disagree with you there, young man, and Alexander, as well."

"No, you don't understand what I'm—"

And the fire in the sky grows brighter, coalescing into a whip of red-gold scales and ebony spines, the dragon's tail to lash the damned, and *Every one of us is damned,* Machen thinks. *Every one of us, from the bloody start of time.*

"I have the texts, Avery, and the aegis of the seven, and all the old ways. I cannot very well set that all aside because you've been having nightmares, now can I?"

"I know these things, Father. I know them like I know my own heart, like I know the number of steps down to the deep place."

"There is a trouble brewing in Coma Berenices," his wife whispers, her eye pressed to the eyepiece of the big telescope in his library. "Something like a shadow—"

"She says that later," Avery tells him. "That hasn't happened yet, but it will. But you won't listen to her, either."

And Machen Dandridge turns his back on the sea and the dragon, on the battlefields and the burning cities, looking back towards the house he built twenty-five years ago; the air in the library seems suddenly very close, too warm, too thick. He loosens his paper collar and stares at his son sitting across the wide mahogany desk from him.

"I'm not sure I know what you mean, boy," he says, and Avery sighs loudly and runs his fingers through his brown hair.

"Mother isn't even at the window now. That's still two weeks from now," and it's true that no one's standing at the telescope. Machen rubs his eyes and reaches for his spectacles. "By then, it'll be too late. It may be too late already," Avery says.

"Listen to him, Father," Meredith begs with her mother's voice, and then she lays a small, wilted bouquet of autumn wildflowers on Ellen Dandridge's grave; the smell of the broken earth at the top of the hill is not so different from the smell of the trenches.

"I did listen to him, Merry."

"You let him talk. You know the difference."

"Did I ever tell you about the lights in the sky the night that you were born?"

"Yes, Father. A hundred times."

"There were no lights at your brother's birth."

Behind him, the sea makes a sound like a giant rolling over in its sleep, and Machen looks away from the house again, stares out across the surging black Pacific. There are the carcasses of whales and sea lions and a billion fish, bloated carcasses of things even he doesn't know the names for, floating in the surf, and scarlet-eyed night birds swoop down to eat their fill of carrion. The water is so thick with dead things and maggots and blood that soon there will be no water left at all.

"The gate chooses the key," his wife says sternly, sadly, standing at the open door leading down to the deep place beneath the house, the bottomless, phosphorescent pool at the foot of the rickety steps. The short pier and the rock rising up from those depths, the little island with its cave and shackles. "You can't change that part, no matter what the seven have given you."

"It wasn't me sent Avery down there, Ellen."

"It wasn't either one of us. But neither of us listened to him, so maybe it's the same as if we did."

The sea as thick as buttermilk, buttermilk and blood beneath a rotten moon, and the dragon's tail flicks through the stars.

"Writing the history of the end of the world," Meredith says, standing at the telescope, peering into the eyepiece, turning first this knob, then that one, trying to bring something in the night sky into sharper focus. "That's what he kept saying, anyway. 'I am writing the history of the end of the world. I'm writing the history of the future.' Father, did you know that there's trouble in Coma Berenices?"

"Was that you?" he asks her. "Was that you or was that your mother?"

"Is there any difference? Do you know the difference?"

"Are these visions, Merry? Are these terrible visions that I may yet hope to affect?"

"Will you keep him locked in that room forever?" she asks, not answering his question, not even taking her eye from the telescope.

Before his wife leaves the hallway, before she steps onto the unsteady landing at the top of the stairs, she kisses Meredith on the top of her head and then glares at her husband, her eyes like judgment on the last day of all, the eyes of seraphim and burning swords. The diseased sea slams against the cliffs, dislodging chunks of shale, silt gone to stone when the great reptiles roamed the planet and the gods still had countless revolutions and upheavals to attend to before the beginning of the tragedy of mankind.

"Machen," his wife says. "If you had listened, had you allowed me to listen, everything might have been different. The war, what's been done to Avery, all of it. If you'd but *listened*."

And the dream rolls on and on and on behind his eyes, down the stairs and to the glowing water, his wife alone in the tiny boat, rowing across the pool to the rocky island far beneath the house. The hemorrhaging, pus-colored sea throwing itself furiously against the walls of the cavern, wanting in, and it's always only a matter of time. Meredith standing on the pier behind him, chanting the prayers he's taught her, the prayers to keep the gate from opening before Ellen reaches that other shore.

The yellow-green light beneath the pool below the house flickers and grows brighter by degrees.

The dragon's tail flicks at the suicidal world.

In his attic, Avery screams with the new mouth the gate gave him before it spit the boy, twisted and insane, back into this place, this time.

The oars dipping again and again into the brilliant, glowing water, the creak of the rusted oarlocks, old nails grown loose in decaying wood, and the shafts of light from the pool playing across the uneven walls of the cavern.

The dragon opens one blistered eye.

And Ellen Dandridge steps out of the boat onto the island, and she doesn't look back at her husband and daughter.

"Something like a shadow," Meredith says, taking her right eye from the telescope and looking across the room at her brother, who isn't sitting in the chair across from Machen.

"It's not a shadow," Avery doesn't tell her, and goes back to the things he has to write down in his journals before there's no time left.

On the island, the gate tears itself open, the dragon's eye, angel eye and the unspeakable face of the titan sleeper in an unnamed, sunken city, tears itself wide to see if she's the one it's called down or some other. The summoned or the trespasser. The invited or the interloper. And Machen knows from the way the air has begun to shimmer and sing that the sleeper doesn't like what it sees.

"I stand at the gate and hold the key," she says. "You know my name and I have come to hold the line. I have come only that you might not pass—"

"Don't look, Merry. Close your eyes," and he holds his daughter close to him as the air stops singing, as it begins to sizzle and pop and burn.

The waves against the shore.

The dragon's tail across the sky.

The empty boat pulled down into the shimmering pool.

Something glimpsed through a telescope.

The ribsy, omnivorous dogs of war.

And Machen woke in his bed, a storm lashing fiercely at the windows, the lightning exploding out there like mortar shells, and the distant *thump thump thump* of his lost son from the attic. He didn't close his eyes again, lay very still, sweating and listening to the rain and the thumping, until the sun rose somewhere behind the clouds to turn the black to cheerless, leaden grey.

VI

August 1889

After his travels, after Baghdad and the ruins of Ninevah and Babylon, after the hidden mosque in Reza'lyah and the peculiar artefacts he'd collected on the southernmost shore of Lake Urmia, Machen Dandridge went west to California. In the summer of 1889, he married Ellen Douglas-Winslow, black-sheep daughter of a fine old Boston family, and together they traveled by train, the smoking iron horses and steel rails that his own father had made his fortune from, all the way to the bustling squalor and Nob Hill sanctuaries of San Francisco. For a time they took up residence in a modest house on Russian Hill, while Machen taught his wife the things that he'd learned in the East – archaeology and astrology, Hebrew and Islamic mysticism, the Talmud and Quran, the secrets of the terrible black book that had been given to him by a blind and leprous mullah. Ellen had disgraced her family at an early age by claiming the abilities of a medium and then backing up her claims with extravagant séances and spectacular ectoplasmic displays, and Machen found in her an eager pupil.

"Why would he have given the book to you?" Ellen asked skeptically, the first time Machen had shown it to her, the first time he'd taken it from its iron and leather case in her presence. "If it's what you say it is, why would he have given it to anyone?"

"Because, my dear, I had a pistol pressed against his rotten skull," Machen had replied, unwrapping the book, slowly peeling back the layers of lambskin it was wrapped in. "That and knowledge he'd been searching for his entire life. It was a fair trade."

And just as the book had led him back from Asia to America and on to California, the brittle, parchment compass of its pages had shown him the way north along the coast to the high cliffs north of Anchor Bay. That first trip, he left Ellen behind, traveling with only the company of a Miwok Indian guide who claimed knowledge of "a hole in the world". But when they finally left the shelter of the redwood forest and stood at the edge of a vast and undulating sea of pampas grass stretching away towards the Pacific, the Miwok had refused to go any farther. No amount of money or talk could persuade him to approach the cliffs waiting beyond the grass, and so Machen continued on alone.

Beneath the hot summer sun, the low, rolling hills seemed to go on forever, and the gulls and a pair of redtailed hawks screamed at him like harpies warning him away, screeching threats or alarum from the endless cornflower sky. But he found it, finally, the "hole in the world", right where the Miwok guide had said that he would, maybe fifty yards from the cliffs.

From what he'd taught himself of geology, Machen guessed it to be the collapsed roof of a cavern, an opening no more than five or six feet across, granting access to an almost vertical chimney eroded through tilted beds of limestone and shale and probably connecting to the sea somewhere in the darkness below. He dropped a large pebble into the hole and listened and counted as it fell, ticking off the seconds until it splashed faintly, confirming his belief that the cavern must be connected to the sea. A musty, briny smell wafted up from the hole, uninviting, sickly, and though there was climbing equipment in his pack, and he was competent with ropes and knots and had, more than once, descended treacherous, crumbling shafts into ancient tombs and wells, Machen Dandridge only stood there at the entrance, dropping stones and listening to the eventual splashes. He stared into the hole and, after a while, could discern a faint but unmistakable light, not the fading sunlight getting in from some cleft in the cliff face, but light like a glass of absinthe, the sort of light he'd imagined abyssal creatures that never saw the sun might make to shine their way through the murk.

It wasn't what he'd expected, from what was written in the black book, no towering gate of horn and ivory, no arch of gold and silver guarded by angels or demons or beings men had never fashioned names for, just this unassuming hole in the ground. He sat in the grass, watching the sunset burning day to night, wondering if the Miwok had deserted him. Wondering if the quest had been a fool's errand from the very start and he'd wasted so many years of his life and so much of his inheritance chasing connections and truths that only existed because he wished to see them. By dark, the light shone up through the hole like some unearthly torch, taunting or reassuring but beckoning him forward. Promising there was more to come.

"What is it you think you will find?" the old priest had asked after he'd handed over the book. "More to the point, what is it you think will find *you*?"

Not a question he could answer then and not one he could answer sitting there with the roar of the surf in his ears and the stars speckling the sky overhead. The question that Ellen had asked him again and again and always he'd found some way to deflect her asking. But he *knew* the answer, sewn up somewhere deep within his soul, even if he'd never been able to find the words. Proof that the world did not end at his fingertips, or with the unreliable data of his eyes and ears, or the lies and half-truths men had written down in science and history books, that everything he'd ever seen was merely a tattered curtain waiting to be drawn back so that some more indisputable light might, at last, shine through.

"Is that what you were seeking, Mr Dandridge?" and Machen had turned quickly, his heart pounding as he reached for the pistol at his hip, only to find the old Indian watching him from the tall, rustling grass a few feet away. "Is *that* the end of your journey?" and the guide pointed at the hole.

"I thought you were afraid to come here?" Machen asked, annoyed at the interruption, sitting back down beside the hole, looking again into the unsteady yellow-green light spilling out of the earth.

"I was," the Miwok replied. "But the ghost of my grandfather came to me and told me he was ashamed of me, that I was a coward for allowing you to come to this evil place alone. He has promised to protect me from the demons."

"The ghost of your grandfather?" Machen laughed and shook his head, then dropped another pebble into the hole.

"Yes. He is watching us both now, but he also wishes we would leave soon. I can show you the way back to the trail."

The key I have accepted full in the knowledge of its weight.

"You're a brave man," Machen said. "Or another lunatic."

"All brave men are lunatics," the Indian said and glanced nervously at the hole, the starry indigo sky, the cliff and the invisible ocean, each in its turn. "Sane men do not go looking for their deaths."

"Is that all I've found here? My death?"

A long moment of anxious silence from the guide, broken only by the ceaseless interwoven roar of the waves and the wind, and then he took a step back away from the hole, deeper into the sheltering pampas grass.

"I cannot not say what you have found in this place, Mr Dandridge. My grandfather says I should not speak its name."

"Is that so? Well, then," and he stood, rubbing his aching eyes, and brushed the dust from his pants. "You show me the way back and forget you ever brought me out here. Tell your grandfather's poor ghost that I will not hold you responsible for whatever it is I'm meant to find at the bottom of that pit."

"My grandfather hears you," the Miwok said. "He says you are a brave man and a lunatic, and that I should kill you now, before you do the things you will do in the days to come. Before you set the world against itself."

Machen drew his Colt, cocked the hammer with his thumb and stood staring into the gloom at the Indian.

"I will not kill you," the Miwok said. "That is *my* choice and I have chosen not to take your life. But I will pray it is not a decision I will regret later. We should go now."

"After you," Machen said, smiling through the quaver in his voice that he hoped the guide couldn't hear, his heart racing and cold sweat starting to drip from his face despite the night air. And, without another word, the Indian turned and disappeared into the arms of the whispering grass and the August night.

VII

July 1914

When she was very sure that her father had shut the double doors to his study and that her mother was asleep, when the only sounds were the sea and the wind, the inconstant, shifting noises that all houses make after dark, the mice in the walls, Meredith slipped out of bed and into her flannel dressing gown. The floor was cool against her bare feet, cool but not cold. She lit a candle and then eased the heavy bedroom door shut behind her and went as quickly and quietly as she could to the cramped stairwell leading from the second story to the attic door. At the top, she sat down on the landing and held her breath, listening, praying that no one had heard her, that neither her father nor mother, nor the both of them together, were already trying to find her.

There were no sounds at all from the other side of the narrow attic door. She set the candlestick down and leaned close to it, pressing her lips against the wood, feeling the rough grain through the varnish against her flesh.

"Avery?" she whispered. "Avery, can you hear me?"

And at first there was no reply from the attic and she took a deep breath and waited a while, waiting for her parents' angry or worried footsteps, waiting for one of them to begin shouting her name from the house below.

But there were no footsteps, and no one called her name.

"*Avery?* Can you hear me? It's *me*, Merry."

That time there was a sudden thumping and a heavy, dragging sort of a sound from the other side of the attic door. A body pulling itself roughly, painfully across the pine-board floor towards her, and she closed her eyes and waited for it. Finally, there was a loud thud against the door and she opened her eyes again. Avery was trying to talk, trying to answer her, but there was nothing familiar or coherent in his ruined voice.

"Hold on," she whispered to him. "I brought a writing pad," and she took it out of a pocket of her gown, the pad and a pencil. "Don't try to talk anymore. I'll pass this beneath the door to you and you can write what you want to say. Knock once if you understand what I'm telling you, Avery."

Nothing for almost a full minute and then a single knock so violent that the door shivered on its hinges, so loud she was sure it would bring her parents to investigate.

"Not so *loud*, Avery," she whispered. "They'll hear us," and now Meredith had begun to notice the odor on the landing, the odor leaking from the attic. Either she'd been much too nervous to notice it at first or her brother had brought it with him when he'd crawled over to the door. Dead fish and boiling cabbage, soured milk and strawberry jam, the time she'd come across the carcass of a grey whale calf, half buried in the sand and rotting beneath the sun. She swallowed, took another deep breath, and tried not to think about the awful smell.

"I'm going to pass the pencil and a page from the pad to you now. I'm going to slide it under the door to you."

Avery made a wet, strangling sound and she told him again not to try to talk, just write if he could, write the answers to her questions and anything he needed to say.

"Are you in pain? Is there anything I can do to help?" she asked, and in a moment the tip of the pencil began scritching loudly across the sheet of writing paper. "Not so hard, Avery. If the lead breaks, I'll have to try to find another."

He slid the piece of paper back to her, and it was damp and something dark and sticky was smudged across the bottom. She held it close to her face, never mind the smell so strong it made her gag, made her want to vomit, so that she could read what he'd scrawled there. Nothing like Avery's careful hand, his tight, precise cursive she'd always admired and had tried to imitate, but sweeping, crooked letters, blocky print, and seeing that made her want to cry so badly that she almost forgot about the dead-whale-and-cabbages smell.

HURTSS ME MERY MORE THAN CAN NO
NO HELP NO HELLP ME

She laid down the sheet of paper and tore another from her pad, the pad she used for her afternoon lessons, spelling and arithmetic, and slid it beneath the door to Avery.

"Avery, you *knew* you couldn't bear the key. You knew it had to be me or mother, *didn't* you? That it had to be a woman?"

Again the scritching, and the paper came back to her even stickier than before.

HAD TO TRY MOTER WOULD NOT LISSEN SO
I HAD TOO TRIE

"Oh, Avery," Meredith said, "I'm sorry," speaking so quietly that she prayed he would not hear, and there were tears in her eyes, hot and bitter. A kind of anger and a kind of sorrow in her heart that she'd never known before, anger and sorrow blooming in her to be fused through some alchemy of the soul, and by that fusion be transformed into a pure and golden hate.

She tore another page from the pad and slipped it through the crack between the floor and the attic door.

"I need to know what to *do*, Avery. I'm reading the newspapers, but I don't understand it all. Everyone seems think war is coming soon, because of the assassination in Sarajevo, because of the Kaiser, but I don't *understand* it all."

It was a long time before the paper came back to her, smeared with slime and stinking of corruption, maybe five minutes of Avery's scritching and his silent pauses between the scritching. This time the page was covered from top to bottom with his clumsy scrawl.

TO LATE ~~IF~~ TO STOP WAR TOO LATE NOW
WAR IS COMING NOW CANT STP THAT MERRY
ALL SET IN MOTION NINTH WAVE REMEMBER?
BUT MERY YOU CAN DONT LISSEN TO FADER
YOU CAN HOLD ~~NINE~~ THEE LINE STILL TYME
YOU OR MOTHER KIN HOLD THEE LIN STILL
IT DOEZ NOT HALF TO BE THE LADST WAR

When she finished reading and then re-reading twice again everything Avery had written, Meredith lay the sheet of paper down on top of the other two and wiped her hand on the floor until it didn't feel quite so slimy anymore. By the yellow-white light of the candle, her hand shimmered as though she'd been carrying around one of the big banana slugs that lived in the forest. She quickly ripped another page from the writing pad and passed it under the door. This time she felt it snatched from her fingers and the scritching began immediately. It came back to her only a few seconds later and the pencil with it, the tip ground away to nothing.

DUNT <u>EVER</u> COME BAK HERE AGIN MERRY
I LOVE YOU ALWAYTS AND WONT FERGET YOU
<u>PROMISS</u> ME YOU WILL KNOT COME BACK
<u>HOLD THEE LINE HOLD THE LINE</u>

"I can't promise you that, Avery," she replied, sobbing and leaning close to the door, despite the smell so strong that it had begun burn her nose and the back of her throat. "You're my brother, and I can't ever promise you that."

Another violent thud against the door then, so hard that her father was sure to have heard, so sudden that it scared her, and Meredith jumped back and reached for the candlestick.

"I remember the ninth wave, Avery. I remember what you said – the ninth wave, greater than the last, all in flame. I *do* remember."

And because she thought that perhaps she heard footsteps from somewhere below, and because she couldn't stand to hear the frantic strangling sounds that Avery had begun making again, Meredith hastily gathered up the sticky, scribbled-on pages from the pad and then crept down the attic stairs and back to her bedroom. She fell asleep just before dawn and dreamt of flames among the breakers, an inferno crashing against the rocks.

VIII

March 1915

"This is where it ends," Merry, her mother's ghost said. "But this is where it begins, as well. You need to understand that if you understand nothing else."

Meredith knew that this time she was not dreaming, no

matter how much it might *feel* like a dream, this dazzling, tumbling nightmare wide-awake that began when she reached the foot of the rickety staircase leading her down into the deep place beneath the house. Following her mother's ghost, the dim glow of a spectre to be her Virgil, her Beatrice, her guiding lantern until the light from the pool was so bright it outshone Ellen Dandridge's flickering radiance. Meredith stood on the pier, holding her dead mother's barnacle- and algae-encrusted hand, and stared in fear and wonder towards the island in the pool.

"The infinite lines of causation," the ghost said. "What has brought you here. That is important as well."

"I'm here because my father is a fool," Meredith replied, unable to look away from the yellow-green light dancing across the stone, shining up from the depths beneath her bare feet.

"No, dear. He is only a man trying to do the work of gods. That never turns out well."

The black eye set deep into the flesh of Meredith's palm itched painfully and then rolled back to show its dead-white sclera. She knew exactly what it was seeing, because it always told her, knew how close they were to the veil, how little time was left before the breach tore itself open once and for all.

"Try to forget your father, child. Concentrate on time and space, on the history that has brought you here. All the strands of the web."

Meredith squeezed the ghost's soft hand and the dates and names and places spilled through her like the sea spilling across the shore, a flood of obvious and obscure connections, and she gritted her teeth and let them come.

On December 2, 1870, Bismarck sends a letter to Wilhelm of Prussia urging him to become Kaiser. In 1874, all Jesuits are ordered to leave Italy, and on January 8th, 1877, Crazy Horse is defeated by the U.S. cavalry at Wolf Mountain in Montana. In June 1881, Austria signs a secret treaty with the Serbs, establishing an economic and political protectorate. and Milan is crowned King of Serbia—

"It hurts," she whispered; her mother frowned and nodded her head as the light from the pool began to pulse and spin, casting counterclockwise glare and shadow across the towering rock walls.

"It will always hurt, dear. It will be pain beyond imagining. You cannot be lied to about that. You cannot be led to bear this weight in ignorance of the pain that comes with the key."

Meredith took another hesitant step towards the end of the short pier, and then another, and the light swelled angrily and spun hurricane fury about her.

"They are rising, Merry. They have teeth and claws sharp as steel and will devour you if you don't hurry. You must go to the island now. The breach is opening—"

"I am afraid, mother. I'm so sorry, but I *am* afraid."

"Then the fear will lead you where I can't. Make the fear your shield. Make the fear your lance."

Standing at the very end of the pier, and Meredith didn't dare look down into the shining pool, kept her eyes on the tiny island fifteen or twenty feet away.

"They took the boat when you crossed over," she said to her mother's ghost. "How am I supposed to reach the gate when they've taken the boat away?"

"You're a strong swimmer, child. Avery taught you to swim."

A sound like lightning, and *No*, she thought. *I can't do that. I can do anything except step off this pier into that water with them. I can stand the pain, but—*

"If you know another way, Merry, then take it. But there isn't much time left. The lines are converging."

Merry took a deep breath, gulping the cavern's dank and foetid air, hyperventilating, bracing for the breathless cold to come, all the things that her brother had taught her about swimming in the sea. Together they'd swum out past the breakers, to the kelp forest in the deep water farther offshore, the undulating submarine weald where bat rays and harbor seals raced between the gigantic stalks of kelp, where she'd looked up and seen the lead-pale belly of an immense white shark passing silently overhead.

"Time, Merry. It is all in your hands now. See how you stand alone at the center of the web and the strands stretch away from you? See the intersections and interweaves?"

"I see them," she said. "I see them all," and she stepped off into the icy water.

October 30th, 1883, an Austro-German treaty with Roumania is signed, providing Roumania defence against the Russians. November 17th, 1885, the Serbs are defeated at the Battle of Slivnitza and then ultimately saved only by Austrian intervention. 1887 and the Mahdist War with Abyssinia begins. 1889 and a boy named Silas Desvernine sails up the Hudson River and first sees a mountain where a nameless being of moonlight and thunder is held inside a black stone. August

1889 and her father is led to the edge of the Pacific by a Miwok guide. August 27th, 1891, the Franco-Russian Entente—

The strands of the web, the ticking of a clock, the life and death of stars, each step towards Armageddon checked off in her aching head, and the water is liquid ice threatening to freeze her alive. The tiny island seemed miles and miles away.

1895 August and Kaiser Wilhelm visits England for Queen Victoria's Golden Jubilee. 1896, Charles E. Callwell of the British Army publishes Small Wars – Their Principles and Practice. *February 4th, 1899, the year Aguinaldo leads a Philippine Insurrection against U.S. forces—*

All of these events, all of these men and their actions. Lies and blood and betrayals, links in the chain leading, finally, to this moment, to that ninth wave, mightier than the last, all in flame, and Meredith swallowed a mouthful of sea water and struggled to keep her head above the surface.

"Hurry, child!" her mother's ghost shouted from the pier. "They are rising," and Meredith Dandridge began to pray then that she would fail, would surrender in another moment or two and let the deep have her. Imagined sinking down and down for all eternity, pressure to crush her flat and numb, to crush her so small that nothing and no one would ever have any need to harm her again.

Something sharp as steel swiped across her ankle, slicing her skin, and her blood mingled with the sea.

And the next stroke drove her fingers into the mud and pebbles at the edge of the island, and she dragged herself quickly from the pool, from the water and the mire, and looked back the way she'd come. There were no demons in the water, and her mother's ghost wasn't watching from the pier. But her father was, Machen Dandridge and his terrible black book, his eyes upturned and arms outstretched to an indifferent Heaven; she cursed him for the last time and ignored the blood oozing from the ugly gash in her right foot.

"This is where I stand," she said, getting to her feet and turning towards the small cave at the center of the island, her legs as weak and unsteady as a newborn foal's. "At the bottom gate, and I hold the key to the abyss."

The yellow-green light was almost blinding and soon the pool would begin to boil.

"The ebony key to the first day and the last, the key to the moment when the stars wink out one by one and the sea heaves its rotting belly at the empty, sagging sky. The blazing key that even angels fear to keep."

For an instant, there was no cave, and no pool, and no cavern beneath a resentful, wicked house. Only the fire, pouring from the cave that was no longer there, to swallow her whole, only the voices of the void, and Meredith Dandridge made her fear a shield and a lance, and held the line.

And in the days and weeks that followed, sometimes Machen Dandridge came down the stairs to stand on the pier and gaze across the pool to the place where the thing that had been his daughter nestled in the shadows, in the hollows between the stones. And every day the sea gave her more of its armour, gilding her frail human skin with the limey shells and stinging tentacles that other creatures had spent countless cycles of Creation refining from the rawest matter of life, the needle teeth, the scales and poisonous barbs. Where his wife and son had failed, his daughter crouched triumphant as any martyr, and sometimes, late at night, alone with the sound of the surf pounding against the edge of the continent, he sometimes thought of setting fire to the house and letting it burn down around him.

He read the newspapers.

He watched the stars for signs and portents.

When the moon was bright, the women still came to dance beside the sea, but he'd begun to believe they were only bad memories from some time before and so he rarely paid them any heed.

When the weather was good, he climbed the hills behind the house and sat at the grave of his dead wife and whispered to her, telling her how proud he was of Meredith, reciting snatches of half-remembered poetry, telling her the world would come very close to the brink because of what he'd done, because of his blind pride, but, in the end, it would survive because of what their daughter had done and would do for ages yet.

On a long rainy afternoon in May, he opened the attic door and killed what he found there with an axe and his old Colt revolver. He buried it beside his wife, but left nothing to mark the grave.

He wrote long letters to men he'd once known in England and New York and Rio de Janeiro, but there were never any replies.

And time rolled on, neither malign nor beneficent, settling across the universe like the grey caul of dust settling thick upon the relics he'd brought back from India and Iran and the Sudan a quarter of a century before. The birth and death of stars, light reaching his aging eyes after a billion years racing across the vacuum, and sometimes he spent the days gathering fossils from the cliffs and arranging them in precise geometric patterns in the tall grass around the house. He left lines of salt and drew elaborate runes, the meanings of which he'd long since forgotten.

His daughter spoke to him only in his dreams, or hers, no way to ever be sure which was which, and her voice grew stronger and more terrible as the years rushed past. In the end, she was a maelstrom to swallow his withered soul, to rock him to sleep one last time, to show him the way across.

And the house by the sea, weathered and weary and insane, kept its secrets.

GLEN HIRSHBERG

Flowers on Their Bridles, Hooves in the Air

GLEN HIRSHBERG IS THE author of a novel, *The Snowman's Children*, and the International Horror Guild Award-winning collection of ghost stories, *The Two Sams*, both published by Carroll & Graf in the United States.

His short fiction has appeared in numerous anthologies, including *The Mammoth Book of Best New Horror* and *The Year's Best Fantasy and Horror* series, *Dark Terrors 6: The Gollancz Book of Horror, Trampoline: An Anthology* and *The Dark: New Ghost Stories.*

He is currently completing a new novel and a second set of ghost stories.

Hirshberg returned to Southern California almost a decade ago, but has not written about it until this story, as he reveals: "Too little of the man-made landscape of this region encourages the sort of aesthetic experience Ramsey Campbell, for one, has always believed crucial to the creation of a satisfying ghostly tale, unless your nearest Banana Republic gets you good and crawly.

"But a few years ago, my wife and I stumbled onto what was

left of the old pier near downtown Long Beach and discovered
the last open establishment there. 'Flowers' is an homage to the
people we saw and met, and to that now-defunct place, which
really was a place, at the very least."

> *Mechanical constructions designed for pleasure have a special*
> *melancholy when they are idle. Especially merry-go-rounds.*
> >   —Wright Morris

ASH CAME IN LATE, on the 10:30 train. I was sure Rebecca
would stay home and sleep, but instead she got a sitter for our
infant daughter, let her dark hair down for what seemed
the first time in months, and emerged from our tiny bathroom in the jeans she hadn't been able to wear since her
cesarean.

"My CD," she said happily, handing me the New York Dolls
disc she'd once howled along with every night while we did the
dishes, and which I hadn't even seen for over a year. Then she
stood in front of me and bobbed on the clunky black shoes I
always loved to see her in, not because they were sexy but
because of their bulk. Those shoes, it seemed to me, could hold
even Rebecca to the ground.

So all the way across the San Fernando Valley we played the
Dolls, and she didn't howl anymore, but she rocked side-to-side
in her seat and mouthed the words while I snuck glances at her
in the rearview mirror. The last time I could remember seeing
her in this mood was on her thirty-first birthday, over a year ago,
right before her mother died and the homeless person's
political action committee she'd been serving on collapsed
in the wake of 9/11 as charitable donations got siphoned to
New York and she finally decided to give up on the rest of the
world long enough for us to try to have a child. I had thought
maybe this Rebecca – arms twitching at her sides like folded
wings, green eyes skimming the night for anything alive – had
vanished for good.

As usual, even at that hour, traffic snarled where the 101 and
the 110 and the 5 emptied together into downtown Los
Angeles, so I ducked onto Hill Street, edging us through the
surprising crowds of Chinese teens tossing pop-pops in the air
and leaning against lampposts and chain-shuttered shop windows to smoke. Rebecca rolled down her window, and the car

filled with burning smells: tobacco, firecracker filament, pork and fish. I thought she might try bumming a cigarette from a passing kid – though as far as I knew, she hadn't smoked in years – but instead she leaned against the seatback and closed her eyes.

We were pulling into Union Station when she turned the volume down, caught me looking at her in the mirror, and said, "A flowered one."

I grinned back, shook my head. "He's a new man, remember? Official, responsible, full-time job. Brand new lakefront bungalow. He'll be wearing grey pinstripes. From a suit he bought but hasn't worn."

We were both wrong. And of course, the funniest thing – the worst – was that even with all that green and purple paisley flashing off the front of this latest vest like scales on some spectacular tropical fish, I still didn't see him until I'd driven ten yards past him.

"Hey, dude," he said to both of us as he approached the car, then dropped his black duffel to the curb and stood quietly, leaning to the right the way he always did.

He'd shaved off the last of the tumbling dark brown curls which, even thinning, used to flop over both his eyes and made him look like a lhasa apso. Even more brightly than the new vest, the top of his head shone, practically winking white and red with the lights from passing cars. His shoulders, big from the boxing classes he took – for fitness, he'd never gotten in a ring and swore he never would – ballooned from either side of the vest. His jeans were black, and on his wrists were leather bracelets studded with silver spikes.

"Ash, you, um," I said, and then I was laughing. "You don't *look* like a nurse."

"Wait," Rebecca said, and her hand snaked out the window and grabbed the side of Ash's vest, right where the paisley met the black polyester backing. Then she popped her seatbelt open and leaned to look more closely. "Did you do this?"

Ash's blush spread all the way up his head until he was red all over, and his tiny ferret-eyes blinked. It was as though Rebecca had spray-painted him.

"Do what?"

"What *was* this?" Rebecca said. "Was this a shirt?"

"What do you mean?"

"Look, El. Someone cut this shiny paisley part off . . .

curtains, maybe? Something else, anyway. And they stitched it to the rest. See?" She held the edge of the vest out from Ash's sides.

Ash's blush deepened, but his smile came more easily than I remembered. "No wonder it cost a dollar."

Rebecca burst out laughing, and I laughed, too. "Been way too long, Ash," I said.

Still leaning, as though he were standing in some invisible rowboat in a current, Ash folded himself into our Metro's tiny back seat. "Good to be here, Elliot." He pronounced it "El-yut", just as he had when we were twelve.

"You get all dolled up for us?" I said, nodding in the mirror at the vest, and to my surprise, Ash blushed again and looked at the floor.

"I've been going out a lot," he said.

Both he and Rebecca left their windows open as I spun the car out of the lot and, without asking, turned south. With Chinatown behind us, the street corners emptied. I couldn't see the smog, but I could taste it, a sweet tang in the air that shouldn't have been there and prickled the lungs like nicotine and had a similar sort of narcotic, addictive effect, because you just kept gulping it. Of course, that was partially because there wasn't enough oxygen in it.

"Where are you going?" Rebecca asked as we drifted down the white and nameless warehouses that line both sides of Alameda Street and house the city's *other* industries, whatever they are.

"Don't know," I said. "Just figured, between that vest and your mood, home wasn't an option."

Rebecca twisted her head around to look at Ash. "Where's all this out you've been going?"

"Meditation classes, for one," Ash said, effectively choking Rebecca to silence. She'd forgotten about Ash's professed Zen conversion, or discovery, or whatever it was. He'd told us about it in a particularly cryptic phone call that had struck both of us as dispassionate even for Ash. Yet another 9/11 by-product, we both thought at the time, but now I actually suspected not. Even back in our Berkeley days, Ash's sense of right and just behavior had been more . . . inward, somehow, than Rebecca's.

Also less ferocious – he hadn't actually believed he could affect change, or maybe wasn't as interested, and was therefore less perpetually disappointed. And now, as we floated between late-night trucks down the dark toward the freeways, a series of quick, sweet feelings lit up inside me like roman candles. I was remembering Friday nights lost in Oakland, gliding through streets emptier and darker than this in Ash's beat-up green B-210, singing "Shoplifters of the World," spending no money except on gas and double-doubles from In-N-Out. We always got them animal style even though Rebecca hated the grilled onions, because it never got old knowing the secret menu, declaring it to cashiers like a password.

"I've been going to music, too. Lots of clubs. My friends Rubina and Liz—"

"Long Beach," Rebecca said over him, and I hit the brakes and paused, right on the lip of the onramp to the 10. Whether out of perceptiveness or meditation training or typical Ashy patience, our friend in the back went quiet and waited.

"Rebecca," I said carefully, after a long breath. She'd been taking us to her sister's almost every weekend since her mother died. She'd been going during the week, too, of late, and even more than she told me, I suspected. "Don't you want to get Ash a Pink's? Show him that ant at the Museum of Jurassic Tech? Take him bowling at the Starlight? Show him the Ashy parts of town?"

"Starlight's gone," Rebecca said, as though she were talking about her mother.

"Oh, yeah. Forgot."

Abruptly, she brightened again. "Not my sister's, El-yut. I have a plan. A place in mind. Somewhere our vested nurse-boy back there would appreciate. You, too." Then she punched play on the CD-player. Discussion over. Off we went.

All the way down the 110, then the 405, Rebecca alternately shook to the music and prodded Ash with questions, and he answered in his familiar monotone, which always made him sound at ease, not bored, no matter what job he'd just left or new woman he'd found and taken meditating or clubbing or drifting and then gotten dumped – gently – by. Ash had been to more weddings of more ex-girlfriends than anyone I'd ever met.

But tonight, he talked about his supervisor at the hospital, whose name apparently really was Ms Paste. "She's kind of this nurse-artist," he said. "Amazing. Hard to explain. She slides an I.V. into a vein and steps back, and it's perfect, every time, patient never even feels it. Wipes butts like she's arranging flowers."

Rebecca laughed, while Ash sat in the back with that grin on his face. How can someone so completely adrift in the world seem so satisfied with it?

We hit the 710, and immediately, the big rigs surrounded us. No matter what hour you drive it, there are always big rigs on that stretch of highway, lumbering back and forth between the 405 and the port, their beds saddled with giant wooden crates and steel containers newly gantried off incoming ships or headed for them, as though the whole city of Long Beach were constantly being put up or taken down like a circus at a fairground. As we approached the fork where the freeway splits – the right headed for the Queen Mary, the left for Shoreline Village and the whale watching tour boats and the too-white lighthouse perched on its perfectly mown hilltop like a Disney-land cast-off – I slowed and glanced at my wife. But Rebecca didn't notice. She had slid down a little in her seat, and was watching the trucks with a blank expression on her pale face.

"Rebecca?" I said. "Where to?"

Stirring, she said, "Oh. The old pier. You know where that is? Downtown, downtown."

Just in time, I veered left, passing by the aquarium and the rest of the tourist attractions to head for the city center. Not that there was much difference anymore, according to Rebecca. Scaffolding engulfed most of the older buildings, and as we hit downtown, the bright, familiar markings of malls every-where dropped into place around us like flats on a movie set. There were Gap and TGIF storefronts, sidewalks so clean they seemed to have acquired a varnish, fountains with statues of seals spouting water through their whiskers. Only a few features distinguished Long Beach from the Third Street Promenade or Old Town Pasadena now: a tapas bar; that eighty year-old used bookshop with the bowling alley-sized backroom that seems to exude dust through the wood and windows, even though the windows are painted shut; and, just visible down the last remaining dark blocks, a handful of no-tourist dives with windowless doors and green booths inside for the more tradi-tionally minded sailors.

"Go straight through," Rebecca said. "Turn right at the light. God, it's been years."

Given her tastes and the sheer number of days she'd spent with her mother, then with her sister, ever since we'd moved down to L.A., that seemed unlikely. But Ash's patience was soothing, infectious, and I waited. And as we edged farther from the downtown lights, through sports cars and S.U.V.'s skimming the streets like incoming seagulls and squawking at each other over parking places, Rebecca shut off the music and turned to us. "My dad used to take us here," she said.

I hit the brakes harder than I meant to and brought the car to a lurching stop at the road that fronted the ocean. For a few seconds, we hung there, the lights of Long Beach in the rearview mirror, the ocean seeping blackly out of the jumbled, overbuilt coast before us like oil from a listing tanker.

"Your dad," I said.

"Left, Elliot. Down there. See?"

I turned left, slowly, though there was no traffic. Neither tourists nor sailors had any use for this road anymore, apparently. "It's been a long time since you mentioned your dad." In fact, I couldn't remember the last time. She talked about her school commissioner mother – stable, stubborn, fiercely loyal, nasty Scrabble player. Also her recovered junkie sister. But her father . . .

"I've never heard you mention him," Ash said, detached as ever, just noting.

The frontage road, at least, did not look like new downtown Long Beach or Third Street, or Downtown Disney. To our left, the scaffolded buildings loomed, lightless as pilings for some gigantic pier lost long ago to the tide. To our right lay the ocean, without even a whitecap to brighten its surface. Few other stretches in the LosAnDiego megalopolis were still allowed to get this dark. We'd gone no more than a few hundred yards when Rebecca sat up in her seat and pointed.

"Right here. See?"

I punched the brakes again and brought the car to a stop. Just behind us, a signless, potholed drive snaked between the black iron posts of what must once have been a gate. Beyond that, a parking lot, then the old pier, lit by too-dim streetlights on either side. And beyond those, right at the end of the pier . . .

"What is that?" Ash said.

It seemed to hover above the ocean, a dark, metallic, upside-down funnel, like a giant magician's hat. Beneath it, dim and scattered lights flickered. If there were ocean rather than pier beneath it, I would have assumed we were looking at bioluminescent fish.

I glanced toward Rebecca, whose smile was the wistful one I'd gotten used to over the past year or so. When I reached over and squeezed her hand, she squeezed back, but absently.

"What's the smile for?" I said, and turned us into the drive. Past the gateposts, we emerged into a startlingly large parking lot that sprawled in both directions. A handful of older cars – an orange Dodge pickup, a '60s-vintage Volkswagon van, a U-haul trailer with no lead-vehicle attached to it – clustered like barnacle shells near the foot of the wooden steps that led up to the pier. Otherwise, there were only empty spaces, their white dividing lines obscured but still visible, rusted parking meters planted sideways at their heads like markers on anonymous graves.

"There used to be a billboard right next to that gate," Rebecca said, staring around her. "A girl dressed in one of those St Pauli Girl waitress uniforms, you know what I'm talking about? Breasts like boulders, you felt like they were just going to pop loose and roll right off the sign and smash you when you drove under them. She was riding one of the merry-go-round horses and holding a big beer stein. Her uniform said LITE-YOUR-LINE on it, and in huge red letters over her head, the sign read, LONG BEACH PIER. GET LIT."

Ash laughed quietly as I pulled into a spot a few rows from the van and pick-up, and Rebecca got out fast and stood into a surprising sea wind. Ash and I joined her, and I had a brief but powerful desire to ditch our friend, never mind how good it was to see him, take my wife by the elbow and steer her to the dark, disused stretch of beach fifty yards ahead of us. There we'd stand, let the planet's breath beat against our skin until it woke us. The whole last year, it seemed to me, we'd been sleeping. Or I'd been sleeping, and Rebecca had been mourning, and something else, too. Retreating, maybe, from everything but her child. Shaking free of something old, because she had *not* been sleeping, even before our daughter was born.

"I think this is the only place I remember coming with him," Rebecca said. "For fun, anyway." She moved off toward the steps. We followed. Ash's vest left little purple trails of reflected streetlight behind him. His gaze was aimed straight up the steps. Rebecca had a deeper hunger for these spots, I thought, these night-places where people washed up or swept in like sharks from the deep sea. But Ash could smell them.

"You came here a lot?" I asked. I considered taking Rebecca's hand again, but thought that would be crowding her, somehow.

"More than you'd think." She mounted the stairs. "Some days, he hadn't even started drinking, yet. He'd wait until we got here. Buy my sister and me three dollars each worth of tickets – that was like fifteen rides – and plop us on the merry-go-round while he—"

The hands closed around us so fast, from both sides, that we didn't even have time to cry out. One second we were alone at the top of the leaning staircase and the next there were filthy fingers clamped on all of our wrists and red, bearded faces leering into ours. The fingers began dragging us around in a sickening circle.

"*Ring around the funny*," the face nearest to me half-sang, his breath overwhelming, equal parts bad gin and sea salt and sand. "*Pockets full of money. Give it. Give it. Give it* now*!*"

Then, as suddenly as they had grabbed us, they let go, a hand or two at a time, fell back a step, and we got our first good look. If we hadn't been on a glorified dock at the edge of the Pacific, a hundred yards that felt like fifty miles from anywhere I knew, I think I might have laughed, or wept.

They stood before us in a clump, five decrepit men in ruined pea-coats with their noses running and their beards wild and their skin mottled with sores red and raised like octopus suckers. Probably, I thought, Long Beach – like the former People's Republic of Santa Monica, and every other Southern California town I knew – had passed and enforced a new set of vagrancy laws to keep all that fresh sidewalk pavement free of debris. And this particular quintet had scuttled down here to hide under the great steel magician's hat and sleep with the fishes and pounce on whatever drifted out to them like marine snow.

"Here," Ash started, sliding a hand into the pocket of his vest, just as Rebecca stuck an arm across his chest.

"Don't," she said.

It shouldn't have surprised me. I'd watched her do this before. Rebecca had worked with the homeless most of her adult life, and felt she knew what they needed, or at least what might be most likely to help. But I was always startled by the confidence of her convictions.

"Nearest shelter's on La Amatista," she said, gesturing over her shoulder toward the frontage road, town. "Five, maybe six blocks. They have food."

"Don't want food," one of the men snarled, but his snarl became a whine before he'd finished the sentence. "We want change."

"You won't get ours."

"*Change.*" The five of them knotted together – coiled, I thought, and my shoulders tensed, and I could feel the streaky wetness they'd left on my wrists and their breath in my mouth – and then, just like that, they were gone, bumping past us down the steps to disappear under the dock.

For a good minute, maybe more, the three of us stood in our own little clump, and there were unsettled feelings seeping up through my stomach, and I could neither place them nor get them quiet. Finally, Rebecca said, "The most amazing merry-go-round," as though nothing whatsoever had occurred.

I glanced down the pier toward the magician's hat, which was actually the roof of an otherwise open pavilion. There were lights clustered beneath it, yellow and green and red, but they seemed to waver above the water, connected to nothing, until I realized I was looking through some sort of threadbare canvas drapery suspended from the rim of the overhang like a giant spider web, generations in the making. Between us and the pavilion lay maybe fifty yards of moldy wooden planking. Shadows of indeterminate shape slid over the planks or sank into them, and on either side of the streetlights, solitary figures sat at the railing-less edges and dangled their legs over the dark and fished.

"Is this safe, Rebecca?" I asked.

She'd seemed lost in thought, staring after our would-be muggers, but now she brightened again, so fast I felt myself get dizzy. "We'll let Ash go first. Drive everyone back with the vest." She flicked his front with her fingers, and I felt a flicker of jealousy, couldn't believe I was feeling it, and made myself ignore it.

Of course, Ash did go first. The lights and the pavilion and the curtain floating on the wind drew him. Me, too, but not in the same way. Rebecca waited for me to return her smile, then shrugged and stepped off behind our friend. I followed.

"They used to sell T-shirts from a stand right there," she said as we walked, gesturing at the empty space to her left. "Army camouflage. American flag prints. They sold candy popcorn, too. My dad always bought us the Patriotic Bag. Red cherry, blue raspberry, vanilla."

"Are there such things as blue raspberries?" Ash asked, but Rebecca ignored him.

"Lot of patriotic stuff, come to think of it. I wonder why. Bicentennial, maybe?"

If she was asking me, I had no answer. Periodically, one of the streetlamps buzzed or flickered. No moon. Our footsteps echoed strangely on the wet wood, sounding somehow lighter than they should have. Not one of the fishermen glanced our way, though one twitched as we drew abreast, hunched forward to work furiously at his reel, and yanked a small ray right up into the air in front of him. It hung there streaming, maybe a foot across, its underside impossibly white, silently flapping. Like the ripped-out soul of a bird, I thought, and shuddered while the fisherman drew the ray toward him and laid it, gently across his lap. It went on flapping there until it died.

We'd all stopped in our tracks at the fisherman's first movements, and we stayed there quite a while. Eventually, Ash turned to us and nodded his head. "I have missed you, Rebecca," he said. "You, too, Elliot." But he meant Rebecca. He'd always meant Rebecca, and had told me so once, the night before graduation, on one the rare occasions when he got high, just to see. "Count on you," he'd told me. "Worship her."

Tonight, Rebecca didn't respond, and eventually Ash started toward the pavilion and the lights beneath it. We followed. I walked beside my wife, close enough for elbow contact but not manufacturing any. Something about the flapping ray reminded me of our daughter, squirming and jerking as she scrabbled for a hold in the world, and I wanted to be back at our house. In spite of the calmer, sadder way Rebecca had been this past year – maybe even because of it, though I hated thinking that – I loved our home.

"What made the merry-go-round so amazing?" I asked.

"The guy who designed it – Rooff, I think? – he's like the most famous American carousel builder. Or one of. He did this one in Rhode Island or Vermont, when they broke it up and sold off the horses, they went on eBay for $25,000 a piece. But this one . . ."

In the quiet of the next few seconds, I became aware, for the first time since we'd reached the pier, of the sounds. That wind, first of all, sighing out of the blackness to crash against the fortified city and then roll back. The ocean, shushing and muttering. The boards creaking as fishermen shifted or cast and seagulls dropped out of the dark to perch on the ruined railings. And, from straight ahead, under that darkly gleaming steel hat, an incongruous and unidentifiable tinkling, almost musical, barely audible, like an ice cream truck from blocks away.

"You should have seen their faces, Elliot. You would have loved them."

I blinked, still seeing the ray. "Really?"

"Rooff – the designer – he made them after his business partner died. His best friend, I guess. To keep him company, or something. I met this older man from the Carousel Preservation Assemblage who—"

"The Carousel what?" I said, and smiled. It really was astonishing, the people Rebecca knew.

"I met him at that open city planning meeting down here a couple years ago. The one about the development of the rest of downtown? The one I came home so upset from?"

"That would be every city planning meeting," I said. My smile faded, and the musical tinkling from the end of the pier got just a little louder.

"Anyway. These horses, Elliot. They were just . . . the *friend-liest* horses I've ever seen. They all had huge dopey smiles on their faces. Their teeth either pointed out sideways, or else they were perfect and glowing. Their sides were shiny brown or black or pink or blue. Their manes all had painted glass rubies and sapphires sticking out of them, and the saddles had these ridiculously elaborate roses and violets carved into the seats. Hooves flying, like they just couldn't stand to come down, you know? Like it was too much fun just sailing around in a circle forever. The Preservation guy said Rooff installed every single one of them, and every cog of every machine down here, by himself, at night, by candlelight. As some kind of tribute to his friend or something. Said he was a total raving loon, too. Got involved in all kinds of séances trying to contact his friend after he died. Wound up getting publicly ridiculed by Harry Houdini, who broke up one of his little soirées, apparently. Died brokenhearted and penniless."

"Your kind of guy," I said. And I thought I understood, suddenly and for the first time, just how badly Rebecca's father had hurt her. Because he'd been her kind of guy, too.

Unlike me.

"Yep," said Rebecca, and her face darkened again. Her mood seemed to change with every breath now, like the pattern of shadows on the pier around us. "Anyway, this is where we came. My dad'd plop us on the merry-go-round, hand the operator a fistful of tickets, and there we'd stay while he went and . . . well. I'm not going to tell you."

Ahead, Ash reached the hanging drapes, which, up close, were stained and ratty and riddled with runs. Without turning around or pausing, he slipped inside them. Instantly, his form seemed to waver, too, just like the lights, as though he'd dived into a pool. I stopped, closed my eyes, felt the salt on my skin and smelled fish and whitewater. And smog, of course. Even here.

"Why won't you tell me?"

"Because I'm pretty sure you're going to get to see." She passed through the drapes, and I followed.

I don't know what I was expecting under the hat, but whatever it was, I was disappointed. The space under there was cavernous, stretching another thirty yards or so out to sea, but most of it was empty, just wood planking and the surrounding shroud flapping in the wind like the clipped and tattered wings of some giant ocean bird. Albatross, maybe. At the far end of the space, another white curtain, this one heavier and opaque, dropped from rafters to dock, effectively walling off what had to be the last few feet of pier and giving me uneasy thoughts about the Wizard of Oz behind his screen. A mirror-ball dangled overhead, gobbling up the light from the fixture-less hanging bulbs suspended from the rafters and shooting off the red and green and blue sparks I'd seen from down the pier.

Spaced around the perimeter of the enclosure, and making the tinkling, bleeping noises we'd heard from outside, were six or seven pre-video arcade games, and stationed at the one directly across from us, elbowing each other and bobbing up and down, were two kids, neither older than seven, both with startlingly long white-blonde hair pouring down their backs like melting wax. I'm not sure why I decided they were brother and sister. The one on the left wore a dress, the one on the right jeans. Of Rebecca's grinning horses, the only possible remnant was the room's lone attendant, who was hovering near the kids but looked up when we entered and shuffled smoothly away from them, head down, as though we'd caught him peeping at a window.

"Come here," Ash said, standing over one of the machines to our left. "Look at this."

We moved toward him, and as we did, the attendant straightened and began to scuttle over the planking toward us. Despite his surprising grace, he looked at least a hundred years old. His skin was yellow and sagging off his cheeks, and his hair was white and patchy. His shoulders dipped, seemingly not quite aligned with his waist, and his fingers twitched at the fringes of his blue workman's apron. It was as though nothing on that body quite fit, or had been his originally; he'd just found the shed exoskeleton and slipped inside it like a hermit crab. I couldn't take my eyes from him until he stopped in the centre of the room.

"Hey," Rebecca said to Ash. "You're good."

"Sssh," Ash murmured, "Almost got it. *Shoot.*" There was a clunk from the machine, and I stepped up next to him.

"We had one of these at the 7–11 by my house," I said.

Simple game. You stuck your hands inside the two outsized, all-but-immovable gloves on the control panel. The gloves controlled a sort of crane behind the glass of the machine. You tried to maneuver the crane down to the bone-pile of prizes encased in clear, plastic bubbles below, grab a bubble in the jaws of the crane, then lift and drop it down a circular chute to the left. If you got the bubble in the chute, it popped out to you, and you claimed your prize. I couldn't remember ever seeing anyone win that game.

"Let me try," said Rebecca, and slid a quarter into the slot and her hands into the gloves. She got the crane's jaws around a bubble with a jiggly rubber tarantula inside and dropped it before she got it anywhere near the chute's mouth.

"I'm going again," Ash said, jamming home another quarter.

Behind us, the attendant wriggled two steps closer. His hands fumbled at the work apron, and I finally noticed the change-dispenser belted around his waist and rattling like a respirator. The thing was huge, ridiculous, had to have housed fifty dollars worth of quarters, and could probably accommodate ten years worth of commerce on this pier, given the traffic I'd seen tonight. The man looked at me, and a spasm rolled up his arms – or maybe it was a gesture. An invitation to convert some money.

"Fucksickle," Ash said, kneeing the machine as another plastic bubble crashed back to the pile.

"Now, now," I said, reaching for both his and Rebecca's shoulders, wanting to shake free of the change-man's gaze, and also of the mood I could feel rolling up on all of us like a tide. "Is that the Middle Path? The elimination of desire or whatever—"

"Don't you mock that," Ash snarled, half-shoving me as he whirled around. His face had gone completely red again, and at his sides his fists had clenched, and I wondered if some of the assumptions Rebecca and I had been making – about whether he'd actually been in a boxing ring, for example – weren't years out of date.

Startled, shaking a little, I held up a hand. "Hey," I said. "It's just me. I wasn't—"

"Yes, you were," Rebecca said, and my mouth fell open, to defend myself, maybe, at least from my wife who had no right, and then she added, "We both were. Sorry, Ash."

"I'm used to it," he said, in his normal, expressionless voice, and wandered away toward the next machine.

For a while, Rebecca and I stood, not touching, watching our friend. I hated when Rebecca went still like this: head cocked, hands in her pockets, green eyes glazed over. At least right now she was doing it during an argument, and not over breakfast coffee, in the midst of reading the paper, just because. Daphne, having sickened of being chased, turning herself into a tree.

Finally, I blew out the breath I hadn't realized I'd been holding and said, "You're wrong, Rebecca. You both are."

"Oh, come on, Elliot. Even when he's not around, what do we talk about when we talk about Ash? His vests, and his inability to land a life-partner, and his refusal or whatever it is to hold a job, and the crazy situations he seems to wind up in without even trying, and—"

"There's a difference between enjoying and mocking."

That stopped her, and even unlocked her, a little. At least she re-cocked her head so it was facing me. "You enjoy us too much," she said, and followed Ash.

I was angry, then, and I didn't go after them immediately. I watched Rebecca approach Ash, stand close to him. They were at the back of the space, now, both seeming to lean forward into the towering white curtain, almost pressing their ears against it. Briefly, it occured to me to wonder where the blonde kids had gone. Fifteen feet or so to my left, the attendant shifted, stared at me, and the change-dispenser rattled against his waist. I started forward, got within five steps of my wife and my oldest friend, and became aware, at last, of the new sounds.

Actually, the sounds had been there all along, I think. I'd just assumed that the murmuring was coming from the ocean, the bursts of rhythmic clatter from the arcade machines. But they originated on the other side of this curtain. For the second time, I thought of the Wizard of Oz crouched in his cubicle, furiously pulling levers to make the world magical and terrible. More magical and terrible than tornadoes and red shoes in green grass and dead or disappearing loved ones and home had already made it.

Ash glanced over his shoulder at me. I stepped forward, uncertainly, and stood behind him. Reaching out slowly, he brushed the curtain with his fingers, causing barely a stir in the heavy material.

"Crawl under?" he muttered. "Just push through?"

He bent to lift the curtain's skirt, and my wife turned briefly toward me, so that I caught just a glimpse of her face. Her lips had gone completely flat, and all trace of color had leached out of her cheeks.

"You know what's back there, don't you?" I said, as the attendant rattled closer, and Ash disappeared under the curtain.

"It's why we're here," said my wife, and followed him.

What struck me first as I struggled through the curtain and shrugged it off was the motion. Even before I made sense of what I was seeing, the whole space seemed to tilt, as though we'd stepped onto some sort of colorful, rotating platform. The color came courtesy of a red neon sign that hissed and spat blue sparks into the air. The sign was nailed to a wooden pillar that had been driven through the planking of the pier right beside where we emerged. I didn't even process what it said for a few seconds, and when I did, the words meant nothing to me, anyway.

LITE YOUR LINE LITE YOURS

"Change?" murmured a voice, right in front of me, and I jerked back further still, bumping against the curtain and feelings its weight on my back.

The girl who'd spoken couldn't have been out of her teens. Her skin glowed translucent red in the tinted neon like sea-glass. Her eyes were brown and bright, her lips full but colorless and expressionless. Her brown hair swept up off her scalp and arced in a slow inward curl to her shoulders, but where it brushed her black turtleneck, the tips had turned white, like a breaking wave upside down.

Before I could say anything, she was floating away, the smoothness of her movements terrifying until I realized she was on rollerskates. Her wheels made bumping sounds between the planks.

"Hi, Dad," Rebecca whispered, shoulders rigid, arms tucked tight to her sides, and I shuddered, my eyes flying around the space.

Mostly, what I saw were machines. Ten stubby, silver pinball tables jammed together end to end at awkward, irregular angles like dodge-em cars between rides. Hunched in identical poses over the glass tabletops were the players, and none of them looked up. They just kept pulling what I assumed were the ball-release levers and then pushing and patting at the flipper controls on the sides. Straight across the space from us, his ass to the drapery that hung from the magician's hat and divided this space from the night and the open ocean, a fifty-ish, red-haired guy with tufts of wiry beard sprouting from the cracks in his craggy face like weeds through pavement bent almost perpendicular over his machine, whispering to it as his fingers pummeled the buttons. I could just see the ripped, faded American flag design on his T-shirt when he rocked back to jack another ball into play.

"Oh my God, Rebecca. That isn't—"

"Huh?" she said, still rigid.

Of course it wasn't really her father, I realized. I'd seen pictures. And anyway, she wasn't looking at the red-headed man, or any of the other players. She was watching the electric board that hung, like the LITE YOUR LINE LITE YOURS sign, on another wooden pillar across the space from us. It was flashing the numbers 012839. Every few seconds, the numbers blinked.

Abruptly, a bell dinged, and the display on the electric board changed. #5, it read now. And then, CONGRATULATIONS! YOU'RE LITER! Then bumping sounds as the rollerskate girl swept the room, removing quarters from atop each player's machine, and dropping a single red poker chip at the feet of the red-haired man.

"Change?" she said to us, gliding past without looking or stopping, and abruptly Ash was out amongst them, assuming a place at a table kitty-corner to the American flag man's. On the board, a new number flashed. 081034. The lever jerking and button tapping resumed in earnest. American flag man never even looked up.

I watched Ash glance at the numbers board, down into his machine, across to American flag man. Then he was pulling his own lever, nodding. There were now five players: two stick-thin older women in matching bright red poodle-skirts, twin sets, and bobby socks, who might have been sisters; a kid in skater shorts with some kind of heavy metal music erupting from the sides of his headphones, as though everything inside his head were kicking and screaming to get out of there; American flag man; and Ash.

"What planet is this?" I murmured, and a bell dinged, and the rollerskate girl circled the room once more while Ash rocked back and laughed and dropped another quarter on his machine-top for the girl to collect.

Closing her eyes, Rebecca surprised me by taking my hand. Then she leaned in and kissed my cheek. "This is where he came. Before he walked out. It's been just like this for . . . God." She shuddered. "He'd put us on the merry-go-round, and he'd come in here, and he'd spend his hours. One quarter at a time. Most days, he wouldn't even take us home. My mom had to come get us."

Another ding, and the kid in the skater shorts flipped his hands in the air and moonwalked a few steps to his right, then back to his machine to pop a quarter in place just as the rollergirl passed and dropped a red chip at his feet. One of the women in the poodle skirts laughed. The laugh sounded gentler than I expected, somehow. The board flashed, and a new round began.

"Ever played?" I said, holding my wife's hand, but not too tight. Whatever tension there had been before between the three of us tonight, it was fading, I thought. Around us, the canvas outer draping undulated in slow motion as the sea breeze pushed against and through it. There was another winner, another burst of quiet laughter from somewhere as some lucky soul got *liter*, another new number flashing. One more sad-magic night with Ash and Rebecca, so long after the last one that I'd forgotten how it felt.

A good while after I'd asked, Rebecca sighed and leaned her head against me. "I miss our daughter," she said.

"Me, too."

"Should we call?"

"She's alright."

"Look at him," Rebecca said, and we did, together.

He was bent almost as far over his machine as the red-headed man, now, and when he played, the lights inside it and the red neon from the LITE YOURS sign reflected off his skull, and his vest beat and twitched with the rhythm of his movements, as though we were looking straight through his skin at the mechanisms that ran him.

"Poor Ash," I murmured, though I wasn't sure why I felt that way, and suspected he'd be furious if he heard me say it.

"I'll bet you a bag of Patriot Popcorn I can win before he does," said Rebecca, and she straightened and let go of my hand.

I thought of the fisherman on the empty pier behind us with the ray dying in his lap, the gaggle of beggars, and beyond them, the too-bright streets of downtown Long Beach. "And where will we find Patriot Popcorn, wife of mine, now that the Gap has come?"

"I think I know a place."

"I bet you do," I said, and let her go. On every side of us, at all times, at least one person was laughing.

"Change?" said the rollergirl, gliding past, but she executed a perfect stop even before Rebecca got her hand to her pocket. She took my wife's dollar, nodded. Her turtleneck clung tight to her, and there were tiny beads of sweat along the mouth of it like a string of transparent pearls. The tingle that sizzled through me then was more charged than any I'd felt since adolescence but sadder and therefore sexier still, and I had to bend over until it passed. Whether it was for my wife, the rollergirl, or just the evening, I had no idea.

When I next looked up, Rebecca and Ash were side by side, both bent over their individual metal machines, fingers pushing and pumping while the lights on the metal board flashed and the rollergirl rolled and the ocean breathed, in and out. Not wanting to distract them – and also, for some reason, not wanting to play – I stepped just close enough to see how the game worked.

Inside each machine was a ball chute and a simple, inclined

wooden playing board, with metallic mushrooms sprouting out of the center and impeding or – if you were skilled enough – directing the path of the ball. Across the top of the playing board were ball-sized holes numbered one to ten in plain black lettering. The object was to sink one ball in each of the holes corresponding with the flashing numbers on the big board. When you dropped a ball in the correct hole, your machine dinged and the number lit up. First person to light up every required number got a visit from the rollergirl and a red chip dropped at his or her feet as the quarter antes were collected for the next round. Then, with no pause, no stretch-break, no breath, the big board flashed again and the game resumed.

I settled into my spot between Rebecca and Ash, close enough to touch both but a step back. I was watching my wife's frame rattle as she bounced up and down in her big black shoes, leaned left and then right, and I thought of the new, permanently puffy space on her stomach where her scar was, and where, she said, she could no longer feel anything, which for some reason always made me want to put my hand there. To feel the dead space, where the life inside her had been. I watched her watch Ash between games, heard her gleeful-competitive murmurs.

"Feel that, Ash? That would be my breath on your neck. That's me passing you by. Again."

Ash kept shaking his head, staring into his machine and seeming to drag it closer to him with those outsized, out-stretched arms. "Not this time," he kept saying. "Not tonight."

And I found that I knew – that I'd always known – that Rebecca was in love with him, too. That I was merely the post she and Ash circled, eyeing one another from either side of me but never getting closer than they already were. The knowledge felt strange, heavy in my chest, horrible but also old. As though I hadn't discovered but remembered it. Also, I knew she loved me, in the permanent way she'd loved her mother, who she'd stayed with, after all. Not that she'd had a choice.

In the back, the man in the flag shirt lit his line, closed his eyes, and slapped the sides of his machine with the heels of his palms. Then the kid in the headphones won again, did his dance. Occasionally, one of the poodle-skirt women won, but mostly they didn't, and their laughs punctuated each round, regardless. Rebecca bobbed, swore, taunted Ash. Ash leaned over further, grim-faced, muttering, the machine bumping and dinging against him, almost attached to him now like an iron lung. Between and amongst them, the rollergirl skated, collecting quarters, strewing victory chips. At one point, tears developed in my eyes, and I wiped them away fast and thought of the perpetual sprinkles of dried milk that dotted the corners of my daughter's lips like fairy dust. The stuff that brought her to life.

It was the poker chips, I think, that finally alerted me to how long we'd been standing there. My eyes kept following the rollergirl on her sweeps, tracing her long fingers on their circumscribed, perfectly circular path from machine-top to black change-purse at her waist, white tips of her hair barely caressing the slope of her shoulders. And at last my gaze followed one of those chips as it fell to the floor amidst maybe a thousand others strewn around the ankles of the flag-shirt man like rose petals after a rainstorm.

My head jerked as though I'd been slapped.

"Change?" the rollergirl said as she breezed past me on her path through the players. Had she said that to me every time? Had I answered? And where was the music coming from? I could hear it, faintly. I was moving to it, a little. So was Ash. A gently bouncing fairground whirl, from an organ somewhere not too near. Under the dock? On shore?

Inside me? Because I appeared to be singing it. Sort of. Breathing it, so it was barely audible. We all were, I thought. It was everywhere, floating in the air of this makeshift room like a sea breeze trapped when the curtains dropped. Dazed, I watched Rebecca fish ten dollars out of her jeans pocket without looking up. The rollergirl took it and stood a bankroll of quarters, wrapped tight in red paper like a stick of dynamite, on the rim of Rebecca's machine. Both of them humming.

"Rebecca?" I said, then said it again, because my voice sounded funny, slurred and slow, as though I were speaking under water.

"Just a sec," she told me.

"Rebecca, come on."

"Might as well," Ash murmured. "I'm almost there. No hope for you."

My wife glanced up – slowly, smoothly – and caught my eye. "Hear that? You'd think he'd beaten me all his life. Or ever. At anything."

"I think we should go," I said, as Rebecca's head sank down over the metal tabletop again and her hands drifted to the ball-

lever and buttons. I said it again, and my words got tangled up
in that tune, and I was almost singing them, and then I smashed
my jaws together so hard I felt my two top front teeth pop in
their sockets. "*Rebecca*," I snapped.

And just like that, as though I'd doused her with ice water,
my wife shivered upright, and there were shudders rippling all
the way down her body. Her skin seemed to have come loose. I
could almost see it billowing around her. Then she was weeping. "Fuck him, Elliot," she said. "Oh, fuck him *so fucking much.
God*, I miss my mom."

For one moment more, I stood paralyzed, this time by the
sight of my weeping wife, though I could feel that tune
bubbling up again in the back of my mouth, as though my
insides were boiling, threatening to stream out of me like
steam. Finally, Rebecca's fingers found mine. They felt reassuringly bony and hard. Familiar.

"Let's go," she whispered, still weeping.

"Come on come on come on *Yah!*" Ash screeched, started to
hurl his arms over his head and stopped, scowling as the board
flashed the number of the winner and the American flag man
closed his eyes and popped the sides of his machine with his
palms once more. "I had it," said Ash, already hunching
forward. "I really thought I had it."

"Time to go, bud," I told him, pushing my fingers against
Rebecca's so both of us could feel the joints grinding together.
She was still shuddering, head down, and the rollergirl glided
up and swept a new quarter from Ash's machine and reached
for the top one on Rebecca's stack and Rebecca swatted the
whole roll to the floor. The rollergirl didn't look up or break
her hum as she passed.

"Right now," Rebecca said, looking up, letting the tears
stream down. "It's got to be now, Elliot."

"Come on, Ash," I said. "Let's go get tapas."

"What are you talking about?" he said, and the big board
flashed, and he was playing again. The kid in the headphones
won in a matter of seconds.

"Ash. We need to leave."

"Almost there," he said. "Don't you want to see what you
win?"

"Elliot," Rebecca said, voice tight, fingers like talons ripping
at my wrist.

"Ash, come—"

"Elliot. *Run.*" She was staring up into the magician's hat, then at the American flag man, who didn't stare back, hadn't ever seemed to notice we were there.

Another number on the board, another flurry of fingers and rattle of pinballs, another burst of laughter from the poodle-skirt women. Then we were gone, Rebecca yanking me behind her like a puppy on leash. Low humming sounds streamed from our mouths as we struggled through the white curtain and just kept going.

"Hey," I said, trying to shake her fingers just a little looser on my arm, but she didn't let go until we were through the outer canvas, standing in the biting air on the wet and rotting dock. Instantly, the tune was gone from my mouth and ears, as though someone had snapped shut the lid of a music box. I found myself trying to remember it, and was seized, suddenly, by a grief so all-engulfing I could barely breathe, and didn't want to. Tears exploded onto my cheeks.

Rebecca stirred, let go of my arm, but turned to me. "Oh," she said, reached up, stuck her finger in one of my teardrops and traced it all over my cheek, as though finger-painting with it.

"I don't know why," I said, and I didn't. But it had nothing to do with Ash, or Ash and Rebecca, or Rebecca's dead mother, or our strange, loving, incomplete marriage. It had to do with our daughter. So new to the world.

"Come on," she said.

"What about our friend in there?"

"He'll follow."

"What if he doesn't?"

"He knows where we live. He's a big boy."

"Rebecca," I said, but realized I didn't know what I was going to say. What came out was, "I don't know. There's something . . ."

Around us, the sea stirred, began to slap against the shore and the pilings beneath it. We could feel it through our feet. The reassuring beat of the blood of the earth. There was a mist now, too, and it left little wet spots on our exposed skin.

Rebecca shrugged. "It's just where my dad is. Where he'll always be. For me."

Then we were walking. Again, our footsteps sounded strange, made almost no sound whatsoever. There was still no moon overhead, only grey-white clouds, lit from behind from millions of miles away. The fishermen had remained in their places, but they'd gone almost motionless, leaning over their lines into the night as though every single one of them had gone to sleep. I saw the guy who'd caught the ray, but the ray was no longer in his lap, and I wondered what he'd done with it. Looking up, I saw the blacked out buildings of old Long Beach, seemingly further from us than they should have been, wrapped in mist and scaffolding like mothballed furniture in an attic. By the time we reached our car, the feeling in my chest had eased a bit, and I was no longer crying and still couldn't figure out why I had been. Rebecca was shivering again.

"Let's wait here for him," I said, and Rebecca shivered harder.

"No."

She got in the car, and I climbed in beside her. I turned on the ignition but waited a while. When Rebecca looked at me next, she was wearing the expression I'd become so familiar with, this last, long, sweet year. Eyes still bright, but dazed somehow. Mouth pursed, but softly. "Take me home to see my girl," she said.

I didn't argue. I stopped thinking about Ash. I took my wife home to our tiny house.

That was Friday. Saturday we stayed in our neighborhood, took strolls with our child, went to bed very early and touched each other a while without making love. Sunday I got up and made eggs and wondered where Ash had gone and whether he was angry with us, and then we went hiking up the fire trail behind our subdivision into the hills, brown and strangled with drought. I didn't worry, really. But I started calling Ash's Oakland bungalow on Monday morning. I also called the hospital where he worked, and on Thursday, right when he'd apparently told Ms Paste he would return, he turned up as scheduled for his shift on the ward. I got him on the line, and he said he had rounds to do and would call me back. He didn't, though. Then, or ever.

After that, I stopped thinking about him for a while. It wasn't unusual for Ash to disappear from our lives for months or even years on end. I already understood that adult friendships operated differently from high school or college ones, were harbors to visit rather than places to live, no matter how sweet and safe the harbor. Rebecca never mentioned him. Our baby learned to walk. The next time I called the hospital, maybe six months ago, I was told Ash no longer worked there.

Last night, late, I climbed out of my bed, looked at my daughter lying sideways, arms akimbo, across the head of her crib-mattress like a game piece that had popped free of its box slot and rolled loose, and wandered into the living room to read the newspaper. I opened the *Calendar* section, stared at the photograph on the second page. My mouth went dry, as though every trace of saliva had been sucked from it, and my bones locked in place. I couldn't move, couldn't breathe, couldn't even think.

Staring out at me was a photograph of a merry-go-round horse, tipped sideways as it was hauled out of its storage closet by movers. Its front teeth were chipped and aimed in opposing directions below the oversized, grinning lips, and its lifted hooves seemed to be scrambling frantically at the air.

LAST ROOFF HORSES SOLD AT AUCTION, read the caption.

I flew through the story that accompanied the photograph, processing it in bits and pieces, while fragments of that tune – the one from the pier – floated free in my head but never knitted themselves into something I could hum.

Once, these vibrantly painted, joyous creatures spun and flew on the soon-to-be-razed Long Beach Pier . . . The last great work of a grieving man . . . His final carousel, populated with what Rooff called "The company I crave" after his longtime business partner and reputed lover, Los Angeles nightclub owner and legendary gambler Daniel R. Ratch, took his own life following a decades-long battle with a degenerative muscular disease in September of 1898.

The reclusive Rooff and notorious Ratch formed one of the more unlikely – and lucrative – financial partnerships of the fin-de-siecle era, building thousands of cheaply manufactured carousels, fortune-telling machines, and other amusements of the time for boardwalks and parks nationwide. They envisioned the Long Beach Pier as their crowning achievement, a world unto itself for "All the laughing people . . .," in Rooff's memorable phrase at his tearful press conference following Ratch's death . . .

Rooff completed only the carousel and the now-infamous Lite-Your-Line parlor before being fired for erratic behavior and the agonizingly slow pace of his work . . . He disappeared from the public record, and his death is not recorded.

There was more, but the words had stopped making sense to me. Shoving the paper away, I sat back in my chair. The trembling started a few seconds later.

I can't explain how I knew. I was thinking of Rooff under that hat, hidden by curtains, working furiously in the candlelight, chanting his dead lover's name. I think maybe I'd always suspected, hadn't admitted. But Ash had made it back to Oakland, hadn't he? And we'd made it here?

Then, abruptly, I was up, snatching my keys off the hook next to the kitchen sink and fleeing toward our car, while that incomplete tune whirled in my head and the whole last night with Ash spilled in front of my eyes in kaleidoscopic broken pieces. I don't remember a single second of the drive down the freeways, couldn't even tell you whether there was traffic, because all I was seeing were the homeless men and the sores on their arms and the way their mouths moved as they chanted their rhyme. Then I was seeing the ray flapping in midair, lifted out of the waves just as we passed, as though the whole scene had been triggered by our passing. The disappearing blonde children, the arcade machine attendant's graceful shuffle and the sound he made. The rose-petal poker chips. The tinkling machines. The glide of the rollergirl, and the skater kid's moonwalk, and the American flag man. And the poodle-skirt women's perpetually smiling faces. Most of all, their faces, and it was their laughter I was hearing as I skidded into that giant, empty parking lot and jammed my car to a stop and leapt out, hoping, praying.

Even the streetlights were gone, and the dark pier jutted crookedly over the quietly lapping water like the prow of a beached ship. No magician's hat. Nothing on the pier at all. Overhead, I saw stars, faint and smeared by the smog, as though I were viewing them through a greasy window. Behind me, the new old city, safely shut down and swept clean for the night, rocked imperceptibly on its foundations. A wind kicked up, freezing cold, and I clamped my arms to my chest and crouched beside my car and wished I'd remembered a jacket, at least.

Finally, I let myself think it. Sort what I'd been hoping. Which had been what, exactly? That I'd find the auctioneer still here? That the movers would still be emptying the last pieces out of the warehouse, and maybe I could . . .

"What?" I said aloud, and slammed my palms against the pavement and scraped them badly. *Do what?* Pick up my friend's body like a cigar store Indian, tie him to the top of the car, bring him to our house, which he'd never seen, and prop him on our little porch in our choice of vests? Maybe bring along a poodle-skirt woman so we could make set-pieces?

Staggering to my feet, I took a huge breath and let the ocean air cut my lungs. In my pocket, I realized, I'd jammed the newspaper article, and I removed it now, uncrumpled it, ripped it to pieces, and set the pieces flying. Rebecca could never see that article, could never know what I was thinking. It was bad enough – it was flat, fucking murder – that we'd left Ash down here. I didn't even want to imagine how she'd react when she realized what really might have happened to her father.

How did it work, I wondered? Were Rooff's ghosts, or machines, or whatever they were, *selective* about the company they brought him? Had they let us go, or had we refused? Had Ash known, before it was too late, that he had a choice? Had the rest of them – the rollergirl, the flag man, the kid, maybe even Rebecca's father – chosen to stay, because it was bright and musical and happy in there, and smelled of the sea?

It was almost light when I fumbled my car door open and collapsed back into the driver's seat. I could be wrong, I thought. I could go home right now and find Rebecca with the kitchen phone dangling from her ear, smiling in the way she didn't anymore as Ash told her where he'd vanished to this time and she spooned minced carrots to our child. But I didn't think so.

Not until I was off the freeways again, just pulling into our little driveway, did it occur to me to wonder where, exactly, Rooff's last merry-go-round stopped. At the edge of the white curtain? Or at the end of the pier? The ray could have been part of it, and the fishermen, and the beggars, too. Or maybe they'd just wanted to be.

I stepped out of the car, felt the stagnant L.A. air settle around me. The rising sun caught in my neighbor's windows, releasing tiny prisms of colored light, and somewhere down the street, wind-chimes clinked, though there was little wind. And the feeling that whispered through me then was indeed magical, terrible, and also almost sweet. Because I realized I might be underestimating the power of Rooff's last carousel, even now. We could be on it, still – Rebecca, me, the whole crazy, homogenizing coast – bobbing up and down in our prescribed places as our parents die and our friends whirl past and away again and the places we love evaporate out of the world, the way everyone's favorite people and places inevitably do. Until, finally, we are just our faces, smiles frozen bright as we can make them, hands stretching for our children because we can't help but hope they'll join us, hope they'll understand before we did that there really may be no place else to go or at least forgive us for not finding it. Then they'll smile back at us. Climb aboard. And ride.

KIM NEWMAN

Amerikanski Dead at the Moscow Morgue or: Children of Marx and Coca-Cola

KIM NEWMAN HAS WON the Bram Stoker Award, the British Fantasy Award, the British Science Fiction Award, the Children of the Night Award, the Fiction Award of the Lord Ruthven Assembly and the International Horror Critics Guild Award.

His novels include *The Night Mayor, Bad Dreams, Jago, The Quorum, Back in the USSR* (with Eugene Byrne), *Life's Lottery* and the acclaimed *Anno Dracula* sequence – comprising the title novel, plus *The Bloody Red Baron* and *Judgment of Tears* (aka *Dracula Cha Cha Cha*). *An English Ghost Story* is currently being developed as a movie from a script by the author, while *The Matter of Britain* is another collaboration with Byrne.

As "Jack Yeovil" Newman has published a number of novels loosely inspired by the heroic fantasy "Warhammer" and Apocalyptic "Dark Future" role-playing games. These include

Drachenfels, Beasts in Velvet and *Genevieve Undead. Silver Nails* is a recent collection of five stories set in the Games Workshop universe and featuring the author's recurrent character, vampire heroine Genevieve Dieudonné.

Under his own name, Newman's extremely clever short fiction, which is often linked by recurring themes and characters, has been collected in *The Original Dr Shade and Other Stories, Famous Monsters, Seven Stars, Unforgivable Stories* and *Dead Travel Fast. Where the Bodies Are Buried* contains four interconnected novellas, and *Time and Relative* is a prequel to the BBC-TV series in Telos Publishing's "Doctor Who Novellas" series. Newman has also edited the alternate history music anthology *In Dreams* with Paul McAuley.

As the author recalls, "Once, long ago and far away, John Skipp and Craig Spector edited an anthology called *The Book of the Dead*, of mostly fine stories set more or less in the world of George A. Romero's 'Living Dead' films. It was so well-received that the editors produced a further volume, *Still Dead*. Then, remembering that there were three Romero dead movies, they set out to do a third volume, which may well have been called *Deader Than Ever* or *Deadest Yet.*

"Since, in my other life as a movie critic, I had written extensively about Romero in my book *Nightmare Movies*, I was pleased to be asked by John to come up with something for this third book. I did a little rewriting at Craig's suggestion, got paid (as I remember it) and waited for the story to appear.

"Years passed. I'm not really privy to what happened, but various publishers and editors fell out with each other and, though the third dead book nearly happened at least twice (I once received page proofs of the story) it never managed to stumble into print. If you've been picking up recent anthologies of original horror stories, you've already read quite a few ship-jumping tales from the collection (Douglas E. Winter's wonderful 'The Zombies of Madison County' is one).

"For a while, 'Amerikanski Dead' was due to come out as a chapbook – but that never quite happened either. Then, with the bogus Millennium looming, I was asked by Al Sarrantonio if I had anything he might look at for what was then called *999: The Last Horror Anthology*, intended to be one of those genre-summing, uber-collection doorstops that the field needs every so often to stay alive. I dug out this, and it wound up as the lead story in the somewhat more modestly-titled *999: New Stories of*

Horror and Suspense. For that appearance, the story lost its subtitle (a quote from Jean-Luc Godard) to keep the list of contents tidy, but I'm restoring it here.

"Though the rising of the dead is supposed to be a global phenomenon, Romero's movies – *Night of the Living Dead* (1968), *Dawn of the Dead* (1979) and *Day of the Dead* (1984) – are all about America. One or two of the stories in the dead collections are about foreign parts (Poppy Brite's 'Calcutta, Lord of Nerves') and Clive Barker was connected with a comic book spin-off that had dead folks (including the Royal Family) in London. But Romero's films belong now to the era of the superpower face-off, and I thought it would be interesting to see what might be happening in the then-Soviet Union during the time between *Dawn* and *Day* and, more importantly, what it might *mean.* The title is a riff on *The Living Dead at Manchester Morgue,* the British release title of the Spanish-Italian movie *No profanar el sueño de los muertos* (1974) – known in America as *Don't Open the Window* or *Let Sleeping Corpses Lie* (rarely has one film had so many great titles).

"The business about reconstructing faces from skulls is mentioned in Martin Cruz Smith's *Gorky Park,* but I remembered it from a 1960s BBC-TV science documentary (*Tomorrow's World?*) in which the skull of Ivan the Terrible was used as a template to recreate his head. For Rasputin details, I drew on Robert K. Massie's *Nicholas and Alexandra,* Sir David Napley's *Rasputin in Hollywood* and various unreliable movie and TV performances by whiskery scenery-chewers like Lionel Barrymore, Boris Karloff, Tom Baker and Christopher Lee."

AT THE RAILWAY STATION in Borodino, Yevgeny Chirkov was separated from his unit. As the locomotive slowed, he hopped from their carriage to the platform, under orders to secure, at any price, cigarettes and chocolate. Another unknown crisis intervened and the steam-driven antique never truly stopped. Tripping over his rifle, he was unable to reach the outstretched hands of his comrades. The rest of the unit, jammed half-way through windows or hanging out of doors, laughed and waved. A jet of steam from a train passing the other way put salt on his tail and he dodged, tripping again. Sergeant Trauberg found the pratfall hilarious, forgetting he had pressed a thousand roubles on the private. Chirkov ran and ran but the locomotive gained speed. When he emerged from the canopied platform, seconds after the last carriage, white sky poured down. Looking at the black-shingled track-bed, he saw a flattened outline in what had once been a uniform, wrists and ankles wired together, neck against a gleaming rail, head long gone under sharp wheels. The method, known as "making sleepers", was favoured along railway lines. Away from stations, twenty or thirty were dealt with at one time. Without heads, Amerikans did no harm.

Legs boiled from steam, face and hands frozen from winter, he wandered through the station. The cavernous space was subdivided by sandbags. Families huddled like pioneers expecting an attack by Red Indians, luggage drawn about in a circle, last bullets saved for women and children. Chirkov spat mentally; Amerika had invaded his imagination, just as his political officers warned. Some refugees were coming from Moscow, others fleeing to the city. There was no rule. A wall-sized poster of the New First Secretary was disfigured with a blotch, red gone to black. The splash of dried blood suggested something had been finished against the wall. There were Amerikans in Borodino. Seventy miles from Moscow, the station was a museum to resisted invasions. Plaques, statues and paintings honoured the victories of 1812 and 1944. A poster listed those local officials executed after being implicated in the latest counter-revolution. The air was tangy with ash, a reminder of past scorched earth policies. There were big fires nearby. An army unit was on duty, but no one knew anything about a timetable. An officer told him to queue and wait. More trains were coming from Moscow than going to, which meant the capital would eventually have none left.

He ventured out of the station. The snow cleared from the forecourt was banked a dozen yards away. Sunlight glared off muddy white. It was colder and brighter than he was used to in the Ukraine. A trio of Chinese-featured soldiers, a continent away from home, offered to share cigarettes and tried to practise Russian on him. He understood they were from Amgu; from the highest point in that port, you could see Japan. He asked if they knew where he could find an official. As they chirruped among themselves in an alien tongue, Chirkov saw his first Amerikan. Emerging from between snowbanks and limping towards the guard-post, the dead man looked as if he might actually be an American. Barefoot, he waded spastically through slush, jeans-legs shredded over thin shins. His shirt was a bright picture of a parrot in a jungle. Sunglasses hung round his neck on a thin string. Chirkov made the Amerikan's presence known to the guards. Fascinated, he watched the dead man walk. With every step, the Amerikan crackled: there were deep, ice-threaded rifts in his skin. He was slow and brittle and blind, crystal eyes frozen open, arms stiff by his sides.

Cautiously, the Corporal circled round and rammed his rifle-butt into a knee. The guards were under orders not to waste ammunition; there was a shortage. Bone cracked and the Amerikan went down like a devotee before an icon. The Corporal prodded a colourful back with his boot-toe and pushed the Amerikan on to his face. As he wriggled, ice-shards worked through his flesh. Chirkov had assumed the dead would stink but this one was frozen and odourless. The skin was pink and unperished, the rips in it red and glittery. An arm reached out for the corporal and something snapped in the shoulder. The corporal's boot pinned the Amerikan to the concrete. One of his comrades produced a foot-long spike and worked the point into the back of the dead man's skull. Scalp flaked around the dimple. The other guard took an iron mallet from his belt and struck a professional blow.

It was important, apparently, that the spike should entirely transfix the skull and break ground, binding the dead to the earth, allowing the last of the spirit to leave the carcass. Not official knowledge: this was something every soldier was told at some point by a comrade. Always, the tale-teller was from Moldavia or had learned from someone who was. Moldavians claimed to be used to the dead. The Amerikan's head came apart like a rock split along fault lines. Five solid chunks rolled away from the spike. Diamond-sparkles of ice glinted in reddish-grey inner surfaces. The thing stopped moving at once. The hammerer began to unbutton the gaudy shirt and detach it from the sunken chest, careful as a butcher skinning a horse. The jeans were too deeply melded with meat to remove, which was a shame; with the ragged legs cut away, they would have made fine shorts for a pretty girl at the beach. The Corporal wanted Chirkov to have the sunglasses. One lens was gone or he might not have been so generous with a stranger. In the end, Chirkov accepted out of courtesy, resolving to throw away the trophy as soon as he was out of Borodino.

*   *   *

Three days later, when Chirkov reached Moscow, locating his unit was not possible. A despatcher at the central station thought his comrades might have been reassigned to Orekhovo Zuyevo, but her superior was of the opinion the unit had been disbanded nine months earlier. Because the despatcher was not disposed to contradict an eminent Party member, Chirkov was forced to accept the ruling that he was without a unit. As such, he was detailed to the Spa. They had in a permanent request for personnel and always took precedence. The posting involved light guard duties and manual labour; there was little fight left in Amerikans who ended up at the Spa. The despatcher gave Chirkov a sheaf of papers the size of a Frenchman's sandwich and complicated travel directions. By then, the rest of the queue was getting testy and he was obliged to venture out on his own. He remembered to fix his mobility permit, a blue luggage-tag with a smudged stamp, on the outside of his uniform. Technically, failure to display the permit was punishable by summary execution.

Streetcars ran intermittently; after waiting an hour in the street outside central station, he decided to walk to the Spa. It was a question of negotiating dunes of uncleared snow and straggles of undisciplined queue. Teams of firemen dug methodically through depths of snow, side-by-side with teams of soldiers who were burning down buildings. Areas were cleared and raked, ground still warm enough to melt snow that drifted onto it. Everywhere, posters warned of the Amerikans. The Party line was still that the United States was responsible. It was air-carried biological warfare, the Ministry announced with authority, originated by a secret laboratory and disseminated in the Soviet Union by suicidal infectees posing as tourists. The germ galvanised the nervous systems of the recently-deceased, triggering the lizard stems of their brains, inculcating in the Amerikans a disgusting hunger for human meat. The "news" footage the Voice of America put out of their own dead was staged and doctored, footage from the sadistic motion pictures that were a symptom of the West's utter decadence. But everyone had a different line: it was . . . creeping radiation from Chernobyl . . . a judgment from a bitter and long-ignored God . . . a project Stalin abandoned during the Great Patriotic War . . . brought back from Novy Mir by cosmonauts . . . a plot by the fomenters of the Counter-Revolution . . . a curse the Moldavians had always known.

Fortunately, the Spa was off Red Square. Even a Ukrainian sapling like Yevgeny Chirkov had an idea how to get to Red Square. He had carried his rifle for so long that the strap had worn through his epaulette. He imagined the outline of the buckle was stamped into his collar bone. His single round of ammunition was in his inside breast pocket, wrapped in newspaper. They said Moscow was the most exciting city in the world, but it was not at its best under twin siege from winter and the Amerikans. Helicopters swooped overhead, broadcasting official warnings and announcements: comrades were advised to stay at their workplaces and continue with their duly-delegated tasks; victory in the struggle against the American octopus was inevitable; the crisis was nearly at an end and the master strategists would soon announce a devastating counter-attack; the dead were to be disabled and placed in the proper collection points; another exposed pocket of traitors would go on trial tomorrow.

In an onion-domed church, soldiers dealt with Amerikans. Brought in covered lorries, the shuffling dead were shifted inside in ragged coffles. As Chirkov passed, a dead woman, bear-like in a fur coat over forbidden undergarments, broke the line. Soldiers efficiently cornered her and stuck a bayonet into her head. The remains were hauled into the church. When the building was full, it would be burned: an offering. In Red Square, loudspeakers shouted martial music at the queues. John Reed at the Barricades. Lenin's tomb was no longer open for tourists. Sergeant Trauberg was fond of telling the story about what had happened in the tomb when the Amerikans started to rise. Everyone guessed it was true. The Spa was off the Square. Before the Revolution of 1918, it had been an exclusive health club for the Royal Family. Now it was a morgue.

He presented his papers to a thin officer he met on the broad steps of the Spa, and stood frozen in stiff-backed salute while the man looked over the wedge of documentation. He was told to wander inside smartly and look out Lyubachevsky. The officer proceeded, step by step, down to the square. Under the dusting of snow, the stone steps were gilded with ice: a natural defence. Chirkov understood Amerikans were forever slipping and falling on ice; many were so damaged they couldn't regain their footing, and were consequently easy to deal with. The doors of the Spa, three times a man's height,

were pocked with bullet-holes new and old. Unlocked and
unoiled, they creaked alarmingly as he pushed inside. The
foyer boasted marble floors, and ceilings painted with classical
scenes of romping nymphs and athletes. Busts of Marx and
Lenin flanked the main staircase; a portrait of the New First
Secretary, significantly less faded than neighbouring pictures,
was proudly displayed behind the main desk.

A civilian he took to be Lyubachevsky squatted by the desk
reading a pamphlet. A half-empty vodka bottle was nestled like
a baby in the crook of his arm. He looked up awkwardly at the
new arrival and explained that last week all the chairs in the
building had been taken away by the Health Committee.
Chirkov presented papers and admitted he had been sent by
the despatcher at the railway station, which elicited a shrug.
The civilian mused that the central station was always sending
stray soldiers for an unknown reason. Lyubachevsky had three
days' of stubble and mismatched eyes. He offered Chirkov a
swallow of vodka – pure and strong, not diluted with melted
snow like the rat poison he had been sold in Borodino – and
opened up the lump of papers, searching for a particular
signature. In the end, he decided it best Chirkov stay at the
Spa. Unlocking a cabinet, he found a long white coat, muddied
at the bottom. Chirkov was reluctant to exchange his heavy
greatcoat for the flimsy garment but Lyubachevsky assured him
there was very little pilferage from the Spa. People, even
parasites, tended to avoid visiting the place unless there was
a pressing reason for their presence. Before relinquishing his
coat, Chirkov remembered to retain his mobility permit, pin-
ning it to the breast of the laboratory coat. After taking
Chirkov's rifle, complimenting him on its cleanliness and
stowing it in the cabinet, Lyubachevsky issued him with a
revolver. It was dusty and the metal was cold enough to stick
to his skin. Breaking the gun open, Chirkov noted three
cartridges. In Russian roulette, he would have an even chance.
Without a holster, he dropped it into the pocket of his coat; the
barrel poked out of a torn corner. He had to sign for the
weapon.

Lyubachevsky told him to go down into the Pool and report
to Director Kozintsev. Chirkov descended in a hand-cranked
cage lift and stepped out into a ballroom-sized space. The Pool
was what people who worked in the Spa called the basement
where the dead were kept. It had been a swimming bath before

the Revolution; there, weary generations of Romanovs had
plunged through slow waters, the tides of history slowly pulling
them under. Supposedly dry since 1916, the Pool was so cold
that condensation on the marble floors turned to ice-patches.
The outer walls were still decorated with gilted plaster friezes
and his bootfalls echoed on the solid floors. He walked round
the edge of the pit, looking down at the white-coated toilers
and their unmoving clients. The Pool was divided into separate
work cubicles and narrow corridors by filmsy wooden partitions
that rose above the old water level. A girl caught his eye, blonde
hair tightly gathered at the back of her neck. She had red
lipstick and her coat sleeves were rolled up on slender arms as
she probed the chest cavity of a corpse, a girl who might once
have been her slightly older sister. The dead girl had a neat,
round hole in her forehead and her hair was fanned over a
sludgy discharge Chirkov took to be abandoned brains. He
coughed to get the live girl's attention and inquired as to where
he could find the Director. She told him to make his way to the
Deep End and climb in, then penetrate the warren of partitions. He couldn't miss Kozintsev; the Director was dead centre.

At the Deep End, he found a ladder into the pool. It was
guarded by a soldier who sat cross-legged, a revolver in his lap,
twanging on a jew's harp. He stopped and told Chirkov the
tune was a traditional American folk song about a cowboy killed
by a lawyer, "The Man Who Shot Liberty Valance". The guard
introduced himself as Corporal Tulbeyev and asked if Chirkov
was interested in purchasing tape cassettes of the music of Mr
Edward Cochran or Robert Dylan. Chirkov had no cassette
player but Tulbeyev said that for five thousand roubles he could
secure one. To be polite, Chirkov said he would consider the
acquisition: evidently a great bargain. Tulbeyev further insinu-
ated he could supply other requisites: contraceptive sheaths,
chocolate bars, toothpaste, fresh socks, scented soap, suppressed reading matter. Every unit in the Soviet Union had
a Tulbeyev, Chirkov knew. There was probably a secretary on
the First Committee of the Communist Party who dealt disco
records and mint-flavoured chewing gum to the High and
Mighty. After a decent period of mourning, Chirkov might
consider spending some of Sergeant Trauberg's roubles on
underwear and soap.

Having clambered into the Pool, Chirkov lost the perspective
on the layout of the work-spaces he had from above. It was a

labyrinth and he zigzagged between partitions, asking directions from the occasional absorbed forensic worker. Typically, a shrug would prompt him to a new pathway. Each of the specialists was absorbed in dissection, wielding whiny and smoky saws or sharp and shiny scalpels. He passed by the girl he had seen from above – her name-tag identified her as Technician Sverdlova, and she introduced herself as Valentina – and found she had entirely exposed the rib-cage of her corpse. She was the epitome of sophisticated Moscow girl, Chirkov thought: imperturbable and immaculate even with human remains streaked up to her elbows. A straggle of hair whisped across her face, and she blew it out of the way. She dictated notes into a wire recorder, commenting on certain physiological anomalies of the dead girl. There was a rubbery resilience in the undecayed muscle tissue. He would have liked to stay, but had to report to Kozintsev. Bidding her goodbye, he left her cubicle, thumping a boot against a tin bucket full of watches, wedding-rings and eyeglasses. She said he could take anything he wanted but he declined. Remembering, he found the bent and broken sunglasses in his trousers pocket and added them to the contents of the bucket. It was like throwing a kopeck into a wishing-well, so he made a wish. As if she were telepathic, Valentina giggled. Blushing, Chirkov continued.

He finally came to a makeshift door with a plaque that read V.A. KOZINTSEV, DIRECTOR. Chirkov knocked and, hearing a grunt from beyond, pushed through. It was as if he had left the morgue for a sculptor's studio. On one table were moist bags of variously coloured clays, lined up next to a steaming samovar. In the centre of the space, in the light cast by a chandelier that hung over the whole Pool, a man in a smock worked on a bust of a bald-headed man. Kozintsev had a neatly-trimmed beard and round spectacles. He was working one-handed; long fingers delicately pressing hollows into cheeks; a glass of tea in his other hand. He stood back, gulped tea and tutted, extremely dissatisfied with his efforts. Instantly accepting the newcomer, Kozintsev asked Chirkov for help in going back to the beginning. He set his glass down and rolled up his sleeves. They both put their hands in the soft face and pulled. Clays came away in self-contained lumps: some stranded like muscles, others bunched like pockets of fat. A bare skull, blotched with clay, was revealed. Glass eyes stared hypnotically, wedged into sockets with twists of newspaper. Chirkov realised he had heard of the Director: V.A. Kozintsev was one of the leading reconstruction pathologists in the Soviet Union. He had, layering in musculature and covering the results with skin, worked on the skulls tentatively identified as those of the Former Royal Family. He had recreated the heads of Palaeolithic men, murder victims and Ivan the Terrible.

Chirkov reported for duty and the Director told him to find something useful to do. Kozintsev was depressed to lose three days' work and explained in technical detail that the skull wasn't enough. There had to be some indication of the disposition of muscle and flesh. As he talked, he rolled a cigarette and stuck it in the corner of his mouth, patting his smock pockets for matches. Chirkov understood this was one of Kozintsev's historical projects: high profile work sanctioned by the Ministry of Culture, unconnected to the main purpose of the Spa – which, just now, was to determine the origins and capabilities of the Amerikans – but useful in attracting attention and funds. While the Director looked over charts of facial anatomy, puffing furiously on his cigarette, Chirkov picked up the discarded clays and piled them on the table. On a separate stand was a wigmaker's dummy head under a glass dome: it wore a long but neat black wig and facsimile wisps of eyebrows, moustache and beard. Once the skull was covered and painted to the correct skin tone, hair would be applied. He asked Kozintsev to whom the skull belonged, and, off-handedly, the Director told him it was Grigory Rasputin. There had been trouble getting glass eyes with the right quality. Contemporary memoirs described the originals as steely blue, with pupils that contracted to pinpoints when their owner was concentrating on exerting his influence. Chirkov looked again at the skull and couldn't see anything special. It was just bare bone.

Each evening at nine, the Director presided over meetings. Attendance was mandatory for the entire staff, down to Chirkov. He was billeted in the Spa itself, in a small room on the top floor where he slept on what had once been a masseur's table. Since food was provided (albeit irregularly) by a cafeteria, there was scarce reason to venture outside. At meetings, Chirkov learned who everyone was: the ranking officer was Captain Zharov, who would rather be out in the streets fighting but suffered from a gimpy knee; under Kozintsev, the chief coroner was Dr Fyodor Dudnikov, a famous forensic scientist often consulted by the police in political murder cases but plainly out of his depth with the Spa's recent change of purpose. The Director affected a lofty disinterest in the current emergency, which left the morgue actually to be run by a conspiracy between Lyubachevsky, an administrator seconded from the Ministry of Agriculture, and Tulbeyev, who was far more capable than Captain Zharov of keeping greased the wheels of the military machine.

Chirkov's girl Valentina turned out to be very eminent for her years, a specialist in the study of Amerikans; at each meeting, she reported the findings of the day. Her discoveries were frankly incomprehensible, even to her colleagues, but she seemed to believe the Amerikans were not simple reanimated dead bodies. Her dissections and probings demonstrated that the Amerikans functioned in many ways like living beings; in particular, their musculature adapted slowly to their new state even as surplus flesh and skin sloughed off. Those portions of their bodies that rotted away were irrelevant to the functioning of the creatures. She likened the ungainly and stumbling dead creatures to a pupal stage, and expressed a belief that the Amerikans were becoming stronger. Her argument was that they should be categorized not as former human beings but as an entirely new species, with its own strengths and capabilities. At every meeting, Valentina complained she could only manage so much by examining doubly-dead bodies and that the best hope of making progress would be to secure "live" specimens and observe their natural progress. She had sketched her impressions of what the Amerikans would eventually evolve into: thickly muscled skeletons like old anatomical drawings.

Valentina's leading rival, A. Tarkhanov, countered that her theories were a blind alley. In his opinion, the Spa should concentrate on the isolation of the bacteriological agent responsible for the reanimations, with a view to the development of a serum cure. Tarkhanov, a Party member, also insisted the phenomenon had been created artificially by American genetic engineers. He complained the monster-makers of the United States were so heavily financed by capitalist cartels that this state-backed bureaucracy could hardly compete. The one common ground Valentina held with Tarkhanov was that the Spa was desperately under-funded. Since everyone at the meetings had to sit on the floor, while Director Kozintsev was elevated cross-legged on a desk, the procurement of chairs was deemed a priority, though all the scientists also had long lists of medical supplies and instruments without which they could not continue their vital researches. Lyubachevsky always countered these complaints by detailing his repeated requests to appropriate departments, often with precise accounts of the elapsed time since the request had been submitted. At Chirkov's third meeting, there was much excitement when Lyubachevsky announced that the Spa had received from the Civil Defence Committee fifty-five child-sized blankets. This was unrelated to any request that had been put in, but Tulbeyev offered to arrange a trade with the Children's Hospital, exchanging the blankets for either vegetables or medical instruments.

At the same meeting, Captain Zharov reported that his men had successfully dealt with an attempted invasion. Two Amerikans had been found at dawn, having negotiated the slippery steps, standing outside the main doors, apparently waiting. One stood exactly outside the doors, the other a step down. They might have been forming a primitive queue. Zharov personally disposed of them both, expending cartridges into their skulls, and arranged for the removal of the remains to a collection point, from which they might well be returned as specimens. Valentina moaned that it would have been better to capture and pen the Amerikans in a secure area – she specified the former steam bath – where they could be observed. Zharov cited standing orders. Kozintsev concluded with a lengthy lecture on Rasputin, elaborating his own theory that the late Tsarina's spiritual adviser was less mad than popularly supposed and that his influence with the Royal Family was ultimately instrumental in bringing about the Revolution. He spoke with especial interest and enthusiasm of the so-called Mad Monk's powers of healing, the famously ameliorative hands that could ease the symptoms of the Tsarevich's haemophilia. It was his contention that Rasputin had been possessed of a genuine paranormal talent. Even Chirkov thought this beside the point, especially when the Director wound down by admitting another failure in his reconstruction project.

With Tulbeyev, he drew last guard of the night; on duty at 3:00 a.m., expected to remain at the post in the foyer until the nine o'clock relief. Captain Zharov and Lyubachevsky could not decide whether Chirkov counted as a soldier or an experi-

mental assistant; so he found himself called on to fulfil both
functions, occasionally simultaneously. As a soldier, he would
be able to sleep away the morning after night duty, but as an
experimental assistant, he was required to report to Director
Kozintsev at nine sharp. Chirkov didn't mind overmuch; once
you got used to corpses, the Spa was a cushy detail. At least
corpses here *were* corpses. Although, for personal reasons, he
always voted, along with two other scientists and a cook, in
support of Technician Sverdlova's request to bring in Amerikans, he was privately grateful she always lost by a wide margin.
No matter how secure the steam bath might be, Chirkov was
not enthused by the idea of Amerikans inside the building.
Tulbeyev, whose grandmother was Moldavian, told stories of
wurdalaks and *vryolakas* and always had new anecdotes. In life,
according to Tulbeyev, Amerikans had all been Party members:
that was why so many had good clothes and consumer goods.
The latest craze among the dead was for cassette players with
attached headphones; not American manufacture, but Japanese. Tulbeyev had a collection of the contraptions, harvested
from Amerikans whose heads were so messed up that soldiers
were squeamish about borrowing from them. It was a shame,
said Tulbeyev, that the dead were disinclined to cart video
players on their backs. If they picked up that habit, everyone in
the Spa would be a millionaire; not a rouble millionaire, a
dollar millionaire. Many of the dead had foreign currency.
Tarkhanov's pet theory was that the Americans impregnated
money with a bacteriological agent, the condition spreading
through contact with cash. Tulbeyev, who always wore gloves,
did not seem unduly disturbed by the thought.

   Just as Tulbeyev was elaborating upon the empire he could
build with a plague of video-players, a knock came at the doors.
Not a sustained pounding like someone petitioning for entry,
but a thud as if something had accidentally been bumped
against the other side of the oak. They both shut up and listened.
One of Tulbeyev's tape machines was playing Creedence Clear-
water Revival's "It Came Out of the Sky" at a variable speed; he
turned off the tape, which scrunched inside the machine as the
wheels ground, and swore. Cassettes were harder to come by
than players. There was a four-thirty-in-the-morning Moscow
quiet. Lots of little noises; wind whining round the slightly-
warped door, someone having a coughing-fit many floors above,
distant shots. Chirkov cocked his revolver, hoping there was a

round under the hammer, further hoping the round wasn't a dud. There was another knock, like the first. Not purposeful, just a blunder. Tulbeyev ordered Chirkov to take a look through the spy-hole. The brass cap was stiff but he managed to work it aside and look through the glass lens.

A dead face was close to the spy-hole. For the first time, it occurred to Chirkov that Amerikans were scary. In the dark, this one had empty eye-sockets and a constantly-chewing mouth. Around its ragged neck were hung several cameras and a knotted scarf with a naked woman painted on it. Chirkov told Tulbeyev, who showed interest at the mention of photographic equipment and crammed around the spy-hole. He proposed that they open the doors and Chirkov put a bullet into the Amerikan's head. With cameras, Tulbeyev was certain he could secure chairs. With chairs, they would be the heroes of the Spa, entitled to untold privileges. Unsure of his courage, Chirkov agreed to the scheme and Tulbeyev struggled with the several bolts. Finally, the doors were loose, held shut only by Tulbeyev's fists on the handles. Chirkov nodded; his comrade pulled the doors open and stood back. Chirkov advanced, pistol held out and pointed at the Amerikan's forehead.

The dead man was not alone. Tulbeyev cursed and ran for his rifle. Chirkov did not fire, just looked from one dead face to the others. Four were lined in a crocodile, each on a different step. One wore an officer's uniform, complete with medals; another, a woman, had a severe pinstripe suit and a rakish gangster hat; at the back of the queue was a dead child, a golden-haired, green-faced girl in a baseball cap, trailing a doll. None moved much. Tulbeyev returned, levering a cartridge into the breech, and skidded on the marble floor as he brought his rifle to bear. Taken aback by the apparently unthreatening dead, he didn't fire either. Cold wind wafted in, which explained Chirkov's chill. His understanding was that Amerikans always attacked; these stood as if dozing upright, swaying slightly. The little girl's eyes moved mechanically back and forth. Chirkov told Tulbeyev to fetch a scientist, preferably Valentina. As his comrade scurried upstairs, he remembered he had only three rounds to deal with four Amerikans. He retreated into the doorway, eyes fixed on the dead, and slammed shut the doors. With the heel of his fist, he rammed a couple of the bolts home. Looking through the spy-hole, he saw nothing had changed. The dead still queued.

Valentina wore a floor-length dressing-gown over cotton pyjamas. Her bare feet must be frozen on the marble. Tulbeyev had explained about the night visitors and she was reminding him of Captain Zharov's report. These Amerikans repeated what the Captain had observed: the queuing behaviour pattern. She brushed her hair out of the way and got an eye to the spy-hole. With an odd squeal of delight, she summoned Chirkov to take a look, telling him to angle his eye so he could look beyond the queue. A figure struggled out of the dark, feet flapping like beached fish. It went down on its face and crawled up the steps, then stood. It took a place behind the little girl. This one was naked, so rotted that even its sex was lost, a skeleton held together by strips of muscle that looked like wet leather. Valentina said she wanted that Amerikan for observation, but one of the others was necessary as well. She still thought of capturing and observing specimens. Tulbeyev reminded her of the strangeness of the situation and asked why the dead were just standing in line, stretching down the steps away from the Spa. She said something about residual instinct, the time a citizen must spend in queues, the dead's inbuilt need to mimic the living, to recreate from trace memories the lives they had once had. Tulbeyev agreed to help her capture the specimens but insisted they be careful not to damage the cameras. He told her they could all be millionaires.

Valentina held Tulbeyev's rifle as a soldier would, stock close to her cheek, barrel straight. She stood by the doorway covering them as they ventured out on her mission. Tulbeyev assigned himself to the first in the queue, the dead man with the cameras. That left Chirkov to deal with the walking skeleton, even if it was last in line and, in Moscow, queue-jumping was considered a worse crime than matricide. From somewhere, Tulbeyev had found a supply of canvas post-bags. The idea was to pop a bag over an Amerikan's head like a hood, then lead the dead thing indoors. Tulbeyev managed with one deft manoeuvre to drop his bag over the photographer's head, and whipped round behind the Amerikan, unravelling twine from a ball. As Tulbeyev bound dead wrists together, the twine cut through grey skin and greenish-red fluid leaked over his gloves. The rest of the queue stood impassive, ignoring the treatment the photographer was getting. When Tulbeyev had wrestled his catch inside and trussed him like a pig, Chirkov was ready to go for the skeleton.

He stepped lightly down to the skeleton's level, post-bag open as if he were a poacher after rabbit. The Amerikans all swivelled their eyes as he passed and, with a testicles-retracting spasm of panic, he missed his footing. His boot slipped on icy stone and he fell badly, his hip slamming a hard edge. He sledged down the steps, yelping as he went. A shot cracked and the little girl, who had stepped out of the queue and scrambled towards him, became a limp doll, a chunk of her head dryly gone. Tulbeyev had got her. At the bottom of the steps, Chirkov stood. Hot pain spilled from his hip and his side was numb. His lungs hurt from the frozen air, and he coughed steam. He still held his bag and gun; luckily, the revolver had not discharged. He looked around: there were human shapes in the square, shambling towards the Spa. Darting up the steps, unmindful of the dangers of ice, he made for the light of the doorway. He paused to grab the skeleton by the elbow and haul it to the entrance. It didn't resist him. The muscles felt like snakes stretched over a bony frame. He shoved the skeleton into the foyer and Tulbeyev was there with his ball of twine. Chirkov turned as Valentina shut the doors. More Amerikans had come: the skeleton's place was taken and the little girl's, and two or three more steps were occupied. Before bolting the doors, Valentina opened them a crack and considered the queue. Again, the dead were still, unexcited. Then, like a drill team, they all moved up a step. The photographer's place was taken by the officer, and the rest of the line similarly advanced. Valentina pushed the doors together and Chirkov shut the bolts. Without pausing for breath, she ordered the specimens to be taken to the steam baths.

Breakfast was a half-turnip, surprisingly fresh if riddled with ice-chips. Chirkov took it away from the cafeteria to chew and descended to the Pool to report to the Director. He assumed Valentina would make mention at the evening meeting of her unauthorized acquisition of specimens. It was not his place to spread gossip. Arriving at the cubicle before the Director, his first duty was to get the samovar going: Kozintsev survived on constant infusions of smoky tea. As Chirkov lit the charcoal, he heard a click, like saluting heels. He looked around the cubicle and saw no-one. All was as usual: clays, wig, shaping-tools, skull, samovar, boxes piled to make a stool. There was another click. He looked up at the chandelier and saw nothing unusual. The tea began to bubble and he chewed a mouthful of cold turnip, trying not to think about sleep, or Amerikans.

Kozintsev had begun again on the reconstruction. The skull of Grigory Yefimovich Rasputin was almost buried in clay strips. It looked very much like the head of the Amerikan Chirkov had secured for Valentina: flattened reddish ropes bound the jaws together, winding up into the cavities under the cheek-bones; enamel chips replaced the many missing teeth, standing out white against grey-yellow; delicate filaments swarmed round the glass eyes. It was an intriguing process and Chirkov had come to enjoy watching the Director at work. There was a sheaf of photographs of the monk on one stand but Kozintsev disliked consulting them. His process depended on extrapolating from the contours of the bone, not modelling from likenesses. Rasputin's potato-like peasant nose was a knotty problem. The cartilage was long-gone, and Kozintsev obsessively built and abandoned noses. Several were trodden flat into the sloping tile floor. After the Revolution, the faith healer had been exhumed by zealots from his tomb in the Imperial Park and, reportedly, burned; there was doubt, fiercely resisted by the Director, as to the provenance of the skull.

As Chirkov looked, Rasputin's jaw sagged, clay muscles stretching; then, suddenly, it clamped shut, teeth clicking. Chirkov jumped, and spat out a shocked laugh. Kozintsev arrived, performing a dozen actions at once, removing his frock-coat and reaching for his smock, bidding a good morning and calling for his tea. Chirkov was bemused and afraid, questioning what he had seen. The skull bit once more. Kozintsev saw the movement at once, and asked again for tea. Chirkov, snapping out of it, provided a cupful and took one for himself. Kozintsev did not comment on the appropriation. He was very interested and peered close at the barely animated skull. The jaw moved slowly from side to side, as if masticating. Chirkov wondered if Grigory Yefimovich were imitating him and stopped chewing his turnip. Kozintsev pointed out that the eyes were trying to move, but the clay hadn't the strength of real muscle. He wondered aloud if he should work in strands of string to simulate the texture of human tissue. It might not be cosmetically correct. Rasputin's mouth gaped open, as if in a silent scream. The Director prodded the air near the skull's mouth with his finger and withdrew sharply as the jaws snapped shut. He laughed merrily, and called the monk a cunning fellow.

The queue was still on the steps. Everyone had taken turns at the spy-hole. Now the line stretched down into the square and along the pavement, curving around the building. Tulbeyev had hourly updates on the riches borne by the Amerikans. He was sure one of the queue harboured a precious video-player: Tulbeyev had cassettes of *One Hundred & One Dalmatians* and *New Wave Hookers* but no way of playing them. Captain Zharov favoured dealing harshly with the dead, but Kozintsev, still excited by the skull activity, would issue no orders and the officer was not about to take action without a direct instruction, preferably in writing. As an experiment, he went out and, half-way down the steps, selected an Amerikan at random. He shot it in the head and the finally dead bag of bones tumbled out of the queue. Zharov kicked the remains, and, coming apart, they rolled down the steps into a snowdrift. After a pause, all the dead behind Zharov's kill took a step up. Valentina was in the steam baths with her specimens: news of her acquisitions had spread through the Spa, inciting vigorous debate. Tarkhanov complained to the Director about his colleague's usurpation of authority, but was brushed off with an invitation to examine the miraculous skull. Dr Dudnikov placed several phone calls to the Kremlin, relaying matters of interest to a junior functionary, who promised imminent decisions. It was Dudnikov's hope that the developments could be used as a lever to unloose vital supplies from other institutions. As ever, the rallying cry was *chairs for the Spa!*

In the afternoon, Chirkov napped standing up as he watched Kozintsev at work. Although the jaw continually made small movements, the skull was co-operative and did not try to nip the Director. He had requisitioned Tulbeyev's jew's harp and was implanting it among thick neck muscles, hoping it would function as a crude voicebox. To Chirkov's disgust, Rasputin was becoming expert in the movement of its unseeing eyes. He could suck the glass orbs so the painted pupils disappeared in the tops of the sockets, showing only milky white marbles. This was a man who had been hard to kill: his murderers gave him poison enough to fell an elephant, shot him in the back and chest with revolvers, kicked him in the head, battered him with a club and lowered him into the River Neva, bound in a curtain, through a hole in the ice. The skull bore an indentation which Kozintsev traced to an aristocrat's boot. In the end, men hadn't killed the seer; the cause of his death was drowning. As he worked, the Director hummed cheerful snatches of Prokofiev. To give the mouth something to do, Kozintsev stuck a cigarette between the teeth. He promised Grigory Yefimovich lips would come soon, but there was nothing yet he could do about lungs. His secret dream, which he shared with the skull (and, perforce, Chirkov), was to apply his process to a complete skeleton. Regrettably, and as he had himself predicted while alive, most of the monk had been scattered on the wind.

Lyubachevsky barged into the cubicle, bearing a telephone whose cord unreeled through the maze of the Pool like Ariadne's thread. There was a call from the Kremlin, which Kozintsev was required to take. While Chirkov and Lyubachevsky stood, unconsciously at attention, the Director chatted with the New First Secretary. Either Dr. Dudnikov had tapped into the proper channels or Tarkhanov was the spy everyone took him for and had reported on the sly to his KGB superior. The First Secretary was briefed about what was going on at the Spa. He handed out a commendation to Kozintsev and insisted extra resources would be channelled to the morgue. Chirkov got the impression the First Secretary was mixing up the projects: Kozintsev was being praised for Valentina's studies. The Director would be only too delighted to employ any funds or supplies in furthering his work with the skull.

Following the telephone call, the Director was in excellent spirits. He told the skull a breakthrough was at hand, and insisted to Lyubachevsky that he could hear a faint twang from the jew's harp. Grigory Yefimovich was trying to communicate, the Director claimed. He asked if he remembered eating the poisoned chocolates? After the jaw first moved, Kozintsev had constructed rudimentary clay ears, exaggerated cartoon curls which stuck out ridiculously. Having abandoned any attempt to simulate the appearance in life of the monk, he was attempting instead to provide working features. Since Rasputin's brains must have rotted or burned years ago, it was hard to imagine what the Director aspired to communicate with. Then, over the loudspeaker, Dr Dudnikov reported that there were soldiers outside the Spa, setting up explosives and declaring an intention to dynamite the building. Grigory Yefimovich's glass eyes rolled again.

*   *   *

Engineers were packing charges around the foyer. Entering the Spa through the kitchens, they had avoided the Amerikan-infested steps. It appeared a second queue was forming, stretching off in a different direction, still leading to the front doors. The officer in command, a fat man with a facial birth-mark that made him look like a spaniel, introduced himself as Major Andrey Kobylinsky. He strode about, inspecting the work, expressing pride in his unit's ability to demolish a building with the minimum of explosive matter. As he sur-veyed, Kobylinsky noted points at which surplus charges should be placed. To Chirkov's unschooled eye, the Major appeared to contradict himself: his men were plastering the walls with semtex. Kozintsev and Captain Zharov were absorbed in a reading of a twelve-page document which authorised the demolition of the Spa. Dr Dudnikov protested that the First Secretary himself had, within the last minute, commended the Spa and that important work to do with the Amerikan invasion was being carried out in the Pool, but Kobylinsky was far more interested in which pillars should be knocked out to bring down the decadent painted roof. As they worked, the engineers whistled "Girls Just Want to Have Fun".

Satisfied that the charges were laid correctly, Major Koby-linsky could not resist the temptation to lecture the assembled company on the progress and achievements of his campaign. A three-yard square map of Moscow was unfolded on the floor. It was marked with patches of red as if it were a chessboard pulled out of shape. The red areas signified buildings and construc-tions Kobylinsky had blown up. Chirkov understood the Major would not be happy until the entire map was shaded in red; then, Kobylinsky believed the crisis would be at an end. He proclaimed that this should have been done immediately the crisis begun, and that the Amerikans were to be thanked for prompting such a visionary enterprise. As the Major lectured, Chirkov noticed Tulbeyev at the main desk with Lyubachevsky, apparently trying to find a pen that worked. They sorted through a pot of pencils and chalks and markers, drawing streaks on a piece of blotting paper. Under the desk were packages wired to detonators. Kobylinsky checked his watch and mused that he was ahead of his schedule; the demolition would take place in one half an hour. Lyubachevsky raised a hand and ventured the opinion that the explosives placed under the main staircase were insufficient for the task of bringing down such a solidly-constructed structure. Barking disagreement, Kobylinsky strutted over and examined the charges in question, finally agreeing that safe was better than sorry and ordering the application of more explosives.

While Kobylinsky was distracted, Tulbeyev crept to the map and knelt over Red Square, scribbling furiously with a precious red felt-tip. He blotched over the Spa, extending an area of devastation to cover half the Square. When Kobylinsky revisited his map, Tulbeyev was unsuspiciously on the other side of the room. One of the engineers, a new set of headphones slung round his neck, piped up with an observation of a cartographical anomaly. Kobylinsky applied his concentration to the map and gurgled to himself. According to this chart, the Spa had already been dealt with by his unit: it was not a building but a raked-over patch of rubble. Another engineer, a baseball cap in his back pocket, volunteered a convincing memory of the destruction, three days ago, of the Spa. Kobylinsky looked again at the map, getting down on his hands and knees and crawling along the most famous thoroughfares of the city. He scratched his head and blinked in his birthmark. Director Kozintsev, arms folded and head high, said that so far as he was concerned the matter was at an end; he requested the engineers to remove their infernal devices from the premises. Kobylinsky had authorisation to destroy the Spa but once, and had demonstrably already acted on that authorisation. The operation could not be repeated without further orders, and, if further orders were requested, questions would be asked as to whether the engineers were as efficient as Kobylinsky would like to claim: most units needed to destroy a building only once for it to remain destroyed. Almost in tears, the bewildered Major finally commanded the removal of the explosives and, with parental tenderness, folded up his map into its case. With no apologies, the engineers withdrew.

That night, Valentina's Amerikans got out of the steam bath and everyone spent a merry three hours hunting them down. Chirkov and Tulbeyev drew the Pool. The power had failed again and they had to fall back on oil lamps, which made the business all the more unnerving. Irregular and active shadows were all around, whispering in Moldavian of hungry, unquiet creatures. Their progress was a slow spiral; first, they circled the Pool from above, casting light over the complex, but that left

too many darks unprobed; then they went in at the Deep End
and moved methodically through the labyrinth, weaving between the partitions, stumbling against dissected bodies, ready
to shoot hatstands in the brain. Under his breath, Tulbeyev
recited a litany he claimed was a Japanese prayer against the
dead: *sanyo, sony, seiko, mitsubishi, panasonic, toshiba* . . .

They had to penetrate the dead centre of the Pool. The
Amerikans were in Kozintsev's cubicle: staring at the bone-and-
clay head as if it were a colour television set. Rasputin was on his
stand under a black protective cloth which hung like long hair.
Chirkov found the combination of the Amerikans and Rasputin
unnerving and, almost as a reflex, shot the skeleton in the skull.
The report was loud and echoing. The skeleton came apart on
the floor and, before Chirkov's ears stopped hurting, others
had come to investigate. Director Kozintsev was concerned for
his precious monk and probed urgently under the cloth for
damage. Valentina was annoyed by the loss of her specimen but
kept her tongue still, especially when her surviving Amerikan
turned nasty. The dead man barged out of the cubicle, shoul-
dering partitions apart, wading through gurneys and tables,
roaring and slavering. Tarkhanov, incongruous in a silk dressing gown, got in the way and sustained a nasty bite. Tulbeyev
dealt with the Amerikan, tripping him with an axe-handle, then
straddling his chest and pounding a chisel into the bridge of his
nose. He had not done anything to prove Valentina's theories;
after a spell in captivity, he simply seemed more decayed, not
evolved. Valentina claimed the thing Chirkov had finished had
been a model of biological efficiency, stripped down to essentials, potentially immortal. Now, it looked like a stack of bones.

Even Kozintsev, occupied in the construction of a set of
wooden arms for his reanimated favourite, was alarmed by
the size of the queue. There were four distinct lines. The
Amerikans shuffled constantly, stamping nerveless feet as if
to keep warm. Captain Zharov set up a machine-gun emplacement in the foyer, covering the now-barred front doors,
although it was strictly for show until he could be supplied
with ammunition of the same gauge as the gun. Chirkov and
Tulbeyev watched the Amerikans from the balcony. The queue
was orderly; when, as occasionally happened, a too-far-gone
Amerikan collapsed, it was trampled under by the great mov-
ing-up as those behind advanced. Tulbeyev sighted on indivi-

dual dead with binoculars and listed the treasures he could distinguish. Mobile telephones, digital watches, blue jeans, leather jackets, gold bracelets, gold teeth, ball-point pens. The Square was a paradise for pickpockets. As night fell, it was notable that no lights burned even in the Kremlin.

When the power came back, the emergency radio frequencies broadcast only soothing music. The meeting was more sparsely attended than usual, and Chirkov realised faces had been disappearing steadily, lost to desertion or wastage. Dr. Dudnikov announced that he had been unable to reach anyone on the telephone. Lyubachevsky reported that the threat of demolition had been lifted from the Spa and was unlikely to recur, though there might now prove to be unfortunate official side effects if the institution was formally believed to be a stretch of warm rubble. The kitchens had received a delivery of fresh fish, which was cause for celebration, though the head cook noted as strange the fact that many of the shipment were still flapping and even decapitation seemed not to still them. Valentina, for the hundredth time, requested specimens be secured for study and, after a vote – closer than usual, but still decisive – was disappointed. Tarkhanov's suicide was entered into the record and the scientists paid tribute to the colleague they fervently believed had repeatedly informed on them, reciting his achievements and honours. Tulbeyev suggested a raiding party to relieve the queuing Amerikans of those goods which could be used for barter, but no one was willing to second the proposal, which sent him into a notable sulk. Finally, as was expected, Kozintsev gave an account of his day's progress with Grigory Yefimovich. He had achieved a certain success with the arms: constructing elementary shoulder joints and nailing them to Rasputin's stand, then layering rope-and-clay muscles which interleaved with the neck he had fashioned. The head was able to control its arms to the extent of stretching out and bunching up muscle strands in the wrists as if clenching fists which did not, as yet, exist. The Director was also pleased to report that the head almost constantly made sounds with the jew's harp, approximating either speech or music. As if to demonstrate the monk's healing powers, Kozintsev's sinus trouble had cleared up almost entirely.

Two days later, Tulbeyev let the Amerikans in. Chirkov did not know where the Corporal got the idea; he just got up from the gun emplacement, walked across the foyer, and unbarred the doors. Chirkov did not try to stop him, distracted by efforts to jam the wrong type of belt into the machine gun. When all the bolts were loose, Tulbeyev flung the doors back and stood aside. At the front of the queue, ever since the night they had brought in Valentina's specimens, was the officer. As he waited, his face had run, flesh slipping from his cheeks to form jowly bags around his jaw. He stepped forwards smartly, entering the foyer. Lyubachevsky woke up from his cot behind the desk and wondered aloud what was going on. Tulbeyev took a fistful of medals from the officer, and tossed them to the floor after a shrewd assessment. The officer walked purposefully, with a broken-ankled limp, towards the lifts. Next in was the woman in the pinstripe suit. Tulbeyev took her hat and perched it on his head. From the next few, the Corporal harvested a silver chain identity bracelet, a woven leather belt, a pocket calculator, an old brooch. He piled the tokens behind him. Amerikans filled the foyer, wedging through the doorway in a triangle behind the officer.

Chirkov assumed the dead would eat him and wished he had seriously tried to go to bed with Technician Sverdlova. He still had two rounds left in his revolver, which meant he could deal with an Amerikan before ensuring his own everlasting peace. There were so many to choose from and none seemed interested in him. The lift was descending and those who couldn't get into it discovered the stairs. They were all drawn to the basement, to the Pool. Tulbeyev chortled and gasped at each new treasure, sometimes clapping the dead on the shoulders as they yielded their riches, hugging one or two of the more harmless creatures. Lyubachevsky was appalled, but did nothing. Finally, the administrator got together the gumption to issue an order: he told Chirkov to inform the Director of this development. Chirkov assumed that since Kozintsev was, as ever, working in the Pool, he would very soon be extremely aware of this development, but he snapped to and barged through the crowd anyway, choking back the instinct to apologize. The Amerikans mainly got out of his way, and he pushed to the front of the wave shuffling down the basement steps. He broke out of the pack and clattered into the Pool, yelling that the Amerikans were coming. Researchers looked up – he saw Valentina's eyes flashing annoyance and wondered if it was not too late to ask her for sex – and the crowd edged behind Chirkov, approaching the lip of the Pool.

He vaulted in and sloshed through the mess towards Kozintsev's cubicle. Many partitions were down already and there
was a clear path to the Director's work-space. Valentina pouted
at him, then her eyes widened as she saw the assembled legs
surrounding the Pool. The Amerikans began to topple in,
crushing furniture and corpses beneath them, many unable
to stand once they had fallen. The hardiest of them kept on
walking, swarming round and overwhelming the technicians.
Cries were strangled and blood ran on the bed of the Pool.
Chirkov fired wildly, winging an ear off a bearded dead man in
a shabby suit, and pushed on towards Kozintsev. When he
reached the centre, his first thought was that the cubicle was
empty, then he saw what the Director had managed. Combining himself with his work, V.A. Kozintsev had constructed a
wooden half-skeleton which fitted over his shoulders, making
his own head the heart of the new body he had fashioned for
Grigory Yefimovich Rasputin. The head, built out to giant size
with exaggerated clay and rubber muscles, wore its black wig
and beard, and even had lips and patches of sprayed-on skin.
The upper body was wooden and intricate, the torso of a
colossus with arms to match, but sticking out at the bottom
were the Director's stick-insect legs. Chirkov thought the body
would not be able to support itself but, as he looked, the
assemblage stood. He looked up at the caricature of Rasputin's
face. Blue eyes shone, not glass but living.

Valentina was by his side, gasping. He put an arm round her
and vowed to himself that if it were necessary she would have
the bullet he had saved for himself. He smelled her perfumed
hair. Together, they looked up at the holy maniac who had
controlled a woman and, through her, an empire, ultimately
destroying both. Rasputin looked down on them, then turned
away to look at the Amerikans. They crowded round in an
orderly fashion, limping pilgrims approaching a shrine. A
terrible smile disfigured the crude face. An arm extended,
the paddle-sized hand stretching out fingers constructed from
surgical implements. The hand fell onto the forehead of the
first of the Amerikans, the officer. It covered the dead face
completely, fingers curling round the head. Grigory Yefimovich
seemed powerful enough to crush the Amerikan's skull, but
instead he just held firm. His eyes rolled up to the chandelier,
and a twanging came from inside the wood-and-clay neck, a
vibrating monotone that might have been a hymn. As the noise

resounded, the gripped Amerikan shook, slabs of putrid meat falling away like layers of onionskin. At last, Rasputin pushed the creature away. The uniform gone with its flesh, it was like Valentina's skeleton, but leaner, moister, stronger. It stood up and stretched, its infirmities gone, its ankle whole. It clenched and unclenched teeth in a joke-shop grin and leaped away, eager for meat. The next Amerikan took its place under Rasputin's hand, and was healed too. And the next.

DAVID CASE

Among the Wolves

DAVID CASE WAS BORN in upstate New York and since the early 1960s he has lived in London, as well as spending time in Greece and Spain. His acclaimed collection *The Cell: Three Tales of Horror* appeared in 1969, and it was followed by *Fengriffen: A Chilling Tale*, *Wolf Tracks* and *The Third Grave*, the latter appearing from Arkham House in 1981. More recently, a new collection entitled *Brotherly Love and Other Tales of Faith and Knowledge* was published by Pumpkin Books.

A regular contributor to the legendary *Pan Book of Horror Stories* during the early 1970s, his powerful novella "Pelican Cay" in *Dark Terrors 5* was nominated for a World Fantasy Award in 2001.

Outside the horror genre, Case has written more than three hundred books under at least seventeen pseudonyms, ranging from mild porn to Westerns. Two of his short stories, "Fengriffen" and the classic werewolf thriller "The Hunter", were filmed as *And Now the Screaming Starts!* (1973) and *Scream of the Wolf* (1974), respectively.

Ramsey Campbell has suggested that "Case's problem as a writer was that he was ahead of his time: the gruesome violence of his tale 'Among the Wolves' can hold its own against the most extreme of today's horror fiction, partly because rather than encouraging the reader to gawk at the spectacle, the gruesomeness of Case's tale seeks to make one feel what the victim feels."

Last published thirty years ago, I am delighted to present this disturbing novella to a new generation of horror fans . . .

THERE WAS SOMETHING ABOUT the killings which went beyond horror. All murder is horrible enough, of course, but one recognizes contingencies, one comprehends motivations and provocations and circumstances, and can understand, objectively, how a man may be driven or guided to murder. I feel I can glimpse into the dark minds which direct murder for profit, can dismember the warped violence of hatred and revenge, can pity the remorse of a killer swept helplessly along on uncharted currents and even, with a chill of grisly perception, understand the mangled patterns of a madman's mind reflected in mutilation or the insane fear of punishment which drives a sex maniac to destroy his innocent victim in the wake of satiated lust. These things are horrible, indeed, but they are conceivable – are no more than a distortion of normal human emotion, ambition, passion, greed – a magnification of urges which all men feel and most men keep bound and imprisoned in the deepest dungeons of the subconscious, shackled by the sensibilities. Sometimes – all too often – these shadowed impulses strike off the fetters of restraint and burst ravening from the corporal cell to stalk their prey, to command their former gaolers to violence. And then the crime is done. But somehow these murders were different. They invoked a feeling beyond such motivations as rage and fear, beyond even insanity as we have come to define it. It must have been a madman, there can be little doubt of that. No sane mind could have directed such crimes, no creature of chemical balance could have committed them. And yet – how can one express it? – the specific horror of these murders was that they seemed so utterly *natural* . . .

I knew rather more about these crimes than the average person, through mere circumstance – was in at the start, so to speak; for the morgue was an extension of the museum in which I was pursuing my research. The museum was attached to the university, and the morgue was in a wing of the university

medical centre. One supposes it was a convenient arrangement. The medical students required cadavers, and unidenti-
fied and unclaimed bodies gravitated to the morgue; and for
the good of medical progress – but I have no wish to moralize
on this point. Things are done, things often are necessary, an
accomplished fact is a fact, no more. I mention it only to set the
scene, as it were, for my casual and superficial involvement – an
involvement, I must admit, due more to morbid curiosity than
any more elevated motives. I am a scientist and, quite naturally,
I am curious about behaviour which does not fit the natural
patterns, which floats suspended at some unexplored level of
the sentient sea and defies the tides and waves of society.

I had been doing my research for some time – far longer
than originally intended, for research, by its very nature, feeds
upon itself and grows, extends and spreads strange and devious
branches from the fundamental roots – and so, quite naturally,
I came to know a number of people connected with the
museum and the university and, by extension, the morgue. I
became acquainted with Detective-Inspector Grant of the
homicide squad and with Doctor Ramsey who performed
the autopsies for the police. With Ramsey, in fact, an arrangement had developed. We found that our homes were quite
close, in the same suburb, and in time we began to share the
task of driving into town, alternating our motorcars to lessen
the traffic and parking difficulties on the campus grounds. He
proved an interesting and congenial fellow and the arrangement was very satisfactory. We became more than acquain-
tances, if less than friends. And it was through Ramsey,
indirectly, that I came to see the first body . . .

It was my day to drive and I'd left the museum library and
walked across the campus to the medical centre. It was a fine
autumn day with brilliant leaves floating like colourful barques
on a gentle breeze. Young couples strolled hand in hand across
the lawns, and students reclined in the lee of oak and elm,
talking of philosophy and love. It was a pleasant setting, slightly
tinged with nostalgia – not at all the sort of time and place in
which to encounter horror. I went into the medical building
and down resounding corridors to Ramsey's office. He wasn't
there, and his secretary told me he had been summoned to the
morgue. She wrinkled her nose at the word and I didn't blame
her. I had no liking for the morgue myself. It was not a place to
spend an autumn day. But I went on down the stairs and along

a corridor and entered the antechamber, a stark room with a tiled floor and a ramp leading up to street level and large metal doors. It was down this ramp that ambulance and hearse descended to disgorge their still burdens before rising, lightened once again, into the sunlight. It was a place of grim silence and foreshadowing. Worst of all, to me, was the smell – that sharp antiseptic scent. Does any odour smell as much of decay and corruption as antiseptic? It eats at the very core of sensation, invoking the essence of death – of more than death, of that which has never known life. The scent of decay and disease is foul but natural, that of antiseptic carries the stench of sterility. It parted like morbid mist before my passage and dampened my footfalls on the tiles.

I stopped at the glass cubicle.

The attendant looked up reluctantly from a lurid paperback, recognized me and nodded. The nod served to lower his eyes once more to the novel and he was already pursuing his pleasures as he gestured me through. I passed on to the operating-room, where Doctor Ramsey was washing his hands at the sink. His white gown was splattered with dark stains and he washed his hands carefully, rubbing them together like struggling serpents in soapy froth. There was a slab in the centre of the room and a shrouded form on the slab. Ramsey looked up with a solemn face and nodded. I advanced, avoiding the slab.

"Will you be long?" I asked.

"No. The necropsy is finished. I'm waiting for Grant to arrive. Identification." The way he said it you could tell he didn't like that part of it. Maybe he didn't like any part of it. He took off the blood-stained gown and stuffed it in the hamper.

"No sense letting them see the blood, eh?" he said. "Somehow the relatives always react more to seeing blood on a gown than to seeing the corpse."

"Accident case?" I asked.

"It was no accident."

I looked at him. He shrugged.

"The man was strangled," he said.

"Oh. Hence Inspector Grant of homicide."

"Exactly."

"I'll wait outside."

Ramsey moved his head.

"Yes. An unpleasant case. The only relative is a niece. Young,

I gather. I hope they weren't very close. It's always rough when they were. And pointless."

I raised my eyebrows.

"We know who the man was. No doubt of that. But legal procedure demands positive identification by a relative. It's funny how authority must always punish the innocent in the search for the guilty. Or maybe not funny."

"Indicative maybe."

"Maybe," he said, and showed a sad smile. I turned to leave, and just then Grant came through past the cubicle. A uniformed policeman and a girl followed. Grant's face was set and the cop looked stern. The girl was quite young and gazed around the room with big eyes. She seemed frightened. Of authority, perhaps. She was also rather pretty – pretty enough for the attendant to raise his attention from the vicarious thrills of his novel and regard her bottom. It struck me as a reaction perfectly suited to an attendant at a morgue. It annoyed me, too. But the man was young and had seen a good many bodies wheeled past his cubicle. Perhaps the sum total of his experience rested in the passage of death, and one must be tolerant.

Grant spoke softly to the girl, gestured to the cop and crossed the room. I noticed that his countenance was set more rigidly than normal and a lock of hair had fallen over his brow. He looked very much the way a police detective is supposed to look.

"Finished?" he asked Ramsey.

"Yes."

"Lab boys been here?"

"Yes. I sent my report round with them."

Grant seemed to notice me for the first time. We exchanged quiet greetings and he turned back to Ramsey.

"Anything that will help us?"

"I shouldn't think so. Must have been in his seventies. Hardening of the arteries, chronic . . ."

"Skip that. We know who he was, we can get those details from the reports. Not that they'll mean a goddamn thing. I mean any clue as to who did it? Or why?"

"Nothing. Nothing I could see. Not my job."

"It was strangulation, wasn't it?"

"Oh yes. Definitely."

Something in the doctor's tone caused Grant to look sharply at him.

"I mean his neck wasn't broken. He was asphyxiated. Must have been a rough death."

"They're all rough," said Grant, and his eyes shifted towards the girl. She was standing just inside the door, very pale, very frightened. The attendant was still regarding her. "This is the rough part for us. The identification. The girl's only nineteen, hardly knew the old boy, and we have to put her through this. Well . . ."

He gestured. The uniformed cop took the girl's arm and led her forward. Ramsey walked over to the head of the slab and Grant stood beside the girl. His shoulders shifted. I had the impression he wanted to put his arm around her. But he didn't. He was a policeman and he couldn't. He nodded and Ramsey drew the sheet down. He drew it down only enough to expose the face and I heard the girl draw her breath in with a sort of whimper. I looked down. I was surprised to see how old the man had been. I'd heard Ramsey say he was in his seventies, but somehow it hadn't registered – age seems irrelevant in discussing a corpse. But seeing him was different. Ramsey had obviously done his best to make the face seem relaxed and natural. But even so I could tell he'd died hard. The lips were forced upwards by the pressure of a swollen tongue and the eyes bulged beneath closed lids. The girl stared for a moment and then covered her face with both hands and turned away. Ramsey drew the sheet back over the old grey face.

"Miss?" Grant said gently.

She nodded behind her hands. It wasn't exactly a positive identification, but it satisfied the formalities, and Grant turned to the cop and said, "Take Miss Smith outside." He waited until they had left, then sighed.

"This will be a bad one," he said. "There's always so much public outrage when some old guy gets knocked off. So much interest and interference. And there seems to be no motive behind this one. Just a nice old guy. Killed in his own room. His landlady sort of took care of him, I guess. Anyway, she found the body this morning. Bringing him a pot of tea. He was on his bed and she thought he was sleeping. Then she looked down . . . well, you know how they look with their tongues sticking out black and their eyes popping. She dropped the teapot, I can tell you that. The killer must have entered by the front door. Just walked in. Had to go right past the landlady's room, too, but she heard nothing. I think she's a bit deaf, although she got

annoyed when I asked her about her hearing. Must be deaf or
she wouldn't have been annoyed, eh? Just walked in cool as a
cucumber and strangled the old boy and walked out again.
Obviously not robbery. Nothing missing. Hell, he had nothing
worth taking as far as that goes. Lived on a pension. Trimmed
the hedge in return for his meals. Had a few friends his own age
and drank an occasional glass of beer with them. No enemies as
far as we know. No opportunity to make an enemy, the way he
lived. Just a quiet old chap waiting to die . . ."

"Well, the waiting is over," Ramsey said.

"For him, yeah."

Ramsey and I both looked at Grant.

"For us, it's just beginning," he said. "A crime without
motives. Well, you know what that means. We wait for the next
one."

"You think he'll kill again?" I asked.

"The mad ones always do," Grant told us. He pursed his lips;
became aware of the displaced lock over his brow and brushed
it back impatiently. "They kill and they kill again, and all we can
do is wait until a pattern develops, a general motivation rather
than a specific motive. Oh, we get them in the end. The pattern
always emerges. But it isn't a line on a graph or a pin stuck in a
map. The pattern is made by the corpses of the victims. A man
can have nightmares about that, you know. Any man. You
dream of a tapestry, and it's all vague shapes and forms and
then you get closer and see the design is made up of dead men.
It isn't a tapestry then, it's a filigree of intertwining limbs and
arched torsos. And faces. The faces staring out from the
pattern, mouths open in silent screams of accusation, eyes
wide in sightless fear. A man . . . well, he dreams."

Grant broke off abruptly; looked rather ashamed of the
intensity with which he'd been speaking and jammed a cigarette in his mouth. It was the first time I'd ever thought of a
policeman as human, I think. He puffed on the cigarette, his
cheeks sinking in, his eyes thoughtful.

"Would you say it was the work of a madman, Doc?" he
asked. "I mean, from the examination . . ."

Ramsey looked troubled.

"I'm not sure," he said. "Some aspects . . . and yet . . . Well,
it's all in my report, Inspector. Black and white. It will mean
more if you read it than if I talk about it. A report is always more
objective and logical."

"Sure. I'll read it."

Grant turned as if to leave and then turned back, the cigarette in his teeth, his cheeks hollow.

"I'm delaying," he said. "I don't want to face that kid again. Have to, of course. But what if she asks me why the old man was killed? People ask cops things like that, you know? And will she feel better if I tell her it was a maniac? That there was no purpose, no reason; that nothing was gained by his death? Oh, I'm supposed to tell her I can't discuss it at the present time. Against regulations. Not allowed. But will that make her feel better? You drag some kid in and make her look at a dead body . . . ah, hell. It's not pleasant, Doc."

Ramsey nodded; looked at his hands thoughtfully. His hands had been scrubbed spotlessly clean, and there was nothing there to see. But he looked. I stepped back, feeling I was intruding. Grant's eyes had gone blank and his brow furrowed. The ash dropped unnoticed from his cigarette, a long ash that disintegrated when it hit the tiles and looked very improper in that sanitary and disinfected chamber. Somehow the ash looked too clean on that sterile floor.

"I hope to God it wasn't a maniac," he said very softly.

Ramsey lowered his eyes. I took another step back. Then Grant turned sharply and walked out with his shoulders square. The attendant did not look up from his book, and it was some time before Ramsey looked up from the floor . . .

We left the building and walked across to the parking lot. Most of the motorcars had gone by this time and the big concrete space looked strangely abandoned and neglected and forlorn. Ramsey hadn't spoken; he seemed to be pondering something – something both disagreeable and interesting – his expression that of a little boy using a stick to poke at the decaying carcass of a dead animal. He was thinking about the murder, of course, and I sensed he was considering that part which was in his report and which he hadn't wanted to talk about. It had captured my interest and, by this time, we were close enough to speak openly.

"Well? Was it a madman?" I asked, when we were in the car.

Ramsey shrugged.

I made an elaborate task of fitting the keys into the ignition but did not start the engine.

"There was something – some aspect – in your report, which troubles you, wasn't there?"

"There was, yes."

"None of my business, of course . . ."

He waved a hand.

"Oh, it isn't that. It troubled me because . . . well, because it was unusual. And gruesome. I've been a doctor too long to get upset by violence and bloodshed, John. But this was different. It was . . . well, calculated. Ghastly but calculated. The fact itself implied frenzy and rage, and yet there was none of that in evidence. It was as if the killer had coldly and deliberately set about his ghoulish act . . ."

The term startled me.

"Ghoulish?" I asked.

"Oh, perhaps I'm being too dramatic. But . . . well, when behaviour normally associated with maddened impulse and blind fury is suddenly transposed to an act of rational logical expedience . . . well, it shakes a man. We are all prisoners of our own perceptions, you know. We have all learned to see things in a certain way and to interpret them in the light of our training and experience. And when a familiar object or action is suddenly glimpsed out of context . . . seen from a different angle . . . it causes turmoil within our preconceived limitations. It takes a while to get our bearings, to adjust our stance, to focus properly . . ."

"What on earth happened?" I asked.

Ramsey didn't seem to hear my question.

"When I was younger, I used to ice-skate," he said, speaking slowly. I blinked. I thought he was deliberately, and rather discourteously, changing the subject, and I reached for the ignition keys. But Ramsey continued. "I learned to skate quite well," he said. "I was never particularly adept at sports or games but in ice-skating I seemed to be more talented than most. I enjoyed it enormously. I learned to figure-skate, to cut designs across the ice. People used to watch me, admiring my abilities. But there was one strange thing. I wouldn't skate when it was dark. All the young people used to go to the rink at night, but the very thought gave me a chill. I had a vague dread – a fear even – of what lay beneath the ice at night. I visualized it – saw it in cross-section, as it were. There I was, cutting my smooth figures across the flat, predictable surface of the ice, and beneath that level there was the dark body of unfrozen water. The ice and water were related and yet they were not the same. I fashioned my designs at one plane while beneath me lay uncharted depths and inconceivable forms. So it is with life – with the human mind. We live our allotted years and carve out patterns upon a solitary level of existence, content and satisfied perhaps, and then something happens which opens a window, just for an instant, through the surface and allows us to glimpse the deeper, darker dimensions with which we share existence. We peer through this hole, we see cowled shapes and mal-formed concepts bloated in the waters and we shudder and look away until the ice freezes over once more and our world is smooth and flat again. Our world is as we know it, as we wish it, and we skate off and leave our pitiful little etching under our runners. And yet, from time to time, those broken areas of open waters appear to disrupt our placid world. Most men shun the glimpse, ignore the depths, pretend the ice is solid. But not all men. In the minds of a few, the hole does not freeze over quickly enough, they stare too long through the break – long enough for something to rise and crawl from that hole and take possession of the upper levels . . ."

Ramsey coughed and looked out through the windscreen.

"Madness?" I said.

"Who knows? Not sanity, surely. But madness belongs to our surface ice. After all, it is we who have defined it. It is our minds which have hardened into ice. What may come up from below, from those regions we have not labelled and named because we have not conceived of them . . ."

He shrugged and we sat in silence for a time. I began to feel uncomfortable and once more reached for the ignition. Ramsey's eyes slid sideways at the motion.

"Yes, I am surely being too dramatic," he said. "I was reacting to a personal awareness. The facts scarcely warrant such imagery. And yet they are disturbing. I expect I owe you an explanation."

I was far too curious to decline. I waited. The keys still waited in the ignition. Ramsey, who seldom smoked, asked for a cigarette. He inhaled and then studied the smoke, as if won-dering whether he were doing it properly. Then, his voice very matter-of-fact now, he said, "The remarkable aspect of the murder is this: the victim was killed by human teeth." And he stared at me.

"Good Lord," I said.

Ramsey nodded.

"But you told Grant he'd been strangled . . ."

"And so he had. Indeed he had. He had been strangled by the pressure of human jaws."

I shook my head.

"That is the extraordinary thing – the combination of the two. I've seen corpses who had been strangled by human hands before. I've heard – although I've never encountered it, thank God – of instances where a man, in a fit of blind rage or insane passion, had committed murder with his teeth. But the combination is quite unique. The flesh was not even broken on the throat. There had been no attempt to tear or slash, nor even any bloodshed. The pressure of those jaws had been applied slowly and carefully. Thoughtfully, even. Obviously, the killer did not want his clothing stained by blood. It appears he had used his teeth strictly for convenience. For efficiency."

"But why?" I asked.

"I can only surmise . . . you see the object of my rambling talk of darkness beneath the ice? Of course. It is exactly that. It is alien to me and I can only draw conclusions within my own frame of reference. They are undoubtedly inaccurate. But this is what I assume. The killer, for some unknown reason, wished to kill this old man. He had no desire to torture the man, for every action was designed to bring death. There were no bruises or contusions to imply a beating, no signs of any attempt to cause suffering, no wounds other than the death grip. The killer, again for unknown reasons, did not use a weapon. I can reconstruct the scene within my own scheme of deduction. The victim was probably sitting or lying on his bed. It was a small furnished room with only a straight backed chair, and I think it likely he used the bed to relax. He was, after all, an old man. He would have wanted what comfort was available to him. But that is irrelevant. The murderer came in through the door. Whether he was known to the victim or not would, of course, alter the preliminary movements. But that, too, is irrelevant here. Whether already there, or forced there, the old man wound up on the bed, on his back. The killer knelt over him, one knee on either side of his chest and placed his hands on the man's throat. The man struggled – his fingernails were broken where he clawed at the killer's hands and forearms – but he was old and weak. The killer tightened his grip remorselessly. I feel sure there was no haste, no frenzy. He merely closed his hands with great deliberation. But perhaps this was the first time he'd committed murder with his bare hands. This seems likely. And it always takes a long time, relatively speaking, to choke a man to death. It must seem very long indeed to the killer . . . and to the victim. The old man's tongue came out, his eyes ballooned, and yet he did not die. It undoubtedly seemed, to the killer, that he had been strangling the man for sufficient time to kill him. And his mind was working, calculating. It occurred to him that he was not able to bring sufficient pressure to bear with his hands – that some air was still passing into those lungs. At this point, most men would surely have panicked. They would have shaken the man violently and snapped his neck, or seized a heavy object – there was a large glass ashtray beside the bed, I understand – and bludgeoned him into unconsciousness. But not our killer. There was no panic, no frenzy. He misjudged the time factor and then he sorted all the aspects out quite logically in his mind and decided that more pressure was necessary to complete the act. And when he had decided this, he followed the rational course . . ."

"Rational," I whispered.

"Absolutely rational. He lowered his head and placed his mouth upon the man's throat and proceeded to close his jaws. He didn't snap, he didn't tear, he used his teeth not as fangs but as a vice. The human jaws are very powerful. They are capable of exerting incredible strength. And so, after a while, the old man was dead and the killer unclenched his teeth and that was that."

I stared at Ramsey. I could feel the blood draining from my face, heavy and sluggish. He read the contortion of my countenance and nodded.

"Oh yes," he said. "It was horrible."

"To use his teeth for . . . *efficiency*!"

"Exactly. That was the point that disturbed me."

"It must have been a maniac," I said.

"Or a philosopher," said Ramsey, and he looked at me and I looked at him and after a while I started the motorcar and drove away. The traffic was light. The wind blew and the leaves fell and as the sun slipped down behind the afternoon angles I felt a distinct chill at my spine.

The second murder occurred several days later.

I wasn't present at the identification this time, and came to hear of the crime through a particularly sensational newspaper story – a borrowed newspaper, as it were, belonging to one of the regular visitors to the museum. Museums seem to be addictive. They each have a set of regulars who have formed the habit of frequent visits, and in the course of my research, I came to meet several of these people time and time again. One of these was a middle-aged gentleman who walked with a stiff leg and used a malacca cane, a quiet and dignified man who always nodded pleasantly, wore well-cut tweeds, and seemed a trifle lonely. I usually encountered him wandering through the natural history rooms but in this instance we met in the library. I had just finished my book and was about to go to lunch when he entered, his cane tapping through the resounding silence of leather and oak. He took a seat next to me and placed a folded newspaper on the table. I glanced over to nod and happened to notice the headlines.

"So the killer has struck again," I said.

"It would appear so."

"May I see your paper?"

"Of course."

He handed it to me and I unfolded it.

"Not the paper I usually take," he said, smiling, as if to apologize for the gutter press. It did not, in fact, seem the sort of paper this rather dignified gentleman should subscribe to, and I had always avoided it. But it carried a very detailed account of the crime, stressing the sensational aspects. The story had been written from the point of view of one of the children who had discovered the body. He was twelve years old. It was the sort of thing that sold newspapers, no doubt of that.

"It's a terrible thing," I said.

"What's that?"

"These deaths."

"Death? Oh, death is natural."

His attitude surprised me.

"Death, yes. But not murder."

He shrugged and tilted his hand in a gesture.

"Murder? But what is murder other than a form of death? It is only unnatural in legal terms, you know. Murder did not exist before we came to define it; before we made laws against it. It is law which is unnatural, not murder."

I looked at him, wondering if he were serious. He seemed so.

"I'm sure it didn't seem natural to the victims," I said.

"Oh? I should think it did. It may have seemed unjust, but

certainly natural. But then, at the moment of death, one does not think in forensic terms." He smiled slightly. "Death is a jealous concept. It will not tolerate other thoughts to exist with it envelops the mind, it refuses to share with alien sensations."

"You seem well acquainted with the subject, sir."

He smiled again.

"Oh, I've held the concept of death," he said. "I've been very very close to dying and, I assure you, it was the most natural thing in the world."

"What manner of death?"

"By violence," he said. "By violence."

I could not picture him in conjunction with violence. I waited for him to continue, but he said no more; sat there with that slight smile. After a moment I turned to the newspaper.

The twelve-year-old boy and several other lads had been playing by the river at the old disused wharf. There was always a great deal of debris in the water at that point. The docks and pilings had collapsed over the years and timber and planks had broken away to float in the river while the pilings which still stood acted as a bottleneck, gathering the various flotsam of the river. The children had developed a game in which the debris was an enemy fleet of warships and they were a defending shore battery, using rocks and stones for ordnance. It was an exciting game. The object was to sink the enemy ships before they came into contact with the pilings and the youths were positioned along the embankment and on the dock. They were laughing and shouting and having a fine time. Their artillery was proving accurate and effective and they had already sunk an orange crate destroyer and scored several crashing hits upon an empty oil can escort vessel. Suddenly one shouted a warning. The enemy fleet was being reinforced by a new ship which came floating out from beneath the pilings in treacherous sneak attack. It appeared to be a gnarled log dripping with moss and sea weed and it floated just below the surface. The children decided it must be a nuclear submarine and posed a most serious threat; knew they had to sink it before it could release its missiles and turned the full force of their lithic ordnance on it. They bombarded it from all sides and with every calibre. Small stones cascaded around the object, and larger rocks hit the water with great splashes, causing the submarine to roll and sway in the riled waters. But all the awesome might they unleashed proved ineffective. The submarine was actually

rising to the surface. In desperation three of the youths joined
forces to lift a huge slab of stone and carry it out on the dock,
directly above the menacing ship. The slab was an aeroplane
piloted by a suicide pilot willing to give his life for his country.
They took careful aim and tilted the stone from the edge of the
dock. It fell, turning in the air, and scored a direct hit amid-
ships of the submarine. The vessel seemed to crack in half. The
bows and stern rose up and the children howled in victorious
glee. And then, very very slowly, the log rolled over and spread
out arms and it wasn't a log at all. The children fell silent. They
stared in shocked disbelief. This was something unique, beyond
the rules of their game, and for some time they stood lined
along the dock, gaping down at the body. It was an old woman.
Her body bobbled about and her grey hair spread out like moss
around her bloated face, writhing on the surface. And then
comprehension came and they ran for help with shouts which
were not of gaiety . . .

The police were summoned and they dragged the body out.
It was the old flower seller who had a stall on the embankment,
not far from the wharf. Investigation showed she had been
dragged to the water and immersed until she drowned. There
were no injuries on her body and she must have been conscious
the whole time. The time of the murder was estimated at nine
o'clock the night before, about the hour she usually closed her
stall. There was still light at nine o'clock. There were invariably
people strolling on the embankment and along the docks and
perhaps young lovers had stood, hand in hand, directly above
the old woman dying beneath the pilings. It was an eerie
thought. One could not help but wonder what thoughts had
screamed through her mind during those eternal instants of
silent struggle, while the water felt like an avalanche of hard
rocks pouring into her erupting lungs. It was far easier to
imagine her thoughts than to conceive of those dark concepts
in the mind of her killer – the mind of a man who killed without
motive, without reason, without passion.

It seemed obvious that the killer was the same man who had
strangled the old pensioner a few days before. The two murders
fitted the same pattern of having no pattern. The woman had no
known enemies and no one could possibly have profited by her
death. The killing had been cold and efficient. The police had
no clues and asked anyone who might have been in the vicinity
to contact them whether they had heard or seen anything or not.

Anyone who had noticed a man with wet clothing anywhere in the city was asked to notify the authorities. The theory was that it was the work of a maniac. It seemed the only solution. The thought of a madman is always terrifying and this was magnified by the fact that the victims had been old and helpless and had died without reason. The police stated it was likely the man would kill again – would go on killing at regular intervals until he was captured. I had a sudden image of Detective Inspector Grant poring over all the details of the two crimes, trying desperately to project and predict and prevent, and knowing with painful frustration that he had insufficient data – and that there was only one way in which to acquire more data and that implied more victims. He would be chain-smoking cigarettes, pacing across his office, snapping at his subordinates, cross with his wife. But they would understand the great unrest of his thoughts, and would tolerate his surly behaviour. And thinking of tolerance, I found myself contrasting Grant with this gentleman whose newspaper I held – who looked at the murders in such a calm and unexpected way. I looked up from the paper; glanced sideways at him. He was turning the pages of a large volume with vague disinterest. I placed the paper on the table and he closed the book; folded the paper neatly.

"Thank you."

"Why of course," he said.

"Say what you will, it's a gruesome business."

"Oh, I daresay the papers make it seem worse than it is, you know. Circulation and all that. The human fascination with the macabre. I find myself fascinated with that strange fascination. As a scientist . . ."

"A scientist?" I said, interrupting him with an abrupt impulse to change the subject. I did not wish to hear his opinions on human failings – if indeed he thought them failings, for he had a tendency to make the unexpected statement; to view from unconsidered angles.

He nodded slowly.

"What is your field?"

"I am a naturalist."

I raised my eyebrows slightly at the old-fashioned term and he interpreted the gesture correctly; nodded and repeated the word. "Yes, a naturalist. I use the old word deliberately – to imply that I have spread myself over the natural sciences rather than specializing. A fault of modern thinking, specialization."

"But surely knowledge is accumulating too quickly for a man to encompass everything?"

"Ah, but is that valid? If all knowledge is related – and it must be, if there is any basic law to the universe – then isn't a shallow immersion in a wide subject better than penetration to blind and limited depths? I have always wished to form conclusions which draw all the branches of natural science into a tighter pattern. An ambitious goal, certainly, and yet in some ways curiously limited." He paused, peering at me sharply. I had the impression he was judging my comprehension and his glance was curious – his countenance resigned and placid on the surface, yet with sharp inquiry coming through. It was like a flash of sudden lightning exposing the inner fabric of the storm clouds for a brilliant instant. Then it faded. "Oh, I fully understand the necessity for specialists," he continued. "Men – men of that sort of mind – must probe the depths of limited fields and form little cones of knowledge – little submerged and isolated studies from which more well rounded scholars may draw as they grope for a totality. Necessary, yes. But it seems a shame that knowledge has outpaced the evolution of the mind, does it not?" And again that keen glance probed me.

"You interest me."

'Yes? I've always believed that a man who has wide interests will prove interesting."

"And are you pursuing your interests here at the museum? I've seen you quite often and wondered if you might be doing research of some nature."

"Nothing specific. In point of fact, I come to the museum for pleasure. As some might go to the opera or the theatre. I dearly love to wander through the natural history halls. But research – no, my research is in the field. It was, at least, until my accident. Now I must content myself with less strenuous studies. Although recently I have been able to do a bit of field work. Just a bit. An application of former conclusions."

"Accident?"

"My leg. I lost my leg, as you may have noticed.'

He glanced down.

"Oh, I didn't realize," I said, a trifle embarrassed.

"I've managed to adapt myself to it. One does, you know. I have an artificial limb, of course, but I'd have adapted without it. That's the story of survival. But it hinders field research, nonetheless."

This fact seemed to sadden him. He fell into a thoughtful silence. Then he looked up and smiled.

"But we've not been introduced," he said. He held out his hand. His grip was firm.

"Claymore," he said. "Edward Claymore."

I told him my name. His name had a familiar ring and after a moment I placed it; said, "I believe I've read one of your books. Dealing with ecology, was it?"

"You please me. One has vanity, of a sort. Of a sort. One hopes one's ideas are of value. And valid, of course. Yes, ecology has always been my prime study, dear to my heart. The linking of relationships between creatures within the scope of their environment, the incredibly complex interplay between organisms, subtle, slowly emerging as one gathers experience, and in no other way. These relationships cannot be predicted in the laboratory nor projected in the library. One must be there. One must observe and record. A falsehood may be written but what one has seen is truth – the conclusions may be wrongly drawn but one cannot argue with the basic premise of objective fact, eh?" I nodded agreement. A certain intensity had come into his voice as he spoke of his work and I felt a new respect for the man. His book, as I recalled it, had been lucid and straightforward and unpretentious; had been an early work which, in its simplicity, had stood the test of time. It was no longer read much, for the theory had advanced beyond its scope, and yet the material had been proved correct and had greatly affected later research along those lines, foreshadowing understanding. I had read it long ago, and yet found myself able to recall certain passages of bright illumination and even simple eloquence in his descriptions of the wild reaches of our northern forests, the perfect balance of nature, the harmony of life and death. Seen in the context of his work, his unusual method of looking at events was no longer surprising. I determined to look up his book and read it again, in the new light of our acquaintance.

Claymore was thoughtful now; seemed to be looking back into the past, looking northward to the forests of former times. I stood up and excused myself. He nodded absently. He was still sitting at the table, staring at far places, as I left.

I did not encounter Claymore for the next few days, and forgot my intention to look up a copy of his book. He may well have been at the museum but my research had taken a sharp turn which kept me in the library through the day and he did not appear there. I did not, in fact, see him again until after the third crime had been committed. This third crime was different. It did not fit the pattern of the preceding murders and, at first, appeared to be an accident. It was far more horrible, in its quantitative effect, than the other crimes and yet did not excite as much public outrage because it was impersonal. It caused anger rather than morbid fascination. The facts were these: the home for incurables on the outskirts of the city caught fire and, in a great inferno, burned to the ground. Twelve men and women died in the flames, including a heroic nurse who had rushed again and again through sheets of fire and saved half a dozen lives; then, making a last desperate attempt, she had been trapped as the walls collapsed and had died in the incandescent ruins. When her charred body was found she still held an old man shielded to her breast, their flesh melted and then annealed together so that the corpses were inseparable. It was some time before the embers had cooled and a proper investigation carried out and then it was discovered that the fire had been deliberately set, a case of arson; some further time before connections were made and the authorities believed it might have been the work of the same madman who had killed twice before. But it was impossible to be sure. The police were keeping an open mind and investigating the background of every patient, both victims and survivors, in an attempt to discover if anyone would have gained by the death of one of them. It was a ghastly thought, but valid in these times when bombs are placed on aeroplanes, killing dozens as a side effect of collecting insurance on a solitary passenger. Nothing came of this line of investigation, however, and I, for one, felt certain it had been the maniac.

When next I saw Claymore, I recalled his calm attitudes concerning the former murders; was interested in what he thought in this instance. I asked him whether he considered this crime natural. I'm not sure what reaction I expected, but he surprised me by screwing up his face in obvious internal conflict, a genuine attempt at decision. I was amazed. I would not have been shocked had he taken an attitude opposed to normal morality, but had not foreseen this struggle within himself. Several times he opened his mouth to speak, and then hesitated. I watched his face, my interest greatly aroused.

Our meeting had taken place in the Hall of Saurians, a great vaulted room of silence with implications of vast and imponderable time. The skeletons of brontosaurus and allosaurus loomed over us. A high skylight sent filtered illumination dropping from the dome, washing the bones and casting Jurassic shadows across the floor, articulated adumbrations of the eons. Presently, without speaking, Claymore moved on, still shrouded in thought. I followed. He moved, as it were, through the path of prehistory; came to the Cretaceous period and sank down upon the edge of a platform with a tyrannosaurus rearing above, the great jaws in the gloom of the arched roof. I sat beside him. It seemed that even the shadows of those bleached bones had a great weight – that they lay upon us with the burden of knowledge, not insight to the mind but some truth known only in our most primitive cells, long forgotten to the magnifying mind but remaining dormant in the glands, the secretions of primordial instinct. I could not understand why this strange mood had come upon me; wondered if, somehow, it could have emanated from my companion by some basic transference, as a dog senses fear in a man.

At last, he spoke.

"The nurse should not have died," he said, quite simply.

"The nurse? Why only the nurse?"

"The nurse. Her actions were so very human and so very unnatural."

"But surely noble?"

"Nobility is unnatural. That, like law, has been created outside nature. Created by man. And man stands at some undefined point between nature and logic. Only man, you know, and possibly the elephant who is mighty enough to afford it – or was until man came along – show concern and respect for the aged and infirm, tolerate the useless elements of the pack, the tribe, the species. It was quite natural for the nurse to risk – and give – her life, but only in the framework of human terms. Not natural science but philosophy. The fault lies deeper than behaviour, it is in the system itself – a system that flaunts and reverses nature and creates homes for incurables, protects the helpless, preserves the weakest units to clutter the species."

He looked sideways at me.

"You can't believe the nurse's sacrifice wrong?"

"Not by human judgements."

"Well then . . ."

"But I am speaking objectively. I am standing outside the system and wish I had a lever long enough to move it. But one man cannot, there is no fulcrum, a man can do his little part and nothing more."

"You speak objectively. But don't you feel human sentiments?"

"Of course. With my human mind, I must. But I can also look through them, penetrate the veil of emotion, and attempt to act accordingly. If man were natural, you see, he would let the useless die, as our ancestors abandoned them to the lion and the hyena. And if man were logical he would, for instance, form his armies from the ranks of the cripples, the defectives, the malformed. War is quite natural – perhaps necessary – to our species. It is a safety valve for the pressures of survival. But it would be a far more effective valve if the casualties came from the weak, allowing the strong to live. But man lies somewhere in the void, groping upwards for elusive logic while his feet are slipping from their purchase on the natural. We are driven by false instincts we term rational – instincts created within ourselves long after nature had finished imprinting her pattern. We weaken ourselves by tolerance and, at the same time, destroy other species by inverse selectivity. Only man – man, the hunter – seeks the finest trophy, the largest antlers, the beast in the prime of life. We kill the best specimens and spurn the weak; we plunder nature as we follow our own descent."

"You have strong views," I said.

Claymore nodded. His slight shadow slipped across the floor, within the dinosaur's vaulted ribcage, as he shifted his position; crossed his leg over the artificial limb.

"Yes, the dichotomy has long troubled me," he said. "As these conclusions first solidified during long winter nights in the open, I often lay awake in my sleeping bag and saw the cold starry sky as a background to my concepts. How implacable that sky seemed, how pitiless. It was then that I saw natural science cannot be isolated, can never be an enclosed sphere of knowledge, for even the non-objective sciences are inextricably linked to ecology. Man is unique. He stands above nature and imposes his half-considered concepts on the natural scheme – forces them in where they do not fit. It seems that the experiment with the big brain has taken a wrong turning – a turning nature never intended but is powerless to correct – to guide us back to the proper channel. Nature has created a Frankenstein's monster which threatens to turn upon its creator. And to destroy nature is suicidal. Far better, perhaps, if homo sapiens had been allowed to survive by virtue of thumb and upright spine, and never granted the gift and curse of vocal cord and concept; to survive like the cockroach which, I daresay, will outlast us yet."

He stretched out a hand towards the tower of bones behind us, the lesson of the extinction of the mighty, the roaring rulers of earth for millions of years reduced to skeletal silence on a platform.

"I planned a book on this subject," he said. "I never completed it, however. It would never have been published. It would merely have invited outraged attacks."

"The idea certainly invites attack," I said.

"You don't agree with me?"

"I see your logic. But surely man is above the laws of the jungle. We have mastered survival and now it is curiosity which directs us, governs us, brought us through dark ages and may yet take us to the stars."

"Curiosity? Ah yes. That will take us – somewhere . . ."

For a time we did not speak.

"However," said Claymore, at length, "all this is conjecture. I am truly sorry about that nurse . . ."

Following this remarkable conversation in the Hall of Saurians, I took the trouble to locate a copy of Claymore's book. I reread it. It was the book I had remembered and none of his anti-social ideas were expressed there. It dealt with observation and obvious conclusions and no more; implied nothing hidden beneath the level of his writing. I found it difficult to see Claymore, as I knew him, as the author of this book and decided he was not – that something had caused his outlook to alter in the interval so that the man who had written so expressively and objectively in the past was not the same man who had spoken with such intensity in the shadow of dinosaur. I could not imagine what this might have been, what experience could have warped and embittered his mind – perhaps the loss of his leg, I wondered. And yet he'd seemed to have adjusted easily enough to that loss. I was curious and would have been most interested to know about it, but could think of no way to bring the subject up; decided to wait and hope that, in the course of our meetings, the truth would come to light.

As, indeed, it did.

But first the maniac struck again.

In many respects, the next attack was the most perplexing of all. The strangest aspect was that the victim survived – was allowed to survive the ordeal. And certainly the most horrible aspect was that the poor fellow was blind, his affliction adding to the monstrous nature of the unprovoked assault. These facts added a new twist to the emerging pattern, complicating and confusing the issue. But what really struck me was purely subjective.

I was acquainted with the victim.

His name was Bill, a big jovial sort who refused to let his blindness change his cheerful nature. He'd lost his sight in the war, spent some time in hospital, and emerged with complete selfconfidence and a fierce independence. He refused even the assistance of a guide dog and was frequently seen roaming the familiar streets with a firm and steady step, behind dark glasses and a fibre-glass stick; pausing at kerbs to listen for approaching traffic or halting for a moment at a corner, head raised and senses alert as he got his bearings. I was appalled when I read of the vicious attack which had taken place in his own basement flat. It is always so much more shocking when it is someone one knows. Bill had been brutally battered and beaten and then left alive on his floor. And that was the extraordinary thing. He had not been supposed dead, for he was still conscious. The maniac had simply walked off and left him, and that behaviour was so far removed from the other attacks that the police were not ruling out the possibility of a second madman amuck in the city. However the method of attack, until it had ceased, fitted the pattern. It was calculated and efficient.

I phoned the hospital immediately and inquired about his condition; found, to my relief, that he was recovering and asked how soon he would be able to have visitors. Apparently he had already been demanding that visitors be allowed in, which was very much to be expected of Bill, and I went to see him in the morning.

He was sitting up in bed, a white bandage around his head and a cigar in his teeth. His big solid shoulders sloped down beneath the sheets, he greeted me in a loud voice and roared cheerfully at the nurse who told him he must be quiet. She turned her eyes upwards and smiled despite herself. Bill was able to make people smile that way. He was pleased to have a visitor, we chatted for a few minutes and then, without urging or suggestion from me, he told me what had happened. He seemed more angered than frightened by the attack, his self-reliance had survived and he did not, in his dark world, understand how one with sight would project and magnify the terror of his position.

"Well, Johnny boy," said Bill, "I don't know if this bastard was waiting inside my flat or if he followed me home. The coppers think he was already inside, on account of one of my neighbours, old widow down the street, got an idea she's got designs on me, you know? – well, this widow saw me come home and says there was no one following me. But I'm not so sure. Seems I would have sensed his presence if he'd been waiting there. Maybe the old gal don't see too well. Anyway, don't matter which way it was. I'd been out for my afternoon walk and I never bother to lock the door so it was a simple matter for him to get in before me or behind me, whichever. I went right into the kitchen as soon as I got home and put a pan on for coffee. I leaned my walking stick against the stove and stood there, waiting for the water to boil. Then I heard him. Just a faint sound, at first, but we blind guys get used to listening for those soft noises. I turned around real sharp and heard his foot scrape as he stepped back in surprise. "Who's there?" I asked. Y'see, I wasn't worried at that point, I thought it might have been a friend or maybe even that old widow come to tempt me. Maybe even one of the younger gals on the street. Plenty of gals like to call on a blind guy, Johnny. Gals that don't like it known they're passionate – figure they can get me to give 'em some lovin' and never even speak, see, so I won't know who they are. Happens all the time. 'Course, once they gets to pantin' and snortin', why, straight off I can tell who it is, long's I've heard their voice before. Easy to tell by the way they pant, how long their hair is, how wide they are in the hips. But, 'course, I don't let on I know, 'cause then they won't come back. I just go along with it, askin' who they are even after I know and then they think they're on to the perfect set-up and come back again. Yeah, this bein' a blind guy got some advantages. An' if their husbands find out, why I got the perfect excuse. Ha ha. Not a bad old game. Got some real fine unfaithful wives on that street, real fine.

"Anyhow, that's what I thought – thought it was one o' them passionate wives, so I wasn't worried. Just asked who it was and sort of smiled. Then when there was no answer, I was sure it must be a gal. I stood there, waitin' for her to come up and start snugglin'. But nothing happened for quite a while. The water started to boil, still nothin' happened. I guessed the gal was shy – figured it was her first visit, see? So I said, 'Want some coffee, whoever you are?' and then I heard the bastard take a deep breath, real quick, and I thought: Oh ho, Billy boy, that ain't no gal . . . What I thought was it was an irate husband, come to rant and rave. That was when he jumped on me . . .''

Bill paused. His brow furrowed beneath the bandage and I noticed several scratches on his face and neck, parallel rows that looked like fingernail marks. His big shoulders shifted as he recalled the violence of the attack and his heavy jowled face was set. I stared at him with great respect – saw that he was reliving only the violence, not the horror. Blindness has always seemed so ultimate a handicap and I had already imagined the scene – imagined Bill cringing, asking who and why, his sightless face questing at the strange sounds, unguided hands groping before him protectively, helpless and terrified, all this in the darkness of his affliction . . . This I had imagined; had pictured with my vision. But this was not the way it had been for Bill. He remembered only his anger and rage.

"He grabbed me by the throat," Bill said. "Well, Johnny boy, that was a mistake. Pretty strong fellow, I could feel his strength in his fingers, but 'course with both his hands on me I knew just where he was. I didn't panic. I got my feet set right and then gave him a couple of good belts in the belly. Good short shovel hooks. Bang bang, just like that." His shoulders rolled, his arms moved under the sheet, the long muscles in his jaw tightened. "He let go real quick then, boy. Real quick. I heard his wind rush out hard as he stepped back. But I hadn't caught him in the solar plexus like I planned and he didn't go down. I took an almighty swipe at where I reckoned his jaw oughta be, but I misjudged it. Missed the bastard. But I followed up, pulling my shoulder around and tuckin' my chin down behind it and coiled into a hitter's crouch. I still sort of suspected it was one o' them irate husbands. Wasn't worried much. I got both fists cocked and my head down and I said, 'Come on, you bastard! You want a fight, you found the right blind fellow. Just come in here, let's see what you can do!'

"Well, he didn't do anything for a while. I could hear him gettin' his breath back and sort of feel his eyes on me. Weird feelin', that. I could tell he was sizing me up, plannin' his attack – could tell he was a pretty cool fellow. He was standin' just out of reach. I thought about lungin' for him, but figured it was better to wait – try to time a haymaker as he came to me. So I feinted a couple of times, to get him to make some sounds movin' but he stayed real calm. I guess we stood like that maybe two minutes. Then I heard him move to the side, very quiet. I thought he was leavin', that he'd had enough. But then I heard the cupboard door open and straight off I knew what the sonabitch was doin'. He was looking for a weapon. Well, there were bottles and things there he could use to club me and I didn't like that idea; tried to play on his pride; said, 'Hey, you need a weapon against a blind fellow? What sort o' man are you?' But that didn't work. He started movin' towards me again. Then I got a little worried. I reached behind me and got the handle of the pan and held the pan in front of me. The water was boilin' away real good by then. I could feel the steam. He hesitated and I swung the pan across my chest, waitin'. I figured if I could give 'im a face full of steam I'd have a chance to get my hands on him. That's all I wanted. Just to get my hands on the bastard. Should've grabbed him straight off when he was chokin' me, 'course, but at that point I didn't know how serious he was and figured a couple o' belly hooks would be plenty. But he was cautious now. I couldn't hear him movin' at all. Then somethin' hit the pan and tilted it and the hot water ran down my forearm. I threw the pan away and missed him and somethin' smacked me alongside the head. In the temple. The coppers told me it was a whisky bottle. How about that? Smacks me with my own Scotch, the swine. Anyway, it was a pretty good wallop and I had to cover up and he hit me again, behind the neck that time and the floor slammed against my knees. I kept trying t' get a hold on him but he stayed out of reach and belted me a few more times in the head and neck and then, for the first time, I realized he wanted to kill me. Not much I could do, just kneel there and dart my hands out in different directions hopin' to get him. He was a cool one. No hurry at all. Wasn't even breathin' hard enough to hear now. Couple o' times I thought he'd gone, even, and then whop! he clubs me again. Would've killed me, I guess, 'cept I touched the handle of my cane then as I slid to the side and I got the cane and made a great wide sweep in front of me, low down, and felt it whip against his leg. Good snappy cane, fibre glass, gave him a helluva slash. Heard him yelp. So I saw that was my only chance, and I sat there with my back against the stove and swung the stick back and forth in a low arc in front of me, fast enough so he couldn't get close without gettin' hit. I was in a bad way by then. Sort of dizzy and sick from the hammerin' I'd had. But the only thing I could think was: Grab the cane, you dirty bastard! Just waitin' for him to grab it so I'd know where he was and could lunge at him. Just wanted him in my hands, y'know. I'd have broken every bone in his body.''

Bill shook his head; shrugged. Then he passed a hand along his jaw. The anger left his countenance and a look of perplexity replaced it.

"Then he left,'' Bill said, simply, and he shrugged once again. "Hard to figure out. I was pretty helpless by that time. And there's no doubt he wanted to kill me. Only thing I can figure is that when I hit him with the cane I hurt him pretty bad. Worse'n I thought. Took the heart out o' the bastard. I guess maybe that's what happened, 'cause he was limpin' when he left. I heard him go. Thought maybe he was trying to fool me – that he'd wait by the door an' then come sneakin' back after I stopped whippin' the cane about. But he left all right. He wasn't breathin' hard and he walked calm enough but he seemed to be favouring one leg. I heard the front door close. I sat there for a long time, holdin' the cane ready and listenin' but he was gone all right. Then I crawled out to the street and called for help. And that was that. Hard to figure. The coppers said it might have been the guy who killed a couple of other people, too, so I got to think he bit off more'n he could chew with ol' Billy, eh?''

"I expect you're right,'' I said.

"Guess so.''

He nodded. His cigar had gone out while he spoke and he lighted it again, holding the match cupped in his hands to guide the flame. The leaf had started to uncurl and there was white ash on the bed. He held the cigar in his teeth. He was very much alive. We chatted for a few more minutes and then I left. As I was going out several other visitors came into the room. They nodded to me the quiet way one nods in a hospital and went over to Bill's bed. They were all women. Widows and unfaithful wives, no doubt. Bill greeted them cheerfully and I went out and walked to the museum.

I found it impossible to concentrate on my research.

I sat in the library and ran my eyes over the pages, again and again, without comprehension. My thoughts kept drifting back to Bill's account of the attack. The most remarkable aspect was that he had been left alive. Whether or not Bill actually believed he had driven the attacker away with his cane, it seemed obvious to me that was not the case – that Bill had been helpless at the end. He'd been terribly battered and must have been nearly unconscious. And yet, even in that brutal beating, there was an element of calculation related to the murders. The blows all appeared to have been struck with the solitary purpose of causing unconsciousness and subsequent death – not pain. There seemed no element of sadism in the method of attack. There had been pain, certainly, but not deliberate, not as an end in itself, the agony no more than a side effect of an amateur attempt at striking a mortal blow. And this created a paradox for, when the end was in sight, the maniac had broken off the attack. It had not been panic. He had not fled and, by Bill's own account, had been cool and calm. And still he had left the job unfinished. Or was it unfinished? Was there some purpose which escaped me? If the goal had been death, why should the man have settled for less? And if the goal had not been death, why had his blows been so obviously intended as lethal?

My mind spun over these disturbing questions again and again, as my eyes moved back and forth across the page and the text failed to register. At last I pushed the book away and looked at my watch. I decided that research was impossible at the time; that I might as well have an early lunch and try again in the afternoon. I replaced the volume on the shelves and left the library. At the main doors, however, a notice caught my eye and I remembered that the new natural history exhibit had been opened the day before. I'd not yet had a chance to visit it and had been eagerly awaiting the pleasure and this seemed an excellent opportunity. I turned back and took the elevator up to the new hall.

It was there I once again encountered Claymore . . .

The new exhibit was the Johnson Memorial Hall of North American Mammals and I knew it had been planned somewhat differently to the other rooms. Johnson had been a wealthy industrialist who had, in later years, found great peace and pleasure in the Canadian wilderness and had left a large sum of money for the express purpose of creating the new hall. He had also stipulated conditions. It was to be as natural as possible. The whole room was to be fashioned into a simulated forest and there were to be no straight corridors, no display cases, no guard rails. There were not even signs to identify the various flora and fauna, on the principle that the animals in the wilds did not wear labels. Johnson's desire was to create a room where one could wander at random, in simulated solitude, in the mood of the far-reaching forests. It seemed a fine idea to me, and I was anxious to see how well it had been carried out.

I was pleased as soon as I entered the hall.

The plans had been well executed. The entrance was irregularly shaped with roughly plastered walls so that one had the impression of passing through the mouth of a cave. The forest stretched away within, the walls hidden behind backdrops of distant mountains which conveyed a sense of great distance and taped music softly repeated the forest sounds, birds and breezes and vague cracklings. Water dripped rhythmically from an artificial cataract. I stood beside the entrance for a time, letting myself fall into the mood, and then advanced. It was very realistic. Narrow paths wound about between arbours and brush and rock, seemingly at random as I turned my head from side to side. At first I saw no animals. Then abruptly the vegetation opened out and I found myself looking at a colony of beaver beside a plastic pool blocked with fallen timber. The animals were there, but one had to look. I strolled on; glimpsed a lynx stretched along an overhanging limb, tufted ears laid back, snarling; turned as the path angled and stopped short as a Kodiac bear reared up. The taxidermy was excellent, the animals were realistically grouped in lifelike positions, often I caught just a flashing glance as I passed some small mammal peering from the undergrowth. I thought Johnson would have approved.

Then, turning on to a secondary trail, I found myself face to face with Claymore.

"A splendid hall, this," he said.

I nodded. Somehow, seeing Claymore, my thoughts left the artificial wilderness and returned to reality . . . to the crimes we had discussed before. I mentioned I'd just come from the hospital where Bill was and Claymore appeared interested.

"Ah yes. The blind gentleman. How is he?"

"Recovering."

"Ah. The newspapers stated his condition as critical. But then, one learns never to have faith in journalism."

"He's a tough one," I said.

"Tough? Yes. Yes, I should imagine so. Obviously he had the will to survive. Admirable and natural. He will undoubtedly live until his time to die."

"Unlike the others."

"Others?"

"The other victims."

"Oh. Oh, no doubt it was their time to die."

I made no comment. Claymore nodded. "No doubt," he said again and then turned and strolled on. I followed. The path was too narrow to walk side by side and I trailed behind him. His limp seemed more noticeable and he seemed very interested in the exhibits, very alert, as if this were truly a wilderness and he were keeping an eye out for dangers or prey. From time to time he paused and used his walking stick to part the growth, revealing some secreted animal I hadn't even noticed, looking up and down. Fox and wolverine and badger lurked on every side. Presently the path opened into a clearing and Claymore halted. He sighed. A deer was bounding tangentially from us, white tail bobbed in graceful flight. At first glance I imagined the deer had been positioned as if fleeing from the visitors' approach down the path, but then I looked sideways and saw differently. Emerging from the opposite side of the clearing charged a pack of timber wolves, frozen in an instant of action, lean and fierce. I was about to point them out to Claymore when he spoke.

"Ah, it makes me long for the wilds," he said. "Books . . . books can only teach what other men have learned, not what each man must learn for himself . . . the sensations, the moods, the tone of nature. The totality."

He leaned on his stick.

"Well, I'm just as pleased these brutes are stuffed," I said, jokingly. "How would you like to face that lot in the flesh?"

Claymore turned, his eyebrows lifting. He saw the wolves. His reaction was startling. He cried out and took a staggering step backwards, raising his walking stick like a club. I stepped forward, afraid he would fall, but he caught his balance: lowered the stick. His face was white and he was sweating.

"Good heavens, man. What is it?" I asked.

Gradually he relaxed. The blood returned to his face and he looked embarrassed.

"Forgive me. A thoughtless reaction."

"What's wrong?"

He shook his head; moved towards the wolves and regarded them, then motioned at the pack with his stick, holding it like a fencer.

"You ask if I should like to face them," he said.

"A silly comment," I said.

"Ah, but I have," said Claymore.

I waited, hoping he would continue, sensing the past trauma in his sudden reaction. I noticed he had raised his stick more in a position of attack than defence and that even now his eyes were bright as he looked at the wolves.

He said, "They are fine specimens. Very fine. That big fellow must have weighed well over a hundred pounds, I should think. It saddens me to see a wolf which has been killed in his ferocious prime. I love wolves. I hate them but I love them for they have taught me so much. Everything is there to be learned in canis lupis. Territorial instinct, the pack urge, monogamy. And mystery. People have always thought the wolf as different from other predators. Finer somehow, and yet inspiring fear far greater than its size and strength should warrant. Why, there is even a disease in which one believes himself to be a wolf. Lycorexia. I wonder if there is a philosophy, as well?"

He shrugged.

"You have been attacked by wolves?" I asked, hoping to hear the tale.

"No. Not attacked. But I have faced them. I faced the pack and therefore they did not attack me, you understand? And facing them, I learned to face all – to face the past as well as the future and to see myself with humility, a small part of existence, of little importance in the total scheme of life . . . and of great importance in that I learned to act as nature intended."

"You stared them down, you mean?"

He gestured vaguely.

"Oh, one might say that. But it was far more than that."

"You interest me greatly."

"Ah, it was . . . interesting. You wish to hear the story?"

"Very much. If it won't disturb you to remember . . ."

"No, not at all. I constantly remember it. You take your knowledge from books – from still lives, as it were – and perhaps you should know how my knowledge came to me."

"I should like to know."

He nodded and glanced at the wolves once more. Then he moved away with a sideward step. A fallen tree had been propped against a stump across the clearing and Claymore took a seat on the log. I sat beside him. For some time he collected his thoughts while I waited. A man passed, pausing to look at the wolves and then looking at us. Then a middle-aged woman with three children crossed the clearing. They, too, observed us for a moment. We must have looked as out of place as they did. But our ectopia was of a different nature, and I felt I belonged there, listening to Claymore as a sceptic might have listened to Socrates, knowing one need not agree to learn. The taped sounds played on and the waterfall rustled and presently Claymore spoke.

"Several months after publication of my book I returned to the north," he said. "The book – I believe you mentioned reading it? – dealt with ecology in general and now I had decided to make a study in depth on a specific relationship. For several reasons I selected that existing between wolves and moose. The most important reason was expediency, for both are territorial animals. The wolf pack sticks within its own boundaries and will tolerate no others there and the moose, in deep snow at least, remains in his own small area or yard. Well, this territorial instinct enables an observer to define the limits of the area and use the square miles within as a field laboratory with checks and controls far more accurately than if the observer had selected his own boundaries at random. I have little patience with those who set aside a tract of land without regard for the animals' own limits . . . less with the modern practice of observing from aeroplanes. This may be a scientific prejudice on my part, and I've considered that sort of work since losing my leg, but cannot see it leading to accurate conclusions. However, I didn't have that problem. All my research was done on snowshoes with a pack on my back, far from the world of society. It would have been difficult to be farther. It was a world of true desolation and abandoned beauty, and my base camp was a little cabin of rough logs beside a stream which opened out, some miles below, into a river. The river was ringed by fir trees and frozen

in winter. I had but one companion – my guide – a man of
dubious ancestry called Charles. He had spent his life in the
wilderness and was a rough, silent man with vast practical
knowledge and experience. He hadn't the faintest idea what
I was studying and did not care at all. He was paid and that was
sufficient. That was the way I wanted it, as well, for all men are
susceptible and I might well have let my conclusions be affected
by a companion who understood the subject. I could ask
Charles questions and he would answer from his experience,
accurate and precise, not knowing what answer I sought and
therefore unable to commit the common error of slanting the
answer to give me satisfaction. We carried all our supplies with
us and relied on Charles to provide fresh meat. I have always
believed in travelling light and Charles was the sort to regard
even my meagre equipment as luxury.

"We went into the wilderness in the late autumn and prepared the base camp. I made preliminary investigation and
identified the wolf pack I would study – a pack some twenty
strong – and the outline of their territory, where they would
remain as long as the food supply permitted. Then it was
necessary to wait, for wolves seldom hunt the moose until
winter. In open water an adult moose can wade out so far that
the pack must swim to reach him, and that is not a pleasant
prospect for the wolves. But in winter the water is frozen, the
beaver keep to their lodges, the snowshoe hares are insignificant meals for pack strength, and then there is the moose.

"Well, winter came.

"Charles and I followed the wolf pack. It was a time of great
physical hardship and exhaustion, of dogged perseverance.
Often we were away from the cabin for weeks at a time, as the
pack ranged over the outer limits of their land, describing a
wide and predictable circle which allowed us to anticipate them
and often wait for them. This was necessary for they travelled
far faster than we could follow. I learned many things but my
main goal was to witness the confrontations between the pack
and the moose. Seldom did I manage to be present at the actual
kill, although often we arrived before the remains were de-
voured. This was important. It was absolutely essential that I
gather data about the victims – to do an autopsy on the
remains. This was no simple matter. For one thing, a healthy
wolf will eat about fifteen pounds of flesh a day and, if we were
far behind the kill, there was little left to examine. On the other

hand, when we managed to arrive before their first hunger had been satisfied, the pack was understandably reluctant to surrender their feast to science. These were wolves of the wilds, they had not yet learned fear of man, and to shoot them would have completely ruined the natural balance existing there. The pack regarded us with curiosity and, when they sensed no fear in us, with respect. Undoubtedly they saw us as fellow carnivores, but not as rivals, as they would have another wolf pack or a fox, and territorial defence seldom extends beyond the genus. So my findings were difficult and not extensive, but I persevered and gradually certain aspects of the relationship began to take form.

"Have you ever seen a moose, full grown in the forest? The wolves had a healthy respect for their prey, and it is understandable. Seven feet tall at the shoulders, weighing a ton and a half, unpredictable in mood and often changing from docile grazing to a thundering charge without a period of transition . . . they are formidable indeed. Often a moose in deep snow can outdistance the wolves with that awkward, long-legged stride. More often they choose to stand defiantly against the pack and invariably the wolves move on in these cases, searching easier prey. I witnessed this several times and came to the conclusion that the pack tested at least ten moose for every one against which they pressed the attack. This conclusion led me to predictions which only sufficient autopsy examinations could prove and I pressed on, faithfully inspecting gnawed bones, scraps of hide, uncoiled lengths of intestine. Eventually it was enough to convince me my predictions were correct – that the wolves' depredations were essential to the moose's survival as a species; that they systematically culled the old and the infirm and left the finest specimens to benefit from limited winter food supplies. Invariably my examinations of the remains showed the same results. The victims suffered from bone disease, cysts in the lungs, tapeworm. Their teeth were worn with age and an abundance of ticks implied they suffered from a weakened condition due to innumerable other diseases. And every victim I examined, discounting calves, proved to be more than seven years old – beyond their prime. Without the wolves these old moose would have lived for a good many years yet, consuming vast amounts of food and depriving the young members of the species."

Claymore had begun to talk rapidly, warming to a subject

dear to him. Now he paused, glanced sideways at me, and shrugged; smiled thinly.

"But all this is common knowledge now," he said, apologetically. "I must not bore you with this. Another aspect of vanity, eh? In my day it was just coming into acceptance and I shamelessly feel pride in my own small role in bringing it to light; in bringing it, perhaps a trifle sooner than it would have been. Still too late, of course. Too late against ignorance. I fear we shall both live to see the day when the last wolf is mangy and cowed in a zoo, when these exhibits are labelled extinct, or the museum equips an expedition to seek the last remaining pack. Perhaps. Still, they fight for survival. This is the first necessity. On the day a creature ceases to flee or to snarl, then it must die . . .

"But enough of this rambling theory. Theories hold true for all, but I must tell you my own experience."

I waited. When again he spoke his tone had changed. He still spoke with intensity, but it was a subjective quality now and there was terror lurking restrained in the timbre of his voice . . .

"There came the day when circumstances forged the links of events – events engraved in the receptive awareness of aroused sensations. There were two separate disasters, insignificant in themselves but combining to form a sum greater than the parts. The first disaster came when Charles broke through the ice. We had travelled far from the base camp, skirting the frozen lake, and night came. We stopped to make our camp. I regretted the delay and was impatient to continue for the pack had not killed in several days and they were lean with hunger. I knew they would press an attack very soon, and hoped to be present. I was standing in the trees, looking in the direction the pack had taken, when I heard Charles cry out. I rushed back. A segment of the bank had collapsed beneath him and he had crashed through the ice. I saw his head bob in the cold water, one hand gripping the jagged splintered edge. I threw myself flat to spread my weight and grasped him; managed to haul him from the icy waters. He was gasping and shaking. The instant the air touched his clothing it began to crackle and harden. Fortunately we had already made the fire and I helped him to strip his clothing off, wrapped him in a blanket and gave him a stiff shot of brandy. For a long time he lay still beside the fire, shivering, his eyes pressed closed. Finally the chill left him and I saw he was all right. But he had a strange look in his eyes. The first words he spoke were, 'My rifle . . . I've lost my rifle.' Well, I assumed he was worried about the loss alone, and offered to replace the weapon when we returned from the field trip, but that was not what troubled him. He had lost his pack, including the tent, but it was the rifle which distressed him. He said that he would have to return to the cabin – to get his other gun before we continued on. I argued. Fate brought out my stubbornness, an ally of disaster. But Charles couldn't conceive of going on without a weapon. I felt greatly frustrated. I knew the wolves would kill soon, and could not bring myself to miss the opportunity to witness the kill. I refused to go back. He refused, at first, to continue – did not even want to stop the night, but to go back in the darkness. He had completely changed. It was as if he had lost a vital organ instead of a rifle and all his taciturn confidence had vanished. Objectively, it was more interesting, a strange twist of the personality of a man who has come to rely on something apart from his own body. But subjectively I could not tolerate it. I could not bear to miss the opportunity ahead. I became angry and Charles, completely out of character as I'd known him, hung his head sullenly and accepted my abuse. I even, I fear, spoke of cowardice. Even this did not sting him to reply, other than to mutter, shaking his head, that a man could not stay in the woods without a gun. I carried no weapon, of course. But I saw no danger. I recalled his own assurance that he'd never known wolves to attack a man. 'Not a man with a rifle,' he mumbled. 'But these wolves don't know what a rifle is, how can that make a difference?' I asked. He shrugged. 'Maybe we might smell different without a weapon,' he said. He kicked at the ground and swung his head from side to side and behaved like a spoiled child. But I was adamant and, after a long while, he reluctantly agreed to go on in the morning. Very reluctantly. And even then he continued to mutter about how impossible it was to go on without rifle and tent. I let him ramble on after he'd agreed; got into my sleeping bag beside the fire. His bag was lost but there were sufficient blankets and my groundsheet and he wrapped up in these. He was still muttering when I drifted into sleep.

"His sullen, fearful mood continued through the next day. The wolves were moving fast and far and, the farther we moved from the extra rifle at the base camp the more frequently he paused to look back over our trail, his eyes longing to retrace our steps. Still, we advanced. In the afternoon we were able to leave the pack's spoor and cut at an angle across the predict- able circle, moving over rolling hills with deep snow between the slopes and stark pines on the crest. Evening was approach- ing. Charles was lagging and I had to urge him on, often walking well ahead of him; turning to find him gazing back- wards; shouting to him, whereupon he would come forward, head down and shoulders hunched. Then sunset struck with golden shafts across the western sky and it was in this violent glow that we came upon the wolves . . .

"I topped a ridge and saw them like a string of dark slugs advancing across a rippled snowfield. I took my binoculars from their case and focused. Charles came up to stand beside me, breathing harder than usual. The wolves moved like a single segmented organism, in a perfect twisting line. Then suddenly the line broke up, the pack formed a semi-circle, sitting back on their lean haunches. Charles grunted and pointed and I turned the glasses along the line indicated, saw a copse of dark trees and, after a few moments, saw the moose.

"He was a huge fellow, completely motionless, facing the pack. He'd not yet shed his antlers and they spread like two giant hands as wide as his great height. His ears were laid back, his mane erect. The wolves rose and advanced a few paces; settled on their haunches again. The moose moved then. The bell beneath his neck swung as he turned his head. He pawed the ground with great platter feet. The wolves showed pru- dence despite their hunger. Their tongues lolled out and their flanks rose and fell. Finally the leader rose and advanced cautiously, turned sideways to his quarry, testing the moose's temper and resolve. The moose didn't wait. He came with a sudden rush, awkward and mighty. The wolf leaped sideways, turning in the air and the pack spun and scattered. The moose halted, snorted and pawed, and then backed into the trees again. The wolves came silently back and drew together, exactly like a conference, heads lowered, muzzles close. From time to time one raised his head to gaze at the moose. The moose pawed spurts of snow and did not look worried or reluctant . . . looked as if he would welcome an attack. I watched, fascinated. This was an important observation. I knew the wolves had not eaten in days and wondered how much hunger was necessary to override caution. A great deal, apparently, for they rose abruptly and trotted off, shoulders rising and falling in a rhythm uncannily like a human shrug in time of resignation. They crossed the snowfield and vanished from sight. The moose began to peacefully strip bark from the trees. Charles snorted and went back down the ridge, wondering what I had seen worth seeing and I stood there for some time, watching the moose in the deepening shadows. The sky had reddened, the tallest trees gathered the last light and darkness fell spreading over the ground. When I could no longer distinguish the moose I turned and started back down the incline, picking my steps carefully. Not, however, carefully enough.

"And then the second disaster struck . . ."

Claymore winced slightly.

"The definitive disaster," he said. "I had just settled my weight on my leg when something struck me just above the ankle. It didn't hurt. I thought the limb of a tree had somehow fallen on me and there was what seemed a great interval before I heard the solid clang of metal – seemed a great time lapse, although I was still suspended in the midst of falling when the sound reached my brain and as I dropped into the snow I already knew what had happened – that I had stepped on the pan of a trap. I had fallen on my back, twisting the imprisoned leg. I sat up, brushing snow from my arms in thoughtless habit, and leaned down to inspect the damage. I still felt no pain, no feeling at all, but the moment I saw the trap I knew I was severely damaged.

"It was a huge trap made to hold a bear. The vicious jaws had sunk deeply into my leg – so deeply it seemed the toothed edges must nearly meet between torn calf and shattered shin. I inspected it very calmly; found it was old and rusted and must have lain there for years, forgotten by some long departed trapper. I looked at it from every possible angle, tilting my head this way and that, and then took the jaws in my hands and tried to open it. I could not budge it. I sat back, wondering what to do – I'd completely forgotten Charles and was undoubtedly in some form of shock. But then he called from the shadows below, asking what had happened. I felt a sense of relief as I heard his voice and shouted to him. A moment later, in a spray of snow, he was kneeling beside me.

"He winced as he saw the wound; bent over my leg and inspected the trap. His hands moved slowly at first but gradually his face darkened and he began to jerk and haul violently. His efforts twisted my leg and the first tingling of pain advanced past my knee. I clamped my teeth shut and watched him without protest, with complete confidence in his experience and ability. But then his face changed again, he cursed and squatted back. He looked sick. His forehead was glistening with sweat. He told me in slow, thoughtful tones that the release mechanism had become jammed or broken during the long untended time and that he wasn't able to open the jaws. He repeated the last several times . . . 'Can't open it, won't open, can't get it to open . . .' Then he cursed some more. I still felt no real panic. It seemed impossible that I was hopelessly trapped as long as I had a companion with me. I asked what we should do, quite calmly, I believe. Charles didn't answer. He wiped the back of his hand across his brow and leaned over the trap again, digging in the snow until he found the chain. He followed the chain, lifting it from the snow foot by foot, like some clanking serpent with a frozen spine; found the end secured to a large tree, encircling the bole and fastened with a stout padlock. I watched as he took the chain in both hands and hauled on it, bracing one boot against the tree and winding the links around his wrists. His shoulders heaved beneath his heavy mackinaw. Sounds came brittle on the cold air. His heel scraped the bark, he grunted and snorted, the chain rattled. At last he gave up the effort and bent to the padlock, inspecting it carefully, turning it over in his hands. His breath hung about his face like a halo. He straightened and rubbed the back of his neck, then came clumping back to where I sat. He moved behind me without a word and began fumbling with my pack; eased it from my shoulders and laid it open, searching for a tool. But there was none. Whatever we had possessed which might have proved effective had been lost through the ice. Presently he returned to the tree. He seemed to have difficulty crossing the deep snow and paused, breathing deeply, before drawing his hand axe. It was a short-handled affair, the blade flat backed, and he struck the padlock several times with it. It clanked dull but distinct and did no good at all. From his posture, the way his shoulders sloped and his head hung, I got the impression he hadn't expected the blows to be effective – had tried them for mere formality. Once more he returned to me. He knelt, cleared the snow away and struck the spring and release mechanism several sharp ringing blows. The axe rebounded and the lock refused to yield. Flakes of rust splintered from the steel and bright marks scored the metal but it would not break. Charles shook his head. The pain was increasing now. He reversed the axe and attempted to use the handle as a prying bar, but could get no leverage between the tightly clamped teeth. After a moment he chopped the axe into the earth in a gesture of frustration; grasped the jaws in his hands again and pulled. I leaned forward to help. Together we applied all our strength. But that trap was fashioned to hold a bear. We could not budge it.

" 'It's no use,' he said.

"I looked searchingly at him.

"His face clouded with anger, he scowled at me. 'Well? What do you expect? It's no use, I tell you!' He gestured at the trap. 'The big brown bears can't open these, what can I do? Eh? What can I do? Sometimes when a bear is caught like this they escape. You know how this is, eh? They escape by gnawing their foot off. That's how. The big bear chews his own paw through, so what do you expect me to do?' I said nothing. Gradually his anger lessened. He glanced towards the tree. 'I might chop the tree down,' he said, but even as he spoke we both knew it was impossible. He had only the hand axe, the tree was large, even if it were possible it would take far too long. 'Even then, you would still be trapped. I would have to carry you, dragging the trap and chain. Or build a litter and haul you behind me. If one had a rifle, the spring could be shot apart, of course. But one does not have the rifle.' He looked sharply at me as he said this. Despite the growing pain, I felt indignant at this reproach; said, 'That's right. We haven't the rifle. So what shall we do?' He didn't answer for a while. Then he shrugged. 'I will need tools. The hacksaw, the crowbar. Also the first aid kit. The spare first aid kit . . .' He nodded to me, to himself. 'Yes, that will be necessary, your leg must be treated before you can be moved.'

" 'But those things are at the cabin,' I said.

"Charles looked away.

"Then I felt the first awful weight of panic . . .'"

Claymore looked at me almost with challenge. I was staring, open mouthed, completely absorbed in his tale, caught up in the complex mood behind the words.

"He left you?" I asked.

Claymore nodded.

"Yes. He left me. It was the fact of not having his rifle, you see. I feel certain that, had he not lost the weapon, he would have found some other solution; wouldn't have abandoned me.

But he had lost the gun and, with it, his courage, his confidence. All his experience was related to the possession of a firearm, and without it he could not function, he could not relate circumstances to past experience. Standing over me he seemed to have no more substance than his shadow; could no more direct his own behaviour than that shadow could defy the commands of the fading light. And then, of course, there were the wolves . . .

"All our efforts, although they seemed to have lasted a long time, had passed quickly. Time had been suspended by stress. The sky was still violent with gold and fire behind stratocumulus formations. I distinctly remember turning to look at this flaming sunset; noticing it without relation to my plight, as my mind turned away from reality in self-defence. I thought quite composedly how beautiful the colours were with the dark pines thrusting up like a palisade. And then, gradually, I became aware of other broken silhouettes above the ridge. It was as if the tournure of the land had shifted subtly, as if during our suspended period of time the world had continued to age and upheavals had altered the contours. I shielded my eyes and stared into the incandescent sunset and gradually the objects took form and became the wolves.

"The pack sat on top of the ridge and regarded us in silent hunger. I spoke – I used my voice, although the syllables were broken and did not take verbal form – and Charles turned to look; jerked up sharply, his face mangled by fear. The wolves followed his motion with their yellow eyes. 'They never attack humans,' I said. And Charles knew this as well as I, but he did not have his gun. He whispered, 'They have no fear of us. You would not let me kill them . . .' Trying to shift the responsibility on to me, of course; to justify his act even before he committed it. And then I knew, definitely, that he would leave me.

"Charles began making preparations then, without another word. I watched him in silence with the fires of agony spreading through my thigh and hip, eager for fuel. He made a fire. He gathered all the wood in the immediate vicinity and stacked it beside me. He took the blankets and sleeping bag from my pack and wrapped them carefully – tenderly even – around me. His actions were stiff and jerky and he could not look at me; could not bring himself to tell me he was leaving. Strangely enough, I felt I should make it easier for him, since it was an irrevocable decision. I asked, 'How soon can you be back?' He looked at me then; seemed relieved that I was not pleading or arguing; that I accepted the necessity. He assured me he could travel very fast alone and unencumbered; that he could be back in two days, maybe less, no more. 'All right.' I told him. 'Obviously you must have tools to free me.' 'And the other rifle,' he added, quickly. The axe was still jammed in the ground and he drew it out; looked at it for a moment, reluctant to part with his only weapon. Then he handed it to me. He held it out by the handle, as if still undecided – as if he might snatch it away at the last moment. But when I grasped the blade he let it go. He tied his snowshoes on, fumbling with the laces and glancing sideways at the ridge. Then he stood up and nodded. 'It is the only way,' he said. 'Yes,' I said, 'it is how it must be.' 'I will hurry. I will return with the rifle.' The way he said it, I could tell he believed he would be returning not for rescue, but revenge. Then he moved off, swinging the big snowshoes wide and moving fast. I watched him until he had passed into the trees. Then I turned and watched the wolves and they watched me . . .''

"My God," I said, the exclamation forced from me as Claymore paused. He was looking at the mounted wolves across the clearing. It was lunchtime now and no one else had passed through the hall for some time. We seemed very much alone and, somehow, I got the impression that Claymore was talking more to himself than to me. I had no wish to destroy the mood with which he spoke, and stilled the urge to comment. He lowered his eyes and regarded his legs then looked at the wolves once again. They stared back with glass eyes.

"I took stock of the situation," he said. "I felt, at first, that I would be able to survive until Charles returned. I kept telling myself that there are few, if any, recorded instances of wolves attacking humans in North America. I had the axe and my sheath knife and the fire. I had a plentiful supply of firewood. I tried to look upon my plight as an experiment, a chance at first hand observation, and actually managed to feel almost cheerful for a short while. But it could not last. I don't suppose I'd expected it to, really. There was the pain and there were the wolves. The pain had become unbearable and the wolves were hungry. I told myself the wolves would not approach the fire and fashioned a tourniquet for my leg, using one of the groundsheets and turning it tight with the axe handle. I was able to cut off the pain this way, but was afraid of stopping circulation too long and each time I released the pressure the agony flooded back worse than before, increasing with each turn of the axe. Time passed with incredible slowness. The sunset lingered, the wolves waited. Then, at last, it was night. I shifted another length of wood on the fire, raising the flames and increasing the circle of light. I could no longer see the wolves, but I could hear them panting. And then, suddenly, I could see them. They had come down the slope to the very rim of the firelight, formless grey shapes with glowing eyes. I threw small flaming sticks at them and they backed away calmly. I held the axe in one hand and the knife in the other, turned my back to the fire and waited. Panic faded into a stupor. I blacked out.

"I couldn't have been unconscious long, only minutes perhaps, certainly less than an hour. The fire still burned brightly. But when I awoke it was with a cold and certain resolve, as if my mind had fashioned a formula while my consciousness was gone. The situation was very clear. I knew that if I remained there I would die. The pain, the cold, the wolves – by one or all I would die. And I was determined not to die; thought of the moose driving the pack away with his charge and then thought of the bear for whom this trap had been designed – the bear who would devour his own leg to escape, governed by a natural instinct far deeper than pain could delve. I saw the only possibility of survival quite objectively.

"I had the axe.

"I had to remove my leg.

"It was decided. I considered no other course of action; refused to contemplate the blinding agony and the unspeakable horror of the act. I used only one rationalization – telling myself my leg was hopelessly mangled already and would never be of use to me again; that I would be cutting away a thing already dead. But I didn't really need to convince myself of this, for I was merely an animal in a trap. Very carefully I began to plan the operation.

"I placed the blade of my knife in the hottest embers of the fire. It was a large triangular blade, very keen, which I used to dissect the remains of the wolf pack's kills. I tested the blade of the axe with my thumb. It seemed sharp – it had to be sharp enough, for I had no way to hone it. Then I waited for the knife to heat. I was very calm. I took out my pipe and tobacco and

lighted it with a burning twig. I smoked slowly and contempla-
tively, watching the smoke rise against the flames. I timed it just
right, so that when the pipe had burned out the knife had
begun to glow. I knocked the ash out and put my pipe in my
pocket, then tightened the tourniquet just above the knee. I
raised the axe with both hands and marked an imaginary line
across my shin; lifted my torso, threw my shoulders back, and
brought the axe down.

"But my nerve failed.

"At the last instant, involuntarily, I twisted the stroke to the
side. The blade bit into the earth beside my leg and the
concussion leaped at my elbows and shoulder sockets. I cursed
myself for a coward. And, as if the wolves could sense the failure
of my courage, they moved nearer. One wolf advanced ahead
of the pack – the same, I thought, that had advanced to test the
moose. Anger surged up in me. I screamed loudly and the wolf
retreated, lowering his muzzle. The anger helped. It purified
my perceptions. I took one of the blankets and draped it over
my leg, smoothing it around the calf so that the contour could
be seen. I was very annoyed with my leg. But, covered with the
blanket, it ceased to be a leg, it was a lump beneath a blanket,
no more. I drew the axe edge across this lump at the proper
spot, wrinkling the blanket to leave a visible line. I raised the
axe once more. I looked at a wrinkle in a blanket. Just a wrinkle
in a blanket in the wavering light of a fire. And then, very
accurately and very hard, I chopped down.

"This time I did not fail.

"The blow did not sever the leg, but it broke through the
slender shin bone and cut deeply into the flesh. I stared at it. I
tried to raise the axe but it was stuck. I had to heave with all my
strength to withdraw it, and the blood spurted behind. There
was more blood than I had imagined and it rose with incredible
force, towering above me and then splattering in all directions.
The blanket turned instantly dark. I was seized by frenzy. My
mind rushed from my body and I saw myself from above, a wild
madman broken in dancing flames, spewing heavy blood in
wide arcs, roaring and jerking and lifting the axe. I had but one
thought: I had to finish the task. I fell upon my leg, hacking
savagely time and again, no longer capable of accurate strokes
but chopping and slashing with insane fury, sawing the blade
back and forth across parting tendons and pounding the edge
through convulsing muscle.

"I have no recollection of when the leg finally parted. I did not know at the time. But it did and I found myself pounding the earth, digging great furrows in the soaked ground, separated from the trap and from the grisly burden it held.

"A semblance of sanity snapped taut in my brain then. I dropped the axe and grasped the glowing knife; clamped the flat blade against the ghastly stump. The odour of charred tissue and boiling blood sprang up in overpowering waves. I held my breath and held the knife and the bleeding stopped. The pain, too, had stopped. My nerves could not convey this message of horror, this agony beyond sensation's scope. I sat there, gasping and gaping. I stared at the trap. Blood bubbled and coiled from the shapeless, lifeless lump in the clamped jaws. It was hideous. I did not want this monstrous object near me. I leaned forward and raised the trap, swung it and threw it from me with all my might. It flew, the chain clanking, and the blanket dropped away. The trap bounced twice when it landed.

"Again I blacked out.

"And again awoke.

"I awoke with a sense of relief and with the wolves making sounds very near. I gripped the gory axe and surged upwards. Every trace of fear had left me, severed as surely as my leg, and I rose to fight. But the pack were not attacking me. They were clustered about the trap. They snarled and growled and their powerful jaws snapped. The wolves were devouring that useless scrap I had abandoned, and somehow that fact was more terrible than the amputation. I shifted back, my arm brushed a burning log and the flames leaped higher. A wolf raised his jowls, his muzzle dark with blood, his eye reflecting the flames. His jaws worked slowly, crunching down, and the flesh disappeared. Some part of my mind insisted it was just flesh and some other part knew it had been my leg and I vomited into the fire . . ."

Claymore's head jerked.

"And so it was," he said, and spread his hands.

I stared at him. I felt like vomiting myself. He turned and ran that searching glance across my face.

"You do understand?"

"I . . . My God . . . I don't know what to say . . ."

"Oh, the horror of it, yes. But you do understand why I did not die . . . why I am alive to tell you this macabre little tale?"

I didn't answer.

"The wolves did not attack, of course. I was too . . . aroused . . . for fear. They tested me and I waited with the axe and they drew back and squatted and then they moved off to seek easier prey. I did not shout at them, did not depend on the fire; I drove them off by the instincts they sensed within me. I daresay they would have found the moose better quarry that night. I was more than a man, because I had become less and it was more than a leg that I cut away. I waited until dawn. I remember little of that time. I believe I ate a bit of food from my pack and systematically loosened the tourniquet. At any rate, I did whatever survival demanded. In the morning I began to crawl. I hardly thought about directions; knew my instincts would guide me. As they did. My mind was free for other thoughts, for concepts. I envisioned revenge upon Charles for a time, but not seriously, for I realized he had acted in accord with nature. The pack does not wait for the injured individual, the species does not risk survival for the organism, the body does not pause for the loss of a cell. Hatred and rage dried up in the basin of my brain, emotion evaporated and laid bare the true fabric of the mind. And in this dry bed all my experience flowed together, all branches met and shared the same natural roots. Some might say I went mad in the long hours of my ordeal, but whatever I lost it was not sanity . . .

"And that was that.

"Charles found me later that day, the next day, whenever. He had his rifle and his confidence and, when the first shock had passed he respected me greatly for what I had done. He did not understand, as a man reasons, but he sensed, as a man should. And do you?"

I could not answer.

I don't believe Claymore expected an answer, beyond what he saw in my face. That was sufficient. Presently he stood up; leaned on his stick for a moment, then nodded pleasantly and moved away. I remained on the log and he went down the trail between the trees. I wondered where he was going. He had told me that lately he'd been doing a bit of field work. Just a bit, he'd said. An application of former knowledge. But that could mean anything. I watched him as he came to a bend. His limp was more noticeable as he turned. The man who had attacked. Bill had favoured one leg when he left. But Bill might have injured him. And Bill, of course, had survived. He had been tested and he survived. Then Claymore was gone and I sat there for some time. Presently, just as if this had been a real forest, a chill seemed to move through the trees and caused me to shiver, there among the wolves . . .